BLOODLINE

A Historical Novel

ANTHONY THOMAS DiSIMONE

ARCHWAY
PUBLISHING

Archway Publishing books may be ordered through booksellers or by contacting:

Archway Publishing
1663 Liberty Drive
Bloomington, IN 47403
www.archwaypublishing.com
1 (888) 242-5904

Because of the dynamic nature of the Internet, any web addresses or
links contained in this book may have changed since publication and
may no longer be valid. The views expressed in this work are solely those
of the author and do not necessarily reflect the views of the publisher,
and the publisher hereby disclaims any responsibility for them.

Any people depicted in stock imagery provided by Thinkstock are models,
and such images are being used for illustrative purposes only.
Certain stock imagery © Thinkstock.

ISBN: 978-1-4808-5821-3 (sc)
ISBN: 978-1-4808-5822-0 (hc)
ISBN: 978-1-4808-5823-7 (e)

Library of Congress Control Number: 2018902222

Print information available on the last page.

Archway Publishing rev. date: 03/24/2018

My inspiration to create anything in this world began when I met my Nancy. All the good things that flow from me come through her. She is my love and my partner, and she has inspired me to be much more than I ever thought I would be.

From the time I met this exuberant, cute little freckled-faced kid, Eric Bulson, I knew he was a special person. Now as Professor Bulson, he was a guide and editor who took a great personal interest in making this book a worthy effort.

Through the years, members of my staff devoted numerous hours to working on the book and took an interest in its success—in particular, Theresa Rafter, my right-hand man!

Members of my family supported me and encouraged me, including my wonderful aunt Pauline Urus and Marie Vazzana, who helped me with some historic background, as well as my *cugini* in Corleone.

Thank you all.

PROLOGUE

THE SICILIAN COUNTRYSIDE is a contrast in landscapes, as well as people. There are lush, fertile areas where fine fruits and vegetables grow in such abundance that it was valued in pre-Roman days. The Roman soldiers transported the cornucopia of goods on well-worn donkey paths that exist to this day.

In contrast, the barren, rocky areas compare closely to desert landscapes. Thus, too, the people vary in physical and cultural aspects. The wealthy, privileged class assumed the vacuum created when the imperial Roman Empire collapsed and a weak monarchy eventually expired.

The island, however, with its superb olive groves, fine vineyards, and notable citrus and vegetable production kept the island's economy intact. Through the invasions that plundered and caused internal strife, including the Moors' occupation, the people survived.

Century after century, the island and its people endured. Vestiges of the past, including Moorish influenced architecture and the dark or olive skin of the descendants of the invaders, left their marks not just on the landscape.

The brutality visited on the people by the invaders, bandits, and mainlanders gave rise to the system where the strong and wealthy were relied upon to defend the weak. Thus, the feudal system where the leaders, the *patrones*, who as a point of respect were called "Don," forced their subjects to fall into place in a strict order.

CHAPTER 1

IN THE TOWN of Corleone, the pecking order was clear. Il Padrone, Don Tomasso Scalisce, was leader. He was likened to a duke or earl—not of royalty but of another kind of power. While some respected the monarchy, such as it was, it was foreign to this *paese*, and Roma might as well have been a world away. Few people ventured beyond their small towns in the hills of inner Sicily. In fact, it was only for a really important reason that a person would even venture to Palermo, the hub of Sicilian commerce. The so-called Palermitani were thought of as godless city dwellers, swindlers, and users. The city swelled with the *scunizi*, the street dogs, which lived by their wits. These street urchins, whether in Palermo, Naples, or Rome, were nonetheless bold and clever. Some were bastards, left in orphanages, churches, or nunneries by a *mala femina*, a bad woman. One who became pregnant without the benefit of marriage was *una puntana*. Since fear of mortal sin and condemnation, excommunication, and even perhaps a deadly stoning were uppermost on these unfortunate women's minds, they discarded these children. They survived the nine-month ordeal but ridded themselves of the child at birth. There were no single mothers, only whores with bastards.

These unwanted children eventually strayed from their virtual servitude in orphanages or nunneries and took to living on the streets in packs, *come i cani*, like the dogs. They preyed on any available mark and could easily surround an unknowing greenhorn from the countryside, beat him, and steal his money and clothes. Merchants were constantly on guard, lest a pack of these animals convened all at once on a shop. As the bewildered shopkeeper chased one away, five others would rob him blind.

These urchins grew up to be the kind of hard-core street thugs that plied their craft in every major city and even some of the smaller ones. Because they were raised and bred on larceny, few ever became "men of respect". Only the ones from recognized families with a lineage and social status became "men of respect". Those boys were taught by their parents, their elders, and indeed their priests from early on. Even in a *scuola*, the school, rules demanded obedience and, of course, respect. The dumbest child was never tolerated if he broke the rules. Composure was demanded, always. Restraint and patience were understood as proper conduct. An elder, even a poor farmer or peasant, was spoken to by a child with respect, for old age had its accumulated value. The richest man, the most powerful man, would not compromise his pride by demeaning a lowly farmer or servant publicly. If there was no reason to show rank, those in the upper class were not eager to make a display of it. There was no need. It was simply understood. The practice of bowing or just even nodding to a person of higher rank was done without thinking. Should a peasant farmer be walking along the road and a car or carriage approach with a person of higher rank, the peasant would turn, remove his hat, and, as the vehicle passed, slightly bow or nod his head in recognition. The remnants of these courtly gestures remained and still to a degree continue throughout many areas of Italy. While it is not so prevalent in the hustle and bustle of major cities, time is not as urgent in the countryside, and a moment lent to a courteous gesture is not thought to be ill spent.

Una porta chiusa, un altra porta aperta (one door closes, and another door opens). The saying has multiple meanings. An era or time passes, and a new one begins; an opportunity diminishes, but a new one appears; a way is blocked, but another opens.

So it was from the transition from the old ways to the new.

The history of each family and each town changed little from century to century. The way of life, and indeed of death, had been well defined, so there was no great rush to change things. In fact, in many ways, it was predictable but pleasant.

The little towns like Corleone had a daily cadence. The church bells rang, the shops opened each day, the men went about their work, the children went off to school, and the world turned.

Signora Trentino would send her two children off to school. The children, Dominic, age nine, and Ramona, age seven, dutifully dressed, ate a piece of bread with a bit of cheese and drank a small cup of milk and then went off to school. La Signora, a robust woman of twenty-eight years, had her chores. She was always a little sad, however, since she had miscarried one child and then a year later a second child. The midwife and then the doctor told her she had to strengthen herself before she could have more children. Her husband, Donato, was a good but simple man. He tended a small herd of lambs and sheep on a plot of land on the mountainside he rented from Il Padrone, Don Scalisce. He also tended a few olive and lemon trees and a small garden where he grew vegetables. He and his family survived on the things the earth provided. La Signora left the house each day and went to the shops near *la chiesa* (the church). There she bought a loaf of bread from the baker. Depending on the day, the butcher might have slaughtered a calf or pig. There was, therefore, some veal or liver or even a piece of pork. She would bring with her some eggplants, olives, lemons, and other things her husband had grown and either trade with someone for eggs or leave the items for sale or barter. Though there was paper money and coins, bartering still had its place. She would also buy some flour and maybe some wheat or barley. If a special feast day approached, she would seek the ingredients for a special dish or special bread or pastry. There, in the square, was a large old stone water fountain. The water, fresh and cool, tumbled over the old stone tower and trickled down into a large round pool. One could sit on the solid stones that were laid end to end. They were carefully cut and placed about the fountain. Anyone could bring their donkey, ox, or horse to drink there as well.

The women of the town congregated each morning, said their hellos, shared a word or two (unless there was some major object of gossip), and were off. All had been to the morning Mass and heard the priest, Father Cataggio, warn the women that their husbands were failing in their duty to the Lord by not coming to church regularly and not supporting their pope. The good priest would announce from time to time the birth of a child, the betrothing of some couple, or up-and-coming special services or feasts.

This day, Signora Trentino heard very unsettling gossip from her cousin Filomena Duchetti. It seemed that young Guilemo Scalisce, the son of the powerful Don Tomasso Scalisce, was rumored to have "been with" the poor Castellucci girl, Bettina. The girl, who was now nearly eighteen years old, never really could learn much more than a ten-year-old child. She was cared for by her parents. Her mother, Beatrice, had had her by breech birth. Filomena was a midwife and had been called by Beatrice's husband, Donato, as soon as labor began. Try as she might, Filomena feared she would lose both child and mother. She used large metal calipers and a set of tools she had had her blacksmith and metal-worker husband fashion by her design. Still, she could not turn the infant. In a fit of pain, Beatrice turned just as Filomena was using calipers to turn the infant by the head. A doctor was sent for and arrived the next day. Beatrice was in terrible pain and had lost a great deal of blood. It wasn't known if the infant was getting a good supply of blood and, thus, much-needed oxygen. Finally, after nearly forty hours, the child was born. The infant was bruised and battered and extremely listless. It took several days before both mother and child were thought to be able to survive and on their way to recovery. Little Bettina stopped breathing at least two times during the first night. Filomena, sensing her problems, massaged the infant and resuscitated her, saving her life. Because of Filomena, her head had been squashed and malformed. There were also deep indentations all over her body, and she was black and blue from head to toe. Her mother wept at the child's plight each time she lifted her to her breast and coaxed the infant to feed. Filomena was a diligent woman with a sense of responsibility and heartfelt sympathy for this poor woman and her family. She stayed by Beatrice's side for nearly two weeks, all the while cooking and cleaning and tending to the needs of both the child and the mother. As the weeks passed, Beatrice was finally able to get out of bed and walk around, and soon thereafter she was also tending to the child.

"Guarda la testa!" she said excitedly to Filomena. "Look at the head!" The child's head, which had been deformed by the pressure of the metal calipers, had, as if by a miracle, become perfectly round. The bruises melted away day by day. As they did, it seemed her appetite increased, and the little infant gained a voracious desire to feed nearly every hour. Soon she was gaining weight on the skeletal frame that had weighed, at birth, just over six pounds. Each night, Filomena, who had been sleeping on a chair next to Beatrice, heard the cadence of the mother's prayers. In the dark of the night, the prayers of the rosary to many saints and many Roman Catholic creeds, spoken so quietly they were barely audible, were like the sound of a whispering wind to Filomena, familiar but nearly inaudible.

"Jesu ringrazia, Jesu ringrazia, Jesu ringrazia, Maria-Madre di Dio ringrazia, Maria-Madre di Dio ringrazia, Maria-Madre di Dio ringrazia …" On and on, hour after hour, she thanked Jesus and Mary for the salvation of her child and the strength she was given to survive and nurture the child. Filomena was in awe and nearly a bit embarrassed to be in this woman's presence when she made her most private pledges to the Lord and the blessed mother and the saints. She had the feeling that she was witnessing some kind of miracle.

Beatrice began referring to Filomena as *mia sorella* (my sister) and for the rest of her life treated her as her closest and most loved family member. Filomena gave her a nickname, "Sorellina" (Little Sister), and the love that was forged during that childbirth lasted the rest of their lives. Filomena was childless. She was married to Guisseppe. She doted on him, and the attention she gave him was no less than a mother with a child. Each morning, she would rise before he got out of bed; silently she would prepare him coffee and lay out biscotti for breakfast. Then she would hang his clothes on a closet door. After he used the bathroom, she would bring him a cup of coffee. He sat on the chair, and she would put on his socks and shoes and chatter about what was to be done that day and if it was hot or cold outside, if he should bring something with him or attend to some matter at work where he managed a butcher shop in town owned by his father.

Filomena's maternal instinct led her to learn quickly the ways of a midwife at the early age of twelve years old, when her mother began labor. She was sent to fetch the midwife and then attend to getting towels, pillows, water, and other things during the delivery. She felt she was present at a miraculous event, since, as she knew well from her upbringing as a devout Roman Catholic, every birth is one of God's miracles. It gave her the feeling that the Lord was somehow involved in this process. She revered life and felt it was a God-given event, as holy as the sacrament. Thus, she felt a particular sentiment for Beatrice and her child. In a way, you could say, she even felt responsible for their lives. She was unaware of some ancient concept that when you save a life, it is then your responsibility to preserve and nurture that life. In this case, there were two lives, and Bettina indeed needed all the attention and nurturing she could get.

"Bella Bettina," Filomena would call as she approached the doorway of the little home where the Castelluccis lived. The villages in this southern region were clustered, little, white stone and cement houses, one on top of another, up the hills and mountains. The rich, fertile valleys and fields surrounded them.

The Castellucci family
Beatrice Castellucci (left), Donato Castellucci
(right), and Bettina Castellucci (center)

The town centers with their water fountains, usually of ancient vintage, were prominent in the center of town, where a large piazza was the hub of activity. The church, the municipal offices, the police station (if it was a large town), shops, stores, offices, and other commercial operations all spurred off this hub. The narrow streets winding up the hills were studded with the old masonry houses occupied generation after generation by the same families, many of them for centuries.

As little Bettina would appear at the doorway, "Bella," Filomena would say. "Dove la dolce?" Where are the sweets? Little Bettina would smile widely and hug the woman, but as she did so, she would slip her hands into the pockets of her housedress and search until she felt the two or three pieces of candy, which were always there. She then stood on her toes and kissed Filomena on the cheek. Filomena and Beatrice would visit each other at least once a week, and always the child was there.

Bettina grew from the time she first gasped for air as a rumpled and bruised waif. Within those first few weeks, however, it was clear that she had not endured the trauma of childbirth unscathed. She would seek to feed from her mother's breast but was physically lethargic. She rarely uttered a sound and hardly ever cried, and when she did cry from some major discomfort, it was momentary. She was sedate when awake, and when sleeping, she lay motionless. Her mother would often press her ear to the child's face to hear and feel her breathing just to reassure herself the child was all right.

As the months passed, the child grew, but there was little change in her activity. She wasn't learning about the world around her, and this continued for the first year of life. Both mother and father spoke to the child, encouraged her, and spent time playing with her. She was physically healthy and responded to activities that encourage physical movement, but her capacity for learning was diminished. Somehow the head injuries had damaged the part of the brain that permitted some learning abilities. Her ability to learn abstract concepts was impaired. While her motor skills and alertness were normal, in fact superior, she had difficulty understanding and learning, most particularly emotions. She showed little reaction to distress, pain, or fear, unless it was extreme. She finally began to speak at age six and had a limited vocabulary by age eight, when she first attended school. She was put with younger children and allowed to learn at her own pace. Her personality, however, was a different matter. What she lacked in intelligence, she made up for in unbridled joy. She smiled constantly and was always mindful of her manners. She was reverent to elders and never treated her classmates with anything but a sister-like regard. She loved everyone and everything.

"Mama!" the girl called out loud to her mother. "Mama!" She lay in bed with just a sheet covering her. There on the bed was a small pool of blood.

The frightened sound of the girl brought the mother rushing from the kitchen. "Che su chesa?" Beatrice asked. Then she saw the pool of blood between the girl's legs. "Oh, bella non ti fare paura" (don't be afraid). The mother took her hand and calmly explained that when a girl reaches her age, that happens every once in a while. She knew Bettina could not grasp the concept of a week or a month; future events were either close or *lontano* (far away). The girl calmed some and told her mother she felt like her chest hurt a little. She pulled the sheet down and exposed her breasts. She asked why she had such globes when her father did not but her mother did. It was all very confusing. Her mother just said that girls are different, and they have breasts. That was enough for her to grasp, and she never asked again. She understood that boys were different from girls. They were stronger and talked with deeper voices. Some had mustaches and beards, but girls did not. She understood, to some vague concept, the difference in genitals since she saw the boys by the farms peeing behind the sheds, and when they were naked, they looked so different.

Bettina grew into a beautiful young lady. Her features were reminiscent of the Renaissance masters. She had dark blond hair flecked with red highlights and cream-colored, smooth skin, but when anyone met her, they were astonished by her light blue eyes. They shined, nearly glowing and sparkling at the same time. Her features were rare in Southern Italy. Her body was straight, slim, and athletic and perfectly proportioned. Here in this human body was the model of an angelical form so often ritualized in the paintings and sculptures of the old masters. But here too was what the Sicilian heritage contained. She had full red lips punctuating a perfectly rounded chin. Her soft pink cheeks were outlined by a muscular facial structure. Her nose, noble, straight, and slender at the bridge, was graceful to its tip. Her hair, thick and swirling in curls, belied the typical pitch-black, shiny mane of her mother and ancestors. Taller than most Sicilians, she was slender in appearance yet willowy and voluptuous at the same time. Her torso curved to the waist, flattened at her belly, and framed out with ample hips. Her body was akin to mythological goddess figures whose broad and strongly structured hips and ample breasts emphasized imagined fertility and childbearing prowess. Bearing children and the supreme image of motherhood, beauty, strength, and sexual attraction was indeed the revered image of mythological women of the ancient world, whether it be Roman, Greek, Germanic, or Oriental.

Bettina's physical attributes were perhaps nature's consolation for her mental shortcomings. One was mesmerized by her luminous eyes and her sweet words, respectful but often incongruous, like those of a child, but she was not ignorant or slow to learn. She had a strong body and angelic voice. Though not exactly dull or dumb, she was not able to connect things in a normal way. She learned her language and spoke with symmetrical articulation; in fact, she spoke in a distinctly clean and nearly melodic cadence reminiscent of the Barese, those people from the Italian town of Bari, noted for their singsong speech pattern. She also had a very special relationship with things of nature. Animals trusted her, even those in the wild. She had no fear of any animal. In fact, she had not ever really displayed the capacity to exhibit a fear of anything. While she might be displeased, even then, she rarely made it noticeable. It was as if she just accepted things as they were. She dealt with life as it came to her each day, each moment. She became more animated about things she liked, whether it was the warm sun shining on her face, a warm night to gaze at the stars, or eating a ripe tomato off the vine. Conversely, she did not exhibit much displeasure at things that were not pleasant—removing a splinter, being inoculated by the doctor when there was a cholera scare, or her father's punishment of being confined to her room when she strayed too far or did not return home on time. Her emotional makeup was surely different. Hidden beneath the beautiful, thick mane of hair were the scars and disfigurations on her scalp and skull, the evidence of the damage suffered during her difficult birth. Sometimes she would finish her mother's sentences, exhibiting a strange sense of telepathic knowledge. Without words, she was able to detect things her mother was thinking. It confused both of them since she began to react before her mother even completed her thoughts. She had an ability to predict rainstorms and lightning, windstorms and excessive heat. At times she became distracted when she knew suddenly that someone was ill or someone had died.

Her mother told her never to tell anyone of these things or let anyone know of her abilities, for fear that they would think her witch-like—or worse, crazy.

Some of the Italians, most particularly in Sicilian villages, believed in *il mal' occhio,* the evil eye. The belief was that someone could put a curse on you. There were, however, those who could, through a certain ritual, dispel the evil. The curse could begin with headaches, upset stomach, or some other malady. The cure involved certain prayers and incantations over a bowl of water with olive oil poured in the center. The oil, of course, stayed together and centered as "the eye." If the ritual was done correctly, the oil and water mixed, dispelling the evil eye. However, as superstitious as these town folks were, when they sought help from such a curse, they were much less able to accept someone with Bettina's strange behavior, and they might think she was indeed possessed. When she approached some women with small children, they were uneasy and shied away not so much from fear but a kind of uncertainty. Others knew her to be unusual but acceptable, again a paradox.

CHAPTER 2

ON THIS PARTICULAR day, the young, prince-like second son of Dom Tomasso Scalise, Enrico, encountered the beautiful Bettina in the hilly olive grove. He halted his horse by the tree where she stood. "Bella Bettina, come sta?" (Beautiful Bettina, how are you?) he asked her.

He looked down at her, drawn to her iridescent blue eyes, and was hypnotized. "Oh," she replied as if she hadn't been engaged in conversation for quite some time. "I wish I could be that little yellow bird in the tree so I too could fly to the top and look out over the land. I wish I knew the bird's song." And with that, she sang a song so sweet it could be the envy of the Sirens.

Enrico was captivated. His horse became a bit restless, gently baying and its head and hoofs shifting as Enrico held back the reins. Leading his horse to a nearby tree and tethering the reins firmly to a low branch, he asked Bettina what she was doing in the grove. "We need more olives," Bettina answered quickly. "Mama needs more olives." She hadn't expected him to get off the horse, let alone so quickly. She stepped back nervously. Bettina was much more comfortable sitting beside a tree or sifting through the base of the ravine for a treasure like a shiny stone. She was much happier in the country than in town. Enrico sensed she was uncomfortable and apologized. Bettina knew who he was and had seen him pass by on his big horse several times. A fully mature animal, the horse was larger than most in the region and a rarity. Donkeys were the usual beasts of transportation, so this shiny, chestnut-colored horse was a sign of status and wealth. Enrico had noticed her gathering olives and collecting wildflowers but never gave her a moment's thought until now. "What do you want?" she asked.

"I don't know really," Enrico replied. "I just saw you there and thought you might want to talk." Bettina didn't answer but simply smiled. Enrico looked into her blue eyes and again told her how beautiful she was. Again she smiled. She had never been spoken to like this before.

"What's in the basket?" he asked. It was a wicker basket covered with a white linen cloth.

"Olives, of course," she answered just as a dry leaf from a tree fluttered down and landed in her hair. She reached up to remove it, but it was already tangled.

"Let me help," Enrico said and stepped to her side. He could smell the sweet scent of her hair and, after he removed the leaf, began to stroke it. "Your hair is very soft and nice," he murmured.

Bettina froze; she had never had anyone she didn't know touch her. Enrico began stroking her cheek softly with the back of his right hand. He lost all sense of surrounding, seeing only her exquisite beauty. Something stirred in him he had never felt before. He just stood there stroking her cheek. Bettina, still frozen, didn't know how to react. Still stroking her cheek, Enrico grew closer to her and found himself standing in front of her, his chest against her bosom. His left arm circled her waist and drew her closer. Not understanding what was happening, Bettina decided to concentrate on the little yellow bird in the tree pecking at his wing. Enrico's left hand wandered down her cheek. Her neck was warm and firm. He could feel the muscles and tendons in her neck and shoulders. Her laced peasant dress, typical of the region, exposed the top of her breasts. His hand drifted slowly down and rested there. Bettina saw the little bird had been joined by a friend. They were turning to face each other, then turning away and pecking at their wing and breast feathers. His hand moved inside her bodice, and he cupped her breast. He guided her slowly to the back of the olive tree. She could still see the two birds. Enrico put his left hand behind her knee and moved her slowly to a sitting position. When Bettina reached the ground, she felt strange. She wondered why he was so close to her. Enrico began to loosen her bodice. She tried to move his hand away but could not. Enrico persisted and put his hand back and laid his full weight on top of her. Confusion was replaced by uneasiness. Why was he doing this? Enrico pulled down his pants and groped at her undergarments. Suddenly, she felt his hands exploring her genitals. He inserted his fingers in her. She was stunned and froze. He continued to be aroused, then got on top of her. Then with a flash of pain, she felt him enter her. She tried to push him aside, gasping for air, but Enrico was too strong and kept pushing, pushing, pushing. He groaned, and as quickly as it began, it was over. Enrico jumped up quickly. His face was flushed, and his genitals glistened with a mixture of blood and semen. Bettina was relieved it was over but wondered about the blood. She pulled her dress down and stood up, still feeling pain between her legs. She felt a warm trickle of blood running down her legs. Enrico looked at Bettina. She stood before him, a bewildered, wide-eyed woman-child. He was at once appalled, guilt-ridden, and fearful. He knew what he had done was wrong. The magnitude of his actions kicked in. He had raped a helpless, innocent virgin, a cursed act.

Bettina's dress clung to her body, and blood saturated her skirt. She reminded him of the traditional slaughtering of the lambs he saw during his youth. He felt sick and disgusted with himself. Then he panicked. The enchantment had disappeared. He looked around quickly to see if anyone had witnessed the encounter. Enrico didn't know what to do next. How could he hide what he had done? Looking at her, Enrico was overcome with a sense of dread. His mind raced. He knew he had to cover up his crime.

He grabbed a linen cloth from her basket and approached Bettina. She stepped back, head turned down and away so as to not look at him. She had been silent during the encounter except when she let out a small whimper when he pounded his pelvic bone against hers. Enrico took her hand in an effort to comfort her and knelt down to wipe off her legs, trying to erase the evidence. He rubbed her dress with the cloth until it was nearly dry. She stood like a statue, not so much in fear as in bewilderment. What had just happened? Bettina had never been told anything about sexual intercourse. "We don't talk about things like that," her mother had said when Bettina questioned her one time about the farm animal's actions during mating season.

"Don't be afraid," said Enrico. "This is only between you and me. Don't tell anyone, and I'll make sure not to tell what you did." Enrico's logic was to convince Bettina that it was her fault. She had flirted with him, and she would have to keep quiet about the attack. He looked her over again. And with that, Enrico straightened his clothing, mounted his horse, and rode a few yards down the path. When he glanced back, Bettina had not moved. He rode out of sight.

Bettina stood there for quite some time just staring. Finally, she looked up into the tree. The birds had flown away. Silently, she picked up the basket and began to gather more olives.

CHAPTER 3

"**BETTINA, COME TU** stato tardi?" (Why are you late?) asked her mother as Bettina placed the basket with the olives on the kitchen table.

"I'm late because I gathered lots of olives today, Mama," she replied.

Beatrice Castellucci looked into the basket. It was filled to the brim with olives. "Grazie, Bettina," said Beatrice.

Bettina smiled and went to her bedroom. She undressed and laid her soiled clothing at the foot of her bed. Bathing, she ran her hands over her genitals. They were still sore. A sticky, bloody substance smeared on her hands. But bathing felt good. It washed away his smell and his touch.

Beatrice walked into her room and picked up her clothing for washing. The dress was still a mess, and Beatrice noticed Bettina had folded her undergarments inside. First, Beatrice noticed the blood smear. Then she smelled an odor distinctively male. Beatrice looked more closely and realized it was semen. She was stunned. How could this be? Bettina never associated with men or even boys. She never seemed to have an interest, and Beatrice attributed this to her daughter's slowness. The only time the subject had been broached was a couple years ago when Bettina, then fifteen, had witnessed two of the cows mating. And she remembered her answer. Now, at age seventeen, Bettina had experienced a sexual encounter—but with whom? Where? And how did it happen? Sickened, Beatrice was determined to find out.

"Bettina, now that you have bathed, tell me, did you enjoy the grove today?" asked Beatrice.

Bettina stared off briefly and said, "I saw two yellow birds."

"Did you see anything else?" her mother questioned.

"The man on the horse," Bettina replied.

"Do you know this man on the horse?" Beatrice pressed on.

"I'm not sure, but I've seen him before on the horse," she answered.

"Does he have a name?"

"I don't know, Mama. What are we eating tonight? I am very hungry."

Beatrice looked at Bettina. She seemed calm enough, but there was an unusual tiredness in her eyes. Bettina was not bounding about with her tireless energy.

Over the next few days, Beatrice received bits and pieces of information about the man on the horse. There were a few young men who rode the countryside on large grand horses. Eventually, she narrowed it down to two men, brothers in the same family.

CHAPTER 4

THE SCALISCE FAMILY had lived in the Sicilian countryside for well over four hundred years. They were well known from Palermo to Messina, and some Scalisce families in Corleone and Messina were said to be of Roman ancestry. They owned land and businesses, and with that, their power and wealth were reason alone to command respect and apprehension, if not fear. Most of the family history was known not only in Sicily but beyond, on the mainland as well. The family was regarded, for the most part, as wielding its power and influence in a fair and just manner. While some families of similar wealth and stature used their influence to abuse and take advantage of others, the Scalisce family did not. When a fair bargain was made, it was honored. They did not exploit the poor, forcing them into servitude, but paid fair wages for work and fair prices for goods. The family was extremely loyal as well, and those under their protection, a friend, family member, or business associate, could always count on their help. But as much as they were fair and honest, the Scalisce clan could also be fierce and vindictive. Anyone who stole or cheated a Scalisce knew their penance would be swift and harsh. The family acted as the old padrones had taught them. Their system was feudal, benevolent monarchs, little princes, dukes, and barons in little fiefdoms.

They lived on old family homestead compounds harkening back to the days when monarchs lived in castles and their realms included those who lived within their sphere.

When a matter went before a magistrate, it was very likely the judge had the Scalisce family to thank for his position and knew he must serve his benefactors. His decisions, no doubt, were in the interests of the Scalisces. When necessary, the magistrate would seek the padrone's advice. This held true for the mayor, the police officers, and postmen as well. Thus, the rule of law and decisions affecting everyday life were at the will of the Scalisces.

Dom Tomasso Scalisce had two sons. Pietro was the firstborn and heir. He would inherit social status and power much as the firstborn of a king would inherit his father's throne. He bore the name of his grandfather in the tradition of his ancestors. His second son, Enrico, two years younger, was given the name of his maternal grandfather. This too was a sign of respect for his wife's family, with whom they retained close ties. There was also another reason. His wife, Sophia Scalisce, referred to as "La Donna" Scalisce, had two younger sisters but no brothers. Her mother, Maria Carmela Scalisce, was surprised and humbled that her son-in-law would honor her husband in such a manner. Showing such a sign of respect had a number of benefits. Not only did it please his wife and family greatly, but it also sent a message to the people in the *paese*, the town and countryside, of what a generous soul he was. The priest who baptized Enrico also made a special blessing to Don Tomasso for his honorable gesture.

Pietro was constantly at his father's side. He was well schooled in both the traditional sense as well as with the ways of the family's business and heritage. Enrico, on the other hand, was an uninspired student at best. One year, on their birthdays, Don Tomasso presented each of his sons a foal. Twin foals were quite a rarity. Both were chestnuts with white markings down their foreheads, regal from notable bloodlines of horses owned by the Scalisce family for generations.

As the sons grew, Pietro studied and eventually graduated with honors from the Università di Bologna, a most prestigious school and one that his father had attended and later was a benefactor. Enrico, too, attended the university but was ambivalent about his classes. He loved being in Bologna, free from the confines of the Sicilian countryside. He enjoyed himself so much, in fact, that he failed to show up for most of his classes. In his third year, Enrico came to an impasse. During his first two years, the hierarchy had looked the other way. Enrico was now only occasionally attending classes and never taking the required tests. Professor Adrio Specchio of Carini, an elderly, well-respected member of the faculty who had taught Don Tomasso, himself, was concerned.

He sent a message to Don Tomasso in a delicate and diplomatic manner, and a visit was arranged.

"Professor Specchio, con piace and honore," said Don Tomasso as the professor was led into the study.

"Grazie."

"I received your letter," said Don Tomasso as he offered café and biscotti to him.

"Si, si," he said.

"Enrico has been helping me with my business in Bologna. He oversees the shipments of our citrus fruits," Don Tomasso lied. "Perhaps Enrico should withdraw for this year and begin another time when he's not so busy," he suggested.

"Bene," said Professor Specchio with relief. A most uncomfortable situation was now diffused by Don Tomasso's good perception and solution. "I think this is a very good idea," he continued. "Enrico is a very smart and respectable young man. He has his family's honorable traits. Enrico is also well liked by the other students, a most popular young man. A hiatus will refresh him, I'm sure."

"Grazie," said Don Tomasso, feeling his anger building.

He ordered his son to return home immediately. He was embarrassed by Enrico's behavior and shortcomings at school. "Allora tu non piace a scuola, fare lavoro," he told Enrico. (Now you don't like school, you will work.)

Enrico was petrified. He remembered working on the farm, tended by peasants growing produce and raising animals. As a small boy, he had witnessed the slaughtering of the lambs. They brought the animals to the barn, and as one man held the animal, another took a sharp blade and slit his throat. Blood would gush to the ground and splatter on the men's leather aprons. He understood livestock was raised for food, but watching the life run out of the animals caused a lump in his throat and his stomach to knot. As he grew, his father took his two sons to the farm at Easter. There his father performed the traditional slaughter of the baby lambs and baby goats. Later, he had the two young men perform the task. Enrico knew it was the Sicilian way of life, one that would carry on through the ages, but Enrico always felt his knees go weak with that first slice to the neck. He knew better than to give away his discomfort. His father, brother, and the laborers went about the procedure in solemn gesture. A sacred duty, one emulating the sacrifices told of time and time again in the Old Testament.

Fortunately, his father assigned him the duty of traveling to village farms and vineyards to transfer funds and relay information. "His fine horse was fine transportation through the hills," said his father.

Enrico was extremely unhappy leaving Bologna. He enjoyed city life, the excitement, the activity, and various diversions, including the bistros and the willing girls. With friends, Enrico found the seedy side, particularly places where they drank wine and found the *putana*, the whores. The few girls at the university were nearly all virtuous, except the ugly ones, but "le prostitute," the prostitutes, simply had a price for their affections.

Back home and under the watchful eye of his father and older brother, he felt confined, and he was also known in every town and village nearby. He ventured to various towns looking for any sort of entertainment, but it was useless. He longed for the freedom he had found at the university. The girls of the towns were virtuous and were virgins until their wedding nights. There was no place for the *putane* in the villages and towns of the countryside. Enrico had no outlet for his suppressed desires. Then, that one fateful day, he saw Bettina in the olive grove.

CHAPTER 5

SIGNORA BEATRICE CASTELLUCCI was not educated beyond grade school. After graduating, her mother, a seamstress, put her to work. She still felt, however, that it was important for Beatrice to keep learning; she worked hard to earn extra money so Beatrice could read books, newspapers, periodicals, and even technical manuals. She had her read operas and would occasionally send Beatrice to the local opera house where her mother made costumes. Beatrice was also exposed to a wide range of authors and artists, including Machiavelli, Da Vinci, Michelangelo, Dante, Puccini, and the masters of music and politics. Her mother quizzed her on philosophy and history at a time when women, it was thought, should learn to keep a house, marry, and raise children. Husbands provided for wives, and that was that. But she had a thirst for knowledge and instilled that in Beatrice.

Beatrice was bright and a quick learner. She never accepted things at face value and was very analytical. Beatrice turned events and matters over and over in her mind, examining cause and effect from various angles and perspectives. Perceptive and patient, she chose her words carefully to both opportunity and adversaries.

Now, the signora had a problem with Bettina and "the man on the horse." She knew she had to be very cautious accusing a Scalise of anything, especially something this terrible. She saw Enrico several times in various places and found that it was he who usually rode the big horse through the hills. She learned his brother accompanied his father every day and traveled mostly by train or boat to important meetings in Palermo, Naples, Rome, and to other foreign countries, so it was more than likely it was Enrico Scalisce who had taken advantage of her Bettina. But she had to be sure.

The train was the major form of transportation, and the stations bustled with activity. Beatrice knew the train on Wednesday was bound for the port of Messina, and the Scalisce goods were usually loaded on this particular train. That would be the place to find Enrico.

The sun had shown bright that Wednesday morning. The sweet-smelling breezes of a Sicilian day and the bustling about the station made for a carnivalesque atmosphere. Beatrice took her daughter by the hand and walked slowly down the platform by the station. Bettina was dressed in a dress strikingly similar to the one stored and rumpled in the bottom of Beatrice's wooden blanket chest. They walked down the platform steps and along the track and stopped where some men were loading boxes onto the train. Enrico stood next to a man holding a sheaf of papers marking shipment quantities. He didn't notice the two women approaching. "Signore Scalisce!" called Beatrice as the man, a load master, turned to look at the boxes before him.

"Si?" he asked absentmindedly. "What do you want?" Then he saw the girl standing a few feet behind the woman. He froze. In his eyes, Beatrice saw what she had come to confirm, panic.

At first, Enrico thought he was seeing an illusion. Then his throat tightened, and his knees went weak. "Si, si?" he stuttered.

"When does the train leave?" asked Beatrice, knowing Enrico would be aware of the train's schedule.

Enrico couldn't take his eyes off Bettina. "I don't know," he managed to say, his heart beating wildly, and his face flushed red.

Beatrice turned to leave, calling, "Vieni, Bettina," but Bettina just kept staring at Enrico. "Vieni," she called again (Come!). Then the signora looked directly into the eyes of Enrico with an anguished face, lifted her right hand, made a fist, and bit it. She turned to Bettina, gently took her hand, and walked away briskly.

Enrico was astonished. He knew now that what he had done was coming back to haunt him. All the repercussions he dreaded about that day rushed back at him. He felt a sharp pain in the pit of his stomach and began to quiver and sweat.

Signora Castellucci and Bettina reached the far side of the loading area. The signora made the sign of the cross. She was shaking yet felt a sense of extreme clarity. She knew exactly what she had to do next.

CHAPTER 6

BEATRICE'S HUSBAND, DONATO, was a good man and always concerned about providing for his family. He made sure his household was never wanting. He knew how the poor lived. He remembered how difficult it was for his own mother and father to provide for their large family—ten children, his widowed grandmother, and his elderly uncle who had been born with a birth defect, leaving his left leg nearly crippled, causing him to use a crutch. This vision burned in his mind's eye. He would never allow his family to sink to the poverty-ridden social order of town. He had far too much pride.

His wife, Beatrice, was his refuge, his support, and the love of his life. He felt he owed her everything.

Beatrice loved Donato equally. She had kept quiet about Bettina's rape during her investigation but now felt she had to tell him. It was only fair. Gathering her courage that night, Beatrice said to Donato, "Bettina has been disgraced. It was the son of Don Scalisce. Your daughter is no longer a virgin."

Donato was shocked and angered. He could not speak for some time. He began to weep. He wept for his daughter. He wept for his wife's pain. He wept for himself. Finally, he said, "Mi pieda u scubetta e mazzare!" (I will get my shotgun and kill him!)

"No, Donato, no," Beatrice replied. "That is not the thing to do. I have a plan. I think I should tell Don Scalisce what his son Enrico did to Bettina, and then he will do that which is just." Donato understood his wife's reasoning. He knew if he shot the boy, he himself would be hunted down and killed. His family could suffer the same fate.

The next day, Beatrice and Bettina made plans to meet with Don Scalisce. Beatrice was calm and confident as she walked the roadway leading up to Casa Scalise, over the stones on the roadway placed in the ancient way the Romans laid on the still active Appian Way. Each side of the road was lined with lush palm trees. The road was a mile long up the hill to the house grounds. At the entrance to the estate was a large circular piazza with a fountain in the center. The fountain, with its sculptures of dolphins and sirens lined with stone-carved ropes of flowers and fruit, rivaled the artwork fountains of Rome itself. There was a center, huge, sweeping stairway to a three-tiered deck leading to a columned portico with two sets of bronze doors, and in the center, there were gigantic marble columns and an archway, which led to a deeply recessed set of even larger bronze doors with artistic reliefs of angelical figures. The building was three stories high with balconies and columned features overlooking the valley below. It was indeed a fortress of stone. The gothic windows of stained glass were deeply recessed and covered with artistic wrought iron. The rear of the house was less artistic but with more functional protection, simple stone pillars on all windows.

Three men on the front deck watched as Beatrice and Bettina made their way up the hill. Once they got to the top, the older of the three men, Pino, walked down to her. "Signora, che cosa fa qui?" (What are you doing here?) she was asked.

"Volere vista Don Scalisce. Io sono Signora Castelluci. Mi volere dici una cosa tanto importante da su figlio" (I want to see Don Scalisce, I am Signora Castellucci. I want to tell him something very important about his son.), she answered.

Pino looked her over and said, "Rimanere ca" (Stay here), and he lead her and Bettina to a stone bench. He went up the stairs and disappeared.

The two sat and waited. After about twenty minutes, he reappeared. He again looked the two women over and asked, "Che sono nella tua mano?" (What's in your hand?)

"Una comisa" (A dress). She opened the cloth bag she carried and showed him. He nodded and led them up the stairs, into the last pair of doors, and into a sitting room. He asked the women to sit. Again, they waited about twenty minutes.

Don Scalisce entered the room, and his eldest son followed him. "Signora, con piacere" (Signora, I am pleased to see you), Don Scalisce said as he entered the room. "Che cosa volere a me?" (What is it you want of me?)

Beatrice stood up. "Questa e mia figlia Bettina" (This is my daughter, Bettina), she said. "E questa e una chamisa de Bettina quando tu figlio Enrico ha visita mia figlia nella albero di olivo nella montagna" (And this is the dress Bettina wore when she saw your son Enrico in the olive trees on the mountain), she said calmly. She unfurled the dress and the undergarments pinned to it. The bloodstains and marks were seen by the two men. "Ora mia figlia non e un virgine (My daughter is now not a virgin). Enrico ho fatto questa cosa de questa biccerede (Enrico has done this thing to this little child). Mia figlia non ha troppo intelegenzia normale (My daughter does not have normal intelligence). Enrico fatto questa cosa con forza (Enrico forced her to do this thing). Pero mi sensa una cosa violentare (I think it may be rape). Ma, tu figlio ti amo mia figlia?" (Does your son love my daughter?) she said.

The Don looked closely at the girl and then back at the mother. He was totally unprepared for this confrontation. She folded the dress, put it back in the bag, and said, "Scusare Signor" (Excuse me, sir). She took Bettina's hand. Her flashing blue eyes and quiet demeanor beguiled the old man. He stood there with his mouth open.

"Signora ha pazienza la se stare ora. Mi io mi chiamo a lei" (Signora, have patience; let things be now. I will call on you), the Don said.

With that, she left, holding onto Bettina's hand.

Enrico watched from behind a bush as Signora Castellucci and her daughter left the house. He felt trapped. His first thought was to mount his horse and flee. He would ride as far away as he could. But to where? And how would he survive?

The Don sent his elder son to find Enrico. He was scheduled to be at the citrus groves, but after searching, he could not be found there. He finally saw him near the house. "Enrico, il Don volare tu va alla casa subito" (Enrico, the Don wants you to come to the house immediately), said the brother.

Then he heard his father calling his name. "Enrico, we need to talk," boomed the voice of Don Scalisce. His conscience began to set in.

Ever since the encounter with Bettina, his guilt had been tremendous. Enrico was having a hard time sleeping, and when he did, his dreams served only to wake him. They were nightmares, dreams of blood, whips, chains, jail, and death. He had committed a terrible crime, and now it was time to face it like a man. Suffer the consequences whatever they may be.

Slowly he walked up to the front door. His father was in his study. The Don sat in his study alone. He thought long and hard on the visit of these two women. He also rolled over again and again in his mind all that Signora Castellucci had to say, particularly her last words. "Does your son love my daughter?" He knew that the woman would not come to him with a false story. He also noted that she had little to say; she merely stated in a few sentences the entire concern and issue. The young girl, a virgin with an abnormality, had been with her son, and that was the Don's focus. What to do? This was his dilemma: what to do? Enrico was irresponsible in schooling and conscientious at work. The Don knew that he had indulged himself both at school and when he would be a few days late returning from business in Palermo or another city. He also knew that this was his second born and that second sons had a particular burden to bear since they were always second to the firstborn in so many ways. Now the Don was faced with being both a father to his son and the Don, "un humane di rispetto" (a man of respect). He had to uphold a code of honor expected of his social position. "Enrico, tu sedere prossimo di me" (Enrico, sit here next to me), said Don Tomasso. "Do you know the two women who visited me?" Don Scalisce asked. "Signora Castellucci and her daughter, Bettina?"

He felt the weight of the question as if suddenly a hundred pounds had been lowered on his shoulders. "Si," answered Enrico. He knew that was how he was expected to respond directly and without banter.

"The daughter, she is very beautiful?" asked the Don.

Enrico was convinced the entire episode had been exposed. "Si," he replied again. Bluntly, Don asked Enrico if he had ever "visited" with Bettina.

Enrico knew he had to answer directly but carefully. "Bettina sono una femina differente. Bettina e molto gentile. Ho vista quando era nella le albero di olivo. Mi sono inamorata e fare sesso. Io non conosce perche Io una poco amore per questa femina. Io non ti sapaere che egli sono una virgine. Ti voula stare con Bettina ma la sua mamma de domanda qualche cosa de Bettina" (Bettina is a different woman. Bettina is very gentile. I saw her when I went through the olive groves and had sex. I was infatuated with her. I did not know she was a virgin. I want to be with her, but her mother always demands many things of Bettina), said Enrico.

"Ti amo?" (You love her?) asked the Don.

"Si," said Enrico.

"Allura tu ha fatto una infominia con una giovina, una virgine. Questa cosa sono terrible. Ma ora io pensa qualche cosa di fare" (Now you have committed a hideous thing with a young girl, a virgin. This is a terrible thing, but I will think about what is to be done), stated the Don.

The Don nodded, and Enrico rose and took his father's hand and kissed it. "Mi dispiace qualche cosa che io ho a fare (I am sorry for what I have done). Era una cosa stupido. Io non conosci perche io ha fatto questa cosa (It was stupid. I don't know why I did this thing)," Enrico said. His eyes turned red and watery, but he held his composure.

The Don sighed and took a deep breath. He was tormented and torn. This boy of his was fascinated with a young, virgin town girl. He said he loved her. The Don knew how beautiful and attractive this girl was. If she was slow, she might be easy prey for his worldly son. What to do?

Several weeks passed, and the Don still had not come up with an acceptable solution.

CHAPTER 7

"BETTINA, CHE COSA?" (Bettina, what is it?) Bettina and her mother were walking to church when suddenly Bettina lurched to the side of the road and vomited.

After the girl composed herself, she stood there. "Non sta bene. Sono mala stomaco (I don't feel good. I have a stomachache). Sono tre giorni (It has been for three days)," she responded.

Her mother looked at her and had the look of shock and concern on her face. "Noi andare a casa" (We go home), her mother said. When they arrived at home, Beatrice told Bettina to remove her dress. She began to grasp her ankles and noticed that when she did so, the flesh remained slightly indented for some time. She then pulled her slip and bra down and examined her breasts. As she squeezed, the girl retracted and said she was sore. Bettina's nipples were reddish and enlarged. Beatrice said to Bettina, "Fare a vestire" (Get dressed).

She took the girl in hand and then walked to the house of her friend, Filomena, the midwife. "Signora," she began, choking back tears. "Filomena," she began again, but her throat closed, and she began to weep.

"Vene ca" (Come here), Filomena said. She sat the two at the kitchen table. "Che suchesa? Una cosa da mala a Bettina?" (What is it? Is Bettina ill?) she asked. The mother nodded her head. "Vene figlia" (Come, daughter), said Filomena and led the girl into a room off the kitchen. This room had been an extra room, but she used it when she brought pregnant women to her house, some to examine and some to give birth and some to stay with their newborns.

Nearly an hour passed when the two emerged from the room. "Bettina, tu figlia, sono con bambino, gravida" (Bettina, your daughter, is with child, pregnant), Filomena whispered to Beatrice.

She gasped and wept again. Pregnant! The girl was pregnant. She could hardly believe her ears. "Come?" (How?) asked Filomena quickly to Signora Castelluci. "Una Scalisce u figlio Enrico, Enrico, Enrico Scalisce ho fatto questa da mia bicheredu questa dolce bambino" (Scalisce the son, Enrico, Enrico, Enrico has done this to my little daughter, this sweet little baby), said her mother.

"La se stare con me. La se stare con me per qualche giorno" (Let her stay with me. Let her stay with me for a few days), Filomena whispered.

Beatrice shook her head. "No!" She knew that Filomena was willing to risk herself by aborting the child. If she was caught, she would be considered a murderess. Also, the act itself would automatically condemn her daughter and Filomena to excommunication from the church. More importantly, Filomena would be condemned in God's eyes. Beatrice could not live with that prospect. Beatrice walked over to Filomena. She took both her hands, looked into her eyes for several seconds, lowered her head slightly, and wagged it side to side. She knew of the friend's gesture of support, her loyalty, her love of the child and for her, but she could not agree. There she stood for several minutes.

Filomena looked up at her and clasped their hands together. Then she nodded as if to say, "I understand."

"Filomena, per piace, vene con me alla casa di Scalisce. Io ho bisogno ti dice questa cosa di Signore Scalisce" (Filomena, please, come with me to Scalisce house. I need to tell Mr. Scalisce of this thing), she said. The woman nodded again.

"Don Scalisce che sono due donna alla porta Signora Castelluci e la donna che fare naiscere il bambini" (Don Scalisce, there are two women at the door, Signora Castelluci and the woman who does childbirth), announced Vittorio, the houseman and one of the Don's trusted friends and bodyguards.

"Fare entrare" (Let them in), said the Don.

The two women entered the Don's study, which was a room off the main entry hall of the grand house. There the walls were lined with books, maps, drawings, a large globe and telescope, and elaborate furnishings gathered from all over the world. "Signora voule una café?" (Ladies, would you want a coffee?) said the Don.

Signora Castelluci hesitated, then spoke in nearly a whisper. "Mia figlia sono con bambino, Signor (My daughter is with child, sir). Questa bambino era fatto a tu figlio (This child was done by your son)."

The Don looked at her and then the other woman. "Vero, me sapere questa cosa e vero" (True, I know this is true), said Filomena, with her eyes darting at the Don, nervous but in control.

The Don turned away for a moment. He was concerned that he would reveal his embarrassment with a reddened face. After a few moments, he regained his composure. "Ti sono vero? Ma questa bambino, non se possible ha un altro padre?" (You are sure? But this baby, are you sure there isn't possibility another father?)

"No! Bettina era una virgine. Nessuno, Nessuno ma tuo figlio ha fatto sesso con Bettina" (No! Bettina was a virgin. No one, no one but your son had sex with Bettina), said Beatrice emphatically. "Solo tu figlio!" (Only your son!) She looked the Don straight in the eyes as she said that.

"Allora mio figlio ho ditto a me che questa ragazza di te e un amore. Questa bambino e' una bambino d'amore. Allora ti fare sposare" (My son told me that he loves this girl and this child is a child of love. So now they will marry), said the Don in a matter-of-fact way.

Filomena looked at Beatrice. Both were stunned. The Don had considered this problem for some time, but in that moment, the solution was clear. These two were together. His son said he loved this beautiful girl. Now she carried his child. The judicious end to the situation was marriage.

Signora Castelluci said, "Signore, volere un poco di acqua" (Sir, I'd like a little water.) She was considering now what he had said: marriage? She thought, well, here was a chance for her daughter to be provided for, cared for the rest of her life. Here the child would also be cared for and be a Scalisce a noble name. At some point, Bettina would have to be alone. The Castellucis did not have long lifespans, and she had some health problems. This might just be a way that would ensure poor Bettina's future. She drank the water, cleared her throat, and said, "Si-Sposare" (Yes, marry.)

"Allora noi sono accordarsi" (Now we agree), said the Don.

The fate of her daughter was about to change.

CHAPTER 6

"ENRICO," THE DON began. "Questa Signora Castelluci ho fare una visito. Ti dice che la sua figla sono gravida. Ti dice che il bambino sono tu. E vero?" (That Signora Castelluci came to visit me. She told me her daughter was pregnant. She said that the child is yours. Is that true?) the Don asked.

Enrico was stunned and panicked. Pregnant? The girl was pregnant from just one quick episode together? How could that be? Enrico wanted to say no, but he knew that his father would be extremely angry if he lied. He did not have time to think of anything to say. "E possibile" (It's possible), he said, pretending to remain calm.

His father took a deep breath before repeating, "E possibile, E possible," and then closed his eyes. He wanted to be composed, to ward off the extreme anger and frustration welling up inside of him. "Tu sapire che lo fatto?" (You know what you've done?) he asked. Enrico hung his head and nodded. "Tu sono in amore con questa ragazza?" (Are you in love with this girl?) he asked.

Enrico was now so panicked and ashamed of the shame that he had visited upon his father, his family, his name, and the girl that he knew he could only answer, "Ti amo" (I love her).

"Allora tu desiderio fare sposare!" (Then you want to get married!) the Don exclaimed in a voice much louder than he intended. "Allora finite (Then it is done)! Noi ti dice tu madre a la familia e la familia de Castellucci, pero questa ragazza voule te anche (We will tell your mother and the family and the family of the Castellucis, if this girl wants you also)."

Enrico just stood in silence. Marriage! He was supposed to marry this girl? He began to sweat, his throat closed, and his stomach convulsed.

"Allora ti chiamo tu madre qui" (Now call your mother here), the Don ordered. Enrico knew this to be his most stringent expression of a command. He also knew that he could not object to his father's request. He was trapped.

Enrico did not say much when his mother came into the room. She already knew about the earlier visit of Signora Castellucci and her son's admission of what he had done with her daughter, Bettina. Now the father had explained that because of this pregnancy and the desire of Enrico and the girl's mother, they agreed to marry for love and the sake of their unborn child. It was not said but understood that they were also marrying for the honor of both families. This girl was no putane (whore). She came from a good, God-fearing, churchgoing family and was known to be righteous even if a bit strange. Signora Scalisce said nothing; she knew the matter had already been settled by her husband, and she would not dare question his judgment, even where her son was involved. A wedding there would be.

The Don sent Vittorio to the Castellucci house that evening to ask if Mr. Castellucci would visit him the next day. He agreed.

"Signore Castellucci, piace," the Don greeted Signor Castellucci with an outstretched hand at the front door, not the typical entrance for a visitor. The Don nearly always had someone else show a visitor to the appropriate meeting room, usually the study. Castellucci put his hand out, but only three fingertips touched in a momentary gesture, and they both quickly withdrew their hands. Bettina's father looked stoic. He was dressed for the meeting and wore a starched white shirt, a short black jacket, and ironed pants. The Don, as was his tradition, wore a custom-made linen shirt slightly bloused at the shoulder with mother-of-pearl buttons and wide black pants with leather boots. His family crest was monogrammed on the right cuff of this sleeve. He led Castellucci into the large living room, a sprawling combination of furnishings, a piano, and fine artwork. The room's large windows allowed expansive views of the landscape. The Don led his guest through the large room and to the veranda. There, set on a small table, was a silver coffeepot, demitasse cups, a crystal bottle, which contained anisette, and a silver plate with biscotti. "Sedere" (Sit). The Don offered a chair. Castelluci sat. "Mi dispiace io non ha parlare di qualche cosa di il noi ragazzi primo di stagiorno" (I am very sorry that we have not spoken about our children before today), the Don said. "Allora noi volere sposare" (Now they want to marry), added the Don as he poured two cups of espresso coffee. Castellucci nodded, unsure of what Scalisce was thinking but somewhat more at ease having been greeted by the Don himself at the door and being offered coffee. "Tu moglio volere fare tutti cosi con il mio moglio per la chiesa e la festivale" (Your wife will want to do all the things with my wife for the church and the festival), said the Don.

"Vero, Signore" (That is true, sir), said Signore Castellucci.

"La ragazzi e la famigla ho bisogno di parlare e decidere una giorno di spasato" (The children and the families will need to talk about deciding on a wedding day), said the Don.

"Si, si" (Yes, yes), said Castellucci. He had not been sure of the Scalisces' reaction to the whole idea, but now he knew that the Don, at least for now anyway, was accepting that a marriage would occur. Castellucci was suspicious of the "padroni," as were most of the town folk (ruling class leaders), and never felt sure that they did not have some other motives than what they presented at first. Castellucci was a simple man but with a fearful conviction. His family was always his prime concern. He sipped his coffee but refused the anisette.

The Don arranged a time when both families could meet, and at the end of the conversation, he stood up and clasped both hands over Castellucci's. "We agree," he said. "Now your family is with mine. Now we make a family for our children." He looked Castellucci straight in the eye and could feel his sincerity. It was done.

On the way home, Castellucci thought about the marriage. He knew his family, including his friends, was now "with" the Don. The benefit of this alliance was as much economical as it was social. Even more, it was a security pledge. The Don had bestowed his blessing on the marriage as well as accepting the Castellucci family. There would be no scandal, no embarrassment to either family. They had done the right thing. *E bene di Dio* (It's God's blessing) he thought as he neared his doorway.

CHAPTER 9

"LA CHIESA DI Santa Lucia, AD 1430" read the old sign at the base of the steps leading up the large carved wooden doors of the ancient church at the north end of La Piazza di Santo Pietro. The builders had proclaimed the church would still be standing when Christ returned to earth on judgment day. This church was a befitting place for the plethora of marriages performed inside its walls through the centuries, vows withstanding the test of time. Here Bettina and Enrico would wed. The whole town would turn out on that day, and Father Cattaggio would read the bonds at Sunday Mass so the marriage ceremony could begin. He would need to see the couple both together and separately and discuss the marriage with the parents. The archbishop from Palermo would perform the ceremony, and a reception for the town folk, all of whom were invited, would be set up in the large piazza. Thereafter, a family reception would take place at the Scalisce estate.

But before the announcement was made in church, the priest had a late-night visitor. Father Cattaggio's housekeeper, Yolanda, was a bent and crooked elderly peasant woman who was as much a housekeeper as she was a charity case taken in by the priest. She had sufficient help since the rectory staff also included the cook, the bell ringer, the maintenance man, and house manager. Often, a young priest would be assigned for a few months as well before moving on to another parish, and sometimes a nun would stay for a few months in order to help with particular projects. That evening, all the guests enjoyed a bountiful dinner and a bit of wine before retiring. Yolanda had just finished sweeping the kitchen and was about to go to bed when there was a knock on the big wooden door at the front of the living quarters of the rectory. "Padre, io vene" (Father, I go), she called, as she scurried to the door.

"Signora, I am Vittorrio of the house of Scalisce," he said, bowing to the old woman. "I know it is very late, but I must meet with Father Cattaggio for a few minutes."

"*Si*, stay here," Yolanda ordered and shuffled to the priest's parlor.

"*Fa be*ne, I'll see him," said the father tiredly. The man was escorted to the priest's parlor.

"Padre mi dispiace di disturbare a questa ora ma Signor Scalisce dire che cosa importani."

Over the next ten minutes, the man explained to the priest that the Don wanted the bonds, the vows, and all the protocol to be done exactly as he directed. There would be no educational period, simply the rosary and the stations of the cross. There would be no questions at confession, only the directive to live under the rule of God and the church's mandate to attend Mass. And there would be general absolution in the confessional and a blessing. Though Father Cattaggio raised an eyebrow at the request, he knew he must do as Scalisce wished. He was a powerful man within the church and had enough influence to have him recalled if he wanted. "Si," said the priest. "As you wish."

When Vittorrio finished, he handed the priest a small heavy sack. "Signore Scalisce has a great deal of respect for you," Vittorrio told him. "This gold is for the poor. Grazie."

"No," said Father Cattaggio. "This is not necessary," he protested quietly.

"The Signore knows there are many who could benefit from this money," Vittorrio said as he pressed the sack into his hand. "You're the one who can help them."

The priest stared at the sack for a few seconds, sighed, and finally said, "Si, grazie. Tell Signore Scalisce thank you." Vittorrio bowed, took the priest's hand at the fingertips, and pressed them.

After he left, Father Cattaggio sat in the parlor for a long while. Finally, he opened the sack and laid the contents on a small table. "Ventiottio, ventinovo, trenta," he counted. Thirty pieces of gold! He shook his head and returned the gold to the sack before taking one last sip of wine.

CHAPTER 10

THE MIDMORNING SUN was high in the sky; only a few wisps of white clouds drifted by. The town piazza was already abuzz with activity. During the night, a group of men had come to the piazza with brooms, brushes, shovels, and buckets. They cleaned the stone and the foundation. They also put pots of flowers and palms all around the square. Chairs were set up near the steps leading to the church. Banners with red streamers, some bearing the Scalisce family coat of arms, were hung along the outside of the church walls.

The inside of the church was also decorated with flowers, and each pew had a white linen ribbon and bow tied to it. Thus, the scene of Bettina and Enrico's wedding was set.

Father Cattaggio made all the church arrangements. Archbishop Delano would officiate.

Those gathered in the piazza chatted amongst themselves. Most questioned each other, Why? Why was the Scalisce son marrying beneath himself? Beautiful as she was, it was highly unusual. The buzz grew louder.

Suddenly, the sound of a street band was heard in the distance. The chatter turned to smiles as they began the march from the edge of town toward the square. The band was an announcement of the arrival of notable figures. An entourage of Catholic hierarchy rode in elaborate horse-drawn carriages following the band. Slowly they traveled up the hill. Those still at home opened second-story windows and balcony doors, waving and cheering. Some threw flowers. As the carriage drew closer, the cheering grew louder. Father Cataggio readied himself and appeared at the front door of the church, positioning himself as the official greeter. The parade gained followers as it traveled toward the church. As the carriages began to arrive, the priest was shocked to see Cardinal Calogero Pumilia sitting next to Archbishop Delano. It was no wonder everyone was so excited. This cardinal was the person closest to "Il Papa" (the pope) and was his ally, friend, and confidant. In Rome, he was known as "Il Martello" (The Hammer), and the pope counted on him to enforce his vision of the church. Also seated next to him was none other than Don Scalisce, chatting easily with the cardinal and occasionally waving to the crowd. The impact of the scene struck the priest, and at that moment, he realized how much power and influence the Scalisce family had. The cardinal was not only a stand-in for the pope, he was also the pope's anointed successor. Father Cataggio was absolutely stunned that the cardinal was attending a wedding here in the little town of Corleone.

Cardinal Pumilia stood over six feet tall and sported a grand mustache but no beard, something few cardinals ever wore. He was broad shouldered and blue eyed, unusual for a Sicilian man, as most were short and stocky with dark eyes and olive-colored skin. He was well educated and self-taught in the study of art and music. He also had the uncanny ability to solve even the most difficult of mathematical problems in little time. The cardinal was gregarious and humorous at times but kept strict to the vows of his office and priestly duties.

As the carriage arrived in front of the church, a loud cheer went up from the crowd. The cardinal and Don Scalisce waved. The cardinal, in his own true style, waded through the throng of people, making signs of the cross on foreheads and giving each one close to him a benediction. Some reached for his hand and kissed his ring, the sign of his office, their eyes streaming with tears of joy. "Grazie, grazie tutti" (Thank you, everyone), the cardinal shouted to the crowd. "Si beneriga" (Bless you).

In response, they chanted, "Cardinale Pumilia, Cardinale Pumilia." He was truly revered.

The procession moved into the church, and Father Cataggio led the way into the sacristy behind the marble altar, built in the old tradition. The structure, with its multilevels, compartments, columns, carved figures, elaborate vines, and florals, was truly an ancient work, massive yet intricately carved. The floor of the church was marble with large yellowed blocks cut and placed randomly. The stone was worn down by the knees that had knelt on the altar rail since 1430. A crucifix of marble hung near the rear door. Its front foot was also worn by untold numbers of lips kissing it in reverence. Anyone who saw this figure was moved. A cut ruby was inserted in the figure's side, and it was rumored that some had actually seen blood drip from it. As the priests passed the crucifix, they made the sign of the cross.

The church began to fill with people. The Scalisce young men lined up inside the doorway. The nephews, cousins, and Enrico's brother, Pietro, led the attendees to their pews, each according to their rank in social order or importance as decided by the Don. The church was bedecked in wildflowers, large vases of orange and lemon-blossomed boughs, and multitudes of floral pieces. The church smelled of the floral perfume, especially near the altar.

The father of the groom had seen to it that Father Cataggio was shown all due respect and told other "men of the cloth" who would be attending him during the ceremony and Mass to do so as well. He hadn't expected this prestigious entourage; however, he was reserved and gracious at the scene unfolding before him. The Don, in an effort understood by the priest to be of great deference, clearly explained that Father Cataggio would indeed be directing the day's ceremonies and thanked him for all his help preparing for the day. The priest, a bit surprised he would be heading up the day and not the cardinal, never lost his composure; in fact, he relished it and assumed the role bestowed upon him by Don Scalisce.

CHAPTER 11

THE MORNING HAD begun for the Castellucci family with the signora sobbing loudly in bed. Signore Castellucci tried to console her but with little success. Bettina was awakened by her sobs. "Mama! What is it? What's wrong?" Bettina asked as she ran to her parents' bedroom.

"Oh, Bettina, do you remember you are getting married today?" wailed Beatrice.

"Si," answered Bettina, looking at her without a change of expression. Beatrice wondered if her daughter truly understood what it meant to be married. Though she had talked with her day after day trying to explain, Beatrice still didn't think Bettina realized the enormity of the situation. This would be the day she would leave everything she had known behind. Bettina listened but said nothing. She simply had her own view of life and was not understood by others. As with the smile of the famed *Mona Lisa*, so it was with Bettina; her glorious face, the perfect skin, those astonishing eyes, yet a total mystery, and so it would be the day of her wedding.

Beatrice helped her bathe and braided her long hair into a crown. After putting her wedding dress on, Bettina stared at herself in the mirror, quizzical but unquestioning. She had a light breakfast of milk, biscotti, and some figs and went along with the course of the morning. Her mother looked for a sign. Was she excited, sad, distressed? Nothing. Bettina simply went around the house as usual, just another day. Then the carriage arrived.

Enrico, on the other hand, had a fitful evening. He awoke in a sweat in the middle of the night after tossing and turning so violently he woke himself up. He got up and opened the curtains. There was a full moon, and the night was so clear the stars seemed to swirl and move as if they were cascading from a celestial cornucopia. His mind raced. *What can I do? I can't run, can't hide. I am being forced into a marriage with a girl I do not love. My father tricked me into thinking I had feelings for a girl I don't even know, someone who doesn't even understand what is happening. My life is not my own. Pietro is the prince, the heir. I am simply a pawn.* He wrestled with this anguish. Then he remembered he had a bottle of grappa in his cabinet. At first, he sipped it, but then he drank deep and hard. Finally, the alcohol took effect, and after finishing more than half the bottle, he fell asleep again.

His brother, Pietro, had to shake him several times to rouse him from an unconscious state. "Enrico, wake up!" Pietro shouted.

"Basta" (Enough), Enrico murmured.

"Father wants to see you in half an hour," Pietro told him and walked out of the room disgusted.

His suit of clothes for the wedding had been carefully hung by his closet cabinet. Enrico bathed in cold water to clear his fogged head. Then he dressed and appeared at the large table in his father's study.

"So, Enrico," Don Scalisce said. "Today you honor your family."

Enrico nodded. In his father's voice, he heard the warning not to embarrass the family name, another admonishment.

The breakfast table was crowded with family, including a few first cousins, Enrico's aunt and uncle, and their three children. Enrico was quiet. His father had left immediately after breakfast to greet the cardinal at the train.

Enrico sat in his room awaiting the call that the carriage had arrived. He finally resigned himself to the marriage but still had fantasies of escape. If not today, then soon, very soon.

CHAPTER 12

THE SMELL OF flowers and the amicable attitude of those invited to the church made the scene inside the old cathedral almost surreal. Times were changing. There was the longing of many to break free from the restraints of the old feudal system evident even in remote Sicilian towns. Yet here was a caricature of the traditional wedding of long ago honored and revered in this paese for centuries.

The service began with the high-pitched soprano voice of a choir member singing "Ave Maria." The hymn flowed through the building as the bride, accompanied by her father, made her way to the altar. Enrico, accompanied by his brother, the best man, waited. The clergy watched the procession, smiling. The bride was astonishingly beautiful. She carried a small bouquet of calla lilies. Her face was serene without a hint of expectation or excitement, almost as if she had done this many times before. At the altar, they stopped and faced Enrico. Her father kissed her cheek, took her hand, and placed it on Enrico's arm. Signore Castellucci uttered a barely audible sigh, and his eyes filled with tears. Though she had remained composed up until this point, Beatrice, seated on the edge of the front pew, also began to cry.

Father Cataggio recited the bonds of betrothal and at the proper moments received the responses. "Yes," said one, and then hesitating, the bride said in a low voice, "Yes."

Father Cataggio read Latin incantations, a children's choir sang, and the ritual of the Roman Catholic Mass and wedding ceremony, for century upon century, continued. Outside, hundreds of townspeople tossed flowers and grain and offered words of benediction and good wishes as the bride and groom emerged. Two children approached the bride carrying a basket filled with the traditional confetti, white sugar-coated almonds wrapped in cloth and tied with a bow, gifts for well-wishers. Enrico and Bettina, with her mother at her side, walked through the crowd handing out the little packets and nodding to each person offering congratulations as they made their way to the carriage adorned with white streamers and large bows. The carriage proceeded around the piazza, Enrico waving now and then, Bettina staring at the spectacle. Carriages filled with family, clergy, and guests followed them as the procession made its way through town to the Scalisce estate. The band played the traditional music of the region with the sun reflecting off their white uniforms. The crowd listened and watched as the last carriage moved out, followed by the band, down the hilly streets to the edge of town. The stairway, front patios, and balconies at the estate were decorated with vases of flowers, and at the front door entry, huge marble columns were festooned with large white banners fluttering in the breeze.

The prepared feast rivaled any royal event. Carved melons and a plethora of fruits and nuts lay on one table. On another was an assortment of vegetables with an arrangement of roasted artichokes in the center. Others boasted roasted meats of every kind, fire-roasted *spendini* (rolled herb-spiced veal), choice chunks of lamb and beef, roasted milk-fed baby goat stuffed with onions and herbs, baby racks of lamb chops, baked lamb's head, stuffed rolled pork skin (*cudene*), rolled beef (*briciola*), pork liver (*figato arrezza*), stuffed veal breast (*petto a vitale*), and whole, boneless, roasted chickens. Still others held broiled fish of various kinds brought in from the coast overnight, octopus salad, clams and steaks of tuna and swordfish sautéed with tomatoes, garlic, and herbs and topped with fresh parsley. The family's bakers offered an assortment of breads, semolina, *cicciola*, *panettones*, and pastries of all kinds. A variety of homemade wines held in small casks had been set inside and outside the house along with grappa, whiskeys, sparkling wines, mineral waters, and homemade aperitifs and anisettes. The entire staff wore *comisa bianca*, ballooned white shirts and blouses, with bright gold sashes and black pants on the men and wide, long black skirts on the women.

Don Scalisce sat with the bride and groom, his wife, Pietro, and the wedding party at a raised table set in the back center of the fifty-foot dining room with its grand stone fireplace. Two other tables were set, one for the Castellucci family and another for the clergy. The servers meticulously attended to every request. The musicians played on the outside patio, and after, dinner couples danced on the stone way. "Supedu" Scalisce, Enrico's cousin who had studied voice in Palermo many years before, sang a few folk songs and opera pieces. As the night ended, more than a few guests noticed Bettina and Enrico were more interested in the festivities than each other. The couple waited as each guest came to wish them well before they left. Enrico thanked them. Bettina was agreeable but seemed as if she was merely going through the motions.

"Allora noi e tutte la famiglia, Bettina sono una figila de te, un parte di famiglia di me" (Now we are all one family. Bettina is your daughter and now is part of our family), the Don told the Castelluccis. The Don expressed his gratitude to Bettina and her family for their help in greeting guests and said that he would always remember the day. He also said that if there was anything the Castellucis needed where he could help, they should not hesitate to ask. This proclamation of sorts of the Don's alliances with them was a pledge of protection and acceptance not lightly given.

The couple looked at each other. Enrico rose and said, "Allora se parte" (Now we will leave), and he smiled at his bride and shook hands with her father and mother. Mr. Castelluci shook his "hand" but really just took the end of his fingers. Mrs. Castelluci barely touched his hand, then withdrew, and both managed a feigned smile. The couple had a horse-drawn carriage waiting for them. It was festooned with white ribbons and bows. Enrico took the reins and urged the beast to move. The trip to the little house at the edge of town gave him, for the first time in the day, time to speak to Bettina alone.

While Enrico thought he might run away, he would not, given the fear he had of his father. He knew he had to obey his father's command. Also, he knew he would never benefit from his father's support financially or, in the event of his father's death, even inherit anything.

General Giuseppe Garibaldi

CHAPTER 13

THE DON WAS pleased with the day's events. All had gone as he had planned. He wanted to speak with the cardinal now, so they retreated to his study.

"Eminensa, come si va il causa di Garibaldi?" (Eminence, how are things going with Garibaldi's cause?) asked Don Scalise.

The Don was very concerned about the move to unify Italy. At that time, the country was divided into several autonomous regions. The Don had considerable influence in the Sicilian region, which involved both business and political power. The Roman Catholic Church held the Papal States in the midregion, and the cardinal was himself a major political power.

Thus, the Don, presented with the opportunity of hosting Cardinale Pumilia on the day of his son's wedding, could take the liberty of indulging in some business and political matters, as it was the custom that such action was acceptable on a wedding day, even if not an official visit was scheduled. Cardinale Pumilia knew the leader of the unification movement, Guiseppe Garibaldi, well. Garibaldi had conferenced with him a number of times, seeking his support and the support of the pope and the church.

The unification of most of the formally independent states, which actually were several individual kingdoms, was being orchestrated in large part by Generale Giuseppe Garibaldi. The old Roman Empire had been shattered long ago. The peninsula that was to become the unified Italy was now broken into eighteen separately administered kingdoms. Garibaldi and his revolutionary army, the Camicie Rosso, Red Shirts, had struggled for several decades and fought battles in his country as well as overseas to unify Italy. Garibaldi was born in Nice,

France, which was at the time part of the Sardinian kingdom. However, the French ultimately took over control, and Nice became a part of the French kingdom. Garibaldi, it was said, became so inflamed with the loss of his homeland that it sparked the burning and never-ending desire in him to see a single political unit under a unified flag of Italy. He envisioned a united country harkening back to the glory of the Roman Empire. History records Garibaldi as "La Spada" (the Sword) aided by Giuseppe Mazzini "Il Cuore" (the Heart) and Count Camillo Benso di Cavour "Il Cervello" (the Brain), who inspired and then fought to unify and create what is now the sovereign country of Italy. Garibaldi lived the life of a romantic figure. In 1848, there were revolutionary activities on the island of Sicily. The Kingdom of the Two Sicilies was really a segment of nearly one-third the entire Italian land mass, including the lower end of the peninsula as well as the island of Sicily. There were vibrant and important cities and seaports in this kingdom: Naples, Messina, and Palermo. War was not unusual, as it was the way the powers in Europe of that era settled their disputes. The French, the Austrians, and others in the region were constantly at war. The region was at war in 1859. The Armenian War made wartime diplomacy a major issue. The French, led by Napoleon III, sought to rule over Europe. As Napoleon I before him thirsted for a French empire, Napoleon III, however, was dealing with a far different world than his namesake predecessor. He would resolve many of his ambitions with greater caution than Napoleon I. He had indeed learned the lesson of history lest it repeat again. He sought by diplomacy to avoid a Waterloo in his leadership period. The French became deal makers and not war makers in the 1860s and ended up agreeing to permit Piedmont to gain power and control several areas, including Tuscany, Parma, and Medina, instead of going to war. For his trouble, Napoleon III, when he agreed to let the Piedmontese control these territories, got in exchange the Kingdom of Sardinia, which encompassed most of the top half of the Italian peninsula.

The carving up of the "boot" and consolidations resulted in the political entities of Venetia controlled by Austrians, the Kingdom of Piedmont, Sardinia, and the Papal States and, in the south, the

Kingdom of the Two Sicilies. Time and again, the royal control of these areas had to contend with unrest and use of force to retain control.

Garibaldi hated the French and sought to liberate his home city of Nice, but timing was not on his side, nor did his band of immigrants, "Il Mille" (The Thousand), provide military support to take on the French. Garibaldi, in concert with the Piedmontese, was convinced that the allies of Piedmont's leader, Charles Albert, the French, as well as the British were not to be incited.

Instead, at Charles Albert's direction, Prime Minister Count Camello Benso di Cavour convinced Garibaldi to look south to the Kingdom of the Two Sicilies, an easier conquest militarily. Gaining this kingdom would provide a more strategic military naval force and strengthen the numbers in the army. With the help of the British, he succeeded and declared these lands for King Victor Emmanuel. He then went on from Sicily to Naples, solidifying the conquest. Thus was born the "Risorgimento" resurgence. The victory was short-lived for Garibaldi. He had worked in concert with Guisseppe Mazzini, the "Pen" of the Risorgemento, as Garibaldi, who was the "sword," and Cavour, "the brain," were the leaders of this movement.

Antonio Meucci

Their plan to invade and annex Rome fell short. The winning of Naples and Sicily in 1861 with the goal of a unified Kingdom of Italy was an inspiration to the movement to move forward. In 1866, they joined with Prussia against their common enemy, Austria. They gained the Kingdom of Venetia in 1866. Venice, a great prize, in the aftermath of the Seven Weeks War not only was added as territory but also enhanced Garibaldi's reputation. The Prussian Alliance was pivotal for the unification since the French by 1870 were engaged in war with the Prussians (Franco-Prussian War of 1870), forcing Napoleon III to withdraw his troops from Rome. Hence, Rome was left unprotected. Italian troops marched on Rome and took it over unopposed. The Roman Repubblica (Republic), the birth place of a representative government experiment with the ancient Roman Senate, chose to vote for union with the emerging Italy by the end of 1870. Roma, the center of the Ancient Empire, was recognized as the hub of the Italian peninsula, and in July 1871, Rome was acclaimed the capital of the unified Italy.

Garbaldi reflected on the decades he spent seeking unification. He had left Italy for foreign shores time and again. He spent time as a soldier and leader. Then again in 1848, he was forced to flee Italy by enemies who tried to orchestrate his assassination. He ended up in Staten Island, New York. His exile was even harder to bear as he lost his beloved wife, Beatrice, to illness (likely small pox). He spent some time with his friend and supporter Antonio Meucci, the great inventor. Meucci has been since credited with the actual invention of the telephone (Alexander Graham Bell was discredited of the invention by revelations of illegal action, and an act of the United States Congress now has Meucci credited with first inventing the telephone).

The bucolic life of candle making and growing vegetables did not end Garibaldi's ambition to return to Italy. His exile did not dim his hope. He sought aid in America to finance his military venture to unify Italy. He received support and funds from his American friends. He returned to his homeland after nearly two years of exile and began where he left off, promoting unification.

By 1871, only the Papal States separated the already unified Italy. The Scalisces had been supporters of the power in the Kingdom of the Two Sicilies. They supported the two brothers from the city of

Simone in France, both generals in the French Army who had been appointed by Napoleon III to protect the royal hierarchy who ruled the Sicilian kingdoms. General Antonio DiSimone settled in Naples, and General Vincent DiSimone settled in Palermo along with their military units shortly after Napoleon III took power. The DiSimones associated closely with their new land. They were suspicious of the ability and legitimacy of Napoleon III. They quietly questioned his choice of diplomatic envoys. They felt Napoleon III had failed in properly equipping and training a strong military force that could defend the French Empire. They harbored a dislike for the man himself (Napoleon III), who they saw privately as weak and inept. However, they kept their feelings quiet. In the meanwhile, they went about making personal alliances with those in power in the regions they controlled. The Scalisces were among the most influential patrones.

The DiSimones chose instead to assimilate with the people in their region, and indeed they married local women and encouraged their men to do likewise. They became part of their communities. They became "autonomies" themselves, without direction from Napoleon's leaders. They personally had protected the local people as much as the royalty. Eventually they became leaders of the ruling order of the Kingdom of the Two Sicilies, not allying with the French. The people pledged their allegiance to their leadership. The French, for their part, so preoccupied with the wars with which they were engaged, took little notice of the defection and thus lost control of those territories to the DiSimones and their associates.

The Scalisces had become so friendly and allied with the DiSimones that they helped recruit members in their communities to support their leadership of the kingdom. The DiSimones reciprocated by assisting the Scalisces in their business interests.

The eventual unification movement was, of course, opposed by the Scalisces and those patroni (leaders) who controlled various areas. Unsettling the current order only served to undermine their power and influence. Democracy in any form, with a Roman Republic or leadership by some distant king, Victor Emmanuel, who had no ties to their social order, was a threat to their power.

Since only the Papal States remained autonomous after Garibaldi had success, the Scalisces and many others who saw what was happening also played both sides at the same time. They supported and befriended Garibaldi publicly but sought to empower the Papal States and the pope to be the eventual political power in the New Italy. They had curried favor with all the popes from the late 1830s on. They had some of their own people join Garibaldi and his forces. They also had members in the leadership of the DiSimones' forces as well. The DiSimones' military power was not overlooked as a stabilizing force in Southern Italy and deferred others from trying to exert power in the region.

The papacy commanded the respect, if not the support militarily, of many European kings. The Scalisces considered that support of the papacy could only serve their interests, regardless if the unification succeeded or not. The Roman Catholic Church still would command a certain unilateral power. Since the church was both spiritual and moral, leaders of the many families of the royal lineages, including the French, German, Austrians, and Spanish families, with sufficient influence with the Swiss and others as well they commanded considerable power. No other force crossed so many lines.

So that was why Don Scalisce was inquiring as to Garibaldi's movement from this high-power church member. The progress was of great importance to the Don. He valued the point of view of this cardinal. The unification of Italy, with the exception of some small northern territories, had been *un cosa fatto* (a made thing) by 1871. Now several years later, it was curious to discuss the "Garibaldi movement" as if the matter was still unsettled.

The Papal States, taken by force from the church, ended the unifications by an active military action. While the action was proclaimed a "merger," with acceptance of the new order, there was reluctance to accept the loss of power by the papacy.

The climate after the fall of the Papal States was one of resignation, but the leaders in the old system, "I Padroni," the Dons sought to establish another line of power, their line of power, within the political organization of the new unified Italy. They would resume control by controlling local and regional government, and their ally could be the church. They sought to continue the papacy as if not in control of territory but of the souls and hearts of the people and the politicians. They still had popular power, and they controlled the pulpits across the land. They also were an influence in business operations.

Don Scalisce had both the money and the web of influence throughout Southern Italy to promote specific agendas of various regents of society. Now the fractionized systems of the various political leaderships had fallen either by force or by agreement. Then there was a consolidation of most of the land mass of what was now a cooperating single country, Italy. Yet the power within the power, the Roman Catholic Church, still held the moral ground with the Italians. Scalisce also had the backing of the military led by the DiSimones.

"Cardinale, tempo in tempo, noi fare tutte cosa anche giorno per tu e il Papa" (Cardinale, time in time, we shall do all that the things each day for you and the pope).

Scalisce's ally, this cardinal and this church, was the only way to have influence on the political power, but it was now necessary to be more clandestine. His relatives and fellow patrones cooperated in his knowledge, even to the points of providing help, influence, and money to the very organizers of the unification, as it would provide the patrones a dialogue with the new order and a place at the table when decisions were made. Thus, the Scalisces became a powerful force as the pivotal go-betweens with the new government and the old patrones and the DiSimones.

CHAPTER 14

"BETTINA, TU E molto bella," said Enrico. He then took her hand and kissed it. Bettina smiled but did not respond. She looked out over the countryside and sighed. She was relieved the day had ended.

They got to the little cottage, and Enrico brought the carriage into the little stable in back of the building. Bettina got out and walked into the house. Enrico brought the horse in the stable and then went into the house.

It was extremely quiet. Their place was furnished by Enrico's mother, mostly with furniture that had been stored at her own house, not being used. It had a small kitchen, dining room, parlor, and two bedrooms, each with a bathroom. Apparently, the place had been built with the concept that two people who were employees were to occupy the house. Only one bedroom was furnished; the other had a few chairs and a small table. It was an obvious action by Signora Scalisce that this couple would share a bed.

Bettina decided to bathe. Her mother told her that she must bathe that night. She lit a fire and warmed a few buckets of water. She found that the bathroom had been stocked with soaps and towels. She filled the metal bathtub with a few inches of water and entered. She washed herself thoroughly and then dried her hair and rolled it tight with a ribbon. She then put on a lace, cotton nightgown. Enrico bathed in the other bathroom. Bettina towel-dried her long hair and then went to the bedroom.

Enrico wore a long night shirt. She got into the bed. Enrico turned off the oil lamp and went to her side of the bed. He kneeled beside her and brushed his hand alongside her face as she lay on the pillow. He then went over to the other side of the bed and got in.

He moved his body close to her. She lay with her back to him. He slowly put his hands on her shoulders and back, then rubbed her hips and belly. He put his lips to her neck and lightly began to kiss her. Bettina stayed completely still. He continued to caress her body for nearly an hour; his breath labored, and finally he moved close and lifted her nightgown. She was still but not rigid. He moved her legs apart easily, almost willingly. Slowly he entered her. The room was dark, and he could not see that she had bitten her bottom lip and that her face was red with anger. He did not know that what he assumed was a welcome to his advances was not received in acceptance but in contempt. She lay there and accommodated his movement until at last he gasped and retreated. Indeed, the marriage was consummated by this act. However, since Enrico had already taken her virginity, this act was one of simple lust.

So it was, and so it was to be. Over the next several weeks, Bettina gained weight. People, of course, did not question the pregnancy but did murmur that Enrico must be a very potent young man to have impregnated his young wife so quickly. Only a few knew the truth. Enrico worked each day at his father's charge and was dutifully providing for his new wife. Bettina's mother and Filomena visited most days, and Bettina spent a great deal of time with her mother, shopping, setting up a nursery in the empty bedroom, and sharing dinners with both families at the Scalisce residence.

Enrico hired a local woman, Margarita, as a housekeeper and cook. Bettina had learned to cook from her mother as well, so the two of them shared the chores of meal preparation. However, since *la prima colazione* (early breakfast) was usually just bread or biscotti and coffee for Enrico, this was left to Bettina, since Enrico left for his work early. Her experience at night did not influence her sense of duty in the morning, or so it seemed.

Bettina still took her walks in the countryside and visited her parents as well as Filomena. She went to the shops in the village with Margarita. The pregnancy was difficult for the first two months or so, but then it became easier. She was nearly five months pregnant before the size of her stomach was noticeably enlarged but still not profound.

Enrico worked six days a week, and on Sunday they visited the Scalisces. Enrico left in the morning but was home for dinner most nights, unless he had to go away on business for one or two days. He sometimes went to Palermo for longer. He expected her "cooperation" in bed at least three times a week. She cooperated but did not welcome the sex. She did not reach orgasms.

One evening over dinner, Enrico announced that he had to go to Palermo in a few days on business. Bettina looked at him with a puzzled expression. "Andare assieme; volere comprare qualche cose per il bambino. Non che stare veste proprio per il piccolo qui" (We will go together. I want to get some things for the baby. There are no appropriate clothes for a little one here).

Enrico hesitated, then agreed. They would pack their things and travel by train. He would help her shop. Three days later, they left by train. The train ride was uneventful but bumpy and unsettling to Bettina.

They reached Palermo and went to a fine little hotel. They had a room on the third floor, with a balcony that had a fine view and permitted the sun to come in first thing in the morning. Enrico went to see his father's clients early in the day and returned midday. He took her to shop for baby clothes, and they stopped for lunch at a café. The next day, Enrico left early again, so Bettina decided to take a walk. She found a street with a number of shops, including one that had a perfumery and a large apothecary, where she spent several hours. She asked the chemist many questions and finally made several purchases.

Enrico had given her some money, and she was very careful in the way she spent it. Enrico completed his business in four days, so they decided to take a late-afternoon train home after lunch. The sun was just setting. They had a compartment toward the back of the train that was several cars long and had a good number of passengers. At the back of each car was a railed standing platform. Bettina said she'd like to watch the world go by from outside the car. They shared a little cheese and bread. Bettina prepared a small bottle of wine and some water for the trip back. Enrico and she spoke of the shopping and the *citta* (city) as the train made its way back.

CHAPTER 15

ABOUT A HALF hour on the way back home, Enrico opened the corked wine bottle and drank from it. He drank again after eating a piece of *cicolla* bread. They spoke about the baby. Bettina then said she wanted to go out to the platform. Enrico, now feeling the effects of nearly a half bottle of wine, was reluctant but agreed. They went toward the rear of the car and opened the door and went out onto the platform. Enrico seemed to stumble and complained about his head aching. The train was at an area of flat, straight track at the edge of a series of hills known as the Sheep's Back (Pecora Spade). Enrico became a little dizzy. Bettina held his arm. Suddenly, he doubled over and began to shake violently. Bettina held tight to his arm as he vomited and shook. The train was nearing a slight bend. Enrico leaned over the metal railing. Bettina said she would get someone to help. His vision blurred, and he felt a hand pushing at his back before blacking out.

Bettina ran through the train car yelling, "Aiuto me, aiuto me!" (Help me, help me!)

She had gotten to the car behind the engine when the conductor appeared. "Che su chesa?" (What is it?) he said.

"Mia marito e malato" (My husband is sick), she cried in a hysterical voice.

The conductor ran back to the compartment and stopped.

"No, no, e al fuori" (No, no, he's outside), she said. The conductor got to the half-opened door and stepped out. The side of the platform nearest the gully was covered in a spray of vomit—a strange, frothy vomit speckled with red gobs of blood and purple wine. Enrico was nowhere in sight. He ran back to the engineer and had him stop the train. It took over a half hour to organize a few groups of male passengers led by four conductors to walk back up the tracks. It was dusk, but there was enough light to see along the track. After an hour, one group who saw a spatter of vomit on one of the rocks near the rails ventured down the rocky gully with a group of men. Now kerosene lamps were signaling to find the others. When they found Enrico, his neck was twisted in a bizarre angle, obviously broken when he fell. His skull was split open, and the gray of his brain was visible. There was no question he was dead. The men carried the body up the hill to the tracks and signaled the engineer to back up the train.

"Signora, me dispiace dire ma tu marito ... tu marito e morte" (Signora, I am sorry to tell you, but your husband ... your husband is dead), said the conductor. Bettina's eyes widened, and she put her hand over her mouth before slumping against the backside of the car at the very platform he had fallen from.

"Vene" (Come), said the conductor, and he led her back to the compartment.

"Lasciare me" (Leave me), she said and closed the door. Once the door closed, she breathed a sigh of relief.

The body was wrapped in a few canvas mail bags and placed in the mail car. The train began to move again. Bettina sat quietly in the compartment. Her face was stoic; she was quiet. As the train rocked to and fro, she fell asleep. Perhaps it was more than the trip and the accident overwhelming her or even her pregnancy.

In a brief moment before she fell asleep, she made the sign of the cross and said, "Allora, sono bene fatto" (Now, it's well done). The train made its way to Corleone Station. When it stopped, the conductor knocked on her door several times before she awoke.

The trainmen jumped from the train and ran into the station. Bettina watched through the window as two excited conductors waved their arms and spouted out the tragic circumstances to the official behind the counter.

Within fifteen minutes, the train station was filled with men, and many others were on the train. The voices of the men yelling orders and the sounds of men getting off and on the train continued. Suddenly, all the activity stopped.

Bettina looked out on the platform and saw the Don approaching, with his eldest son just behind. The crowd of men parted, and the two men walked down the platform and onto the train. Within a few minutes, the men walked back, and four men were behind them, carrying the wrapped body of Enrico in a makeshift shroud of blankets.

The Don spoke to the conductor, and he pointed to the train car where Bettina was still inside. He got into the car and in a moment tapped on the door. "Bettina," he called. She opened the door to the compartment. The Don looked at her flushed face and wild eyes. She seemed agitated but strange as well. She was not crying but seemed to whimper now and then. The Don beckoned to her with his hand. He put his hand on her back as she walked carrying a small carpet bag. He took her arm as she walked down the few train stairs to the platform. He put his arm around her shoulder and escorted her through the crowd to a waiting carriage. Not a word was spoken between them. The old man was visibly shaken, and his eyes were red and watery. His son rode in the back of the carriage with the body as they headed to the Don's compound.

When they arrived home, a throng of people were waiting. The Don's wife rushed to the carriage. The Don simply shook his head and closed his eyes at the sight of his wailing wife. She put her hand out to the girl to help her out of the carriage, but Bettina grasped the hand rails at each side and quickly was on the ground. The old woman was overcome with emotion. She clutched the girl, and Bettina could feel the old woman convulsing and whimpering. She merely stood stone still for what seemed to be a long time. Finally, the Don took his wife's hand, then put his arms around her and walked into the house. Bettina followed, but as she got to the stairs, she turned around. She could see the body being removed from the carriage. She entered the house. The servants stood by the entry, their faces emotionless.

The Don emerged from his library. He walked over to Bettina. "Bettina, tu rimanere qui per questa sera; noi parla domani" (Bettina, you stay here for tonight; we will talk tomorrow), he said. He waved his hand to a housekeeper, who walked over to Bettina and then escorted her to a bedroom. The Don disappeared into his library.

Bettina heard the door close behind her. She saw by the candlelight a pitcher of water and a basin in a bureau, and she washed her hands and face, then removed her shoes and lay down in the bed, eyes wide open. Those deep, dazzling eyes were now staring skyward, seeking some answer to some complex question, perhaps too complex for her to understand or perhaps so simple that the answer was all too obvious. She struggled to recall all the events of the day as if, in recollection, the answers could be found. She fell asleep still gazing at the ceiling, eyes wide open.

CHAPTER 16

THE OLD CHURCH on the piazza filled with mourners, some from as far away as Rome and Milano. Father Cataggio officiated at the solemn Mass for the Dead, and the pallbearers were directed by the Don and his son.

The procession from the edge of the cemetery to the mausoleum of the Scalisce family weaved through the hilly, hallowed ground, and the procession of hundreds was silent. All that could be heard was the shuffle of shoes against the dry, rocky soil. The event lasted the entire morning, and the Sicilian sun was high in the sky as the priest uttered the final prayer before those in the throng filed past the bronze casket to pay their last respects.

The Don stayed by his wife's side. She seemed almost semiconscious by the end of the ceremonies. She clung to the Don's arm and simply followed where he led her; her oldest son was just a step behind. "Allora Mama" (Now, Mama), the Don said, urging her to move forward to touch the coffin.

She hesitated, then put both hands on the casket, shaking her head. As she did so silently, her tears sprinkled the shining metal so that they glistened in the sunlight. "Mio figlio, mio figlio" (My son, my son), she whispered, and in a moment, the Don led her away.

The week after the funeral, little was said. The old woman went to church each morning with two of her nieces and her sister. The Don went about business with his eldest son. Bettina became a member of the household, but really she was left to herself except at mealtimes when the table would be set for the relatives, mostly those close to the wife, who would intermittently join the Don's family for dinners in the evenings.

Several weeks after the funeral, the Don had a housekeeper tell Bettina to meet him in his library. There he asked her what had happened on the train. In a very calm voice, she told him: he drank some wine, ate, felt sick, went out onto the rear deck, lurched forward when the train made a sudden turn, and the jolt tumbled him over just as they reached a deep ravine. He watched her face and eyes closely as she spoke. She was serene and showed little expression, as if relating a story she had been told by another. He could see, however, that she trembled a little relating the more morbid details of the fall. She turned away. "Morte ti dice me—morte, morte" (Dead they said to me—dead, dead).

They sat in silence for a little while before the Don stood up, walked over to her, took her hand and kissed it. "Tu si familia. Non ha paura" (You are family. Do not be afraid). This was a grand gesture, and it had far-reaching meaning that she could not pretend to comprehend at that moment.

The Don sat quietly sipping his coffee in the library. Most mornings, he arose, washed, dressed, and was sitting at his desk in the early morning as the sun shone in through the windows. On this morning, just a few days after he buried his youngest son, he had his man wake his eldest son and told him to come join him in the library. The Don had not slept much over the past few nights. He was understandably tremendously distraught over the loss of his son and the concern for his wife's extreme grief. He had considered what needed to be done for his business and for his family. Sleepless nights were filled with calculating his positioning a nephew, Vincenzo Terranova, to do the work of his deceased son, Enrico. He also spent part of his night in deep depression and remorse. Though he was not a deeply religious man, he believed that the Roman Catholic Church was handed down by Jesus Christ to his disciple Peter; Pietro, the Rock, who had organized the church as Christ had directed. Rome was the residual home of the church and the crucible for the church. Scalisce held the church in high regard. He deemed the Roman Catholic popes God's heirs to the Vatican throne and moral leaders. He respected the pope as much as the leader of men of business as a spiritual leader. But it was not the man himself who wore the robes at this time he held in *respetto* but the robes, the office. The probability of a friend becoming the next pope greatly pleased the Don.

In the middle of the night and in complete solitude, the Don prayed for the soul of his dead son, and tears of guilt fell from his eyes. While the boy did not live up to his vision of the life he should have lived, the Don was remorseful that he had not given him better direction. He questioned himself. Had he spent more time teaching the boy, would he still be alive? Had he taken more time to teach the boy more self-control and act more conservatively, his life may have been drastically altered. He would have enjoyed a more powerful position at home and may not have been so impetuous with that young girl, which caused the awkward circumstances ending in the boy's marriage—a marriage meant to save the dignity of the family and avoid a scandal and perhaps criminal charges. All this preyed on his mind as he grieved the loss of his son.

"Papa, buon giorno," his son said. Then he walked over to his father and kissed his hand and sat in the chair beside the desk. He could see the weariness in the eyes of his father.

The Don took his son's hand, held it for a moment, and looked up at him. "Figlio mio. Tu sapere il moglie da tu fratello state alla casa. Allora che sono una cosa necessario quando la moglie da una fratello morte di dovere da fare. Tu ha ragione da sposare questa vedova sono tradizione; sono una cosa imperativa, sono uno obligazione a tuo fratello. Sapire?" (My son, you know that the wife of your brother is staying here. Now there is something you must do for the wife of a dead brother. You need to marry her. It is traditional, it is imperative, and it is an obligation to your brother. You know?)

The look in his son's eyes revealed that he had been waiting for the moment when his father would be bringing up the question that everyone expected him to answer. He understood, whether he liked it or not, that he was leading the life of a man of honor and had to follow the tradition. He thought that Bettina might resist. He just did not know how. "Io sapire, Papa" (I know, Papa). He nodded his head. The Don was relieved that the heir to his position understood what had to be done.

Later that morning, the Don asked Bettina to come to his library. There, with his son standing beside him, he told her that his son had an important matter to discuss with her. His son spoke of their family and his sorrow for the loss of his brother. He understood that Bettina, a mother-to-be, was in mourning. He said that he wanted to protect her and her child, a Scalisce child. Then he paused and said, "Voule sposare" (I want to marry you).

She did not respond immediately and seemed as if she was even daydreaming. Within a few minutes, however, she turned to his father and said, "Si" (Yes).

On a Sunday, after thirty-one days, Father Cattagio and the few people from the Scalisce house, as well as Bettina's parents, went to the church. It was just as the sun was setting. Few people were out of their homes, and the small number of people going to the church seemed to have no interest. The Don had arranged for a quiet wedding.

Vows were exchanged on the altar. It took only a few minutes. They went back to the Don's compound for dinner. The scene was reminiscent of the recent funeral instead of wedding. The mood was somber. The polite and necessary ceremony ended by mandatory acknowledgment of what had transpired earlier.

Months passed. The baby within her grew larger. She seemed even healthier, if that was possible. Even after a few weeks of sleeping with her new husband, in his bed, he had not approached her sexually.

However, in the middle of one night after he consumed a bottle of wine and some grappa, he put his arms around her, and she turned her back and just exposed her lower body as if to acknowledge his need. That night, they consummated the marriage. He was not forceful or aggressive. In fact, it was his nature to be methodical, even in a situation as intimate as this.

So it was that he had her periodically. The months passed as the families settled into their routine.

The child was born, a healthy boy. The name was given to honor the Don's father, Nicholas, and within the next few years, two more children followed, one named Giuseppe after Bettina's grandfather, and Antonio named after the child's maternal grandfather.

The loss of a son receded some in memory, but there was always noticeable somberness. It was a much different atmosphere than before his death.

CHAPTER 17

THE EXPANSION OF the unified Italian government forced changes in Don's business, particularly on the mainland. The power and respect for the padrones, the "Dons," waned, and the old vestige of the feudal system where these men were like princes and dukes diminished as the monarchies diminished and disappeared. Alliances between the padrones were made with a single member of a royal family, or old alliances formed within the intricate systems of control of areas weakened and began to dissolve.

The concept of a governing power in Rome made the system a shadow of what it once was. Still there were the alliances with the leaders in the Vatican, but that too had less immediate power and in a real sense could not compete with the political power the unification had brought.

Little by little, the many business operations of the Don diminished. His contracts for shipping fruits and vegetables from the farms he controlled in Sicily nearly disappeared over a ten-year period. He had no control over the new order on the mainland. The Sicilian island, however, was set in a system that could not diminish. The Sicilians had seen political systems come and go over the centuries, and in many ways, they still clung to the old ways. Problems arose, however, when those in Sicily with the strength and determination tried to maintain their economic and political power. Rivalries grew where once there were great opportunities all over the Italian peninsula to reap a benefit of age-old alliances. Now they were gone. Messina and Palermo, the financial hubs of the island, saw the insurgency of old, powerful families pitted against one another in the ever-shrinking financial and political pond. As the law of nature would have it, the big fish were eating the little ones. Territorial altercations, which were always ongoing, increased dramatically. The level of violence and corruption was constant, and so too the rise of secret alliances between strong families eager to preserve the heritage of their empire.

The Don was powerless to stop the change. He did not have the wealth or the power and could not withstand being pushed out of business situations in these major cities. He was forced to withdraw to the areas of the smaller cities and towns where he still maintained some influence. His son, who was schooled in recognizing the ways of change, also realized the problem the unification created for their way of life. He had always felt secure since he was the firstborn and would ascend to the leadership of the family as a birthright. Now he saw the empire, built generation after generation, crumbling. Encroachment into the business interest in the mainland cities was impossible to control. However, they would resist attempts in Sicily. Once their business agreements around the island were threatened, they sought out those who were responsible and sent emissaries to meet with them to demand they cease. This was particularly true of the wholesalers and shippers of their produce and fruit.

The lack of markets on the mainland forced the Don to give up many of his leases for the farms where he grew oranges, lemons, and other products. He still controlled the major production of artichokes and some of the more delicate farm products that demanded the warm Sicilian temperatures and rich volcanic soils.

The Triamonte family was involved in similar operations and business interests. They were based in Palermo and known to be an aggressive and a vicious bunch. Whenever they met with resistance, they resorted to violence and relied on their relationships with some of the most ruthless gangs in Palermo and Corsica. The Triamonte were suspected in a number of bombings and disappearances of adversaries when they refused to give up markets or abandon dealing with other suppliers.

The Don was distressed when he was informed that one of his wholesalers, located near the Messina port, had cancelled a large order. He was nearing seventy years old. He had lived under the stress of being patriarch of the family, and the years had taken a toll. His outward appearance had changed. Though he once had a large broad frame, muscular and barrel-like, with thick, strong hands, he now appeared pale and drawn. He needed more and more sleep in order to function for a full day, and his habit of getting up at dawn changed, and on Sundays and holidays, he would not appear until midday.

Bettina had been somewhat insulated from the concerns of day-to-day business problems of her husband and father-in-law. However, she saw the effect on them and her mother-in-law, whom she had grown close to and with whom she learned how to manage the households for the compound. She understood that her position as the wife of the heir would result in her eventually taking over the house management of the family once her husband took complete control. More and more, he was taking over much of the old Don's responsibilities and operations. When the old Don developed a persistent case of the gout, he was unable to travel, and the son had to assume all business outside the compound. He often traveled to Messina.

The Triamonte problems had to be dealt with. They had intimidated two of their largest wholesalers and made contact with distant family members in Palermo who were suffering from the loss of the Scalisce businesses in Palermo and they were to meet with him in Messina. This branch of the Scalisce clan also had relatives in Corsica and Sardinia. These isolated islands were as much autonomous socially and politically as the old kingdoms and independent states of a century before. The meeting between Leno Scalisce and his two cousins Pietro and Paolo at the train station was a brief exchange of embraces and kisses on the cheek. "Leno, tu pare bene" (Leno, you look good), said young Pietro Scalisce. They then left hastily, looking around to see if anyone recognized them on the crowded station platform. They knew that their enemies had spies always looking to see what strangers came and who they met with. Thus, they were very cautious. There was a small window where a ticket master peered out onto the platform. The ticket clerk rarely sold a ticket, as there was a larger ticket counter inside the station. He did make a note of three strangers waiting and alerted another man in the station to go to the platform to watch who they were meeting with once the train began to approach. Pietro Scalisce had been to Messina regularly on business over the years.

The little man was off to one side of the platform observing the four men. He followed them to a hotel near the train station. The hotel was primarily a traveler's *pensione*, with a small café on the bottom floor near the lobby. Here the Scalisces would meet with others to consider a plan to deal with the Triamonte threat.

The café in the hotel lobby area was a room with neat little tables with starched white cloths and comfortable, cushioned chairs. Scalisce had checked with the front desk for a key and directed the bellman to take his one suitcase to his room. He told him to return the key to him in the café since his cousin had already checked in. They all went directly to the café and sat at a table in the back corner.

"Tu dice a Triamonte una propizione a laboro insierme. (I want to give the Triamonte a proposition to work together.) Now my family has many towns with fruit and vegetables, artichokes, tomato; all things. I have spoken with the padrone of these towns, and they want to continue to prosper. The Triamonte have the distribution. Together we have a strong opportunity for the entire south of Italy," said Scalisce.

The cousins understood but were also wary. "Il Triamonte sono cane. Voule tutti solemente" (The Triamonte are dogs. They want everything for themselves), they responded.

"They know my father and the name Scalisce. For more than two hundred years, the Scalisce have done things in this land. The Triamonte will listen," said Scalisce. The cousins nodded. They would set a meeting with the Triamonte to talk with Scalisce. They also would have the Corsicans stand by as a precaution.

The meeting was set in the hotel café. The Triamonte sent word with one of their most trusted family managers, Giancarlo Benotti Triamonte, to discuss the meeting. He agreed to meet at the café and suggested that only the three Scalisces and three of the Triamontes meet. Vincenzo Triamonte and Scalisce would sit alone, and the others would wait in the adjoining lobby. They decided on a midmorning meeting when there would be few, if any, people in the café. The meeting was set for two days later.

Scalisce then met with the Corsicans. They had been in the hotel lobby or out in front of the hotel in the café's outside tables watching day and night. Scalisce instructed them to keep vigilant and also told them that he would await the meeting and the Triamonte response. Once that happened, he would give them further instructions.

The meeting began as scheduled. Giancarlo Benotti Triamonte arrived at ten thirty in the morning, and he and Scalisce walked from the lobby to the café and a table set with coffee and biscotti. No one else was in the room, and the waiter had been instructed to enter only if called.

"Signore Triamonte sono piacere da parla con te. (Signore Triamonte, I am pleased to talk to you.) Your family and my family go back long ago. Now we have an opportunity to do something together, a good thing. I have the production, you have the distribution. It's a chance to make a lot of money." Triamonte sipped his coffee and seemed to be silently thinking over the proposition.

The four men in the lobby sat facing each other in pairs. They neither spoke nor moved about.

"My family is very large, Mr. Scalisce. All we do we do with family. But you want us to do a thing together. I want to talk with my brothers about the things you said," said Triamonte.

The meeting was brief and to the point. Scalisce had already considered that the Triamonte knew full well why he had personally come to Messina to talk to them. He knew that the Triamonte had already decided if they would choose to partner with the Scalisces or try to expel them from the business. When Triamonte indicated that he needed to talk the deal over with his brothers, Scalisce knew he had no deal.

The Triamonte left the hotel, and one of the Corsican brothers sat with Scalisce almost immediately. They spoke for several minutes, and then Scalisce called his cousins into the café.

"We are done here. Thank you for everything that you did, but the Triamonte, as you say, are dogs and will not listen to me. But don't be afraid; be quick. Leave here and go back to your town. Tell all your family of this problem. These words with Triamonte are dead. Understand?" said Scalisce.

The cousins nodded. They understood that the Triamonte were now enemies and that the family had to defend against them. Scalisce knew that the Triamonte would never be reasonable.

The next train back to Palermo was later that afternoon. The cousins had already left the hotel. Scalisce went to the desk and told the clerk that since his friends were kind enough to take care of things, he would now pay the bill two days in advance and would not need a maid later. A little while later, Scalisce slipped out a back door, went to the train station, and boarded the train back. The ticket master nodded to the small, thin man on the platform who boarded the train at the same time.

Pietro Scalisce had entered a small private compartment when one of his cousins tapped on the door.

He sat beside Scalisce and in a quiet voice told him that, just a short time before, he was told by one of the Corsicans that the body of Giancarlo Benotti Triamonte was seen naked lying over his desk at the Triamonte offices. He went on to describe the strange scene. Apparently, his head was twisted in an awkward angle, indicating he had his neck snapped. There was an even further oddity; the body was laid stomach down over the desk, a large artichoke had been inserted in his rectum, and his mouth had a bright yellow lemon in it. It was a message.

Pietro Scalisce eased back in his train seat and nodded.

The train made a stop in less than an hour. Scalisce waved to his cousin, who had left the train and was on the platform.

He then closed his eyes and began to consider how to explain all that occurred to his father. Scalisce wanted to tell him without alarming him. He retired to a small sleeping cabin and slid the door closed. He went over and over the words in his mind and finally fell asleep.

He did not hear the click of the sliding compartment door at first.

Suddenly, he felt a sharp pain in his stomach as he awoke to find a man standing over him holding the lapel of his jacket in one hand and a bloody, short-bladed knife in the other. The man pushed him against the seat and plunged the knife into Scalisce's belly. "Morte scunizi, morte!" (Die, you street dog, die!) he whispered. He turned and was gone.

Scalisce grasped his stomach. The blood was oozing out, and a large red patch grew on his white shirt, then another. He panicked for a moment and then yelled at the top of his voice, "Auito, auito me!" (Help, help me!)

He waited and yelled again. Finally, a conductor arrived, his eyes wide and shaking. "Madonna!" he exclaimed. He bolted to the front of the train and within a few minutes returned with a roll of cloth bandage. By this time, the floor was spattered with Scalisce's blood, and the poor conductor slipped and fell but arose quickly. Scalisce grabbed the cloth and pressed it to the two puncture wounds just a few inches apart on his belly. He pressed the cloth into the two small holes and kept his fingers against the wounds. "Signore, Signore, che da fare?" (Mister, Mister, what can I do?) said the conductor.

Scalisce shook his head and said, "Piede il grappa" (Get some grappa). The conductor scurried off in search of anyone with the alcoholic beverage. Scalisce was feeling a bit faint now. He could feel himself slipping from consciousness. Minutes passed. The conductor returned with a small flask of whiskey. "Mette ca!" (Put it here!) said Scalisce. He pointed to the wounds. The conductor was shaking as he poured some of the liquid into the wounds. The red liquid leaked down Mondellas pants legs and onto the gray floor.

Scalisce grabbed the flask and took a long drink. "Quando to arrivare al Palermo?" (When do we get to Palermo?) he asked.

"Un altro ore" (Another hour), said the conductor. Scalisce closed his eyes and in his pain tried to recall the image of the little man who stood before him earlier with his knife. He became semiconscious and tried to cope with the extreme pain, periodically drinking the grappa. The alcohol stemmed the flow of blood.

When the train stopped, the conductor jumped off and darted to the station master, yelling as he went. Within several minutes, other train men rushed to the train and carried Scalisce out onto the platform. There within a few minutes, a man with a large leather bag ran to the scene. He pulled gauze and a bottle with alcohol from the bag and applied it to the wounds of the man who now lay unconscious. He finished applying a bandage, and Scalisce was carried to a carriage waiting nearby. Someonè gathered his bag and searched to find identification, a passport. He gasped, "Scalisce. Una Scalisce."

By the time the doctors had treated the wounds and discussed his injuries, word had gotten to Scalisce's uncle in Palermo. The uncle, a man in his eighties, had then appeared. "Don Scalisce," the doctor said. "Questa e il nipote?" (Is this your nephew?)

"Si," said the old man. He went into the room and held the younger man's limp head and shook his head.

Dominic Scalisce had lived in Palermo from the time his father decided to leave the countryside when he was a child. His brother, the Don, was the father of this boy who lay in the hospital. He had shared a bed with his brother as young children. The old man said a silent prayer, then made the sign of the cross over the boy's head. "Porto a sui padre" (Bring him to his father), the old man said to the doctor. Scalisce was given medication for the pain, and his wounds were cleaned and stitched. But stomach wounds always carried the severe threat of infection, and Scalisce's body temperature rose and remained there. They packed him in a blanket with ice to cool the fever and, as the old man directed, put him on a train for home.

He arrived hours later. The entire family was at the station, his father, his mother, and Bettina with the children. They rushed him home. He was delirious during some of his waking period and was unconscious the first day home. He lingered for ten days as the infection from his wounds contaminated his internal organs and spread to his bloodstream, then to the rest of his body. There were times, however, that he was conscious and lucid, giving false hope that he would recover. He spoke with his father. "Questa cosa di Triamonte e difficile. Benotti Triamonte e morte. Una cosa che di voule mazzare io" (This thing with the Triamonte is difficult. Benotti Triamonte is dead. That is one reason why they wanted to murder me), said the dying man.

His father told him not to concern himself with anything but getting better. He told him, "Of course your children and your wife are here with us and will be cared for." The old Don knew that regardless of what was told to him, he had seen too many men die from similar wounds. His assurances that his children and family were well cared for was his way of saying that if he did not survive, his family would be fine. The last few days of his life were miserable.

His wife and children came to his room several times a day. Occasionally, he would be lucid and tell them he cared for them and not to worry. The afternoon of the tenth day, he fell asleep and never awoke again.

CHAPTER 18

THE FUNERAL PROCESSION wound through the same streets from the church to the graveyard, as it had with his brother, Enrico. The Don could hardly believe that he had lost both his sons. A month after burying his son, the Don had to cope with yet another funeral. He considered it so ironic that both would meet their fate on a train coming home. The Don's wife became a recluse, hardly ever leaving the house except to sit out by the gardens. She lost all reason to live, even when she was with her grandchildren.

They believed she died from a broken heart. The old woman suffered a heart attack while sitting in the garden. The Don had feared that she would be unable to sustain the grief of the loss of her other son, and when told of finding her dead, he simply hung his head, walked into his library, and locked the door. He stayed in the room for several hours, and the sounds of his wailing and frustration could be heard through the closed doors.

The Scalisces had become such a forceful and prominent family over the centuries. How, in the stretch of just several years, was all this waning, loss of family, loss of business, and loss of wealth and prominence? The deterioration was overwhelming for the Don. He had always been a careful steward of the family. He had lived a cautious and well-planned life and had thought that he raised his children to do the same. He was perplexed and frustrated, and although he had had a vision that his family, his sons and his grandchildren, would continue as a legacy, it had vanished. It struck him that this despicable sequence of events coincided with the arrival of Bettina, that strange, exotic creature. The Scalisces, he began to believe, were cursed because of her.

After his wife's death and burial, the Don stayed long hours in his library. He summoned the priest, Father Catanzzaro, to elicit his thoughts on life and the concepts that the Lord was either a righteous, fearful God or a forgiving and loving God. He also sought answers to these age-old questions from his friend Cardinal Pumilia.

He had Bettina fetch the midwife, Filomena, who was also known to be consummate in the understating of "il malocchi" (the evil eye). This was thought to be a curse perpetrated by an enemy. It would manifest itself in physical ailments, such as headaches, stomachaches, or worse. It could bring bad fortune, loss of money, and bad luck. It was an evil spell that could be detected when a knowing person conducted a procedure by dropping olive oil in a dish of water. The larger the co-agulation of oil, the bigger the curse. Dispelling the curse required a strong intercession of prayers and incantations and the powers of the person conducting the ritual. The Don had the old lady brought to his house, and the two went into his library.

There, she conducted the ritual, saying prayers and having the Don kneel before her so as to make the sign of the cross again and again on his forehead once she discovered a huge blot of oil in the water. Try as she might to have the water consume and mix with the oil, a sign the spell was broken, she could not. She told the Don, "Questa e un infamnia. (This is a disgrace.) I have never seen such a thing. I have no prayer or thing to make this evil eye fly away." Try as she might, hour after hour, it was to no avail. In the weeks to follow, he had the old woman come several times, even bringing others to help her. Still, with no success.

Bettina watched these women come and go. She immediately sensed that they were unsuccessful, though the Don never spoke of this to her.

He would see the children and enjoyed time with them in the evenings or after Sunday dinner, but it was more and more infrequent that Bettina's parents would join them.

The Don continued to isolate himself in his library and have his managers come in daily to discuss his failing businesses. Without his son, and being personally unable to continue working with his buyers, competitors edged into his business base. Much of the commerce he had generated was because he and his family were seen as powerful, wealthy, and capable—indeed even feared. That aura of invincibility was gone, and even though his managers were loyal, they could not maintain the appearance of the Don's power. Without that power, his operations were no longer seen as critical. Nor was it critical to continue favor with him or his organization. The businesses shrank to where his main interests sustained only in olive oil and some produce—artichokes, asparagus, tomatoes, and some citrus fruit. The expansion of the olive oil's production and his old leases on the olive groves as well as the groves he owned ensured the production. He also sought direct purchase from a number of the small villages around the area. He did the same concentration of effort—controlling the artichoke growers market.

However, his health continued to deteriorate. Bettina noted his lack of appetite, and as he grew weaker, he slept later and tired easily. She assisted in either preparing or bringing him his daily meals. Finally, he was unable to rise from bed and became so thin and frail that he could not walk. Meals were brought into to him by Bettina. "Signore, mangia un ove" (Sir, eat an egg), said Bettina. He looked down at the tray and plate of food placed before him and then up at Bettina. For the first time, he looked straight into those mysterious and luminescent blue eyes.

Carlo Terranova

Suddenly, he had a startled look on his face. His legs jumped, forcing the tray of food to fall off his lap. He gasped and brought his thin, boney arms and hands out in front of him. Bettina stood there, petrified. He trembled with fear, his face contorted and mouth agape. "Tu, tu (You, you!) he uttered in a raspy, choked voice. He saw her serene face and a slight turn from the side of her mouth, perhaps a grin or a smile, perhaps a grimace but something else. Somehow, at this moment, it all made sense. He knew that the destruction of his dynasty was inexorably tied to her, but it was too late He expelled one great gust of breath and expired.

Bettina arranged for the Don's burial next to his wife and sons in the mausoleum. Since the old man had the only direct blood heirs in his grandsons, they inherited the estate. However, since the businesses had so deteriorated, there was not much of value beyond the two houses and the land, some of which were in the joint names of his brother's children. Few liquid assets remained, and there was a great deal of debt.

With the help of her father, Bettina settled most of the financial situations, sold the Scalisces' houses and interests to his distant relatives, and moved in with her parents. The children grew, and she, despondent with her life as it had been with the Scalisces, felt emancipated by finally being free of them. She felt as if a weight had been lifted. She was still a young, strong, and beautiful woman even after bearing three children. She spent her days going to the town market for food she needed for the family and occasioned the local *salumeria* grocery. There she met a man, Carlo Terranova. He was close to her thirty-eight years in age and single. He struck up a conversation with her and over several months began visiting her and her family at their home. Within a year, in a quiet church ceremony with just Bettina, Carlo, their parents, and her children, she married again.

Some rumors circulated around the town that Bettina engineered the demise of Don Scalisce by putting a curse on him. The priest, Father Catanzarro, warned Bettina that members of the Scalisce clan had discussed this with him and were upset.

Afterward, Bettina never felt at ease in the town. Her husband, Carlo, had word from relatives that had gone to America that there was more opportunity there.

Bettina had been helping Carlo and his father, Tomasso, who owned the produce shop with the business from time to time. She had her boy cleaning up and doing small tasks as well. Carlo was only making a meager living and with this new family depended on Bettina's help financially. Within a year, both her father then her mother passed away, and they decided to leave and seek a better life in America.

A minor complication had to be overcome once they learned that Bettina was again pregnant. The child would be born nine months later, delaying their departure. Trying to save enough money and have some residual funds for his family of six required careful planning.

Nearly five years went by before they could accumulate enough funds for the move. During that time, the child named Enrico, after the Scalisce great-grandfather, was born. Also born was a daughter Salvatresa, named after Salvatore, Bettina's great-grandfather. Bettina also selected the name Enrico because she felt that to name the child after her late husband could dispel any rumors about his death. Antonio, Giuseppe, and Vincenzo maintained their ancestral names of Scalisce.

Bettina gathered and packed the things that were of the greatest importance, a photograph of her mother and father at their marriage and one of her in her communion dress standing with her parents. When she came upon one photo taken that same day with Filomena Trentino and her mother and another with Filomena with her arm around her, she suddenly felt an urgent need to visit her old mentor. She immediately prepared herself and dressed in her best clothes. She arranged her hair carefully, and with little Salvatresa, she journeyed off to the house where the old lady lived. Filomena was a widow now but well respected and indeed well loved by many of the local people whom she helped. Each day there would be food, fresh vegetables, and bread left anonymously at her door. Bettina knocked at the door. The little Salvetresa fidgeted with the bow in her hair. She resembled her mother but was a far different personality. She was vivacious and mischievous. Her father would say, "Solemente Salvestresa un piccolo con poco di cativo, siscina una siscina" (Only you, Salvetresa, little one with a little badness, scoundrel, a scoundrel).

After a few minutes, the wood plank door at the white cement and stone-front house opened slowly. The old woman stood there, cane in hand and hunched over due to a spinal curvature, and looked up. Her eyesight had been failing, but her face lit up. "Bettina! Bella Bettina!" she exclaimed, throwing her arms around the smiling Bettina. Filomena took her hand in her gnarled, arthritic, bent hand and kissed it. The little girl watched intently. "Vene, vene!" (Come, come!)

They entered and sat at a table in the little kitchen. Bettina eventually explained that soon she and her family would sail off to America. The old woman nodded as tears ran down her face. "Buona, buona" (Good, good), she said. "Che niente ca per te America sono miraviloso. (There is nothing for you here. America is marvelous.) Bene di Dio figlia. Bene di Dio. (Go with God's blessing, my daughter. Go with God's blessing)," said the old woman.

Bettina became slightly confused. She could not quite understand why her eyes were tearing. "Bella Bettina to fare me molto felice. (Beautiful Bettina, you make me very happy.) Fare a vita nouva. (Make a new life.) Ma non di rescored me. (But never forget me.)"

Bettina felt a surge in her breast and hugged the old woman. "Mommina nessuno riscordare te (Little Mother, no one forgets you)," said Bettina. Salvetresa sat quietly maybe for the first time in her life.

"Allora me fare andiamo di America (Now I can go to America)," said Bettina. She then reached inside her dress and pulled out the photograph of her and Filomena taken those many years before. She had written on the back "Mommina Ti Amo, Bettina" (Little Mother, I love you, Bettina).

CHAPTER 19

THUS, IN THE late 1890s aboard a fully loaded "immigrant" transport ship, the Terranova/Scalisce clan uprooted and headed for America. The move also was done in consideration of other concerns.

The Triamonte were not done with the murder of the son of the Don. Before his death, the Don had become a recluse, in part because of his illness but also because he was informed by his cousins that the Triamonte had a vendetta against the Scalisce family. In fact, there were murders of two Scalisce family members, one in Messina and one in Palermo. The Don, mindful of his weakened position, had warned his entire family of the threats. Bettina was well aware that her small children were in danger since they carried the Scalisce name, but it was unusual that a vendetta would prompt the murder of a child. Vengeance of the type sought by the Triamonte could rage for decades, sometimes generations, allowing them to wait until a child became a young man to dispose of him. This vendetta did not exclude women, although in many instances if a widow did not display any threat, she was passed over. Thus, the family of Bettina Scalisce-Terranova still had serious concerns that someday the Triamonte would seek additional vengeance. There was an added benefit to continuing the vendetta. Inspiring a fear of violence can be powerful. The Triamonte's vendettas worked this way: never forget, never forgive.

As this immigrant-filled vessel steamed into the bustling port of the greatest city in the world, the sight was awesome to behold. The entire visual panorama of the harbor after such a long, monotonous voyage with nothing to see but ocean was more than a welcome sight. A verbal description of the size and grandeur of this sight was never sufficient preparation for actually being there. Ships and boats passed across the skyline of Manhattan, with the Statue of Liberty protruding upward, and as the vessel passed, many of those standing silently on the deck looked upward and made the sign of the cross. It was as if they interpreted the figure of this monumental woman as a Catholic deity. This lady who exuded the word they had heard over and over again in their homelands—Libertà, Libertà, La Donna di libertà (Liberty, Liberty, and the Lady of Liberty). Coming from a land that was the home of the pope and the Roman Catholic Church, the Italians had a habit of attaching religious importance to everything, and this statue was no exception.

The decision for some Italians to immigrate to America was an extremely difficult one. Though they faced poverty and persecution at the hands of the upper class and had no real freedom, they knew no other place, no other life. If they got even the sheer minimum of knowledge by chance, it only served to help them understand even more how desperate their condition was compared to someone living in a democracy like America. Those who had educated a relative or friend might teach a child. The irregular formal schools in places like the internal countryside of Sicily might be organized and supported by the townspeople who had a means of participating by paying a tax or simply by paying a teacher to educate their children at home. The wealthy, some with a social conscience, also helped to support the church. In fact, many of the schools were church run, and it was the most important source for organized education.

A poor peasant could learn that the way foreign governments operated was a far cry from the neo-serfdom under the control of patrones, but they also had the land, their family, and traditions. They would have to decide, in a real sense, to leave all that behind. Most, with meager possessions and without knowing what the future held, had to convince themselves to leap into the abyss, leaving their paese (town) behind. It was all made more difficult by the fact that there was little chance these voyagers would ever return since it was difficult enough just to buy tickets for one voyage across the seas to America, let alone to get money for a visit back again.

When a family said its last goodbyes, the mood felt as if they were dying, and in a sense, they were. With the exception of writing a letter home now and then and perhaps sending photographs, all ties to one's family, town, and country were severed.

Life in Sicilian Italy seemed to have had an effect of rooting people to the land, to the place of their birth, and it still does. The ancestral history of those people created an invisible bond. They were indeed people of that place, that earth, but more than that, there was a sense of ownership to this land, these towns, and the cities. More than just a feeling of familiarity, they were part of a common history and landscape, and each generation felt as close to the land as the next for centuries. When the soil did not produce, some felt as if it was a personal insult from this *terra amaro* (bitter earth). If the vines were poor producers or the weather wreaked havoc with the grapes, it was considered anger expressed by nature against them in an extremely personal manner. "Dio Aiuto" (God Help Me) and therefore the church was a place of communication as much as it was for communion, and here in this silence of the stone edifice lit by candles, they could have a conversation with God.

The dons and padrones were given special places within the church pews at the front of all others, closer to the priest, the altar, and the sacraments and to God himself. They could dispense *una benedizone* (a benediction) as they saw fit. Roman Catholic doctrine recognized that benedictions were the province of a man of the cloth. These pseudo icons who had influence with the church somehow converted the gesture of the kissing of the hand, the bowed back or bent knee, the sign of the cross and a benediction statement completed a Don's form of eliciting a special benefit to the recipient. Or perhaps it grew out of a sense of acquiescence to his power and as a sign of respect and compliance. These acts by the mock pope were taught regularly by those under the protection of the leader, the padrone, the don. This tradition became part of the rituals of the Mafia, incorporating religious symbolism and utilizing the Roman Catholic tradition of obeying and having reverence for the higher power, be it priest, bishop, padrone, or don.

Many of these pseudo-demagogues took the perception to heart. Though ruthless, and most bloodthirsty, they would wear the Christian cross hung from their necks much like a monk or a priest. They sought acknowledgment by their chosen church as benefactor and supporter, perhaps in the hope that they could con the deity into some benefits in the afterlife by some good works to offset their villainous lives. The incorporation of Renaissance era religious symbolism lent a time-honored essence to these rituals. Seeking the blessing by the father of a proposed bride, a position the father shared with the old padrone, as well as through life with rituals at the birth of children and finally at death contained elements of the old ways and rituals were incorporated into the modern-day authority of the padrone. The rules of morality were interpreted and decided by these ritualistic concepts as well as by the padrone's authority. While infidelity was not in itself *una infamia* (a disgrace), cohorting with the wife of a man of honor, a relative of the don, or with one's own blood-related woman was a transgression sure to be ruled the worst of offenses. The list of intolerable acts did not necessarily incorporate the Ten Commandments, only where there was specific application or where the commandment could not be convoluted or interpreted. "You are the Lord, thy God, there shall be no other strange Gods before you" was clear and accepted. The dogma of the Holy Trinity of the Roman Catholic Church was not disputed, although one could argue that the Mafia's rules put one's life in the organization in their rule as primary upon pain of death. Was this a perversion of the commandment? The act of burning an image of a saint was part of the Mafia ritual of reciting, "May I burn in hell like this image if I betray my oath."

The coveting of thy neighbor's goods and wife might be permissible as long as it was not a fellow member's wife or the goods of a relative, the church, or another interpretation barring the act.

The idea that the Sabbath should be kept holy only applied when there was no serious work to be done.

"Thou shalt not kill"? Well, again, this was modified with few exceptions; murder when necessary was surely an option God would just have to understand. If we kill in war or in self-defense, then surely there were exceptions to the commandment. Did not the Lord permit the "slaying of the enemy" in biblical interpretations? So, if someone encroached on your territory, was it not war, an affront permitting retaliation? Homosexuality between men or women was considered a perversion of God's meaning of life and was denounced in the church as a curse and an intolerable sin. Yet, if it did not directly affect one, it was simply ignored, if not tolerated. Thus, the mentality was not to disobey God but to employ an alternative explanation of how to employ the rules in God's commandments as well as one's own rules.

Should a made man become senile and unable to control his mouth about the business, he forfeited his rights to a protective shield.

The Mafia members distilled, and at times distorted, the lessons learned from generation to generation. The traits that lived on included patience, cunning, silence, thought planning, wariness, distrust, loyalty, obligation, and respect. They understood that religion played a large part in the lives of the people in their own families. With their women, they kept the religious holidays, the major ones and the minor ones, and they celebrated the feast days and the saints' days. They had an ally in the church due to their generosity, and by their observances, others followed, acknowledging the importance of the church and those ordained by the church.

Those in the church had no alternative but to accept all comers regardless of their reputation. The church's doctrine of forgiveness of sins, all sins, was the hallmark of their teaching and the purpose of the confessional. Absolution was a mere penance in this life.

While the motives of most church leaders were righteous, those who sought to use their association with the church were surely not as committed. The appearance of propriety and being an intricate part of the religious life at the church was yet another social shield and layer of insulation, and it transferred that image of power, to some degree, to those who sought to impose their will on others. Consider that in the middle and end of the 1900s, political and business leaders sought to further their careers by doing the same thing. The Kennedys' historic relationship with the Catholic Church and its cardinal is one notable example. Presidents sought out Billy Graham, the nationally revered evangelist, for council and support, and others did the same. Their dual sense of morality, one for public life and one for a private one, made no difference. The mistresses, adultery, thievery, money laundering, and other illegal acts tainted the personal reputations of presidents of the United States from FDR to Eisenhower, Kennedy, LBJ, and of course Clinton. England's "Profumo Affair" and those of the French and Canadian politicians were no less sensational. All hid behind a feigned righteousness and a close association with the church, but only after their moral indiscretions were publicly exposed did we learn of the true fabric of these leaders.

CHAPTER 20

CARLO HAD AN uncle who met the Terranovas at the port. "Carlo, Carlo," Zio Giuseppe called through the fence as the Terranova family exited the treadway off the vessel. Carlo immediately recognized his old uncle and ran to the fence. "Zio!" (Uncle!) Carlo said excitedly as they touched hands.

The rest of his family followed behind. An immigration official directed them to a nearby ferry ramp that took them to Ellis Island to be formally processed. Although it only took three days, it seemed like months.

Once released, they were met by Zio Giuseppe when the ferry from Ellis Island landed at Manhattan's Battery area ferry dock in New York City.

The crowded conditions on the ship from Italy gave the family its first glimpse of what they could expect in America. This was confirmed when they all had to squeeze into one small cabin for the voyage. This was at least better than steerage, where hundreds were jammed in a large area in the bowels of the ship. Next, the experience of the processing at Ellis Island, waiting in lines and threading their way through crowds hour after hour, was new for all of them. Bettina and Carlo had been to the cities of Palermo and Messina, but they had never experienced the huge crowds so crushed together. To the children, this was all new as well, having seen only the countryside in their town. Bettina's children obeyed her implicitly.

The uncle was fortunate to have found the family an apartment in a five-story tenement building on Grand Street near Mulberry with two bedrooms, a kitchen, a bathroom, and a dining room. It also had a small storage room that doubled as another bedroom. The quarters were tight but adequate. Zio Giuseppe had a small produce shop re-selling fruit and vegetables from this shop on Grand Street. The three older boys, Antonio, Giuseppe, and Nicholas, sought work wherever they could get it and ended up with odd jobs hauling furniture or cleaning a store. They even found that they could make a few cents by helping some of the local street gangs case nearby neighborhoods for potential targets. Robbing stores and reselling the stolen goods were good ways to make money. This introduction to the street gangs led to being more acceptable, as time went on, to the more established crime lords.

The family moved north from Grand Street to a larger apartment after Bettina had another male child, Giovanni. It was a three-bedroom tenement in the lower Harlem area, and it was here that the Scalisce boys learned quickly and became members of one of the most powerful street gangs in the entire city.

Ciro Terranova   Ciro Terranova

CHAPTER 21

YOUNG CIRO TERRANOVA quickly learned the ways of the New York gangs. Because of his experience in the fruit and vegetable stores, he was introduced to the wholesalers in the produce markets and became knowledgeable about the commerce at the piers in the Red Hook area of Brooklyn and up in Yonkers just north of Manhattan. Since most of the olive oil in New York was imported from Europe, it came through the piers from Italian ships with huge cargos unloaded by immigrants. Ciro was clever enough to devise a scheme to bribe the crew bosses to slow down the unloading of the cargo in order to frustrate the shippers. However, if these buyers and the shippers wanted help speeding up the work, Ciro was there to provide the service. Since the so-called tribute wasn't a great deal of money at the start of his scheme, they paid it. The more they paid, the greater his influence on the piers.

Eventually, he became a principal entity for controlling the off-loading of olive oil in the city. He kept in contact with the friends and family he left behind in Sicily and had them deal with the olive oil producers the Scalisces had done business with. By importing their oil at a slightly higher price than the local distributors, he cut out the commissions of the middle men, controlling all of the olive oil importation into New York City and backing it up with the force of local street gangs when necessary. Since the majority of olive oil was sent through the port of New York, he controlled the product nationwide.

He had also concentrated his efforts on the railways in the Lower West Side of Manhattan where the railroad cars arrived with the produce intended for the different distribution centers. Here, his contacts in the market and the transport of the goods from the rail yards inspired another scheme. Since artichokes were primarily grown and consumed by Italians, he quickly learned how to control the stocks of artichokes before they even got transported to market.

If the produce wasn't moved quickly, it would rot. The growers in California were under his control.

He even bought the product before it was shipped and then inflated the price in the market to wholesalers and vendors. Any competition was dealt with harshly. Thus, after several years, Ciro earned the nickname "Artichoke King" as well as "Olive Oil King." These rackets kept him in close and constant touch with the street gangs in East Harlem since he provided them with work and a source of income. He recalled his boyhood days as a street gang member and could relate easily to these young men. As his influence and wealth grew, he also became well known with several local politicians. He used those contacts to help elect councilmen and in return got their assistance in introductions and eventual friendship with the police and dock security. He also had friends in security at the rail yards and piers and was recognized by one of the leading gang bosses, Geosue Galluci.

Galluci, an immigrant as well, had to learn his way on the streets and eventually built a racketeering empire. He operated a numbers racket and was also involved in hijacking, loan sharking, and small operations bringing in narcotics, a commodity sold in the colored districts of Harlem for big profits. Ciro had a unique way of easily fitting in with anyone, whatever their social class. He was a short man, about five feet five, and though not overweight had a rotund appearance. While his mother, Bettina, was slim and graceful, he resembled the short and stocky Sicilians with rounded faces and protruding, prominent noses. While his skin was not really a deep olive color, he seemed to have a perpetual suntan. Unlike his mother, whose mesmerizing blue eyes were immediately noticeable, Ciro's hazel colored eyes favored the Terranova genes. He had a very easy manner but could be, in an instant, forceful and foreboding.

He knew every block of Harlem, and when Galluci was murdered, Ciro easily moved to take over the numbers racket.

He also derived some income from the narcotics trade and became well known to the upper echelon of organized crime leaders and assisted them when they needed a trusted ally. Thus, he met the leader of the Lower Eastside Mafia, Ignazio Lupo, known as "Iggy the Wolf." Iggy had also done well as an immigrant. He controlled a very lucrative immigrant area. The Sicilians had the control now. A rival organized crime organization, Il Cammora, was made up of primarily immigrants born in the Naples area who had imported their brand of criminal enterprise to the new world, as had the Sicilian Mafia. However, the sheer numbers of Sicilians didn't bode well for these Cammoristas. Yet they remained vicious and deadly.

Iggy was introduced to Ciro's sister, Salvatrese, and an instant, romance blossomed. With the marriage of his sister to Iggy, Ciro became his close ally, and the Terranovas and the Mondellos and Iggy became more and more powerful.

Giosue Gallucci   Ignazio "Iggy" Lupoo

The rackets were expanding into Brooklyn, the Bronx, and Queens as more immigrants came and spread through the city. Though their influence with law enforcement was considerable, some of the Cammoristas had come to America even before the Sicilians and had established their organization Il Mano Nero (The Black Hand) with ruthless power. They bought the influence of corrupt police as well.

Thus, when Iggy Lupo and Giuseppe Scalisce ventured to Brooklyn to compete with the Cammora in their home territory, members of the Cammora kept close watch on their activities. Through paid informants, they were able to tie Giuseppe Morella and Iggy the Wolf to a series of beatings of local merchants and a string of fires at those bakeries that would not comply. Both were arrested, convicted, and sent to Sing-Sing prison, appropriately known as being sent "up the river" since the prison was located in Ossining, New York, and was built on the banks of the Hudson River north of the city.

When Iggy's influence and presence was gone, Ciro and his brothers had to maintain the organization without him. Nicholas and Antonio Scalisce and Vincent Terranova with Ciro's leadership tried to maintain what control they had but also get even with the Cammoras who had set up Iggy and Giuseppe. Ciro continued the fledging racket in the Brooklyn neighborhood controlled by them.

In retaliation, however, Nicholas Scalisce was accosted on the street going home one evening in East Harlem, and two men stabbed him to death.

The news of the death of one of Iggy's lieutenants was a signal that Iggy, the Scalisces, and the Terranovas were unable to maintain their grip on the organization.

Ciro recognized the problem. The concern grew, as did opportunity. With the passage of federal legislation's Volstead Act prohibiting sales of alcoholic beverages, the roaring twenties began in earnest.

A short, fat stump of a man, Joseph Masseria, had managed through murder, extortion, loan sharking, and then bootlegging liquor, to rise to the pinnacle of having one of the most powerful organized crime gangs in the city. He had built a formidable name in the Mafia, and Terranova considered that aligning his group with Masseria would preserve his organization. It was likely "Joe the Boss," as he was nicknamed, would end up running the entire city's crime organization.

Within a few years, Masseria and Terranova did solidify their grip on organized crime and took control of the bootlegging racket. Terranova's knowledge of transportation distribution and his connections with law enforcement combined with Masseria's huge cadre of men resulted in rival gangs coming under their control.

Ciro still had concerns. He knew that his family, through its history, had many members murdered. He recalled the stories his mother told him of his half brother's father and the murder of those in Italy and the Triamonte vendetta and the murder of Nicholas. Now that he had attained leadership status, he knew he was more a target than ever.

He also had a new concern. He had decided to marry a nice Sicilian girl, Vincenzia Marchetta. She too had come from Corleone, and he knew her family. He found a quiet neighborhood in the Bronx in the Pelham Manor section, a tree-lined, almost rural setting, and purchased a large home with a large garden. He brought his new bride and his mother out of the threats in the city to this safe haven.

His concern elevated when two of his men were gunned down by machine gun fire in front of a warehouse in Harlem. He purchased a big Packard limousine and had the doors lined with thick lead shields and doubled the glass with sheets of bulletproof glass.

By the close of the roaring twenties, Ciro's family had grown. He had three children, and with his longevity as a mob leader, he had become a target for federal and state law enforcement. Local police were wary of being implicated in dealings with the mob once state and federal authorities showed interest, so Ciro began to lose his alliances with the police and judges.

The immigration from Italy intensified, and a new crime organization imported from the town of Castella del Mare del Golfo appeared in the late 1920s. This Mafia gang had a longstanding rivalry with the Corleone Mafia. Masseria "Joe the Boss" saw their emergence as a threat. They had once been rivals in Sicily and were now enemies in America.

Giuseppe Masseria

Salvatore "Charles
Lucky" Luciano

Meyer Lansky

CHAPTER 22

SALVATORE "CHARLIE LUCKY" Luciana and his gang had also come to prominence in New York. While he and Ciro maintained a tentative truce, neither trusted the other. Luciana associated with Masseria from time to time, and there was a tentative truce or at least unspoken understanding. Luciana's group of friends included allies in the Jewish mob as well, including Meyer Lansky and Benjamin "Bugsy" Siegel. Lansky was a brilliant financier, while Siegel, aptly nicknamed "Bugsy," had a violent streak and would kill without hesitation. Since Masseria had exhibited strength, both Luciana and Terranova continued their alignment with him until it became clear that the Castella del Mare group sought an all-out war. This breed of immigrants hungered for power and was more ruthless and bloodthirsty. Soon the streets of New York became a killing field. The Castella del Mare group was run by an astute, educated leader, Salvatore Maranzano, a man more suited to be a mayor or professor than a mobster. He dressed in tailor-made suits with formal starched white collars and spoke in a measured voice. He was tall for a southern Italian, six feet, and squarely and somewhat athletically built. He had a thick handlebar moustache, and his build, carriage, and voice made him look and sound like one of the leaders of the old Carabinieri, the elite Italian army that was athletically built, educated, and well trained. These men were the cream of the Italian army in the late 1800s and were seen as romantic figures, elite, and dedicated to duty, dressed in uniforms with large elaborate swords hanging from fancy sheaths. Maranzano emulated that behavior.

Maranzano liked to quote the great authors of Italian literature and had serious admiration for the Roman emperors and their empires. He prided himself in his knowledge of Roman history and surrounded himself with sculptures and paintings by Italian artists and sought to live a lifestyle mimicking that of seventeenth-century Italian noblemen. Yet he commanded the respect of the most ruthless Mafia members and through bootlegging and other criminal rackets accumulated great wealth. The fate of "Joe the Boss" was eventually decided by his allies, Luciana and Terranova. Ciro felt a sense of kinship with Masseria. They had both grown up together in a small rural Sicilian town and struggled in the streets of New York as kids before rising above the numerous street gangs. They had no opportunity at schooling, and beyond reading and writing, they were mostly self-taught. Maranzano represented the old world of Il Patrone to a large extent.

Ciro, however, was a practical man. He knew Maranzano had command of more men and more vicious and ambitious immigrants willing to crush life to win.

Luciana also knew Maranzano would emerge over Masseria and that one would eventually be killed.

He informed Terranova of his concerns and enlisted Ciro to assist in the elimination of Joe Masseria. It made good business sense. Ciro agreed, fearing that if he did not side with Luciana, he too would end up dead. They planned for Masseria's assassination to take place in his office. Ciro was told to enter Joe's office first along with "Charlie Lucky" Luciana and Antonio Scalisce.

On the morning of April 15, 1931, the three men came to the building where Joe had his office. Luciano thrust a revolver into Ciro's pocket before muttering, "You do the shooting." That wasn't the original plan. Ciro was not supposed to be the one to pull the trigger, but it was too late to back out. They opened the door, went through a hall, and saw Joe sitting at his desk. He rose. Ciro began to speak to him but seemed nervous. "What is it?" asked Joe. Suddenly the room filled with the sound of a revolver firing, and a hole appeared in Joe's forehead. Luciana fired three more times into his chest. Luciana glared in anger at Ciro because he had failed to help since he never raised his gun to shoot. It was to be a huge error for Ciro.

Maranzano was quickly told of Joe's demise and was cautiously pleased since he now dominated the organization without opposition.

Ciro, on the other hand, had mixed feelings about what he'd done. The last-minute hesitation revealed an unconscious unwillingness to execute a man who was his friend. Luciana had no such feeling. Masseria was merely another mob acquaintance who, as far as "Charlie Lucky" was concerned, was expendable if it served his purposes. Since he was one of the *giovani* (young men), he learned the harsh reality of living a life with street gangs and hoodlums. His run-in with an opposing gang resulted in his being slashed across the face, shot, and left for dead. He survived with that huge scar, a daily reminder of the life he had chosen, thus his cheating death earned him the nickname "Lucky." Ciro and Luciana had a very different upbringing. Ciro, one of several children, was exposed to the needs of siblings and family. Luciana was a loner and self-centered. Likely, Luciana's ambition to excel at any cost was never balanced with genuine regard for anyone else. Ciro married and had children. Charlie's female companions were generally prostitutes.

In the eyes of Luciana, Ciro was weak, and he would never attain his confidence. As a result, Charlie saw him as a person to be exploited. Soon after Lucky systematically undermined Ciro's authority with his men, and out of fear and loss of faith in Ciro, they then turned to Luciana for leadership. Ciro's wealth and prestige deteriorated; he lost more and more power. In the life of a Mafia boss, one either excelled and advanced or spiraled downward but never stood still. Within the next few years, Ciro's position declined to where he lost his other rackets, including olive oil. Finally, under direct attack by orders of the tough antimob mayor, Fiorello "the Little Flower" La Guardia, he banned artichokes in New York just to stop distribution. By 1935, Ciro was broke, and by 1937, he lost his Pelham Manor homestead. The mental pressure and failing in his life during the 1930s resulted in his suffering a massive and fatal stroke in 1938. Meanwhile, Lucky Luciano and his cohorts planned and executed Maranzano, and Luciana formed the "Commission," bringing the five Mafia families in New York together, ending the so-called Castella del Mare War. Luciano's ability to eliminate the existing bosses earned him the leadership role, both out of admiration for his skills and fear of his ruthlessness. He set up territories and organized the families in orderly regimes that harkened back to the Roman legions' sequential order of ten units to a crew and creating the titles the leadership would carry, a capo (boss), a sotto capo (underboss), a consigliere (counselor), and then captains and soldiers, a chain of command that had well served the Roman emperors' army for centuries.

Bettina Terranova, a widow from the sudden death of her husband from a mysterious illness, lost her son Vincent Terranova in his early twenties, a victim of a drive-by shooting by rival bootleggers. Her other son, Nicholas Scalisce, was also murdered. She now had only her daughter and two sons left.

The children, Antonio, Vincenzina, and Franco, moved back with their mother, Bettina, when Antonio and she found a quiet place, a large apartment away from the day-to-day threat in East Harlem. Antonio moved himself and his family along with his mother to the Bronx with his three children and wife, Paolina.

The children found that life in the mainstream of America tradition was pleasant and rewarding; they rejected the life organized crime demanded.

Vincenzina met the Merendinos, a family in the same building. Their son Vincenzo and she were of the same age and were Corleonese. The attraction was mutual and resulted in marriage. Vincenzina had six children from this marriage: Frank, Vincenzina, Sara, Bettina (called Bessie), Maria, and Salvatore. There was a large family in Italy, and other Merendinos came to America as well.

Vincenzina was born when her mother, who returned to Italy several months before the child's birth, went back to Corleone for an extended visit. She had gone back to settle some unfinished business of her former husband's estate.

Mayor Fiorello "Little Flower" LaGuardia

CHAPTER 23

ENRICO MERENDINO'S LIFE was spawned of those times. The monarchy still had some influence and was perpetuated by the padrones and landholders, while a new regime and government force was struggling to create a more unified and democratic society. The desire to be a person of importance stirred in every man's heart. Enrico sought to make his way in America, the land where money could come to anyone. Then he landed in New York City. He found that there were also barriers similar to those that existed in his native country but in a different way in America. Here, being an Italian put you in the low caste, similar to the peasant class back home. Enrico was the product of a thousand years of Roman history. His Sicilian roots and heritage provided him with a keen intelligence. Had there been IQ tests at that time, he would have scored off the board—a genius! But without much formal education and a limited social and community background, Enrico had to rely on what he learned at home and his own instincts. He was a quick learner and an eager student. Thus, the history of the Italian immigrant in America began by underestimating the intelligence and abilities of these foreigners to succeed in an American society. But succeed they did.

He was the one who left his family in Italy and began a new generation in America of Merendinos.

The immigrants in America also suffered the indignity of a government that ignored them. Thus, the immigrants fell back upon their own kind of social order, opening a new chapter of secret government, this time not in Italy but in America. The Neapolitans transported their La Cammora; the Sicilians brought their Mafia.

And thus, Enrico Merendino found that life and its challenges remained, regardless of where one chose to live.

These organizations easily brushed aside the new and modern theory of a revolution for one that has stood the test of time. Change is the standard if indeed change can be acknowledged as a standard.

Enrico Merendino grew up in the feudal history that was centuries old. Little change occurred, as little change was needed or wanted. The society was homogenous. The old Italian and in fact European-style order shunned outsiders. That was no truer than in Sicily. "Omerta," the code of secrecy, was a way of life for these island dwellers, though the word never existed in their common language. There was no need for the word. The concept was understood. Outsiders were never to be accepted, never to be included, never to know what the locals knew, and what they knew they kept in secret. So it was for centuries; the invaders of Sicily left their mark and their legacy written on the island's winds and infused in the soul of its people.

The Moors' influence, still evidenced by their style of architecture and the grand arches and facades and towers, was the neo-Islamic testament to their past presence. More sanguine, however, was the olive-dark and black-skin Sicilians, the inheritors of the Moorish blood. The rape and comingling with the Sicilian women on an immense scale over centuries by these invaders from the south told a more significant story. People's coloration varied from fair-skinned, black-eyed beauties to black-eyed, black-skinned, mysterious-looking creatures who were all Sicilian. The need for these people to protect themselves was the catalyst for secret societies and unions. Since there was a continual history of invasion from the French, the northerners, the Greeks, the Africans, Moors, and other Arabs had an ingrained sense of necessity to self-preserve.

So it was with the formation of the Cammora in Naples, since the history of invasions there were similar to Sicily. The so-called Black Hand (I Mano Nero) grew in this port city, a city of riches, by way of their harbor attracting commerce from all over the Mediterranean Sea and a world of import goods. Sicily offered a different wealth, fertility—fruit, figs, citrus, nuts, lamb, goats, cattle, olives, grapes for wine, spices, and so much more, not to mention the fertility of the women.

The young Sicilian women were sturdy, proportionate, passionate, supple, and condescending to the male. These women, predominantly with their dark eyes and black hair, with robust healthy complexions, sensuous, full lips and intriguing demeanors, were as desirable as were the other spoils of conquest.

So the protective societies flourished for centuries. Even after World War I, little changed. The advent of World War II and the alliances made by the Mafia and the US government created an easy opportunity for the Mafia to gain a kind of nominal acceptance as an organization, sufficient to make a deal to assist the war effort.

The legendary gangster Salvatore "Charlie Lucky" Luciana and his cohorts assisted the US war effort, the invasion and subsequent fall of Mussolini, and, by the way, Hitler. The war solidified the connections between the Mafia and the US government in an unholy alliance but an alliance all the same. That alliance would spur the growth and protection of the mob in the US for decades. It also helped to win the war. There was Mafia influence and reconnaissance at US ports and elsewhere to protect the American war effort.

However, the true noble aspects of the "Men of Respect" that their forefathers conceived gave way to the more decadent aspirations of the American society, the society of change that fed on profit. The control of these societies' more noble aspects and more creative minds eventually ended up in the hands of men who had no great moral codes but those self-conceived.

Salvatore Maranzano

CHAPTER 24

DON SALVATORE MARAZANO and the last vestige of the old-world code of honor expired when Salvatore "Charlie Lucky" Luciana took the reins of the American mob. His clever manipulation of the two old-world dons, Salvatore Marazano and Guiseppe Masseria, resulted in both of them being deceived, betrayed, and killed by Luciana and his cohorts. It was an enviable plot by any criminal standard but the end of an era for the historic Men of Respect. The old dons lived and died with their lust for revenge, a revenge passed on from generation to generation. But even this activity had a set of rules, and as ruthless and bloodthirsty as the forefathers of La Cosa Nostra were in the old country, they acted with a sense of balance fitting the retaliation to the offense. While the actions of foreign invaders, the army, or the Carbeniere were rarely seen as humane or at least judicious, the old dons at least sought out a more pious route.

There was a ritual when one was admitted to this secret society. The ritual was a passage from a mere "associate" to a "made man." It was the manner in which a new member was brought into this Mafia organization. The secret ritual, participated in and witnessed only by made members, took place once the candidate had reached a certain level of acceptance. The controlling commission in the United States dictated when the books could be open. The making of new members could only occur when the leadership of the commission, the ruling heads of the American Mafia families, agreed to do so. There was no set schedule, and someone could wait years for the books to reopen and to be inducted. The ceremony involved a circle of men as witnesses bringing the candidate to the forefront and having him place his hand on a Bible and swearing his allegiance to the organization. The dagger was then used to cut a finger and swear a blood oath, and an image of a saint on a paper card was set in the candidate's hands and set afire. As it burned, he swore an oath that he would burn in hell as the image of that saint in his hands was burning if he betrayed the oath. This induction committed the man to an oath for life. As a made man, he could never renounce his membership or retire. He was committed to obey the rules of the organization above all other rules or obligations by any other authority or commitments to anyone or anything, be it his family, his government, humanity, his church, even the laws of God. Thus, even the Ten Commandments were no longer his to uphold. The ritual incorporated elements that many did not even consider or chose not to. The ritual itself was an affirmation of a union, of an obligation, of an authority, of an acceptance, and of a religion. It was also a paradox. The symbols, a dagger and a Bible, were clear, as was the reference to the saints, albeit not in the normal sense. The burning of an image of the saint spoke to punishment but also, importantly, to the existence of the saints and the religion and the mortal soul. Somehow this organization thus acknowledged God and church. The drafting of the oath by those who structured this society much in the way as ancient brotherhoods, such as the Knights Templar and the Masonic Order, considered their charge to follow a noble cause, and as much as there was a time when these Men of Respect, the dons, conducted themselves accordingly, the meaning deteriorated, and the baser elements of power, control, and fear overwhelmed their more noble intentions. The seeds of destruction of any order or society are sewn within it. Driven by power and greed, this society's respect deteriorated bit by bit with its exportation to America. As these men became Americanized, they lusted after an accelerated life, and they had a voracious appetite for change and renewal in the American core, with little reverence for history.

"Papa" Merendino

CHAPTER 25

RARELY DID PAPA Merendino raise his voice above a quiet, conversational tone. Then again, Merendino rarely spoke unless it was absolutely necessary. The late 1890s were excellent years for those like Merendino who owned properties and estates in the crop-growing regions of Sicily. The olive groves produced such profits that patrones like Merendino sought to buy even more holdings. Spaced near the olive trees were groves of lemon, orange, fig, almond, chestnut, pine nut trees and more and, of course, vineyards.

The mild winters with periodic rains followed by the warm, sunny growing periods were like *i bene di Dio* (a blessing from the Lord). Silverio Merendino had another blessing as well. His wife had given birth to ten healthy children, seven of them male and the last three female. He envisioned his own family as a budding dynasty.

Francesco, the eldest son, was already directing crews of peasant workers in the fields, and by age fourteen, he had won their respect. As a result, he was able to organize the planting, transport, and harvest without a hitch, and his crew had the shortest daily schedule of all twelve work crews. It helped that he had his father's temperament: quiet, cool, insightful, and strong. These were the traits of Sicilians in these fields and mountains. They planned and worked and prospered.

They were still part of a feudal system. Il padrone was addressed in the formal title of don, and depending on a laborer's association with the padrone, it was customary to use only his last name if there was anyone else within listening distance. The use of a first name after the title was reserved for those of greater stature and importance. This social order suggested not only who was in the higher echelon but also where one fit in that order. Even when addressing the padrone by his first name, however, the title don was always necessary to show respect.

Don Merendino's wife, Sophia, and sons, Francesco, Salvatore, Enrico, Giovanni, Giacomo, Silverio Jr., and Benito, kept a close eye on all the happenings in their paese and were particularly concerned with the goings-on of Nuinzia, Giacenta, and Yagenta, the three little girls. The boys were born two or three years apart, but the girls seemed nearly all the same age. The last two looked like twins since they were born barely ten months apart.

Francesco had a tall, wiry frame, which was unusual in this family. In fact, in this entire region, there weren't many tall men. Few, in fact, were really large framed except those whose ancestry included the bloodlines of the conquering African Moors or other such invaders. The Moorish bloodlines had a way of accentuating the deep olive skin color as well. Francesco's physical traits were a far cry from the figure his father cut. Papa Merendino was a short, stout barrel of a man. His skin was burnt by the sun, but he was still much lighter than his son. The dark olive skin and jet-black hair of his wife, Filomena, were the commanding genes of Francesco's physical attributes. She was thin and slightly taller than her husband, which in itself was unusual. She was extremely dexterous and quick. She could sew, though she left ordinary sewing to servants and housekeepers. She would, however, crochet and embroider grand appliqués on the clothing of her little girls and could play *il mandolino* and *la concertina* as well as sing. She was strikingly beautiful with a straight, elegant nose, high cheekbones, and big black eyes. She might have been taken for a gypsy had it not been for her courtly manner, keen intelligence, and trusting eyes.

Salvatore was just ten years old, but he was beginning to look more and more like Francesco. Though still somewhat shorter, he was built like his older brother and mother. He had, however, much lighter skin and shock of red hair. He was also a very attentive student of his older brother's actions and would strive to emulate Francesco down to the way he held his fork. The two brothers were inseparable, and Salvatore seemed more like Francesco's twin than a younger sibling.

Enrico was another story. He was short and stout, even more bulky than his father, with black skin and black hair. His rotund face and deep-set eyes gave him a lightly menacing quality even as a child of eight years. He was even more serious than his father. On Sundays after *chiesa* (church), the family would spend a few hours in the late morning visiting relatives, the Delasantes. More often, though, Silverio would visit his aging father and mother. Usually Silverio's younger brothers, Angelo and Francesco, or his sister, Lena, would stop by too and bring part of the day's meal. The town, Carini, was about three miles from the Merendinos' properties and had several little shops and cafes. There were some 1,200 residents in the maze of little streets of stone and concrete houses that wound through the hillside. The church and a huge cobblestone piazza stood at the top of the hill. The bell tower and its bells could be seen as one approached the town. Now the Merendinos had so many mouths to feed that they started making larger and larger stocks of pasta. They also had stores of grain, which they ground into flour, and semolina and even some rice. Over time, they grew a large surplus.

Thus began Silverio's small retail enterprise. He found an empty shop near the church and convinced the owner, an elderly tailor, to rent it to him. In time, the little shop did well, and Silverio also purchased the shop next door when the widow who owned it lost her only son to influenza. The main products were their pasta, grains, flour, nuts, seeds, and such, but Silverio would also send other items when the abundant season's crops were harvested. The one thing that generated attention was the few liters of olive oil that he had specially filtered and refined. Silverio had learned how to do it from his great uncle when his father sent him to help him, since the uncle had no children. The brightness of the gold-green color and clarity came through a secret and special filtering process the uncle had devised with help from an old Spanish farmhand who lived with his family. A small amount of this oil went a long way, and it remained flavorful and rich. The other secret was knowing when the olives were ripe and how to combine various strains of the olive fruit as well as the proper pressing process and extraction of the water. It was costlier since only about 75 percent of the normal yield would end up as part of the final product.

Over the next ten years, Silverio Merendino bought more and more olive groves and purchased what he could from the neighboring groves as well. Francesco and Salvatore learned all there was to learn from Papa Merendino, and that became part of the secret to their success. Silverio and his two eldest sons grew in other ways as well. The wealth and land holdings brought respect. Protection by the Merendino aura was known in the surrounding towns. The Merendinos brought prosperity to these areas by maintaining alliances to purchase not only olives but also other locally produced products. They steadily maintained their purchases and stabilized the price of several products, particularly the olives. Even if the olive harvest was not as good from season to season and the olives were not up to the highest standard, they would still maintain the usual growers' price. In addition, they would occasionally lend a fellow grower some men to help out if there was a shortage of workers, or a little money if there was some kind of problem in their family. For this generosity, they would not only receive respect but also genuine loyalty. They took care of their flock in more than a biblical sense. They were patrones in the social as well as the economic sense, as well as general mediators and benevolent protectors.

This role was particularly important because of the bandits, which were a part of life in Sicily. These marauding bands of men were a constant threat to the wealthy and the weaker people of the region. If a household had no protection, they were helped by the Merendinos, who made sure that if anyone encroached on their extended family or friends, they would be dealt with in the most severe way and with vivid expression of brutality. As a result, the bandits avoided the paese around the Merendinos.

The legends of the village of Corleone date back centuries, including the one about the rape and murder of a young girl during the raids on Corleone. The poor distraught mother went berserk and ran screaming in the streets, "Mia figlia, mia figlia" (My daughter, my daughter). The town people identified with the centuries of invasion and oppression by the word "Mafia" (symbolic of the cry "mia figlia"). Thereafter, the townsmen of Corleone joined in organizing a plan for self-protection and vowed that since justice and protection eluded them, they would join together for the mutual protection. While there was no concept of an enterprise, the cooperation grew into more than just a method for physical protection. The settlement of disputes, the welfare for *e meschino* (an unfortunate), and the judicial and social orders evolved around this core sentiment of mutual protection and justice. It became the only equitable system of law and order, but it was more like a benevolent dictatorship.

The Merendinos understood this theory well and followed its principles. Their extended influence was considered a force of good that benefited the entire area. Others were less beneficial to the peasants with their power, but Merendino saw things differently.

Young Enrico did not have the same eagerness about operating the land interests. He was bored with the bucolic life of the farm and the groves and found any opportunity to go to the town and village. When there was opportunity to set up new transportation routes or new markets, Enrico would implore his father to permit him to take on the task. Over the period of adolescence and young manhood, Enrico not only excelled at problem solving and deal making, finding faster and safer routes for products, but he also became a virtual innovator. He made deals with the operators of the trains to make unscheduled stops at points close to Merendino product depots and had goods picked up for markets in other towns. In order to placate the train passengers, he had his men pass out fruit and wine to crew and passengers and provided some lira to bribe the conductor. His father appreciated his ability and gave him the authority to fully manage and operate the shops in town with his uncle. Soon, not only was Enrico increasing the sales in the shops, he was also making deals with other suppliers to export the special Merendino olive oil to other parts of Sicily and eventually to the mainland.

He began to bring huge quantities of olive oil cans and had a metal stamp made with a Dino imprint that would be printed on every can that was sold or exported. Soon crates of Dino oil were being shipped to Palermo by train, wagon, and eventually the more primitive motor trucks. The ferries from Sicily across the straits of Messina brought the Dino oil to competitive markets at the edge of the mainland. Word reached Enrico that since these were large shipments, competitors on the mainland were becoming annoyed with the competition. Soon, shipments by railroad disappeared before they reached Palermo. Some shipments did leave shipping ports but disappeared thereafter. Something had to be done.

CHAPTER 26

ENRICO ARRANGED TO follow a very large shipment of oil, some two hundred crates, to Palermo. He anticipated trouble and had ten of his most aggressive men dress in disguise as poor laborers to accompany him. He wore peasant clothes and looked very much the part of a workman. Each of his men carried a cut-down shotgun and pistol carefully hidden under their baggy peasant shirts and bloused-out *pantalone* trousers and shoulder sacks that they slung over their shoulders and backs.

Enrico got on the train alone as it loaded the goods. The rest got on the train at the two nearby stations. Nearly two and a half hours passed as the train made its way through the Sicilian countryside. Not far from Palermo, the train suddenly stopped by a desolate crossroad. Waiting there was a group of twelve men and eight horse-drawn wagons. The men boarded the flat car and began unloading the crates of oil. After twenty or thirty crates were removed, there was some noise in the rear part of the flat car. Suddenly, one of the half-loaded wagons began to move. The horses walked up to the front of the train, but the wagons had no men on them. The crew leader, a short, stumpy man on horseback who was directing the crew in the front of the flat car, spurred his horse toward the back of the flat car. The other men stopped to look. Suddenly, a barrage of shots rang out, and one by one, the men fell, screaming and yelling. The bandits were all finally executed. Enrico emerged from the center of the crates, and the other men from various parts of the train cars along the rails. They shot every one of the interlopers multiple times, then loaded the bodies onto one wagon and reloaded the oil crates back on the train. The uniform of the "conductor" was clearly visible on the man on top of the heap. There were forty or fifty other people on the train, some passengers and some crew members. No one said a word, and all, quite nervously, avoided looking out. Soon the train lurched forward and resumed its journey to Palermo. The wagons were loaded. Five or six men were left behind to dispose of the wagons and their bloody cargo. Enrico and his men boarded a separate train car and changed into conventional travelers' clothes and tossed the peasant garb out the windows. Enrico turned to one of his trusted men and calmly said, "Finito" (That's done).

Within a few days, he heard rumors in the city of a massacre by a train stop. There were never any details regarding location and not a single witness. The shipment went by ferry through the straits of Messina to Calabria. There the cargo was loaded on another flat car bound for Naples. Enrico returned to Palermo and stayed several weeks. Soon, word got out that somehow the train, the olive oil shipment, and the Merendinos were connected to the rumored massacre. While there was no newspaper publicity, the whispered rumors in the cafes, piazzas, and shops persisted for weeks. Enrico and two of his men stayed at an old hotel near the train station frequented by travelers.

There was a little café off the lobby. Enrico had spent his time meeting and talking with several businessmen who did business with the Merendinos for several years. One evening, Enrico was in the café enjoying an espresso when a well-dressed man sat down at the table next to him. The man didn't appear to take any notice of Enrico and his two men sitting nearby. "Che bella note" (what a beautiful evening), he said to no one in particular. Enrico didn't respond, but he began to feel uneasy. The man looked over to Enrico's table and asked, "Si piace espresso con anisette o strega?" (You like your espresso with anisette or with strega?) Again, Enrico did not answer but looked over to the man who had raised his cup of coffee in a sort of toast and sipped it down. "Pero, se piace un poco pane con oglio di olivio?" (Maybe you like a bit of bread with olive oil?)

Enrico immediately turned his eyes to his two men and in a quick, upward glance signaled them to be alert. He rose from his chair and slowly moved to the next table, seating himself directly in front of the stranger. His eyes searched the lobby and glass windows around the café, but no one else seemed to be of concern.

Enrico said, "Scusare, ma io non capisco quello che lo ditto" (Excuse me, but I did not understand that which you said).

"Far niente" (It's nothing), the older man said. "Tu piace u café?" (You like the coffee?)

"Si, mi piace." (Yes, I like it.)

"Ma penza che tu piace il oglio di olive piu meglio." (But I think you like olive oil more.)

Enrico leaned in close to the man and said quietly, "Che voglio a me?" (What do you want of me?)

In the course of the next hour, the man explained he was also a businessman who had many connections throughout Southern Italy. He said it was a shame how some businessmen could not ply their trade because greedy thieves sought to steal from them. In fact, he said, he heard of a recent case where a respected family had bandits try to steal their goods when they tried to transport them to this area. He had similar problems and was very interested in finding someone who could help him protect his shipments. His name was Carmine "Turrido" Scalise, and he lived in Palermo. He brokered various goods from all over Sicily and across to the mainland as well. Enrico offered assistance.

After a series of meetings, Merendino and Scalise devised a plan where Merendino would stamp his Dino imprint on all of Scalise's goods, including the crates of dried fruits, vegetables, and nuts from Central Sicily to Palermo. Some would be shipped to the mainland and some to other countries, including America. By this time, the Dino stamp had gained enough respect that the bandits avoided trying to steal those goods.

CHAPTER 27

ENRICO HAD LEARNED a great deal as he moved around the docks and in the city. The bandits responsible for the theft of his father's goods were employed by a fellow in Palermo known only as "Il Grigio" (The Gray One), a former street urchin who had survived his formative years of criminal enterprise by taking refuge in alleyways, under bridges, and in vacant buildings. It was rumored that he was one of many newborn infants left just after birth in a church by one of the many whores and prostitutes in the city unwilling or unable to care for them. Usually these youngsters survived with the help of the church until they grew old enough to escape to the streets. Perhaps he never had a real name, but because of his gray skin pallor, he became known as the "Bambino Grigio" (the Gray Baby). There was an entire subculture of these *scunezzi* in the poorest sections of many Italian cities. They lived by their wits and usually did not grow old.

Il Grigio had made a deal with some local merchants who had little concern over who supplied goods or where they came from. *Il prezzo* (the price) was their only concern. This was just one of Grigio's low-level enterprises. He had survived for more than forty years working these kinds of schemes and deals. "Sales" was his forte—stolen goods, information, even flesh. There were always eager buyers for all his wares.

Grigio had no loyal cadre of men. Simply hiring a fellow scunezzi in Palermo was an easy feat. The younger ones were more desperate and more eager. The risks were of little concern if they could fill their pockets with lira. Boys of just seven or eight years old were accomplished thieves and swindlers and could perform all the necessary tasks, which included pickpocketing, stealing from shops or carts, and slipping into the rooms of travelers to lift that had not been tied.

Those now dead bodies piled up in the wagons at that railroad crossroad slaughtered by Enrico and his men were the nameless and faceless, innocent *picciotti* (boys) of the street, the deprived *proietti* (the orphans), *il povaruzzu* (the poor ones), but in reality, they were *briganti* (brigands), thieves, and as thieves live, so do they die—that is, with no one to weep or mourn them except those who depended on them for sustenance, the hangers-on and parasites. Soon they latched onto another host and forgot their meager benefactions.

Enrico felt no remorse. When he understood who was behind the theft, he sought to learn more. After several weeks, however, word reached him at his hotel that he was needed home as soon as possible. He met one last time that evening with his new business associate and departed with his two men the next morning.

He brought with him the astonishing news of the progress of Garibaldi's unification movement as well as his "adventure" with the train bandits and his new venture with Turrido Scalise.

When the train pulled into his hometown station, his brothers Francesco and Salvatore were waiting for him. They led him from the station in haste with a brief hug and kiss on the cheek.

"Enrico," Francesco began as he led him to a roofed black motorcar, "tu padre ha pauda per te. (Your father is afraid for you.) Ascolta, fratello mio! (Listen, my brother!) There are some men who want to do you harm." Enrico realized some of the scunezzi dead had some friends. Grigio also had learned more about the mishap on the train, and he was part of this scheme for revenge.

They sped off to the Merendino estate. They entered the long, winding side road leading to the father's home. Enrico noticed that several of the men walking the edge of the fields and woods had *lupari* (shotguns) slung over their shoulders. The car in front of his was occupied by four Merendino workmen, also armed. His father was sitting out on the stone terrace in front of the house.

"Enrico," he called out. "Buon jamieli mani! (Welcome home!) Veni, ven (Come, come)," and he directed his son into the house.

Enrico could not recall when his father had been so talkative. In fact, he could not recall any occasion when his father actually greeted anyone outside the confines of the house.

"Figlio mio, dici me quale che ba fatto." (My son, tell me what you have done.)

In a quiet and measured tone, Enrico relayed the events of the past several weeks to his father. When he was done, his father explained that the hills were swarming with enemies. Some were those who sought revenge for a few of the scunezzi who saw their end at that lonely railroad crossing, and some were associates of the corrupt buyers of Grigio's ill-gotten goods. These were a concern. Word had gotten out to the local warlords that the Merendinos were becoming influential and supported by Garibaldi and his followers. It was known that the Merendinos had brought money and men to Garibaldi. In part, this was fine; however, Enrico himself had been identified as the leader.

CHAPTER 28

BACK IN THE mid-1840s, Napoleon's (Napoleon died in 1821) legions marched on Rome against Garibaldi's forces. He had become a hunted man after the French won the battle and, under the cover of night, boarded a ship to America.

Papa Merendino was aware that those who supported Garibaldi were loyal to him as well.

"Enrico, che sono qualche cosa ti fare in America." (Enrico, there are things to do in America.) Papa Merendino had already had Francesco, his firstborn and heir, as his chief administrator. He knew also that Francesco and his brother Salvatore were much too close to separate. Enrico, however, was different. He was a loner and yet still worldly. Though it also served his purpose to have Enrico as his emissary overseas, he also reasoned that he was the most qualified. Papa Merendino still abided by the traditional *primo figlio* theory; the first son was the heir apparent and leader of the family. But Papa Merendino also felt Enrico would be in less danger going on an extended trip far away. Enrico also knew this, and much of the work he did was training for when he would eventually strike out on his own. He was ready. This was just the opportunity he needed.

"We do it quickly," his father said. Within five days, he was traveling, this time to Naples where he would easily be able to board a ship unnoticed and unknown to the United States.

Once aboard the ship, he and his travel mate and erstwhile bodyguard, Checco, kept a private profile. The long voyage went smoothly. It was August, and the warm breeze on the ship's walkways agreed with Enrico. While the limited food supply was less than appealing, Enrico found solace in studying the many faces of the other Italian immigrants on the ship. This was not a luxury liner for vacationers. These passengers were the ones desperate to leave Italy so they could start a new life in America. Checco had made sure he brought a bountiful supply of wine, dried salamis, and pepper biscuits.

After three rather uneventful weeks, the ship entered the New York Harbor. Visible were the lines of piers that stuck out like a centipede's legs along the north side of the island. These immigrant passengers landed on Ellis Island, a small island in the center of New York Harbor where they could be registered. Papa Merendino had seen to it that his son would be identified by "amici" (friends) who had influence there. As a result, Enrico and Checco were released; they made it through all the checkpoints within forty-eight hours while the other tired souls waited several days, sometimes weeks. During a short boat trip to Manhattan, he was approached by a young fellow named Achille Mora. Achille was a distant cousin who had gone to America a few years earlier to study at university. Mora's mother, Maria, was an extremely wealthy widow who lived in Rome, where it was rumored that she was linked by blood to the historic Borgia family.

From the ferry, they took a horse-drawn wagon several blocks to a two-room flat near Mulberry Street. This was an area of mixed immigrants, some Jews, Chinese, and Eastern Europeans, but a large majority of them came from Ireland and Italy, and together they dominated the Lower East Side of Manhattan.

Once he settled into his cramped apartment, Achille explained to Enrico that he had traveled to Staten Island on many occasions to bring packages to Guiseppe Garibaldi. Sometimes it was a small wood crate sent to a rail station; other times it was just an envelope with a few papers. Nearly every week, he received newspapers from Italy, France, Spain, and New York, with occasional dispatches from Argentina. Achille did not specify the exact contents of these packages or envelopes, but it was obvious Signore Garibaldi was keeping well informed of the ongoing organization of supporters of the unification of Italy. Such unification would create a new commerce and economy in Italy and would be especially beneficial for trade as well as a new political stability and openness.

The Merendinos learned much through their conversations with friends and relatives in Palermo, Messina, and Rome, and particularly the many tradesmen who knew he had given support to the unification movement at its earliest beginning. Support included lira, paper from which leaflets were printed, access to buildings and storehouses, and conduits for communication. They also quietly let others know of their support so that they could enlist new sympathizers.

Achille arranged to meet Enrico and Checco a few days later and advised them to be extremely cautious in the meantime when they traveled the neighborhoods. The Manhattan ghettos were a dangerous place for Italian immigrants. These so-called greenhorns who had been here for several years were preyed upon by their own kind as well as the other unsavory element in their metropolis.

The Irish had particular scorn for those immigrants. The Irish immigrated to America in the 1880s following the devastating potato famine. Those Irish who could find sufficient passage money to escape an inevitable fate of dying from famine, illness, the scorn of religious persecution, or a desperate life in a political system controlled and dominated by the English, who despised and exploited them, came through the port of New York or Boston in huge numbers. Mothers would sell what valuables they had to get passage money so that they could get a wee bit of steerage space for their children, but this was no bon voyage. Most said their goodbyes to loved ones knowing they would never see each other again.

The Irish found all the work they wanted in the bustling economy of the American Northeast. Every menial task needed an immigrant worker, and the pay, though small, was steady. Never had America experienced such an influx of one nationality in such a compressed time period. Eventually they spread across the country as they worked building railroads from coast to coast, many of them settling down along the way. The Irish saw particular opportunity in the public sector as they filled positions in firehouses, police stations, city offices, public works, and immigration. They resented these "Dagos" and "Wops" invading their territory since now they would compete for the menial jobs. They did not speak English and were ridiculed at their attempts to learn the language. While the Irish were not exactly accepted with open arms during their main immigration, they were tolerated and could easily be trained and directed. The Italians, some with their dark skin colors and more suspicious and cautious nature, were not to be trusted. The original settlers were mainly English and Irish, and their traditions were known as common. These Italians were dramatically different. They ate pastas and polentas. They smelled of garlic, onion, and peppers fried in olive oil. Surely, they did not smell like boiled potatoes, ham, and cabbage or roasted meat.

Enrico had a great deal to learn about this land. He had a particular problem since his physical appearance made him seem even more foreign.

He had a thick, rubberlike "hide," and that made his skin seem as if it had several thick layers. His dark skin glistened with an overabundance of skin oils. Consuming large quantities of olive oil just added to the look. His looks belied his keen mind; in fact, he was a genius.

CHAPTER 29

THE MERENDINOS, SCALICES, and other families had a stake in Giuseppe Garibaldi's success. The story of the ascension of Garibaldi was the stuff of legend both in Italy and in America. This product of a fragmented collection of fiefdoms and papal domains had the inspiration and vision that he could be the driving force to reunite part of what was the great and historic Roman empire's homeland. His life was as much tragic as it was triumphant. His first attempts at organizing unification resulted in his becoming a wanted man. He could not muster the support needed, and the opposition sought to kill him. In desperation, disgust, and disillusionment, he and his wife fled to America in search of refuge. Instead, Garibaldi met with even more heartbreak. His beloved wife became terminally ill. The chilling vision of his arrival at the home of Antonio Meucci, his genius friend who lived in Staten Island, became etched in history and memorialized by a painting of Garibaldi rushing up the stairs of the house with his wife draped lifeless across his arms, her life's blood running from her mouth. There she died. Meucci had invited his friend to this place of pastoral beauty overlooking the mouth of lower New York Harbor but a world away from the great metropolis that was a short distance across the bay. The house with its wide porches and French doors overlooking the harbor was both a home and a place where Meucci could earn a meager living and still work on his inventions.

Both Garibaldi and Meucci were men of extraordinary intelligence, but neither was able to coordinate the complexities of earning a living, providing a family life with some reasonable continuity, and eventually accomplishing the monumental achievements that would mark them both as historic figures of maximum consequence. Garibaldi remained at the Meucci house for a few years, ostensibly as a part-time candle maker, but in his little second-floor bedroom, he worked feverishly on his unification plan. Poor Meucci, at times penniless and nearly having his family starve, forged ahead with his inventions. History would finally record that it was he, not the fraud Alexander Graham Bell, who invented and perfected the first telephone. Italians, who had known the truth for decades, were frustrated by the adulation of Bell.

Garibaldi, the candle maker, fisherman, and cacciatore (the hunter) of rural Staten Island, with a view of the big city across the bay on one side and little fishing docks on the other, still burned with the desire to make his vision of a reborn Italian peninsula a testament to the grandeur of the ancestral Roman Empire. Finally, Garibaldi left his old friend Antonio Meucci and returned to his homeland, now a widower. History would be kinder to Meucci than life. He would, generations later, be credited with inventing the telephone. The next several years saw his efforts and vision turn tragedy to triumph. With the help of other historic Italian figures and the support of families like the Terranovas, Scalisces, Merendinos, and others, the Garibaldi finally succeeded. The new constitution and parliament promoted a renaissance of Italian economy as well as renewed international interest in Italian culture, modern as well as ancient. Garibaldi took his rightful place as a senior statesmen and member of parliament, perhaps somewhat parallel of the great general George Washington, whose transition from military leader of the revolution to political leader and statesman helped to build a new nation. So, in fact, did Garibaldi and those friends and successors of the Garibaldi regime continue through the generations to incorporate their mentors, including the Terranovas, Mondellos, and Merendinos, their extended families, and others who had helped the unification efforts and the building of a new Italy.

CHAPTER 30

THE ELDEST SON of Silverio Merendino sent word to Enrico via cable. "Fratto mio, tu Papa sono molto milato. Vieni subito. (My brother, Papa is very ill. Come quickly.) Franco."

Enrico had communicated with his father and siblings regularly via cable. Generally business matters were stated in a way that the part-Sicilian, part-English ramblings were not discernible by others. He received the cable at eleven o'clock at night. The next morning at eight, Enrico went to the nearby Western Union cable office and sent a response. "Franco se videmo." (Franco, I will see you.) He also sent a sealed note to Cosmo Marchiani through his valet to meet him immediately. Enrico continued to maintain a small flat on the Upper West Side of Manhattan but generally only used it for business purposes for private, discrete meetings with his managers. Few people knew he owned an eight-story building on the Upper East Side on Park Avenue just midway at the corner of Park Avenue and Eighty-Sixth Street. The security in the building was of his own design. Actually, the building had an unusual feature that first attracted Enrico. The building was U shaped with a small courtyard entry in the center guarded by a foot-high wrought iron fence with closely linked fence points. There was a small doorman's cubical built out from the fence line so that the doorman, who actually occupied a ground-floor apartment, could see all that was passing by both sides of the building as well as the entry at all times. There was also a buzzer by the gate with a gatekeeper known simply as Lillo, who was over six feet tall with huge shoulders and an athletic build.

The buzzer sounded. Lilo looked out a window and immediately went out a door to the courtyard and to the metal gate to the fence.

"Buon Giorno, Mr. Costino," said Lilo and quickly opened the gate by turning a key and a geared lock device. Cosmo was shown to the center lobby where the steel and glass elevator was located. Lilo pulled out a small silver key, turned it in a lock, and pushed open a scissor gate and door to the elevator.

"Cosmo viene ca," he heard from the rear of the apartment.

Though he had been in this apartment several times, he always marveled at the feel of the place. It was as if he had been transported back to a luxurious villa in Italy. The place was done with rich appointments, marble columns, and great detail.

"Don Enrico," Cosmo began, "I came as quickly as possible."

"Cosmo, I must return to my father as soon as possible. There is a freight ship from Italy that is just about to finish unloading at the North River Pier. I have sent word to the ship's captain to refuel and get his crew set up to leave on the evening tide. I also told him not to take on much weight so we can cut our travel time. The charter officer of the Isbrandsten Shipping Line, the American Isbrandsten, knows how easily our friends can resolve labor problems and control pilferage. He has provided me with a cabin and instructed the captain to assist me with whatever I need. I want you to continue things here. There is no need for anyone to know where I am. I will send you a cable when I arrive. There is no need to respond unless there is a problem or a need you can't handle," said Enrico.

"Capisce," said Cosmo.

"I want you to drive me to the ship. I'm just about packed here," said Enrico. He put on a thin raincoat over his dark suit, picked up his large leather briefcase, and they left. Little was said as they drove through the Central Park crossroad and under the overhead structure on West Street. The cobblestone street under the elevated highway caused a constant hum to the tires. Enrico, however, was preoccupied and hoped he would get back before his father died.

CHAPTER 31

ENRICO'S TRANSPORT BACK was the *Northern Star,* a typical freighter. It had six passenger cabins. Enrico went to the wheelhouse. The captain, a tall, beefy, middle-aged Norwegian, said, "I am Olaf Kreigstead, captain here. You must be Mr. Terranova. We are just about ready to sail. Is there anything you need now? I have had cabins A and B cleaned up for you. I will give you a tour of the ship and main crew members when you ask."

Enrico said, "Thank you. I am anxious to leave as soon as you are ready."

Enrico settled into the stateroom and soon felt the rumble of the ship's engines. He lay on the bed and for a moment let his mind wander. He recalled his father's strength and perception of being invincible. He could not have imagined his father ever dying. He removed his suit and put on a pair of khaki slacks, boat shoes, and a pullover shirt. He put the contents of his suitcase in a pull-out wood locker under the bed. He went out to take a last look at the harbor and felt that the ship was beginning to pick up speed.

"Captain Olaf, can you show me the communication room?" asked Enrico. Olaf beckoned to another man with a peak cap, and the two men went out the doorway to a communications room located just behind the wheelhouse.

"Peter," said the captain, "this is Mister Tee. He shall have full access to everything on the ship. If he needs your help anytime day or night, it is my order to do so. Peter is in crew quarters one, behind the cabin."

"At your service, sir," Peter responded. "We have fairly good communication for at least two days out and when we get about two days to port. The time in between is hit and miss."

The two men stepped out to the rail. "The captain's dining room is just down that staircase. I informed the cook to accommodate you at any time. He serves my breakfast at 7:00 a.m., lunch at 1:00, and dinner at 6:00. I usually have my first mate, communication officer, and a second man for dinner. However, I can arrange any schedule if you wish and can have whatever you need brought to your cabin," the captain advised.

Enrico nodded. "Thank you. I'll take coffee at 7:00 a.m. in my cabin but will join you later." Enrico retreated to his room and arranged some papers on the desk top in his cabin. He reviewed the papers and general contracts. The midday sun was waning. It was nearly four o'clock. He wet a towel, put it over his eyes, and fell asleep for half an hour. He used a short nap two or three times a day, sometimes for only twenty minutes or so, so that he could continue at a full pace for twenty-four hours a day for several days in a row.

He awoke and spent the next few hours with the captain, first mate George, second man Dolph, and Peter. Dinner consisted of steamed vegetables, a hearty, thick bread, and a slab of fresh fish.

Enrico enjoyed the thick, strong coffee. He made a mental note of each of these men. They were serious, strong fellows who knew what needed to be done. They followed their captain's orders and direction without question. Enrico was comfortable in their company since he had grown up in the company of serious men. He had a respect for them but always felt aloof and superior. They recognized that this strange-looking barrel of a man was a very strong person of obvious command. The captain's deference to Enrico was noted immediately. Surely he was a man of stature and importance since it was rare that the captain treated anyone, particularly a passenger, with this much deference.

Enrico would rise at six each morning, shower, dress, shave, and work on paperwork for a half hour before he received his coffee and a chunk of the thick grain bread. He then walked the deck for an hour. He returned to his cabin and worked until lunch. Some days he would simply take a bowl of soup or piece of dried meat or fish and some coffee. He did send few messages to his brother, simply saying, "About six days out," "About four days out," though he wondered if the messages were getting through.

The entire trip seemed like one long day. The weather, the hum of the engines, the sound of the ocean, and the roll of the ship all repeated and repeated. Enrico grew increasingly anxious and after a few days was completely bored. About four days out, he brought a deck of cards to the communication room and taught Peter the Italian card game briska.

Two days from port, late in the afternoon, Peter tapped on Enrico's cabin door. He awoke from his short nap startled and rose quickly. "I have a wire," said Peter.

Enrico opened the door, and Peter handed him a note: "Fratto mio. Questa citta non e buono, fare un altra porto, e chiama me." (My brother, this city is not good. Do another port and call me.) It was unsigned, but Enrico knew full well it was Francesco. He had expected to disembark near Palermo since it was the closest port to his father's home.

He went to the captain and told him to change his plans and head for Messina.

CHAPTER 32

ENRICO'S INTUITIONS ABOUT matters of security were keen. He had been staying in cabin A and occasionally used cabin B during the day to work or nap. This night, however, he arranged the bedding in both cabins so it appeared as if someone was occupying the bunks.

Enrico took a blanket and pillow and found a small cubicle below deck used as a store room. It had a door with a large wheel-operated lock that could be manipulated only from inside and applying a steel bar. Since he only had two nights to port, he wanted no problems, even if he did not sleep more than a few hours.

The final day was a particularly anxious time. Enrico recalled a shipping agent in Messina who could be counted on as a friend. He had visited his father's house and had sought the elder Terranova's protection when some gang in Messina was ravaging the goods on many ships.

The ship pulled into the docks of Messina at midnight. The warm Mediterranean breeze of June made Enrico feel as if he was being welcomed by nature herself. However, reaching someone that night would be a problem. Enrico decided that he would pack up and leave his suitcase in cabin A. Peter stopped by after the captain to say farewell to his new friend, bringing with him a bottle of Danish liquor, a kind of vodka. Peter said he did not know anything about Messina. Enrico knew of some cafés and brothels along the waterfront, but that was it. Peter had been ship bound for over a month and a half and only had a day or so off the ship. Enrico felt perhaps a little diversion might ease his tensions as well. "Peter, I think we can find a place nearby to get an excellent meal and perhaps meet some interesting ladies. Would you like that?" asked Enrico.

Peter answered, "It would be wonderful. I expect we will leave as soon as we refuel tomorrow, and I'll be stuck out at sea for a few more weeks."

The two men left the ship, and within a half hour, Enrico had ordered a meal and some wine at a café just a block off the waterfront. Soon, a few women, likely employed by the innkeeper, came in. Enrico and Peter were aware of the many people in the café but noted at least four single women who appeared slightly overdressed with heavy makeup on their black eyes. Enrico went over to the one in her late twenties, and Peter noted that she seemed very friendly. She was seated alone at the table but had been talking to the innkeeper and a waiter. After a few minutes, another woman, slightly older, perhaps in her early thirties, joined her, and the three came over to Peter's table.

Peter's English was passable, but he did not speak a word of Italian. Enrico apparently had already let the ladies know they were to spend their evening with the two of them. Enrico told Peter, "Lora, this one with the blue eyes, and I will leave you and Dina when we return to the ship. I think I am going to use cabin A. If you need some money, let me know. At the last moment, Lora told Enrico the innkeeper had a fine room in the back of the inn they could use.

Enrico gave his key to cabin A to Peter, and he retreated with Lora to the room in the back of the café. Peter walked back to the ship with Dina, occasionally trying to communicate, but it was useless. She giggled like a schoolgirl at his ramblings but didn't understand a word.

Enrico reveled in the relaxation and barely slept as dawn approached. When he was not finding the charms of this lady inspirational, he was finishing the wine. Lora was encouraged by the wad of lira placed near her side of the bed and flattered by the attention, conversation, and physical and sexual attention that Enrico bestowed on her. She could not recall when she had been treated so gently by an Italian customer. Usually, most of the foreigners were a little less rough, but most of the Italian seamen were crude, even if some were a little lighthearted or comical. They lacked manners.

In the morning, Enrico left her after the innkeeper sent up some coffee and biscotti. He showered, dressed, and said his goodbyes to Lora, who remained in bed.

Upon boarding the ship, Enrico sensed something was wrong. No one was stirring, and it was already seven o'clock. Enrico went to the door of cabin A to retrieve his suitcase and briefcase, which he had hidden beneath a loose wall panel. He noted the door was just slightly ajar, unlocked.

He peeked in and saw the forms in the bed, but the sheets were covered with blood. He quickly slipped in and walked over to the bed to see the gash in the side of Peter's neck where a knife had cut his carotid artery. The woman's throat was slit so severely that her head was nearly severed. Enrico knew that their ill fate was the case of mistaken identity. The knife was meant for him.

He pulled the bedspread over the two and quickly left, locking the door behind him. He walked directly across the ship dock and up a narrow street until he reached the second block. He saw a man standing next to a car. "Piasano il mio padre sono molto milato; per favore porte me alla citta." (Piasano, my father is very ill; please take me to the city.) With that said, he pulled a large roll of lira from his briefcase.

The man, who apparently was caught by surprise by the request, stood still for a minute, thought about it, then said, "Si" (Yes).

CHAPTER 33

ENRICO GAVE HIM the address of the shipping agent whose office was just five minutes by car. Enrico handed the man some lira in silence and rushed into the shipping agent's office. Fortunately, Signore Girando Dito was in his office early. He rose and exclaimed, "Don Enrico come sta?" He had a big grin and outstretched arms.

Enrico hugged him and said, "Dito, I need your help. I must get to my father immediately. He is very ill. There are people here in Messina that want to do me and my family harm. Be discreet. Find me a fast car and good, trustworthy driver, and I will be sure you are rewarded."

"Ma che cosa?" said Dito. "Of course I will help you. My son, Paolo, will be here in a moment. He just went to get us some coffee. He loves to drive. In fact, he has a hobby driving in these local road races with a car he built with some friends. Your father helped me when I needed it most. It will be my privilege to help you now." He had hardly finished this sentence when a bright, shining red Lancia pulled up to the front of the office.

Dito said a few quick words in his son's ear, and Enrico hopped in. The young man was an expert at the wheel of the car. Though the roads were narrow, winding, and at times rough, Paolo kept control even at extremely high speeds. The car roared through the straightaways always at over one hundred miles per hour. He knew the roads and exactly when to slow down or let it out. At the last hill, his father's estate was a welcome sight.

Enrico noted men every hundred yards on either side of the roadway and up the driveway to the house and knew immediately that the problem was grave.

He was met at the front door by Francesco. They hugged and kissed each other on the cheeks. There in the hallway was his mother with tears in her eyes. Enrico took her in his arms and said, "Mama, Mama." She led him to their upstairs bedroom. His father lay in the bed. His breathing was labored and rough.

"Enrico, figlio mio," said the old man. His face was thin and drawn and had a dark look, the look of a man whose inevitable end was coming near. But for now, his face lit up, and his eyes brightened. Enrico bent over him and held him. He could feel the skeleton and bone joints as he embraced him. Enrico, who was always in control, suddenly felt a dry lump swell in his throat, and his eyes watered. The men looked in each other's eyes for a long moment. Enrico knew without words that his father's usual distant exterior had faded, and maybe, for the first time in his life, he knew that his father loved him.

After a few minutes, everyone left the room except for Francesco and Enrico.

"Enrico, we have been seeing things go from bad to worse here," the old man said. "The renegades in Palermo have organized with some others in Messina. They are under the leadership of that pig Tino Rebozze. He is a ruthless murderer and has created problems everywhere. He has not come at us directly, but he has gone after some of our friends, suppliers, and transporters.

"He knows I'm sick and has gotten bolder. He even has started a rumor that he has men looking for Francesco since he is the oldest son. We need to end this now," said Silverio.

Francesco added, "He has assassins all over Sicily. Now he is offering huge rewards for the murder of any Terranova."

"He is associated with some of the renegades from Sardinia and as far as Corsica," Enrico said. "I know there is a problem. A friend on my ship was mistakenly murdered because they thought I was in my room instead of a crew member," he said.

"Papa," Francesco said, "we will find a way, don't you worry. This fellow will show himself. Now rest. We will talk some more and be back to have dinner with you."

Enrico and Francesco spent the next three hours with three of the other boys making a plan. "Look," said Enrico, "we have our friends in

Rome and those here in Sicily. I will organize and finance units in each Sicilian city and smaller groups in the towns around Palermo, Messina, Reggio Calabia, and Sciacca and form a communication each day to my place in Palermo. Let's see just who Rebozze is aligned with. This Tino will surface soon enough. We will put a bounty on his head of several million lire. If he thinks he can destroy us, he is a fool. A smart man would seek an alliance."

When they went back to Silverio's room, he was sleeping. "Don't wake him. He needs rest. Let's talk to him in the morning."

The next day, the six eldest boys sat around their father's bed. He addressed each one and advised them all of his wishes when he was gone. He turned to Francesco and said, "My eldest son, you are and have been the strength of our family as I have weakened. Your brother Enrico has added a new branch to our great tree. Each of you, Don Franco and Don Enrico, have your place as equals here. Share with each other and protect the rest. Our family and our friends will go on with you."

Soon after the rest of the family came in, Silverio held his hand out like a groom to a bride. His wife smiled and kissed his cheek. He whispered something to her and then left. It took a few minutes for all in the room to realize he was gone. He made not a sound. He willed his death as he commanded his life.

Francesco finally said, "Jesue, auito" (Jesus, help him).

CHAPTER 34

WHILE SILVERIO WAS never a very religious man, the priest from Corleone, Father Tomasso, had given him last rites two days before when he had fallen unconscious for several hours. Now the priest who stopped by at noon each day went to the bedside and offered prayers and left a gold crucifix after a short service witnessed by the entire family.

He joined the family in the main room downstairs and said he had arranged for the funeral. The body would lie in a coffin in the main living room of the house for three days. Many from all over Italy would come to pay *rispetto* (respect). On the third day, they would bury him. Enrico kept out of sight. He also did not let anyone except immediate family see him.

A fine wood casket lay in the main room. Basket upon basket of flowers lined the room. Wreaths of grape vine wrapped with flowers and ribbon were placed around the room. The men wearing black arm sashes and the veiled women dressed all in black stood vigil for the three days. Finally, with a Sicilian band playing a sad dirge, the casket was taken to the local church. The Mass was said, and a long procession walked to the church yard where a Gothic style, granite mausoleum, which had stood for many years, was opened, and Silverio was placed inside. Carved in the stone over the entry was the family name, Terranova.

Enrico stayed home. As the procession dispersed, two men came up to Francesco. "Don Francesco, Tino Rezolla is in Palermo. He has called on his friends in the cities and towns around Southern Italy to join with him by offering them parts of the Terranova organization as reward. He also knows about the price we placed on his head. He has a dozen armed bodyguards with him at all times, even when he sleeps," said the messenger. Later, the men came back to the Terranova house.

Enrico and Francesco asked the two men to spend the night.

Enrico said, "This Tino wants our organization. We shall offer it to him. If the price is right, we will offer to sell him a large portion of our business interests. When we lure him in, we may have a chance to get him."

Francesco agreed. "I will offer to meet him and lay out the deal. He expects, as far as we still know, that you are dead in that stateroom on the freighter. We made sure the ship left before anyone got any word of what occurred. No one knows exactly what you look like now after these years you have been away. Yes, and without shaving for a few days and some padded clothes, no one will recognize you."

So it was necessary for Enrico to keep out of sight. Family and friends were advised not to mention him. A rumor was spread he was missing, never attending his father's funeral. A few days later, Francesco traveled to Palermo and in a contrite and businesslike manner met with and laid out an offer to Tino Rezollo. He placed a price on each business operation separately, except for the immediate estate land, olive and vineyards.

This fellow, whom they called a "pig" indeed, resembled just that. He was a short, fat slob of a man. His shirt could not button since his neck size was far too large for a shirt collar, so his tie hung around his neck and loosely to one side.

The meeting, held in the center of the municipal railroad station in Palermo at nine at night, was a little noisy but apparently acceptable to both partners as safe since each could monitor the area and it was far too public a place with policemen and witnesses all around. There were benches rounded in a semicircle so each could face the other.

Tino and Francesco sat. Each had one bodyguard. They spoke as if they were two traveling businessmen. Tino appeared reserved but was convinced he had intimidated the Terranovas now that their leader had died. However, he was clever enough not to place his trust in anything or anyone. He had already been seated when Terranova arrived. Francesco explained, "My father's business connections are now a problem for us. It was his business. We helped, but now it may be best for us to sell some of our holdings because we may lose our edge since our business was created by my father." He listed out each operation and a price and deal for each. Tino listened and finally said he would get back to him. With that, Tino boarded a nearby train for his exit. His bodyguard, obviously armed, stayed behind. Franco had left two backup men outside by his car.

Tino Rozello had grown up on the streets of Palermo. His family was there for many generations. Little that they did was ever legitimate. He started his crime career as a street hustler and through the years organized cooperation with group after group of street gangs. He had found a safe place to live in the rectory of a large church, Saint Christoforo in Palermo. A new rectory had been built on to the old church. He had a friend, through whom he donated money to the church, get him this new addition. The old rectory was in fact a very elaborate residence once occupied by a cardinal. It was now a fortress within the city, safe enough for Tino. He lived there with a group of his henchmen in the old section.

A priest friend of another priest in Corleone, Father Tomasso, visited him and told Tomasso of this strange arrangement, knowing full well who Tino was. Father Tomasso invited the Terranovas to meet. Enrico and Francesco met with the priest. "So, Father, what is it you want to tell us?" Enrico asked. They sat in a small office in the rectory of the church in Palermo late one evening; in fact, it was after midnight when no one was around.

"I have a friend who tells me Tino Rozello and some of his men occupy the old rectory at Saint Christoforo Church in Palermo. The men are armed bodyguards. The rectory is an old stone building."

Enrico looked at Francesco and then back at the priest. "Father, this man is known to be a murderer, defiler of children, young girls, a kidnapper, and worse. He is scum. You know this."

The priest nodded. "Yet to get close to him, one would need divine providence to prevail. We have known each other for many years. You know the ways of these towns. Your cousin Toto Merendino was my father's close ally, God rest their souls. Now we need to do something," said the priest.

The priest, now fifty years old, looked back at Enrico. "I am tired of seeing the problems of this area. I have been thinking about America for several years. Maybe I should talk to my friends in Palermo and the Vatican to get a transfer to America. Maybe you have friends in America whose church needs a priest who speaks Italian."

Enrico said, "Father, why don't I arrange for you to take a trip to America, maybe to New Orleans. You can see if you like it there, and you can relax there without commitments. We have some friends in the church there, and of this Tino fellow, I will send you something, which you can deliver to him."

This priest was suspected to have turned his collar around regularly on his visits away from Sicily. He grew up in the Corleone area and knew well the stories and saw the results of vendetta. He was indeed tired of trying to help those in constant poverty, tired of the needs of these families and a mundane existence and vendettas. He longed to leave. This was a chance for his exit. Exit to America.

A day later, a package was delivered to Father Tomasso. He opened the paper wrappings and found two thin six-inch steel spikes sheathed in thin leather cases with points as sharp as pins.

Father Tomasso arranged a retreat in Palermo for ten local priests and himself. Since it was near a feast day, the church rectories were full. The priest at St. Christoforo mentioned to Father Tomasso that he could arrange temporary rooms at his old rectory. Since there were some fifteen rooms there and only six or seven occupied, the priest told Tino Rozello of his problem, and Tino responded, "Father, you have need of some rooms for some priest friends. I'm sure they will be comfortable here for a few days. They won't bother my boys."

Father Tomasso had received tickets for his passage on a ship to New Orleans before the retreat. The feast day had started. The guests arrived over the day. The priests settled in for a four-day retreat. On the night of the last day, Father Tomasso had already met all the men in the house and knew the layout of the sleeping quarters for each man. They even shared some meals and bottles of wine together with the priests. The priests made fine wine and even a little grappa.

Tino enjoyed these bottles of wine with dinner, most times consuming a bottle himself, followed by the strong grappa with his espresso. Father Tomasso brought five fine bottles of wine this night. Each a little different, the fine ruby color of each was tested and drank by the six men and three of the priests that night. The other priests were guests of the main parish house. He followed the wine with two bottles of grappa. Father Tomasso positioned his seating next to Tino and kept his glass full of the grappa.

By midnight, all were well relaxed. Tino made his way to his bedroom a bit uneven on his feet after having finished a bottle of wine and half bottle of grappa. He collapsed on his bed.

Father Tomasso's door opened slightly at three in the morning, and quietly a hooded figure in a black monk's robe slipped down the hallways and through the rectory to the rear new wing. The figure stopped at Tino's door and opened it. The shiny steel spike was withdrawn from its leather sheath a second before it was driven into Tino's fat neck. His body jolted as the second spike slid across his throat and split open his windpipe. He grasped as his throat, spattering blood all over the white cotton sheets. His body writhed and jolted for what seemed to be quite a while, but it was less than a minute. Finally, he slumped still. The shadowy figure disappeared back to the priest's room. All was silent. The next morning when Tino's men finally went into his room to rouse him, they found him dead. All the priests had left and were in church praying, as was customary on these retreats each morning at dawn.

Father Tomasso stowed his things in his ship's stateroom, dressed in a conventional gray suit. He locked his door and took out some maps of the United States, looking closely at the southern coast and New Orleans. He had arrived on the ship at dawn.

The priest in the church hardly missed Father Tomasso. The church began to fill early since it was the feast day of a saint, and parishioners arrived at church early as well.

Tino's men searched the rectory and the nearby street, to no avail. They found nothing, not even the knife or wire that they suspected had been used to cut his throat. Over the next months, one by one, Tino's men disappeared from sight. Some said they fled the area; others knew better.

Father Tomasso found it rather easy to shed the persona of a priest and just be Tomasso, another of the ship's passengers. He enjoyed the uneventful ocean voyage, particularly the social aspect. He strolled the deck and came upon others either walking or relaxing on deck chairs. He was not conspicuous, nor was he reclusive after a few days out to sea.

After dinner, he enjoyed the ocean breezes out on the wide decks of the promenade. One evening, he approached two ladies, both in their forties, also enjoying the evening voyage along the railing.

"Good evening, ladies," he began. "It is a beautiful evening."

The taller of the two responded, "Oh yes, it is very nice." Tomasso recognized the distinctive southern Italian accent.

The other lady, a bit shorter and younger, resembled the taller one. She eyed this tall, distinguished, middle-aged man and was not concerned he might think her rather bold as she stared at him, until she broke into a smile. "My sister and I find the evenings on this ship very enjoyable, if not a bit lonely."

Tomasso was a bit surprised at the woman's response but was quick to respond, "Well, perhaps I can fill in a few minutes of the time this evening."

The shorter one said, "Maybe. I am Corina, and this is my sister, Gia. We are returning to New Orleans. Our home now is in New Orleans, but we had to return to Italy to settle some business affairs."

"I am Tomasso Marino, and I am also on my way to New Orleans on business or maybe more than that. I am pleased to meet you."

The trio continued the conversation through the evening and then shared coffee and cordials as the night wore on. The breezes were warm, and the fragrance of the sea, warm salt air, and gentle roll of the ship all seemed to make for an exotic setting and invited romantic thoughts in the passenger Tomasso. The ladies were more than interested in sharing their time with this man. They both had great experience in travel and in life.

"So, Gia, now that you are a widow, do you think of remarrying?" asked Tomasso.

"I'm not sure. After the first few years, I learned to sustain myself and rather enjoy the freedom. Corina has always been the eccentric, never interested in marriage. Maybe she has influenced me some. Now being a widow of over ten years, I have found life can be an adventure."

Gia turned to Corina. "Sure it's an adventure. That fat little man you married left you a fortune. She is living like a queen now. He would turn over in his grave. The husband saved every bit of money he made. His family was wealthy as well, and he was the sole heir. He wouldn't even spend money on a doctor when he fell ill, the fool. Now Gia has it all, and good for her. She had to lay in that little pig's bed for years. She was a beauty at eighteen years old; even the artists in Palermo wanted her as their model. My father, as is the way things are with those old Sicilians, arranged for Gia to meet Don Feuego because he was rich and his family was related to the family of the king, Victor Emmanuele. But he was a fool," she finished.

"Now, Cara, you don't have to speak so ill of the dead. Carlo had his good points too. He wasn't a prince, but he had his good points. He was very obedient, and he never looked at another woman," said Gia.

"Sure, you would have castrated him. Who knows? Maybe the little fat man was chasing the young boys instead. I wouldn't put it past him," said the sister.

"Oh, please, let's leave this talk alone. It's old history. So, Tomasso, were you ever married?" she asked.

"No. I have had too many obligations in my life," he responded. As the night wore on, the trio returned to the dining room where the ship's band was playing and the passengers were dancing. Tomasso was physically in excellent condition and, as a child, had learned all the dances from his mother. He looked at the two ladies, and his interest seemed to direct him to the widow. It seemed his thought was dancing with a widow was justified even for a man of the cloth, although he had removed his collar and broken his vows on several convenient occasions, perhaps even this evening. "*Con permesso, signora*, would you care to accompany me on the dance floor?" he said to Gia.

"Thank you. Yes, I would," she answered. Corina rolled her eyes at her sister when Tomasso turned away. Corina made an O with her lips, then squinted at her sister. Gia could not help herself and giggled a little. Corina had turned away so her laughter could not be heard by Tomasso.

The dance was slow and rhythmic. Gia immediately pressed her body close to her escort, and he could feel her legs, belly, and breasts pressing against him. He tried to concentrate on the music and his steps, but his mind and body began to react to the woman he held in his arms. "You dance very well," he told her.

She answered in a coy and wispy voice, "Oh, I do many things well. Try me."

Tomasso smiled and tried to restrain himself from trembling a little. He took a moment to compose himself, then answered, "Lovely lady, I would surely like to try anything with you." They lingered on the dance floor for a while after the tune was over, caught in the moment.

When they returned to the table where Corina was seated, she smiled broadly and said, "Well, did she step on your feet?"

"No," said Tomasso, "she is a wonderful dancer."

"Compared to whom?" said Corina. With that, she rose and took Tomasso by the hand and said, "Let us give it a try." The music was a lively "Mazurka," and as they walked out onto the middle of the dance floor, Corina already had a rhythm to her step. She glided across the floor and twisted and turned with Tomasso. She was an expert dancer. Actually, she had trained as a professional ballerina but never completed her training.

The musicians blended the "Mazurka" into a slow waltz, and Corina seamlessly stepped into the slower rhythm as Tomasso followed. Again, he felt the warmth of a woman close, and the smell of her perfume filled his senses. "You are an excellent dancer," he said.

"Thank you. You do very well yourself. You have strong hands and are very agile," she responded. He looked down at her, and she looked back with a little grin on her face as she rubbed his right hand between the thumb and index finger.

Tomasso was confused. Suddenly he had an opportunity to share the charms of two women but was torn as to making a decision. On the one hand, Gia had been married and was a widow. She had been with a man but was now unattached. Corina was obviously a free spirit and had chosen not to be married to any man but felt free to be with whomever she chose.

Corina said, "Why don't you and I ask Gia if she wants to do something." Tomasso was really confused. She led him to Gia and said, "Why don't we go back to our stateroom. We have a fine bottle of anisette there." And off they went. They drank, and things got hazy after that.

Tomasso awoke at midmorning, naked, lying between these two women. He could hardly believe the evening's events and felt strange in the place and indeed in his own body, as if he were a stranger to himself. New Orleans would confuse and change him even more.

CHAPTER 35

THE COOPERATION BETWEEN the Copolla and the Merendino families and their extended associates in both the United States and Italy was important to their mutual friend, the Catholic archbishop, as well.

The appointment of church leaders was mired in Vatican politics and was an extremely complicated matter. The old alliances and historic cooperation between the old monarchs of the eight city-states still had a great impact on the internal operation of the church in Rome and worldwide as well. The original Papal States, which compromised a relatively large land mass before the unification had been a major force, continued to be on the Italian peninsula.

Enrico Merendino was acutely aware of the power and influence that an American Roman Catholic archbishop position commanded. He was very careful as to how he presented himself to Copolla when they first met. The meeting was one of several meetings.

This meeting was arranged at St. Louis Cathedral at Jackson Square in the middle of the French Quarter. There was a small doorway on the south side of the building. The meeting time was eleven o'clock on a Saturday morning. Since it was September, the humidity and midmorning heat was just beginning to peak. The temperatures reached above eighty degrees. The humidity was even higher.

Enrico had learned that the heat in Louisiana was especially great as the day wore on. He dressed in a thin off-white linen suit and cotton shirt with muted, tan, silk tie. He made sure that his shoes, a light tan, were carefully polished. He had the barber, in a shop just a few doors from his hotel suite at the Maison DePuy, carefully shave him that morning and give a trim to his hair, as well as his ears, eyebrows, and even his nose hair. He paid meticulous attention to his personal appearance, as he had always noted that his father and other elders and men of respect and dignity in his community in Italy always looked well manicured. Only a *cafone* would be sloppy or slovenly. He also disliked those who did not take care of their personal appearance since it was the outward sign of inner disorganization and laziness. If a man or woman did not take care of their body and personal health, then they could hardly be trusted in a business or any special matter.

Enrico walked several blocks to the church with his "valet," actually a bodyguard and messenger, a *piciotto* (young man) named Tino Barzie. Tino was born in the French Quarter to an Italian father, Alfredo Barzie, and a mother, Jolie, whose heritage was a mixture of cultures with more flavors than a Cajun jambalaya (fish stew). He was a tall, lean, wiry fellow. His father was a Palermitano (Palermo born), sent to Louisiana to assist Bishop Coppola and act as a messenger and bodyguard.

Tino led Enrico to the prescribed doorway and knocked. An old priest in black vestments shuffled to the door after several minutes. "Hello," said the priest. "The bishop is expecting you. Please follow me."

Enrico nodded, and Tino said, "Thank you, Padre. I shall wait here inside the doorway for Mr. Merendino to return." Tino knew his place and just when and where he should be.

The doorway opened to a courtyard, and the priest led Enrico along an open corridor to a small office. He knocked twice on the thick, arched, wood door.

"Come, come," he heard.

He entered and said, "Bishop, Mr. Merendino." Enrico bowed at the waist in the most formal manner and stepped around the old priest and stood directly in front of the bishop, who had stepped out from behind an ornate French Empire carved wood desk. Enrico extended his right hand to the bishop and grasped just the tip of the fingers of his right hand. The bishop had seen that Enrico began to extend his hand in what he assumed would be a handshake but was a bit surprised when Enrico knelt fully on his right knee and brought the bishop's ring to his lips and kissed his ring.

Coppola knew the reputation and stature of this man and had not expected his action in such a courtly and reverently subservient manner.

"Reverend Father," Enrico began, "it is my extreme honor to be with you. My father sends his greetings and best wishes. Eminence, I can't express enough the gratitude that I and my family have for your friendship, your assistance, and your vigilance on our behalf. We shall ever be in your debt. We offer our prayers and unquestioned support to you. Grazie, tante grazie." Enrico spoke and acted in a classic Sicilian style, which overwhelmed the bishop.

Coppolla raised his hand as he grasped Enrico's thick, rubbery fingertips, which caused Enrico to rise to his feet. He took a step forward and kissed Enrico on each cheek and said, "Su Beneriga, bless you and bless your wonderful family. I am so pleased to finally meet you. Please sit here next to me."

The bishop guided Enrico by his hand to a red velvet armchair that looked like a small throne with its carved lion head, arm ends, huge seat, and plush cushion back. The bishop sat alongside him in a matching chair. There was a small table in front of them.

"Please, let us have a little something for our esteemed guest, Father John," the bishop said to the old priest. He turned to Enrico and said, "Father John is famous for his espresso special. It would please him to prepare some for us."

Enrico nodded and said, "Thank you. It would be very nice, Father John." The old priest shuffled off and closed the huge door behind him. Though it was getting warmer outside, the small office with its thick stone walls and stained glass gothic window remained relatively cool inside. Enrico was a little relieved since he sweated profusely during the heat of the day, particularly when he drank a hot cup of coffee.

"Tell me, son, things are going well for you here in Louisiana?" the bishop inquired.

"Your Eminence, due to your intercession and constant help, our affairs here have run smoothly and are constantly growing. There is little interference from any competition or law enforcement. In fact, the local police are most friendly and helpful. They are to be commended for their watchful eyes since we know how there are many thieves and burglars to keep under control here. The operations in Baton Rouge and the north are progressing well, and we even have some activity in the Mississippi ports of Gulfport and Biloxi. We are just beginning to research a location on the coast of Texas, just over the Louisiana border. Alabama, however, has not been so hospitable. We had an incident in Mobile, and we had to remove our operation to a smaller operation further out from the city to the small village called Bon Secour."

The bishop inquired, "What seems to be the problem in Mobile?"

"Well, two of our men stopped at a food distributor, a major distributor, in the city and explained that they would like them to try some samples of our Dino olive oil, some of our vinegar, and a few other products. The manager, a large white-haired man named Bobby Gest, told our men that they were not interested in any of our products. Our man said he would leave the products anyway just in case he might reconsider trying them. Mr. Gest got a bit red faced and said, 'Listen, your kind isn't welcome down here. We don't like you and don't want you to try to do business here. You best pack up and leave now.' The Italians were polite but rather upset, so they repacked their samples and walked out toward their truck. Two men stood between them and the truck. It was obvious that Mr. Gest had summoned them to create a problem. The two men began to swear at my men and threaten them. Still they kept themselves under control. They tried to move into the truck to leave when one of Mr. Gest's men pushed our man, a fellow named Rigo. Rigo dropped the box of samples. He bent to pick them back up, ignoring the push, but Gest's man started toward him again, this time with a billy club in his hand. Rigo pulled a small knife from his shoe and cut the man's hand across his fingers so that he dropped the club. Then the two Gest men stepped back. Our men left the city two nights later.

"Then our warehouse was broken into, and everything inside was smashed. Our men cleaned up the mess and a few days later had more merchandise brought in. The next two weeks passed by without incident. Then the police came and said that our operation did not have proper city licenses, and they nailed steel plates and bolted the doors. They posted a citation on the door and arrested Rigo. When they got him to the jail, Rigo saw Mr. Gest with two plainclothes police officials in the station. Rigo was put into a cell. That night, two men in street clothes came in, unlocked the cell, and beat Rigo with baseball bats.

"He was released the next morning, and the cops told him he should think about leaving town with the rest of his friends. They said they would be back. Rigo and his man left that night after emptying the warehouse.

"The newspapers had no information about any incident or even a recent story. Rigo moved the small operation to Bon Secour to a small warehouse owned by a friend of one of the Bertucci family members in Biloxi.

"Nearly a month later, there was a newspaper story about a particularly brutal murder and theft at the Gest Company. It seems Billy Gest, nephew of the owner Robert Gest, was found with his knees cut, stomach slit, and elbows cut, lying on the floor of his office on a Monday morning. It was reported that he had paid his workmen on Saturday but was not seen after that. There was some two thousand dollars missing."

The bishop said, "Such tragedy, but that area is known for its violent crimes, particularly since there were so many poor Negros there, and they are harassed by the local Ku Klux Klan and others who hate them. It's a shame that they hang these black men and have no hesitation about such murder. Sometimes these Negros strike back. There are very few Catholics in Alabama, and our church has never been very welcome there. Perhaps, in time, things will change, but it is not likely to happen soon."

Enrico understood the excusatory tone of the conversation, essentially dismissing Gest's execution as a racial crime. He also understood that some areas still did not present the opportunity to make profit.

The bishop then offered his further assistance in the areas where he had friends and influence. He basically laid out a regional boundary where he could be of major influence with those in power. Enrico was attentive.

The old priest knocked twice on the door, then entered with a tray. "Ah, our coffee," said the bishop.

The tray had a chrome coffeepot, well known throughout Europe. The coffee grounds were put in one end, and boiling water in the other. The pot was then flipped over, and the water dripped through the grounds. Alongside was a basket with an assortment of biscotti and cookies. "Please, help yourself," the bishop said to Enrico. There were some small stem glasses about the size of a wineglass. "There is some homemade anisette, some excellent Napoleon brandy, and my own homemade grappa. The grappa is made the way my grandfather taught me."

Enrico noted that the bishop filled his glass and drank down the grappa in one gulp. Enrico poured out some coffee and rimmed his cup with a bit of lemon rind that was in the saucer. He then poured a glass of anisette and poured some off into his cup of espresso. The aroma of the coffee and liquor filled the room. Enrico sipped from the coffee cup and then the glass. "Molto bene," he said, acknowledging the old priest. "Molto bene," he said again. The old priest smiled and shuffled off, closing the door.

Enrico felt the warmth of the anisette in his mouth, nose, and throat. This drink was as strong as brandy and extremely aromatic. "Your Eminence, this is exquisite anisette, most excellent."

The bishop poured another glass of grappa and drank it down, then poured some in his cup of espresso. "Enrico, there are opportunities that will be available soon that could be beneficial to both of us. The Vatican is considering expansion of new positions in the United States. There will be a need for the holy father to consider someone to oversee his flock in various parts of the United States where our church is growing larger and larger. Such an appointment will come after a great deal of maneuvering and review within the Vatican and outside as well. Many forces are at work here. There is a need for us to use all our resources and all our friends to communicate any information about this so we can assess what is happening. Our many friends can help us here in the United States, and those families in Italy and the border countries know what they must do to promote my name. Your father and mother and the friends and family that they are close with need to move now. I know your family has been with Garibaldi and his movement from the beginning. His support is needed as well. It can be the most important part of our quest. A cardinal can be of extraordinary influence." The bishop's quest to become a cardinal needed all the help he could get.

Enrico hesitated for a moment, then answered, "Your Eminence, every resource that we have will be used to help. I will devise a systematic plan so that each and every possibility is addressed, and everyone who can help us will be alerted and enlisted both in Europe and here. I promise you that."

The bishop smiled and nodded and took Enrico's hand in both of his and said, "I know you will, *figlio mio* (my son). I know."

The old priest showed Enrico back to where Tino was waiting by the side door. Enrico thanked the old priest as they left.

On the walk back to the hotel, Enrico instructed Tino to deliver messages to a long list of people in Louisiana, Texas, Atlanta, Georgia, and Boston, Massachusetts, and further north of there. The information concerning the position of cardinal made Tino extremely attentive. He was aware that this was an extremely important mission, and he felt good about being trusted by Enrico Merendino.

When Enrico returned to his hotel, he was told by the clerk at the front desk that he had a cable message. He received the written cable and read the sentence. The cable was from his eldest brother. It was written in his colloquial Sicilian language in a phonetic manner.

"Fratello mio, che sono qualche cosa, che la fatto una problemma. Chiddu che fare un scenario nella il trano vicino Palermo sono arriva a New York. Sta tendo. Chiddu voule cuisa la porta, fare un a cosa a te. Non che sono neri colore, ma una poco di bianco, alora che sono grigio. Parlare con tu amico, il carnetieri. Salute Fratello." (My brother, there are some things that have become a problem. He that did the scene in the train close to Palermo has arrived in New York. Be careful. He wants to close the door and do a thing to you. There is no black alone but has a little white, and therefore, there is gray. Talk with your friend, the butcher. Salute, your brother.)

Enrico understood that his old nemesis, Grigio, the thief, had made his way to New York. It was not unlikely he was being paid as an assassin. His likely taste for revenge for the Palermo train event, orchestrated and managed by Enrico, convinced him to finally try to even the score and close the door on Enrico literally. Mr. Gray was indeed neither black nor white but the color of red, blood red. He would have to return to New York as soon as he had an opportunity to find out what the butcher could tell him.

Early the next day, he made a phone call to Vincenzo Delmonte, *il carnetieri* at Columbia Market, the butcher shop in New York. Delmonte's family connections in Palermo knew the movements of all of their adversaries, especially those who sought vessel passage to America. His cousins ran the bursar's office and got the name of every passenger. If someone sought passage on a freighter, one of the Delmontes would be alerted as well. Grigio was notorious, and word soon got to the Delmontes that he had boarded a freighter for New Orleans. Enrico said, "Piasano, come sta? Che sono con una a cugini de le, e vicino a Dio." (Piasan, how are you? I am with a cousin of yours, close to God.)

Vincenzo understood that he was close to Bishop Coppolla and responded, "You should have a visitor within the next day or two. Mr. Gray has made inquiries here and was able to find out where you are and intends to pay you a visit, a final visit."

Enrico needed to find out just where this fellow was going in New Orleans. He had Tino contact his sources, including the bishop, to check train manifests and passenger lists at the ports. He sent a message to Rigo in Bon Secour to come to New Orleans immediately. The police stations were given Grigio's travel plans and alerted to report any sighting of this man immediately. All of the friends of the Merendinos were alerted to search all transportation centers and likely entry points for this man.

Enrico kept his room at the Maison DePuy but put Rigo and his man in the room and moved to a ground-floor room that had a view to the front entry of the hotel. The suite had two rooms and a bedroom on the second floor with a small stair as access to the second floor. Tino moved in. He stayed downstairs. The next step was simply a waiting game.

After nine days, one of the train station's clerks was questioned by a street cop about a passenger he saw come in on a late-afternoon train that dressed like a foreign traveler. He had a foreigner's look and a gray pallor. He had boarded the train near a commercial dock, near where a freighter had just docked, that had come from Palermo, Italy.

The net began to close. The man was identified at the front desk of the small Iberville Hotel at the edge of the French Quarter.

Enrico was told, and he alerted Rigo and Tino. They had a young lady, a friend of Tino's, go to the hotel and check into a room close to the lobby corridor. Also, there was a small shop across the street. Tino arranged to have a series of shifts of different men there to watch the front door.

Grigio was hardly a tourist visitor. He left his room for a very short time each day after he arrived at midday. He was followed to a nearby grocery store where he purchased some bread, salami, cheese, and olives and then a bottle of wine; then he returned to his room. He had a visitor the next day, likely an informer.

The next night, Enrico and Rigo, dressed in dark workmen's clothes, took a walk to the Iberville at about two in the morning. The town was still active, but there were fewer people in the streets.

They quietly entered a rear door to the hotel, conveniently arranged to be left unlocked. Rigo walked the hallways in the vicinity of Grigio's room. No one was stirring. He reported back to Enrico. Enrico made sure that no one was outside and that Rigo had brought two garrotes with him. He had also placed a small .32-caliber revolver in his pocket earlier in case the garrote could not be used. He asked him for one of the garrotes.

They both moved slowly down the hall to the door to Grigio's room and listened for any activity. It was quiet. This fellow likely was sleeping. He sent Rigo around outside of the building to see if he could see through the single window to the room. The drapery was drawn, and the window was securely closed. Although Enrico wanted to enter the room, he decided there was not enough known about Grigio's location in the room to make a move. They decided to wait in the stairway down the hall and watch the room.

At about eight in the morning, Grigio finally stirred and left the room. Enrico and Rigo found their way into the room and found, after a brief search, ammunition for a .45-caliber handgun, lengths of piano wire, and a small leather travel case with a few personal items. They found that the full-length draperies were thick and triple layered; they were the perfect cover.

The next two hours were tense, but eventually they heard someone at the door. The door opened and closed, and they heard the rustle of a paper bag and the sound of the springs of the bed. Enrico slowly pulled a cloth handkerchief from his back pocket. He waited for a minute or two, then quickly emerged from behind the drapes and rushed over to a startled Grigio. Grigio, who was seated on the bed, had just taken a mouthful of wine. He tried to get up but was immediately pinned to the bed by Rigo. Enrico grabbed Grigio by the back of his neck and stuffed the handkerchief in his mouth. His arms were pinned to the bed by Rigo, but his legs were flaying wildly. Enrico pounced on his legs with his full weight, and a cracking noise was heard. He grabbed at Grigio's waistband and removed the weapon, a .45-caliber revolver. Enrico took Grigio's head in both his hands and squeezed his eye sockets, blinding him. Wine leaked out of Grigio's nose. Grigio arched his back in pain and shuddered and collapsed back onto the bed. Enrico pulled a garrote from inside his shirt, wound it around Grigio's neck in one swift motion, crossed the ends, and pulled each end tight. Again, the body arched up, and Enrico, who was on top of the man, lifted his right knee and jammed it against the center of the victim's chest. The mouthful of wine poured out of the pinned man's nose mixed with blood. In an instant, Enrico pulled the garrote ends and saw blood swell from the welt that the garrote had caused. Enrico took the victim's head and spun it from side to side, snapping the neck and collapsing the right eye socket. Blood now poured from the limp neck and nose, and the body relaxed. Rigo knew the man was dead. He heard the last exhale of air release through his mouth along with the gurgle of blood. He released his hold as Enrico, rose to his feet, and wiped his hands on the bed cover. They began to wrap the body in the thick floral bed cover. Rigo had additional lengths of rope, and soon the bedspread looked like a cocoon. Rigo carefully forced the window open. It led to a very quiet narrow side street. Enrico and Rigo slid the body out the window and carefully gathered all of the personal effects and the bags of food and wine. They exited the window and dragged the body to an alley in the rear of the building. Within a few minutes, Rigo walked quickly out of sight. A few minutes later, a small delivery truck pulled up to the alley, and Tino and Rigo came out, grabbed the cocoon and the other things, and loaded them into the truck and drove off. Enrico, who was now drenched with sweat, composed himself. He wiped his face with his shirt and walked off toward the hotel. As he walked, he ran his left fingernails under his right fingernails. Bits of skin, dug out of the victim's face, were under his nails. He removed them.

He finally got back to his hotel, entered through a back door, and quietly made his way to his suite. He had a pitcher of water and cloth in the bathroom, and he washed away the evidence of his night's work. He felt a sense of great relief and was satisfied that he had eliminated this Grigio himself, in front of Rigo and Tino. As much as it was necessary, it was also an illustration of his power, cunning, and strength. These men would relate to others that Enrico was a serious and dangerous man, smart and ruthless, the qualities these men understood in a leader.

The truck pulled up to a deserted section of the levee below the French Quarter, and the body was slipped with its cocoon into the muddy water. First there was a large splash, the body, and then two smaller splashes from the bags of stones tied to each leg. The package disappeared, in just a few moments, in the muddy ooze below. A package was wrapped in a hotel towel. It had Grigio's gun, papers, and an item wrapped tightly in oilcloth and in a leather wallet. Inside was one grayish ear, evidence of the demise of its owner.

Eventually the package made its way back to Palermo and was left on the doorstep of Grigio's ally, the second in command of his gang. This was a proclamation of the strength of his enemy and a warning.

CHAPTER 36

THE DELMONTES HAD the humblest of beginnings. The cramped space in the three-room flat seemed to be even more confining and unlivable when the El went by and vibrated the brick walls of the building, which was located near the Allerton Avenue station in the bustling neighborhood of that part of the Bronx. Vincenzo had thought that he and his little family would get used to the rumble over time and that would be solace enough for the six-dollar discounted rent per month he negotiated with the landlord, a cousin of a paesano from Corleone. Now that he had been in the States for three years, he was able to save enough money and accumulate enough confidence that he could surely prosper in America. The trip from Italy on the ocean liner that they took with their young baby, Antonio, was full of promise. As he passed the statue in New York Harbor, Vincenzo's wife whispered to him as they stood along the rail, "La Donna pare come una Madonna ma pui forte" (The lady looks like a Madonna but much stronger). He thought to himself that maybe this country could be strong, even stern, but beautiful and righteous. Though he loved his family and his little town, there was limited opportunity. He was the third son born to Marisa and Antonio Delmonte. His oldest brother, Salvatore, nicknamed Toto, would inherit his father's holdings. Giuseppe, the next in line, was not focused on exactly what he wanted to do or where he wanted to live but continued working in his father's shop as a butcher. Giovanni and Tomasso worked there part-time but also attended the little school in town and would be in that school until they graduated. Carmine, the youngest son, also attended a school that was geared to the age group below adolescence. His sisters, Sarah and Maria, were still too young for school, so Marisa had to keep them occupied at home while she tended to all her household duties. She had a little help from Concetta and Rosa, two ladies who were paid a small sum each week to wash clothes, keep the house clean, prepare meals, do some of the shopping, tend to the few chickens on the property, and generally help out with a million little tasks, including preservation of the garden tomato crop, putting up jars of various foods, and making specialties, such as was customary around so many of their religious holidays.

Vincenzo worked for over three years both for the local meat market and also in off hours traveling downtown to the New York City wholesale meat center, the Gansevoort Meat Market next to Manhattan's sprawling Washington Market, where he processed whole beef cattle carcasses and whole calves, lambs, goats, and pigs, and down in the Lower West Side on Little West Twelfth Street in the shadow of the construction of the elevated highway, which was to be called the West Side Highway.

Now he had accumulated both money and enough knowledge to open his own small retail meat market. He learned that a relative owned a building with a store for rent on 102nd Street in the Bronx. Vincenzo decided that he could move his family uptown and open a store. There was enough money to afford a two-bedroom rental above the store as well. He could not afford, however, to pay a salary to another butcher. His wife had enough experience and knowledge of the butcher business and some experience in keeping the books to be of great help. Vincenzo eventually made a deal with the landlord and within a few weeks moved uptown. The landlord, his cousin, interviewed the prospective tenant before making a handshake deal. Vincenzo had only met his cousin a few times when he was a young boy, but he never forgot his stern and strange appearance. The meeting was held in a warehouse on an alley close to 102nd Street. The sign on the building simply had the word "NOVA" on It. He was led by two large men to the barrel of a man who sat behind a desk in a cluttered office in the back of the warehouse. Vincenzo introduced himself, and his host simply nodded while looking him up and down. Vincenzo was unsure of this fellow.

"Don Terranova, piacere," Vincenzo began, "ringrazia da Corleone mio padre Antonio Delmonte" (Thank you for myself and I bring salute (good health) from my family, my father Antonio Delmonte).

He went on. "I appreciate your consideration of my being your tenant. I promise to pay you the rent every first Monday of the month. If you can see your way clear to rent the apartment and the store to me, you have my word that I will operate in a proper and diligent manner."

Don Terranova listened and watched Vincenzo's movements and facial expression. He also noted that this fellow had a familiar temperament, a Sicilian temperament, *come piasano de Corleone a piase.*

Enrico responded, "Signor Delmonte tu sei molto gentile e accomedo. Mi penza che tu e me che fatto una cosa buona. Salute a tu famigia tu padre. Mi non te rescordare a te. Su beneriga vascera." (Mr. Delmonte, you are very kind and a gentleman. I think you will do a good thing and good health to your family and your father. I will remember you. God be with you.)

"Allora quando tu fare tutti csa che necessario per u 'businesse' in un altro settimana passatta chiamo me, per piace, e insemo ti fare un altro cosa," said Enrico. (After you get all the things done necessary for your business, come see me in a few weeks, and we can do other things together.)

"Grazie," Vincenzo said as he nodded and left the office.

Vincenzo had hardly expected an invitation to come back in a week to "speak of other things." His rental of the store and apartment was to bring him a great opportunity. Enrico Terranova had an instinctive feeling about the fellow that he was a man who could be trusted. He also had studied his smooth and easy manner and pleasant Sicilian features. Vincenzo had an engaging and pleasing smile, one that exhibited trust, confidence, and strength. He had a moderate frame that was measured at five foot seven and was very dexterous and agile. His oval face had a rounded, straight nose and moderate cheekbones complemented by a thin, handlebar moustache. His perfectly rounded head had a flat, thin crop of hair already receding although he was only twenty-eight years old. His green eyes were true and trustworthy, and he never spoke to anyone unless he looked them straight in the eye.

Enrico was a good judge of character, and he recognized these traits in Vincenzo, his woodpile *cugino* (cousin). He did expect that Delmonte knew of the history of the Terranovas in the old country and was showing the respect for the name as well as the man. Vincenzo wasted no time in setting up his new home and shop. Within a few days of moving in, he arranged to have a sign put up over his shop proclaiming "Columbia Market, Finest Meats and Poultry." He had many paper signs in the window for every item sold from beef *bracciola* to *salsiccia* (sausage). He prepared the Italian pork sausage with hot pepper or with wine, fennel, parsley, and cheese. He had a full line of steaks, chops, and even several salamis and cheeses, all the best quality, many of them imported from his native Italy.

Soon his little shop gained a local following.

His wife, already busy keeping the books, also became a full-fledged butcher, handling a meat cleaver as easily as the cash receipts. As the months passed, the shop prospered, and another boy was needed to help with cleanup and other menial tasks. There was even enough profit to hire one more boy for the busy weekends and another for deliveries. In fact, to speed up the deliveries and increase sales, Vincenzo bought a used bike. It seemed that the sales increased along with his wife's girth. Vincenzo knew that the expanding business and his wife's expanding belly meant he would soon have to get more experienced help. From time to time, he also received letters from home about local news and family matters. While not being too explicit, it was clear that his brother Toto and Giuseppe were not getting along, and it was beginning to disrupt the stability of the entire family.

Since there were now two bedrooms, Vincenzo decided to bring his brother Giuseppe over to the States to help in the butcher shop.

Vincenzo suggested the plan to his father, who responded favorably, and it was all quickly arranged. Within six weeks, Vincenzo was greeting his brother at the same ship dock he had once arrived at. Within a few days, Guiseppe became "Joe," and Vincenzo was being called "Vince." It seemed that the timing was perfect as the shop's sales began to grow faster and bigger week by week, and Vincenzina began to slow down due to the pregnancy.

When Enrico Terranova went through the neighborhood in one of his NOVA trucks, he would occasionally stop in and watch the commerce at the Columbia Market.

He recalled his early days arranging his business in the States. Soon after, he and his new manager, Achille, found a small warehouse in the Bronx and began bringing in NOVA olive oil.

Guiseppe Garibaldi, back in Italy after his few years in Staten Island, had stayed at his friend Antonio Meucci's house. After the unification of Italy, he had a commanding place in the new Italian government. He was successful in swaying his colleagues and even brought in local supporters to help in the reorganization of government affairs. The Terranovas were prominent in that reorganization. They also assisted, along with the Merendinos, in setting up government regulation for domestic and foreign trade for the new nation of Italy. They saw to it that the approvals for any trade in olive oil, particularly in export to the US, were under their control and approval. Eventually any producer of olive oils had to have an agreement with the Terranovas or they would not be granted export or trade rights. Thus, the control was complete. Eventually all the oil sent to the States was shipped to one of the NOVA distribution centers in New York, Boston, or New Orleans.

Enrico had done well organizing these reception and distribution centers. When he ran into resistance from a local operator, he would present an offer to buy him out. If that failed, more drastic methods were employed, such as from purchasing his competitor's building, and if that failed, burning it.

Soon Enrico had hundreds of men to support his efforts, many of them Italians sent to America for this purpose alone. His first complete coup was the solidification of control of the business in New York; from there, he branched out to Boston and Louisiana. Boston had an Italian ghetto, which was expanding rapidly, and control was under the watchful eye of a cousin, Lido. He also solidified the other New England cities in Connecticut, New Hampshire, northern region of New York, Vermont, and Maine.

Louisiana was not as easy to control. The Cajun influence was notable. Many of the men there were fiercely independent and could use a rifle or a knife with equal ability as using a cooking skillet or barbeque fork. New Orleans and Boston Italians had long traditions of operating fine restaurants with knowledgeable chefs as well as the ruthless Cajun bayou men.

The Merendinos had a relative who was a monsignor at the Vatican. Through proper communication channels with the church and their government influence, the pope appointed Monsignor Federico Cappolla to New Orleans as the assistant to the bishop there.

The bishop, Dino Santagorda, was not well, and given his advanced age and poor health, he was not expected to be able to carry out his office for much longer. Within six months, Cappolla took over for the ailing bishop and within a year was elevated to archbishop of the city of New Orleans. In 1918, the pope saw to it that full authority was given to the bishop of all the Catholic parishes in New Orleans and the rest of Louisiana. It all came under the authority of the archbishop. Cappolla helped the Terranovas consolidate operations with many of the parish leaders who, most incidentally, wielded ultimate political power.

Thus, the control of the olive oil and some other import products fell to the control of NOVA, the Terranova company.

Enrico particularly enjoyed his visits there. The city was more European than American, and the atmosphere was less intense than New York and offered a great deal more than a stoic Boston. There were many fine restaurants and clubs, gaming halls and gambling dens, and an incredible red-light district known simply as Storyville. New Orleans catered to every vice in an elegant yet informal and easy manner. Indeed, the nickname "the Big Easy" was really appropriate. It was easy to indulge yourself.

The profits in the olive oil and imports did not depend simply on this Italian ghetto since the entire southern region used Italian goods. Eventually, Enrico had operations supplying not only several food products but also Italian wines and liquors, clothing, artworks, marble, and more. Eventually he purchased store houses and a pier to ship direct. Profits rolled in, and he and a small contingent of his Sicilians were brought in, headed by Giovanni "John" Bertucci and his cousin Franco Marcello, to run things. They bought restaurants and clubs in the French Quarter along with a bunch of whorehouses in Storyville. Eventually they operated liquor store distributors and an import company as well. Having the protection of the parish leaders and the cooperation of Archbishop Cappolla meant their business could flourish unimpeded. Their interests spread to the Gold Coast of Mississippi as well and to the border of Texas. Eventually they operated numbers racket and loan-sharking. They got control of politicians and the cooperation of the leadership of the police department. While the city was known for its French Cajun culture, the real power, the economic power, eventually rested with the Italians. Their main competition was from the Irish who had gotten there decades before and wielded considerable governmental power.

CHAPTER 37

THE INTERESTS OF the Terranovas and associates with other families in Italy and the United States were extremely profitable over the years. From the late 1800s to the early years of the next century, the ventures expanded with the economies of the two nations. The Terranovas and their associated families and friends cooperated closely, and nearly all of their ventures were successful and served to further advance their wealth and power.

The production and sale of home-grown or manufactured Sicilian products produced a partnership in the expanding trucking operations between the towns in Italy and the markets in Palermo, Messina, and other cities. The manufacture of tin containers eventually became one of the businesses the Terranovas partnered in with a firm in Milan, their major partner up north. The tin can manufacturing firm was operated by a relative of the Borga family. Enrico had been in Rome for a family christening and reception and struck up a conversation with Silverio Borga and his son while the ladies were fussing over the newly christened family member. Most of the business interactions occurred through some connection with a relative, friend, or business associate. The Terranova family members had a reputation for being very clever. They knew that once their pasta manufacturing operations in Sicily began to grow, the cardboard and wood packaging already needed for their olive oil export would soon follow.

In the US, Enrico expanded the family's holdings by investing in several small businesses that included packaging firms, crate makers, trucking firms, and others. They would seek out a small operation and with their web of connections expand the sales and client base in a very short period of time. While there were certainly legitimate opportunities to be found, they did not pass on illegal operations as well. One of them involved the lending of money. It was not possible to lend through a bank or some other institution either in Italy or the US, particularly for these relatively unsophisticated small operations.

The age-old trade of private money lending was the best source of immediate capital for any purpose, particularly the illegal pursuits.

The ghettos and slums of Lower Manhattan had a long history of illicit activities. From the mid-1870s, the formation of predatory gangs gave this city a reputation for being a dangerous place. Gambling, prostitution, and virtually every other vice could be satisfied here. All one needed was money, and the easiest and quickest way to get it was to steal, swindle, or kill for it.

Without knowing the danger, some unfortunate travelers would venture into some areas of the city, particularly near the transportation centers, docks, ports, train stations, and liveries, without ever being heard from again. Bodies stripped of every stitch of clothing were found in the rivers, on train tracks, and in cellars all around Manhattan on a daily basis. Some were stabbed, others strangled. The Hudson River and East Rivers would become the favorite dumping grounds for bodies later in the century by gangs and the mob. Manhattan's notorious reputation stemmed from the early days of the infamous "Five Points Gangs" in the 1890s, which was made up primarily of Irish immigrants, to the 1990s when the "Capo" of the Gambino Mafia family was gunned down in the wide-open streets. The violence never relented as the home location of the most fearsome and bloodthirsty criminals. The history of New York City, many say, was written in blood.

CHAPTER 38

WHEN HE FIRST arrived, Enrico Terranova's connections with the money lenders, thieves, gamblers, and owners of houses of prostitution in New York was to him just another aspect of the life of the times, an opportunity to make money.

When a businessman borrowed money and could not pay it back in time, he put himself in jeopardy and was in danger of being physically attacked or losing his business. When Enrico became aware of such a situation and felt it could be profitable, he could finance the deal and become a partner.

This was how Enrico became a part owner of several businesses, and as his NOVA company's operations expanded, so did the Terranovas' interest in other operations, such as financing gamblers, loan sharks, fencing stolen goods, and being silent partners in prostitution rings and robberies. Since the NOVA company's operations permitted Enrico to have advanced knowledge of when certain cargo ships would arrive and what cargo they carried, it was not a difficult task to have it hijacked or robbed. The many New York gangs were more than anxious to deal in such goods, and there was such a tremendous influx of them that it was not unusual to have several opportunities each week.

Eventually the extended Terranova family had an extended network of customers for their contraband. If there was some concern that a particular cargo, which was "acquired" in New York, might be too recognizable locally, Enrico would arrange to send it to the south or north, and from there it would get redistributed. The same situation might also arise from these destinations, so it would frequently happen that when these same trucks returned to New York, they were not empty.

This commerce required Enrico to travel continually between New York and a number of other cities from the northeast to the south as well as back to Italy.

Enrico did not want to start a family until he felt more established in the US. He traveled to Italy once or twice a year and spent time with different women. As forceful and impenetrable and fearless a Sicilian as he was, he had a particular weakness for women regardless of their age.

Enrico's enjoyment of the more aesthetic things in life was from time to time limited by the time constraints that business and travel required. He found opportunities when he could to pursue his many interests. He was so regimented with his time, in fact, that he hardly needed more than four or five hours of sleep per night to feel fully rested, and when he could, he took short naps during the day, perhaps just dozing off for three or four minutes to feel rested.

The expansion of the family holdings meant Enrico was responsible for protecting all of the financial enterprises. The acquisition of part or full ownership of the illegal operations required the creation of an intricate system of protection, communication, insulation of principles, supervision, hierarchy, and a trustworthy accounting and collection system. Enrico found himself constantly interviewing more and more prospective employees locally as well as welcoming those sent in by the operations in Sicily.

"Bon jamalie mani" (Good day), said Enrico as he spotted a tall, wiry, thin, middle-aged man coming down the gang plank of the massive ship, *Conte di Savioia*, which had just docked that morning at Pier 38 on the Hudson River. The man removed his dark gray fedora and hugged Enrico as he kissed him on both cheeks.

"Piace, piace Don Terranova," said the man in a tone of voice that exclaimed genuine affection.

Cosmo Marchiani was relieved that he finally reached his destination and was being met by a friendly face. Though he appeared to be just another Italian immigrant, his appearance belied the man under the modest suit and demeanor. Cosmo Marchiani was a relative of the Merendino family but had been a loyal friend and visitor to the Terranova estate in Sicily. He was educated in Rome and had the equivalent of a professorship in finance. He also had studied in Bologna and for a time even considered becoming a physician. He was a genius with any mathematical problem and had created an intricate system of accounting, banking, and schedule of investments many years earlier.

Enrico had been traveling and working at a feverish pace for weeks. He had his associates in America that he saw each day and generally dined with one or another of them. He was extremely pleased to have Cosmo Marchiani assist him and genuinely enjoyed his company. He respected him as an intelligent and learned businessman but also as a raconteur and sophisticated, worldly gent, truly a man to respect in many ways. Cosmo's knowledge of business matters was extensive, only equaled by his knowledge of fine arts, fine wines, and fine foods.

"Porta la machine" (Bring the car), Enrico exclaimed as he beckoned to Tino standing near a big, four-door Packard sedan just at the entrance to the pier. A porter had loaded two huge steamer trunks and several leather traveling cases on a dolly and had wheeled it out to the street after it was offloaded as one of the first items off the ship.

"Paesano," said Enrico. "I can do what you like today. We can go directly to the apartment or we can go to a nice hotel nearby and relax for a day or so."

Cosmo opened his hands and in a mild Italian accent said, "Don Terranova, I would enjoy spending my time with you, and I could surely use a little relaxation. The last few days on the ship were rough. The seas did not relent day or night, and I am not the sailor I used to be. It took a bit out of me. I didn't sleep or eat well and am still a little weak. I have stiffness in my joints and back."

Enrico smiled. "I know just the remedy," he said. "Take us to the Saint George," he ordered Tino.

Tino eased away from the curb and proceeded south along West Street. There was construction in the center of what was a very wide, multilane boulevard. There were concrete and steel columns and an overhead roadway, the West Side Highway, which was being constructed. Enrico said, "This new highway is really a marvel. It is suspended above the street like the Roman viaduct."

After a short drive, the Packard slowed down in front of a massive building. There were several people outside, and Cosmo noticed the canvas canopy with the name "St. George Hotel" emblazoned in red on the side. Enrico said, "We can have the trunks brought to your apartment if that is convenient and bring your essential luggage into the hotel."

Cosmo answered, "That would be fine." A doorman opened the door as two bellhops got their direction from Tino. The two men walked into the stately old lobby arm in arm.

Enrico went to the desk clerk and said, "Please tell Mr. Talbot that Mr. Terranova has arrived." The clerk behind the front desk lobby disappeared behind a door at the end of the counter.

In a few minutes a tall, thin man in a dark gray suit and tie emerged. "Mr. Terranova, how good to see you. Your suite is ready. Please let us know what we can do for you. I have spoken with George at the health club, and he has prepared a private section for your needs. Please let me know if there is anything you need." He handed Enrico two key rings, and after raising a finger, two bellhops rushed over. "Boys, please assist Mr. Terranova and his guest."

They took the elevator to the eighth floor where the bellboys directed them to the two doors at the end of the hall. Enrico said, "I took the liberty of having these rooms prepared for us. Please let me know when you have settled yourself in, and we'll take you to the health club to ease that back."

In Cosmo's, there was a sitting room with two love seats, a chair and desk, and some tables with lamps. The carpets were deep, plush, and soft. Off to one side was a large bedroom, and next to it a white tile bathroom. The bathroom had a large pedestal sink, deep bathtub, and a tiled shower cubicle with row upon row of metal rings, which produced hundreds of pinpoint streams of water from head to toe. The drapery, bedcovers, and linens were perfectly matched. The several towels had the St. George name in red embroidery embossed across each one. Cosmos inspected the rooms as the bellhop brought in the luggage and then asked if it was permissible to unpack. Cosmos nodded, and the bellhop placed all the contents of the two bags in a closet and two bureaus. On one table were two bottles of wine and a bucket of ice along with a seltzer dispenser and a bottle of scotch whiskey. There was also an embossed card edged in a floral framed note: "Welcome to America, Commandatore Cosmo Marchiani." He also noted some confetti sugar-coated almonds and a variety of chocolates and small biscotti (biscuits) near the tray.

Enrico had his personal effects and clothing brought to the hotel a day earlier and was at the desk reviewing some notes when there was a tap at the door. The bellhop brought in a tray with wine, figs, and biscotti. He handed the boy two dollars. The freckled-faced boy's eyes widened, and he said, "Oh, thank you, Mr. Terranova. Oh, thank you very much. Please ring if there is anything you need at all, sir. Thank you," and he backed out the door.

Within an hour, Enrico rung up the bellhop and told him to deliver Mr. Cosmo a note next door. The boy tapped on the door and handed Cosmo the note and left. Cosmo went to the phone, and when the attendant answered, he asked for number eighty-one. Enrico answered, "Yes?"

"Don Enrico, per piacere" (I am at your direction).

Enrico responded, "Grazie. I will come over." In a few minutes, he was at Cosmo's door, and the two went down the hallway to the elevator.

When the elevator stopped, the men proceeded down a carpeted hallway to a double set of wooded doors. Enrico opened the door. There was a rush of hot, humid air and the buzz of male voices. A big blond-headed fellow in a white T-shirt and white canvas pants came over to Enrico. "Mr. Terranova, pleasure to see you. I assume your guest will need directions to our facilities. So I told Franco here to help us out."

Just behind the blond man was a large black-haired fellow with huge biceps, standing six feet six inches tall. Enrico said, "Thank you, George. This is Mr. Marchiani. He just arrived. He's having a bit of a problem with his back and limbs. Maybe a massage, steam, and hot shower or salt bath can help."

George said, "I'm sure we can find a solution. Please, sir, follow me. Franco will attend to you."

Each man was massaged for about two hours. Occasionally, warm oils or cool, aromatic waters were applied to their bodies, scalp, face, and feet. The masseurs used their hands, forearms, and elbows to thoroughly massage each muscle ligament and tendon in their bodies. Enrico had become accustomed to a weekly massage. George had, over time, gotten to know exactly where Enrico had a tightened muscle or a pulled tendon. He was fierce in his pummeling of the muscles of the back and shoulders, nearly reaching the bone in his manipulations.

Two hours of vigorous massage can take a toll on a man's endurance. The two men led them to a huge steam room with twenty other men barely visible in the hot mist. This room was the smallest of three steam rooms. An attendant with a bucket of ice water and pewter cups circled the room from time to time with four or five towels hooked at his waist. Occasionally, he would pour a cup of water for a man who beckoned to him or hand them a cup of ice-cold water to drink. Enrico pointed to a bench at a corner, and Cosmo sat down next to him. "Feel any better now?" inquired Enrico.

"Yes, much. It's like the Roman baths, very good, very good," said Cosmo.

After the hot mist had gotten to the two men, Enrico said, "Let's go," and they left the steam room wrapped in terry towels. George and Franco were waiting outside and led the men to yet another small room with a few thick, padded, soft cots. The men lay down and were covered with three thin, cool, cotton sheets. Within a few moments, they were both asleep.

Enrico awoke first and quickly noticed it was six thirty in the evening. Cosmo was still fast asleep. Enrico walked out to the tiled shower room and went into a shower cubicle.

Twenty minutes later, Cosmo appeared red eyed and a little dazed. He heard the rush of water from the shower and found a shower cubicle himself. The dressing room down the corridor had a small vanity area and bathroom with combs, brushes, alcohol, towels, razors, shave cream mugs, soaps, and powders. The men completed their personal regiments and dressed.

Enrico said, "If you like, there are many types of food at fine restaurants nearby, or I can have something brought to the hotel as you prefer."

Cosmo thought for a moment, then said, "I have been confined on a ship for many days. It might be nice to walk on terra firma for a while and see something instead of the rolling sea. I will dress and be guided by you."

Enrico said, "Fine. I will call you shortly."

Cosmo returned to his suite and reviewed the clothes the bellhop had hung in his closet. He chose a shirt, suit, and tie and dressed, making sure his black leather shoes did not have any dust or mark on the toe. Enrico walked across the hall and tapped on the door.

Cosmo opened and with a sweep of his hand invited him in. Both felt in excellent humor. The health club had relieved their tensions and nuances, and each had an expectation of enjoying the evening in the great town that lay before them, New York City.

Cosmo took note of the small hotel lobby, observing the interior layout and the activity of the hotel staff when Enrico said, "So, my friend, *andiamo*!" and ushered him outside. They strolled slowly along the sidewalk. Each was meticulously dressed in a tailored, dark suit, Cosmo in midnight blue, Enrico in dark gray. The springtime evening air was welcome though just a bit cool. The odors of the city changed from block to block.

Cosmo's eyes darted from building to street to window and back again. "I'm sure these buildings could tell us many unusual stories if they could speak." The masonry facades, some with ornate floral or statuary designs, row after row, seemed to go on beyond the extent of vision.

"Paesano," began Enrico, "this country is a marvel. Everything I could imagine is somewhere within its borders. It is the continent of Europe compressed into one country. The many immigrants who came here before us, however, resent the newcomers. They will deal with us, take advantage of the cheap labor, discriminate, take our money, and still hate us. Even if we become wealthy and powerful, they still believe they are superior. At once I am comfortable in this land and still feel like an orphan, *una proietta* (an orphan)—*capisce*?" Enrico asked.

"Si," responded Cosmo. "Ma per io tutti il mio vita chi sono una prioetta (Yes, but all my life I have been an orphan). Far niente (It's nothing). We just go on," Cosmo ended.

Both knew well the feeling of being an outcast.

Enrico typically had little to say, and yet it was a comfort to have Cosmo beside him. They were the new invaders in a hostile land whose riches and opportunity begged to be exploited, even in the face of a hostile society suspicious of these swarthy newcomers. Those who had come before did not trust them, but they could not get rid of them.

Enrico directed Cosmo to a storefront doorway and into a long, narrow, tiled floor trattoria.

A short, stout, balding fellow with a white apron down to his shoes rushed over. "Don Terranova, *piacere*. Please come in. It's wonderful to see you. Giovanni," he called to another aproned fellow at the back of the room. "Get the table ready for Don Terranova and his guest." "Signore, I am honored to have you here," he said to Cosmo. "I am Vito. Please let me know what I can do to make your visit with us comfortable." Vito ushered the two men to a table at the very back corner of the restaurant, a large round table, and quickly had three chairs removed. This area was the most private inside the place but afforded a view of the entire restaurant.

The men sat down. Almost immediately, Giovanni and a young boy came back out from the kitchen in the rear with a pitcher of water and carafe of red wine. "Don Terranova, this is Vito's homemade wine," said Giovanni.

Within a few minutes, Vito had visually checked the rest of the guests in the restaurant and directed three other waiters so he could devote his time to the two men.

Vito and Giovanni began bringing out flat platters; first a salad of various greens, some pasta pomodoro, and then the main courses accompanied by small dishes of roasted peppers and onions, crisp, sautéed potatoes, spinach, and roasted mushrooms. The men ate heartily and hardly spoke.

Vito, Giovanni, and the boy quickly cleared the table and rushed back out with trays with assorted fruits and endives. Soon after, they reappeared with bottles of anisette, grappa, and Strega. They placed a pot of espresso on the table still brewing and steaming. Thereafter, a tray with *dolci* (sweets) with cannoli, *sfogliatella*, baba rum, cookies, fig bars, dry figs, and dates and nuts were placed on the table.

Vito fussed around the table from time to time clearing chunks or changing silverware or glasses, then disappeared.

"Cosmo, this fellow has become a good friend. He had some problems when he first opened this place. It seems he and a brother-in-law had worked in a restaurant on Mulberry Street for some time when they first came over. They saved a few dollars and borrowed money from Vito's uncle. After a year or so, Vito wanted to begin to repay the loan. The brother-in-law resisted, telling him if their loan was being repaid, it should come out of Vito's end. One night they ended up in a fight. The brother-in-law threatened to kill Vito. Vito explained the story to me. 'Vito, if you like, I think there may be a way out of the problem. I will buy out your uncle's debt.' It was some two thousand dollars. 'I'll look for a small payment back, say fifty dollars a month, and, of course, when I want to eat here or bring people, you will accommodate.'" He agreed. As soon as the brother-in-law heard who the new partner was, he left the business. Cosmo smiled broadly and nodded.

Vito came over. "Don Terranova, the delivery olive oil and pasta this week were much too much. It is excellent. I thank you. What else can I bring you?"

Enrico just nodded, rose from his chair, and ushered Cosmo out to the street with Vito at the front door waving goodbye.

Enrico walked Cosmo down the street into a small grocery store. There he spoke to the man behind the counter. The fellow handed him a set of keys, and they went around to the back door of the store where in the alley a small Ford sedan was pushed in at the back entry.

"Let's go for a little ride," said Enrico as he slid behind the wheel and started up the car. It bucked a bit, then rolled away. Enrico drove, bounding along the cobblestone street for about twenty minutes, then pulled off into a dark alleyway and shut off the lights. It was totally dark except for the streaks of light just peeking out from drawn shades.

Enrico walked first down a few steps to a wood cellar door and knocked. A big, beefy fellow peered through the crack of the door and then, recognizing Enrico, opened it wider and let him in without saying a word. Enrico led Cosmo up two sets of stairs and into a wide main hall.

To the left and right were two ornate parlors, and Enrico entered a rear door to one. A small wood bar was at the rear with eight large velvet sofas. There was a group of men at the small bar with five elaborately dressed women talking to them. There were four ladies sitting on the sofas next to three men.

Cosmo's eyes darted around the room and took notice of all he saw. A middle-aged woman came up to Enrico and said, "Mr. Terranova, how nice to see you and your friend. Please let me know what I can get you to drink or anything else you like."

Enrico said, "Cecilia, this is my very good friend Cosmo." He nodded.

"Well, sir, please let me know whatever you like," she responded.

Enrico entered a small alcove off the center of the room. There were sofas and tables there with terraces that looked out onto the street a story below.

Enrico explained, "Cosmo, we have investments of this kind here in Boston and New Orleans. We have a very good relationship with the local police."

Then a young woman came with a tray with three bottles and glasses and set them down in front of Enrico. "May I get you something else?" she asked.

"Not at the moment, but please ask some of the ladies to stop by and introduce themselves to my friend Mr. Cosmo," Enrico said.

The young lady said, "Sure, Mr. Terranova." She turned and said, "I am Mary, Mr. Cosmo. Anything you need, please call me," and she left.

Within the next few minutes, several ladies stopped by and introduced themselves. "Hi, I'm Annie." "Hello, I'm Delia." "Hello there, I'm Lenora." "Hey there, I'm Anna," and on and on. The piano player in the next room started to play.

Enrico turned to Cosmo. "Please stay here as long as you like; just tell Cecilia what you need. If you want to return to the hotel later, she will provide a car and driver. Relax. Enjoy yourself."

Cosmo responded, "I thank you for your hospitality. I am at your disposal. I will be anxious to see what business needs you have tomorrow, but I will spend some time here tonight first." Cosmo rose and walked over to the next parlor where the piano player was playing. He took a dollar from his pocket and said something to him. He began playing a slow Italian melody. Cosmo walked over to a particularly tall, slim woman seated near the door, and within a minute, they were talking quietly.

Enrico caught the eye of Cecilia, and she came over. "I noticed a lady here a few times. I just never got her name. She has brown hair and green, sad eyes. She was very beautiful."

Cecilia thought for a moment. "I'm sure you must mean Doria. She is a very nice person. Actually, she helps me operate here—keeps accounts and helps instruct the girls and the maids. I think she is in the bookkeeping office. I'll get her." Soon she reappeared with a woman of medium height and slim waist. Her bright brown hair was thick and wound in a neat bun at the back of her head. She wore a dark blue dress, straight with gold trimming and a set of small white pearls. The dress revealed the plump pink flesh of her cleavage.

She smiled. "Don Terranova, it is a pleasure to meet you at last. I am Doria."

Enrico responded, "I have seen you several times and always enjoyed your smile. It's perfect." He again noted that although she had classic high cheekbones, a long, straight Mediterranean nose, and dark green eyes, though bright and clear, they had a definite sadness.

Enrico could only imagine that this *bella robba* (literally "nicely dressed") lady would use her body to support herself. He felt at once attracted and just a bit repulsed.

She had perfect olive skin, and her body movements were fluid and easy. Her deep red lips were accented by glistening red lipstick, but she had no other makeup. She did not need any. Her thick, flowing eyebrows and long eyelashes were a gift of nature. Her bright white teeth had an iridescent, pearly caste. Her lower lip was thick and full and moved in nearly a quivering motion when she spoke, which caused the eye of the person she addressed to go directly to her mouth. It was nearly a magnetic reflex that drew a person to gaze at her face and lips. Her voice was a full soprano but reserved and reassured, and it was all complemented by a slight, knowing smile.

Enrico seemed a little uneasy with his words. "Signora, you have been here for a while, but we've never had an opportunity to talk to each other. It's a pleasure finally to talk with you."

"Don Terranova, you are very kind to say that. I am flattered by your notice," responded Doria.

Enrico continued, "You're Italian, right?"

"Yes, I was born in Napoli, but I have been here several years. I have known Cecilia for quite some time, but it's just been a few months that I have moved into the house here."

"I see," said Enrico. "You speak English wonderfully. I still have a little trouble, as you can tell." Enrico's English had improved over the years, but he still had a distinctive foreign accent and was self-conscious whenever he had to use words in English that he found difficult to pronounce.

"How long has it been since you left Italy?" Enrico inquired.

"Oh, quite a while I guess. Some fifteen years ago, my late husband and I came to New Orleans to make a new start. Unfortunately, he contracted diphtheria within a few months of our arrival, and due to several complications, he died," she responded.

"So," said Enrico, "then as a widow you decided to come here?"

"Well, I got work at a house down the street as a cleaning lady with hope of earning my boat passage back home. My husband was not a wealthy man; he left me very little money and very pregnant. My daughter was born six months after my husband passed away."

Enrico was a bit surprised that she had a child. "Where is she now?" he asked.

"Well, I have a local woman who lives on the street a few blocks over from here where there is a little place for us. This woman was the mother of my second husband. He was from New York, so we moved here. He was murdered several years ago. His mother and I have only each other, and she loves my little Rosa. There is no one else here for either of us."

"So now you work here?" said Enrico.

"Well, I tried to provide for the child on my own, but it was very difficult with the few dollars I made as a cleaning woman in New Orleans, especially since the local women who work these houses resented a foreign white woman taking money from their pockets. Eventually I found I needed to find another kind of work." She smiled and lowered her head. Enrico could sense the embarrassment and pride in this woman. Life had been an effort to survive, and for the good of her child as well as keeping herself sound and safe, she turned to selling herself.

"Why don't we go somewhere a little quiet, Doria, if you can leave your bookkeeping," Enrico said, trying to put her at ease. She realized he was trying to acknowledge that her bookwork was a source of her income more than the sordid endeavor of servicing men with her body. It was a kind and gentle gesture she rarely experienced and certainly never expected from a man of such great wealth and power. The men she usually met were self-impressed pigs with large bankrolls who treated the women in the house like chattel. They did not abuse the women, but it was clear that most of these men simply sought to use the flesh they purchased for the time allotted, much as one would hire a horse and carriage or spend on an elaborate meal. It was an indulgence to be savored as a rich bottle of wine or brandy and nothing more.

Doria took Enrico's hand and led him up to the third-floor room. She opened the door and, when he entered, locked it. She went to a small table and lit four large candles and one small one and pulled the drapes closed. Then she poured a little water from a white pitcher into a large ceramic basin and touched a small cloth and dabbed it in the water and then dabbed her eyes.

"The men smoke those cigars, and it never fails to cause my eyes to tear and burn a little. I apologize but just give me a moment." The cabinet was at the edge of the alcove. There was a large brass bed with piles of pillows on it and a thick, goose-feathered comforter on it. There were two chairs, one big chaise with a velvet back and a thick, heavy, tapestry-cushioned base some seven feet long and a large overstuffed armchair. Next to it was a high wood cabinet with several bottles of liquor, wines, and some glasses.

Enrico walked over to the cabinet, poured some whiskey, and drank it down. Doria was still dabbing her eyes when she felt a hand gently touch the back of her neck. Enrico stood just behind her and with his huge, thick fingers gently traced the angular line from the back of her left ear to the base of her neck, once and then again. Doria stood perfectly still, just a little concerned but also somewhat surprised at the light and gentle touch of such a strong man. Because of his big barrel chest, rotund, puffy face, and fierce looks, Enrico usually made anyone retreat after the slightest glance.

She stood still as she now felt his right hand on her shoulder as he moved closer and closer behind her. She could smell the faint aroma of a man's shaving soap mixed with alcohol. Again he traced the line of her neck and shoulder but placed his hand lightly on her waist. "Why, Mr. Terranova, you are very kind. I am a simple, plain woman who, as fate would have it, finds myself in a strange place in a very bizarre life. But you are very kind," Doria whispered, almost out of breath. He led her away from the cabinet; at the same time, she turned around to face him. He turned back and blew out all but one small candle. The room grew dark with just the flickering of the tall, thin candle for light and a little glow from the window drapery. He returned to her.

Enrico faced her and ran the back of his huge hand against her right cheek, down to the end of her chin, her neck, and then her chest very slowly, seeming again to trace the fine lines of her features. He was completely under the spell of her face, lips, and soft skin. "You should not be concerned this evening about anything. I hope you can just feel at ease and comfortable here with me. I do not want you to feel you must do anything you don't want to do." She felt her usual resistance to being touched by a stranger melt away and sighed quietly.

Enrico bent and touched his lips to her bare shoulder and drew in the scent of her perfume. Doria nearly fell into his big muscular arms as she leaned forward against his frame for support. It was as if she had drunk the whiskey.

The two stood there for what seemed like hours, quietly embracing and gently feeling the warmth of each other.

In time, Doria, her weary eyes now bright and soft, loosened her dress and slipped out of it. "Would you like something to drink?" asked Enrico.

"Some sherry please," she answered. He poured a glass and handed it to her, and he finished the whiskey he had poured for himself. Doria drank half the glass and then, still in underclothes, pulled back the bed covers and lay back on the bed in a sitting position. Enrico removed his suit and shoes and sat next to her.

Again he began to trace the line of her face and then her body as he removed her undergarments and undid her pinned hair. She reclined and, after finishing the wine, lay back on the bed, stretched out. She uttered a sigh from time to time, hardly conscious that she had done so.

She began to stroke his neck and shoulders and could feel the thick, sinuous muscle of his powerful upper body. His chest and stomach were like thick coils of muscle covered with a human hide. In time, she reached his abdomen and then grabbed his large swollen penis. The night turned into dawn, and they were still embraced as the first hint of daylight shown from behind the shades.

He rose, dressed, and was gone before Doria woke.

Bringing Cosmo Marchiani into his business operations as his financial controller would give Enrico the peace of mind he needed now that his expanded interests needed one person to concentrate efforts solely on finances. Cosmo was the perfect fit. Making Cosmo feel wanted was also part of Enrico's strategy to enhance loyalty. The elaborate reception would ensure benefits of his new associate being obligated to Enrico in a manner that was known in the old country.

CHAPTER 39

ENRICO TERRANOVA LIVED in a homogeneous feudal society that was centuries old. Little change occurred, as little change was needed or wanted. That was not truer than in Sicily. *Omerta*, silence, and secrecy was a way of life for these island dwellers. Outsiders were never to be accepted, never to be included, never to know what the locals knew, and what they knew they kept secret.

So it was for centuries that the invaders of Sicily left their mark. The Moors' influence is still visible in the architecture that survived. More sanguine, however, was the olive, dark, and black-skinned Sicilians, the inheritors of the blood. The rape of the Sicilian women by invaders from the south told a more significant story. The need for these people to protect themselves was the catalyst for secret societies and unions since there was a continual history of invasion. The French, the northerners, the Greeks, the Africans, Arabs, and such took turns. There grew an ingrained sense of necessity for self-preservation by the indigenous Sicilian population.

So it was with the formation of the Cammora in Naples. The so-called Black Hand grew in this port city, a city of riches by way of their harbor attracting commerce from all over the Mediterranean. Sicily offered a different kind of fertility—fruit, pasta, vegetables, lamb, goats, cattle, figs, olives, grapes for wine, spices, and so much more. The Sicilian women were sturdy, proportionate, passionate, supple, and deferential to the men. They with their dark eyes, black hair, sensuous, full lips, and intriguing demeanor were as desirable as were the wealth of the spoils of conquest.

These protective societies flourished for centuries. Even after World War I, little changed. The advent of World War II and the alliances made by the Mafia and the United States government created an easy opportunity for the Mafia to gain some kind of nominal acceptance. The legendary Salvatore "Lucky" Luciana and his cohorts assisted the American effort to protect the ports during World War II, which solidified an unholy alliance between the Mafia and the United States government, one that would spur the growth and protection of the mob in the United States for decades.

The true noble aspects of the Men of Respect that their forefathers had conceived gave way to an American society of change that fed on profit and ended up in the hands of men who had no great moral codes.

Don Salvatore Marazano and the last vestiges of the old-world code of honor expired when Salvatore "Charlie Lucky" Luciana (he changed his name to Luciano when he emigrated) took control of the American mob. His clever manipulation of the two old-world dons, Salvatore Marazano and Joseph Masseria, resulted in both of them being deceived, betrayed, and killed by Luciano and his cohorts, an enviable plot by any criminal standard that marked an era for these Men of Respect. The old dons lived and died with their lust for revenge, a revenge that passed from generation to generation. But even this activity had a set of rules, and as ruthless and bloodthirsty as the forefathers of La Cosa Nostra were in the old country, they acted with a sense of balance, matching the punishment with the crime.

The people, who lived in that era, including the Delmontes, knew this history all too well. Others, including Guiseppe Bonanni and Calogero Gambini, also knew the history and indeed were to become part of its continuation. Many of them, in fact, were related. These blood relatives would inherit their place as the next generation.

They were also aware of why the families left Italy between the 1890s and 1930s in the 1920s when the changes in Europe ushered in a whole new era. During this period, offspring of the families in Sicily were immigrating to the United States, many to New York. They came to Manhattan, Brooklyn, and the Bronx. The streets in the Italian neighborhoods, particularly in Manhattan, Brooklyn, and the Bronx, were teeming with these people.

The Terranovas were part of that movement also. As such, they were acquainted with the families of those who were now coming to New York.

From time to time, Bettina would get a letter from a paisano of someone she knew in Sicily asking information about finding rooms or inquiring about employment. When these immigrants arrived, they naturally congregated close to areas where they knew other Sicilians had moved.

Through the early 1900s and up until 1919, many that had seen the horrors of World War One decided Europe was not the best place to live. Even though they were not in the middle of the conflict, the economic upheaval affected every place in Europe. This was less noticeable in the Sicilian countryside, but the news of the war as well as the continued caste system convinced many to seek a new life in America.

The Volstead Act (National Prohibition Act of 1919), which allowed for the reinforcement of the eighteenth amendment, banned the transport, manufacture, or sale of intoxicating alcoholic beverages. This action created an entirely new criminal enterprise. There was never a reduction in demand for alcoholic beverages. The effect of the prohibition was essentially closing a public market and transferring it to an underground one. While bootleggers and moonshiners in the south had plied their trade for years, this action banning alcoholic beverages became a nationwide illicit market. Those in command of the organized crime operations in the major cities across the country immediately seized the opportunity. The legendary crime bosses, "Scarface" Al Capone in Chicago, Salvatore "Lucky" Luciana in New York, the factions in Los Angeles, New Orleans, Boston, and Miami, almost immediately came to prominence and made fortunes.

The Terranovas had missed out on those fortunes due to Enrico's mistake. However, now that the crime organizations were well funded as well as more organized, the Terranova boys, Enrico's sons, at least had money-making opportunities.

Throughout the Roaring Twenties and into the 1930s, crime flourished. Using the profits from illicit liquor sales, the mob kingpins expanded their loan-sharking and prostitution operations. As they became wealthier, they infiltrated politics and even law enforcement.

When the Terranovas were asked to find additional help for various tasks, the newly arrived immigrants were a ready source of power. Also, these "greenhorns" had to kick back part of the monies they got to the Terranovas if they expected to ever get that work again. While most of the work was physical labor, the newcomers became acquainted with some of the more influential members of the gangs they were working with.

These associations gave rise to even more interaction between these newly arrived destitute immigrants and the gang crews. The glory days of the 1920s were, however, followed by the devastating economic chaos brought about by the 1929 stock market crash. The legends of the Roaring Twenties were by this time being bounded by a new faction of law enforcement created by the US federal government. The "G" men were not corruptible local cops but well controlled by those in Washington whose political careers were being tested by the seemingly out-of-control crime enterprises that had spread out around the nation. It was clear, however, the prohibition experiment did not work. It merely created an alcoholic subculture. Then in 1933, the Volstead Act was repealed.

The structure of organized crime grew and expanded into the smaller cities, and the fortunes made by some of the families bankrolled them into both legitimate and greater illegitimate businesses.

The Depression and now the repeal of Prohibition were felt across the nation but no more so than by those new immigrants who during the past decade had come to America with high hopes. They had heard that this was the "land of opportunity," but just as they were about to get on their feet financially, the opportunities dried up. Having lived in hardship back in the old country, however, they persevered. They also took note that times were changing. Perhaps their instincts in leaving Europe weren't so ill-founded after all, as the rise of fascism became known. In Germany, Adolph Hitler had risen to the point of controlling the entire country by the mid-1930s, and Francisco Franco became dictator in Spain.

In their own country, the Italians were swept away by the promises of Benito Mussolini, another fascist. Mussolini, the benevolent dictator, was in the early 1930s seen as the way to economic as well as political prosperity. He rebuilt the Italian army and indeed was the architect of a new social order. He was cheered as the one "who made the trains run on time." However, in time, he would be seen in a much different light by his countrymen.

CHAPTER 40

THE STORIES OF financial success by those who had decided to make their way from the countryside villages in Sicily, indeed throughout Italy, were a compelling enticement for others to leave. While those who were born and raised in these areas were part of that culture, the urge to better themselves overshadowed that nostalgic notion that they were part of an unbroken generational lineage tied to the land.

Thus, even those who had found a measure of success and respect in their area still had the desire to seek their fortune in this new world.

Calegero Pumilia was always an introspective individual, even as a young child. His mother would lay him down in a huge gray leather carriage as an infant, and he would peer out over the edge at the trees as she took him for a stroll. He marveled at the birds flying by, the flowers in the neighbors' yards, the smell of the freshly mown grass and lilac bushes. She would then park the carriage on the upper deck in front of the house and pull out a large cloth carpet bag and either crochet or knit while sitting on a small chair beside this little one-year-old, her third child, her third male child, content with life, simple in the existence that would be the continuing foundation of her patient attitude and calm and collected nature. She had learned that patient manner from her father, a fairly educated man who had a brilliant mathematical mind. While he was not formally schooled, he attended each grade of the little stone schoolhouse in Corleone. He worked in his father's bakery as well. He learned his lessons well.

The recruiters from the Carabinieri traveled the countryside in search of those in Sicily that could reach the "gigantic" height of six feet or more and could read and write. They were hard-pressed to find many. In the early 1900s, few Italian men were taller than five feet six inches. The need to organize a cadre of such imposing-looking figures was difficult. It was paramount to the military. The military and the police were close in order. Sending people out to fetch recruits fell on all the governmental authorities.

Calegero grew to over six feet by the time he was sixteen, as he finished the last year of his local formal education, the last teachings the little town school could offer. Now he was seventeen but appeared to be a mature man. He was robust and big boned, twice the size of his father, and with the thick moustache and thick, wavy hair, he looked like a throwback to the ancient Sicilian warriors who resisted the Moors. He had learned all of that history as well. He was a student, a conscious worker for his father, and an extremely patient Sicilian. Sicilians, by nature, were a patient lot in any case. The many hundreds of years of their history of oppression made it so. Invasion after invasion of foreign armies simply changed the populace into a vengeful and resistively quiet cadre of those who chose to survive or be exterminated. Over the centuries, the people of the land learned to communicate with each other without saying a word. They feared for their lives, but their inner fiber, who they really were, simply chose the right time to exact vengeance. How foolish would one be to try to oppose the inevitable invasion of those who had superior power and masses of weapons? Seething inside, they watched as their town was pillaged, their goods and food confiscated, their animals taken, their women defiled, and even their churches burned. Hundreds of thousands of armed soldiers set on the few hundred in these little villages. Resist? No, be slaughtered.

However, when night fell and the stars and moon shone, revenge came. A piece of rope, a small thin sliver of a knife, a smooth, palm-sized stone, a spear-shaped shard of sharpened bamboo, an ice pick, and a razor-sharp piece of honed metal all became instruments for their vendetta.

The drunken, invading hordes that had murdered and plundered and raped by day were exhausted by night.

And it was then that the little bands of short, stocky Sicilians would steal away from their little abodes and gather in the night. With hardly a spoken word, a leader would emerge, and the night's plan would be put into deadly action. They met in an olive grove or a wheat field or by a certain lemon tree. Each man would tell his wife or his family, "Fare un cominata" (I'm taking a walk), and steal away into the night. Nothing would be said. The women, knowing full well what was in their hearts and minds, would simply wait patiently in their beds, listening for the creak of the door or the wind from a window opening, hoping that they returned safely. Some did; others did not.

With the morning sun, the soldiers' leaders would rouse their men. A few of them, however, could not be awakened. It would be a strange red mark on the neck that made it unclear if a fellow soldier had killed his comrade. If two men had been stabbed to death, it appeared as if they had fought. Some appeared to have died from overindulgence, eyes popping from their heads, bellies full to bursting with wine, laying in their own excrement.

However, finding a dead farmer or wine maker or baker was a telltale sign. The leadership knew of the raids at night by these little bands and set out watchmen, but all too often they were also killed or bypassed. And so it went. After years of invasions, they learned patience and the ingraining of vendetta.

When the western world opened up in America, these souls sought to escape to freedom, only to find they had exported their culture.

So Calogero was pressed into the king's army and served in the special ceremonial corps that required a man to be over six feet tall and robust and sport a handlebar moustache and formidable demeanor to serve his land. He and his family were proud that he had reached so high in the ranks and was commissioned. He served his term in this elite military corps and distinguished himself by always being prepared and attending to his duties. He spent four years in service and then chose to be discharged, as was his right. Then, when he could leave, he did, on the chance of a better life across the sea. He took his family and his culture with him. He had patience and intelligence, tools that would serve him well in this new world. His children watched and listened as well. His dutiful wife followed him to this new land. She bore him two children. Fearful that he could not afford to support more than the four of them, he told his wife she was not to bear any more. Thereafter, they lived a semicelibate life, learning from midwives and home practitioners the ways to avoid pregnancy by following a natural course of sexual activity only when the female was infertile. The concepts were not foreign to those who lived on the land. Knowing a lot about the cycles of life, of animals and humans, wasn't foreign to these people. Knowing if a woman was defiled by a ravaging horde or bandits or a group of soldiers when the woman had no eggs could mean the difference between allowing the victim to be treated, harbored, and taken care of and telling that there was a chance for a pregnancy or not. Rape victims, innocent though they might be, bore the burden of shame and degradation simply because they were defiled. What logic is that? one asks. Sicilian logic is a code of its own. The farmer and the butcher slipped away at night to murder the murderers and rapists, to avenge, to get revenge. Herein the elements of the Sicilian codes began. Trust no one. Keep fresh memory of those who chose to oppose or harm you. Be patient, not foolish. Do not express your feelings. Seek opportunity to your advantage and always, always seek revenge, vendetta.

Young Carolina, with her little boy, sat patiently knitting and watching and hoping. The young woman, much in the tradition of the old ladies who sat by the water fountain in the town square in Corleone, practiced patience and restraint. Could her example be sensed by the child? Could he too learn the patience of the age-old history of his culture? Or would he be a hothead, a throwback to the outraged temperament of the imperial nature of the Roman Empire? Time would tell, but young Anthony seemed ready to embody both worlds.

As a child, he marveled at the world around him yet somehow by instinct knew that his mother would attend to all his needs. From time to time, when it seemed he could simply not contain his emotions, the rare occasion occurred, and he would burst out in rage, turn red faced and scream. He was indeed a metaphor for all those who were part of the same Sicilian heritage.

The Egyptians and the Greeks raised statues to certain virtues and personalities.

The Sicilian once was beautiful, cunning, resourceful, vengeful, hateful, defiled, defeated, quiet, intelligent, steadfast, oppressed, raging, ill tempered, and patient. Thus the child of this heritage could embody all of these traits and more. Carolina wondered just what lay in store for her, for her husband, and family and for this last child of hers, this smiling, exuberant cherub.

Anthony grew and learned from her and absorbed that which was around him. He, sometimes in wonder, saw the many sides of the same view of the world, not always comprehending each element at the time but absorbing the collective knowledge to be used at some future time.

CHAPTER 41

THE DEATH OF Enrico Terranova in 1938 had a devastating effect on his family. Earlier he had lost the confidence of the mob leadership and, in particular, Salvatore Luciana. He was eventually stripped of every financial operation he had. Having lost nearly everything before he died, his death just added to the misery of his family. Bettina, now an old woman, relied on her sons to take care of her.

Enrico's boys, however, had learned that in order to survive tough times, they needed to be self-reliant. They worked at any job that was available. Most were menial tasks that involved things like loading and unloading freight from trucks, doing cleanup in the markets in Manhattan, or working construction jobs as day laborers.

Some of Enrico's old associates sought their help for prospective jobs from time to time, whenever they needed people who could be trusted. Although Enrico had failed at his appointed task, some still remembered him from his glory days as the artichoke king and olive oil king.

His kids were sharp and industrious as well. So, when they were asked to help with looting a store, assisting in the hijacking of a truck, or transporting stolen goods, they could be trusted. They learned well under the tutelage of the young bosses who used them as hired help. Within some three years after Enrico's death, these boys had earned reputations as reliable guys and always made themselves available when they were called upon. Their mother lived out her days in New York, never again returning to Italy.

The political climate in the 1920s in Italy, and in fact throughout Western Europe, was in transition. Strong men who had a military rearing and spoke fiercely of nationalism were attracting popular support. Benito Mussolini would rise to power in Italy in 1922 and was one who found popular support by denouncing the Communists and Socialists, who, following World War I, were also finding popular support in Europe, Russia, and even in the United States.

Mussolini sought to crush *i mafiosi* in Sicily and around other areas in the south because he perceived them as a threat.

He was an unabashed nationalist whose rhetoric played well with the Italians. They sought their national pride as much as the French, Germans, and Spanish. Mussolini articulated the rich heritage of these Italians and harkened the spirit of the Romans and the empire. He also "made the trains run on time," an axiom that was pervasive with his ability to make government services actually efficient in a country, which, heretofore, had a weak monarch with a parliament that really had no accountability. No matter that the Italian unification had a really recent history. Mussolini had successfully seized his opportunity to take power.

Giuseppe Bonanno

The shadow government was run by the generations of Mafia that were easily identified in each community, town, and village as well as in the major cities. It was no secret that the Bonannis, Gambinis, Magaddinos, Profacis, Buccelatos, and others in one region, and the

Delmontes, Rienas, and others in other Italian towns and regions were the forces of the order of things.

This order underwent drastic changes as Mussolini's troops began hunting down, arresting, and indeed killing some of the princes of this old order.

Hopes of transplanting this organization, one that had served these paesi (towns) for so many years as the only law and order when a decades-old republic had failed to do so, grew. It was about to expand in a new place but again primarily among the southern Italians. Instead of the order anchoring itself in Sciacca and Palermo, it was the Bronx, Manhattan, Brooklyn, New Orleans, and other American cities with enclaves of immigrant Italians far from the oppression of the fascists.

The Volstead Act had ushered in criminal enterprises, which would long outlive Prohibition and would become the catalyst for Mafia growth in the generations to come. No other nation had seen a private, illegal enterprise flourish like this, except perhaps the pirates of yore who made their mark centuries before but never really formulated expansive bands like the bootleggers.

Mussolini's systematic attack on Mafia families in Sicily got worse from year to year, and the Bonnani family knew that there was no way to stop the onslaught. They chose America, the home of the free, but this freedom also meant they would try to reestablish the same order and culture Mussolini sought to destroy.

Giuseppe Bonanni, an immigrant from Castella di mare Del Golfo, a little Sicilian citadel, had come to New York as a small boy with his father. A close English translation of his name was "Good Year," but as he rose to prominence in the underworld, he became "the Good Guy." During the early 1920s, Calogero Gambini also arrived in New York and would later be referred to as "Mr. C" or simply "the Little Guy." Gambini stood only five feet in height and was slim. These two men would become the most powerful Mafia bosses of the era, far more than their rivals.

CHAPTER 42

OTHER FAMILIES IMMIGRATED to New York City as well, settling in all five boroughs, including the Profacis, the Persicos, and the Genoveses. All would rise to power.

Some old country family ties between these families made communications easy. Some of these immigrant families had been doing business in Southern Italy for centuries, and it was a natural order that they would find each other and generate ties to these families in the United States. "Joe" Bonanni was extremely intelligent and resourceful. He came to America as the offspring of a well-to-do family with some money and connections. He eventually returned to Italy, where he was educated in his hometown and then at the university. Young men whose families were financially well off sought to have their children educated with varied backgrounds. Joe, however, was a bit of an enigma. Though he was educated in schools, he also had a well-rounded education in the old ways as well. He learned how to protect himself. He was fairly tall for a Sicilian and was physically fit and wiry. Mentally, he could be a reserved business type or revert to a tough street guy if the occasion arose. He returned to America with ambition, but he also had the knowledge of the old ways. The ways of Sicilian Mafia were well ingrained in the young man long before he crossed back over the Atlantic Ocean, as it was with others who had decided to make their way from the semifeudal societies of the old European countries where the monarchy systems were still fresh in memory and whose vestiges still survived to a land where no monarchy, in the royal sense, ever established a ruling head or leader. Thus, the ones who emigrated still understood the class system, and though not acknowledged by government, there was surely a hierarchy, if not by royal sentiment, then by the informal rule of others.

Giuseppe "Joe" Bonanni was educated in the best Italian schools. His father, Salvatore "Turrido," was a well-established wealthy man, a man of respect. He raised his family in Castellamare Del Golfo along with other prominent families, some of whom were affiliated with Mafias. One of the most powerful families was the Buccellatos. A blood feud arose between Turridu and the Buccellatos. During this period, Benito Mussolini had risen to power and created even more friction as he vowed to shut down the Mafia. Turridu, feeling the pressure from both the Bucellatos and Mussolini's forces, decided to leave Italy for America. He brought his family to Brooklyn. Joe, nicknamed Peppino, spent the next five years there, where he learned the way of the streets. From a boy of privilege to a tough guy on the streets, Peppino learned how to handle himself after several years. Eventually, Turridu thought that the events in Italy had calmed over sufficiently, so he could return. However, the Buccellato vendetta never ceased, and when he went back to his home, the assassins were waiting and murdered him. Then Joe returned to America.

Peppino understood firsthand what his kind of leadership meant. Papa Bonanni also knew the world was changing, even his world. He understood that the need to educate his offspring was as much a necessity as his teachings, and Peppino was eventually sent off to the university. Joe did avenge his father's murder later when it was reported that leadership of the Buccellatos had been killed.

The Bonanni family moved on after the deterioration of their power base in the old country. Joe became an educated young man both in school and on the street.

Bonanni found he could make money and gain important connections with many who knew his family in Italy and those who had immigrated to America as well. Over the decades, Bonanni gained notoriety as one of his cousins, Stefano Magaddino, who had arrived in America several years before, became an important Mafia leader. This blood relationship was of extreme importance to Joe's future. While his pedigree as a Bonanni and his relation to other Castellammarese was extremely important for his acceptance into the Castellammarese family, his friendship with Salvatore "Turridu" Maranzano was one ultimate relationship of importance. Maranzano had known Joe's family in Italy and, upon his immigration to America, soon had Joe as one of his friends, disciples, and associates. Maranzano was well educated, prosperous, and extremely clever. As a non-Castellammarese, his friendship with Joe gave him the opportunity to be accepted into their clan.

The 1920s and 1930s thus saw the old order in the new country emerge as an organization. While "family" was a term coined as these clans formed centuries earlier, such men of respect of the old feudal tradition or of the family reformed it and took on a more central motivation. It indeed became an American Mafia.

The power in New York City was divided into five "families." The Gambinis and Bonannis eventually became the largest and most powerful. After Salvatore Luciano was first jailed, because of his help with the war effort during World War II, he was released and deported. He remained a force in New York until his death in 1962 from a heart attack.

After Hitler began his invasions across Europe, those who had left Italy were concerned about those they left behind. Business as usual between the United States and Italy ceased. The Italian Mafia, now hounded by Mussolini, retreated and became less and less visible, as well as less and less powerful. However, they still maintained their organization and even communicated with their associates in the United States, though now cautiously. Mussolini had no patience for anyone who would sabotage his plan to assume complete control.

The prospect of another world war invigorated the United States' economy. The lend-lease program President Franklin D. Roosevelt entered into with the British meant converting peacetime manufacturing to war materials, ships, planes, tanks, guns, and such that were needed immediately, and there was a rush to retool factories and shipyards. Work for everyone from laborers to engineers became abundant. The recession was indeed over as federal monies began flowing profusely. Material suppliers were deluged with orders for everything from canvas to steel, and these so-called war years were now the new economic boom years.

When the shipyards began hiring, the hot dog vendors, which were located near the yards, put on extra help.

The "organization" began to capitalize on the new prosperity. Suddenly there was money flowing. Flush with cash, workers looking for a good time had the cash for booze and prostitutes. The mob accommodated. Gambling too increased, all to fill the pockets of the Mafia crews.

When America finally entered the war, there were more opportunities than ever to make money, both legally and illegally.

Vincenzo Delmonte had been lucky in his life, and it came by going fearlessly forward. He related to his sons and daughters that leaving Corleone in 1918 was an incredibly difficult thing to do. You were leaving behind those you loved, and it was rare that you would ever return to or even speak to them again. The thin blue and red-lined postal envelopes with tissue-paper-thin letters were the only opportunity to keep any communication alive.

Antonio, Vincenzo's eldest son, had heard these stories of the old country as a boy, but the harsh reality of everyday life as a child in the Italian ghetto in New York City had a way of obscuring their poignancy. Just venturing out on the streets each day was a concern. Crime was commonplace, and eking out a living in the competition of a vastly overcrowded city took a strong will, quick mind, and physical stamina. Vincenzo had a slight build. He was a wiry fellow who grew up to be most like his father, a man of intelligence and moderation.

Vincenzo's son, Antonio, named after his grandfather, had his father's intelligence. He was curious and a risk taker, but unlike his father, he was also prone to taking chances. He had grown up on the stoop in the front of his tenement building in the Lower East Side of Manhattan just outside his father's meat market. As the family grew, he had the responsibility of watching over his siblings, which included his younger brother, Salvatore, and sisters Giacinta, Paolina, and Maria. Unfortunately for his mother, Tony disappeared more often than he stuck around. "Gia, I have to go down the street for a few minutes. Make sure the others stay in the house and don't let Mama know. She's in the shop and won't be back until tonight. If I can, I'll bring you back a charlotte-ruse," Tony would tell Giacinta. The charlotte-ruse was the clincher, and Tony knew it. Gia loved food and especially the whip-cream-laden cupcake with the cherry on top rounded in a white paper. It was a bribe that could never be refused by a seven-year-old. By his twelfth birthday, he was one of the best street fighters on his block. He had to be. On his first day in first grade, he really learned a lesson. He spoke English but still had a slight Italian accent. A boy half his size and probably only one year older pushed in line ahead of him. He pushed the boy back. The little guy hauled off and punched him in the jaw with a swift upper cut that sent Tony reeling into the school yard fence and then down on the pavement, with his teeth still rattling. The other kids laughed and howled at him. From that point forward, he made sure that he would not be sucker punched again.

Occasionally on a Sunday morning, they would entertain visitors in their sprawling second-floor flat above the meat market. It may not have been fancy, but it was always neat as a pin, even with the large family that occupied it.

Vincenza would spend the first few hours every Sunday morning preparing a traditional meal. The Italian feast, as it were, always started with a huge pot of tomato sauce and an assortment of meat specialties, such as *braciole, pulpetto, salziza, pede de porco*, and occasionally *caldene*. A pot of espresso coffee and Italian cookies as well as a bottle of anisette were placed on the dining room table whenever visitors would drop by.

The click of leather heels on the terrazzo floor to the stairs foretold that someone in dress shoes approached.

"Don Vincenzo, come sta?" shouted Signor Petrosino from the stair bottom.

"Come, Don Petrosino. Come up," called Vincenzo.

Giuseppe (Joseph) Petrosino was one of Vincenzo's friends. The fact that he was a policeman with the New York City Police Department was a testament to the respect he had earned in and around his neighborhood over the years.

Petrosino was a tall and very broad Italian man, an imposing figure with his thick shock of salt and pepper hair and a large handlebar mustache. He had known Vincenzo for a number of years. In fact, their families were acquainted and did business in the old country.

Petrosino was in his fifties and had quite a career. After attending college in New York, he had started as a beat cop in New York. He worked Little Italy and had knowledge of every major character that mattered, including the criminals, priests, and businessmen. He quickly rose through the ranks and became a detective. When organized crime took off, his knowledge of the Italian mob became crucial. He ended up heading the detective division that handled the organized crime investigation and put away more of his crooked countrymen than any other cop in the city's history.

Vincenzo knew that his friend was a relentless anticrime crusader, one who devoted his entire career, indeed his life, to that end. He also knew that Petrosino's motivation was to rid the city of those who besmirched the reputation of all the hardworking Italians. Soon after his visit with Vincenzo, Petrosino had gone to Palermo. His investigation into the Mafia in Sicily that had spread to New York uncovered a connection with La Mano Nero, the Black Hand. This crime gang in New York preyed on the hapless immigrants that streamed into New York City's Little Italy in Lower Manhattan during the turn of the century.

Although his mission to Italy was supposed to be secret, a newspaper reporter broke the story just before he left for Palermo. Undaunted, he decided to go anyway. While he knew the Sicilian Mafia was ruthless, he was not convinced they would attack an American police officer. Policemen in New York were off limits to attacks by the Mafia there but not in Italy.

Petrosino had arranged to meet an informant near a church in Palermo. Instead, assassins emerged and shot him to death.

The public outcry in both nations was notable, and the fear associated with the Mafia grew.

Vincenzo had lost a great friend.

One hundred years would pass after Petrosino's death before the name of the murderer would come to light. The person was Paolo Palazzotto, a mob member. His family continued in the life of crime after him.

The Petrosino name also continued as Giuseppe's brother had family, all of whom distinguished themselves as part of New York City's finest, even one hundred years later.

Vincenzo's connections to Petrosino gave him validity as an honest businessman. His ambition made his luck. He built a thriving butcher shop. Then as the years went by, with the money he made, he built apartment houses and rental stores.

He was respected as a leader of the community, and others came to him for advice and some to ask his help. He was known to be a generous benefactor as well to those less fortunate in his community, well beyond the borders of his Italian neighborhood. When a black woman raising several children had little money to feed them, Signor Vincie helped out. Though only having a few dollars to spend, the woman who worked scrubbing floors at the local hospital walked out of the butcher shop with a cart load of groceries. Thus, Madame Nina would tell all those in the black neighborhood, "We never steal from Mr. Vincie. He helps us. Never let anyone try to steal from him." The poor Polish priest would stop in now and then, and without hesitation, Vince would have a large carton of meats and groceries brought to him, saying some anonymous donor asked him to make up a carton and donate it to the church.

Because of his generosity, Vince was sought out by the local Catholic church, and his wife was among those who attended daily Mass, then changed her clothes and worked as a butcher as well. The children worked as well, except for the youngest, Marie, who was much younger than the others and as such treated as the baby sister even as she grew older.

The boys, Anthony and Sal, learned a lot from their father and knew how well he was respected. The old Italian men who had immigrated years before even referred to him as Don Vincenzo. In a sense, his upbringing back in Corleone helped affirm his role of a padrone, the kind who cared for a multiethnic paese that he called his neighborhood. Anthony knew the old school ways but got a New York City education on the streets as well. Both learning experiences would serve him well later in life when his father became ill and passed away, leaving him as the eldest man in the family. After World War II and Vince's passing from cancer, Anthony and Sal took over the Columbia Meat Market. Mama Delmonte retired after the death of Vincent but still lived in the apartment above the butcher shop. Anthony began other business operations on his own as well as working in the shop. Eventually, he would go out on his own.

The relationships between these families, while they were aggressive in promoting their own success, also had an element of mutual respect. Back when "Lucky" Luciano and his crew eliminated the old bosses, Masseria and Maranzano, Luciano created a new order. He explained to the leaders of these families that there would be a commission to replace a single leadership position. Each family leader would have a vote, and the democratic rule would thus avoid conflicts. It worked. The cooperation between the families actually enhanced their power. Working together, they forged new alliances, and their mutual cooperation expanded their overall control of many industries.

Even families like the Delmontes, though not a Mafia family at all, could work within the framework of the commission. Some of the organizations grew so large that they were permitted to split off and form new families.

Luciano's deportation to Italy created the need for a surrogate leader in New York. Frank "Costello" (Francesco Castiglia) took over day-to-day operations much to the dislike of Albert Anastasia, a "capo" who ruled Brooklyn and had organized a murder-for-hire outfit known as Murder Inc. When an attempt was made on Costello's life, he retired. Not long after, Anastasia was murdered while he sat in a barber's chair. The elimination of Anastasia, which was approved by the commission, paved the way for Mr. C, Carlo Gambini, to become something. Luciano had preferred not to create the "Boss of Bosses." The "Little Man" remained low-key as the Gambini family, as it came to be known, grew. The Dessios, nephews of Mr. C, expanded their operations and also sought new business opportunities. The Bonnanis, also very strong, spread out, and while Joe was seen as a rival, it would be years before an all-out war broke out between these two groups.

The other families saw the consolidations of some different factions with some new families arising, but the power remained with five.

Every major population center had an organized crime family, and every family answered to the commission. This secret society also had its emissaries in Europe and other places as well.

The Dessio family, having such close blood ties to the Boss, enjoyed the prestige and gained power. They were also very clever and had keen minds for illegitimate business.

The price wars on gasoline ignited in the year 1959. One station would advertise thirty-eight cents a gallon one day, and a station across the street would lower their price to thirty-five cents. New Jersey was always the cheapest state to buy gas, and it was a reason to go over into Bayonne or down toward the other end of Staten Island over the Outer Bridge to fill up. President Eisenhower and Vice President Nixon were trying to guess just what Russia's leader, Khrushchev, and his thugs in the KGB were doing to try to infiltrate the US. Eisenhower survived a critical heart attack, and his chief adviser, Sherman Adams, carried on a great deal of the administration policy behind closed doors. He was nearing the end of his eight years in office, and the stark appearance of the man after the ravages of a heart attack and the pressures of world leadership had taken a toll. The problems in Vietnam were escalating, but still it seemed that it might be contained. Space exploration and the Sputnik revelations were causing serious concerns in Washington's security community.

The military draft was fast becoming a fact of life, and most men of draft age simply waited to be called. In New York, the military processing center on Whitehall Street in Manhattan was doing a swift business every weekday. The Dessio family had lost one of its own in battle. Nickey, Johnnie, and Alex had lost their brother Pasquale. In tribute to him, the brothers saw to it that an American Legion post, the Pasquale Dessio / Joe Lennon American Legion Post, was started. It headquartered near a busy intersection in Concord, Staten Island. Here, war veterans gathered together for some social interaction. Though the boys played occasional card games, it was a strictly legitimate organization. Patsy D's memory was elevated to near heroic stature, and it was a source of pride and consolation to the family that he was accorded the status of American patriot and hero with the VFW post as his monument.

Notwithstanding that, gambling, loan sharking, hijacking, union control, fencing stolen goods, shy locking, and a host of other enterprises were under the control of the Dessio family, and these guys were ranking members of the Gambinis, the most powerful family in New York.

CHAPTER 43

"NICKY D" DESSIO wasn't worried about being drafted. His brothers Dom, Johnnie, Pat, and Alex, however, were not immune.

Once the United States began sending thousands of its young men overseas, the entire tenor of the country changed. We were in the war. Suddenly, moms were going off to work in the factories where the young men, who had once had the jobs, were drafted and gone. Reduction in consumer spending was also noticeable. Using raw materials to make items for the war caused companies to produce fewer and fewer consumer goods. Everything became scarce, including gasoline, tires, food, and more.

Thus, the US federal government established the OPA (Office of Price Administration) in 1942, which was responsible for setting up a rationing system. Each person applied and was given a certain number of books of ration stamps, secured at their local county OPA office. Control of these ration books was in the hands of local OPA office personnel.

Nicky pulled up to the back of the Columbia Market in his black Buick four-door sedan. He opened the back door and walked in, shouting, "Hey, Tony, where are you?"

Tony Delmonte came back to the kitchen. "Hey, Nick."

"Listen, I need some steaks, a lot of steaks. I got a bunch of freeloaders coming over. I need twenty two-inch-thick porterhouse steaks. And you better give me about twenty pounds of sausage too and ten pounds of veal cutlets," said Nicky.

Tony said, "Okay, you wanna wait or come back?"

"No, I'll wait," said Nick.

"Okay," said Tony, and he put a bottle of scotch and a glass on the table in the kitchen. "Here, have a drink," said Tony and slid the glass across the porcelain table. "You're really gonna owe me on this. This ration stamp business is crazy. I go to the markets on Little West Twelfth and gotta grease everybody to get meat, but now that might ease up some," said Tony.

"Why is that?" asked Nick.

"Well, my uncle Carmino introduced me to this broad, Connie Odessa. She just took over the OPA office in St. George when the director fell dead of a heart attack at his desk. Connie grew up in Rosebank with Carmino's family and is really close. He had me come over to meet with her. I knew her father, Guiseppe. He was a wine maker during Prohibition and made a bundle of money. He had a whole flock of goats like a lot of others who lived there. They used the milk to make cheese. That area was always known as Nanny Goat Town. Well, Carmino's goat flock and their smell hid the odor of the wine-making business he also had going. Connie told me that the entire office for the OPA was chaotic. Double shipments came in for ration books, and some stacks of the books disappeared when some in the office helped themselves to open boxes. She was in charge of sending the administrator's communications out, including orders for the ration books. She also keeps the accounting of the cases of books as well.

"She told me that she had been shipped double orders on a number of occasions from the distribution center somewhere in Maryland. The center apparently had a handwritten manifest system, and lots of times orders would get misplaced, so a second request was made, but a few weeks later, the original order turned up, and the center would ship a duplicate order. Those cases were just set aside in the warehouse. Some were used, while the others were just left stacked there.

"Her cousin, Carmella, also worked with her. Carmella's boyfriend worked in the warehouse as a delivery man. He had a club foot, but it was his left foot, so he could drive a truck. He was Four F, so he was excused from the draft. This boy, Gino, was twenty-five years old and kind of handsome. He thought the sun rose for Carmella. She was a little spitfire, five foot five, jet-black hair, big black eyes, with big tits bursting out of her dresses. Gino would do anything for her.

"So, I arranged to have Connie get Carmella to have this Gino load up fifty cases of ration books and bring them to Pier 9, where they were handed over to the crew boss to be shipped. Gino had no idea that the manifest signed by my guy, Emil, would end up back to Connie and go missing. So, I got fifty cases of legitimate books. Every case is worth a bundle of dough. The coupons are for gas, tires, food, and everything else. There are a thousand booklets in a case. We can get at least twenty-five bucks a piece for these books. We just have to spread them out. We can wholesale some in other cities with your connections. I think I can get another fifty cases by the end of the year, maybe sooner," Tony said.

Nick began to do the math in his head: fifty cases, twenty-five bucks a book retail, even at a fifty-fifty deal, was more than half a million dollars. It could be the score of his life. He looked at Tony. The two had known each other since they were teenagers, and now twenty years later, they still were doing deals together. But even then, just for a moment, the street instinct got to him.

"So, where you put all this stuff?" he asked. Suddenly he realized that he had been too blunt with the question. He sensed Tony's change of expression immediately. He tried to cover by saying, "If we need a safe place to stash this stuff, I have warehouses with guys there twenty-four hours a day." Tony seemed to ease a bit, but he also knew that he would never leave himself vulnerable to anyone, not even Nicky.

"Oh, I got it covered. No problem there," Tony answered. "I even have a way to transport that is foolproof," he added. "Just line up your end, let me know what you can handle, and I will cut you in for a quarter," Tony finished.

Nicky stroked his chin. "A quarter, huh? Well, I'll tell you what I think I can do with a quarter, but the guys who will move this will have to give pieces down the line, you know, tribute to the big guys. I gotta give them a big enough piece so they can make it move. Tony, I'll need at least a fifty-fifty deal here," growled Nicky.

Tony threw his hands in the air. "Fifty percent! Nick, I got expenses with this deal. I got the broad Connie and her cousin, Carmella. I also gotta cut Carmino in for a piece, as he brought in the deal. I can't do that fifty-fifty. I won't end up with anything. Look, from each end, we gotta figure what makes sense. Getting the goods is the biggest part of the deal. After we got it, it's like having money, real money, not counterfeit. I gotta part with about a third. If I split the rest, a third each, that's actually a fifty-fifty deal. I'll cut you a third from what you can handle of this load. Okay?"

Nicky knew this was a sweet deal no matter how the cut was done. He also knew he could turn the ration coupons fast. In fact, he knew his biggest problem would be who to give the books to. He could make great friends with these things. Nobody had swag like this. For a while, one guy in Brooklyn tried to manufacture counterfeit coupons, but they were so hard to get right that they were identified as soon as they spread the first batch. The ones Tony had were genuine and could not be traced, so long as Connie was straight up about the operation. Nicky would check up on her to make sure that was the case.

"Okay, Tony, we got a deal. I'll let you know what I can handle. Get me some samples so I can show the goods," said Nicky.

Tony reached into his pockets and pulled out a book of coupons. "Here, these are the gas coupons," Tony said.

Nicky looked down at them. They were crisp, flat and the color and number sequences were clear and perfect. "Hum! Hum!" he said. "Okay. Good. I'll be back to you on this right away," said Nicky.

Tony poured both of them a glass of scotch. "Salute," he said, and they touched glasses and drank half the bottle in the next twenty minutes.

A boy knocked on the kitchen door. "Okay, Mr. Tony, I got the order here." The boy came in with four large shopping paper bags loaded with meat.

Nicky stood up and reached in his pocket. He pulled out a thick bankroll of bills, peeled off some, and put them on the table. "Okay, I'll see you soon," said Nicky. He picked up two of his bags, and the boy followed with the rest. Tony smiled, knowing he had at least one outlet to move the coupon books quickly.

Tony had already made his deal with Connie and Carmino. He had already gotten fifty cases and had them safely stored at his brother Charlie's place. Charlie lived up in the Hill Section in the middle of the island. He had about a one-acre compound with several other buildings on it. The main one was built back in the turn of the century. It was a stark block-shaped building, and there were trees and foliage around this house in a middle-class neighborhood, which was the perfect place to operate a business away from prying eyes.

Back when the buildings were being put up by some Italian immigrants, they dug and excavated a full wine cellar. These immigrants were masons. They installed six-inch-thick concrete walls and floor. Thus, the temperature in the cellar never fluctuated very much from summer to winter. It was large enough but could only accommodate fifteen or so full-sized barrels of wine. There was also storage of vegetables and fruit. The building, which stood over the top of the wine cellar, was a wood structure used for storage of various items, from furniture to tools and wine-making equipment. There was a section of floor that seemed normal to an unobservant eye. But the ingenious Italians had rigged a small hook to the underside of the floor frame. A thick rope was hooked to the underside of a floor flap. There was a second hook on the ceiling from which a shovel was hung. However, when the rope was hooked up on top and run through a pulley system, a huge section of floor came up, and the hinged section lay back against the wall, revealing a ten-foot-wide set of stairs and the seven-foot-deep wine cellar below. A series of porcelain light fixtures dimly lit the cellar. This was a perfect place to hide things.

During Prohibition, the cellar was a storage place for illegal wine, liquor, and beer. The adjoining building, a large two-story structure, actually was operated as a speakeasy and liquor store. The long driveway back to the rear building was hidden by a ten-foot stone wall on one side and the three-story house on the other. The cars would drive through the wooden gates, manned by a fellow who hid behind a series of thick evergreens. When a car pulled up and flashed the lights three times, that was the signal to open the gates. He also had a sawed-off double barrel "luparo," a twelve-gauge shotgun, just in case there was need to chase away unwanted guests.

The cars would pull in and park or drop off a passenger and then leave. Those who came by foot had to navigate a well-worn footpath through a thick wooded lot behind the rear buildings. There, they would spend an evening drinking and listening to radio broadcasts from Manhattan and maybe dance a time or two.

The stairs to the second floor had a thick wood door guarding the stairway. The man behind the door would answer the knock and open the door slightly, just his hand out, and say, "You pay before you go up." The rooms upstairs were divided into small cubicles with a bed, a chair, a lamp, and a girl. There were some guests who never even realized what the second floor was all about. Some of the vestiges of those Roaring Twenties were still in the buildings. The wood chairs and steel bedframes were scattered here and there among boxes and other furniture.

The cases of ration coupons were set inside cartons marked "chopped beef" with a weight and other identification codes.

When they had to be moved, Tony would send a meat truck to pick them up. Over the next three months, the coupons were sold off, and a second shipment was put in the wine cellar. Tony and Nicky had made the bundle of cash as promised. Tony, who lived in an apartment above the meat market, put the bills in a leather satchel in a bedroom closet. When that satchel was so full he could hardly close it, he found another leather one to fill. After selling off the second load of coupons, a few months later, the closet had five satchels filled with cash.

He and his brother Charlie went to Great Kills Yacht Club one evening in February. The place was really a meeting place for the shakers and movers on the island. Politicians, judges, lawyers, business operators—the "wiseguys" and the "boy scouts," as the old adage went. They were sitting at the bar when one of Tony's friends came in, Charlie Pizza. "Hey, Tony. How are you, Charlie?"

"Hello," said Pizza. "What are you guys up to?"

"Just came to eat dinner and relax," said Tony.

"Well, this place has really been dead. What with the war and so many guys over by the docks and shipyard on the other side of the island, not too many people drinking here," said Pizza. Pizza owned a wholesale liquor and beer distribution company, White Horse Beverage, so he knew every joint on the island. "In fact, I hear that after last season, the club is really hurting for members."

"Really?" said Tony. "You know I had been thinking about getting a boat. I was just telling Charlie we ought to be doing more fishing. I went down to Miami a few weeks ago and went out with some guys I knew down there; we caught ten big tuna. One was over two hundred and fifty pounds. What a fight! My arms were sore for two days," said Tony.

Deep sea fishing was an obsession with these guys. Bringing in the big fish was considered a sign of strength and manliness. It was also a place, out there in the ocean, where no one would know what else besides fishing was happening. On occasion, a side trip to pick up some women to share the fun was part of the fishing trip. There was always plenty of booze and food as well.

Owning a boat made someone an instant celebrity. It was the goal of many entrepreneurs to captain a big vessel, or at least own one, even if they had to hire a captain.

CHAPTER 44

"YOU KNOW, I did hear of this boat for sale from Woodchuck, the bartender. He said there is a seventy-footer out in the yard, and the guys that own it are broke and can't even pay membership or storage. He said the boat's a beauty. It's got twin diesel engines, big Lycoming engines with only a hundred hours or so on each one. You know, Lycoming makes airplane engines; they're the best. This boat's supposed to cruise at thirty knots and maybe faster. The two tanks take a hundred and fifty gallons each, so it's got terrific range. The problem is the rationing of the fuel," said Pizza.

"Well, actually, that's really no problem for us. We've got that ration thing really covered," said Tony.

"No kidding," said Pizza. The boat was just a bit shorter than seventy feet long; therefore, it did not require a captain.

"Do you think we can see this boat?" said Tony.

"Sure, I'll tell Woodchuck to put the lights on in the yard, and we can take a peek at it now," said Pizza. The three men went out to the boatyard as the lights lit up the rows of boats chocked up on wood frames. He said, "It's down near the roadway, the big one. It's named *The Rebound*."

"There it is," said Tony.

The huge, shining hull and eighteen-foot beam raised up on the wood frame gave the vessel an appearance of being even larger than it really was. "Hey, is this a Staten Island Ferry or a fishing boat?" said Charlie. They all laughed. "Boy, it's big; seems in nice shape too."

They climbed up a ladder onto the rear deck. The deck was dark wood, and the polished wood finish glistened from the light string with single bulbs overhead. "This is worth a second look during the day. Any idea how much they want for this?" said Tony.

"Not sure, but the guys that own it are really up against it. I heard two of them got drafted and the other three guys don't have a pot to piss in," said Pizza.

"Okay, I gotta get my guy, Mike Arbarno, to check the engines. He really knows those diesels. See if you can get Woodchuck to get the keys and to let one of the owners know I might be interested."

They went back to the clubhouse, and Charlie Pizza spoke to the bartender. By the time they finished dinner, the bartender came by the table and told them everything was arranged for the next day.

"You know, I had been thinking about a boat myself. I'd like to go in on the deal if it works out," said Pizza.

"Okay, Charlie. I might have some other guys too, maybe Joe 'Beef' and Marcy 'The Dutchman,'" said Tony.

"Those are good guys too," said Pizza.

Midmorning the next day, Woodchuck, a short, fireplug-shaped guy with light brown hair that stuck up straight, joined Mike, the mechanic, alongside the ship, along with Charlie Pizza, who always dressed sharp. He was wearing a dark gray suit and camel hair overcoat. "Mike here is going to look over the engines; Woodchuck will take the keys," said Pizza. All the men climbed up the ladder to the deck.

"She's a real beauty," said Charlie Delmonte. As they went inside the boat, the boat had an elaborate galley, four state rooms, and a well-equipped wheelhouse. There was a metal stairway down to the engine compartments. They were also accessible from the top. Two big hinged deck plates opened up on top and exposed the tops of the engines. Mike Arbarno climbed down and looked over the engines. He reattached cables to the electric system. He had a five-gallon can of high-octane fuel with him when he went aboard. He also had a large battery with jumper cables.

"I'm going to start these babies up for just a short time. I made sure the shafts were clear. The props are stored here, but no matter. I can tell if they sound right," said Mike. He primed the engines and then started to grind the starter on one. He ground away for a few minutes until suddenly the engine caught and started humming loudly. "She's okay, sounds solid," Mike said after the engine ran for a few minutes. He then shut that one down and started the other. "This one's fine too. These Lycomings at three hundred horsepower will make this boat fly through the water. Hey, they lift airplanes, don't they?" said Mike.

"Okay," said Tony, and they all laughed.

Later that week, Tony met with Gene Ferranti, a lawyer, and with the owner of the boat, Pasquale "Pat" Dantonio, to sign the boat documents. The deal was for seventy-five thousand. The real cost to build the boat was close to four hundred thousand, and it was just three years old. Tony lifted two leather satchels onto the table. "Okay, Pat, we have the cash here."

Tony lined up bound bundles of bills and laid them out on the table. Then Pat went through each stack and counted the bills. "That's it. Thanks," Pat said.

"Here, you can have the bag too," said Tony, and he chuckled as they shook hands.

Back at the yacht club that night, the partners got together for dinner. Joe "Beef" Bufalino was a six-foot-tall redhead with huge shoulders, eighteen-inch arms, and a big head to match. Marcy "the Dutchman" was over six feet tall as well, with a huge, ugly head and a large bulbous red nose. He weighed over three hundred pounds, and when he laughed, which was often, his big belly shook his whole upper body.

"We're going to do some real fishin' now with that baby," said Marcy. "We can almost fly out to the canyon in a couple of hours." It was over eighty miles to the Baltimore Canyon, the deep ocean trench off the Atlantic coast. They enjoyed a big dinner together. The weather in late February was unusually mild. Charlie Pizza had Woodchuck round up two guys who he hired to clean the boat and get it ready for the water.

As advertised, March came in like a lion with a late and very wet snowstorm. Tony and his pals were spending more and more time at the yacht club. By mid-March, he had sold off most of the cases of ration coupons, and his bedroom closet was piled high with satchels of cash.

On a particular Saturday night in mid-March, there were a half-dozen or so guys drinking at the bar. Tony was with Pizza. "Hey, Woodchuck, give me another scotch," said Tony.

Pizza leaned over to Tony. "You know I have to cut the club off because they haven't paid their bill to me for three months. They are in really bad shape here. They are going bankrupt," said Pizza.

"Really!" said Tony.

"They will go to tax sale soon, and they owe everybody and his brother," said Pizza. "The taxes haven't been paid for years. It's a large debt."

Tony said, "Well, maybe there is a way to get this place. I got some friends at Borough Hall in the tax department. Who is the treasurer here?" asked Tony.

"Dom Santore. You know him," said Pizza.

"Sure, he's from the neighborhood. I'll call him," said Tony.

Tony met Santore in the back of the butcher shop two days later. "You want coffee, Dom?" asked Tony as he poured himself a cup at the table.

"Yeah, fine, thanks," said Dom.

"Listen, I know the Great Kills Yacht Club is in trouble. Maybe there's a way to do something here. The taxes are unpaid, and I'm told there is going to be a tax sale. Eventually the place will be sold off because of all the debts. I want you to go to the guys on the board and convince them to sell the place to me before the tax sale. Tell them there is no way to save the place anyway, and I will buy up all the shares for a hundred grand and assume all the debts. There is about twenty-five grand in debts before the taxes, isn't there?" said Tony.

"Yeah, maybe thirty," said Dom.

"You'll get ten grand cash from me if you can get this done fast," said Tony.

"Okay, Tony. I'll try," said Dom.

"Dom, you also have to get rid of the tax debt on the books. Capisce?" said Tony.

Four days later, Tony got a call. "Tony, it's Dom. I spoke to the board. They're in. They said to contact their lawyer, Louis Arano, in

St. George and make arrangements. I'll be at the club tonight if you can come."

"Okay," said Tony. The next call Tony made was to the lawyer, Gene Ferranti, and he laid out the details for him and had him contact Arano.

Within thirty days, the deal was closed, and Tony became the new owner of the Great Kills Yacht Club. He didn't waste any time getting a crew in and the place cleaned up. He had new furniture brought in and had a full-time electrical crew install new lighting. He paid off all the debts in cash. He could not reduce the taxes but got a deal to have all interest and penalties waived when he paid off the entire tax liability. He also contacted all the vendors and got discounts from all of them once they knew he would pay off all debts in cash. Once Dom Santore erased the tax debt in the borough office, he owned it free and clear.

By mid-April, he had the grounds cleaned up and the main clubhouse totally repainted, with new furniture, new draperies, and a new top on the bar. He had Nicky come in to look the place over. "Tony, the place looks great. I've got to get my brother Al over here. He has just the thing you need, a jukebox. He's also got this cigarette vending machine," said Nicky.

"Great! We need the music, and it will bring in extra cash," said Tony.

"Yeah, he'll outfit the whole place with speakers too and give you a fifty percent cut," said Nicky.

By May, the club had become a regular stop for all the wiseguys and boy scouts in town. He also instituted a very liberal drink policy for good-looking women. They ended up paying for one drink at most. Tony had to bring in an experienced chef to run the kitchen. His friend Ally Capeletti owned a big restaurant, the Town Tavern. He and his two sons operated the place. Tony and Ally's son, Frankie, were about the same age, thirty. Ally spoke broken English. Frankie came to the yacht club, which was about five miles down the main road and off on the waterfront from the tavern. Tony told him he needed to get some help in the kitchen. "Tony, I got a good guy for you. We have a chef, Tom. He came over from Italy with my father around 1915 and has been with him ever since his *cugino* (cousin) got here a few months back. He's a *siggie* (Sicilian) who had his own restaurant but had some kind of trouble over there and had to come here. His family is still back there, and he wants to bring them over. I know you got an apartment on the second floor of the club. Maybe you can use this guy and his son and wife to run the kitchen for you," said Frankie.

"Yeah, maybe," said Tony.

"I'll tell Tom to send a message to his brother Santo to give you a call and stop by to see you," said Frankie.

Once Santo was hired, he sent for his wife and son. Within a few weeks, he reorganized the kitchen and immediately started putting out incredible meals. The fishing had been good in April and May, and Santo specialized in seafood. Soon the word got around about how good the food was, and a steady crowd poured in. Several boat owners began renting slips, and by the end of May, the entire club was buzzing with business. Tony also got another shipment of ration coupons. With all the people in and out of the yacht club and the need for fuel for their boats, he had found a ready-made outlet to sell off the coupons.

The yacht club featured a band on the weekends, and not only boat owners were attracted to the club; businessmen, politicians, and wiseguys became regulars. Tony had instituted a social membership as well and didn't discourage nonmembers from coming in to eat and drink, so long as they spent enough money. Of course, the abundance of ladies drew the men in like flies to sugar. By midsummer, his bedroom closet was stacked to the top with satchels of cash.

CHAPTER 45

CHARLIE PIZZA CAME into the club late one Saturday night in August. Tony was at the bar with his brother Charlie. He sat next to Tony. "When are we gonna go on that fishing trip?" he asked.

"Soon. I saw some big tuna come in on the dock today and a load of nice-size bonita and albacore. I had Woodchuck tell the guy over at Milton's Dock to get ready to load up with buckets of chum and gas up the boat," said Tony.

"Great," said Charlie. Then he said, "Hey, Tony, I know you know this guy, Sammy Talarico. He owns the Log Cabin Inn on Forest Avenue, over on the other side of the island near the bridge to Jersey. He's going through a rough time. His brother is his partner. His brother started gambling really heavy. Nicky 'D' knows the story; he owes Nick a bundle! He's into the loan sharks for a big number. Sammy said he's too old to deal with the problems. He wants to sell the inn and pay his brother's debts and retire. I think he will bail out for fifty grand, lock, stock, and barrel," said Pizza.

"Really? That's a pretty good size place. It has a big bar and dance floor area in the showroom. It could be a real big joint, and it's on the Avenue, which is always busy," said Tony.

"I know. I was thinking if you, me, and maybe your brother and Joe Beef put up the dough, we can buy him out," said Charlie.

"That sounds like a good deal. Do you have some idea what the place makes in a week?" said Tony.

"I think they do a grand or so, but I think it's not well run, what with the brother and all."

"Okay, let's talk to him."

"Joe Beef is going fishing with us too," said Tony.

"I'm in," said Charlie.

"Okay, Charloutz, this could be a lot of fun," said Pizza.

They would charter boats in Miami and then go all over the Caribbean, sometimes spending weeks fishing, drinking, chasing women, and seeking out new business deals. They trusted each other as much in this deal as they did in others. They grew up in an atmosphere where watching a friend's back was necessary for survival. They spent a great deal of time working out the details of business deals, but they also spent a lot of time having fun. When it could be arranged, they went on extended business trips to Miami, Florida, Cuba, and the Caribbean. Those trips were the most exciting times, as they were really fishing expeditions mixed with other kinds of debauchery. They also opened up worlds of new opportunity.

On one of their adventures, Tony and his friends, Doc, Charlie, and Brisk, traveled from New York to Miami in that large fishing boat, *The Rebound*. They hired a fellow, Cap'n Bob, a no-nonsense boat captain of over forty years. Bob knew many of the great fishing spots. They also hired his young mate, a sandy-headed fellow named Scotty who followed Bob around and took his orders easily. Scotty, however, was partial to two things: women and whiskey. He would drink gin or rum or whatever there was and would spend time with middle-aged, soused, alcoholic broads or young, innocent, black chambermaids; it made no difference to him. Whatever there was was okay. The guys knew that and teased him, saying he would screw a snake if someone held it.

After spending some time in Miami, they would travel over to Cuba. In Havana, there was always a good time to be had, fishing, gambling, beautiful women, and great food. The atmosphere was cordial, and the people were grateful for the tourist dollars. Tony made the trip several times and stayed at the same marina. There were several serious fishermen that used the marina.

"Papa" was Tony's friend there. He was always welcome at Papa's table because he always brought with him some great specialties—Italian cheeses and dry sausages, salamis, great wine, and some frozen, thick beef steaks. There were always a few nights to feast from the food lockers on *The Rebound*. Papa had the locals bring in lobster and tuna.

He was a legend who could drink all night, take two women to bed, then go fishing at five o'clock the next morning.

Tony and his crew were also serious fishermen and businessmen as well as fun-loving rouges, not quite polished but world-wise. Papa respected men who had that strength and confidence and enjoyed their company.

The next morning, Tony made his way down to *The Rebound*. The other men were already on board. Scotty had a cup of strong black coffee in his hand as Tony boarded and handed it to him. "You want to sweeten it?" he said with a bottle of rum in the other hand.

"Yeah, a touch." He poured a shot of rum into the black Cuban brew. "Where are we going?" Tony asked.

Cap'n Bob said, "I think we will head east a bit, and since the locals say the current there brings some great catches, we can try it." He had already filled the big twin tanks with diesel. The vessel had a long cruising range due to the special oversized fuel tanks the boat had been retrofitted with. The converted twin Lycoming engines made this large vessel one of the fastest for its size.

The Lycoming engines were World War II vintage airplane engines, which were in heavy production at the end of the war. Then, at war's end, so many of these engines were no longer needed by the military, so they ended up as surplus. The extreme high-quality, high-performance engines made the wood-hulled *Rebound* fly through the water at over thirty-three knots. The color of the water changed visibly as the vessel approached the change of current at the east end of the island.

Cap'n slowed down, and the mate, Scotty, began setting out four lines at varying depths, trolling at a slow speed. Cap'n kept looking out with binoculars, hoping to spot some surface movement. The big, feathered, metal, weighted plugs skipped along the top, and the lower lines were fitted with live bait. Suddenly, Cap'n spotted movement and a strike as the line tightened on a deep runner, and the reel started whining. Tony was nearest the rod. He grabbed it, and by the time he backed into the fighting chair, Scotty had a leather harness on him and strapped it across his back.

"Geez, look at this," exclaimed Tony. The rod bent, and he had to hold on with all his strength. Tony, a seasoned fisherman, eased the rod tip up to be sure the hook was well set and used his arm and back strength to begin the arduous process of pumping the rod, tiring the monster at the other end of the line. Once he could get that fish up to the surface, he knew he would win the battle. The reel was hot from the pressure, and Scotty cooled it, careful not to spill water on Tony's hands. As he poured the water on the reel, he concentrated his focus on the area of the reel, not realizing he had poured it not only on the reel but on Tony's crotch as well. "What the hell, Scotty, I don't need the cold-water treatment on my pecker. I've caught big fish before, so I don't get a hard-on anymore," bellowed Tony.

Everybody, including Cap'n, was laughing so hard he had tears in his eyes. "Tone," said Doc, "you look like you pissed those nice linen pants."

Scotty said, "Boss, you bring that fish in, and I'll make sure you get that wet cock sucked dry." Again they all were roaring with laughter.

"Cut it out! I won't catch this fish if I can't stop laughing," said Tony. He eased the rod, tip up, and reeled time and again. After more than an hour, the blue back of the fish, a huge tuna, surfaced. Tony kept the pressure on now and nearly stood straight up raising the rod.

"Easy, Tony," said Cap'n, who kept maneuvering the boat as the fish would back up or dive. "Just get him up so he'll bloat with air." The pull and take continued on and on. Another hour passed as Tony strained to regain line with each run by the fish.

"Joe!" Tony yelled. "Pull those two port lines in now. I got one hooked on the jig. It's big." Tony maneuvered himself with the rod into the fighting chair bolted to the deck.

"Marone! It's really big," said Tony as the rod bent and the line streamed out. Charlie, back her up!" Tony yelled. Pizza was in the wheelhouse with Doc. He put the engines in reverse slowly and stopped the forward movement of the big boat, then slowly backed up, turning in the direction of the rod tip.

Tony started to reel in the slack. "Charlie, Santo, get gaffs ready on either side just in case. Sammy, pull those chum cans away."

Everyone scurried as Tony continued to strain at the rod. The boat slowed and finally stopped. The fish at the end moved from port to starboard and then back again. Tony kept the line tight and the rod tip up. The line streamed out again as the fish plunged again. "Jesus Christ, back it up, back it up!" Tony yelled, his face red with sweat pouring down. "It's a friggin' monster," said Tony as he grunted. Charlie poured a pail of water on the reel as the line streamed out. Then he grabbed a big terry towel and wiped Tony's hands and his face.

"Lead him in, and I'll hit him with the gaff," Scotty yelled, holding a long-handled hooked gaff. Scotty leaned over the side. The others had gaffs as well, and Doc grabbed Scotty's belt and hooked a rope around him so Scotty wouldn't be pulled over.

The battle lasted for over two hours when eventually the big fish began to tire. "I think he's coming up!" yelled Tony. He began reeling in now with a slow but steady pace. The water began to churn as the familiar torpedo shape of a tuna began to come to the surface. "He's gonna surface on the port side!" yelled Charlie. Charlie and Santo, with long pole gaffs in hand, bent over the rail.

"There he is, and he's huge, Tony!" said Charlie. "Bring him back slow, and I'll gaff him."

"Santo, you hit him with the gaff on the other side once I got him firm to the boat. It's gonna take both of us to pull him over. Unclip that rail and pull it back!"

Santo moved quickly and positioned himself.

"Okay, here he comes," Charlie said.

The captain idled the engines. The mate, Pizza, and Sammy had come to the rail too. "Okay, Tony, ease him alongside," said Charlie. Tony told the mate to unclip him from the chair, and he stood up, wobbling a little when he got to his feet. The veins in his neck and arms were clearly visible, and his face and chest were bright red. The thin cotton shirt he wore was open to his waist and soaking wet. Tony made his way over to the side. "Okay, I'm gonna hit him now," said Charlie.

He swung the gaff down just as Tony lifted the huge head of the fish, breaking the surface. "I got him." Santo had simultaneously positioned his gaff and hit the fish just below the gills. They looked at each other, and Charlie nodded and grunted. The water turned red when the gaff hook found its mark.

Suddenly, the huge fish burst from the water, resisting the pulling, but the two men were able to lift the big fish up out of the water. It flopped and wriggled. Pizza had grabbed a baseball bat and swung it down, hitting the fish on the top of the head. The fish was pulled against the rear of the boat. "Got him!" yelled Scotty. With that, Doc and Cap also hooked the fish at the gill with the gaff. The fish was nearly ten feet long. "I don't think we can pull this one over," Scotty yelled to Cap'n.

He saw the size and yelled, "Just tire him out." He clamored down the stairs and threaded a rope with harpoon.

He had made this rig himself just in case he came across a huge fish. He got to the side. "Doc, pull the mouth up, and I'll run the harpoon through the gill. Scotty, hand the gaff to Cap'n and take another gaff and pull the rope up." It worked like a charm. The rope was slid up to a stanchion and wrapped. "Okay, Scotty, pull the block and pulley out." Scotty pulled out another of Capn's inventions, a pulley and block, and he locked through a port in the gunnel. It had a ball-bearing reel handle and an open end to hook in with a big handle.

"Okay, you guys, crank slowly." The fish still had a bit of strength left and began flapping against the side of the boat, causing it to rock a little.

"Jesus!" yelled Scotty. Slowly the head of the monster came higher and higher. "Now lasso the tail so he's high enough." Scotty and Doc kept cranking, and Tony dropped the rod, and he and Cap lassoed the tail. "Okay, on three, we all pull him in—one, two, and three." The big fish slid up and finally flapped onto the deck. The boat pitched under the weight, blood squirting all over the deck.

"Watch out! He'll break your leg," yelled Cap'n. With that, Cap grabbed a long, round, steel baton. He swung it and smacked the fish on the top of the head. The fish shuddered and then flapped a little but without much strength.

"Wow, look at this thing. I'll bet he goes over 1,500 pounds," said Doc.

"Yeah, we eat tonight," said Tony. They all laughed again, as much out of relief to have boated the big fish as the humor.

"Jesus Christ! Look at the size of this thing! I'll bet he weighs more than 1,500 pounds," said Pizza as the fish calmed down and was quivering and still flapping around. He hit it a second time, and it really stunned the fish. By this time, the deck was covered with blood. The mate grabbed the bucket with a rope attached and threw it over the side, filling it with seawater, then pulled it back up and washed down the deck. Doc took a long, thin knife and punctured the brain through the eye socket.

"To-neeee!" yelled the captain. Then everyone started yelling. The big tuna was over ten feet long, end to end, and seemed to be as wide as a car.

"It's a beauty, Tony!" said Santo. They secured a rope canvas around the fish and lashed it to the side. The blood kept oozing out, and the mate kept pouring buckets of seawater, rinsing the fish off as well as the deck. The whole event took over three hours.

"Okay for today. Let's bring the big boy home," said Cap'n. Cap'n went into the cabin and pulled out a tuna flag. He then tied a red handkerchief on the same grommet and hauled it high. "The trailer is for you, Tony. Nice going." With that, they all applauded and headed back. They arrived early in the afternoon. The big fish was hung up at the dock on a rack. As all the other boats came in, the look on the faces of those others, awestruck, said it all. They checked the weight on the broad side of the fish: 1,783 pounds.

A large fishing boat approached the marina. Papa Hemingway was sitting in the rear of the boat in the fighting chair, whiskey glass in hand and talking to two men leaning on the gunnels, when he spotted the tail of the big fish. His boat was moving toward the rear of the marina, but it suddenly slowed. The six men on the boat all converged on the port side and gawked. Hemingway raised up both hands as the others applauded. Tony and his gang waved back.

That night, the menu was tuna.

Pizza slapped Tony on the back. "Great Job. Unfucking believable."

"Yeah but I think I got a hernia," said Tony.

Santo handed Tony a big schooner of ice-cold beer he retrieved from the galley. "Boy, can I use that." He gulped it down.

"Well, I think we did a real day's fishing now. We got twenty albacore and eight bonita, some blues and two other tuna, and then this bigshot here," said Pizza. "Let's go eat."

CHAPTER 46

THE EARLY-MORNING SUN was already blazing, and the overhead fan simply blew the air downward onto the bed and mosquito netting like a furnace. The subtle morning breezes made the long white netting bellow out and back like a fanciful, wistful dancer turning and twisting. The twelve-foot-high ceiling was spotted with small flying creatures, which occasionally changed position on their ceiling perch.

Tony rolled over, and the stale taste in his mouth from too much rum and spiced foods made him roll out of a bed in search of water in a pitcher on the dresser. He poured a glass of water and rinsed his mouth before parting the curtains and spitting out to the veranda below.

Havana was a bustling place in the morning—porters, maids, groundskeepers, waiters, and merchants delivering the day's food staples as they crisscrossed the veranda going to various parts of the hotel, carrying everything from linens to cooled fish and breakfast trays.

Tony walked to the bathroom, showered, and dressed in white linen pants and a cotton shirt with boat shoes. He splashed on a brownish Bay Rum aromatic lotion, which stung his recently shaved face.

He recalled the night before with a large group of men at a nearby café and bar. The little guitar band played quietly as this irregular group traded stories of the day's fishing and what they would do the next day. There were a few brown-skinned, wrinkled men in their late thirties or early forties off to one side, their faces tanned by the many years spent on the sea. They clutched tall glasses filled with local rum. A lily-white, blue-eyed Dutchman with his white straw hat half-cocked seemed uneasy on his chair and nearly fell over each time he reached for one of the several rum bottles on the table. Two middle-aged balding men, who were tall and muscular, had faces that clearly showed they were serious. While the tanned skin indicated they had been out in the sun for some time, they were not fishermen but businessmen and politicians. They spoke Spanish and English when conversing with the man seated in the center of the group. He was a large broad-faced man with a thick shock of black hair spotted with gray. At his side was a small older man who periodically would refill the man's glass and occasionally rush off to the kitchen and bring back a platter of food or fruit.

The big man's rounded cheeks were red with the sun, and he alternately smiled or laughed and then scowled and grunted. They drank over eight bottles of rum. The big man's eyes were red and watery, but he was still animated and spoke with an enthusiastic tone as he told the story of catching a huge tuna that afternoon. He grimaced as he bent backward with an imaginary fishing rod in hand, straining back with both arms outstretched and relating the tale in an animated discourse till finally he stood up, bumping the table, and overturning two half-full rum bottles as his imaginary struggle with the big fish came to an end. He guided the imaginary fish alongside the boat, and the little man jumped up and pretended to man a gaff and secure the fish. With that, they both pulled and strained till the big fish was up and out of the water, on board twisting and flapping. The two turned and spun around the imaginary fish, and the big man roared with laughter as he turned and looked at the wide-eyed audience.

The little man ran off for a few minutes and then returned with two huge platters and struggled to set out the plates stacked high with thick, charbroiled tuna steaks. "Gentlemen, I want to introduce you to my big fish. Enjoy." He then laughed again, his watery eyes twinkling. The dozen or so men took knives and sliced off chunks of tuna and washed it down with rum. The taste of lime, salt, and pepper on the tuna complemented the strong black rum.

The bald man nearest the big man said, "Papa, when are you going to go 'chicken' fishing? We are getting tired of eating fish." The group laughed again.

The big man turned and speaking to no one in particular said, "If I want chicken, it has to be young and tender, slightly browned with large breasts and a nice round ass so I can ride it all night." Again the group roared with laughter.

Tony asked, "Where do the boats head tomorrow?"

The big man turned. "I think we head to the eastern end to catch the current and see what that brings." The night wore on. Tony was surely not a great student of literature and assumed this fellow whom he had met on his several trips to Cuba was more a serious fisherman than a renowned writer. His dress and the company he kept surely was commonplace for the fishing crowd in this part of Havana, and so was the rum consumption, storytelling, and womanizing. Tony did know, however, that the man enjoyed celebrity status even with these folks.

From time to time, a hotel messenger would pop in and walk to the big man the others called "Papa" and address him deferentially. "Sir, a wire for you." He waited to see if there was a reply or a tip. Papa reached into his pocket and pulled out some coins and handed them to the messenger. "Gracias, Signor Hemingway," he said before darting off.

Hemingway would drink most of the day if he did not go fishing. Some of the men who knew him would carry him back to his rented rooms when he could no longer stand up. He eventually bought a ranch near town.

Later in life, he found a house in Key West, Florida, and used it as his home base. The house and Sloppy Joe's bar became legend for that famous author. The political takeover by the Communist Castro regime forced him to abandon Cuba.

A few days after the big catch, *The Rebound* headed back to a marina at Coral Gables, Florida. After securing some provisions, they began the long, leisurely trek back to New York. They reached the yacht club at dusk on the twelfth day after numerous stops along the way.

CHAPTER 47

THE YACHT CLUB was still experiencing activity from the day's operations. Tony went to the clubhouse and arranged with the kitchen manager to have his men unload a huge amount of frozen tuna. The crew ended up at the bar for about an hour, then said their goodbyes.

Tony arrived at his apartment building around six o'clock at night. He never really liked the idea of having to maintain a house. He took a sprawling apartment and refitted it to make a home for him and his wife, Kay. It was Sunday. Tony could smell the aroma of tomato sauce as he climbed the two flights of stairs. His wife, Kay, was at the door. "Hi. How are you?" she said.

He kissed her cheek and said, "Fine, a little *stanga* (tired)."

He saw the table set in the kitchen, anticipating his arrival. They sat down and devoured the home-cooked pasta with a rich tomato sauce with chunks of pork and beef, washing it down with red wine. Kay was attractive, slender, and quiet. Her life revolved around Tony.

The next morning, he was off to Manhattan dressed in a midnight-blue striped suit, starched white shirt, and blue tie. He drove to the Staten Island Ferry and got there just in time to drive straight onto the ferry as it was loading.

His drive from Lower Manhattan's Battery and Ferry terminal to George's Restaurant in the Financial District took only twenty minutes, as the morning traffic had subsided some. He saw his associate George standing in front of the restaurant. George Besham (no relation to the restaurant) was just made vice president of American Iberian Shipping Lines.

"Hey, Tony." George waved and opened the passenger-side front door of the green Oldsmobile and popped in. They discussed Tony's

Cuban fishing trip for a while, and then George said he finally arranged for Tony's company to supply "ship stores" and provisions for three incoming vessels as well as picking up some cargo. Besham handed Tony a folder with the shipping information, and they shook hands.

"George, this is the start of a great deal, and you know you will be well taken care of on this."

"Hey, I gotta go. I'll see you in a few days, Muzzie. Thanks," and he was gone. George had, on one night of drinking at the George's Restaurant bar, began calling Tony "Muzzie," short for "Mussolini," when he barked at two of his men, a waiter and a bartender, all in less than five minutes. Tony did not really like the name much but let it pass.

The idea of owning the Log Cabin Inn had stuck in Tony's mind, and he called Charlie Pizza. "Charloutz, arrange a meeting with Sammy at the Log Cabin. I want to see if we can make a deal." A few days later, Charlie set it up.

Tony, Charlie Pizza, and Joe Beef sat down with Sammy. "Sammy," said Charlie, "I think we can help you out. You need to get this done quickly, and we can come up with fifty to bail you out for the place. I throw in two thousand more for stock and booze. Okay?"

"Well, okay. I got to do something, and I can't wait. I got maybe four or five thousand in bills and still owe some of the help some money," said Sammy.

"Tony, what do you think about another few grand? About fifty-eight all together?" said Charlie.

"Okay, Sam, we can do that. I'll have Ferranti get the paperwork together, and I'll call you. It's a deal," said Tony.

"Deal," said Sam, and they shook hands. Tony now had controlling interest in a hot night spot.

The lifestyle of these men was in a way an extension of the Italian tradition in Sicily. Men, ambitious men, went out in one world and made their way. They lived life on their own terms and were independent thinkers and doers. If they were the product of centuries when the padrones ruled the villages, here in America they were aggressive, business-minded men who also sought to enjoy every vice life had to offer. They also sought to build their own empires; perhaps some Roman blood had something to do with their ambition.

CHAPTER 48

FRANCO MERENDINO UNDERSTOOD a great deal about wines. He not only knew the processes but also had detailed knowledge of its history. His earliest recollections involved the harvesting of the grapes when his family was noted winemakers in Corleone. He also remembered the relatives and friends of his father and their extended *famiglia*.

The elder men, who were the family leaders, included his father, Cossimo, his uncle Tomasso, and an elder cousin, Vincenzo, would be responsible for keeping an eye on the vineyards in late summer. Sometimes Franco would travel with them in a drawn cart his father had while the others walked alongside it. Down the gritty paths between the vines, they would occasionally stop, and his father would hand Franco his razor-sharp pocketknife. "Franco, pieda questa uva" (pick that grape), he would say, pointing to a specific bunch of grapes. Franco would leap from the cart and carefully slice the stem with his extremely sharp, hook-shaped knife in one hand while cradling a robust bunch of deep purple grapes in the other. Then he would hand them up to his father, who would then take the grapes in those big, calloused hands in such a way that it seemed as if he was weighing them. He passed them from one hand to another, looking to see if the movement would cause any of the larger ones to split open or leak their sweet, sticky juice. He would then pass a few grapes to Tomasso and Vincenzo, sometimes handing a few to Franco as well. The serious discussions that followed regarding the softness, weight, color, and condition of the stem would take several minutes. Franco listened intently as if he were learning about a mystical secret. Finally, they tasted the grape. They took a few and squeezed them until the purple skins split and the mucous-like pulp spit out, running the juice down between their fingers. This would be inspected, and then the skin would be put in the palm of the hand and pressed. The rich juice and purple color ran out. Only when the grapes were fully ripened and loaded with juice would they all nod and agree that it was the right time to harvest. "Franco, mette un pezzo di lenya bianco." (Franco, put a piece of white linen cloth.) Franco would rip a strip of white cloth, which was tucked by the seat of the donkey cart, and measure it from his elbow to his hand, then tear the strip and tie it to the top rung of the rack that supported the grape vine.

The vineyards of the Merendinos covered three hillsides and valleys. Along the natural land contours were ancient man-made paths dating back to the days when the grapes from these hillsides were producing the wines for the Roman aristocracy. These hills also produced olives, lemons, oranges and other fruits, almonds, other nuts, and a variety of vegetables. Franco understood his heritage. He was taught well by as his father and remembered it all. "Franco, questa terra e molto bene per noi. Il famiglia mangia ca per molti anni, ma la terra non dimenticare noi. Sono sempre bono." (Franco, this earth is very good to us. The family has eaten from here for many years, yet this earth never forgets us. It's always good.) Franco understood the productivity of the land and, in particular, the wine production. Now, even at ninety, he saw it all clearly! Wine to him was a constant reminder. It varied somewhat in taste and color, but it was always a reminder of where he came from and what the wine was in this life.

"Sangua di Cristo," he would say when, at any gathering, he would open a bottle of wine (Blood of the Christ). The symbols of the Catholic Church, the wine as the blood and the bread as the body, were part of the Sicilian daily life. They lived with these symbols from early childhood to old age. There was a lesson to be learned from generation to generation—respect for that which sustains you and remembrance of the religious lessons as well. God was to be respected, and so were the wine and the bread, the blood and body.

Franco remembered that when his mother was preparing a meal, if a piece of bread accidentally fell to the floor, she would pick it up, kiss it, and say, "Bene di Dio" (Graced by God) and make the sign of the cross as if to purify the bread again against anything that desecrated it.

The world Franco once knew had disappeared, and the old man of ninety, the patriarch of his family, was saddened. Perhaps he had lived too long, he thought. The old ways were all gone now. Even though coming to the United States as a young man changed his life forever, much of that lifestyle was not so different from the way the people he lived with conducted themselves in Italy. He lived in the Italian neighborhoods in New York City and learned the essentials for survival, but there were no vineyards to be seen, only cobblestone streets and buildings. Now it seemed these peasant people of his and even the next generation, including his children and their contemporaries, had faded away. The subsequent generations were growing up with no knowledge of the old country and old ways.

Franco's great success as a businessman in the late 1940s and '50s could only have happened in the United States. Like so many others who found little opportunity by the turn of the century in Sicily, particularly for a picciotto (young man) in Corleone, they left Italy for America. So many others left for the promise of wealth in the United States, only to become a part, again, of the poor class in New York instead of Sicily.

With the help of relatives, including the Terranovas, Franco got a start in the food business in New York, first working in a butcher shop. He had ties to cousins in the business and also worked part-time as a baker at night. He started a side business as well, making homemade wines during the fall of the year, and earned quite a reputation.

The choice of grapes was critical to the quality of the wine. When the grapes were harvested, they were sent in wooden crates or large baskets to the fruit and vegetable market in Lower Manhattan. These areas, Little West Twelfth Street, Gansvoort Market on the West Side by the North River, and on the East Side, Fulton Fish Market, were a beehive of activity in the wee hours of the morning five days a week. Just about anything you could eat was available in these markets.

Franco and a few relatives and friends would drive the old Ford delivery truck to the market. He would go through box after box, crate after crate to find the perfect grapes. The choices of grapes—cabernet, concord, muscat, zinfandel, and more—were important. The difference made dramatic difference in the wine, the reds for body and color, rich muscat for their sugar, which would provide the catalyst for fermenta-tion and alcohol strength.

The process of grinding, fermenting, filtering, and finally trans-ferring to the aging barrels was an ancient trade. The men knew that this process dated back millennia and often joked that the ghosts of the Etruscans would be watching.

Franco now looked to relatives and friends to provide him with homemade wine. The smell of a freshly opened bottle of wine filled his senses with memories.

Franco married Regina Anna Scalise when he was forty, a little late in life by American standards. The Scalises were a very large, well-known family of Sicilian background, many from Corleone, Carini, and nearby towns back in Italy. In the US, they settled in Manhattan, the Bronx, and Brooklyn. The marriage produced three children, Franco Jr., the firstborn, and Cossimo, named for his grandfather. The youngest, Vincenza, a petite baby girl, was a special person in the fam-ily. Even the boys doted on her when she was first born. They marveled at her tiny fingers and little toes and would try, each day, to find some little token to bring to her, a flower, a unique stone, a piece of ribbon.

Franco Jr. was called "Little Frankie" by his mother, who secretly adored Frank Sinatra. She could not, of course, let her husband know she liked another man, even if it was a simple admiration for a celebrity entertainer. "It might bruise his Italian ego," she would tell her sister Maria who lived a few doors down the block with her husband, Nick.

Frank Sinatra

Now that his father was aging, Little Frankie visited his father every day. "You know there have been times when I thought that time would stand still. Your grandfather had his family, relatives, and friends with him all the time. Men in every town, every city seemed to form a core, a group, and dealt with life in a cooperative way. When we came to America, there were changes in the place we lived, but we still had our friends. The law here called us gangs, Mafiosi, and criminals. Maybe we did not follow the laws or the customs of these 'Mericans, but we did have respect for our lifestyle, our people, and our world. Frankie, these times have changed. Men expected to associate with their group of men. We Sicilians grew up understanding life was hard. You needed to learn to protect yourself, your family, and your group, your *pisani*. This was our tradition for thousands of years with good reason. The history of Sicily is a story of foreign invasions and Sicilians repelling them and surviving periodic foreign occupation." Frankie was so much like his father in his curiosity and eager desire to learn everything.

"Frankie," his father continued, "when your uncles and I became part of the Terranovas' network, we knew that there were two sets of rules—those of the American judicial system and the rules we grew up with, the old ways. We did not fear the police or worry about our personal safety even in the worst neighborhoods. We went to Harlem and the Brooklyn ghettos as those to be feared, not fearful. We did not feel invincible but confident and capable of handling ourselves as always. We were careful. This was not unusual for family, businessmen, and friends to be together. Times have changed. What we once took for granted is gone. We have our family, but it seems many others no longer can count on having family around all the time. This America has the children moving from the parents and hardly ever seeing them or other family members. Cousins, uncles, aunts, even grand-parents are becoming strangers. My mother and father visited us here but could not stay. I know they missed the life they had, as primitive as we thought it was compared to New York; it had other things we don't have any more. When I visited my paese (hometown), I saw the physical changes, new buildings, new roads. No more donkey carts. But the people are still very much the same. Frankie, I think the world changes a little too fast."

Frankie nodded. "I know what you say is true, Pop."

Frankie remembered the crew his father had and the other groups of years gone by. They were strong, fearless men. "Frankie, bring us a little wine and some glasses." Frankie brought back an unlabeled bottle and two short-stem wineglasses.

"Salute, Pop," he said as he handed them over to the old man. "Here's to the old times and old friends."

His father smiled, nodded, and sipped down the wine. "Buono, buono," said the old man. By the time he finished the last sip, he was asleep, clutching the glass stem in his fingers. Frankie slowly pulled it away, looked down at him, and smiled. He knew that his father didn't have much time left. As invincible as he had been all his life, the old man's days were running out. Yet, in a way, he was still strong. His thinning gray hair still covered his head. The leathered skin was pink and robust. When he embraced his father, he still felt the sinewy muscles in his arms. The old man walked slower now but had a delib-erate step and was steady on his feet. Occasionally the old man used a silver-capped walking stick that he used more like a pointer than a cane to steady himself.

The grapes that were shipped to the metropolitan area for wine production went to markets in Newark, Hoboken, and Jersey City as well as Manhattan. Union leaders had influence at the train yards in those cities where California grapes were shipped by freight train. A delay in unloading the carloads of grape could spell disaster for the fragile fruit. This was particularly true if the heat of the summer continued into the fall harvest and shipping season.

As Franco's wine production increased, he frequented the smaller markets for a better price.

Franco even began buying shipments from vineyards directly. When it became important to ensure swift unloading, he got to know those men in the unions and in the rail yards where the grapes were shipped in New Jersey. He learned where they ate and drank as well and made himself known to these people.

Franco also learned it was important in the business order of things to have political friends.

Thus, he learned of Dolly Sinatra's influence with local political leaders.

"Hey, Sammy, give me a big beer," the burly railroad yard man yelled over the noise of the crowded bar, "and one for my friend here."

Sammy's was a combination bar, restaurant, and meeting place in the center of the older section of Hoboken that never seemed to close. You could get steak and eggs at five in the morning or a roast beef sandwich at one in the morning.

"Okay, Patsy," yelled back Sammy, "as soon as I see some coin."

Patsy Brio was a tank of a man with a barrel chest, endless thirst, and shallow pockets. Franco put a dollar bill on the bar. Patsy had brought Franco to Sammy's this Friday night to introduce him to his friend and mentor, Dolly Sinatra. Patsy's mother, Donna Celeste, was Dolly's friend. She was also a midwife. Dolly helped Patsy get his job with the railroad. He had four kids and a wife, and Donna Celeste wanted her boy to have steady work. Marty Sinatra let Dolly know when a spot opened in the yards through the fellows he knew. Dolly had her union friend slip Patsy's name on the top of the waiting list for hires.

A railroad job meant benefits and a good pension at the end. Franco had Patsy check the train schedules and loading and unloading docks so his cargos wouldn't get "side railed." He also collected funds from "friends" like Franco for the union's "widows and orphans" fund and, of course, kept some pocket money for himself. Franco was glad to have such a friend.

"She knows how to get things done," Patsy said of Dolly.

When Dolly walked into Sammy's, she was greeted by nearly everyone in sight. They all knew her, and she had the respect usually reserved for a man.

"Hey, Dolly," Patsy called.

He pushed back the crowded bar, which left an opening for Franco to follow, and turned to Dolly. "This is my friend Franco Merendino. He helps us with the fund," said Patsy.

"Hello there," said Dolly. "Glad to meet you."

Franco put his hand out, and in his old-world way, he half-bowed and said, "It's my pleasure, signora."

"Patsy here is a good judge of people. I think his mother taught him well, and if you are his friend, you are my friend as well. Welcome to Hoboken. If I can be of any help to you, let me know," said Dolly.

"Dolly, Franco will take some of the raffle tickets for next month's drawing," said Patsy. Dolly reached in her coat pocket and pulled out a stack. Franco handed her a twenty-dollar bill.

"Why, that's very generous of you."

"Thanks, the money will be well spent. We help support kids and women who are poor, many without husbands, and then there are those who are sick or have some special problem," Dolly said. Franco nodded.

Over the next several years, Franco often visited Hoboken and became part of the well-known patrons of the fund, but more important, a respected friend to Patsy, Dolly, Martin, and eventually their only son, Little Frank.

Franco's wine-making operation expanded as time went on, and his son, Little Frankie, became more and more of a salesman and enjoyed marketing the wine more than making it. He researched all the family connections, including the extended Terranova family and their friends. He secured the names of all those who had restaurants, bars, or some other connection where he could sell their wines. His memory, of course, was a huge asset. His father would tell others, "Once I tell Little Frankie something, he always remembers for me." It was a huge compliment, since Franco confided closely with his son, whom he trusted without reservation. Sons of Sicilian fathers were, if nothing else, unquestionably loyal. Regardless of circumstance, that mutual trust only ended at death of one or the other. It seemed as much as instinctive. A Sicilian son might leave his father's house and go off on his own, even a world apart, but in his soul, his loyalty, maybe even his love for his father, was unshakable. In time, Frankie got the names of several *compari* in Staten Island who were Corleonese and relatives of the Terranovas. One of those families was the Delmontes. In fact, the Delmontes also had intermarried with the Scalisces.

Franco traveled to Staten Island to expand his business. He had traveled to Staten Island with his father. He saw Ellis Island and the Statue of Liberty when he was a young boy.

Frankie pulled his old Buick sedan into the narrow lane on the ferry. It was about three in the afternoon, and the turn in the weather in late April from cool to hot felt good. He opened the windows to let the salt air in.

His list of prospects on Staten Island made him a little anxious. Even more was his father's list of courtesy calls to friends and those who, for some special reason, were to be visited. He knew the reason for some of the stops his father wanted him to make. The old man knew that these people should meet his son face-to-face. Franco had already brought the boy to his paesani when he was a youngster, and he was called upon to keep the personal communication going. Some day he would not be around, and it seemed sooner than later that could be, yet his son should not lose the connections he had made through his life, family to family, friend to friend.

The vessel jolted as it hit the pylons before coming to a stop. It was the unheard signal to start the engine.

His Buick eased down Bay Street near the Paramount Theater. He stopped in front of a large warehouse, 30 Prospect Street, and his photographic mind recounted a boy's vision of a bustling loading dock with men behind trucks unloading and loading crates and boxes. His last visit to the place seemed not that long ago, but it was over twenty years before he stepped up onto the high concrete loading dock and walked up the ramp and into the wide entry, then through the hallway to the office door. He knocked. "Yeah," he heard. He opened the door. Tony and Emilio were seated behind the two desks facing each other, which took up most of the space in the room.

"Yeah," said Emilio.

Frankie offered a half bow as his father would have and nodded. "I am Frankie Merendino, Franco's son," he said. "My father asked me to come by and drop off a little of our wine to Mr. Delmonte."

"Oh, okay. Wait a minute, he's just finishing up on the phone," said Emilio.

Tony was seated across at the second desk. He had been in an intense conversation, but by the time Frankie mentioned his last name, Tony nodded back at him vigorously.

"Okay, I'll meet you at George's on Wednesday at noon. Thanks," said Tony before slamming down the phone and standing up.

"Bon gemilie mani," said Tony as he strolled over to Frankie with both hands out.

"Piace," said Frankie as the two embraced, kissing each other on the cheeks.

"You look just like your father, only more handsome and more American," said Tony as he chuckled.

"My father wanted me to say hello and thank you for all the consideration over the years," said Frankie.

"Fare nente" (It's nothing), said Tony.

"Aspetto un momento. I have something from my father in the car," said Frankie.

He went back out, got a box from the trunk, and laid it on the desk.

Tony opened the box and saw four bottles of Zinfandel wine and two jars of olives. He picked up a bottle and pulled a wine key from the desk draw and opened it. He poured three cups and handed one to Frankie and one to Emilio. "Salute," he said. They drank. "Very nice, real body," said Tony. Emilio gulped down the wine and nodded.

"Thank you. We made eight hundred barrels three years ago. The grape was excellent from a vineyard in California. Don Abramo, I think, your cousin?" said Frankie.

"Sure, he has the vineyard, and the family has tomatoes, the Contadinas," said Tony.

"My father told me that you might have someone you know who's interested in buying some of this wine, or maybe the four or five others we have," said Franco. "I have one very unique wine also. We call it Lacrima Cristo," said Franco.

"Huh. Tears of Christ. It must be something special with that name," said Tony

The two spoke of the wine and prices. Emilio answered the phone, which rang constantly. Occasionally, he would hold his hand over the receiver and nod to Tony and say a name. Tony shook his head no.

"Listen, I have some friends I think you would like to meet. We have a place on the other side of the island, a restaurant, the Log Cabin Inn. Let's go there, and I'm sure we could use this wine there. I have to go there to see these guys anyway. You can follow me over."

"Stick around and close up then come over to the Cabin tonight," said Tony to Emilio.

They went to the cars and drove off.

The Log Cabin Inn wasn't at all what the name suggested. It was a roadhouse. The building fronted Forest Avenue; hence the name Log Cabin. The cars pulled up at the side parking area. Already there were twenty-five cars in the lot. The double-door entrance was at the top of three very wide stairs that ran across nearly the entire front of the building. When Tony opened the doors, he heard the sound of music, the clatter of plates, and the clinking of glasses all combined.

"Some joint, eh?" said Tony.

The place was bigger inside than it appeared from the exterior. There was a large bar, dance floor, and bandstand on one side and a dining room on the other.

"Very nice," said Frankie.

They walked up to the bar.

"Frankie Merendino, meet Charlie Piazza. Charlie has the beer and liquor distributorship here."

"Glad to meet you," said Charlie as Frankie nodded, bowed, and shook his hand.

"This is Frankie C. He and his family have restaurants." Again they shook hands. Tony introduced him to three other men seated at the bar, and then they walked in the kitchen. Charlie followed.

"Frankie, bring in a bottle of that Zinfandel," said Tony. Frankie picked out another bottle from his trunk and quickly returned.

"This is Dominick. He runs the kitchen and bar." They shook hands.

"Dom, open this," said Tony. Dom popped the cork and filled four glasses.

"Charlie, what do you think?" asked Tony.

"Excellent, really full bodied and rich," said Charlie.

"I'd like to make it the house wine," said Tony. "Dom, what do you think?" asked Tony.

Anthony "Big Tony" Delmonte
Charlie Pizza, a friend

Dom took another sip. "This'll sell. It's like the old country," said Dom.

"Okay, Frankie. Set up with Dom, and he'll contact you for what we need. Now let's try the scotch," said Tony. They all laughed and walked out to the bar.

The night wore on, and Frankie was cautious not to try to keep up.

"Charlie also has the White Horse Scotch," said Tony.

Charlie said he had at least five places that could use the wine, including his brother's restaurant.

Around nine o'clock, a piano player and singer took the stage.

"You know, we've got to get some entertainment to draw in the nighttime crowd a little better group; maybe a band."

This got Frankie's attention. He said to Tony, "I know a fellow who is part of a group—Italian too. His father and mother are friends of mine. I understand that there are four players in the band, and they are very good. They have a great lead singer."

Tony looked at Charlie. "Well, let's get them over here for a tryout on an off night," said Tony. "Maybe you can give him my number, and we can arrange something."

"Okay," said Frankie, and Tony wrote the number on a beer coaster.

"The fellow's name is Frank, Frank Sinatra. I'll get in touch with him." The jukebox music began, and a few couples got up and danced.

Emilio walked in and headed for Tony. "Hi, guys," he said, then turned to Tony and in a low voice said, "Nicky D called just as I was leaving. He said to tell you to meet him at the Tavern tonight at ten."

Frankie stood up after finishing his drink. "Tony, I will tell my father how much you did here for us. I greatly appreciate everything. I'm going to make a few more stops tonight."

"Su beneriga," Tony responded. "It was good to see you. Hey, listen, if you are still on the island later, stop by Town Tavern on Hylan Boulevard. The owner, Ambrose, is an old friend and Frankie C's father. Maybe he can use your wine too."

Frankie said, "Okay. Thank you," and left.

Frankie drove to the other side of the island along the only four-lane road, Hylan Boulevard, before turning down Sand Lane. The bright lights over the sign "Crocciottos" were clearly visible in the distance. He parked and walked in. Crocciottos was as much a nightclub as Staten Island had to offer. There weren't too many places like this. They had a full floor show with a comedian, band, dancers, and a headliner of some sort. They also served food. South Beach was well-known as an amusement and recreation area. It had a boardwalk along the beach with rides and games of chance. There was a cluster of bars, restaurants, and shops along Sand Lane and the nearby side streets and boardwalk. It had been more a summer place, but now with the club and restaurants, it had become a year-round attraction. The sound of band music was audible even before the door was opened. Frankie walked in and found an empty seat at the end of the bar, the only empty seat. It was still fairly early, close to nine thirty, but already the crowd was building. Friday was always a big party night on Staten Island.

The young men at the bar were mostly dressed in suits and ties. Their shoes shined in the overhead lights, and each had obviously taken great pains to swirl their hair in a flowing set of curls or a big wave in front, slicked back on the sides, and parted in the back. Pants pleated out at a high waist and gathered tightly at the cuff were all the rage. Some began wearing the black or blue suede shoes as well, and if a suit was not worn, at least fancy shirts were the uniform of the night. The music varied between heartbreaking love songs and hip-hop tunes. The ladies also dressed to impress. The expensive sweaters or linen shirt tops and short skirts showing plenty of leg, and maybe a little thigh as well, were accented by stiletto heels with razor-pointed toes. The girl's hairdos were like huge, puffy clouds thanks to the beer-can rollers used to expand the hairdo to its biggest and widest length. But if you just got out of work and could not spend time building a hairdo, a ponytail pulled straight back in the front would be okay too.

Frank looked around for the familiar face of the owner, Dominick, and ordered a scotch and soda. The bartender slipped the drink in front of him with one hand and lifted the twenty with the other. As he placed the change, Frankie spotted Dominick across the room. He got up and met him halfway as they approached the door to the kitchen.

"Mr. Croccitto, how are you?" asked Frankie. The other man, a stout, medium-built man in his fifties, turned to Frankie. He smiled, but Frankie could sense he did not recognize him. "I'm Frank's son, Frankie. My father told me to stop by with some wine for you."

"Oh sure, Franco, it's been a long time. You look like your father. Come in the kitchen. It's a little noisy out here," said Dom. "How's your father? I hope he's doing okay."

"My dad's fine, getting a little older now and doesn't travel as much. If you have a minute, I'll get something from the car."

"Use the kitchen entrance here," said Dom.

Frankie went to the car and brought back three bottles of wine. "Please enjoy these with my father's compliments."

"Thank you," said Dom.

"We've been wholesaling wines like these for quite a few years. If you like these and want any more, here's my number," Frankie said and handed him a card.

Manhattan had its premier night spots and hangouts. The hottest places were the Copacabana and the Latin Quarter. Some of the biggest entertainers were being booked there. The clubs outside of Manhattan and Brooklyn had not been making a lot of money since the war started. Now those that were still surviving were hardly paying their bills.

Tony still bought supplies in Manhattan and Brooklyn for the meat market, but with all the other business interests, he was not spending a lot of time at the butcher shop. He had his crews make up purchase lists, and he would do the ordering with guys he knew, sometimes over the phone, other times by going to the wholesalers directly.

World War II was won, and the troops were welcomed home. Tony expanded the meat businesses by making customers of his friends in the other restaurant businesses. With war coming to an end, men returned home, and many were looking for jobs. There was no shortage of butchers and delivery men for the meat business. Also, there was plenty of help available for the kitchens and bars at the club and the Tavern on the Green.

Over the next few years, business took a peacetime turn.

By the late fifties, Tony had made connections in Manhattan with some of the executives of some large international shipping companies. Nickey D and some other connected guys got him an introduction to the union bosses who controlled the piers and docks in Manhattan and Brooklyn. They introduced him to some of the leading management people in the shipping companies. One of the meeting places for the shipping managers was George's Restaurant in downtown Manhattan on Pearl Street. It was there that he was introduced to Mel Beaumont. Mel was in the army during the war and had been assigned to a procurement division stateside. He had traveled up and down the East Coast from Florida to New England doing contracts to purchase food products for the troops in Europe.

The army quartermaster division in Manhattan had the task of purchasing some food goods and arranging shipment with the navy.

Mel became familiar with many of the busiest ports along the coast. Now those ports had connected back to nearly all full-time operations by private shipping companies. Also, now as a bursar for the American Shipping Lines, he got to know all the foreign as well as domestic companies doing business on the North River piers in Manhattan, Red Hook, and the Point in Yonkers and Port Newark in Jersey. He also knew all about the shipping traffic from Baltimore to Newport News, Charleston, and elsewhere.

"Mel, I'm Anthony Delmonte. I own Bay Shipping Company and Columbia Shipstores," Tony said as he put his big thick hand out.

"Pleased to meet you, Mr. Delmonte," said Mel.

"I hear you have a lot of connections along the coast and know a lot about the shipping business," said Tony.

"Well, I worked for the army and spent time in ports where any little ship can land and dock, from Maine to Florida. Sometimes it was pretty boring, but I learned a lot during and after the war," said Mel.

"Yeah, but I'll tell you, I don't like the work much now. I oversee the payments going out and sit at a desk all day. After traveling all those years, this is not for me. I really would like to do something else," said Mel.

"How would you like to get back on the road? I need someone to connect with shipping managers to sell ship stores. I bought the old Armour Meat Plant in Staten Island. It's a big plant with several freezers and coolers. We are now doing some large orders for some of the companies in Manhattan and Brooklyn. I have enough capacity to expand tenfold. I can use a savvy guy like you who can sell to the companies in the ports along the coast. You'll get an expense account, a modest salary, and a big commission, ten percent," said Tony.

"Well, that sounds interesting. I might like that. I sure have the connections," said Mel.

"Okay. Why don't you come over next week, and I'll show you the plant. Call my office. My guy Emil is there, and I will have him talk to you too," said Tony.

Tony had bought supplies from the Armour Company for years. When management decided to shut down the Staten Island Plant and consolidate it with the new Newark plant, the building complex was closed and stayed that way for over two years. One of the reasons was a regionalization plan by management; the other reason was the equipment. The old plant was run by an alcohol refrigeration system. The new plant, ten times the size, used the new Freon gas system. Also, Armour had expanded and had a fleet of new refrigerated delivery trucks so they could service their customers throughout the Metropolitan area.

Tony knew the old plant well and made a cash deal to buy it through one of his friends and associates with Armour. He got the place for a song after giving his friend a nice little bag of cash to close the deal.

He could now wholesale across the island, as well as to shipping companies. Mel came on as a salesman. In the first two months, he doubled the ship store's business, and Tony set up trucking to eight new stops along the eastern seaboard.

The big meat plant also provided the versatility with dry storage and a fish storage section and expanded the overhead rail from the coolers to the loading dock, which expedited the loading and unloading. Located just blocks from the local piers, it was perfectly situated for storage as well. By the mid-1950s, business really boomed. Bay Shipping became a hub of activity, some legal, some not so legal.

Nicky D. had operations going all over the city. Bay Shipping was the perfect place to unload a truck of hijacked goods, be it cheeses, wine, or canned food. It was a place to buy, sell, make deals, and always find a good bottle of scotch or brandy. The local liquor stores a block or so away had its best customers from the big plant. Even the local restaurants got a steady lunch trade from the plant. In turn, they bought supplies from Tony.

The longshoremen's union controlled the New York City docks throughout the city. Shippers had to make their deals with the union bosses if they wanted to have their goods loaded or unloaded. This was particularly true of perishable food products.

The heat in late August made the transition from being in a five-below-zero storage freezer to the eighty-five-degree outdoor temperature a rather unique experience. In order to spend more than a few minutes in these walk-in freezers, they wore heavy leather-trimmed lamb wool coats, canvas pants, ear-flapped thick leather Bolshevik fur hats, heavy gloves, and lined boots.

Tony could not waste time dressing properly to go into the cooler and freezers. Instead he kept an old heavy wool overcoat, lined overshoes he could slip on over his shoes, a pair of gloves, and a Bolshevik fur hat in his office.

Tony emerged from the freezer with "E." "Okay, I want to have all these cases brought to freezer two, and get this one cleaned out real good," said Tony. E nodded as they walked through the huge refrigerated working cooler where men were cutting meat, making ground beef, and boxing product.

He emerged from the cooler having pulled off his gloves and hat. Standing in the loading dock entry was Nicky D. "Tony!" Nicky said and put his hand out for Tony to shake.

"Jeez, you're freezing!" said Nicky as he quickly pulled his hand away and rubbed it.

Nicky was nearly as round as he was high and stood about five feet five. The workmen joked that he was Mr. Five by Five, five feet tall and five feet wide, but they were sure not to tell him to his face. He had considerable strength and a legendary temper. It was said someone got him angry when he was trying to give directions to his guys out on one of the piers, and to shut him up, Nicky backhanded him and broke his nose and jaw. He also was known to be a made guy, an inducted member of La Cosa Nostra.

"Well, what do you expect? It's fucking thirty degrees below zero in those freezers," Tony said, and he chuckled as he led Nicky into the office. E followed. "E, close the door and get out."

"Tony, there is a ship coming in from Japan. I got word from my guys in the union that they will be here in about four days. I arranged a little union problem and a walk-off as soon as the ship comes in. After a few days, the trucking schedule will be all screwed up, so the Japs will have to have the shipment unloaded right away and store the cargo. It's all prime swordfish, worth a fortune. The Japs got to pay a big price to the union guys to come back, then arrange new deals with the truckers. Everybody gets greased in this deal. The longshoremen's union guys are with me too, so they got to make a new deal to move the stuff off the pier.

"We will get a fat storage charge and then get all the distribution from here. Of course, having a couple million pounds of prime swordfish here, a few pieces gone here and there won't be missed, especially when their entire distribution comes right from the docks to you," Nicky said.

"Hmmm, I think I can get my main big freezer pretty empty fast, and I got two small freezers I can combine into one. I can do it. I also have two refrigerated trucks and can get more and crews to unload whatever they send here," said Tony.

"Okay, I'll get someone to get back to you with the storage contract and timing of when we start," Nicky said. The deal was set.

The loading dock looked like an assembly line. Four trucks were backed up to it, and each truck had two guys inside bringing up the cigar-shaped swordfish carcasses. There were all different sizes and weights, from 25 pounds to 150 pounds. All were stone cold, frozen solid, wrapped in heavy corrugated paper, and covered with cloth stockinette. Trying to get a hold of the bigger pieces was tricky. Finally handing it off to the guys below took a bit of doing as well. Once they had the piece, the guys stacked it on big metal dollies that they wheeled down the loading dock and into the main big freezer at the end of the building. It went somewhat smoothly at first, as each crew took its time moving and placing the fish and handing them off. The heat and humidity soon caused a cloud of fog in the trucks. It wasn't too easy to see where the next stacked fish was lying. Also, the fish were rounded, and although they had been jammed in almost to the top of the trailer, when the load began to diminish, the frozen fish logs began to slip and tumble down. "Ow! Son of a bitch!" one guy yelled from inside trailer number two. One big fish had slid down just as he put his hand down to get a hold of another fish, catching his hand between the two heavy frozen logs. "Shit! I almost broke my fucking hand. Go slower. Let's pull one out at a time and get away from the stack," he said to the other guy in the truck.

Just as he finished, E yelled, "What's the matter with you pussies? Can't you do a day's work without whining like a bunch of schoolgirls? You'd think you've never unloaded before. What's the big deal? It's only a bunch of fish. Here—hand me that big one." The metal cart was loaded with about six big fish, some weighing over two hundred pounds. They were stacked precariously on the long, low metal dolly lengthwise. "You girls gotta get movin'," E yelled.

E grabbed one side of a big fish. "Hey, let's get this one on top." He ordered one of the guys on the loading dock to get the other side of the fish.

They placed the fish on the top of the pile on the cart. "See—that's not so hard, is it?" said E, and he patted the top fish. Suddenly, the whole load shuffled and slid toward E. He tried to step backward but tripped and fell flat on his ass. The fish seemed to slide in slow motion as they fell on him one after another until he was virtually covered by the huge fish log.

"Help! Help! Get me out of here!" E yelled. The four men quickly removed the fish from on top of him. One fish had hit him in the mouth, and his lip was cut and bleeding. He also split his pants from the zipper to the back during his tumble. The fish banged up both his legs, and red welts rose up. He finally got to his feet with the help of two of the guys. He had lost one of his shoes and socks under the pile of fish, and some of the frozen fish fell off the loading dock and lay under the trailer in the parking area. All the guys were laughing and yelling. The commotion brought Tony out of the office.

"What the hell is going on? E, look at you, you fucking clown. I leave you alone, and look at this. You fucking idiot! Clean up this mess.

That fish is worth a fortune. Don't bang them up, or I'll bang you up. Get back to work!" screamed Tony. E cowered, momentarily forgetting the stinging pain on his lip and legs. Meanwhile, the men were laughing and yelling out to E. His face turned bright red. He lowered his head and limped back inside.

Anthony Delmonte and friends

Nearly two and a half million pounds of prime swordfish were unloaded, stored, and, over nearly a month or so, pieced out into trailers again and shipped off from the Bay Plant. Except somehow by the time the big freezer was emptied, nearly two hundred thousand pounds of fish had found their way to somewhere other than the owner's customers. Nicky had freezers full of swordfish steaks. Tony's restaurant and ship stores customers also bought pounds of them. The storage fees were also a big windfall.

Over the next two years, there were similar situations with boat loads of Italian wines, canned Italian tomatoes, Dutch cheeses, Spanish olive oil, Perrelli tires, clothing from Asia, and more. The three-story plant's entire storage was always full of either dry goods or foods.

Eventually, Bay Storage became a general merchandise wholesaler and was buying legitimate "damaged" ship cargo lots as well. When the cargo in a ship shifted from a rough sea, boxes would tumble and crush the other crates. Buyers would refuse the goods, and insurance companies who insured the goods would set them in locked cages on the piers until someone held a bidding sale, usually an insurance claims man. If a company had a mixed lot of goods, he would sell the entire lot to the highest bidder or in many cases the only bidder. Some of these claims men got to know Tony's men quite well. They were treated to elaborate lunches and dinners and presented with envelopes filled with cash. Whatever bids were made were usually left in envelopes on the pier for the claims man. Strangely, it seemed Tony was either the high bidder or the only bidder on any goods. He and the men he worked with always won.

Eventually they got so many goods that Tony decided to find an old, closed supermarket nearby and opened a store just for nonperishables. He began shipping goods overseas as well, and on one of his trips, he scouted opportunities in the Caribbean islands.

While traveling from Caribbean island to island, he arrived by small private plane on the island of Antigua. He had a friend from New Jersey managing a casino there.

"Bobby-boy, you look great," said Tony as he came down the airline stair, which flipped out the side of the plane onto the sun-drenched tarmac.

"Hey, Big Tony, *come' sta?*"

"How long has it been—two, maybe three, years?" Tony asked.

"More like four, Tony! Sam and the boys got the casino here, and they sent me down here to take care of things. It's gone well but sometimes is a bit boring. You know, you get island fever. There is just so much of a place like this you can take, even with the action, the broads, and good food and drink. It's like living in a place you don't really belong to, but I make the best of it, and the dough keeps comin' in. Come on. The car's over here," said Bobby.

Bobby DiCicco was a middle-aged mobster who had been one of the right-hand men for Sam "the Plumber" De Calandro, boss of the Newark mob and head of his own family in New Jersey. While the

Jersey mob was once, in fact, more a faction of a New York family, Sam actually brought it to family status in the Cosa Nostra. It was, however, smaller and weaker and did not have the same stature as the five families in New York. Because Sam had construction businesses, he earned the nickname "the Plumber."

Bobby had been born in Brooklyn and worked his way through two families in New York and became a made guy, a real wiseguy after he took care of some "buis-a-nessa" in Manhattan with a potential witness in a case involving the Profaci family and some operations at the shipping piers in Red Hook some ten years earlier.

He took a "long vacation" in a little shore town, Ship Bottom in New Jersey, helping a cousin at a shorefront restaurant, Le Bella Mare, for the entire summer. It was a nice place to hide out, and no one would suspect a hit man would be working in a trattoria on the beach.

Bobby recalled his days as a kid going to Coney Island. Ship Bottom did not hold the same kind of action, but it was still a great little vacation town. The biggest crowd came from Staten Island, Brooklyn, and the nearby Jersey towns, including Newark. It was a rather quiet getaway with few prying eyes to worry about.

Sam "the Plumber" had a big beach house tucked away on the bayside with a long dock and two boats, a twenty-foot speedboat and a fifty-two-foot Bertram sedan fishing boat rigged for serious sport fishing.

Sam liked to get away from the city with its constant pressures and surveillance and escape down the shore. He enjoyed the food and the bar crowd at La Bella Mare. Some of the regulars were doing business with one of his crews. The owner, Jimmy Chairello, Bobby's cousin, had been a bookie in Brooklyn. He had made enough money to buy a summer house and use to frequent the Bella Mare. The Old Italian couple that owned the place, the Cellas, let Jimmy know they were getting too old to keep the place and had no kids to take it over. Jimmy loved the shore. They made a deal, and Jimmy quit taking "book" in Brooklyn after a while and moved to the shore after the second summer. However, he did not give up his day job. He turned his street book over to another cousin but retained some of his best customers. He also was running his bookmaking operations out of the

Bella Mare. However, in order to do that, he had to make a deal with
Sam "the Plumber" or at least have the Profacis cut the deal for him. It
was more like a transfer for Jimmy.

Jimmy became a sort of celebrity with the summer crowd. He
had the Cella's head chef return and brought some imports, Italian
cooks, over to help. His seafood menu was a big draw, *zuppa di pesce*,
calamari *siciliano*, *spindola oilio e oilio*, *scungilli* marinara, and other
Italian specialties. His chefs could take off-the-menu orders too.

Sam "the Plumber" became a regular summer customer and came
in whenever he was able to get away. "Sam, I want you to meet my
cugino, Bobby DiCicco," said Jimmy. "He had a little heat in Brooklyn,
so he's on vacation with me down here."

"Pleased to meet you," said Sam. He then looked back at Jimmy.
"How's the calamari today?"

"Very good. I'll make it special for you," said Jimmy as he placed
a bottle of Brunello on the bar. "You've got to try this—I just got it in.
It's the best." Sam had an associate, Pete Montello, with him. Jimmy
poured four glasses of wine. "Centanni" (Salute), said Jimmy, and they
all drank.

"So, Pete, you're a Jersey guy originally? Seems so many people who
come in here now live in Jersey but were from New York," said Bobby.

"I lived in Manhattan, East Side as a boy, and then later I worked
with some of the guys there but had to leave after an incident. Sam
took me in over here," said Pete.

"That's funny. I'm down here because of something up there too.
I've got to find work now. Been enjoying the good life for almost a year
helping Jimmy, but I've really got to do something," said Bobby.

Bobby was not exactly what you would call an imposing figure.
He was about five foot eight but appeared taller. He had a broad
barrel-shaped chest and a thick neck. However, he had arms that measured eighteen inches around and huge ham hands. It gave him an
unusually powerful appearance. From the time he was a kid, he used
a set of dumbbells every morning so that he could pump up his arms
and forearms.

"Well, maybe one of our guys might need help. We are doing some
things at the shore. Even the Newark guys have interest here. You know

it's kind of strange because Philadelphia controls a lot of the shore, Atlantic City and all," said Pete.

"Yeah, I found out. I went down there a couple times and met some guys, all Philly guys. They don't know anybody I know," said Bobby.

"Let me go back in the kitchen and tell Sabatino what to cook up," said Jimmy.

Bobby followed him. "Jimmy, do you think you can put a word in with Sam? I think I'd rather stay here in Jersey. With what went on back there in New York, who knows what can happen. The feds are still sniffing around, and the guy I whacked had family and friends. Maybe his friends will look for revenge. I like it in Jersey anyway," said Bobby.

"Sure," said Jimmy. "I'll get Sam on the side. He's got a bunch of crews, and I'll tell him about you. Then he can check with the Profacis."

Within a few months, Bobby was brought in and introduced around to the crews and to the union guys in Port Newark and the Port Socony waterfront. He ended up working with Pete, and soon Sam was asking for Bobby to handle important communications. Within a year, he became a trusted part of Sam's inner circle. When Sam returned from the vacation in the Caribbean, he brought Pete into his office in Newark.

"Pete, I told you things looked good in the islands. Well, we got a great deal. I got some of my New York friends in the family to go in with me on a casino in Antigua. There is a nice resort hotel and a separate casino. We will be running the casino. There's a guy from New York going there, but I'm sending you as the main man. You're going to be the general manager down here and oversee the operation. You're gonna cut the cash out of the skim every few weeks and bring it up here. I even got them to agree that you're gonna get a little piece of that too, as well as a legit weekly paycheck. They got a nice suite for you at the hotel, so you can take your 'cumard' if you want to. Maybe you should check out the place first, though—lots of vacationers, lots of single women looking for a good time. The place is a paradise. They got this big fishing boat too, nicer than mine. It's always sunny and warm," said Sam.

"Really? Antigua Island, huh?" said Pete. He could hardly believe what he was hearing. Sam knew he could trust Pete. He needed someone he could really trust since he had brought in money from two New York families, and he had to be sure there were no fuckups.

Pete had been Sam's consigliere (counselor) and right-hand man for over fifteen years. He had a special aptitude for numbers and could do mathematical figures in his head quicker than with the aid of a machine or using a pencil and paper. But Pete also had another talent. He was an only child. His mother and father had come to America, to Brooklyn, before he was born. They were from Sorrento near Naples. Pete's father had, as a boy, learned to play the mandolin, then the guitar, and eventually the violin as well. He worked in a music shop in Italy and kept the books for his boss. He too had a gift for numbers. He was a tall, slender man and had a perfect-pitch singing voice. He met his wife at a music festival in Naples. They had both been amateur performers. Pete's mother, Adele, had finished high school and hoped to pursue an opera singing career, but her family could not afford singing lessons to train her voice professionally. She was rather tall and slender for an Italian, with light brown hair and green eyes.

It seemed Pete ended up with the best traits of both. He was nearly six feet tall and wiry and had a thick crop of curly brown hair. He was doted upon by both his mother and father as a boy. His father taught him to play mandolin by the time he was seven, and his mother taught him every song she knew, from the Neapolitan love songs to the great arias of Puccini.

Even with all this nurturing at home, he still became a favorite part of the street guys club in the section of Canarsie where his parents settled. He was a handsome guy who attracted the girls, and his friends became his close companions because of the obvious benefits. He also had an open way about him and could befriend someone or bedazzle a young girl with ease. He organized an a cappella singing group in high school. "Frenchy, let's get the guys together in the third-floor men's bathroom at the end of seventh period. I want to try out this new song I heard on the radio. That bathroom has the best echo."

Frenchy wasn't really French; he was Italian but had this French girlfriend who spoke with a heavy accent. He would mimic her perfectly and consistently, so he got his nickname. Frenchy's real name was John Damiano. He also went into detail about how this girl taught him to French kiss and even went so far as instructing his friends in this fine art with a split-open watermelon.

Pete, even with all this socializing, still did well at school. He did so well, in fact, that his father made him apply to Brooklyn Poly Tech Institute, which was considered an excellent school. Pete, Frenchy, and their crowd, however, had other issues. They all knew how to raise some extra cash. They had some friends who owned a local car lot and body shop. They would stop by the shop, Gino's Car Lot, and take orders for parts, whether it was hubcaps, carburetors, emblems, tires, batteries, or whatever. "Midnight Auto Parts" could supply them; that's what Frenchy dubbed the operation. Pete, Frenchy, Donnie, and Pip could do in a few hours enough thieveries to make up to one hundred bucks a night. When Gino's got slapped with a stolen goods possession charge, the boys changed their venue.

They began breaking into stores and shops in the middle of the night and grabbing whatever cash they could find and fencing any goods they could take with them. It didn't take long before they attracted the attention of the real wiseguys and started doing work for a Bonnani crew, helping to move stolen goods. They also began hanging out at the local bars where the mob guys met. Pete would tell his parents he was singing and getting paid. He did go to their bars, the Blue Moon, Connie's, and the Esplanade, and he did sing. With his mandolin, he would do some of the old Italian songs his father and mother taught him. He and Frenchy and the other guys would do some a cappella too.

But as Pete became more involved, he stopped going to school regularly, and in his third year, he stopped going altogether. His parents were upset but could not control him at that point. When he turned eighteen, he left his parents and rented a room in a private house he shared with Frenchy. They pooled their cash and bought an old '48 Ford coupe. One of the made guys, "Sally" Scalzo, had a book-making operation. He brought Pete in as a runner, sending him to his customers to collect numbers and sometimes horse bets, and gave him a small cut. Pete really had found his niche. He was so personable and knew so many people he soon was bringing Sally more and more clients.

Soon there was so much business Pete brought Frenchy in to help as well. Sally apparently was not informing his bosses of his good fortune, as he continued to send the same cut to his boss.

"Hey, kid, Joey G wants to see you. Be at Connie's tonight at six o'clock and don't be late." Pete stared up at this huge, heavyset mountain of a man. He stood over six and a half feet tall and weighed over three hundred pounds.

"Okay. I'll be there," said Pete.

Pete walked into Connie's Lounge a few minutes before six. There were a few guys talking at the bar but no one at the tables. He sat down at the bar. "Tom, give me a beer," said Pete. He sat there for a half hour.

One of the guys who had been talking went to the pay phone at the back near the bathrooms. Pete could hear a coin drop followed by a muffled conversation, "Yeah, he's here."

He stayed for another half hour and was just about to leave when two men walked in. The guy who had made the phone call went over to them, and they shook hands. Then one went back outside.

He returned with two other men, the big guy who had summoned Pete and a short, thin guy dressed in a black mohair suit, white shirt and tie, and highly polished wing tip shoes. They sat at a back table. The bartender went to the front door and locked it.

The big guy came over to Pete. "Hey, come over here with us," he said. Pete went to the table.

The little guy looked up, smiled, and said, "Hey, kid, sit down, sit down." He put his hand out. "You know who I am, kid?" he asked.

"Yeah, you're Joey G. Everybody knows you," said Pete.

"Heh! Heh! Heh! Everybody knows me. That's good, kid. Well, I hope not everybody, but that's good," said Joey. "I know who you are too, Pete. I know that you've been a good worker for Sally. The other guys said you're okay too. We got a little uh situation. We are a little shorthanded, you see. Sally had to go on vacation. So we need a fill-in for a while. I'm told you're a pretty smart kid, running numbers without slips and things like that. Is that true?" said Joey.

"Well, yeah, I just memorize the numbers and then give Sally the numbers, the bets, and the cash," said Pete.

"Well, I might need you to keep doing that and also bring in your friend's action and some action from Sally's other runners. You bring it all to Buffalo here." He looked over at the big guy. "He's gonna give you a cut. He'll also give you cash if somebody wins. Can you handle that, kid?" said Joey G.

"Sure, Mr. G," said Pete.

"Okay then, you'll work for me, and we'll take care of you. But just a warning: no sticky fingers. It's not good for your health. You got it?" said Joey G.

"Yeah, boss, I got it," said Pete.

"Hey, Buff, this kid catches on quick." He stuck his hand out, and Pete shook it. "Give the kid a drink," said Joey. "I'll have a scotch."

Over the next three years, Pete worked himself up from runner to book manager for Sally, then helped with the loan-sharking operation for Buffalo's crew. When "Buff" moved up to take over union work on the docks, Pete took his slot running the entire crew. For the next two years, he became a huge earner. He headquartered at Connie's.

"Hey, Pete, come quick." Frenchy rushed through the door almost out of breath late one night. Pete was just finishing up counting money and was about to put a slip in with the cash, put it in a canvas bag, and put it in a floor safe in the back room. "Pete, you hear? You hear?" said Frenchy.

"Hear what, Frenchy? What?" asked Pete.

"Joey G got whacked. He's dead. He got it at dinner. He was eatin' at Umberto's Clam House in Little Italy, and some guys blasted him as he had a mouthful of mussels marinara stuffed in his gullet."

Pete looked at Frenchy. "Jeez! Jeez!"

"What'll we do, Pete?" asked Frenchy.

"Calm down, for Christ's sake, will ya," Pete said, tightening his lips. "Calm the fuck down," Pete said again.

Pete tried to think. Who would do it and why? Would anyone else be next in line? His mind was whirling. *Carmie Persipico, Ally, Jay?* There was talk that Joey had something to do with muscling in on the Colombini group. Then the head guy, Joe Colombini, got shot in the head and was in a coma somewhere with half his brain gone. Some black kid was seen with the gun. Pete remembered seeing Joey G with a bunch of black guys a few times and knew he had deals with black gangs. Somebody killed the black kid on the spot, so they could not find out who sent him.

That's it. Joey had to pay for the other guy or shut him up.

"Listen, Frenchy, tell our guys to take a little vacation out of town for now. I don't want any of our group around town." He handed Frenchy a canvas bag. "Here. Spread this around for travel money. Tell them to go tonight," said Pete. "Call Tom with a phone number."

He went over to Tom the bartender. "Tommy, me and my guys have some business out of town. If anyone comes asking for us, let them leave a phone number, and I'll call them. The same goes for Frenchy and the other guys."

That night, Pete and the others left town.

Pete ended up in an Atlantic City hotel. He stayed there for a few days and then took a ride to Newark. He had met a guy with Buffalo who was "associated" in Newark. He knew the guy, Eddie Salerno, had a big construction machine business there. "Is Eddie in? I'm a friend of Buffalo," Pete said at the office counter.

"Let me check," the woman behind the counter answered and left.

Soon Eddie appeared. "Hello. What can I do for you?" he asked.

"Do you remember me? I met you with Buffalo at Connie's in Brooklyn a while ago," said Pete.

"Hmmmmmm, maybe," said Eddie.

"Look, can I talk to you?" said Pete.

"Here, let's step outside," said Eddie.

"Eddie, you heard what happened to Joey G. Buffalo said you were a good guy and well connected. He said you know everybody in Jersey. I was wondering if your Jersey guys could make an inquiry. I have no beef with anybody. Whatever happened happened. I'm just a working guy. So, Joey G did something to someone. It's too bad, but it's none of my business. Now somebody has to have moved in. I just need to know who I got to talk to now. That's all. Here's my phone number," said Pete.

Eddie looked at him. "Okay, kid, I'll pass it along, but why me?"

"Well, I figured if it came from Jersey. There is no one here who is involved, so it is a good contact source," said Pete.

"Hmmmm, okay."

"I'll owe you, and I'll pay you back, Eddie."

"Okay, kid," said Eddie.

Within a few days, Pete got a phone call at the hotel. "Pete, it's Buffalo. It's all done. Come on back. I'll meet you at Connie's tomorrow at six o'clock."

Pete walked into Connie's. Buffalo was there with Frenchy and two other guys.

"Hey, Pete, how are you?" said Buffalo.

"Fine."

"Well, what's done is done. I'm going to be with another group. You come with me, okay?" he said.

"Yeah, okay," said Pete. And that was that. Buffalo actually had made it known that neither he nor his crew sought revenge for Joey G's murder, and none of them had ideas about taking over his business. In fact, Buffalo had spoken with Eddie, and he was needed in Newark to work between the Jersey and New York union guys.

"Pete, I need you to help me," said Buffalo. "I'm going to be spending a lot of time in Jersey. You will too, so find yourself a place near me." Pete wanted to be near New York, so he found an apartment in Perth Amboy, New Jersey, close to the tunnels and bridges. He worked on accounts for Buffalo with the crews who worked the docks for over three years when Buffalo moved up in Sam's organization. Pete was trained by Buffalo and knew all the contacts. It was a smooth transition, and Pete took over the liaison position and also collections of money. He no longer reported to Buffalo but directly to Sam himself. Sam began to have him to his social gatherings at the shore and invite him on fishing trips. Frenchy stayed with Pete all through the moves.

One night at the Bella Mare, Sam, Buffalo, Pete, Frenchy, Jimmy, and some of Sam's other crew, Dom and Gito, were having dinner. "So, everybody has a story about nicknames, but then there are different stories about how that happens," Frenchy said. "Yeah, like Pete the Machine. Everybody thinks the Machine is a math whiz. The truth is Pete had these girls in high school and in the neighborhood. He would set up early dates and late dates, sometimes four a night. And like a madman, he would spend a couple hours early banging one, then move on to the next one, bang that one, then go to the next and finish off staying late with the last one. Thing is he would do that routine sometimes four or five nights in a row, *like a machine*," said Frenchy.

"That ain't true," said Pete. "I only did five nights a few times and tried to take a night off in between," said Pete, obviously very serious about his explanation.

The whole table started to laugh. "So, Mr. Machine, that's the real truth? It wasn't the numbers after all? It was all that zomma-zomma business that got you the name," said Sam. They all laughed again.

Years later, Pete was diagnosed with stage three testicular cancer. It seemed he was fine one day; then he had a constriction. The cancer spread, and he was gone within a year. Bobby took on a lot of Pete's business, and when the Caribbean job came up, Sam felt he had the right person for it. Antigua was wide open, so Bobby landed there.

Tony said, "Where's the car?"

"It's this," said Bobby. He saw what looked like an oversized, glorified golf cart. It had a driver's bench seat and two others and a big luggage platform in the rear. "Open air, my friend. You in da islands now, mon," said Bobby in his best Caribbean accent. Tony laughed and got in. The luggage was loaded, and the vehicle sputtered off down the road. It took about twenty minutes to get to the hotel, and Bobby acted as a tour guide, pointing out all the important sites.

The hotel was nestled in a cover of tall palm trees. The driveway in was lined with sea grape trees and flowering hibiscus. The two-story hotel section was spread out across a few acres and crisscrossed with pathways, alcoves, and well-beaten sandy pathways to a huge lagoon. Off to the side was a large one-story structure with wide porches all the way around the building. There were discrete lighted signs announcing "Casino" in red neon letters. The air had the scent of flowers and the ocean.

Bobby was greeted at the huge porte cochere by three men dressed in starched shorts and short-sleeved white uniforms with epaulets. "Hello, Mr. Bobby!" one tall, smiling, cocoa-skinned man said. "Hello, sir," the man nodded to Tony. "I am Oliver. Please let me assist you." He looked over to the other two men, similarly dressed, and they immediately gathered the luggage. "Would you like a cold refreshment, some pineapple or mango, a bit of local beer or cool wine and juice?"

Tony looked over to Bobby. "Try that wine cooler. It's great, and I will take one too," said Bobby. Oliver turned and opened a large cabinet, and the cool breeze from a refrigerator could be felt nearby. He poured two large goblets and placed a small purple flower on top.

"Chin-Chin," said Bobby, and they drank as they walked through the stone corridor, through the lobby area, and down a long hallway.

Bobby opened the doors to a grand suite. The room was a large salon with a bar and a living room area that opened up onto a large balcony. There were two bedrooms, one at each side, with attached bathrooms and a kitchenette. In the living room was a dining table with a bowl in the center filled with tropical fruits surrounded by lush flowers.

"This is very nice," said Tony.

"Tony, mi casa su casa. There's a stack of chips for the casino in the top drawer of that master bedroom off to the right side," he said, pointing to a double door. "You know you can stay as long as you like. Sam sends his regards," Bobby said.

"Thanks," Tony said as the bellman arranged the baggage.

"I'll see you downstairs. I'll be over in the casino. If it's okay with you, I arranged dinner tonight with some friends and associates and some local color," said Bobby.

"Okay, see you in a bit. I'm going to get a shower. I still smell jet fuel," said Tony.

Tony walked into the entry of the casino wearing a thin, white, half-sleeve linen shirt and thin linen pants with a pair of leather shoes, ventilated with a louvered pattern.

"Tone, you look fresh. Come on. Let's get a drink," Bobby said. His office was just off the entry, and a huge ornate mirror actually had a two-way mirror to his office. He had seen Tony coming in and walked out to greet him.

They sat at the bar, and Bobby ordered a drink. "Scotch-rocks, splash of soda," said Tony.

"Lito is my right-hand man. He is a cousin of one of my buddies from Jersey. He lived in Sicily for most of his life, then decided to come to the States and live with his cousin. He watches my back down here, you know," said Bobby. "He will join us along with Bennett, my bookkeeper, and Jake, my main pit boss. Then there are some local ladies and one of our entertainers, a singer, Maya. She's terrific."

The two chatted for over an hour, catching up on each other's activities. The restaurant was out in the back of the hotel on the terrace overlooking the ocean. The two walked out the side of the casino, down a palm-lined, flowered pathway, and up a flight of wide coral stairs.

At the top of the stairs, the terrace was spread all the way around the ocean side of the hotel. There were tables carefully set with red and white linens and red and white floral arrangements. The terrace had bumped-out balconies at the edges that had foliage in between them, giving a sense of privacy to each balcony. In the center of the two main balconies was a wide set of stairs that had banisters and railings leading over the short stretch of beach down to the sea and into the water. The entire place was lit with huge torches at the top of high metal urns. It was an idyllic spot. When they got to the table, a man seated there chatting with another man and four women arose.

"Lito, this is Tony," said Bobby.

Lito stood, took Tony's hand and, in what could only be described as a half bow, clasped his other hand over Tony's and said, "It is my pleasure, Mr. Delmonte, and an honor." The man appeared to be about sixty years old, with salt and pepper gray hair, a medium build, and a thin waist accented by a tightly pulled leather belt that was over three inches wide. It caused his flowered shirt to blouse out from the thin, white, pleated linen pants.

"Nice to meet you, Lito," said Tony. "This is Mr. Bennett—Robert to you, sir. Over here is the lovely Maya and Santora, Columbia and Teresa." The ladies smiled and nodded. Maya stood up and extended her hand toward Tony. Tony met her hand and held it loosely at the fingertips.

"Bobby tells me you are here on the island often. I am glad to finally meet you," said Maya in a lilting voice that had a slight Caribbean accent but was smooth and full. Maya stood almost five foot nine, an extremely tall woman for the islands. She had a very athletic figure, enhanced by the sleeveless, bright yellow dress with a neckline that plunged to reveal her ample cleavage. Her jet-black hair framed her rounded face, and her honey-colored skin was flawless.

"It is certainly my pleasure," said Tony. They all sat down. Bobby motioned to a waiter, and he brought over two buckets, one with a bottle of Barolo, the other a bottle of a French white. The waiter began to pour for each guest.

"Well, I had the chef prepare us a very special dinner in your honor, Tony. We had some fresh catches come in today, so he prepared a little of this and a little of that," said Bobby.

The two waiters were joined by two more, and soon they were shuttling back and forth to the kitchen, bringing out silver trays filled with lobster, whole blackened fish, pork filets sliced thinly with slices of peach, conch fritters, flattened slabs of tuna barely cooked with chopped chutney garnish, ceviche and iced lemon water, and a whole range of other delicacies Tony had never seen. "Well, that's quite a feast, Bobby," said Tony.

They all ate and chatted. Columbia spoke in broken English with a Spanish accent. She was born in Peru. Her father was an Italian merchant, and her mother a Peruvian of Spanish descent. They had left Peru for a business venture in Puerto Rico. She attended the university there and then got a job in the Tropicana Casino. Bobby met her there and offered her a job at the casino on Antigua Island. Her friend Santora, a cocktail waitress, came along too; they were roommates. Both women were in their early thirties but had taken very good care to keep a youthful appearance and encouraging smiles. The tips came bigger that way.

Bennett was from Boston. He was certified as a CPA and also had a law degree from Harvard. His father was a Boston politician.

"Rob," Lito said, "you should unwind more." Later, Bobby told Tony that Bennett had been the comptroller of a major investment banking firm in Boston that had close ties to the Buffalino family who were legendary as the bosses in New England. The Buffalinos had helped Edward Bennett, who was at the time a young lawyer, get elected to office as United States senator for Massachusetts. Over the years, they were able to help him get through the many difficulties the factions in Boston Democrat politics had jockeying for power. He became a consensus kind of office holder and seemed to have his foot in all camps, no doubt with the help of the Buffalino family. After his son finished school, his father got him a job with Boston Federal Bank. He became an executive in no time and soon a board member. The bank was partially owned by the Buffalinos. When the bank was approached by Banco International of Panama, Bennett, with the guidance of the Buffalinos, headed the merger. After it was all done, the Buffalinos sold most of their stock but still had a great deal of interest in the states. Bennett Sr. was brought to a meeting with the Buffalinos, and a scheme was devised to get a series of loans to various front companies owned by partners of the Buffalinos and take millions from Banco. The plan worked well under the direction of "Rob" Bennett. Then the FDIC (Federal Deposit Insurance Corporation) stepped in when the loans defaulted. They audited every transaction, but records had disappeared, and the data was removed. In the meantime, Rob was diagnosed with acute asthma, and his Boston doctors recommended he move to a dryer climate. He left the bank and literally left Banco holding the bag for the loss of millions of dollars.

Bennett Sr. had met Sam the Plumber at a birthday party in Boston for one of the senior Bartolini family members, Rosario. They sat at the bar and had an hour-long conversation about family, and Rob in particular. Sam was impressed with Rob's credentials and considered him the perfect person to serve as comptroller for his new casino operation in the islands. It also was a perfect job for Rob, who had to leave the country as the Banco paper trail kept leading back to him.

"So, Rob is a really bright boy, huh?" said Tony.

"Yeah, he is but pretty much a Boston type, a real stuffed shirt. You know the type, all business. He also has a little superiority complex with the locals here and sometimes, behind my back, with me. But he's a good bean counter anyway," Bobby said. Tony sensed a little tension in Bobby's voice.

Santora had a vivacious personality. She was truly effervescent, with big breasts that seemed to bounce about. She and Columbia enjoyed teasing Rob, who took their chiding very seriously. Santora, after having finished nearly a whole bottle of Asti Spumante by herself, got up and, as the steel band picked up, did an improvised dance around the table, turning and bumping and grinding until she got directly behind Rob, who was sipping his tea. She pulled the straps down from her dress and put ample breasts on top of Rob's head. He instinctively reached up overhead, not really knowing what was smothering his ears, and ended up grabbing onto both of Santora's breasts. This all happened just as the hotel photographer had come over. She snapped a few pictures just as Rob realized what he had grabbed. "Oh, Meester Robbie! Oh, Meester Robbie! It feels soooo good! Oh, Meester Robbie!" exclaimed Santora. When he realized he had her tits in his hands, Rob finally jumped up. The entire dinner party was laughing so hard they hardly noticed his hasty exit. He nearly fell over as he ran down the stairs and down the pathway.

Lito got up and went over to Santora. "Very nice. You are so silly," he said.

With that, she pushed her breasts together in her two hands and pressed them up to Lito's chin. "Oh, Mister Lito, are you afraid of these too?" she added with a coquettish smile.

Lito bent down and said, "My mother breast-fed me, so I know a lot about these," as he took the nipple of one of her breasts in his mouth and sucked on it.

"Oh, oh, Meester Lito, oh, Meester Lito, don't do that, oh, don't do that. Okay, now about the other one," she added, switching one breast and putting the other nipple in his mouth. She looked skyward and rolled her eyes and hips at the same time. The rest of the group laughed out loud.

"Lito, you got enough air in there," said Bobby, nearly gasping with laughter.

"Ummm, ummm, ummm," gargled Lito, still sucking away as he now had both his arms around Santora and had pulled her closer.

Maya, dabbing her eyes with a napkin, said, "Bobby, maybe we can put them in my show between songs so we can keep everyone's attention."

"Good idea," said Bobby, still chuckling.

Finally, Lito picked up his head. "Oh, Meester Lito," said Santora with a mock frown of disappointment.

"Don't worry, Santora. I'm not done yet. This will continue later, sweetheart," Lito said with a grin.

"Oh, Meester Lito, you're sooo nice," Santora said with a big smile.

Lito put both his hands on her breasts and held them, then lifted them. "Here, sweetheart, let's put them away now. I want to be sure they're okay for later," he said, then bent down and kissed each one as she stuffed them back in her dress.

"I think that calls for another bottle of wine," said Bobby as he motioned to the waiter.

"That's one hot number," Tony said as he leaned over to Bobby.

"You have no idea. She's nonstop in bed. I nearly put my back out many times, but that's the hazards of the job. Hey, you wanna try that?" said Bobby.

"I don't think so. Maybe a little too lively for my taste. I better let your guy Lito calm her down. I might like to hear Maya, though, do a little private concert for me," said Tony with a snicker.

"Bon appetite," said Bobby, extending his open hand.

Maya who was sitting a little distance away couldn't hear everything that Tony said. However, she had heard enough to understand the substance of the conversation. She slid her chair closer to him and put her hand on his arm. "I thought I overheard you say you were a music lover," she said and looked Tony straight in the face with a little side smile.

"Oh, yeah, I am. I am a lover of music and other things too," he said and turned and brushed her cheek with his other hand.

She smiled and rested her head on his arm. "Santoro, come here, baby. Let's see if you can teach me to dance to this music," said Lito, and they left the table. There was a large open space in the middle of the veranda with a few couples dancing.

"Excuse me for a minute. I have to go powder something," Maya said, grinning at Tony, and she left and went into the building.

"She's quite a woman," said Bobby. "She is a great singer. Smart too."

"Yeah, she seems so," said Tony.

"She was educated in some university but always wanted to perform," said Bobby.

"Well, I may be seeing her from time to time. I made a deal to lease the old refrigerated warehouse facility nearby in Santa Lucia. There is a large plant over there that was built during World War II as a supply building for the Allies in the war. It was out of the way, so the enemy wouldn't suspect such a place even existed so far out in the Caribbean. When supply ships went out in that direction, there weren't any subs or planes that followed them. It was a smart idea. But once the war was over, there was no need for it because of the port nearby.

"I met Sir Anthony Eden while I was on a sailing vacation. His sailboat was cruising the islands too. We happened to moor our boat near his. When he reached the port bay in Santa Lucia, he invited me and the eight others on our boat to come over for a cocktail party. Well, we ended up drinking a bottle of Napoleon Brandy and got quite friendly. It seems he had a business on the island. He had four refrigerated cargo ships that received shipments of frozen food and then shipped them to the other islands. He was based in the British Virgin Islands.

"His problem was getting supplies from the States, as most everything is shipped out of ports around Miami or the nearby ports on the coast there. The suppliers really bumped up the prices of just about everything they ship.

"Now I had been to Santa Lucia quite a number of times and was very friendly with the Pompton family there. They hold all the power on the island and have since the British left and the island became independent. They still use BWI money (British West Indies money), but the Pomptons basically hold every political office.

"Old John Pompton and I hit it off real well, especially when I brought him a case of fine single malt scotch. I made a deal with him to take over the plant. It has huge freezer space. I have access to frozen food products as well as other goods at the lowest cost and began shipping to the plant and wholesaling these goods. Sir Anthony and I made up a partnership. I ship in food products, and he distributes. We can supply just about anything. I have my contacts in New York, New Jersey, and Miami as well as other places. Your boss, Sam, had made connections here, and we sell to a lot of places here in Antigua. So now we are spreading out to a lot of the islands.

"I made deals with Pompton, and he gets taken care of. Now I got guys that took over a number of stores in Santa Lucia, so we sell all kinds of stuff I get in New York. We sell clothes, shoes, even general merchandise besides frozen food. I even took over the local taxi cab company.

"When the last hurricane came through, it damaged the local hospital run by the Catholic Sisters of Mercy. They lost supplies, medicine, and a lot of stuff. I got some of my doctor friends to donate a big quantity of medical supplies and other stuff and shipped it over to the Sisters.

"Well, they think I'm a great guy. When I come to the island, they send people to meet me. My plant is about two hours from the airport over those little roads out there, so I stay overnight at the hospital. They laid out a suite for me there. It's just five minutes from the airport. They even said novenas for me. Can you imagine nuns praying for me?" Tony told Bobby.

"Wow, that's some deal. Well, whatever I can do, you know. Sam, let me know if you and your guys got anything you want here, anytime," said Bobby.

"Thanks."

A waiter came over to Bobby and said something quietly to him. Bobby nodded. "Hey, Tony, I got a little problem. I gotta go. I'll see you over at the casino later. Tell Maya to show you around. I'm sure she will," said Bobby.

Lito was still dancing, and Bobby went over to him. Lito nodded, and Bobby left. Lito continued to dance with Santora.

"So where is everybody?" said Maya when she returned. "Is the party over?"

"No, sweetie, it's really just starting. Bobby had to leave but said maybe you could show me around. And when you're done, maybe I can show you around," said Tony, smiling.

Maya laughed. "Okay let's go." Lito waved, and Santora smiled as they continued dancing as the couple walked away.

Maya showed him the rest of the complex, and after her last show, she and Tony spent the night in his suite.

The next year was a profitable one. Tony continued his operations from the States to the islands. He often flew there to oversee the operations and talk business with the Pomptons. His operations became the biggest economic boom the little island had ever seen. He brought in an entirely new economy to an island with very little commerce to offer.

Outside of the three main cities, Castries, Soufriere, and Vieux Fort, the poverty was pervasive. The villages were little more than groups of huts with dirt floors. Most people did not have shoes and cooked their food over fires set in stones arranged like in a campfire. Local men worked for twenty-five cents an hour when they felt they wanted to work at all. The new economy changed that a bit. Shipments of clothing, shoes, and inexpensive items began to show up. The local stores run by Tony would sell the cheapest goods to the locals with little profit but with a huge turnover, so it still was worth the shipping costs.

Men did show up for work and got their twenty-five cents an hour. They were paid in BWI money at the end of the day. The problem was that they would work several days on some project or another, collect their money, accumulate some amount of cash and knowledge of their task, then disappear for a month. Tony still managed to keep the operations going.

Next, he made a deal with the government to be issued the only liquor import license on the island. Prior to that, several suppliers had brought in alcoholic beverages with no real schedule. Once supplies at some retail general merchandise store ran out, there was not much variety on the island. The license gave Tony's company the sole right to bring in liquor, wine, and beer. He converted one of the Main Street shops he owned to a liquor store.

The new supply came in regularly as stock was depleted. The cheapest rum from the other islands was bought and transported duty-free. Thus, it was sold relatively cheaply. Soon, even some of the poorest local men would work long enough to buy a liter of a cheap, somewhat less refined bottle of rum. The alcohol content, however, at over 8 percent, was highly intoxicating.

The island had never experienced drunken men passed out in alleyways and along the roadways, and for a while at least, it was all tolerated with the new economic boom. However, it got to the point that the sisters in the hospital began asking Tony to restrict sales of liquor to local men. The problem was that several of them had been brought in with alcohol poisoning after nonstop drinking bouts.

Tony's staff set more stringent guidelines for sales to locals. They were closed on Sundays and rationed sales to those who they knew by keeping a sales log. Once the problem was resolved, the nuns organized a dinner at the hospital and presented Tony as guest of honor, thanking him for all his good works on the island. Life on the islands was simple and a far cry from New York City.

CHAPTER 49

UNDERSTANDING LIFE IN New York City is difficult. There is no primer to help those who have not been born and bred in this place. You just have to live it to understand. It is a place like no other, a concentric hub whose spokes spread around the globe. The inner core is the greater New York and metro New Jersey and Connecticut fringe areas. The epicenter is, of course, Manhattan, and it is what New Yorkers refer to as "the city."

The fortunes of men like Enrico Terranova and Vincent Delmonte and their offspring were interrelated to the world around them with the center of that world, always "the city." The force of this single metropolis on the entire globe was as essential as the gravity that ruled the tides. Even as the next generations emerged, the vestige of the earlier culture still was there.

Living in New York requires being under constant compression. There are times when one can virtually feel the weight of the city on one's shoulders. Other cities bustle like Chicago and Boston. But "the city" churns and grinds under its own gravity. You learn quickly to accept the strange and unusual and just take it in stride. You live, you fight; you assert yourself even at the expense of others. Cruelty is just life here. You may or may not choose to help or assist a neighbor. It depends on who it is, where, when, and why. It's a qualified society, having its own caste system and rules. Kids and women, in that order, have some priority. Men need to fend for themselves; even the elderly, sick, or handicapped are given little priority.

The transplanted Sicilians function well in this society since they are inbred over the centuries. Self-preservation and protection of the family was paramount.

Anthony Delmonte had no long-range plan for life. He was not like his father in that he had clearly defined goals and a vision. Vince had thought out a simple financial concept that he followed. Accumulate money, buy a business, buy a building, accumulate more money, and become a landlord. Independence and self-sufficiency are primary traits of those Sicilians from time in memorial. They did not have to explain these things to their offspring, for, by example and demand, they lived it. One took care of one's self. With that sense of self-sufficiency came dignity and, if not pride, a satisfaction of being able to cope with anything in this life by finding inner strength to do so. Women could be dependent; men could not.

Anthony's business flourished in these early years. Through the contacts of his family, business associates, and friends and his entrepreneurial spirit, he branched out into several operations. Those operations expanded his world. Now he was dealing in several major US cities, in Europe and the Caribbean, and even Asia and parts of North Africa.

He was charismatic and had a gregarious personality. As a boy and young man, he had fought his way through life, and he had the scars to prove it. Most prominent was a pug nose. It was broken and bent in a barroom fight when he was twenty-one years old and gave him a bulldog-like appearance. His round face, slicked back hair, and barrel chest made him appear taller than he was. Even when he wore a finely tailored, dark blue pin-striped suit and white-on-white custom shirt with silk tie, this businessman commanded respect. Anthony's big smile and inviting manner did not hide his power. Like the leopard, Anthony's good-natured and gregarious smile could change in an instant. He could become a raging animal surely capable of anything, including killing another with his bare hands. He had nearly done so several times. His heavy hands were like sledgehammers when he made a fist, and he had, more than once, broken the jaws of men twice his size. He did so not just with physical strength but by his sheer animal will. His anger was so visible and so intense that one could feel his life force. This was more than simply a Sicilian temper; it was, in a word, diabolical.

Even this dynamo needed recreation, which occasionally took the form of a visit with family or attending the mandatory clan gathering for holidays. Other forms of recreation were combined with some business deal or meeting. Business was seven days a week, 365 days a year. The workday began at seven thirty or eight in the morning, six days a week. Sunday started a bit later, usually after eight thirty, and generally ended by eleven thirty or noon. On some days, the workday included a luncheon meeting in Lower Manhattan's Financial District or in the Markets District. Anthony always had his table at George's Restaurant near Wall Street that doubled as his office. The table could accommodate ten people and took up a semiprivate corner of the place. Anthony held court there at least three days a week. No one else was ever permitted to use it except Anthony and those he sent there. Union bosses, shipping company executives, politicians, police officials, midlevel crime bosses, and even a monsignor or two might be seen there on any given day eating, drinking, and making deals, paying or receiving, or just being entertained. Rarely were there any women at the table or the bar. This was strictly a man's place. George's had a rich and colorful history. With the chestnut paneling and thick, plush chairs, it was more like a movie set than a real place, and even the characters resembled a movie cast. However, it was real, sometimes too real—deadly real. Murder was an everyday reality in the city, another part of doing business.

It was assumed that the place was named after a founding owner. In reality, no one really knew for sure since the place had been a public house since colonial times. There was some credible evidence that, in fact, George Washington had used this, trying to gather men and funds for what would become a revolutionary army. He took rooms above the restaurant and conducted meetings in a corner of the place, the same corner occupied now by Anthony. Manhattan had many iconic restaurants and clubs. Copacabana, Stork Club, and Latin Quarter had the best entertainment. Jack Dempseys and Peter Lugars had the best food.

Anthony sat at the wall side of the table at George's so he could see a bit of the front door entry waiting for Scotty to come in. When he did, he walked straight to Anthony. "Hey, Tone, how you doin?" he said.

"Okay, okay," said Anthony.

Scotty sat next to Anthony and turned so he was facing his right ear. He put his hand to his jaw and rested his elbow on the table as if he were holding his head up with his hand. Scotty was always suspicious and concerned that a lip reader could see him or a hidden camera might capture his conversation. Law enforcement never could be trusted in the city, even those on the pad. "I got word that the feds have been watching every move on the docks all over the city—New Jersey, Staten Island, Brooklyn, all over. They have plainclothes guys and likely even some rats piecing together information and people. This has been going on for a long time, so we don't know where it starts. All of us have a headache here. The word is that it stems from the little prick Bobby Kennedy. He has free reign from his brother to go ahead even though some of our guys put themselves on the line for the old man. We were fucked over after the election even though we made the difference. Some shit, huh?"

Anthony said nothing. He listened and just looked around the room. Finally, he said, "Okay, I'll get my guys to ask around and see what I can find out and back them off any new operations."

"Listen, I'm told it's not just New York either; our friends all over are hearing the same story. I'm not sure what's going to happen or if there's anything we can do about it," said Scotty.

"You want a drink or something?" said Anthony.

"No, I gotta go. I'm staying off the phone. I'm sending messengers and shutting down all the scams."

"Okay, see ya," said Anthony as Scotty got up and left.

Anthony ordered a scotch and a cup of coffee. As he drank it, he tried to recall every deal when swag came into his warehouse, and this included the crates of stuff from hijacked truck cargo, the tons of stuff fenced through his place over the last several months. It was too much to remember. His train of thought was interrupted.

"Hey, big guy. I got the tickets for the plane and set us up at the Fontainebleau Hotel through our friend with the American Export Shipping Line, through their guy in Miami. We leave in five days. I told Beans he had to cover the office for at least a week, and Mr. R will be there every other day. I talked to Marcy. He is gonna be down there around the same time for a day or two. I think Charlie is down there already with some of his guys because he has some of his horses running at the track. I let them know we'll be down. Junior will take us to the airport. Anything else?" said Emil as he waved to a waiter.

"I'll let you know. I think we're set except, since we will be away, that thing with Artie? Maybe it's not good timing now. Tell him to forget it this time," said Anthony.

"Why? I set it up fine, and Junior has the layout. It's okay. It'll work fine. He knows where to stash the stuff until we get back," said Emil with great concern.

"Naw, too many loose ends, and if we're not there, it could be a headache. Tell him it's out." Anthony stood up and with his right hand made a thumbs-down sign. "Finito," he said. Emil slumped in his chair. He knew it would be useless to argue once he got the thumbs-down sign. This deal meant at least five grand in his pocket alone. He didn't understand why Anthony killed it. They had done several deals like this. Just because they wouldn't be there wasn't a reason to kill it.

Junior and Emil parked the car at the curb across from Anthony's apartment building. The three-story building had two stores on the ground floor and apartments on the second and third floors. His father, Vince, built this building and the one down the street on a two-acre lot on the corner of Scribner Avenue and Jersey Street. Junior pressed the bell, and the door buzzed open. "It's me. I'm comin' up," yelled Junior. He walked up the two and a half flights of stairs to the third floor. There was a suitcase and a hanging suit cover on the top of the stairs.

Anthony opened the door, saying, "Bring it down. I'll be right down."

The Oldsmobile was a big car and very fast. At six thirty in the morning, there was no traffic on Staten Island, so they sped along at a fast clip till they arrived early at LaGuardia Airport.

On the plane, Anthony lay back and fell fast asleep. He had been out till three o'clock the night before at the Riviera Chateau Ristorante. He had finished off about a half a bottle of Ballantine Scotch by himself. He met with Nicky D and Johnnie Lucci. Nicky told him to meet this guy "John" in Florida when he was there. John was going to do business but also had some messages for Nicky.

The plane touched down in Miami, and once they got their luggage, they had a cab bring them to the beach. The pink façade of the huge Fontainebleau Hotel reflected the hot tropical sun. Anthony took off his suit jacket, rolled up his sleeves, and loosened his tie as they strolled into the lobby. Emil went to the young man behind the front desk. "Hi, you have a reservation for Mr. Jackson?" he asked.

"Yes, sir, you're all set. Two rooms, ocean view, and poolside. Just sign in here, and I'll get your keys."

Anthony stood back and waited till Emil handed him the key: room 600. He got to the room, went straight to the phone, and dialed. "Hey, John, I bring you a hello from Nicky. He said to touch base as soon as I got in," said Anthony. He got an answer, then called Emil. "This guy will be here around noon at the pool bar. I'm going to take a shower."

The hotel grounds were splendid. Small palms and orange trees, lush greens, and a magnificent beach and ocean view.

Anthony sat on an end stool at the pool bar. The warm sun was now welcome. He felt strangely relaxed in this atmosphere; the weight of the city seemed to be lifted from his shoulders, and he felt he could breathe better even with his semiflattened nose that occasionally made him wheeze. He saw a stocky, middle-aged fellow walk toward the bar and then directly toward him. "Welcome to Miami," said John. "Your trip was okay, I guess?"

"Yeah," said Tony. "Glad to meet you. Nicky sends his best," said Anthony.

"Ronnie, give me a little Anejo on the rocks with a splash of soda, huh?" said John to the young, blond bartender. The boy nodded and quickly brought the drink.

"So, there's news up there. I'm hearing from everyone up there about heat, about problems. Tell Nicky you're not alone. It's all over. We never got this kinda heat before. I know J. Edgar isn't running this show; it's the pipsqueak. He's on a mission," said John. "Tell Nicky to let the guys you know up there that Carlo, the little guy, and Sam talked and will figure out something. Mike says you have guys that have things here, in North Carolina and Baltimore, Jersey, New York, and maybe some on the docks in New Orleans. I have things I can hook you up with after the heat is off. I'll have some guys contact you," said John.

"Okay. My salesman, Mr. Samson, is my contact guy. He runs each location outside of New York and New Jersey. He is in touch with me every day. Whatever you have we can move, whether it's shoes or cars," said Anthony.

"How long you staying in Miami?" asked John.

"I'm not sure. I got my friend Charlie running his horses at the track and another New York guy using Miami as a shipping base for the islands for his equipment business. It depends on what I can do here now. I have a guy in St. Lucia who tells me about a deal there, and then there is something about some deals in other islands, maybe even with the military in Cuba," said Anthony.

"Stay away from Cuba for now. It's bad news," said John, and he winked and closed his eyes. "Have a good time. Tell Nicky hello." John got up, took one more sip, and left.

Miami was an action town. The night never ended, and the atmosphere was supercharged with anticipation of a good time. Charlie, Anthony, and E sat at a rail-front table in the owner's section of the Hollywood Racetrack Clubhouse. "Well, they told me that the fishin' is really hot right now off Lauderdale. Maybe we'll catch a charter up there and see if we do any good. There's always good sailfish and maybe some big tuna." Anthony recalled the look on John's face when they spoke of Cuba. The prior trips to Cuba were always great fun before the regime change and Castro. But, for fishing and fooling around, Cuba was still okay if you had an American bankroll and some contacts there. The island government was restrictive to its own people, but if you had native friends there that survived the revolution, you could live like a king on twenty dollars a day.

Anthony had made many trips to Cuba in the pre-Castro days and had been shipping various goods there for his Cuban casino owner friends from the city. Most of the investments through New York, Chicago, Boston, and the West Coast were lost after Castro took over, but Anthony had a few well-placed government people who were able to make the transition from capitalism to communism without getting their heads blown off. Goods shipped by way of the other Caribbean islands found their way to the tiny Cuban black market frequented by those government officials who had learned to insulate themselves from exposure. Though Castro was a corrupt and tyrannical character who inhaled his rum, cigar, and young *chiquitas* in legendary fashion, he did, by making examples of his own followers and lieutenants, continue a reign of terror and fear, which kept everyone in line. The occasional missing local political leader, party bigwig, or local *commandante* was never spoken about after he was gone. It was assumed he had been taking bribes or hadn't been ardent enough in support of Castro's regime—perhaps even a spy or possible insurgent former capitalist or just too greedy or disrespectful. Over the years, thousands disappeared.

Anthony "Big Tony" Delmonte in Havana, Cuba

Anthony liked a particular place in Havana near a waterfront complex that had been a pre-Castro hangout for New York guys. The suites were luxurious and plush, and there were excellent cooks and wait staff. The manager also could provide the best fishing charters and the most beautiful female companions. Though the revolution had a huge impact on the operations, it still survived, but now most of the clientele were Castro's military elite who paid little or nothing but protected the operation. The foreign travelers from Europe, Soviet Union, the Far East, and other countries who were supportive of Fidel provided enough financial support to keep a moderate operation going. It was a great place to lay back and relax for Anthony, but he wouldn't chance it now that John had warned him to stay away. He would have to find some fun in Miami after all.

"And they're off!" exclaimed the track announcer, causing Anthony to refocus on the here and now. The machine gun voice of the caller cracked through the speakers, complementing the excitement in the crowd.

Charlie stood up. "We got Scotchie White running good now; watch him go," said Charlie. The bunched-up field pounded the earth, and as they made the turn, the jockey, Scotchie's Jockey, went to the whip. The horse accelerated and seemed to blast ahead of the field in no time. The big white animal galloped way out in front, and by the time they reached the finish line, he led by ten lengths. "All right," yelled Charlie, and he walked out onto the field and over toward the winner circle. Anthony had E put three hundred on the horse to win, and it paid twenty-six dollars and thirty cents.

"Hey, Charlie has a hot one there," said E. "I wonder if he was juiced up."

Anthony grinned for just a second and told E, "Go get my money." E left. By the time Charlie got back, Anthony had rounds of drinks brought out, and the celebration began.

Midnight in Miami overlooking the city from the Homestead Bar was a sight to behold. The whole place was glassed in with a 360-degree view. The music was tropical except for the occasional vocalist who did their best to emulate Sinatra or Bennett. The female vocalist, in the mandatory red sequined evening gown, so tight she waddled to the stage, was Monroesque but had very little vocal ability. The three men had already been joined by three ladies, and they had gotten to know each other over a sumptuous dinner at Enrique's, a real rug joint on Los Olas Boulevard in Fort Lauderdale. Henry was a New Yorker who had been a piano player in the Log Cabin Bar and Restaurant owned by Anthony, Charlie, and a few other players. He had made it big and built a great place in Lauderdale's high-rent district. The joint had flourished, and Henry had made some key investments. He bought the entire block, built an apartment and condo complex, and ended up a multimillionaire. But when Anthony and Charlie showed up, he would put on the dog for them, recalling how they always helped him either with finances or with influence, even with the Miami crew. The place had six waiters for each table, a strolling four-piece band, and every fine liquor known to man. Topping off a fine dinner of parchment-cooked pompano or a thick tuna steak was an array of Cuban cigars and Napoleon brandy. The ladies had been arranged by Henry and knew that they were to be particularly attentive to his friends.

Henry had sent over three bottles of Dom Perignon by the time dinner was halfway through. That was preceded by several rounds of scotch and soda. By the time dinner was through, the group had also consumed three bottles of Amarone and two bottles of Frascati. The band hovered over the table, playing one old Italian number after another, each ending with Charlie or Anthony passing the leader a five-dollar bill. Occasionally, Charlie would join in the chorus of "Torna Sorrento" or "Il Marechiare." The ladies loved it. Henry made sure there was one of each, a blonde, a redhead, and a brunette, all of them beautiful, well dressed, and bright. These working girls were surely the big spenders' type.

The moon at midnight over the city cast a cream-colored glow, and between the booze, the music, and the view, the ladies were thoroughly enjoying every moment. In fact, they were still going strong by daybreak when finally Anthony said he needed to get some sack time. So, with the redhead in tow, he left.

Anthony Delmonte and fishing buddies with tuna catch

CHAPTER 50

CHARLIE HAD SET up a charter boat, a fifty-footer, the day before. By eight in the morning, all the lines were out. "Hey, Charlie, you got a whale or what?" yelled Anthony as the reel screamed and the line spun out off the spool.

At home, they had a new sixty-foot Bertram to replace *The Rebound* (this one named *The Q99*) with every fishing accessory possible and a fully stocked bar. They did not have time to bring that boat down to Miami, so they chartered the best one they could find. They knew many boat captains and marinas in the area after having brought the old *Rebound* to Miami (then Havana) many times.

"Pull those other lines in. I think I got a good one here, pal," shot back Charlie. The fighting chair pitched a bit forward, and Charlie pulled the tip of the rod, straining every muscle. The captain and the two mates took note of the bend in the rod. The wheelman was directed to slow to a very slow forward, just enough to keep a tight line. The mates rushed to the other three rods and outriggers, hauling them in and preparing for bringing in the fish.

Charlie yelled, "Turn to port! He's coming around." The wheelman had already gotten the word from the mate in the crow's nest tower and was guiding the boat to ease the line. "He's diving! God, he's diving deep." The reel screamed, and the mate poured half a bucket of fresh water over the huge reel and wiped a wet cloth over Charlie's strained face and the back of his hands. "Geez, he won't stop. Anthony, is this one of your throwbacks?" joked Charlie.

Anthony had been in the fighting chair many times with great results. The marlin he caught in Havana years before was close to or even a world record. Anthony peered over the side and watched the line run one side, then the other. "Charlie, it's your buddy down there, Big Tuna," Anthony joked back. The movement of the line and deep diving patterns meant it was indeed a tuna. The battle took over an hour, and once Anthony could see the line begin to slack a little, Charlie began the long process of hauling the big guy up from the depths. Anthony knew that Charlie had now won. "Hey, Charlie, you want me to cut the line now?" Anthony said, more as encouragement than a joke.

Charlie's arms ached, and his back was in agony. "Wait till I bring him up and put him in your lap," chided Charlie.

The mates yelled to the captain. All four ran to the side with gaffs. "I'm gonna hook a leader line to this big fella before we haul him over," shouted the captain to the mate. All four joined in, and Anthony and E grabbed gaffs as well. They all pulled, and finally the huge fish was flopping on the deck, spewing blood all over.

"My God, look at this monster," said the mate in broken English. "Madre Mia, you got some fish here man."

Charlie said nothing, grinning ear to ear. Fishing these big ones was serious business; the jokes aside, these men knew that the ultimate fishing triumph was to pull up to the dock, fish flags flying, and these monsters gazing back up. "We can't ice this guy much. He's too big. I'll keep him cool and wet," said the second mate.

Charlie finally regained his composure and got up from the chair. Anthony went to his side. "Congratulations, Charlie. This guy is world class. You did a beautiful job for a beginner," said Anthony. Charlie, who taught Anthony to fish, just grinned and nodded.

The day wore on, and several more fish were boated. The captain was delighted. "I thought you fellas were greenhorns; looks like you've been out once or twice before," he said. With that, he broke out a bottle of fifty-year-old scotch. As the sun began setting, they pulled the big vessel into port. Several other boats were already in, many with four or five flags flying. Since there were fourteen flags flying, the dock crowd thought there must be a joker on board.

The captain yelled to a dock guy, "Tell Sam to send me three more hands for a while. We are gonna need some help." The crowd began to build as one big fish after another was flopped onto the dock. Finally, a tow rope and portable block and tackle hoisted the big catch off. The mandatory trophy photo could hardly capture the big haul hanging and laying dockside.

"Hey, Charlie, let's get a hamburger," Anthony joked, and they all laughed.

They sold off most of the catch and tipped the captain and crew handsomely. The mate cut out about fifty pounds of choice center tuna steaks, wrapped them in ice, and packed them in coolers. The mate loaded the big Buick that Henry had graciously sent over, and with that, Anthony said, "Okay, we finished the scotch. Let's go."

The flight back six days later was the quietest time all three had in the last week. Though exhausted, hungover, muscles strained from fishing, screwing, and carousing all night, they hardly showed any signs of wear, except for E. He looked like a ghost. His eyes were sunk in his head, his face white, and he was slurring his speech even in the morning. On the plane, Anthony finally figured it out. "What the fuck have you been doing? Cocaine! Disgraziato, you shit! You fucking dope addict. I should have left you there. You cock sucker. Look at you! Do this again, and I'll crush your fucking nuts." Anthony was seething, and he slapped E across the mouth so hard with the back of his beefy hand that his head spun back and a trickle of blood came from the edge of his mouth. Charlie, sitting across the aisle, shook his head and squinted, his eyes closed. That just added to E's embarrassment. The stewardess, who saw it all, looked away, too frightened to say a word.

Fall was a busy time at the piers.

"E, I'm leaving for the city; we have two truckloads coming in, and we have to have the ship stores for the America out first thing tomorrow, so be sure the trailers are all set up and the boxes, bills of loading, and order forms are done upstairs," Anthony instructed.

Anthony went uptown by cab and met Mr. Roth with the two bankers at CCC (Commercial Credit Corporation). "We'll need about seventy grand, Roth," said Anthony.

The two men looked at Roth and then looked over the papers in Roth's folder. "Okay, that's fine. You got the rates here. You got to sign these forms." Anthony did and quickly left.

When he arrived at George's, the place was packed even though it was early. It was unusually quiet. There was a small TV at the end of the bar and a radio in the center of the dining area. "Is he gone?" one guy at the bar asked the bartender.

Anthony had noticed the streets were unusually uncrowded on his way downtown, with very few people walking the sidewalks. He suspected that something important had happened. Finally, he heard the news commentator say, "It is confirmed the president has been shot and is seriously wounded. Several others in the motorcade were also hit, and the country is on full alert."

"Whew," said Anthony to himself. His mind began to spin. Kennedy shot, others shot. Who? Who else? He noticed things in the place were getting a bit chaotic. He had arranged a meeting that day at his usual spot at George's. "Hey Frankie," Anthony called to the bartender. "I gotta go early. Something came up. Give me your phone." Frankie handed him a phone. "Hello. Hello, Dottie, it's me. Call Paulie. Tell him we're off for today. I'll be back."

E was waiting at the ferry terminal door when Anthony walked off the boat. "Hey, this is something. There's a crew at the place—Nicky, Bobby G, and others. Paulie called in too." Anthony said nothing as they drove off. When he got out of the car, Nicky was on the loading dock.

"Hey, D, let's go inside." They walked into the cooler and then through the cooler into a freezer locker.

"Look, we got guys to move, you know, Miami guys. They need to disappear for a long while with this one," said Nicky.

"Okay. I'll put them through the pipeline with my main salesman down there." Anthony knew then that John's conversation in Miami had been accurate. He knew the entire connection in a moment.

"Who knows what's to happen—heat, shutdowns, whatever, we'll see. I got to go," Nicky said.

"Okay. I'll let you know when it's done. You want me to let one of your guys know over at your place? I can just say tell Nicky 'we got the ribs.'"

"Yeah, okay, see ya," said Nicky.

The next days and weeks that followed resulted in high-security alert on many levels. The piers turned very quiet, and feds were in and out every day. City cops were on alert as well as the entire story

unfolded on television, in newspapers, and on radio. Anthony's operation slowed. The entire nation paused during these days and the
Kennedy funeral. No one wanted to talk to anyone or be seen out
of concern for the heavy police surveillance all over. LBJ, the new
president, had little time to get his staff together, and the US Justice
Department became immediately obsessed with the single issue of the
assassination. Eventually, the months passed, and there was a measurable ease in law enforcement on the daily activities of the New York
crews. But the link was eventually known to Bobby Kennedy. No one
knew exactly what he had learned or how close he was to peeling the
several layers of insulation to the core of the action. The conspiracy
speculations were front-page news every day.

"You know the little guy is friendly with Sinatra. He told him that
Frank thought JFK was a stand-up guy and that his father was like one
of our friends. They were all lying pricks. They all dumped us after
the election, but Bobby was the worst of them all. He used his father's
friendships to learn about some of our operations, even those that
helped the old man and the election effort. Then he turned around and
shoved it up our asses. The fuck had it in mind all the time, to come
after us to make a big name for himself. He had his brother's and his
father's blessing. The old man figured that once his son was president,
they were invincible and insulated. How stupid and arrogant. He did
business with our guys for his whole life and still never understood us.
Maybe it was that little prick Bobby that convinced him. Bad instincts.
Frank liked the guy so much he made him a celebrity with our friends
and his crowd. He even fixed him up with Marilyn Monroe, some
thanks. Frank wasn't stupid. He saw a chance to get in the inner circle,
the big power. I guess he figured he had enough shit on John-Boy that
he would never turn on him, what with the election, the booze, the
broads, and all the rest. It's hard to believe. Roselli sent his thanks by
the way. You know he's close with Carlo and Momo and those guys.
You have friends there. Hopefully things will cool down now unless
the little prick keeps things hot. I'll see you," said Nicky.

Anthony figured that this assassination thing was very dangerous.
These frigs could use it for leverage or hook up with some Sicilian faction in the old country to cause grief. Maybe not. Anyway, keeping a

low profile was smart, even if it hurt business for a while. He began to turn his attention to the connections he had in the Caribbean.

Apparently, things just never really cooled down. One after another, things happened. Within just a few short years, the little guy, Carlo, died, and his son-in-law, Paulie, got the power. Bobby Kennedy had a short run, but finally the political fortunes turned on him as well. His party lost, and LBJ quit, and Nixon was elected. Anthony still couldn't figure out the Sirhan-Sirhan assassination connection, but either way, Bobby, the little prick, was gone. Maybe the Hoffa thing, Marilyn, and all that was just too neat a package to buy, but there were too many business problems to deal with to think about those things that had no effect on the immediate future. Dealing with the changes in the shipping industry was tough enough. Big changes occurred almost overnight. The unions could not stop the changes, as they had lost their juice with both the politicians and the shipping lines.

American shipping in general fell off at an alarming rate. Other countries were much laxer with regulations, so shipping generated around registries in places like Liberia. Then all the shipping of goods became containerized. Very little stock shipped got damaged, so there wasn't much in the line of distressed or salvaged cargo. Even storage fell off, and Anthony Delmonte's business was seriously in decline.

CHAPTER 51

"YOU LITTLE PRICK!" Tony yelled as he lunged at Emilio, who was just walking through the office door. "You thieving little prick bastard," Tony yelled again as he grabbed Emilio by the front of his shirt at the neck. Once he assured himself that he had a firm grip, he swung the back of his left hand across Emilio's face with all his might. Emilio's head rolled to the side, and blood ran from the corner of his mouth and nose. Emilio was so shocked at the attack that he had no time to protect himself. Now stunned and wobbly, he was hardly aware of what had happened. Tony brought his big arm back and this time, with his left hand opened, smacked Emilio's face on the other side, causing blood to trickle out the right corner of his mouth as well. Emilio's face flushed bright red, and he slumped against the top of his desk, sending the phone, papers, pens and pencils, rolodexes, and other things flying in all directions.

Tony's face was contorted in rage. He released his grip and at the same time grabbed Emilio by the throat with his other hand. Almost simultaneously, his clenched right hand dug deep into Emilio's abdomen, and he doubled over. "You steal from me, you fucking prick. I should break your fucking legs," yelled Tony as Emilio slid down onto the floor. Tony wiped the spattered blood from his face, looked down on his white shirt, and saw it too got dirty. This only seemed to anger him more, and he kicked Emilio's writhing legs a few times out of frustration. "Look what you made me do," Tony said disdainfully. "Get up and go get yourself cleaned up before I really beat the shit out of you, *cafone*," Tony finished.

E could hardly breathe, much less stand. He gasped for breath while clutching his stomach. It took him several minutes to recuperate enough to speak "Tone, what the hell, Jesus Christ."

"Shut up, you fuck, or you'll get more. I'll put your cock up your ass. Steal again from me, and you won't be able to walk. Got that?" fumed Tony. E tried to think what he had been careless about when he pocketed money for something he sold, either from one of the dry storage warehouses or food operations. His mind searched through the deals he had recently done. He had pocketed money several times this week alone but was trying to think of a major amount that would be easily missed.

He knew when Tony was in this kind of mood, it was better to leave him alone. Fortunately for E, the phone rang, and it gave him the chance to walk out to the bathroom as Tony answered the phone. E stumbled into the bathroom and looked in the mirror over the sink. His puffed-up face was smeared with blood, and his lips were all puffed up and split at the corners of his mouth. Blood had run out his nose and down his chin and neck onto his shirt. His hair was stuck against his scalp with blood. His gray pants were speckled with blood, and a big wet area was visible from his waist to his knees. Apparently when Tony hit him in the stomach, he peed his pants. His eyes were beginning to swell as well. He had such an ache in his stomach that he could hardly straighten up. He finally caught his breath, but when he bent over the sink, he immediately felt a rush of saliva fill his mouth, and he vomited uncontrollably into the sink. He felt his knees buckling and grabbed the sides of the sink to steady himself. He was sorry he had drunk three large beers with lunch now, since the foaming sludge was choking him as it gushed from his swollen mouth.

"Yeah, I need at least thirty feet of freezer space in the shop for this load. And we'll need enough dry space for about 150 cartons. Get back to me when you know what's available over the next week and how long it will take to sail from New York to St. Lucia."

He had expanded his operations in the Caribbean over the last few years, primarily due to a series of unforeseen events, luck, if there was such a thing. His father had said, "You make your own luck. Fate is a flexible and ever-changing thing, *figlio mio*. The grace of God and your own personal responsibility is the most important forecaster of your success or failure in life. You get up in the morning, and you decide how you can accomplish meaningful things each day. Don't waste your time. Time is like money, and ambition and perseverance are luck. Just be a little cautious. You don't want to tickle the devil's ass."

CHAPTER 52

THE LAST THING Emilio wanted to do was piss Tony off any further, so he kept out of his sight for the rest of the afternoon. Nicky and his brothers, on the other hand, nephews to the big boss, Carlos Gambini, were constantly in and out of Tony's place making deals.

"He's in the office, Nick, but he's in a mood," E yelled back. Nicky waddled in through the anteroom area and into the front office.

"Hi, Nick. Be with you in a minute. I'm on the horn here to make a connection to the islands," Tony explained.

"I got a deal for you, maybe some stuff for the islands too," Nick responded.

Tony finished on the phone and turned to Nick. "What you got?"

"Well, first off, I got a food supplier that can drop off coffee, crackers, canned tuna, can tomatoes, fry oil, and other restaurant supplies four or five times a week. We cut this guy in for a piece, and he'll show up nearly every day. He said he might get two or three other drivers to help too if he can get to the dispatcher as well. If this thing is played right, we can do $300 or $400 a day from each of these guys; maybe five grand a week, and we give each guy $250, and we split sixty-forty but count in $250 for the dispatcher. That leaves $4,000 a week to divvy up. We got the warehouse, and you can do the delivery since you got the men and the trucks. We have the operation covered from inside too. I talked to cousin Carl. One of his guys is wired into the comptroller of the distributor. They do millions of dollars a month. They are a subsidiary of United Foods, US. Leakage like this, with guys inside, the fixing books can never be traced. Their warehouse man and accountants are all on Carl's payroll, so now we are golden. Can you handle your end and retail this stuff?"

Tony looked Nicky in his big, rosy face and noticed, as if for the first time, just how many freckles this redheaded Italian had. Tony's wheels were turning. "Nick, I got to get more trucks and at least two more drivers. I have enough stops to retail the stuff, but I got to reach out probably to the Jersey and Maryland shores, maybe even Virginia and south, but I can handle it. I need to get at least fifty-five percent. I can run guys and do the collection within thirty days and guarantee the cash. That's not easy. If I get stiffed, I will still come up with my end."

Nick looked back. He knew he did not have anyone as clever as Tony with this kind of a deal and with his connections and outlets. He also knew Tony was tough when it came to deals like this, but he respected him because he knew his word was good. "Okay, fifty-five percent to your end. We will likely start in a week. Now there may be something else too. It's not a done deal yet, but I got a connection working on a deal for cigarettes, maybe a carload a week. Getting them in is no problem, but with no stamps on them, they are a problem. The feds, the state—it's a lot of heat. I asked Carl who we had that's good with either the stamp offices or the printer who puts this stuff out, who has the control. Poppy has the vending machines and distribution, but we need a quiet place to store and stamp this stuff, a safe place too, maybe your second-floor dry space or your building next door. The second floor is better, safer; no one can see in, and we can back right up to the loading dock at night and not be seen. You got the elevator, and with three guys, we can get this stuff in and out of here in two or three hours, twice a week, in and out. Then all we need is two guys to lay stamps and repack the cartons," Mike said.

Jimmy Hoffa

Robert F. Kennedy
and Jimmy Hoffa

Tony thought about how he needed to refit the building so that he could have guys work without detection. He already had half the 122 Police Precinct on the pad or doing something for the bosses there. It cost a fortune, but from the stuff he was getting off the docks and the protection he had on the island and even in Brooklyn and the Bronx, it was worth it. He had separate deals in downtown New York (Manhattan) that was a different deal. Then he had to give Nicky something to pass along to Carlo as well to keep him happy and to keep the rest of the dock guys in line. Ever since "Tough" Tony Anastasia got the docks under control and his brother Albert, likely the most feared made guy in New York history, to that point (except maybe for the old guys like Charlie Lucky), all had been set in a very specific order. The lineage transfers from Luciana eventually to Carlos really had been pretty orderly. Now Nick's cousin, Tommy Scotti, was taking over for his uncle Al DiBriggio, who was turning eighty years old. Tommy would keep the unions in line so not only the docks were good, but they had a connection to the truckers, tradesmen, food suppliers, and even the city workers. Carlo and Jimmy Hoffa, the union boss, had an understanding as well, and the whole operation, which took nearly thirty years to put together, piece by piece, worked like a charm. Everybody ate. Sure, there were problems from time to time, but there was a steady stream of goods, cash, and enough scams to keep all the crews in line and finance all the new ones. They had people in every political club, and organized guys were part of the staff of every major political player from Bob Wagner's office to Mario Biaggi in his Bronx congressional office to Abe Stark in the Brooklyn Borough president's office. Donny Manes from the Bronx ended up running Queens. Borough President Alberto Maniscalci ran Staten Island along with "Black" Jack Murphy, the congressman. The Democratic organization had a shadow framework within, and Carlo held the wires to it all.

The wild cards were guys like Mike McQueenan, the Transit Workers Union president. This guy was born in Ireland and spoke very broken English. He had all the Irish, blacks, and Puerto Ricans in his pocket because he was the most difficult guy to control when it came to contract deals for hourly wages. He didn't have the sense to realize he needed some support from the politicians, and his arrogant ravings were just what played well with the Irish. He yelled and screamed, red faced, at the mayor's negotiators and wasn't afraid to do so in front of the news media.

If Al Shanker, the NY teachers' union guy, was Mr. Professional smartass, Mike was a terrorist, round and red faced and known to down a fifth of Jameson's Whiskey in a single sitting. He had big, strong arms and would punch out anyone who crossed him. He was a problem for the union continuity. The other union guys in the city would be looking for the same deal that McQueenan cut for his group. The politicians would get flack because the city could not pay that kind of money unless they raised taxes and made cuts in some other places. It was a vicious cycle. "We ought to slip something into that Irish prick's whiskey cup," Tony Scotti would say since the control of the unions was his responsibility. Carlo would give the orders to Nicky, and then Scotti would line up the guys. Letting Mike McQueenan disrupt the order was a problem that needed a solution.

Anthony had ended up in the island of St. Lucia on one of his fishing expeditions, years before. The island had just left the British Commonwealth but still used BWI currency. Flirting with Fidel's brand of "socialismo" proved disastrous for this small island. The economy failed, food was scarce, and unemployment soared. Men worked for thirty-five cents a day if they could find work. It became a way of life. Abject poverty became nearly an accepted lifestyle for most of the islanders. The island's natural untouched beauty impressed Anthony. While the roads were nearly all dirt paths cut as former donkey cart routes, there were few places to travel to around the island. The two main cities were Contant and Vieux Fort.

These islands were used during the war as supply stations since shipping from the Caribbean was largely noneventful. Supply to the African continent or elsewhere in the world from this area had its advantages. The island had a large concrete supply building complex in Castries. The buildings were actually in good condition since this place, with the exception of an occasional hurricane or earthquake, rarely experienced bad weather of any kind. There was a group of capitalists, including some high-level British businessmen, who noted how the socialist experiment was failing and sensed it would not be too difficult to get support for a team of locals to take over government either through a democratic election or by a coup. It only mattered how quickly it could be done and how much of the socialized confiscated property would be available for snatching up if a friendly government took over.

"I think this guy Pompton has a good chance of taking over the government. His family has been a power on this island for centuries. He has key people in the business community and government who know where well-placed bribes and threats will have the maximum effect," Anthony said to Mel "Doc" Firamosca, his buddy and potential investor. "We can literally take over several business operations as exclusive operators. There is no likelihood of gambling coming here due to the strong Roman Catholic Church influence on government, and really, everyday life on this island has not been much interest to either US or European interests, neither tourist business nor organized crime. Once we have the premier on our side, his word is law." Anthony had already gotten Doctor Tompson, another old friend, to invest months ago. This was an unspoiled paradise. The lure of investing in such a place was irresistible, and a whole range of entrepreneurs did.

The Pompton regime permitted Anthony to secure the island's only liquor import license. The old government warehouses nationalized and owned by the government were leased for an amount equal to the cost of refurbishing these defunct buildings. Refrigeration, electricity, plumbing, sanitation, and other parts to the buildings' superstructures, roofs, windows, doors, and floors all were reworked.

Soon containers full of every kind of domestic product flowed into the warehouses. The boarded-up shops downtown, dozens and dozens of them, were also leased to Anthony for refurbishment costs only. Stores required labor, and even the meager labor rate meant growth to capitalism again. The government was also a consumer. The dormant island began to attract shoppers from the cruise crowd to nearby islanders. A deal was made to install a new dockside petrol station as well, and the island quickly became a fuel stopover.

It was never known exactly how, but the former British prime minister Sir Anthony Eden heard of the economic rebirth of the island. He had seen to it that his friends in the medical community found a way to get donations to the local Roman Catholic hospital, St. Francis of Mercy. Eventually medical supplies worth millions were sent in. The nuns decided in gracious appreciation to have a residential wing built at the end of the hospital grounds. It was a two-bedroom apartment fully equipped with kitchen, dining room, two bathrooms, and, most important, a communications room with a communication radio that had worldwide coverage. It was Anthony's to use whenever he chose to.

"Mr. Anthony, please come to see us," said Sister Maria. She greeted him right there on the tarmac as he exited the small commuter prop plane, which had just landed. The plane had twelve seats and usually was full. This day, there were only five passengers; however, all the seats were purchased by presale to one English fellow. The group of four men occupied the entire back of the plane; Anthony had occupied the two front seats.

There was a small white open canopied vehicle waiting at one side of the stair; on the other side stood a group of men who looked like military. A boy took Anthony's luggage. He got into the sister's vehicle and beckoned the young fellow who was behind the wheel. "Dominic, okay," and off they went.

The hospital in Contant was about a fifteen-minute car ride. The sister spoke to Anthony for nearly the entire trip. She told him how all the supplies and medicine helped the local people, naming each person, their affliction, their treatment, and their cure. The vehicle pulled up to the end of the property, and the mother superior, Helene, stood by the door.

"Mr. Anthony, Mr. Anthony, welcome back. God bless you," said the nun. "We are honored to have you here. I have a small gift for you. We can never repay you for all you have done for this order and the island people," said the sister. "This place is yours whenever you choose. It is now the Mr. Anthony Place. Our sisters will take care of your needs there anytime you need them. They will bring you food and do your clothing. You and your guests are home with us here. God bless you."

Anthony was overwhelmed. "Why thank you, Sister. This is just too much. Your people are so kind to me. Thank you." He opened the door and, followed by the nuns and the young driver, explored the new apartment. There were a few rooms to rent on that side of the island, and most were filthy places over a noisy bar, infested with rats and insects. This place was pristine, white walls, white tile floors, even white rattan furniture. Large fans spun overhead, and the grated and screened windows allowed the breeze and smell of the flower bushes along the outside walls to fill the place with a natural perfume. Tony was impressed.

The Tin House was a combination bar, restaurant, meeting place, news station, transportation station, taxi station, charter boat rental booth, and generally the hub of the town. There were wide verandas and an expansive lobby area with people bustling in and out. Anthony sat at the end of the long wooden bar sipping black rum over ice. "Billy, you have to tell your uncle that if we take over his taxi cabs, he will still have work. I will hire him as a driver and pay him a weekly salary even if he doesn't have many passengers. The cars are old anyway. You will run the cabs for me. I'll give you fifty dollars a week. You pay the driver. I can have six new cars shipped in."

"Yes, yes, Mr. Anthony, I will be sure I see you tomorrow with my uncle. We will do that, yes, yes," said Billy.

Two men walked in that obviously did not fit in with the local color. Dressed in open-collar linen shirts and black linen pants, they strolled around the room, eyeing every person at the tables and bar. Anthony continued his conversation with Billy Bash but watched the men out of the corner of his eye. One of the men sat at an empty table in a corner of the large room, while the other one walked out. Within minutes, he walked back in, and two men followed him. The first three looked like military, the men he saw on the plane. The last man was older with gray hair. He was tall and wore a linen suit. His face was lined and tan, and his mustache was trimmed. He sat with the others, and a waiter went over to them. Words were exchanged, and soon a tray with several bottles was set before them with glasses.

After a half hour, one of the men got up and approached Anthony. "Mr. Anthony, I believe?" he said.

Anthony looked the young man up and down before answering, "Who's asking?"

The fellow's face was blank, but he responded, "Pardon me, there is no one who could have introduced us, and I apologize for just walking up to you like this. However, my superior would very much like to meet you. I can assure you of his earnest intention."

"Well, who is he?" said Anthony.

"Well, I assume you are familiar with our political system in Great Britain. My employer is a former political official. He is Sir Anthony Eden," said the man.

Anthony instantly matched the name and face, the former prime minister, grayer, older but surely him. "Oh, certainly, it would be a pleasure," said Anthony.

The two walked over, and Sir Anthony stood and stretched out his hand. "Mr. Anthony, pleased to meet you, sir," Anthony said.

"My pleasure, Sir Anthony. Please join us," and Sir Anthony held his hand out to a nearby chair.

"I understand that you have been very instrumental in rejuvenating the economy here. You are to be applauded for your efforts. This poor nation was really in need of help," said Sir Anthony.

"Well, I try to help, you know, a bit at a time, and it seems things are a little better," Anthony said. In the meanwhile, he was concerned. Would this guy try to muscle in with some kind of political scam?

"I have been involved in business for many years in these islands. "You have done well here," said Eden.

"Well, I think this end of the Caribbean has great potential. I have considered doing more," said Anthony in an effort to bait the hook.

"Really, my trip here is precisely for the same reason. Perhaps we have some common interests. I'm always eager to explore joint ventures with someone who has proven successful in the islands. Not many make a go of it and succeed," said Eden.

"I have located three refrigerated cargo ships. Every island within a reasonable distance has a market for fresh or frozen foods, meat, poultry, fish, prepared foods, and quality goods. They'll pay five bucks for a quart of fresh milk. I already have operating refrigeration and freezer warehouses. Frozen and refrigerated cargo ships have no problem docking near my warehouses at the end of the island, breaking down these big loads and sending my own smaller ships to the islands, especially those that large intercontinental have a difficult time unloading without large booms or cranes for the containers. My ships can be unloaded either by hand or small motorized lifts right onto the smallest docks. Getting sales and business permits for the various governments is likely my only obstacle," Anthony said, setting the hook.

"Oh, that can be worked out easily, I think, if the right party were to negotiate such treaties. What sort of gross business do you believe can be generated?" asked Eden.

"Well, it would be slow at the start, but I think at least twelve to fifteen stops could generate ten thousand each, and bimonthly stops are possible with growth from there. In a few years, it would be possible to generate millions."

Eden looked over at Anthony and then to the fellow on his right. "Well, Neal, what do you think? Neal here is a fairly bright financial professional, although he only graduated midclass from Oxford," joked Eden.

"I think it is interesting, sir. I'd like to see a *shedyouall* (schedule)," he answered in an extremely thick English accent. This fellow was tall and slim, with a drawn face and wiry frame. He was much older than the other fellows, who were obviously valets and bodyguards. Anthony noticed the younger two had bulges under their waistbands, along with the outline of holsters.

Anthony waved to the fellow at the bar, who jumped off the barstool and scurried over to the table. Billy Bash was a short, thin, dark brown-skinned fellow who had a strange combination of features. He appeared to be Caucasian but also possibly Polynesian or Oriental as well, and his crumbled black head of hair made him seem more Mediterranean. "Yes, Mr. Antony."

"Billy, go to the desk and get me a printing pad and pen; bring it here," said Anthony.

As Anthony sketched out figures and details of various elements of the project, Neal Shoreham peered over his shoulder. The detail of the vessel size, capacity, age, tonnage, power specs, and manufacture yard were all listed. Various other factors included rental cost per square foot of ground storage refrigeration, number of crews, hourly costs, and so on. Within twenty minutes, the first few pages were complete. Mr. Eden was quite astonished by what was unfolding before him as a complete business prospectus, and he kept sipping his Bombay Gin and Quinine water. Less than forty-five minutes passed when Anthony finally looked up and said, "This is just a rough concept but probably will give you a fairly good idea of the hardware needed as well as a customer base to start." Anthony then took a full glass of black rum and gulped down half.

Neal pored over the several sheets before him. He looked up at Eden and said, "This does, if accurate, have potential, sir."

"Okay then, let us meet again tomorrow, late afternoon, say teatime, 4:00 p.m., and if all is well, our deal shall be sealed," said Eden. He extended his hand to Anthony, who took it, and both clasped strongly. "Please consider that a fifty percent partnership is the only possible way to make this deal happen. We have the funds in BWI currency here in the bank. Neal can handle the details of the draws needed to purchase ships and set up a payroll system." They shook hands again, and Anthony left. The others stayed.

Eden turned to Neal, "Well, it seems our background check expenses were worthwhile." Eden's network of friends and associates in the British Intelligence, MI-5, had been relied upon to do a background check on Delmonte. They did reveal that some of his business associates were unsavory characters, but Delmonte's records in St. Lucia and the Caribbean were clean. Furthermore, Eden himself had done business deals with people who had checkered backgrounds, but with Anthony, there were no conflicts of interest. His relationships indeed seem to verify that he and his associates did quite well in the deals they had together. Also, Anthony's caution was noted since the few arrest records he did have were for minor assault, gambling, and lesser charges.

After reeling in this big fish, Anthony felt confident the operation would work within weeks. The ships were purchased, and operations were under way. Neal was the communication point. In fact, it wasn't until several months later that Delmonte and Eden even met face-to-face again. By that time, the operations were up and running and already generating profits.

"We are having a little dinner party on the boat later on. Would you please attend?" Sir Anthony inquired of Delmonte.

Delmonte had been shuttling back and forth between the US mainland and the islands constantly. "Sure, thank you."

Delmonte arrived at dockside. The dress was casual. The small launch brought him out to a huge yacht. A crewman welcomed Anthony aboard and then escorted him to the state dining room. There were about twenty-five people there enjoying cocktails. "Anthony, glad you could make it," said Neal, before leading him to the host.

"Hello there. Neal will introduce you to our guests. Actually, we were a bit surprised to have so large a group. It seems an old friend of mine is filming a movie here, and I bumped into him downtown."

As the party continued, Anthony was introduced to Rex Harrison, Samantha Eggar, and others in the cast. Miss Eggar was a beautiful, black-haired woman who found Anthony's New York accent "most interesting."

"Well, do they call you Samantha, Sam, or what?" Anthony asked.

"You call me whatever you like; just keep talking. I love your accent," she answered. He was over fifty now but still viral.

By midnight, Anthony and Sam, as he finally called her, were out at the end of the bow of the boat, drinking from a bottle of champagne. She had drunk most of two bottles herself and was feeling no pain.

"So, what do you think of my shape?" she asked Anthony, pushing her breasts up and opening her mouth, mimicking a sex pose like Marilyn Monroe or Mamie Van Doren, the sexpots of the day.

"You are beautiful," he answered and laid his right hand over one of her pushed-up breasts. The woman began to squirm and gyrate under his hand and pressed her body against him. She took another swig from the bottle of Dom Perignon and then pulled the front of her dress down, exposing her two perfectly formed breasts in the moonlight.

"You like these?" she asked with her lips rubbing the left side of his face and ear.

"You are a gorgeous woman," he answered before turning to kiss her full on the mouth. She became insatiable and began rubbing his crotch.

"Oh, what a big boy you are. Now what can you do for a poor little wench like me?" she asked. Anthony's instincts took over. He bent her over the rail, lifted her dress, and stripped off her silk panties. She gasped as he entered her. She was at once embarrassed, excited, and wanton. She reached orgasm in less than a minute, then again, then a third time. Anthony pulled away, and she melted down on the ship's deck. "Oh my, oh my," she said. She could not figure out what more to say. She rubbed her genitals and then pulled her dress back into position. "Oh my," she said again. Her face was flush red. She touched the side of his leg, and he looked down at her with a slightly amused look on his face. "You are quite something, aren't you," she said. "Oh my, no one has ever done that to me—I mean I never. Oh, I mean oh, oh I, please hand me that champagne," she finished, nearly out of breath. She swallowed two more gulps of champagne and then composed herself and stood up.

Suddenly, an urge came over her. She locked her arms around him and whispered in his ear "Please, please do that to me again, please," her voice now out of breath, her body pressed against him tight and the nipples of her breasts stiff, showing through the cover of the dress.

He looked back at her and answered, "I think we have to move this somewhere else, not here."

No one in the party could figure out where Samantha had to go when she and Anthony took off in the launch in the middle of the night.

The next day when she did not show up for the morning cast assembly, the director sent three of his people to look for her. They became concerned that night when she had not returned to the rooming house village that the entourage was using.

It was not until the following afternoon that she returned. "My God, what happened to you?" Felix the assistant director asked her as she slowly walked into the area when a scene was being filmed. She had a man's shirt and white pants on, and her eyes were puffy. Her hair was tied back with a thin piece of hemp, and she had no shoes.

"Oh, I just decided to explore the island." She was walking with a strange gait. Felix looked at her.

"Yeah," he said, "I bet. You look like you've been in the sack for the last two days. Don't let the others see you. Come with me. I'll clean you up," Felix finished. Felix was a homosexual, but he loved Miss Eggar. Back at her room, he drew a bath and pulled out some towels. He put bath oils in the water, and as she stripped off her clothes, he wrapped a thin robe around her and led her to the bath. She slipped in. He went to the kitchenette counter and took out a large glass, squeezed out juice from a few oranges and a lemon and poked a hole in a coconut and extracted the milk. He mashed in a banana and added sugar and a shot of rum. "Here, drink this." She gulped it down and smiled back at him sheepishly.

When she rose, he noticed the water had a reddish tint. He looked and saw telltale reddish drops of water in her pubic hair. "Are you bleeding?" he asked.

"Only a little," she answered.

"God, who have you been with?" he asked. She grunted and exited the bath. He wrapped her in the robe, led her to the bed, and rolled her in. Within minutes, she was out, still smiling.

CHAPTER 53

E CAME OFF the plane with a small canvas pouch. "Hey, big guy." he said to Anthony.

"You brought what I need, no problems?" said Anthony.

"Yeah, it was easy," said E as he handed the pouch to Anthony.

He unzipped it, peered inside, flipped the packs of bills over, counted them, and closed it. "Good, very good. Let's go," said Anthony.

They drove off in the four-seater car and ended up by the apartment at the hospital. "Hello, Mr. Anthony," said Billy Bash. "Where do we need to go today?" he asked.

"I need to get to Eden's yacht," Anthony replied. They drove back toward the marina.

"Hey, look at that," said E. There was a large group of people and a jeep and cameras all over the beach cove. There were several animals milling about and people dressed in costumes from the early 1900s.

Anthony spotted Sam in the middle of all the commotion. "Billy, pull in there." The little car slid to a stop, and the three men got out.

"Mr. Harrison, the scene needs to be reshot because of the sun's position at the end," said a fellow dressed in a T-shirt, shorts, leather sandals, and a cap turned backward.

"Shoot again, shoot again. Come on. Let's get it over with. It's too hot!" said Harrison.

Samantha saw Anthony and quickly walked over to the three men. "Hello there."

"Hello," said Anthony. "Sam, meet Emilio and Billy."

"Hi," they said in unison as they nodded their heads in her direction. Anthony and Sam then walked off toward a clump of palms.

While Anthony and Sam kept talking, E turned to Billy and asked, "Do you know what movie they are shooting here?"

Billy answered, "Oh, yes, sir. *Doctor Doolittle*. He talks to the animals, you know." E snickered.

The cameraman had set the camera. "Okay, boss!" he yelled.

"Quiet. Quiet. Quiet!" yelled the director. The camera filmed as Harrison spoke to a large snail figure. "Okay, that's a wrap."

And with that, E walked over to Sam. "Miss Eggar, I'm a big fan. I think I met you before when I was in Florida or California," said E.

"I don't think so," said Sam.

"Well, maybe you and I can get together later to talk about it," said E.

She looked him up and down and in a bland voice said, "Really, I'm very tired."

Anthony returned, and Sam walked over to him. "Your friend is just a little crude, isn't he?" she said.

"Yeah, I'll straighten him out. I have to see Eden. I'll see you later. I gotta go," said Anthony.

They drove out of sight. As soon as they had gotten out of sight of the movie shoot, Anthony turned to E. He swung the back of his hand and hit E on the side of his head, nearly knocking him out of the car. "Jeez, what was that for?" asked E, his ears ringing and his head racked with pain.

"You have to be a fucking pig to every woman you see, you prick?" said Anthony.

Finally, they reached the marina. "Oh, Mr. Anthony, I'll tell Mr. Eden you are here," said the mate at the roped gangway to the huge yacht.

The men sat at a table at the rear deck. "I've made the connection for the refrigerated ships and got the money I need for labor and start-up for my end," said Anthony.

"Well, fine, fine," said Neal, and Sir Anthony nodded his approval.

"Let's go forward then," said Anthony.

There was a sheaf of papers. The two principals signed and dated the agreements. The fish was now mounted. He was "ours."

CHAPTER 54

AS A YOUNG child, Anthony Delmonte learned that though people were permitted to immigrate to America, they were hardly accepted as equals. Anthony understood the order of things by age eight. He knew just what he could do on his own and what authority expected of him. If he was confronted by the nuns in school, he understood the power they had. So, when Donald Ryan, the tallest boy in the class, decided he would challenge that authority, Anthony and his classmates were stunned. During recess in the schoolyard at St. Sylvester's Grammar School, Sister Mary Joseph was watching over the children from first to eighth grade as they played ball or teased each other. Donald, the class bully, was bouncing a rubber ball against the brick wall while Anthony stood chatting with a few friends nearby. His tall size, blazing red hair, and broad Irish face covered with freckles seemed not at all to fit into this class. Also, Donald was held back because he failed so miserably in the prior school year and seemed now, by mid-March, headed in the same direction. His father, George, was a beat cop in Manhattan, and his mother cleaned houses. He had an older brother, Bobby, who had been in and out of jail after dropping out of high school. Through the intercession of his father, the judge in one of his burglary cases, and some friends of his father, Bobby ended up in the US Army.

Donald was arrogant and resentful. His father disciplined him with a two-inch barber's strap, but it made him all the more aggressive. His mother was a quiet, religious soul. She didn't quite know how to control the two tough boys she had nurtured as little babies. She was kind to Donald and tried to cover for him when he ended up in trouble.

The bell rang, and the schoolyard began to clear. Sister Mary Joseph stood out in the center of the playground watching as two other nuns stood at the doors gathering the kids to return to class. But on this day, Donald just kept on throwing his ball. Anthony and his friends were the last in the line going into the building and stood at the bottom of the steps. When the bell rang the last time, Sister Mary Joseph, a short, stocky, athletic woman in her fifties, paused as they began walking toward the stairway, in anticipation Donald would see her and follow her in. He did not. She yelled, "Ryan! Ryan!" He paused but did not look at her, then threw the ball again. The nun visibly stiffened and marched over to him. "Are you deaf, Ryan?" she hollered. He did not acknowledge her. With that, she grabbed his ample crop of red hair in one hand and his arm in the other. Now everyone going into the school stopped and stood still. The two nuns by the door stood with their mouths wide open looking at each other. Ryan struggled as the nun started to pull him in the direction of the doors and steps, but when Ryan twisted and turned, she could not hold her grip on his arm and only had his hair. He twisted his head and pulled back, freeing himself. The nun looked down and saw a clump of red hair still in her hand. She advanced toward Ryan, who was howling. As she approached him, he looked up and was facing her. She raised her right hand to touch his head to determine if he was bleeding. She never saw his clenched right fist. He swung at her with all his might and put his entire body weight into the punch. He struck her right on the nose. She stumbled and fell over, bleeding profusely. The two nuns now pushed the kids aside and rushed over to her. One of the nuns pulled a handkerchief from under her long black robes and put it on the sister's face. Ryan watched, his face red as a beet and his fist still clenched.

Suddenly, a group of nuns and Father Peter came running out to the scene. The priest grabbed Ryan by the back of the collar and put his right arm behind him and half-pushed and half-carried him into the school in a rush as the group of nuns assisted Sister Mary Joseph into the school. One nun commanded, "You kids go to class."

Only then did Anthony and the group disperse and scurry back into the school.

Anthony was shocked by the incident. He had been harassed by Ryan just like so many others in his class. "You greasy wop bastard, get out of my way," Ryan would say to him as he plunged through the line at lunch to the front. Ryan's contempt for the kids with Italian names was well noted. "You wop bastards came here from wopland to murder Americans, you and your Mafia," Ryan would taunt. For a boy about to turn twelve, Ryan had heard much more about New York crime than most kids his age. His father and three uncles were cops, and his grandfather was a captain in the New York Police Department who dealt with dozens of organized crime cases.

Some of Anthony's schoolmates were Italian boys and girls identified as part of Mafia families. The Dalessandros, the Gambarinis, the Casteluccis, and the Dessios had sons and daughters in St. Sylvester's School. Anthony knew these kids, and some were neighborhood friends. When the names appeared in the newspaper on charges of racketeering or union corruption, the other kids would ask questions: "Is your father in the Mafia? Does he kill people?"

Anthony knew the kids, and his family knew theirs. Growing up in the "neighborhood" in Staten Island, it was hardly a secret who was who. Nearly everyone who had family on "the Island" for a few generations somehow touched each other. Even those who had emigrated from the Bronx, Brooklyn, and Manhattan or Queens over the years to Staten Island were interconnected in various ways, going back to the original Italian immigration of the late nineteenth century.

The history of the European immigration from the time of the influx of Irish in the late 1800s, due to the potato famine, to the Germans, and Italians lived on in New York City with new immigrations. Each wave of immigrants brought new prejudices and sometime violent actions against newcomers.

Anthony often recalled the Ryan event. After the playground cleared and the children went back to class, he would sit quietly at his desk looking forward as the nun started teaching. He appeared to be paying attention, but his mind was playing the scene he had just witnessed over and over. He recalled that the nun, Sister Mary Joseph, in her haste to discipline Ryan failed to consider his reaction, even when he gave off signs that he wasn't going to obey authority. When he broke away, she sought to discover if he was injured but did so by exposing herself to his attack. Ryan's rage showed in his body language. He gathered all his body strength and hoisted his fist in a missile-like action, but he also used the shift in his torso and spring like leg motion to propel himself upward. This united effort fully increased the power of this twelve-year-old to equal that of a full-grown man. The sister, though stocky and muscular, was no match for the puncher. Apart from the fact he actually liked Sister Mary Joseph, even though she was gruff, he observed the event also as two forces in action. While he felt just a twinge of remorse for the nun, he also felt a bit of contempt for her lack of discipline.

By the following week, Ryan, having been suspended, had his father at the school advising the principal and the priest of his son's activity. When he got home from his tour of duty in Manhattan, the evening after the punching event, he learned from his wife what had occurred. Mary Catherine Ryan had been at a house nearby. The school was near a very upscale area called Emerson Hill. She was cleaning the mansion of a wealthy shipping company owner when the school principal tracked her down by phone. She rushed to the school, and when she got there, the priest, a police officer, and three nuns asked her to step into an office. There, red faced, sat Donald, his head hung low with a bandage on his head. "What happened?" she exclaimed. The boy never looked up. A young cop, Joe Sistine, took her in the hallway and told her the facts. As he related the incident, tears streamed down Mary's flushed face. She trembled. He then escorted her across the hall. There, in a large upholstered chair, Sister Mary Joseph was laid out, her feet on a chair and an ice pack on her swollen face. In a trembling voice, Mrs. Ryan whimpered, "Oh, Sister, I am so sorry. Oh my God, Sister."

The nun peered out of her left eye, as the right one was swollen shut. Her face was distorted as she lifted the ice pack. "That Donald is a bad one. He really needs help." The nun, though stung by pain, was still feisty.

The following week, George Ryan took a day off from work to bring his son to the 121 Precinct in New Dorp. There the boy was brought to the juvenile officer, who interviewed him for nearly an hour. He then brought him to another office in the building, and he was photographed. He had to fill out a series of papers with his father's help. He was handed a green card. The officer in JD, Tom Simpson, told him, "This is your juvenile delinquent card. You must carry this with you wherever you go. If you are ever involved in any other incident, you will be brought directly to the Juvenile Detention Center next door. Do you understand me?"

The boy, wide-eyed, looked at the cop and whispered softly, "Yes."

"What did you say?" bellowed the cop.

The boy increased his voice volume and with a trembling tone said, "Yes, sir." George Ryan took the boy by the shoulder and marched him to his car.

He drove a few blocks to New Dorp Lane and then turned south on Hyland Boulevard, a direction opposite of his hometown of Dorgan Hills. He drove in silence. The trip took about twenty minutes. Then they approached a semirural area and finally a large fenced-in compound. There was a large sign at the entrance driveway that read "Mount Loretto." This facility was a well-known Roman Catholic facility for homeless children and also a detention center for juvenile delinquents.

Donald began to shiver at the sight of the sign, his red face crunched up, and tears welled in his eyes. He knew well that this place was a prison for bad boys. Mr. Ryan pulled up to the main administration building and opened the passenger door. Donald tried to slide away as his father grabbed the back of his collar and pulled him out of the car. They walked swiftly to the front door and into the hallway. Mr. Ryan knocked at the door of the office with a sign next to it, "Admissions."

Father Douglas O'Brien opened it and said, "Hello, George. Come on in."

"Father, this is my son Donald. I want you to know who he is because I think he will be enrolling in your detention unit very soon. Donald, say hello to Father Doug," said George.

"Hello, Father," the boy said, standing there trembling with tears streaming down his face.

"We will take the forms we need now in case we need to bring him back," said Mr. Ryan.

"That's fine, George. Donald, you understand that your father wants the best for you, but if you get yourself in trouble again, you will come here to stay until you are eighteen years old and on your own. You understand?" said the priest.

"Yes, sir," said Donald.

"Thank you, Father," said George, and he turned, took the boy by the arm, and escorted him back to the car. "You understand that if you get yourself in any trouble again, I'll have you brought right back here. You understand?" said George.

"Yes, sir," said Donald.

After three weeks, George had Donald reinstated at school on a provisional basis. For a month or so, he stayed to himself. Sister Mary Joseph was back after a week. She wore a white bandage over the swollen, blackened side of her face, eye, and nose. Donald would look the other way and hang his head whenever he passed her. She glared at him as he passed. The students in Anthony's class buzzed about Donald until his return but never in front of the nuns or when he returned. Things got back to normal, and within two months, Donald regained his position as the school bully. He continued to push people around but made sure it was out of sight of the nuns.

As the spring days returned, the nuns permitted lunch period to be taken outdoors in the playground yard. Anthony's mother made lunches for him, his three older brothers, and two little sisters each day. Anthony and a few friends gathered at the small picnic style table at one side of the courtyard and opened their lunch packages. "What did you get?" asked Louie Radisson.

Anthony unwrapped the wax paper roll and found his sandwich. "It's a veal cutlet," Anthony said with a smile. He loved his mother's cutlets, and this one was on Italian bread with just a bit of red sauce.

He turned back to Louie when he noticed a shadow behind him. He swung his head around. There with a big, grimacing grin on his face was Donald Ryan. "What you got there, grease ball?" said Ryan.

"Uh, uh a sandwich," stuttered Anthony.

"Oh really? Well, let's see," said Ryan.

Anthony stood up and grabbed the sandwich in the waxed paper, stepped back, and held it in front of him with his left hand.

"Well, I think that's mine now," said Ryan, and he grabbed the sandwich off the paper.

Anthony turned slightly and bent his knees just a little bit. His fists were already clenched. He watched as Ryan turned his attention to the sandwich, and when he looked down, Anthony sprang into action. His right hand was below his thigh. He swung it and propelled his entire body with the swing and hit Ryan flush on the face and nose. Ryan crumpled to the ground, still clutching the sandwich in his hand. He began to bleed profusely from the nose and a cut on his cheek. He lay on his back stunned, his eyes glassed over and his mouth wide open.

"You killed him!" exclaimed Louie in an excited voice.

Just then, Ryan began to moan. Anthony stood motionless for a moment, then bent over Ryan, grabbed the sandwich, and put it on the picnic table. He went back over to Ryan, who now had his eyes wide open. Anthony straddled him, bent down, and with his clenched fist in Ryan's face said, "You touch me again or tell anybody that I hit you, I will find you every day and beat the living shit out of you till you die. You get that?" he said in a menacing voice. Ryan, still flat on his back, looked up at Anthony and saw the fire in his eyes as he spoke. "You tell them you fell running. You hear me?" said Anthony.

"Yeah, yeah okay, okay," said Ryan.

Then Anthony retreated, sat down at the table, and motioned to his three friends to sit. He began eating his sandwich. The entire matter was over in less than a minute.

Sister Mary Joseph was tending to first graders at the other side of the courtyard, so she did not notice what had happened. A few of Anthony's classmates did, however, so he looked around and put his index finger to his mouth. Then he nodded as he looked around and a group of five girls looked back at him. They each did the same, putting their finger to their mouth and nodding. So did the boys at his table and the table next to him. Ryan finally sat up and had blood streaming down his face onto his shirt and pants.

Eventually one of the nuns came out the door and noticed him on the ground. She ran to him as Sister Mary Joseph also noticed him. They both rushed over. "What happened to you?" said the nun. Ryan, still stunned and shaking, started to cry. "Are you all right?" said the sister.

"I think he was running and tripped," said Louie.

Then Angelo, another at the table, said, "Yeah, he was running real fast and stumbled." The two nuns helped Ryan to his feet.

"Ryan, Ryan, look at me," said Sister Mary Joseph. Sister Conceptual looked on.

"I fell, Sister. I fell," said Ryan.

The nuns turned to the others. "Anthony, tell all the others to go back to the classroom and call Father. He's in the office."

She looked at him and then noticed the knuckles on his right hand were cut and a bit swollen and noticed a bit of blood there too. Anthony looked back at the nun with a blank stare. She looked at Ryan and then looked back at Anthony. He shrugged his shoulders and opened his mouth as if to say something but just stood there.

A smirk crossed the nun's face, neither a smile nor a grimace. Then she nodded her head a few times and said, "Go ahead, Anthony. Do what I told you." He left with the others, and Ryan

Vincenzo Delmonte

stood there. He wanted to attack his attacker but now had a sickening feeling in his stomach and felt a weakness in his legs. He was truly afraid, afraid of Anthony and his threats. He also remembered his trip to Mount Loretto and the black barber strap his father wielded so well when he got him back home. His ass had red welts for weeks, and it hurt whenever he sat down.

Anthony said nothing more about the event, but every kid in school now treated him differently. The older girls smiled when he passed in the hall, and the older boys would grin. "Hey, Ant," they would say, or, "Ant, anybody get in your way lately?" or "Hey, Ant, got a sandwich to share?" Even Sister Mary Joseph, who used to put on a stern look as she made her way through the hallways, would stop when Anthony was going by and give him a half smile.

Throughout his life, he continued to consider plans and actions in the same way.

After leaving grade school, he spent the next four years in a much different atmosphere. New Dorp High School was built in the 1930s. The imposing brick structure, a U-shaped, five-story monstrosity, was built to house about 1,200 students. Now past midcentury, the en-rollment topped 3,800. The administrators had instituted a staggered session system when it got to the point that there were just too many students and not enough classrooms or teachers. The sessions began at 7:30 a.m., then 8:30 a.m., then 9:30 a.m. Some lunch periods were 10:00 a.m. to 11:00 a.m., and school let out at 1:30 p.m. for some kids. If a student had an after-school job, he could apply for early release—no gym class, no study hall, no lunch, no health class, five forty-minute classes and out. Anthony was one of those who attended the 7:30 a.m. session as a freshman. His older brother Vincenzo, Vince to his friends, was in his senior year. But halfway through he decided to join the marines and was gone by spring. His other brother Cal, Calegero was his given name, had moved to Manhattan to work with their uncle John as a machinist. Then there was Mario. He was a junior who was also released early to work in the family business, Columbia Market. Anthony escaped each day after class at about noon, took a bus to a transfer stop, then took two more buses and arrived at the shop about 2:30 p.m. He worked there till about 6:00 at night on weekdays and till about midnight on Friday and all day on Saturday. Salvatore Delmonte believed that his boys, like himself, had to carry their own weight to help the family, and it was a good way to keep the boys out of trouble.

The shop was founded by his grandfather, Vincenzo Delmonte, in 1909, and eventually uncles and cousins came over from Italy and opened shops in Staten Island, Brooklyn, Bronx, and Manhattan. Anthony carried the workload of a full-salaried man and was a butcher, accountant, and salesman all in one. There were four other employees and Vickie Fumo, the cashier. The market sold groceries, fresh fish, and cured meats and had a large wholesale business as well. Anthony got to meet a great number of the largest wholesale food suppliers in the greater New York area. He also met associates in trucking, shipping, ocean marine, insurance salvage, lawyers, and politicians, all of them with some kind of connection to the business.

Anthony's uncle Tony, another Anthony Delmonte, was now a large national wholesaler. He had major shipping lines as clients as well as clients in wholesale businesses.

Anthony decided shortly after enrolling in his first year in college that fitting in the general population made one less conspicuous and less likely to be noticed.

He had saved enough money to buy an old Ford sedan. Now, as he pulled into the parking lot at campus, he noticed the shiny new convertibles, foreign sports cars, and fancy coupes driven by students. He wore a sweater and chinos that first day. He then saw the guys dressed in college sweatshirts and gabardine pants, and the girls in crisp blouses and plaid, straight skirts. Some of the upperclassmen wore cardigan sweaters and shirts with ties. He shopped the next day and found the shirts he needed and a few ties.

When he received his registration forms, he Americanized his name by purposely leaving off the last "e" in Delmonte. It was his way to try to mask his ethnicity as best he could. He chose classes that would broaden his abilities not only in business but also in politics and the arts and befriended foreign students to learn about their culture and attitudes. He dated the daughters of airline CEOs and politicians and joined various college organizations and clubs, including the Arts Club and Math Society. He pledged the fraternity with the largest number of chapters in the country, Kappa Tau Epsilon, so he could visit colleges across the country. He found time to work each day and had enough money for gas, clothes, and nights out.

Working with the businesses in Manhattan and Brooklyn involved labor unions as well as other suppliers of various products and the docks where imports were shipped in. He also met those who were involved behind the scenes, the members of the underworld.

The waterfront at the North River piers along Manhattan's West Side was a constant hive of activity. The other hubs of commerce in the city were Red Hook, Brooklyn, Fulton Fish Market and Ganeswoort Meat Markets in Manhattan, and Hunts Point in the Bronx. If a truck was to be parked to pack up supplies, there was a fee to be paid unless you had a connection, someone who could vouch for you that had juice with the hierarchy that ruled the streets of the market.

If you disobeyed the rules, you might go into a supply house after parking only to find your truck nearly destroyed when you came out only a few minutes later. It was easy to tell who didn't follow the rules. The truck windows were smashed and the tires slit. Perhaps the cargo was gone as well. The fish market was the most controlled of all the markets. Here, even product flow and pricing were often set by the mob. There was a classic event that proved the power of the controllers. New Yorkers have a huge appetite for lobster tails. A conglomerate of mobsters in the fish market began buying up all the suppliers of the frozen delivery and holding it. Soon the price jumped from five dollars per pound to ten dollars, then twenty. Restaurants had the item on their menus, and the well-known places around the city had to provide lobster tails on the menu. When the price inflation got to its highest levels, supply began again.

Soon the market saw that shrimp supplies were diminishing. This business was controlled by brokers, and some of the largest of them were in Philadelphia and had New York mob connections. They controlled suppliers in the shrimp-producing areas of the south and the overseas trade. Producers and shrimpers continued to sell their entire product to a broker, who earned a commission of perhaps one-quarter or one-half cent on a pound, given the millions of pounds sold per day in the northeast market alone. Commissions were huge. Prices to the broker for product in Louisiana, Alabama, Florida, Texas, and other areas were also controlled. The mob connections in New Orleans and Florida saw to that.

Market manipulation began by buying shrimp cheaply and then holding the supply back to create demand, then selling it at inflated prices, just like the lobster event, except these brokers controlled the price at the place of supply, at the catch, even before the shrimp were caught. Contracts were not sold to other brokers for fear of serious reprisals and also because the shrimper and local wholesalers had immediate purchase of all the supply and were assured to make money. Those contracts were good as gold to the banks, who would finance shrimp captains and owners to buy more boats and wholesalers to expand warehousing and shipping.

That's how Anthony met the moguls of this underworld empire. He was careful to remain inconspicuous and always acted nonchalant as he went about his duties as a salesman or truck man or even stevedore or longshoreman working unloading ship cargo.

He learned the names of the crew captains in the union and their place in the pecking order. He noted when a man was promoted from cargo handler or simply a "shape-up guy" who did not possess a union card to the next level, then getting a card, so he had a good chance of being put with a permanent work crew who were chosen just when ships came in. Next, a man was promoted by the crew boss and his supervisors to a checker. The checker merely verified the count and matched the crate or box number to a manifest sheet. He no longer had the backbreaking job of actually lifting the cargo boxes. Crews were made up of ten longshoremen, a crew captain, and a checker as designated by union rule. Then, to augment positions, they sometimes added a checker to check the checker. This job involved verifying the work of the checker, a cushy position but also a key to scamming.

These fellows were in the perfect position to have cargo stolen, swag cargo, and often loaded to a vehicle waiting nearby. The local union manager and the hierarchy on the dockside all looked the other way as well and were very well compensated by the mob-run scammers. A call for high water, coffee break, could be a signal to move the cargo to be stolen to the waiting truck while the crew came out of the unloading order for their break. Perhaps the guard at the exit gate would be looking the other way or go out to get his coffee when this vehicle left the dock compound. It was all neatly arranged, and profits were shared by the highest levels of Mafia family members who controlled the processes as well as the union partners in the AFL-CIO.

If a very valuable shipment was scheduled to arrive, there was always great tension at the unloading. Occasionally the FBI would set up an operation to catch the thieves if the cargo had some federal jurisdiction associated with it. The most obvious product was liquor from abroad that would be taxed not only at US customs rate but in the retail end as well. While someone might get away with a bottle or two of fine scotch whiskey, it was a lot more difficult to swipe twenty or thirty cases.

Those operations, however, hardly went unnoticed. The typical FBI agent stuck out like a sore thumb, and a strange car or truck was easily spotted when it was parked in sight of a ship. Even when the Bureau guys stood by a checker to intimidate the entire crew, they simply ignored him till he went away. If there was to be a scam, the entire crew just slowed down. The ship would remain day after day. FBI operations were noted, and finally when they tired of hanging around, they would be pulled out for another assignment. Now when the obvious threat of being exposed while stealing was gone, the scam was back in operation again. The cat and mouse game rarely worked. Occasionally someone would stumble onto a warehouse with swag goods, but mostly those facilities were under the jurisdiction of New York's finest.

The pad rewarded cops, from the lowly beat cop all the way up to the captains, each one of them getting an increasing piece of the action and offering protection in return. It was all an elaborate system, and it worked well, at least for several decades. Anthony's knowledge of the inner workings of such a system was invaluable. His formal college education made him understand the financial systems of business as well as the physiology of men, religion, and art. His interaction was with a cross section of society, the mob kids and those who got to college with little money but great intellectual abilities, sons of noted physicians and daughters of airline presidents. He befriended fellows like Art Silen. Art's father was a noted Long Island neurosurgeon and an extremely wealthy man who had inherited a family fortune as well. Art was unique. He had a photographic memory and could thumb through ten pages of a textbook and then recite it, word for word, after closing the book. He never needed to study, so he often cut classes. But Art had one fatal flaw, alcohol. Art enjoyed a morning breakfast of a cold beer, and there was never an afternoon or evening that he was not at one of the college's nearby waterholes or with some friends drinking.

He also had a great talent as well. He was a mechanical genius and loved automobiles in particular. He did what he needed to do to pass his college subjects, just barely after his freshman year. When he was a dean's list student and competed to be first in his class with straight As his second semester as a freshman, he slipped to three As and three Bs, having increased his class load. His sophomore year was much different. He managed to pass every subject barely with a C average. However, his major accomplishment was not in the classroom but in a friend's garage. He managed to rebuild a 1953 Ford convertible with a massive 1952 Cadillac engine and even modified it by adding dual Carlson carburetors and a Hurst four-speed floor shift. The customized exterior had every piece of chrome removed, even the door handles. The doors operated by a hidden lever system. The car was finished in twenty-five coats of black lacquer, and there were small pinstripe decorations on the side of the fenders near the headlights and on the corners of the trunk. The interior was finished in dark crushed velvet with burgundy features. When the work was finished, Art and several friends, including Anthony, formed a caravan and went out to the end of Hyland Boulevard, a wide four-lane highway. At the south end, it widened out further. This was a desolate, uninhabited area perfect to test the speed of a vehicle on a fine concrete surface, and test they did. Art topped the "Fordilac" out at 115 miles per hour.

All were impressed. Art was on a high and invited everyone to the nearby White Horse Tavern that stayed open all night. Few made it home; most opted to sleep it off in their cars.

Art enjoyed driving at a snail's pace around the college's oval drive in front of the main building of the college. The deep-throated glass pack mufflers would echo off the stone building. Everyone passing and walking would wave or shout, "Hey, Artie," or, "Artie, my man." He became a celebrity and an altruistic one at that. Anyone who had car trouble or needed advice about their vehicle went to Artie. He fixed more cars in the parking lot of the school than the half-dozen auto garages nearby. Anthony often brought Art home to dinner with him. His bizarre lifestyle estranged him from his domineering and serious father. For many holiday occasions, Art opted not to go home at all, so Anthony brought him to his home. He sometimes brought Art to work with him as well. After work, they would end up at a local bar, mostly the Stapleton Chop House, where Art would recount in every detail all that he saw. He was like a movie rerun machine, observant enough to note who was doing what and who was in charge. Anthony learned much from Art's recollections and particularly the order of things in every place they went. Later, under some circumstance or another, Anthony would find a way to meet the principal operators and forge a relationship of some sort or another, though relationships usually turned into friendships.

Danny and Artie had boosted cars regularly and seemed calm, but young Tony Delmonte was jittery.

"Artie, are you sure you can keep the car running after you hotwire it?" asked Tony.

"Eeehhh, whadya think, I'm an amateur?" said Artie. "I know what I'm doing. Caddies are a cinch. First off, they make a hardtop convertible so easy to jimmy I can do it in thirty seconds. Second, the wiring is easy to get to and color-coded. I can slip under the dash, get it started, and be gone in under two minutes," said Artie with pride.

Tony knew his father would kill him if he got arrested. He remembered his brother Cal caught hell for months when the cops pinched him on just a JD charge (juvenile delinquency) for hanging out with a gang of guys one night. They took him from the front of Jake's Soda Shop down to St. George police precinct. The cops there were busy with a messy stabbing and told Red O'Brien, the sergeant who made the arrest, to bring Cal, Georgie, Frankie, and Dennis to the "Tombs" in Manhattan and book them. This was where the worst criminals, the murderers, dope dealers, and maniacs from the five boroughs, were incarcerated to do jail time. None of the Staten Island cops liked O'Brien because he was a smartass "Mick" cop, so they usually found a way to give him a hard time. The desk sergeant, Joe Labrio, told him they were too busy with a knife fight case, where six kids had cut each other up, so no time to book the minor JD case. This was partially true since there weren't many cops on duty in the 120 Precinct at eleven at night. Staten Island was Siberia to most cops, a faraway wasteland. If the few cops were too overloaded and no one at the old 122 in New Dorp was busy (or asleep), they sent arrests to Manhattan. So they put the kids in the back of an old green paddy wagon and took them over to Manhattan on the Staten Island Ferry and then booked them in the Tombs in a Manhattan precinct.

In prison, Cal was allowed one phone call, but by the time he called his home, his father, Salvatore, had already gotten a call from the 121 Precinct that his kid had been pinched. Sal had called Chief Detective Louie Cosenza at his house, actually waking him. Cosenza called the 120 Precinct, but the kids had already been taken to Manhattan. Sal asked Lou to get them back. He knew that Lou and a lot of other cops owed the Delmonte family a lot. This was not a big favor, and really the kids never should have been brought to a place like the Tombs in the first place. True some of them boosted cars, broke into stores, or were part of neighborhood gangs that rumbled now and then, but these kids really weren't doing any of that when Big Red grabbed them and brought them in because he despised Italians.

Lou went up to the Tombs and by three in the morning got the boys released. Sal was waiting at the Ferry Terminal at four o'clock when the four boys and Lou appeared. "You jerks," said Sal. He shook Lou's hand and thanked him and then slapped his son Cal on the head.

For the next several months, Cal was under the gun. He wasn't allowed out for a month even though, at age sixteen, he was doing the work of a man. He finally got a reprieve for Saturday nights when a friendly judge dismissed charges against the boys in a court hearing. Sal's brother, Anthony, had seen the judge, who was a friend, weeks before and told Sal the matter was not a big deal.

Tony had lots of friends. He had also been in many scrapes with the law before, both as a kid and later through his business associates with thieves, shylocks, shysters, swindlers, bookies, mob guys, and crooked politicians. He had a regular payroll for his men and an irregular payroll for cops, from the beat cops all the way up to captains. It was how business was done. Judges for the most part were politician-lawyers who had made the right connections both legally and otherwise to get on the ballot and get elected to a judgeship. Once elected, both political parties tended to back a judge's reelection. The judge had to reciprocate, however, whenever a friend had an issue brought before their court. The judges were also expected never to have to go into their pocket for the cost of a lunch or dinner. If you owned a store, the judges simply picked out what they wanted and never got a bill.

So, Cal and the boys really weren't in too much trouble, except now they were issued JD cards. There were three levels, from simply breaking curfew to some criminal act like burglary, theft, or rumbling (fighting) or attempted murder. The gangs in the other four boroughs were a lot more violent than their Staten Island counterparts.

They were making money by robbery or some other criminal enterprise. They learned how to take a car aerial and a stiff rubber band, some pieces of metal, and electrical tape and make a lethal and accurate .22-caliber zip gun. Some sewed a series of razors and covered them with tape inside their Garrison belts, a wide, big-buckled belt. Then they honed the edges of the belt buckle, razor sharp as well. The belt was a formidable weapon in a gang fight. Held wrapped around a hand, at the one end they stripped off the tape and swung it at great speed. It could slash and cut an opponent with two or three swings so that he was a bleeding mess.

Young Tony wore such a belt and also had the uniform of the day, which included peg pants with saddle stitching, flapjack shoes for daytime, and pointy nosepickers dress shoes for a night's fun. His hair was done in the common flat top with a DA, or duck's ass, in the back. Iridescent shirts with pink collars on black shirts (collar up, of course) finished the ensemble. The perfect "hood," as the cops called these hoodlums.

Boosting cars was fast becoming a commonplace operation for some of these kids. "Artie, I'll walk up Hylan Boulevard, and you do your work. I'll keep Danny in eyesight and give him a high sign by scratching my head if there's a problem. Okay?" said Tony.

"Yeah, okay," said Artie, while Danny nodded. Danny Manichello was a big oaf a kid who was seventeen years old but looked like a man in his twenties. He got the nickname "Egghead" because of his oversized head and goofy mannerisms.

Artie Newman, on the other hand, was thin and wiry with a medium build. He had an uncanny resemblance to the actor James Dean, except he wore his glasses all the time. He had a photographic memory and was nicknamed Artie Candle because he was so bright. He was articulate, though more interested in cars than girls, who still chased him all the time. He resisted most times, but once in a while when out drinking, he would end up with some chick in the back seat of his "Red Rocket," a 1956 Pontiac convertible. The car was special to Artie. He spent over two months tearing it apart after buying it from a dealer. His father was a wealthy doctor who bought him the car after his freshman year at college. Artie added a few goodies to the stock Pontiac V8 engine—triple Stromberg carburetors, modified transmission, a four-speed manual tranny, converted it to a four-speed floor shift, fender skirts, spinner hubcaps, and cut-off pipes wired under the seat, just in reach of the driver's seat. There were also gearing and timing modifications, which enabled the car to do zero to sixty miles per hour in under seven seconds and a top speed of over 150 miles per hour.

He would edge up to a light next to some hot rod and pull the wire attached to the cut-off pipes, eliminating the muffler passage and redirecting the exhaust out the car at midpoint just past the door opening. The engine always growled some, but it looked more like a fancied-up stock Pontiac. When the light changed, the Pontiac would stream out flames blasting from the cut-out pipes, and the "Rocket" would launch, leaving the hot rod driver trying to figure out what had just happened.

Artie's Fordilac was rarely used during the daytime once he got the Pontiac slow car. But the Ford was the quickest and could handle better when a getaway car was needed. He kept it at Skippy Connor's house in his long driveway off campus, but the Pontiac was more inconspicuous. It looked like a conventional car, a stock dealer issue.

The traffic was always constant on Hylan Boulevard, and the activity was not unusual at ten or eleven on most any night. There were two car dealerships close to each other near New Dorp Lane and the Boulevard. Artie walked at a leisurely pace as he turned the corner from the Lane to the Boulevard. Danny and Tony walked on the opposite side of the Boulevard. Artie had parked his Pontiac on the Lane.

Artie and Tony had coasted around the lot earlier that day and saw a black '55 Caddy parked in the second row back in the middle of a line of cars. The dealership closed at nine that night.

Artie slipped between the first row, slowly getting to the passenger side of the Caddy. Danny had crossed the Boulevard and made his way along the first line of cars and the edge of the sidewalk. Tony was on the opposite side of the street. The signal that all was okay was a simple hand at the back of the neck. There were no cops in sight, and so the sign was given.

Artie slipped a thin metal strip with a crooked hook at the end down the door at the window rubber and moved it around for a moment, then pulled it up with a "click" and opened the door. He pulled the jimmy out and slid on his belly across the seat, pulling the car door closed with his foot. He lay still until the interior light dimmed. He held a penlight in his mouth and pulled a cuplike gadget out of his top pocket. The flexible metal gadget had a series of clips attached. Artie pulled at the clump of wires just under the ignition port. He lifted his head up once, pulled an interior window sign away from the windshield, and then went back under the dashboard pressing wires to metal. The engine began to crank, and after one false start, it regrinded and caught. He quickly slid back up and behind the steering wheel, dropped the gear shift into reverse, and popped the emergency brake. The Caddy slowly rolled backward as he swung the wheel sharply, then shifted into drive, easing the car to the exit and out the driveway. He then flipped on the lights, turned up Hyland Boulevard, and onto the Lane. Less than sixty seconds had passed from the time he first approached the car to when he was tooling up the road.

Danny and Tony quickened their walking pace toward the Lane, and by the time they got by Artie's Pontiac, he had already parked the Caddy close behind it but left enough room to slip between his car and one next to it to screw in a set of Jersey license plates he had picked up at Newark Airport's long-term parking lot. He also had a doctored registration in the glove compartment.

The Caddy was running smoothly as Danny quickly got behind the wheel and Tony got in beside him. He pulled out, turned up the Lane, and noted Artie right behind. It all went as planned, or so they thought. About two and a half blocks up the lane, a cop had just come out of Three Jays Restaurant and Bar. He just stood against the building for a moment and looked down the street, the exact moment when

Artie pulled the Caddy into the parking space and got out. He saw Artie go to the Pontiac, open the door, close it, and then disappear in between the cars. Then he saw two other figures approach the car and get in. The cop quickly got in his squad car and told his partner that he had seen a suspicious event. He put the sandwiches he had gotten at the restaurant on the floor and pulled his car up to an open curbside position. When the Caddy and Pontiac pulled out, he told his partner to follow. The three vehicles had gone about five blocks when Artie noticed the cop car behind him. He blinked the floor button high-beam switch device. Tony saw that and told Danny, "We got trouble." Traffic in both directions on New Dorp Lane was always constant in both directions. Artie began to slow the Pontiac down just a little at a time while Danny began to accelerate. The cop driving, a rookie, hardly noticed the slow down. Artie took a tissue from his pocket, opened his window, and threw it out. The cops both turned their heads to the tissue, distracted for a moment, when Artie quickly flashed his high beams twice again.

Danny sped up the lane, and when he came to the next side street, he swung right. The cops never noticed the Caddy turning off, too distracted by the tissue and then the Pontiac breaking abruptly, then speeding ahead.

The Pontiac got to the top of the hill at Richmond Road as the light turned yellow. Artie smiled and gunned it, turning left and roaring away through the intersection.

The rookie cop gunned his engine just as the light changed. Suddenly a station wagon pulled into the intersection. The rookie veered right and just missed the wagon. The left-turning traffic was streaming by as the cops turned on their lights and sirens. Artie had already turned right and was flying away. By the time they got to the next T-intersection, he had turned his lights off. He whipped the Pontiac right and was up to seventy-five miles per hour through the many curves in that deserted road before the cop car reached the intersection. The older cop looked both ways and pointed left since the roadway was a straightaway and the main road. Artie cruised for a few miles, then backed down a little when he finally got to the next intersection and turned left. The Caddy had continued up a series of back streets, then back down to Hyland Boulevard. Artie kept driving until he felt sure he had evaded the cops, then made his way back to the main road, Richmond Road, toward Hills Station.

Danny and Tony got to a strip of old garages in New Brighton and already had the Caddy backed in and the door down.

"So, you think Artie is okay?" Danny asked Tony.

"Hey, Artie probably fished those cops into following the Rocket and then lost them in the dust," Tony answered.

"Yeah," said Danny. They both lit cigarettes and lay back in the comfortable seats of the Caddy. "Hey, turn on the 'Alan Freed Radio Show,'" said Danny. Tony fumbled with the radio dial until he reached the station with the unmistakable loud and raspy banter by Freed.

Tony looked at Danny with a smile. "Artie," he said and got out of the car and pulled open one side of the two garage doors.

Artie stood there with a smirk on his face, hands outstretched. "What did I tell you, eeehhh!" They both laughed.

Alan Freed

The next morning when Tony arrived with Skippy Connors, Artie was under the Caddy. He had already loosened the transmission housing and had a chain hooked around the engine. Skippy had a pickup truck backed up to the garage doors. Tony sat out in the pickup watching the Alley roadway.

About two hours later, the Caddy engine was in the back of the pickup. Skippy handed Tony a wad of bills, and the pickup was gone. "I was able to get a wrecker for a while, so we got to get this junker out of here now; then we can go over to help Johnny," said Artie.

The wrecker was parked around the corner, and Artie pulled it around and backed it up to the Caddy. "Hook her up." Tony crawled under the front end of the Caddy and put the two hooks around the frame. Artie cranked up the lift on the front, and the Caddy was airborne.

"Okay," said Artie, "let's go." He pulled the Caddy out easily. Tony closed the doors and got in the passenger door of the wrecker.

Saturday morning traffic was good cover for moving a dead car. They headed out toward Outer Bridge. That end of Staten Island was noted for its farms, junkyards, and old, deserted World War II-era WPA-built, abandoned roads. They got to a potholed, muddy junkyard and pulled up to a rickety office shack next to a huge crane and a large mechanical structure that resembled a gigantic steel-framed box.

"Blow the horn," Tony said to Artie. About ten minutes later, a vehicle appeared from the mounds of metal and cars and came up to the shack.

"Hey, boys, what we got here?" the driver asked.

"One for the crusher, Harry," said Tony.

Harry raised his eyebrows. "Oh, a little warm, is it?"

"Yeah, real warm," said Tony.

"Okay, pull it over to the crane," Harry said.

Artie got in the wrecker, turned a half circle, and stopped by the huge crane. He got out and went to the rear of the wrecker, lowered the car to the ground, and unhooked the chains. Harry walked up to the crane and climbed into the cab. The motor ground a few times, then sputtered and caught, sending plumes of black smoke from the exhaust stack. He engaged the huge boom with a clawlike apparatus hanging at the end and dropped it on the roof of the Caddy with a crash. The claws bit in, and soon the entire vehicle was airborne. He dropped it into the crusher bay and killed the motor on the crane. Then he went over to the crusher. The sound of the motor engaging sent vibrations through the ground. He engaged the crusher motor, and a variety of metallic noises screamed out as the Caddy slowly disappeared down the conveyor. The finale was a huge block of metal neatly pressed into a rectangular cube.

Tony walked over to Harry, out of voice range of Artie, who was still sitting in the wrecker. After a short conversation, Tony pulled some bills out of his pocket, handed them to Harry, and shook hands.

Artie gunned the engine, and Tony half-skipped over to the wrecker, got in, and they were off. They dropped off the wrecker and took off in Artie's Pontiac. They arrived at Skippy's home and went back to his garage, which was at the end of a long driveway, well back from the front of the house. Pieces of cars, parts, tires, bumpers, and wood support blocks were all around the outside. Skippy was under a car with the hood up.

The car, a black 1953 Ford, two-door sedan was just below the huge Cadillac engine dangling from chains attached to an overhead steel rig. Skippy had made his own lift and even welded the steel frame. Skip had already modified the engine's identification numbers so it was impossible to read.

Artie's eyes widened. "That's quite a bit of power for that little Ford," he said.

Skippy crawled out and stood up with a big grin on his face. "Wait until I get this baby together and fire it up. This will compete with any hot car on the island, even one of those Petey Sinatra specials." Sinatra was the most notable custom car guy on Staten Island. His souped-up cars were even getting attention throughout New York City and beyond. If you wanted to buy one of Petey's specials, you had to wait in line. The chopped and channeled 1950 Mercurys, custom 1955 Chevys, and '32 Ford Roadsters he produced were classically hot cars as well as mechanically superior to any other custom jobs, with the most inventive flame paint jobs and detailed pin-striping.

While Artie and Skippy talked for a while about how to interface the powertrain and four-speed floor shift transmission into the Ford, Tony left.

He had a different ambition from having the fastest or hottest car in town. He preferred to hustle a buck wherever he could make a deal. When Skippy said he was looking around the junkyards for a good Cadillac engine and knew the price would run well over $500, Tony told him he could get one within a few days. Artie was always up for anything, especially if a car was involved. He had plenty of money but was always looking for a scheme. Danny, on the other hand, was always broke, and Tony knew it. After the cost of the crusher and a cut to Danny and Artie, Tony pocketed $300. That would keep him going for quite a while.

He spent his adolescent years with the neighborhood guys. As much as they were spoken of as a gang, they simply were the social order.

Even when they went their separate ways some nights to take a girl out to a movie or a dance, they usually ended up together at some all-night hamburger joint like Cosmos All-Nite Char Grill, or they traded stories about the hot chick they were with when they got together the next day.

As Tony grew older, he needed more money. So he looked out for opportunities. He worked for his uncle, Big Tony, part-time. Most of the work involved tracking and storage from goods that came from nearby pier operations that imported overseas goods.

Young Tony had finished high school and was in his last year of college when Big Tony asked him to spend at least three or four full days a week helping him out. The young man was smart and energetic and could handle himself. He also was another pair of eyes Big Tony could use to keep an eye on the place. Young Tony really could use the extra money as well. He was hustling whatever he could from time to time to get some money in his pocket. Little did he know the education he got was well worth more than the money he got as hourly pay. It was an experience, in fact, that would prepare him for the rest of his life.

Aristotle Onassis

CHAPTER 55

BIG TONY TRAVELED throughout the city and met with various intermediaries for some very serious businessmen, including Aristotle Onassis. Young Tony was sent, after introductions on various business missions, as his representative and trusted nephew. Onassis's ships were constantly in and out of ports in and around New York City. Young Tony made connections with the union leaders at the piers, which led to introductions to the purchase officers, bursars, and even captains in the shipping industry. Occasionally he would meet some of the higher-level executives in Onassis-owned companies. Such was the case when he was told to go to Pier 26 in Manhattan. There at the end of the pier was the most impressive vessel he had ever seen. As he walked the scarred and worn-down wood planking along the pier edge as the hi-lows (power lifts) zipped around with pallets of goods on their forked blades, he looked up at the inscription on this glorious vessel, the *Christina*. He was met by a young man dressed in a crisp white nautical uniform that resembled a US Navy officer.

"I'm Anthony Delmont, representative of Bay Shipping Company. I am here to see your ship stores steward," he told the fellow. "My boss, Tony Delmonte, sends his greetings."

The young man responded in broken English, "Wait here. I will be right back," and ran up the gangway to the ship. There he met another sailor, similarly dressed, and they spoke. One left while the other stood at the post at the top of the gangway. Soon two men in uniform came to the gangway. They pointed to the posted sailor, and he went down the gangway to Anthony.

"Please, sir, please go up." So Anthony got up and went on board.

"I am Anthony Delmont. I'm here to see your steward," he said.

"Yes, yes, you were expected. Come with me." They walked down the outer corridor, and he was led to the entry at midship and to a small office.

"Mr. Delmont, I am Marcus Stavros, the steward. Pleased to see you. Would you like something to drink?" The steward was a young man, perhaps Anthony's age. His dark skin contrasted against the white uniform so that it made him appear even darker skinned than he really was. He was a slim, athletic fellow with an easy smile, and though he had a pronounced accent, he spoke excellent English. Marcus presented a list and questioned Anthony about the quality of his products, his suppliers, availability, and delivery.

"Look, Marcus, I am very familiar with the high quality of food products and meats. We have been dealing with people in the Greek community here in New York and along the East Coast for many years." Anthony recalled having gone to the small auction markets in rural upstate New Jersey and New York and buying live baby lambs and baby goats for the Easter feast for the Greeks and the Italians. "I can supply milk-fed lambs and goats as well as fresh-cut whole lamb, fresh beef, pork, and veal. We use all fresh-killed poultry, and all our other products from extra virgin olive oil to the finest cheeses are direct from Greece and of the highest quality. And the prices are right," said Delmont.

Marcus smiled. "Well, maybe we ought to sample what you have. If I give you an order today, when can I get delivery?"

"I'll have nearly everything you need here tomorrow, except for the baby lamb or baby goat. That will take a few days longer if you want fresh killed," said Delmont.

"Okay," said Marcus. "That's good, very good. You know your family was recommended to us by our friends here, some who have helped our company for years."

Delmont nodded. He knew the longshoremen's union bosses going back to "Tough Tony" Anastasia up to the current president of the union, Tony Scotto. They were close friends of Onassis there in New York, and there were ties in Italy and Greece. Big Tony had been friendly with Scotto and his associates for years. In fact, some of them grew up together. He did business with their families.

"So, Marcus, how do you like New York?" asked Anthony.

"Well, I have been working for the company for a few years, starting just after I finished university. I have been in the Mediterranean on different vessels. Just recently I was assigned to the *Christina*. This is my second trip to New York. I visited the United States a few times with my family when I was younger but mostly for family events here and in Miami. Once we went to Boston. I really can't say much about New York. Usually when we visited, I was with many family members, and we attended some event or another—weddings, business receptions, funerals, whatever. There was business but also a lot of personal activities. Now I really would like to see the city but don't know my way around," said Marcus.

"Well, there is a lot to see here. I think you would really enjoy yourself," said Anthony.

"Look, my father is cousin to Aristotle. I first got my job with the company through our relationship. I grew up outside of Athens but under a very strict father and mother. After university, my father, who is an executive with the Onassis Company, put me to work on oil tankers. Then I worked in his office as a junior accountant. A few months ago, they found out that the former ship steward on the *Christina* was stealing. I should say I found out. I matched the supplies going to our ships and the quantities of goods and average number of people on the vessels. I also kept track of the fuel supply," Marcus said.

"I noticed an erratic amount of supplies sent to the *Christina* but only in certain ports. I saw a trend that indicated very large invoices in some ports, then low inventory afterward even when there was no big event or usage. I showed my father, and he alerted Onassis. They caught the steward one evening at a bar in Lower Manhattan receiving a big wad of cash as a payoff. They waited for him outside and pushed him back to one of the old ships that had just come in to the North River piers.

"After a day or so, locked up in the ship's hold and a few beatings, he admitted everything and gave the names of two others on board that were in on the deal. He also gave up the names of the suppliers who were his connections in New York, Italy, and elsewhere. I was asked to take over his job at a bigger salary, and my personal position in the family became very good. My father brought me to Uncle Aristotle, and he thanked me personally. He wanted to know a lot more about me and my education and social life. It was the first time we really talked even though I had been with him at family events many times.

"Now he always smiled when he saw me and always stopped to say something to me. When my father and he talked, they both thought that it would be good for me to be on the *Christina*. I am the steward, but sometimes he brings me with him to business meetings and introduces me to some of our business connections. Sometimes he has me meet some of our clients, and I help work out some details once a deal is made. I think that this job is my beginning," said Marcus.

"I think I know what you mean. My family does the same thing. That's why I'm here," said Anthony. They both laughed. Both young men were on similar career tracks as the older men sought to build the structure for the next generation to take over when the time came.

Marcus turned to a cabinet behind him, as he was seated at a desk, with Anthony seated in a chair in front of him. He pulled out a bottle and two glasses. "So, we drink to our new deal," he said. He poured two shots of Ouzo. The powerful, colorless Greek brandy burned Anthony's throat as it went down, and the hint of anise and grape seemed to rise from his throat into his nostrils.

"Look, if you want to see Manhattan, I can take you around to some places," said Anthony.

"Yes, yes," said Marcus. "I can go any night, usually if there is no business to attend to, and I can set up the security crew. Actually, we are having some electrical repairs done. I don't think that they will be working Saturday or Sunday because they need to get parts, so maybe we can go Friday," said Marcus.

"Fine," said Anthony.

"I also have my assistant, George, who is a good help to me; maybe we can bring him along," said Marcus.

"Sure, I will meet you here around six on Friday," said Anthony.

"Well, maybe I should meet you someplace so those others here in the crew don't know my business," said Marcus.

"Okay," said Anthony. "I think you would like to see little Italy and Chinatown. We can eat something there and then go around."

"Fine," said Marcus.

"There is a restaurant on Mulberry Street called La Mela. Meet me there at six."

Anthony left and was on his way to his next stop in Midtown. His next stop took him to Forty-Second Street.

When they needed cash to make a fast buy in any market deal, arrangements were made with Sol Zinsky, who was a partner in a company called Commercial Credit Corporation, the CCC. This was an unusual loan company. They would loan money on goods for purchases or assignment goods considered collateral. It really didn't much matter. Now the loan described was based on trust and knowledge. This loan outfit was well connected. It was rumored that Meyer Lansky had a major interest in the company as a silent partner. There was never a robbery attempt or any problems known to have occurred at the location even though Times Square had a notorious reputation for crime. It was likely under the protection of one or more of the New York mob families. The lender knew who he was borrowing from and could trust the debt would be collected. Not exactly a traditional Bank of America Savings and Loan. The loan carried interest that was calculated by the hour. The deals usually were fast, and the loan was generally repaid within twenty-four to thirty-six hours. Occasionally, it was paid in two timely four-hour installments.

Delmont stepped into a small lobby and pressed a bell button. An intercom crackled on the wall. "Yeah, who is it?"

"It's Anthony Delmont. I have a deposit," he said. With that, a buzzer unlocked the electric door lock, and Anthony stepped into the lobby. As the door relocked, the elevator door opened, and he stepped in. There was only one button with an arrow pointing up. He pressed it, the door clunked shut, and the elevator began its ascent.

After a minute or so, it stopped, and the door opened. Anthony stepped out into a small lobby and looked directly into the camera mounted on the ceiling. He said, "Delmont," and pressed yet another buzzer. A steel door opened, and a small man beckoned him in. He began to walk down a corridor with glass partition booths to one side. Inside each booth was a man counting money or writing in ledgers.

The little man wore a green eye shade on his head. He led Anthony to a small room with a solid metal door.

"Okay," he said.

Anthony was wearing a bulky raincoat that he took off. Inside were interior zipped pockets sewn in. He unzipped two of the pockets and pulled out packets of money wrapped neatly and marked. "It's eighty thousand," he said. The man took the money and sat behind the table in the room. There was an odd-looking scale on the table. It had two pans and a series of small round metal weights in various sizes. The man unwrapped a lot of bills and counted them. When he reached $5,000, he stopped and put the bills on the scale. Then he unwrapped the next stack of bills and put it on the opposite pan. He waited, then lowered his reading glasses to the end of his nose and peered at a dial in the center of the scale.

"Okay for now. Tell your boss I am giving him a temporary receipt. I'll finish and check the count." The man pulled a ledger book out from a drawer in the table. He scribbled on a coupon and handed it to Delmont.

"Thanks," said Delmont.

The old man looked at him over the glasses on his nose. "Yeah," he grumbled and pointed to the door. Delmont had been to CCC many times, sometimes with as much as $100,000 in cash. Later that day, he returned to his Market Office with his receipt. He gave the secretary, Ginger, the order for the *Christina* and told her to get the order ready.

Anthony checked every item on the order list as it was loaded onto the delivery trucks the next day and put his initials on each package to be sure everything was in order. He also had a nearby Italian bakery prepare a selection of Greek and Italian pastries and a cake. He had a huge Sicilian Cassata cake made as well. This was a multilayered, cannoli-cream-filled cake laced with Strega liquor and covered in a white glaze, garnished with marzipan fruits. It was a magnificent confectionary and weighed nearly ten pounds.

He wrote a personal greeting on the package in Italian and directed the delivery men to bring the pastries directly to Marcus.

It was still several days before all the work would be completed. Marcus knew earlier that day that his uncle and his daughter, the namesake of the vessel *Christina*, had arrived by plane to spend a few days in New York before the vessel would cruise to Miami. He called up to his uncle's stateroom steward and told him he had some special items and gifts to show him. He was told to bring them to Aristotle's elaborate main stateroom, his uncle's onboard quarters.

He approached the doorway and saw his uncle, Aristotle, and the steward, Giorgio, and an assistant to Christina seated, discussing plans for the trip.

Aristotle looked up and saw Marcus, carton in hand. "Come, come in," he beckoned. Marcus entered and greeted everyone. "Okay, let's see what you have," said Onassis. Marcus carefully took each white box out of the carton and placed it on the table in front of the sofas where the four were seated. He opened each one. The pastries were exquisitely decorated in multicolored icings and then laid in a floral design with multicolored paper doilies under each one. The Cassada cake had replicas of fruit around the outer rim and a large replica of the ship *Christina* in the center. "Bravo," said his uncle. "This is wonderful."

Marcus said, "Well, you have your friend Anthony Delmont's nephew to thank for this gesture."

"Well, tell him I thank him and his famiglia. If he should be here before we depart, I would like to talk to him," said the uncle.

Christina dipped her finger into the icing on the Cassada. "It's delicious." She smiled.

"I expect to see Anthony one evening. He offered to bring me to some places he knows in Manhattan," said Marcus.

"Where will you go?" said Christina.

"Well, Chinatown, Little Italy, maybe the Theater District, and— who knows—maybe a few of the upscale clubs," said Marcus.

"Oh, that sounds wonderful. Papa, would you mind if I decide to leave you alone for the evening and go with them?" asked the girl.

Aristotle thought for a moment, "You take Taki and Georgio with you," said Onassis.

"Wonderful," said Christina.

Marcus smiled. "This will be fun." Anthony knew his way around Manhattan.

Delmont dressed meticulously and headed to meet Marcus on Friday. He took the subway and arrived at about five thirty, a bit early. He had arranged to meet Marcus at a bar in Angelo's Restaurant on Mulberry Street. The streets were bustling with people, diners, delivery men, and taxis.

He walked into Angelo's and almost immediately recognized Marcus at the end of the bar, surrounded by a few people. He walked over. "Hello, Marcus," he said with a big smile on his face.

"Aha! You too are early. Good. I want you to meet Giorgio, my steward, Taki and George, who you met before. And this is my cousin, Christina." Anthony smiled and took Christina's hand first. She smiled back. He then shook everyone else's hand. "My uncle thanks you for the lovely pastries," said Marcus. "Christina here was very impressed also." She smiled. "I hope that the little group is not too large tonight?" said Marcus.

"No, no, not at all," said Anthony.

He had noticed the size of Giorgio and Taki; both men were broad shouldered and bulky. Giorgio was a hulking man in his fifties with a clean-shaven head and salt and pepper mustache. He smiled when addressed, but his eyes were constantly scanning the room. Anthony recognized the sign of a professional bodyguard, although he did not stand out too conspicuously. Taki was a short fireplug with huge shoulders and arms. He was congenial, but his glances over at Giorgio indicated he was taking his lead. George, the steward to Marcus, was a thin, young fellow with a quick smile, and he was constantly positioning himself to be close to Marcus without getting in his way. "George, let's get some more drinks. Anthony, what do you like?" said Marcus.

"Johnnie Walker Black, rocks please," said Anthony.

He purposely leaned back on the bar so that he could see past George and Marcus to his right but could see Christina without her seeing him. He wanted to look at her without being obvious. She was a very pretty girl with jet-black hair and smooth, tanned skin. She wore a plain black dress, which was cut high enough not to reveal any cleavage but smoothly tailored. She had gold earrings and a thin, gold chain with a medallion around her neck. She had sparkling eyes that seemed to show a bit of excitement at the discussion of the night's itinerary.

Anthony sipped his drink and casually walked over to Giorgio. He noticed an odd-looking ring on his right hand. "What is that?" Anthony asked.

Giorgio looked down at the ring and then at Anthony. "It was a gift," he said. "This is a gold coin from the age of Socrates. It was a gift from Mr. Onassis." He smiled and put his hand closer to Anthony's face so he could get a good view.

"Fascinating. Mr. Onassis must have great respect for you," said Anthony.

"And I for him, Mr. Anthony. He is my mentor and my boss. He is my family," said Giorgio. Anthony could tell by the tone of his voice and his expression that the man's loyalty to Onassis was genuine. While he did have an interest in the unusual ring, he also wanted to move closer to Christina now that he had a chance to observe her for a little while.

Out of the corner of his eye, Anthony saw that she was inconspicuously looking him up and down while chatting with Marcus. An unwarranted little hint of a smile appeared at the ends of her mouth. Anthony wondered if it was a sign of satisfaction, amusement, or sarcasm.

"So, Mr. Anthony, you spend a lot of time here in the city?" Christina inquired, tilting her head slightly as she spoke in a playful manner.

"Well, I do a lot of work here in the city," he said.

"Do you do a lot of play in the city too?" she said with a grin, and the others chuckled.

"I guess I do a bit of that as well," he answered, smiling back at her.

"Marcus says you know all the interesting places to go here, and this is one of them," she said.

"This is one of the oldest restaurants in Little Italy. Besides great food, you often see some very notable people here as well." The walls

Christina Onassis

were filled with photos signed by various celebrities, including a few US presidents. That was true of a number of places in Little Italy. "Now Angelo's had the pleasure of having Christina Onassis here, and that is notable as well," said Anthony with a sheepish smile. She did not answer but sipped a drink from a tall-stemmed glass.

After several minutes, Marcus said, "Shall we take a look around outside before dinner?"

Christina looked up at Anthony. "Sure, if you like," said Anthony.

They finished their drinks, and Giorgio nodded to Taki, who walked over to the front door. George paid the bill, and they walked outside.

Marcus and George followed Taki up the street, and Anthony and Christina began walking together with Giorgio close behind. "The sidewalks are very narrow here, so I will take your hand if you like," said Anthony. She slipped her hand in his as they walked. Occasionally, they would stop to look in a store or a shop and chatted about the array of food and other items. The music from one restaurant that had an open front caused them to stop again.

Christina said, "That's nice. I like that." So, they went inside and found a table. The small band had a male singer who alternated between Italian and English lyrics to his songs. They ordered drinks, and George ordered some eggplant, calamari, bruschetta, and other items.

Giorgio sat a bit back from the table while Taki stood up by the bar, between the table and the line to the front door.

Marcus said, "Anthony, what is the biggest moneymaker with your company?"

Anthony answered, "We actually do a lot of different kinds of operations. We deal in distressed cargo and insurance claim damaged goods. We also supply merchant ships, restaurants, and institutions. We buy and sell foreign goods and arrange for storage too. We do some trucking and brokerage as well. Quite a diverse number of operations."

"It sounds like your company has much to do all the time and you are very busy," said Marcus.

"And what do you do when you are not out there making money? What do you do for fun?" asked Christina.

Anthony smiled. "Well, I am having fun now," he answered.

She smiled. "I have been looking over some business matters here for our shipping companies. There are some vessels that are of interest to my father. They are being held by your federal authorities. I am not sure how they acquired them; perhaps your US Marshall's Office got them through some sort of default. However, there are five of them that have our interest," said Christina.

"Where are they?" asked Anthony.

"They are docked at a pier in a place called Red Hook," said Christina. Her ability to speak English was very good, but she had a distinct accent and seemed to exaggerate syllables sometimes.

"Sure, I know the piers there very well," said Anthony.

"Do you have anyone who could look at these vessels and see what condition they're in?" said Christina.

"I think so. I'll check and let you know," said Anthony.

Christina had taken a very different posture and mannerism when she spoke of this matter. She was no longer casual as before. She was very businesslike and straightforward. Anthony sensed that this girl was an experienced businesswoman as well as the daughter of an extremely wealthy man. The group drifted through Little Italy then

Chinatown. They ate and drank in Little Italy in a number of places, then headed uptown to the Cheetah Club. There the place was jumping with live music and a large crowd. They joined in the fun for a while. They took cabs to Studio 54 and found the crowds there so dense they could hardly get to the gatekeeper. He was approached by Taki and, after a brief conversation, motioned to the group to go in. The place was full of people, some dancing, others on lounges and bar chairs. In the darkened corners and recesses, Christina noticed unusual goings-on. Here, men with men and women with women were not strange sights. Nor were the intimacies she saw going on in various places as the group made their way to an alcove with lounges.

Not far away in another alcove framed by curtains, a woman was seated on, or actually straddling, a man and slowly swaying her hips back and forth. Anthony noticed that Christina was glancing over in that direction a number of times, so he inconspicuously turned and saw the activity. Christina then looked at him and instead of speaking merely raised her eyebrows quizzically and shook her head a little, then rolled her eyes.

The gesture sort of caught Anthony by surprise, and he laughed out loud. When he did, she began to laugh too. Marcus, who had not really noticed any of this, looked at the both of them and raised his hands in front of him. "What is this? What did I miss?" he said. By this time, George, who had noticed the scene going on, was trying hard to be inconspicuous by putting his hands over his face. Then Christina pointed at George, seeing how he was trying hard not to show himself, and began to laugh all the more.

Giorgio, who was seated behind the group, glanced around, still solemn faced, but a slight hint of a grin transformed his serious face. By now they had spent some four hours hopping from restaurants to bar to bar, and everyone had had several drinks, except the two bodyguards.

Christina was feeling pretty good but surely had not lost her composure. She had learned to sip her drinks, then leave them more than half-full. She might have had several drinks before but really only consumed two or three. But it was the combination of the drinks, the casual atmosphere, and the events around her that really caused

Christina to find the entire scenario hilarious. She pointed at George and began to laugh hysterically. George did the same.

Finally, things quieted down. George asked, "What will you have?"

Christina, not missing the opportunity to continue the hilarity, blurted, "I'll have whatever they are having," and pointed to the couple who by now were bouncing up and down at a furious pace. Marcus finally saw the action and looked at Christina and Anthony and laughed.

George left and came back with a waitress in tow, and drinks were ordered and brought to them. "I guess there's a show wherever we go," said Marcus.

"Well, if you want to see an unusual show with music, let's go to the Red Parrot," said Anthony.

The club was a huge, wide expanse with lounge pits and bars spread out across a hangar- like, cavernous room. There was a huge, electrically colored, lighted screen that changed scenes as the music played. They settled into a pit lounge, and drinks were brought. The atmosphere was lively. There was a large dance floor, and Christina took Marcus's hand and said, "Let's try this." They went off to the dance floor in front of the large screen while Giorgio lingered nearby with Taki.

"So, George, how do you like New York?" asked Anthony.

"I like it very much; so much to see, very much activity. There are some very lively places in Athens and Rome when we visit, but mostly Mr. Onassis seeks more private places, quiet for me," said George.

"And what does Christina think?" asked Anthony.

"Well, I am not sure. She likes to see everything but also is very private like her father," said George.

After the dance, Christina and Marcus returned. "This place is wonderful," said Marcus.

Christina nodded as she sipped a drink. "Mr. Anthony, are you ready?" asked Christina. She stood up and offered her hand. They went out to the dance floor as a lively song played. When it ended, a slow ballad began. Christina held Anthony's hand and then turned when the music began. "Let's try this," she said. They began to dance close. Anthony had his hand on her back and held her hand. He could feel her skin through what was extremely thin and clinging material. After a little while, she moved very close to him. He could feel her breasts and hips press against him and could smell the hint of fine perfume in her hair as he pulled her a bit closer. She responded by pressing her bosom tighter against his chest. They danced, and when the dance was over, she looked up at him and touched his cheek, softly tracing his jaw line and then across his lips. She then touched that finger to her lips. "Thank you. That was very nice. You are very nice," she said with a smile. He kissed her lightly on the cheek in response, and then they went back to their seats.

Anthony was not quite sure if this woman, this very rich, well-traveled socialite, was really warming up to him or merely playing him for the fun of it.

His upbringing and temperament were always part of his inner conflict. He was, as a child, always forward and direct, even if he had to pay consequences for it. He stood his ground even when the odds were against him and he knew it. While it took quite a bit to get him upset, he was vicious when he was pushed too far, even with his friends and siblings. He was wary of being played by this woman but at the same time found her fascinating. He could tell by their conversations that she was intelligent and clever and that there was a very hard and calculating side to her. She measured her responses, but so did he. He was careful not to show too much of his inner thoughts. He knew he liked her, and she knew it too. Yet she also knew he was not a pushover. Many men who met her would fawn all over her and try to get close. Anthony encouraged her by not being too aggressive. He was gentlemanly, courteous yet warm to her when she sought a response from him.

Likely she was a bit curious about him now as he sipped yet another scotch on the rocks. She noted he had drunk several, but she could not detect any change in his behavior or speech. She noted that the hour was nearing three in the morning. "Marcus, I think we'd better head back shortly," she said.

"Of course," he said.

They rose, and as they did, she took Anthony's hand and entwined her arm around his. They walked, and she said in a whisper, "I really enjoyed this evening, and I look forward to seeing you again very soon.

You are a wonderful host, and I will tell my father that you will look into the matter of the ships in Brooklyn." They went outside, and the doorman whistled for a cab.

"Look, Marcus, you are going back to the ship, and I am going in a different direction, so I will get another car," said Anthony.

"Fine, thank you. It's been fun. I know we will see you before we leave port. Call me. Goodnight." And they were off.

Anthony stood there waiting for the next cab. He had made two important friends that night, maybe three. His mind was racing. He remembered the section of piers that held several vessels under the control of the US Navy. The area was fenced off and had a gatehouse with guards twenty-four hours a day. He also saw New York City Police cars inside that compound as well as maintenance trucks going in and out.

He would find a way to get the information on these ships. He had some friends in the New York Maritime Union. A number of them worked in the Department of Marine and Aviation that was the Ferry Transportation division. Contractors who worked on the city's vessels were all affiliated with a union.

The next day, he went to the office. Big Tony was in. Anthony "Big Tony" was a real tough guy. He learned to fight on the streets of Hell's Kitchen in New York. He also knew how to handle himself with all kinds of people. He had come to America at age five. He built a prosperous business.

"Hey, Uncle Tony, I delivered the order for the *Christina* and last night met the real Christina. I took Marcus, the nephew, out to a few spots, and Christina was with him. She asked me to find out about several confiscated ships under the control of the feds in the Brooklyn Navy Yard. I was wondering if we could ask Alan's connection on the piers if they can give me information on their condition and who's actually in control. If you think it's a good idea, I will work on it too," said Anthony.

His uncle looked at him, leaned back in his chair, and then smiled. "So you have been rubbing elbows with Christina Onassis and the family. Very good, very good. Now you are doing his research. Also very good. I will contact people to see what information I can find out about the ships being held there," said Big Tony.

"I think they are under control of the US Marshall's Office, but I'm not sure. There are supposed to be seven or eight, but Onassis had an interest in the five largest," said Anthony.

"Okay, let me see what I can find out," said Tony.

The streets around the Fort Greene Market in Brooklyn were always chaotic in the morning hours on weekdays. There were trucks pulling in and out honking horns, men in long white work gowns and heavy, cotton, long-sleeve coats with a butcher's apron worn over the front. Men were darting in and out of the vehicles, carcasses of animals being loaded on trucks and boxes of poultry pushed out on hand trucks. The gutters ran with reddish water and smelled from the ice melting inside thin wood crates packed with poultry, chickens of various sizes and weights.

Tony pulled his Oldsmobile in between two large box trucks in front of one wholesale market. As he got out of the car, one of the men loading chickens on a truck yelled to him, "Hey, Mr. D, how are you?" Tony waved and stepped carefully over the flowing creek at the curbside, being careful not to splash his Florsheim shoes or splatter his suit. He wore a thin gray overcoat, and although it was not his usual custom to wear a hat, he was wearing a silver-gray Borsalino fedora. The attire was as much the mark of a properly dressed boss as it was the fashion of the day in those circles when there were workmen and bosses.

He entered the loading dock area, then the office areas. There was a man in a white gown and black fedora, adding slips on a hand-operated manual calculator. He punched in numbers, then pulled a handle, and the white paper rolled out longer and longer. He looked up. "Hello Tony. How are you? What can I do for you?" the man said. He was a middle-aged, stocky man whose gray hair was visible under the hat.

"Hello, Gene. I called yesterday. I have to see Paulie," said Tony.

"Okay, I'll tell him you're here," said Gene and got up and went through an inner office door. In a few minutes, three men walked out with Gene. Gene said, "Paulie's inside. Please go ahead." Tony proceeded through a second office area where a woman and two men were sitting at wooden desks looking over papers. The smell of cigars and meat permeated the air. They walked to a door at the far side of the room and opened it.

"Tony, come in," said Paulie, and he walked over to him and they hugged. "How are things?" he said.

"Good, we're doing good. Always busy like you," said Tony.

Paulie Castelucci was tall and bulky and athletic. His very prominent Roman nose gave him an appearance in his early years of a latter-day matinee idol, but he was not that handsome anymore. He was, however, a very confident man, and he had a sort of all-knowing aura about him, serious but relaxed in his confidence. Being the relative by marriage to Carlos Gambini surely had a great deal to do with that self-confidence. He owned the very successful Blue Ribbon Market.

CHAPTER 56

"HOW CAN I help you?" asked Paulie.

"I have been dealing with a number of shipping lines, including some of the Greeks. One of my contacts saw the ships lined up at the piers at the Navy Yard here. They are confiscated vessels, and I think the US Marshall's Office has custody of them. Usually they will do a survey on each vessel then sell them. Sometimes they go to auction, but sometimes they just get rid of them to any buyers who come along. If the ship is deemed unseaworthy, they might just sell it for scrap. They hire a number of private contractors to do the surveys. The repair contractors are almost always union. I need to talk to the contractor's union connection. If the five largest of these ships are okay, I think I can find buyers for them. If the contractor gives reports indicating these vessels are junk, then they are only worth scrap metal price. I think that we can all make a buck on this. There will be a piece for the union guy and for you. The US Marshall's Office would just as soon get rid of these ships anyway. I was thinking you would have a connection. Those guys who work for the union with the city Marine and Aviation use those piers and know what's what there as they move the ships around," Tony explained at length.

"I think I might have a way. What do you think the deal is worth?" asked Paulie.

"I am not sure until we get some information on the ships, the age and condition of them, the engines and who and when built. Once I know that, I will have a better idea. It could be millions," said Tony.

"Okay, let me see what I can do. Check in with me next week," said Paulie.

Tony had known Paul for many years. He also knew his family and his connection to the highest-ranking boss in the mob. In fact, he had always been invited to their family weddings and attended the funerals. Tony's father was a distant relative of the Gambini family. The branch of that family settled in Brooklyn when they came over from Sicily in the early 1900s.

Tony did business with Paul, but, as with others who were connected, he was always wary of giving out too much information. The connection to Onassis that he had was too important to let others know. In fact, the connection was made through yet another mob guy in Manhattan, Angelo di La Cruce. Angelo did not get along that well with Paul, so there was reason to keep those associations separate. Also, if any of their guys smelled big money, they would want to run the deal themselves and try to cut everyone else out. It was the way many of their guys did business, even with friends. Tony also knew Onassis had his own people who communicated with the organized crime leadership not only in America but worldwide. Onassis used intermediaries so his name was never directly involved.

Tony could get a fairly good idea of the value of the ships from a number of his associates in the shipping industry if Paulie could get someone to get the information he needed. It would not be unusual either for one of his companies to buy the vessels, even just to scrap them. So Tony had a plan. If he was sure they were good, seaworthy vessels, he would suggest to Onassis's people that an intermediate company buy the ships, then move them to a foreign port, where he could sell them to an Onassis subsidiary so there were no links to Onassis's company. This also gave him the edge he needed to cut himself in on a piece of the action.

"Anthony, I want you to get back to your friend and tell her you will have some information about the ships shortly. Also, tell her we will, if the deal is good, find a way to have a neutral party who has a history with these purchases and could possibly have a big influence on the price," Tony told Anthony.

A few days later, Tony got a call from one of Paulie's men for Tony to stop by.

"My guy knows the private contractors that the feds hired who were brought in to survey those ships. They were all part of the assets of a company that was caught dealing weapons and used because they were regular merchant liners that ran between the US and Europe and some of the countries in the Arab Gulf. The CIA uncovered the connection. They are still trying to find the lead guy. He had a deal with this guy, Ken Bosworth, who ran a legitimate shipping company, the Freedom Laetch Lines. The ships were all made in Virginia by the Northern Ship Company. They haven't tested all the systems, but my guy says they're in good shape. Here is a list of sizes and capacities along with the power and so forth. He said he could arrange to have the reports of those good five ships and the other twelve being held there mixed up. He will change the numbers on the paperwork and show that these five good ones are for scrap. He wants a half million to do it," said Paulie.

"Whew, that's a lot of coin. I'm not sure my people are going to go for that. I know the price they will want for the scrap purchase and then they got to get these things towed out. Can you talk to the guy and see what his bottom line is?" said Tony.

"I guess so, but you know whatever happens here, I get two hundred Gs," said Paul. Tony knew that Paul was going to get a piece from the union guy as well but said nothing about it. It was the price of doing business.

"Okay," said Tony, "but let's try to get this done quickly. My contact may need to leave soon."

"Marcus, good to see you again. And, Christina, how are you?" said Delmont.

"Fine. So, how did things go?" asked Christina.

Delmont explained the details, and when done, Marcus left the room and then returned. "I think we will be here for several more days. They are installing some sophisticated new electronics, and it takes time."

"In that case, why don't we take another evening on the town," said Christina, and she turned to Anthony as if he should respond.

"Well, great. Let's do that. Why don't we begin sort of where we left off? There are lots of interesting places to go, and I would be happy to enjoy another evening out," said Anthony.

"I need to attend to some things for the next two days but perhaps after that," said Christina.

"I think I can do that," Anthony replied.

"Then it's settled. Why don't we decide on a place to meet now? Have you a place in mind, Anthony?" inquired Marcus.

"Yes. I think I do. It's an easy place to find as well, the Empire State Building. There is a club on the ground level and the Rainbow Room on one of the top floors with the greatest view of the city," said Anthony.

"Sounds wonderful," said Christina. The days were turning warmer, and late spring was a transformation in New York City.

The mostly gray buildings and leafless trees had changed to a more hospitable view with blooming trees and patches of green here and there now that May was here. Flowers grew in little pocket parks, and even the smell of the fuels that burned to heat the metropolis disappeared. Not that it smelled like a flower garden, but one could walk the sidewalks without nearly choking on the thick, smog-like, dreary winter air.

It seemed to invigorate the people as well, and there was a noticeable change in attitudes. The populace did not change the habit of rustling and bustling about, but the expressions on people's faces were less grim or taut. The warmer weather seemed to soothe the spirit somewhat, or at least people seemed less annoyed with life.

Anthony handed the cab driver some bills and stepped out onto the curb as the cab sped off.

He walked to the revolving door and through the corridor to a stairway, which led down to a black steel door with a bell button at one side. He pressed the button and waited. The door opened, and a small, frail-looking man looked up at Anthony. "Hey, Antonio. Glad to see you," said the little man.

"Alphonso, how are you?" inquired Anthony and walked in. The noise of pots banging and people talking loudly in various languages filled the air. The corridor led to a huge kitchen, and cooks were rushing about.

"You look well, my friend. How is your family, your uncle?" said Alphonso.

"Very well, thank you, and I will tell him you asked for him—that is, if he's not here now. I know he likes to stop in as much as I do," said Anthony.

"And we so enjoy it when he does," said the little man, and he smiled as he led Anthony to yet another door at the end of the kitchen and out to a very upscale bar. Music was playing from the sound system.

"What time does the orchestra begin tonight?" asked Anthony.

"Oh, about nine or so," said Alphonso.

Anthony looked at his watch; it was seven thirty. "Well, I expect some friends to be by shortly," said Anthony.

"I have your table set whenever you are."

Anthony had spent the better part of the day going over the details of the reports his uncle received on the five ships in Brooklyn and had committed to memory the details of each. Big Tony had gotten the call from Paulie to expect a messenger, who brought a large portfolio with blueprint copies and details of each ship.

The club was relatively quiet at this time. There were people at the bar, and only a few tables were occupied. Anthony watched the public entrance doorway, which led to the street side stairs and the sidewalk.

It was his habit to go to the rear entrance after leaving a message with Alphonso that he would be there. Perhaps habit was not the accurate word. During the times when police surveillance was at high alert, certain places were always watched for the comings and goings of familiar faces, particularly those notable places like this club and the Copa as well as Top of the Mark. The surveillance was usually done by a pair of detectives in an unmarked car parked near the entrances. So someone walking into a building from the business entrance was hardly noticeable in the crowds streaming in and out.

Since the sensitive nature of the communication between Anthony and Christina concerning the ships warranted extreme caution, Anthony had plans to keep their association from here on a very low profile.

The patrons at the bar were mostly upper-class New Yorkers. The men were either in business suits or in more upscale attire, spruced up for a night on the town.

The women were well dressed too, some with the obvious trappings of wealth, diamonds and jewels, in designer dresses. One side of the bar had a group of three women, in their late thirties to midforties, sipping martinis and chattering continually. These ladies were obviously moneyed.

One woman, in particular, was a standout. She was in a deep blue cocktail dress that revealed an ample chest and was complemented by her long blonde hair and sparkling jewelry. Dripping from her ears were long strands of gold studded with diamonds, and a necklace with multiple diamonds hung around her neck. She had a classic Nordic profile, straight nose, high cheekbones, and flawless complexion. She could have been a cover girl in her earlier days, but now the hint of a wrinkle about the edges of her eyes and just a slight puffiness around those darting, dark blue eyes gave away her maturity, obviously not yet the subject of the plastic surgeon's handiwork. She also had just a hint of extra skin under her chin, which gave her face a bit more fullness. The men at the bar, even those engaged in conversations with their female companions, would, from time to time, attempt a glance at her.

Marcus entered first, followed by Christina's main bodyguard, and then she walked in followed by two other men. Marcus spotted Anthony at the bar, and all walked over. "Good evening," greeted Anthony as he shook Marcus's hand but also moved toward Christina at the same time. She held out her hand, and Anthony took it as they made eye contact. She had a slight upturn at the sides of her mouth, but her eyes widened, and she looked amused and excited. Anthony took her hand to his mouth and kissed it.

She turned to Marcus as he did. "Your friend is a gentleman to the extreme. The last time I had my hand kissed, it was by one of the sons of the old former Italian monarchy, a prince something or another. But I must say, I am flattered to have the opportunity to tell my Greek friends that I so beguiled an American boy, even though of Italian ancestry, that he kissed my hand," said Christina. They all smiled.

"Well, I can do with a drink after all that," said Marcus. The bar man accommodated as Marcus made the introduction of the two other men. "Anthony, this is Stavros Andopolio and Antonin Vulga Starvos, who is a marine engineer. Tonin is one of our executive mechanics. He is also one of our prize employees. He swims like a fish and drinks like a Russian. That's because he had a Russian father who married a Greek woman who lived on one of our small islands where he grew up. I think he was born in the water," explained Marcus.

Tonin smiled as he shook Anthony's hand. His grasp was strong and vigorous. He was about Anthony's height, but his jacket size was at least three times larger. He had wide shoulders, and his chest bulged. Marcus went on, "Stavros is not simply an engineer; he also designs ships and does retrofit designs. He can turn a battleship into a luxury yacht, and one would never suspect its origins."

Stavros was of average build, a man in his fifties with thick, wire-rimmed glasses that gave his eyes a peculiar beady appearance. He stumbled a bit with his English pronunciation but finally got the words out. "Extremely pleased to meet you."

They chatted about the food in New York, the progress of the work on the vessel *Christina*, and finally Anthony mentioned having spoken with some friends in Brooklyn recently concerning the Navy Yard there. Instead of actually mentioning the ships, he first sought to gauge Christina's reaction about discussing their business before the two men. He gave her the opportunity to open the subject for discussion. "Oh, and have you any information on those ships being held there? I discussed this with Stavros and Tonin, and we'll seek their opinions once we know more," said Christina. This was Anthony's signal that these men had her confidence.

"Well, let's get our table, and I will tell you what I know."

Alphonso had been attending to a series of wine bottles just off the corridor between the kitchen and the end of the bar. Anthony glanced over to him and raised his head. Alphonso saw him and came over. "Good evening and welcome. May I show you to your table?"

After everyone was seated and Alphonso had brought over a bottle of red wine and poured each a glass, Anthony began his report. "Our people have received the mechanical survey reports and spoke to some of the survey team. The five vessels are all in fairly good condition but require a bit of work."

Stavros and Tonin posed a series of questions, some too technical for Anthony to answer. Tonin wanted to know if the hulls were properly surveyed. Anthony knew the reports had detailed each hull. However, he did not want to say he had those reports at the table.

There were a few people on the small dance floor in front of a large bandstand. Anthony said, "The last time we danced, you asked me. Now it's my turn to offer."

Christina smiled and said, "Okay." They rose and made their way to the dance floor. The slow, rhythmic music was loud enough so that Anthony's conversation could not be heard except by his partner.

"I have all the reports and can provide them to you. I can also deliver the vessels to a small yard in Virginia where they will not be noticed. There they can be slightly refitted and disguised so they can be removed with no curious eye about. So many ships are in and out of these piers, so they will never be noticed. If your people are interested, I will be happy to provide information," Anthony said.

She nodded. "Yes, very interested, and what would the cost be?" she said.

"We are working that out, but it will take between five and a half to six million, not including the refitting and changing the ships' profiles."

"Hmmm, seems a bit steep," she said.

"Christina, the one vessel, the three-hundred-foot cargo ship, was built three years ago, but you already know that. It cost over $8 million. It's probably worth over seven today after all the sophisticated equipment that was added to it when it was used to transport weapons." Christina smiled and nodded. "And I need half a million for the transfer and one million for our end," said Delmont.

"I am interested," she said in a whisper, but this time she pressed her mouth against his ear lightly and also pressed her chest against him as well. He reminded himself that this person represented not just a major business connection to his family but was the daughter of one of the world's most powerful men, who had the respect of the leaders of many countries, including America. He and his family assisted the

Allies with supplies during World War II and were influential in the supply of fuel. Hence his hesitation to mix business with his more basic needs. He also considered that she played on that very apprehension to some degree. Anthony, however, was clever in his own way. While he did not respond in an immediate and obvious manner, he moved his legs and his hands so that she could sense the male response, subtle yet arousing. He occasionally brushed his own hair slightly or his chin, always somehow touching her ear or her neck in the process. Thus he probed her sensitivity and noticed she stiffened when he touched the nape of her neck or the exposed area between her neck and shoulder. At the same time, she squinted her eyes slightly at that touch and pressed her body forward. Then the music stopped, and as they parted, Christina looked up at Anthony with a wistful smile.

The evening proceeded as the crowd thickened. Then after dinner, the show began. The attention turned to the curtain on the stage. The house lights were dimmed, almost unnoticed. The stage lights brightened, and a deep, strong voice proclaimed, "Ladies and gentlemen, welcome to the Riverboat. I give you the one and only Doc Severson and his world-famous orchestra."

Doc walked on stage with the gleaming brass trumpet in his hand and waved at the now packed house. Then he began to lead the orchestra in the tune most associated with World War II, "I'll Be Seeing You." The trumpet sound seemed to transform the room into an instant catalyst for the romance of old, perhaps the nostalgia of a bygone, desperate era. Couples seemed to refocus from whatever their workday chatter was to tune into the atmosphere change.

Marcus and Stavros were discussing the music with Tonin, but Marcus seemed to be looking over the two women at the other end of the bar.

More drinks and wine were brought. Marcus excused himself as the others chatted. "Ladies, good evening. I see you are enjoying the wonderful music and wondered if I might ask if you would like to dance," Marcus said smoothly with a warm smile.

The ladies looked at each other, and one, a dark-haired, dark-eyed woman, said emphatically, "I don't think so!"

"Oh, wait just a minute, maybe that would be nice," said the blonde. "I love the music, and we are short on men here." The three laughed, and Marcus smiled and held his hand out to the woman as she rose from her bar seat.

As they began to dance, Marcus said, "My name is Marcus. I believe your friend seemed a little annoyed that I asked."

"Oh, Marjorie has a lot on her mind these days. I'm sorry if she was not very nice. She is involved in a bitter divorce, and I think she has it in for all mankind. That is the male part of mankind. Men aren't her favorite people just now," said the blonde.

"And are you kind to our species?" said Marcus.

"It all depends on how I am treated. I can be very, very kind," she said. As she spoke, the last part of her sentence sort of came out in a lower, slightly deeper tone.

"So, kind lady, what is your name?" asked Marcus.

"What do you want it to be?" she replied. "Shall I be Anita or Maria or simply Kind Lady?" she added with a sly smile and a raised eyebrow as she blinked her eyes excessively.

"You are very clever and amusing. I think I'll call you Joy because you make me happy." She smiled, but it was not a smile of happiness.

"Joy, yes, that's me, Joy. I go around spreading cheer and goodwill. Oh, I'm sorry. I don't mean to be so sarcastic; it's just the name struck me as ironic," she answered. They danced awhile longer, but neither felt very comfortable.

Marcus was trying to consider some more neutral item of conversation. "How do you like living here in New York?" he said.

"Oh, it's fine, I guess. Lots of places to go and things to do," she said, refocusing herself on her dance partner.

She noticed his handsome facial features, and she detected through his accent that he was likely a Greek. "So, what does Marcus do when he's not asking strangers to dance?" she inquired.

"I run a very exclusive yacht from time to time, and I am in the boat business."

"Oh, really, and I suppose you arrived in New York on some magnificent boat?" she asked.

He smiled. "As a matter of fact, yes, that is true."

"Well, Mr. Marcus, you are a very good dancer, and I would guess you are a good yachtsman. What else are you good at?" she said with a throaty voice.

Marcus pulled her closer, and she responded by placing her leg between his legs as they turned. "Oh, many things—many, many things," he answered, whispering in her ear.

Anthony caught a glimpse of the two on the dance. "Seems like Marcus found a new friend," he said to Christina. The other two men were uninterested and kept talking to each other.

Christina replied, "Well, Marcus is a real lady's man. The women love him. He is so appealing that if he were not my cousin, I might give him a second thought," she said and laughed a little. "So, the ships will be good, but can we trust that the surveyors are knowledgeable? Do you have any way we can authenticate their findings?" she asked.

"I can only tell you that the two lead technicians have many years in the business, and their company, Northern Ship Company, builds various vessels under their direction. Also, we have information that they did tests on the main vessel systems and engines to be sure they were okay." Christina nodded. A waiter brought out a tray with several dishes and placed it in the center of the table. There were a number of small plates of various appetizers, grapes, cheeses, and fruits. A variety of breads were brought out as well.

The two engineers looked at each other and then at the food. "Wonderful," said Tonin. He began to eat and was soon joined by the others. The music continued, and Anthony answered Christina's questions regarding the vessels.

After nearly an hour, Anthony said, "Excuse me," and walked to a corridor off the bar to the restroom area. As he entered, he could hear the music loud and clear as it was being piped into the men's room as well. He walked into an area with wall-installed urinals. The floors were rich granite, spotted gray, and the walls were done in slabs of highly polished marble. He proceeded to his business, and as he did, he could hear noises coming from a cubicle behind him, which were accessible through an arched opening. He stepped back and could hear distinct grunting sounds. Curious, he walked slowly and quietly into the area where there were bathroom stalls lined against a wall. The noise emanated from the last stall. He walked down and stood just a few feet away. He stooped down and recognized the shiny alligator skin shoes Marcus wore. He could see his foot placed flat on the floor and a shoeless foot covered in nylon stocking dangling over his leg facing the opposite direction. The breathing sounds and grunts made it very clear what was happening. He also noticed through the small jointed metal stall panels a glimpse of color and movement. He saw the blue fabric of a dress and wisps of blonde hair. There were rhythmic movements accompanying the sounds. He retreated and went back to his table. The three were still chatting.

The music continued after a short break.

During that break, Anthony saw Marcus and the blonde emerge from the corridor near the bar. Marcus had his arm around the waist of the woman, who had a definite red blush about her face. Marcus, on the other hand, seemed cool and composed as he escorted the woman to the table. "I want you to meet my friend, Joy," he declared drily, and two more chairs were quickly brought over.

Christina looked the woman up and down. The blonde observed the looks Christina was directing her way. "So, Joy, what brings you to New York besides this music?" asked Christina.

"Oh, it's home for me," she said. "I'm a lifelong New Yorker. My friends and I get together now and then to catch up."

The music began again, and Marcus said, "Joy, please let's dance to this." They rose and walked off to the dance floor.

"Well, you are more than a great dancer, as you said. I'm still trying to catch my breath," said Joy.

"Well, you are an incredible inspiration," Marcus responded, brushing his mouth across her ear.

"Careful or I'll have to take you back there again to calm you down," she responded. They both laughed.

"You know your friends will wonder why you have abandoned them," said Marcus.

"I don't think so. They are used to my disappearing act if there are good reasons for it."

"Oh, am I a good reason?" asked Marcus.

"Honey, at the risk of being a little coarse, you are a good reason and an incredible fuck," she answered.

Marcus was a little stunned but also flattered. "May I say the feeling is mutual?" he answered.

"My friends do their thing, sometimes with other men, sometimes between themselves. I don't do that, but whatever makes you happy. I'm sure, however, that you have created a great deal of attention with them since we pulled our little disappearing act," she added.

The pair walked back to the bar where the other ladies were chatting. "Oh, you two found your way back. I hope you're not exhausted from all that errh—dancing," said the dark-haired lady in a good-natured tone. "Oh, yes, Marcus is quite a dancer, and I mean quite a dancer. I think he is as good as a professional," she said.

Then the other lady whose marital problems were discussed said, "Well, you should know; you had your share of professionals, sweetie. Dancers that is," she added sarcastically. The other women looked at her and groaned. The little group chatted for a while when Marcus noticed that Christina, Anthony, and the other two were getting up from their table.

"Ladies, it's been a pleasure, and I hope to see you all again sometime. I think my group is moving on," said Marcus.

The blonde slid off her bar chair and got close to Marcus. In a nearly inaudible voice, she said, "The pleasure, my dear, was all mine," and embraced him.

The group gathered, and Anthony said, "I have a little shortcut to upstairs we can take," and they proceeded through the kitchen doors, out to the lower lobby entry, and up the stairs to the main lobby and a bank of elevators. There they entered the elevator and went up to the Rainbow Room and when the doors opened, the sound of the music and the crowd instantly filled the air.

"Good evening," said a man standing by an entry stand. He was dressed in a tuxedo and had the look of an English butler.

"I am Anthony Delmont, and these are my guests, Christina Onassis, Marcus, and Mr. Tonin and Mr. Stavros. The other gentleman is with us as well, but he prefers to stay at the bar," said Delmont.

"Of course, Mr. Delmont. It's a pleasure to see you again. Please come this way." They were escorted to an area that had brass stanchions and red velvet roping. By the time they walked the few steps, another man similarly dressed walked over.

"Sir, it is a pleasure to have you here again at the Rainbow. Please may I show you to your table?" the maître d' gushed. He led the group to a ringside table, one close to the piano and dance floor, which afforded a view of the performance stage. "I hope you like the seating," he said and retrieved the "Reserved" sign from the table.

"Thank you, Carlo," said Delmont.

The waiter came over with a bottle of water and a silver bucket with ice and arranged each guest a glass and then left.

"The place is always special," said Delmont.

"I believe you. I have heard of the history here. Billie Holliday and the French singer, oh, I can't recall her name," said Christina.

"Piaf—Edith Piaf. And many others. It's history all right." The band was playing an old Duke Ellington number, one everyone in America knew by sound but few could name.

There was a pause, and a woman made her way to the center stage. "Is that Eartha Kitt?" asked Christina.

"Why, yes," said Delmont.

Soon the crowd hushed as the intro to the songstress's first tune was struck. The voice was clear and unmistakable. The words were sung with precision and passion. Her facial expression changed with the lyrics.

"She's wonderful," said Marcus.

"Don't get any ideas," said Christina. "You have prowled around quite a bit already tonight, and I don't need you to be chasing the star of the show and end up making a scene," scolded Christina.

Marcus laughed. "A scene? Me? A scene? Why, I never ever make a scene. I am not one to offend, Christina, dear Christina. The one thing I do is make people happy," he answered with a jocular attitude.

"Oh, yes, we know how you make people happy, you gigolo," she said and gently slapped his hand. They all laughed.

The music continued for hours, and the singer did two shows.

As the night wore on, Anthony sensed that the interest Christina had shown in him might very well have just been for sport. She had learned about the vessels and sought the information to review. She had accomplished the task she set out to do and now just relaxed with no particular direction in mind.

"Here I am." Marcus looked over at the two men. Tonin had his eyes closed, and Stavros was leaning back in his chair. "I think we need to get these two some sleep," said Marcus.

Christina said, "I agree. Anthony, you have been a grand host."

"Thank you again," said Marcus.

"We will be in touch," Anthony said to Christina, and they lightly embraced as the elevator door opened. The group bid good-night as Anthony stayed behind. He went to the bar. There, Carlo approached him.

"Thank you, Mr. Delmont," he said and handed him a check, which Anthony signed. He had a drink and then headed for the elevator.

He retraced his path back to the Riverboat and sat at the bar. "Hey, Danny, how are you?" Anthony said.

"Good, Mr. Delmont, real good. Say, that was some group you had with you earlier. Isn't that the Onassis girl?" asked Danny, the bartender.

"No, Dan, but she is a dead ringer for her," said Delmont.

"Well, her pal is a pretty swift mover. He came over to the girls' corner over here. Those ladies are our regular irregulars. They are here fairly often. Giselle is a lawyer, the tall brunette hard as nails. You know, I think she might be a dike. Margorie is married to a Wall Street guy who was a money lender and had lots of money. Some said he's in the top one hundred richest on the street. Then there is Janet. She was married to some advertising bigwig. I think Janet and Margorie live in the same building over on Sutton Place. The real looker is Diane, Diane Cushman. Her husband owns half of the city of New York. His great-grandfather was said to be a partner of J. P. Morgan, they say— old money. You know that Diane is really something. You can always tell when she's on the prowl. She dresses to the teeth. I thought she was going to eat that young guy you had with you alive. She latched onto him real quick. She does her little tour deal around here. She disappears, but more than once she's been spotted in the men's room in one of the stalls sucking some guy's dick. What whores these ladies of fashion are," Danny said with a grin. "You know, I can't figure it out. That woman is so beautiful and rich, and she can have any man she wants, but what does she do? She picks up a guy at our bar, gets him in the men's room, and bangs him. Then she always leaves alone. I guess things aren't so good at home no matter how much money you got. Maybe it's just sport for her. For me, she can lead me to the shithouse or anywhere anytime. *Marone*, what a pair of knockers," Danny exclaimed as he gestured with two hands at his chest. The bar was still full, but the band was done, and the tables had mostly cleared out. "You want another, Mr. Delmont?" asked Danny.

"No, I think that's enough for tonight." Delmont peeled a twenty-dollar bill off his bankroll and laid it on the bar. "Night, Danny." He left.

Big Tony had gotten a hand-delivered tube sent to him personally from his Brooklyn friend. "Anthony, find a way to have someone over there pick this up in an unlikely place," he told Delmont.

After considering a drop-off point, he called Marcus and told him to send a trusted aide to Bill's Market Bar and Restaurant. This place was located in the middle of the downtown Manhattan wholesale meat market district, on the West Side, just off Little West Twelfth Street, by the Gansevoort Market.

At midmorning, the place would still be active but not completely jammed as at four or five in the morning with the crash of trucks and when men in long, white, starched kitchen coats loaded meat products in a rotating frenzy.

Even the streets smelled like animal flesh. The sidewalks were dotted with little splotches of flattened-out, rolled-over chunks of animal fat. Even when wholesale market owners sprayed hot, steaming water on the sidewalks, loading docks' curbs, and gutters, the smell remained.

Bill's was a market bar and restaurant. Men in white coats and greasy fedoras sat at the bar or the tables, eating steak and eggs washed down with strong black coffee laced with multiple shots of rye whiskey or scotch. The ceramic tile floor was spread with sawdust to prevent slipping on grease tracked in by the patrons, and the sawdust was removed and replaced each day.

Delmont knew the place well. He recalled his days as a young boy when he would accompany his father to the market. They would wake at two in the morning and dress quickly, and Mom would have a bowl of oatmeal or farina for each to gobble down. Then off they'd go in the old Chevy panel truck, through the Holland Tunnel to make their rounds to the beef house, the veal dealer, the chicken and poultry and the lamb and pork dealers. Each had a specialty. There was an order to loading the truck. The animal carcasses were laid on just before the thin wooden crate of iced poultry. Boxes of pork loins and shoulders were purchased and loaded first. Then whole lambs and calves. Boxes with livers were wedged in as well, and then four quarters beef chucks and hines (rear quarters) were loaded. Then the poultry. The truck was then not only balanced, but the melting ice would drain out the back as the truck tipped slightly to the rear with the load. Rags and butcher aprons absorbed any other runoff.

Burly men in fedoras with cigars clenched on the side of their mouths would know Anthony by name. "Hey, Antneey, you're getting big. Where's your brother Vinnie?" Going to the market was like visiting old relatives. The market owners and their men lived the job, generation to generation from the turn of the century. At that time, Anthony's father used to go to the market with his father. They started at midnight when the two would get the two horses and hitch them to a huge wood-slatted wagon. If it was winter, they covered up with blankets and then went off to the Staten Island Ferry. There they crossed the Lower Manhattan bay and from South Ferry headed up the West Side of Manhattan. The sounds of the horses' hooves on the cobblestone street sounded like a symphony. Big Bill Kerner had the poultry house. There you could get crates of freshly killed chickens, "New York dressed," with the head and feet and the guts intact.

Not much had changed since those days; only now they had the comfort of the Chevy truck. There were still live chickens, pheasants, and rabbits to be bought, and the heirs to the families were still there. Billy Kerner, old Bill's son, took over when some crazed, irate customer pulled a gun and shot Bill Sr. dead, right on the sidewalk many years earlier. The son had a peculiarity; his ears were nearly double the size, and though no one would say it in front of his face, Big Billy was nick-named "Big Ear."

The rabbit man, Joe Coniglio, always tried to slip a small rabbit in Anthony's coat pocket as a pet, but his father would always catch him doing it. "No, no live rabbits. No place to keep them."

Anthony knew the markets were beginning to disappear and move to the new designated market area at Hunts Point in the Bronx, but some remained. So did the cobblestone streets and Bill's, at least for now.

At eight in the morning, Anthony sat at a table as men wandered in and out. He sipped his coffee laced with Jack Daniels. Eventually, he saw one of Marcus's stewards walk in and beckoned to him. "You have a package for Marcus?" he asked.

"Yes, here. Please be careful with it and tell Marcus to call me immediately when he receives it. You are going directly back. Here's a number. Just tell Marcus to ask for me when someone answers. Ask for Tony," said Delmont. The steward took the tube and left. Anthony sat back down and pulled out a newspaper and waited for the call. An hour passed.

"Hey, Tony, it's for you," the bartender called.

Tony went to the bar and was handed a phone. "Yes," he said.

"Well, these things are very interesting to us. We would like to have someone actually take a look. Is that possible?" the female voice at the other end asked.

"Difficult, but it's not impossible. I'll get back to you," said Anthony.

Queenies on Court Street in Brooklyn was one of the busiest lunch places in the downtown area in the vicinity of the federal courts and law offices, as well as the hub for business and politics. The Queen Restaurant, its formal name, had great food even if it wasn't the fan-ciest place downtown. The crowd thinned around one thirty when Anthony went in with two men who looked like they were workmen. They were dressed in gray workmen's jackets and pants, twill cotton uniforms, and wore fedoras. They proceeded to a rear table where two other men, similarly dressed, had just finished eating sandwiches.

"Anthony, how are you?" asked Sally Deito, who rose and shook his hand.

"Great. This is Steve and Tony," Anthony said, introducing Stavros and Tonin by their new Americanized names. Both shook hands. "This here's Bobby Ceroli. He's one of my top mechanics."

"Okay, if you guys will come with me, I'll get you where you want to go, and all you need to do is follow me. Put these badges on like this." He showed his ID badge pinned on the left side of his uniform pocket. "We will see you later, Ant, about five, I guess, okay?"

Sally said, "Yeah, fine, I'll be here." They left, and Anthony walked out soon after.

He was sipping his coffee and looked down at his watch; it was a quarter after five. Then the door opened, and Sally walked in, followed by Steve and Tony. "Well, I gave them the tour. We even fired up the motors and checked the electronics. All is copasetic."

Steve and Tony nodded. "Yes, yes," said Steve.

"Thanks, Sally. I'll see you soon."

"Okay," Sally said as he turned toward the door.

"These vessels are okay. All he said is true. They need some work, but all the basics are fine, just a little neglected," said Tonin.

"Let's go," said Anthony. "I'll drop you off myself in downtown Manhattan because I have to go there now." The three got into Anthony's green Oldsmobile four-door sedan. Actually, it was Big Tony's car he had borrowed.

Anthony really never got used to driving this car. The gas pedal was like a hair trigger. Just a little pressure, and the rear wheels would squeal, and the car would lurch forward at top speed. The car could reach sixty miles per hour in less than seven seconds. Then there were those power brakes. They were indeed power brakes, for when you touched them just a little bit too hard, you could go through the windshield.

Anthony drove to the Brooklyn Queens Expressway and then veered off at the tunnel to downtown Manhattan. He got just past South Ferry and pulled to the curb at West Street. "Okay, I think you can pick up a cab from here pretty easy," said Anthony.

"Yes, fine," said Stavros. "We will. Okay, see you." And they left.

Anthony turned and headed toward the East Side, threading his way through downtown traffic and pulling up at a parking garage near Pearl Street. He handed the attendant a five-dollar bill. "I'm not sure how long I will be. Hold it out for a while."

He walked around the block and entered George's Restaurant and bar. He spotted Big Tony at a back table and waved and walked to the bar. Tony was talking to a fat, balding, heavyset man with glasses that had a thick stump of a cigar sticking out of his mouth. He recognized the fat man, Mr. Rothstein. He knew he was some kind of accountant but never really knew exactly if he was a CPA or a glorified bookkeeper. He knew he lived on the Upper West Side of Manhattan because he had to pick him up a few times to take him various places, mostly in Westchester.

Anthony ordered a Compari and sipped it slowly. After fifteen minutes, Rothstein got up and left. He noticed Anthony at the bar and nodded to him as he walked out. Anthony nodded back. Then Big Tony looked over at Anthony and raised his eyebrows. Anthony went over to the table. "Everything go all right today?" he asked.

"Yeah, fine. All is in order just like was said," Anthony reported.

"Good. Now we can move on this. Let's make a phone call in about an hour. They should have been briefed by then," said Big Tony.

They called a waiter over, and each ordered a steak. They each ordered a schooner of beer to wash down the steak and potatoes.

An hour later, Anthony went to the phone booth in the corridor near the men's room. "Hello, Marcus. So, we're in good shape," said Anthony. He got an affirmative reply. "Okay, we move in three days. Let me know when your cranes are in, and we will start," Anthony confirmed.

The call came two days later. Documents had already been submitted to remove "salvage." Big Tony had engaged a well-connected lawyer to handle the transaction, Eugene Ferranti. Ferranti had become a lawyer and joined his father, John Ferranti, who had begun his law career by being a conduit for contributions to political campaigns throughout New York, funded by some people whose names could not appear on contributor lists. Eugene's father had bribed the law school admissions officer to approve his application to Brooklyn Law School.

After that, pressure was put on professors to be sure he passed, and another bribe got him a passing grade on his bar exam. The old man knew his son was not capable of passing on his own, but he needed someone to follow his direction, someone he could trust. The powerhouses in the ruling Democratic Party, Adam Clay Powell and his protégés and associates, were keenly aware of the sources of the money. Political influence was priced by virtue of the level of the favor. No favor was too difficult; it just cost more. Men like John Ferranti made a lucrative career not trying cases and not being entangled in long and complicated litigation. He had found the antidote for stress, and its color was green. Thus, he taught his son, "Genie," the ropes. The father was, however, an old-school student. He was smoothly articulate and discreet. He exuded confidence while also knowing how to charm both his clients and his connections. He also had a sense of who he was and what he was doing. He had no delusion. His son, Genie, however, grew up as a child of privilege. While he was doted upon as an only child by his mother, his father did not have too much time to devote to his upbringing. His mother, Clara, taught him to be mannerly, very mannerly. He also picked up his father's mannerisms and his faux charm when he wanted something. He found that he could manipulate his mother at an early age. His father, however, insisted early on that his son excel in school. Genie never forgot his experience when in third grade he had been acting up and not tending to his studies. He had lied to his mother about doing his homework. The old man saw the report card and immediately brought the boy before him, removed his belt, and beat the boy until his squeals were heard a block away. He was confined to his room every night for months and had to handwrite two copies of all his homework, one for school and one to be left on his father's desk. He was thereafter referred to by the nickname his father gave him, "Slacker," or "Slack" for short. Rarely, except in public, was he ever referred to by his given name. It was "Slacker, how are you doing in school now? Slack, what marks are you expecting?" His father was appalled at his son's failure to understand the importance of excelling in school. Memories of the Great Depression were vivid in his father's mind. His family emigrated from Italy at the end of the century in 1898. John had lived through the famine and World War I.

Gene, however, grew up, in contrast, never having to hustle for a dime and a mama's boy as well. Only he feared his father. Should he forget his place and misspeak, his father would be quick with a sharp and stinging smack across the mouth, maybe two. More than once, he attended school with his lips puffed out and red welts across his face; a bicycle accident was blamed. His mother would ice his wounds and remind him not to talk too much when his father was in the house.

"I hate him. I hate him. Someday I'll beat him up," he responded to his mother after a particularly severe beating brought on by his own arrogance with his father. When asked if he was so stupid that he could not bring a B+ to an A, he slipped. Although all other marks were As, his math mark was a B+ from his Irish teacher who he had sassed from time to time. Genie responded with the F word. Out of frustration, he blurted out the one word, "Fuck!"

His father's face turned red, and he grabbed the boy by the arm. "Fuck? Fuck who? Fuck me? I'll teach you. Fuck, you are fucked." He pummeled the boy until he was whimpering. "Here, lady. Take this shit bag out of here," he said to his wife, disgusted with the boy's attitude. Thus, Genie learned the hard way to restrain himself and be cautious. As he grew up, he always sought his father's approval but harbored a burning resentment, which never subsided, even years later when his father suffered a debilitating stroke. He had no compassion or concern. He did, however, see the opportunity to take over the entire financial empire his father had built over the years, apartment houses, some commercial properties, stocks, bonds, and the golden goose, a lucrative legal practice. He clearly resembled his father, nearly a twin twenty years younger. He also emulated his father's mannerisms, having studied his father's manners and voice inflections, hand gestures, and even his style of dress. He even had his father's voice. He easily slipped into the role his father played with those clients who saw him as truly his father's son. He was a good actor. He actually had a rather aristocratic air about him, which betrayed his role as his father's son. The old arrogance he had as a boy welled up in him when he no longer had to be in his father's shadow. He also had an unbelievable ego and a twisted view of life. He felt as if he were the center of the universe. While not an unreasonably attractive man, well proportioned, pleasant features, and well groomed, he envisioned himself a matinee idol and expected not just men but women to see him in that light. He could not understand why his advances to women were rejected. His frustration in attracting women resulted in a deep resentment for all women.

His father had built an office building, and his law firm occupied one half of the second floor. Genie moved into his father's office the day after his father's stroke. After weeks in the hospital, John was released, unable to walk and just nearly able to utter guttural sounds. An invalid confined to home.

About two weeks after his father's return, a woman came to the office. She asked the receptionist to see Mr. John Ferranti. She was told he was not in, out sick. "No," she insisted, "I want to see Mr. Ferranti Jr." The woman had been to the office many times over the last several years. She was in her midthirties, blond, and extremely well dressed, smelling of expensive perfume.

She was shown to the conference room. "Hello," she said when Genie entered the room.

"Yes, can I help you?" he said.

"Well, you know your father handled my affairs, and I heard he isn't feeling well," she said.

"He suffered a stroke and can't talk or walk," he said bluntly with a sort of strange grin or grimace.

She looked up at him and said, "Do you know who I am?"

He said, "You're my father's whore. He has had you around for years. What of it?"

Her face turned red. "No, I'm not a whore. Your father and I have a special relationship. We really care for each other, and I am beside myself about his stroke. I haven't come around, as I did not want to embarrass anyone. However, your father and I have business interests together," she said.

"Oh really? Business interests, is it? Is it funny business, monkey business, or just fucking business?" he said sarcastically.

She sensed how brutal this man could be and took a different track. "Look, I made your dad happy. Whatever he wanted, whenever he wanted it, I was there. He paid my rent and gave me money. I liked him. Now I'm broke. I can't even pay rent. I need a loan but have no-where to go for it," she said.

He looked her over. "Stand up," he said. She did. "Take your blouse and bra off," he said.

"Wait a minute. Who do you think you are?" she said, annoyed.

"Look, if I'm buying something, I want to see the goods. Take your blouse and bra off and drop your skirt," he demanded. She hesitated, then with a reluctant look and a flushed face, she obeyed.

She stood there naked except for her lace panties. "Turn around and drop your drawers." She did. "Spread your cheeks and bend over," he said.

"Now wait just a minute, you pig. That's far enough," she said.

"Look, I want to see if you have any kind of rash or worse." She then complied. As she bent over, he walked over to her and put his hand on her genitals. She gasped but stood still. He felt her private parts, then stuck his finger into her vagina. She could not see his face, which was contorted into a demonic grin. His father's whore, and he had his finger up her cunt. He pushed it further in. She gasped but stood still. She held the back of an office chair as he continued.

"You like that, don't you, you whore," he said. She did not answer. It was slightly painful, and she was enraged but held her tongue. "I said you like that," he said again.

"Yes, I like it, sweetie," she muttered sarcastically as he pushed his finger deeper.

"Okay, then turn around." She did. Standing in front of him naked, she faked a big smile. "Well, I think we are beginning to understand each other," he said. He turned and locked the conference door." Get up on the table and spread those legs," he ordered. She did it as he unbuckled his pants. She knew what to expect next.

In a moment, he was in her, pumping vigorously inside her. He groaned and pushed hard into her. She grimaced. He gasped when he was done. Then he withdrew. "Now that's the way things will be from now on," he said. "You understand, don't you?" he said.

"Yes, sir," she said.

"Now get dressed and tell Vivian to give you your monthly check and leave." This was just what she had done for years. She took a tissue from her purse and wiped her vaginal area and her legs where he had splattered her with semen. "Oh, I know all about that. Nothing will change, but now I will tell you when and where to be. You got that?" he said, still out of breath.

"Yes, thanks," she said and left.

Ferranti was now in full control of everything, and his arrogance grew daily. His encounter with Cat Sorensen stuck in his mind. He reveled in belittling his father's whore and then banging her. He rolled it over and over in his mind.

Katelyn "Cat" Sorensen was the product of a Swedish father and a Sicilian mother, the odd couple in their day. Carmela Risso Messina had come over from Italy in steerage class with her new husband, Enzo. Enzo, unfortunately, contracted some respiratory disease on the way over and died of pneumonia halfway between Italy and America in the middle of the Atlantic. His body was committed to the ocean, and his wife took on the mantle of a widow. She arrived in New York, and with the help of some people from her hometown who had come over a few years before, she got work cleaning for the wealthy. She was fastidious and organized. One of her friends became pregnant and in her later months had to give up a cleaning job for a wealthy shipping company broker, Carl Sorensen, a Swede. Sorensen had been a ship's bursar and had been educated as an accountant in his home country. He rose to the head of the accounting department of the Holland-America Lines but then struck out on his own when he saw the opportunity to broker space on the various freight shippers, any of which came through the Port of New York.

He made a fortune during the shipping heyday just before the world war. Carmela was a clever young woman who was also very astute. She not only cleaned his house but cooked sumptuous meals for Mr. Sorensen, a bachelor. Over time, his employee became a live-in maid. His brownstone home was a large, imposing three-story place. Once she moved in, she had the place running like a top. He enjoyed learning her language, and he taught her English. They grew closer, and eventually she shared his bed. She was entertaining as well. She had learned to play mandolin as a child and would play and sing for him. Eventually his affection turned into a loving relationship, and he looked forward to having his woman there after a day's work.

Then she told him some news one night. "Carl, I love you very much, so I must tell you I think I'm to have a baby," she said in a frightened whisper as the two lay in bed.

He hesitated for a few minutes. Then he said, "Of course you are, and we will have a wonderful child. You will be the mother, and I will be a father and a husband. Now we must marry." She smiled, and so it was. They had a small wedding in the church she chose, St. Helen's. Some nine months later, she gave birth to a girl, Katelin. It was a joyous time. Katelin was raised with the support and love lavished upon her. The war began to erode the Sorensen business, however, and Carl worried. The years passed, and Katelin was never deprived of anything. She went to the best schools, had the finest clothes, and her nanny was also her teacher. She was an English woman who taught her how a proper young lady learns to be a polished woman in café society.

The war dragged on, and afterward, the country went wild.

Katelin was just coming of age, a teenager. She was invited to the finest parties and mingled with the children of the wealthy.

Then, as she turned sixteen during the Depression, suddenly her world was fading. Sorensen's company could not sustain itself and folded. He took a job as a bookkeeper and was forced to sell his fine house. They moved into a small apartment, and Carmela had to go back to work. She found work as a seamstress in a Manhattan clothing factory. Katelin was devastated. The strain had taken a toll on Carl. He was several years older than Carmela, and he began to age rapidly. One night he did not come home. Carmela waited anxiously, wondering what had happened. When a knock came at the door, she hurriedly opened the door. "Mrs. Sorensen," the policeman began, "I have some bad news." He hesitated as the woman held her hand over her mouth. "Your husband passed out at work. He could not be revived. They think his heart gave out." She stared at him but said nothing. She began to shake and then wail hysterically. Finally, the policeman got her to sit down, and she calmed some.

"Where is he?" she said.

"They took him to the Flower Fifth Avenue Hospital. When you are ready, I will take you there," said the cop.

She scribbled a note and left it on the kitchen table: "Papa very sick, I must go to hospital, wait here."

The months following Carl's death were unbearable for Carmela. In her dreams, she had flashbacks of the death of her first husband aboard the ship. Katelin was hardly ever home. She despised the flat they lived in, and she hated the life she now had to endure. She had grown up accustomed to the finer things in life, and suddenly it was all taken from her. She was very much an only child. Spoiled by both her doting parents, and then suddenly they both had no time for her because they had to go to work. She resented her father, having had all she wanted, and then he failed to continue to provide. She was ambivalent about her mother, an unrefined woman, not at all like Miss Cross, the English nanny she grew up with. Miss Cross knew all there was to know about being a fine lady. Her mother was not much more than an immigrant peasant.

Katelin began manipulating her friends. She would find a way to get invited to sleepovers and stay for days in the homes of friends who were well off. She would stay until another invitation came, then go from house to house. She told her mother she needed time to adjust. Her mother, devastated by the loss of her husband and mentor, had no hold or control of their daughter. When she did come home, she often arrived late at night with the smell of alcohol on her and a harried disheveled look. "Tu se putana," her mother said one night after a particularly hard day at work. "You are a whore. Look at you. I'm ashamed," the mother said out of frustration.

"Oh, Mama, what do you know? How am I supposed to live in a place like this?" Katelin scolded.

One day, Katelin arrived home and packed her clothes. She left a note: "Mama, I've been invited to stay with some friends for a while. I will let you know when I am settled," said Cat.

The "friends" was actually a friend. The father of one of her girlfriends had recently divorced his wife and had moved to a fine apartment on the Upper East Side of Manhattan. One night before the breakup, Cat attended a party at the home.

She had been drinking and had gone upstairs to the bathroom. The girlfriend's father waited till she came out and after some conversation escorted her to a nearby bedroom. As the party continued, Cat, fairly drunk by now, did not resist when he approached her and simply allowed him to use her body. He told her he liked her very much and would do anything to help her. She said she had a real money problem, so he handed her a wad of bills.

She began visiting the house regularly, and the man found time to meet her at his office as well. His marriage unraveled, as did her friendship with the girlfriend after an episode when the wife actually caught Cat and her husband in the act in her own bathroom. He moved out, and soon after, Cat moved in.

Cat tired of him after several months and after having found a way to get him to fill her bank account. She moved from time to time, from man to man, till she found one who would pay her rent and provide her with cash. She seldom visited her mother, and when she did, the visits were brief and her attitude cold. Carmela had her own problems. The loss of Carl had changed her. She lost her will to live. She worked and went through the day somber and joyless. She had no friends and kept to herself.

Katelin, however, lived the life of a party girl, attending whatever events around the city she could get into without having to spend her cash. She lived by her wits and her beauty. She was indeed a beautiful woman and used her body as enticement to wealthy men who would have her and pay for it.

She happened upon John Ferranti at an event at the home of a girlfriend whose father was a powerful Supreme Court judge. Ferranti engaged her in conversation, and she immediately came on to him. Ferranti's style was gracious, and she noted he wore a finely tailored suit and expensive shoes. She also learned he had an extremely lucrative law practice and a list of clients that was extremely impressive, including the judge's own family.

That night, Ferranti arranged to meet her a few days later over lunch so she could discuss a legal problem she was having with her landlord. It turned out the problem was nonpayment of rent. She invited him to view the apartment and, once there, to view her bedroom.

He arranged to pay her back rent and also arranged to continue to pay her rent, continuing his visits to her bedroom as well. He was attentive and generous, and she was discreet. She had the security she wanted and a life she chose. He gave her a monthly check. All she needed to do was to cooperate and fulfill his needs a few times a month, a very compatible arrangement.

The day he had his stroke, he was in her apartment. He was in bed on top of her pumping away when suddenly he convulsed. She nearly panicked but kept her wits about her.

She summoned her doorman, who secured a wheelchair, dressed and wrapped Ferranti in a blanket, and called an ambulance. He told the driver the man had been in the lobby and collapsed. Afterward, the doorman was well rewarded for his help.

Now this new arrangement with the son would be all right, although she disliked him immensely. She felt secure for the time being.

Genie Ferranti had made his rounds of the proper offices and secured the salvage documents needed for the five ships. He had gone from each authority to each office to secure the documents and ended up at the US Marshall's Office. The officer in charge of vessel disposal was Dominick Mancuso. Ferranti knew Mancuso from prior dealings with that office.

Mancuso's father came to America from Southern Italy like many others. He got a job driving a produce truck for a wholesale vegetable dealer in Manhattan. He was a shrewd man. He watched as trucks from all over came and went from the market in Lower Manhattan during his loading and deliveries.

He noted how many were from South Jersey, particularly from Vineland to the farmlands north of there, nearly to Camden. Vegetables and fruits that did not make their way to Philadelphia did get to New York. There, the prices were always higher.

He wrote to his elder brother in Italy. If he could accumulate about $6,000, he could get three good trucks and go to the growers, secure their products, and deliver them to New York for higher prices. He would charge only a penny a pound for his service. He promised to repay his brother with interest.

The brother did send the money. Mancuso started his venture, and within a few months, the word got around to many growers. His truck fleet grew in two years from three to twenty, and he financed the trucks by borrowing from the growers themselves. Soon the profits permitted him to pay off his debts, and he invested the surplus in Consolidated Edison stock, the New York Electric Company.

He wrote his brother, offering to repay him. The brother asked him to put his money in the stock as well.

Years went by, and the Mancuso Company made huge profits. The stock increased, split doubled, and with dividends became a considerable fortune.

Fate had a strange turn, however. On his son's twenty-first birthday, Mancuso was just leaving his truck yard when a new driver, not alert when he backed up, hit and killed the elder Mancuso.

When his son read the will, he saw that his father had included his uncle in Italy as heir to one-third of the Con-Ed stock. The stock was worth over $1.3 million. The young man took the will and went to Eugene Ferranti, whose father had drafted the will.

He told Ferranti that his mother, now a widow, was ill, and he had little money to help her. He hated that most of his father's trucks were mortgaged to various people, including the growers. He added that his father had, by mistake, included his uncle in Italy in the will. The original will was never recorded. Old man Ferranti held many wills and would be chosen as administrator when the heirs came to resolve the estates. Ferranti thus insured his cut of the estate.

Genie devised a plan to eliminate the uncle's name and insert the son's name instead. He had knowledge of how to make the documents appear authentic, and it worked.

Now Ferranti needed Mancuso to reciprocate. "Mancuso, I need you to release those five vessels as salvage at three cents a ton. Also, list this company as sale bidder. You understand?" said Ferranti.

Mancuso looked over the documents. He knew he could not refuse, though he felt cornered. "Okay, but get them out of the area immediately," said Mancuso. And so the deal was struck.

The ships were one by one eased out of the harbor by tugboat, then tethered to a large freighter and towed out to sea past the twelve-mile limit. Once there, each was boarded by a Greek crew and under their own power sailed to Virginia.

There they were retrofitted, serviced, and disguised with plates and smoke stacks, then repainted and sent back to Greece. After the retrofit, Anthony met Marcus at Market Restaurant. "Hey, Marcus. How are you. How are things?"

"Very well. All is fine," he said. The briefcase that he held under the table was handed to Anthony, who took it and nodded. He could feel the weight of the cash inside.

"Great. Well, I hope to see you soon."

Anthony drove straight back to Big Tony's office. "Here it is, boss," he said and handed the case to him. He put it up on the desk and closed the blinds behind him.

"Lock that door," he told Anthony.

He snapped open the locks and opened the case. There neatly arranged were stacks of hundred-dollar bills. "Okay, now we have to count this and separate out the pieces we promised."

Thus, the money was distributed. The Onassis flag flew over the ships, whose profile was so obscured they would never be recognized after the metal facelift was completed.

Anthony waited outside Big Tony's office, and he could hear Rothstein's and Tony's voices in a heated exchange for several minutes. Finally, Rothstein opened the door. "Fuck him. He will get what I pay him, that shyster bastard. Let him come talk to me if he doesn't like it," Tony said. Rothstein just walked out. He went down the loading dock stairs, got in his car, and left.

Anthony sat in the outer office waiting for Big Tony to finish on the phone.

The door had a glass panel, but it had been painted over years before. He could hear Big Tony's voice but could not get much out of the muffled sounds of this conversation. Finally, there was silence. Then the door cracked open. "Come, come in," the voice said.

Big Tony sat behind the desk. He held a glass in his hand. "You want a drink?" he asked.

"Okay," said Anthony. Big Tony picked up a glass that was on the windowsill behind him and then picked up a bottle that was nearby on the desk. The bottle had a brownish label.

"Here. This will put hair on your chest." He poured the black liquid into the glass three inches full, then slid the glass to Anthony. "Cento Anni," he said, and they sipped the contents of the glass. Anthony had seen the bottle many times before. It was Fernet Branco, that bitter Italian aperitif. He still was not sure whether he liked it or not. It was far different from any other thing one could drink, except the other bitter liquid in the red-and-white label bottle, Ramazotto. That was equally bitter, and drinking too much would give you the shits.

"Well, I finally connected with Marcy Hageman. That's the connection we needed to get those boats retrofitted and that whole deal done. Marcy still won't come home." Anthony had heard that Marcy had traveled to Europe on what was supposedly a business trip. Here it was three months later, and Marcy was still gone. A few weeks before, Tony had finally gotten Marcy's guy, Al, to track him down.

"Marcy, where the hell are you, you bastard?" said Tony.

"Hey, Tone. What are you up to?" replied Marcy. Tony could hear voices in the background, female voices.

"Sounds like you found some company," said Tony.

"Oh yeah, the mademoiselles are taking good care of me," said Marcy, and he laughed out loud.

Tony could hear female voices giggling in the background. "What have you got yourself into over there?" asked Tony.

"Well, I just wanted a little company for dinner when I got off the plane. I made some deals in London, and my connection there set up a meeting in Paris with an equipment dealer. I flew over here a few months ago. I met this lovely lady on the plane, and being I had no date for dinner, I invited her. She knew all the best restaurants in Paris since she was born there. Well, when we got to dinner, her sister and the sister's friend joined us. Oh, Tony, these broads are something. We ended up drinking all night, and then they joined me up in the hotel suite for a nightcap. Tony, they're still here!" Marcy said, and again he laughed so loudly Tony had to pull the phone away from his ear.

"You got three broads with you?" asked Tony.

"Hey, it just worked out that way, and you know me—there's enough to go around." Marcy laughed again, and so did the girls.

"You fat bastard, you're gonna kill yourself screwing three broads at the same time," said Tony, and now he laughed too.

"Tony, I had them bring me another bed so we could put two together and all sleep together," Marcy replied. "They love it. Of course, it's costing me a fortune, but what the fuck. It's heaven," said Marcy.

Tony could hear the voices speaking French and then Marcy breathing. "Oh, oh," said Marcy.

"What the hell is going on there?" said Tony.

"Well, the little one has her must-not-touch-it pressed against my hand, waiting for me, and the other two are down south taking turns," said Marcy.

"Look, you gotta get serious for a few minutes. I need your help," said Tony.

Marcy's voice changed a little with a bit more seriousness in his tone. "What do you need, Tone?" he asked.

"I need you to get Al to line up shore guys who own the shipyard in Virginia to do a retrofit of a few ships I want to send down there. It's important that it's done very clean, and I know Al can get to those guys quickly," said Tony.

"Okay, Tony. I will reach out to Al and tell him. I will also connect with the guys in Virginia," said Marcy.

"When are you coming back?" said Tony.

Marcy hesitated. "I think pretty soon because my money is running out, and I'm beginning to have trouble getting it up." Marcy then laughed again.

"Anthony, Marcy helped me get the Virginia thing lined up. That fat bastard is still in Paris shacked up with three French whores."

Anthony laughed. He could picture the big Dutchman sprawled out on a bed with three women.

Marcy was indeed a big man. He stood about six foot three and weighed well over three hundred pounds. He had a thick crop of white hair and a huge, bulbous nose that made him look like W. C. Fields. He was known to drink two bottles of rum a day, which explained the redness in that big nose. He had a huge belly but was strong as an ox and could eat a cow. His big, booming voice could be heard a block away. His business connections in the States, the Caribbean, and Europe had been built over some forty years.

Tony had met Marcy when they were just kids, eighteen years old. They hit it off as pals along with several other guys, and they formed a sort of group. It wasn't a street gang, but it wasn't a group of choir boys either. There was not a set leader. About a dozen guys that grew up together were involved. They, through the years, made deals and swindled the unsuspecting. They trafficked in everything that could make them a buck. Eventually, they all evolved into individual business owners. As the years went by, they all accumulated wealth. Charlie Pizza owned liquor stores, Marcy, restaurant and bakery equipment sales, Carlo, a car dealership, Alex, a bar and restaurant, Frankie, a banquet hall and gourmet restaurant, Jack and Fran, a catering hall and bar, Louie, a discount store, Al and Mike, vending and jukebox businesses, Allie, junk yard and salvage yard, Doc, a dentist, Eddie, a physician, Telly, an accountant, John, an insurance agent, Reggi, a cop, and Peter, a surgeon. There were others, but the core group always stuck together.

"Anthony, come in," said Tony. He was sitting at his desk. He had a large hardcover checkbook in front of him. His face was red and slightly perspired. "Those fucking lawyers, they will try to suck the blood out of you. Look, I need you to go to that cocksucker Ferranti's office and deliver this envelope. Just bring it there and say nothing if you're asked. Just say Tony told you to drop this off; you have no idea what's inside. You got that?" Tony said abruptly.

"Yeah," said Anthony.

He tore the check out of the book and put it in an envelope, "Okay?"

Anthony took the check and left. He went from Stapleton to Tompkinsville and then to St. George where the Staten Island Ferry terminal was. The ferry ran to South Ferry in Manhattan. They ran every twenty minutes or so. The fee for foot passengers was a nickel.

He pulled into the parking lot, which was directly across the street from Ferranti's office building. There were only four cars in the lot. He locked his car and walked across the street and up the sidewalk. As he approached the building, he saw a woman coming out the front door.

She stepped out onto the stairs, and as she did, her right leg turned under her, and she fell, sliding down the stone stairs with her leg tucked under her, sort of bouncing on her buttocks. Her high-heel shoe heel was laying on the third step.

Anthony rushed over to her and helped her sit upright. "Are you all right?" he said. Tears were welling up in her eyes, and she gasped for breath. The fall had knocked the breath from her. Her dress was raised and crumpled under her, exposing her knee and the top of her thigh. Anthony held her upright. "Take it easy; just take a little breath at a time and don't try to talk," he said. He calmed her, and in a few minutes, she was able to speak in a wavering voice.

"I hurt my leg and my back," she said. "I'm so embarrassed," she uttered, tears now streaming down her cheeks.

"Don't be. I'll call an ambulance," he said.

"No! No!" she said emphatically. "Please no!" she said with panic in her voice. She started to move to try to get up.

"Okay! Okay! But don't panic. I'll help you. Just take it easy," he said in a slow and calm voice. "Look, I'll get someone inside."

"No, no, don't do that. I'll be all right in a minute, and I'll get in my car. It's parked across the street," she said.

"I'll try to get you up, but you broke the heel off your shoe, so let me take them off for you," he said.

"Okay," she said, sobbing a little. He removed her shoes and picked up her pocketbook, which had fallen off her shoulder. Next, he got behind her and put his hands under her armpits. The late spring day was warm and sunny. He could feel the dampness in his hands from her sweating, certainly brought on by the emotions and panic caused by the fall.

"I'm going to lift you to your feet. Spread your right leg out from under you and try to plant your two feet directly in front of you." She did as she was told, and he lifted her.

"Oh, oh," she groaned in pain.

"Okay, it's okay," said Anthony as he finally got her upright. Anthony had done a great deal of manual labor as a boy and a young man. He lifted carcasses of beef and crates that weighed over sixty pounds all day long. The woman was no strain for him to lift as she weighed only about 120 pounds. She stood there. "Can you stand by yourself?" he asked.

"I think so," she answered. He slowly released her left side and began to release her right side but could feel her beginning to slide down.

"Hold on," he said, and he lifted her straight again. "Shift your body to the left side and lean against me as I turn to your side." She obeyed, and he took her left arm and put it around the back of his neck. "Okay, let's start to the car," he said. She moved her left foot and dragged her right leg. There was no other person in sight. He managed to get her to the curbside across the street from the parking lot. "Look, I'm going to have to carry you across the street. If we try to walk across, some car is going to come up that hill, round the bend, gun it to make it up the hill, and maybe hit both of us," he said.

She looked at him, bewildered and a little frightened, tears still glistening on her cheeks. "Okay," she said in a little voice, "whatever you think." He put his left arm under the back of her legs. Still supporting her and in one quick movement, he scooped her up in his arms and against his chest. He steadied his balance and began to walk across the street down to the parking lot entrance. He got halfway across when he heard a car engine whining up the hill. He quickened his steps and was nearly on the far curb when a big black Cadillac sedan appeared racing up the hill, around the curve and out of sight.

"Whew, I guess I had a premonition," he said. She just stared at him. He could feel a sticky substance on his wrists as his suit jacket sleeves had pulled back. He got her to his car and set her against it. With her feet firmly on the ground and her back supported against the car, he retrieved the car keys from his pocket. He noticed patches of blood on his wrists from where he had carried her. He opened the passenger side door of the Oldsmobile and helped her to sit, her feet and legs dangling out of the car. "Look, I want to see your right leg. I think you cut yourself," he said. She nodded. He lifted the hem of her dress and pulled it up. The side of her calf, knee, and thigh were scraped, and shreds of skin were hanging. It was as if she had been injured by a metal cheese grater from just below her hip to just above her ankle. Apparently, as she slid down the stone stairs, the rough stone stripped away her nylon stocking and scraped her leg. "Well, you got some scrape there. I can tell you that," he said. She whimpered. "Look, it's okay," he said.

"I want to go home. I live just a few miles. Take me over there to my car," she said.

"I'll be right back. Will you be okay if I leave you?" he said. She nodded. "Here are the keys to the car. Lock the door and just wait here, okay?" he said.

"Yes," she responded.

He straightened his jacket and briskly walked back to the building and up the stairs and inside. He bounded up the stairs to the second floor, opened the door to the office, and closed it. He knocked on the door. "In here," he heard a voice say. Down the corridor was a series of offices. The sound came from the last one. He entered.

"What do you want?" said Ferranti, who recognized him after a moment.

"I have this envelope for you from Anthony," he said and took it out of his inside pocket and handed it to Ferranti.

"Okay." Ferranti took the envelope and put it down on his desk. "Anything else?" he said.

"No." Anthony turned and started to walk away.

"Tell him I'll call him," said Ferranti.

Anthony rushed back to the car. Katelin unlocked the door. He got in the driver's side. "You all right?" he said. She nodded, and he started the car.

"Go right up the hill, then left," she said. She directed him through the hilly streets and finally to the top of a steep hill that plateaued. "There at the top," she said. "Pull in the driveway on your right." He drove into a circular driveway and in front of a three-story mansion.

"Quite a place," he said.

"Well, it used to be. Some big shipping tycoon owned it; now it's apartments. I'm on the second floor," she said.

"Okay, you put your arm around my neck, and I'll just sort of lift you when we get to the stairs. Okay?"

"Yes," she said.

He got her out of the car, around the driveway, and up the front steps into the house. There was a wide foyer and a grand stairway. "Up there," she said. He helped her up the stairway, lifting her each step to the top and then down the hallway. She fumbled to open her pocket-book. "Look, let me find your key in there before you fall," he said. She handed him the pocketbook.

"It's on a ring with other keys." He began rummaging inside the pocketbook, and his eye caught the name on a check, Ferranti and Ferranti, but he could not see the amount, as it was folded over. He found the key ring.

She pointed to the key. "This one," she said. He opened the door and resumed carrying her.

The door opened into a spacious living room with a visible corri-dor off to the right that led to a dining room. The thin lace curtains allowed the room to be extremely bright from the sun. There was a large overstuffed sofa. "Put me there," she said, and he eased her down and stood up.

"Where is your refrigerator?" he said. She looked up quizzically and pointed to a hallway. He walked to the kitchen. He went to the re-frigerator and found the freezer. He pulled out two ice trays. There on the counter of the kitchen were kitchen towels. He found the largest, laid it open, pushed the ice cubes out of the metal tray one by one, and then folded the towel over. He went back to the living room. "I have an ice pack here I want to put on your leg," he said. She moved her leg and pulled at her dress. He could see bloodstains and blotches that had seeped through the bright yellow, flowered dress. She raised the dress up to her thigh. He carefully put the ice pack on her leg. "I need to get another for the ankle," he said. He went back to the kitchen and reappeared with another ice pack. She began to regain her composure.

"You're quite a boy scout, aren't you Anthony," she said.

He looked up and smiled. "Look, I saw how you fell like that. I couldn't very well leave you there, could I? All alone in the street?" he said.

"Well, really, you could have, and it is my good luck that you didn't. That was a very sweet thing you did for me," she said earnestly.

"You okay now?" he said.

"My back and my backside are killing me, but the leg feels a lot better," she said.

"Let me see," he said. She uncovered the ice pack on her thigh. It was bright red, and he could see little pieces of scraped skin clinging to spots of dry blood.

"Do you have any first aid things in the house?" he said.

"Yes, go down the hall past the kitchen to the bedroom. Off to one side is the bathroom. There is a closet in there, and inside there is peroxide, creams, and other stuff."

He left and came back with a handful of items, including a tube of antibiotic cream. "I think you need to get some of this on that scrape," he said.

"Okay," she said.

He had a gauze patch and squeezed the cream on it and began applying it to the area just above the ankle. He smeared a thin coat of the cream up to the knee, then squeezed the cream on his finger. "Look, I think the gauze is shredding and will dry in the wound. I'm better off using my fingers," he said.

"Whatever you think, Doctor," she said now with a faint smile. "It feels good," she said. He began working his way gently and slowly up the side of her leg. She moved slightly, spreading her legs apart, and she pulled her dress up to her waist, revealing the rest of the scrape on her upper thigh and near the hip. She also revealed the thin, clinging, silk panties she was wearing. As Anthony moved his hand further up her leg, sort of kneeling by her side, his eye caught the outside of the area between her legs. The extremely thin, silk panties, yellow in color, were somewhat transparent, and he could see the reddish-brown pubic hair curled at the sides of her vagina. He turned his eyes back to her leg and continued to apply the cream. However, he could not avoid turning his head again to view her anatomy as he rubbed her leg. He could see her pubic mound and the fold of her sex.

"See anything you like?" she said in a somewhat comical tone.

His face flushed. "I'm trying to cover all of this," he said.

"I'll bet you are," she said. "Can you move your hand a little this way and put some here?" She pointed to the inside of her thigh, and he obeyed again, head down, not saying a word. As he got to the edge of the silk panties, she took her hand, placed it on top of his, and guided it to the center of the panties. He began to breathe a little heavier.

"That's nice. Rub that please," she said, and he began to rub her. The silk panties easily slid over the outer part of her vagina. "Oh, that does feel very nice," she said.

He looked up at her. Her eyes were closed, and a thin smile was on her face. For the first time, he noticed how beautiful she was. Her hair was flowing over her shoulders, and her lips were full and thick. Her high cheekbones and her ample breasts were now beginning to heave slightly as he rubbed her. She smelled of fine perfume, not overdone but very noticeable, and as she spread her legs wider, he detected the perfume even more.

As he rubbed her, she slowly pulled the panties away and revealed her flesh to his fingers. Instantly, he felt the warm moistness of her, and he became even more excited. However, he continued to rub her slowly. She moved now, turning her body so that he was between her legs, kneeling on the floor. He looked up at her.

"Please do it," she whispered and put her hands on his and gently guided his face to her groin.

She moaned when he began. He continued to move up and down for a while. "Oh, oh please stop, please," she said. "Come up here with me." He removed his pants and shorts as she undressed. He carefully positioned himself so that he had none of his weight on her and entered her. She lifted and moved time and again, and finally as he pushed hard, they pressed against each other tightly. He pressed into her again and again until they both climaxed.

"Oh, oh," she said quietly.

He turned back and sat by her, stroking her face. "You all right?" he said.

"Oh yes, yes, yes." She squeezed his hand and closed her eyes tightly.

They stayed like that for several minutes, not talking or moving. He then said, "I need to use your bathroom," and he got up. He took his clothes with him. Soon he returned dressed. She had repositioned herself on the couch with the ice packs on her leg. He went over to her and took her hand.

She pulled him toward her and kissed his lips. "You are really something, Mr. Anthony. You really know how to save a damsel in distress," she said.

He smiled. "It's my duty, ma'am," he said with a grin.

"Well, you do it well," she answered. "What if I run into trouble again? How do I reach you?" she asked. He reached in his coat pocket, pulled out a business card, and handed it to her.

"Wait, let me put my private number on that." He retrieved it before she could read it. He wrote his number on it and handed it to her.

She looked up at him with a strange smile on her face. "You're Anthony Delmont, and I see you work for the Bay Company. My fiancé does work for that company. What do you do there?" she said curiously.

"My uncle owns the company. I'm sort of a salesman and do other stuff," he said.

"Your uncle is Anthony Delmonte?" she said.

"Yeah, I kind of Americanized the name."

She chuckled a little. "Well, my fiancé is Eugene Ferranti, and I don't think either one of them should know what happened here," she said, laughing. "I know your uncle very well."

"Oh my gosh, you're Ferranti's fiancé. Oh, man," he said, stunned.

"Listen, don't worry, it's no problem. In fact, it really is *no* problem," she emphasized. "You're great, and I enjoyed being with you and will never forget what you did out there for me. Few people in my life treat me with the kindness you showed. What we did just sort of happened I guess, and you know what? I am grateful for that too. It was wonderful. Actually, I really liked it. And so did you. So, what's the fuss?" she said.

"I guess none when you put it that way," he answered.

"Look, Ferranti has his time away from me. Who knows what he does, and frankly, I don't care what he does. If I make a friend, well, that's my business. He doesn't need to know any of that. So maybe if you feel okay with that, I will call you when I get in trouble again, and you can come to my rescue. What do you think?" she said with a wide, naughty smile.

He looked at her. "I think that's fine so long as no one else knows, I guess," he said.

"Okay, then it's settled. No one will know, and we will not be concerned about them. But I am very happy you came by, and I hope you come by again," she said.

"You have my number if you find yourself in trouble," he said. He hugged her and then made his way to the door.

"Bye, Anthony. Thank you," she said.

As he started the car, his mind flashed back to when he first really noticed how beautiful she was. Then too, he noticed that her face had the slight traces of her age. *She must be in her forties*, he thought, *or even fifty*. He smiled. He thought to himself, *I just had Ferranti's fiancée.*

That prick, Ferranti, that arrogant bastard. It serves him right. Every time Anthony was near him, he seemed to exude his own image of superiority. *Here I am screwing his woman.* He smiled again. What was it his uncle had told him? That revenge sometimes is the sweetest when it's served cold. He wanted to tell his uncle, but he dared not. He would not want to put Katelin in jeopardy. He turned up the radio and began to sing out loud as he drove. He could still smell the fragrance of the woman on him.

Ferranti treated everyone with arrogance and condescendence. Anthony had been sent to him when one of the company trucks he was driving was stopped by the police. Inspection of the vehicle revealed some twelve violations, including improper registration and insurance. Somehow the vehicle registration and insurance was never renewed. This was an offense that could result in both suspension of license and jail time.

Anthony went to Ferranti after Big Tony made a call to him. He was left waiting in his office for over five hours, and when Ferranti did grant him an audience, he just told him, "Give my secretary your citations and be in court an hour early, in a suit, and wait for me there." He dismissed him in less than two minutes.

On the prescribed court date, Anthony, dressed in a suit and tie, entered the court waiting area an hour and a half early. He waited patiently for an hour and a half, then went into the courtroom and sat there until his case was called. Ferranti was nowhere to be seen. "How do you plead?" said the judge.

"Your Honor, my attorney, Eugene Ferranti, has been detained," he said.

The judge looked around the half-full courtroom, then down at Anthony. "That's not what I asked you," he said. "How do you plead?" said the judge sternly.

"Guilty, with an explanation, Your Honor, if you please," said Anthony.

"Listen, you, if you're guilty, you're guilty. There is *no* explanation," said the judge. "You sit over there, and the bailiff will call you."

He sat red faced and embarrassed at the judge's admonition.

All the cases went forward, and at noon, the courtroom empty, the judge stood. "Recess," said the bailiff. The judge left.

The bailiff went over to Anthony. "You wait," he said, and he left. There were a few staff people, a stenographer and clerk gathering papers. Anthony sat impatiently. After another hour, the bailiff came back. "The judge wants you. Come with me." He led Anthony down a corridor and to a bench outside an office. "Sit here," he said. Anthony sat. He could, through a glass front door, clearly hear voices.

In about fifteen minutes, a white-haired woman opened the door. "Come in," she said. He walked in, and she pointed to a chair. He sat. There was a half-open office door, and he could see the judge seated behind a desk and the back of a man's head that was sitting in front of him.

"So, Joe, have you been over to Bascilio's lately? I was there last night. The osso buco is the best," said the man, and Anthony recognized the voice. It was Ferranti.

"No, but we have a group going there next month. Gene, what do you want to do with this kid?" the judge responded.

"The stupid bastard, he is an embarrassment to his family. I suggest he be taught a lesson. Put him in for thirty days," said Ferranti.

"Well, I would do that," said the judge, "but his uncle called me and said he has work for him and did not want him jailed."

"So maybe give him thirty days' probation," said Ferranti. Neither man realized that the door was partially open and that their conversation could be heard.

A buzz sounded, and the woman picked up the phone. "You can go in now," she said. Anthony went in.

"I've been talking to your lawyer, and I decided what to do with you," said the judge.

"Yes, Judge, and it is unfortunate that this stupid ass takes up your time and the time of the court. His family tried to guide him, but he isn't very smart. I think he needs some time in jail, but you decide," said Ferranti.

"Well, because of your family, I'm going to give you a break. I can put you away for months, you know," said the judge sternly. Anthony nodded, saying nothing. "I'm giving you thirty days' probation and fines, three hundred for no registration, two hundred for the other violations, and two hundred for costs."

"Can I pay that now?" he asked. "I have a check, Your Honor," said Anthony.

"Well, go down to the pay window and take this with you. I don't want to see you in my court again. You got that?" said the judge.

"Yes, sir," said Anthony. He took the papers and began to walk out. As he got out the door, he pulled it tightly closed. He could hear the two men laughing.

The woman stopped him. "You need this form as well." She began going through a folder.

"That stupid bastard. I don't know why Tony keeps him around. I told him, family or not, this kid is trouble, and he ought to get rid of him. But he said it's his brother's kid. I told him he ought to have somebody beat the shit out of him a few times, and maybe it would smarten him up. He is an asshole just like his father. His mother is an idiot, never could raise kids," said Ferranti in an acidic tone.

Anthony could hear him, and his face flushed red. The woman handed him the paper, and he left.

As he went about paying the fine and getting the receipts, his mind was racing. He thought, *I will wait for Ferranti to come out of the building and get even.* Then he resisted—his uncle, the business, the judge connection seemed too important to upset. He did vow to get revenge.

Now as he looked back on the encounter with Katelin, he smiled to himself.

Anthony learned to have patience through years of encounters with all sorts of people in varied situations. He also became an avid reader and intermittently returned to college for courses in various disciplines. He took law courses, accounting, and psychology. He also became interested in art. He studied Renaissance art, the masters, and sculpture and became quite knowledgeable of their value, often attending auctions around the city at Sotheby's Parke-Bernet, Christies, and other notable houses. He kept a close association with his uncle through the years but by age thirty-three opened his own consulting business. He helped his uncle by brokering deals, arranging financing, and funding projects. He also secured his own licenses in real estate and insurance. He became a licensed talent manager and developed contact in the entertainment industry. He invested money for a few wealthy clients, including a few entertainers, and also collected their fees and other payment for them. He handled their real estate deals and that of others. Soon he became noted in political circles as well. Working with contacts he had in business and family, he was invited to attend various political functions and saw to it that important contributions went to people he knew would help him when he needed it. He was able to cross party lines and was equally respected by both parties. He focused on judicial appointments both on lower levels and eventually through lawyers and judges he knew. He became acquainted with US magistrates and US federal judges. He also became keenly aware of the appointment process.

Thus he had the kind of influence that could ease a real estate deal, secure financing, expedite closings, and clear any legal hurdles. He could, on occasion, influence judicial nominations as well.

His motives were, on the surface, noble and altruistic, but he had an underlying perception that those he helped would be useful allies in the future. Allies not only had a link to him because of his assistance but also because of the blood relationship. He too assisted those close to the family. These too might be people who had more of a stake in being loyal than simple strangers. Family, friends, and their offspring would be more likely to have a concern about their associations than someone who had no ties—a lesson he learned well.

Thus, Anthony was quite pleased when he heard that his cousin, Victor Terranova, was engaged to the granddaughter of an old family friend, Tomasso Mondello. The young lady, Catherine Mondello, was an extremely beautiful girl whose wit and charm made an instant hit with the Terranova family. She was almost immediately accepted, which, for someone who was to marry a Terranova, was quite an accomplishment.

The Terranovas were extremely cautious if not suspicious of everyone, particularly someone who would seek to marry into the family. And even though the two families had an enduring friendship that reached back to Sicily, they still harbored the same nuances. Catherine, however, was so appealing and goodhearted that she disarmed even Donna Nicole Terranova, the ninety-year-old matriarch of the family. "Bella Caterina," said the old woman. Kay, as Vic called her, obeyed and sat next to the old woman.

"What is the best month to marry?" the young lady asked in the old woman's native dialect, asking "the strong and intelligent lady." The question was really a sly way of saying, "Do you approve of me marrying into your family?"

"Very clever," the old woman whispered close to Kay's ear. "Marry soon, as I am very old, and I want to bless you in August. The blood is hot in August."

The old woman was indeed intelligent, and her advice that one's blood was warmest in August was, too, advice that insinuated that a mate would be more accessible when the blood runs hot. Even at ninety years of age, the old woman was clever and mindful of what emotions stirred in those in their twenties.

This impending union gave reason for the entire families from both sides to reunite and convene at introductory parties and what would follow.

The sequence of engagement parties, showers, and other events served to bring the two families and their extended families together.

For Anthony, it was the opportunity not only to reunite with the bride's family, old friends as it were, but with his own family as well. It was tradition to invite every cousin, uncle, and related in-law to every event to showcase the one who would be joining the family. It was reminiscent of the same ritual in Italy where a possible new in-law would be scrutinized and rated by the respective families.

The engagement party was held at the catering hall of choice in Brooklyn near where Catherine's family had settled. The Oriental Manor was the most sought-after location for such events. The food vendors were primarily Italians. In fact, Big Tony's company did sub-contract the supply of beef to their meat supplier. Thus a family discount was in order. Anthony saw to that. The Manor was famous throughout the city for its extravagant Italian weddings.

The family of the bride-to-be chose the menu, the settings, the dishes, the time, the flowers, and more. Victor and his family arranged for the band, chose the wine, and even provided the bride and her immediate family limousine transportation. Even a simple engagement party was a celebrated event as the joining of these two longtime allied families.

Anthony Delmont saw this wedding as a very important opportunity. His own family would attend as well as many families associated with both families. He considered a way to capitalize on this opportunity.

Not far from the Oriental Manor in Bay Ridge was a well-known club, the Terrace. The engagement party was set for Sunday at one o'clock, after church and in time for the midday Sunday dinner, an Italian tradition.

Anthony contacted the owners of the Terrace, who were customers of his uncle's meat supply business and also connected to his liquor distributor, City Liquors. He arranged to book the place for the evening, closing it to the public.

He had Victor call all the young men who were invited to the engagement party to attend an after-party, as it was a pre–bachelor party of sorts following the engagement party. Considering that it would be a great party, it was not difficult to get nearly all the cousins, uncles, friends, and those chosen from the invitation list by Anthony to attend.

Victor was actually eager to be involved and was enthusiastic about the idea. The engagement party was a real family affair. Everyone was invited from each family, including children. Anthony's oldest brother, Vince, had five sons and one daughter, Maria, who was the apple of his eye, and she was a sweet and loving daughter. His wife, Barbara, once an extremely attractive and vivacious young woman, now suffered from a debilitating arthritic condition and joint disease. Vince ran a wholesale food operation, and between helping operate the business and watching over the family, he had little time to do much else. His boys all were grown and working, but still two lived at home; both worked in the family business as well.

The youngest, Michael, was taking courses part-time in college while doing some work for a local body shop. Vince Jr. worked for an insurance title company. Sammy was married with two small children, and his wife, Heidi, had brought the kids, one still in diapers, not even a year old.

Lucia, his younger sister, also had two boys. The eldest was a pharmacist, and the younger had just enrolled in college.

Janette was married, but her husband who was in the US Army was killed in a freak accident when a truck with ammunition exploded while it was being unloaded.

Chippy, another brother, was a musician and never had much interest or ambition, except to play music.

The events went well, and the reconnection with old friends and family reinforced those bonds. Even Big Tony came back from the islands to attend. The business there grew at a steady pace.

CHAPTER 57

THE OFFICE IN the meat plant at Vieux Fort, St. Lucia, always seemed musty, even with the air-conditioning on. That's why Tony always kept the jalousie window behind his desk cracked open. He had spent two weeks on the other side of the island after arriving by plane. He had a large shipment of dry goods come in and was met by E, who he had sent a week earlier to make arrangements for the ship's arrival.

Once everything was offloaded and transported to the stores on Main Street, Tony checked to see that it was out on the shelves. He also financed six used cabs from Zombone, a local driver from the island who was a cousin to President Pompton. Zombone had to get the drivers and care for the vehicles. Tony's deal was simple. He would get a hundred dollars a week per cab. Zombone would give fifty dollars a week to Pompton to take care of the cost of operations. Tony arranged an office in one of the rented stores, and Pompton arranged an exclusive taxi stand at the airport right by the exit of the terminal building.

Gregorio was one of his main men at the plant. He was a big Greek who loved cigars and was never without one in his mouth. "Tony, we got all the ground meat set and ready to go," said Gregorio.

"Okay, we'll send it out tomorrow. Make sure we get all the other parts of the order for Trinidad checked," Tony responded. Just then, Gregorio and Tony heard the motor of a vehicle approaching just outside, along with some muffled voices once it stopped. Although he had Andre, a bookkeeper, who kept a sawed-off shotgun under his desk, Tony had a spring lock installed on the door so it automatically locked. He recognized that it was E talking with someone beside Andre. He had a solid wood door with a peephole so he could see the entry office. He saw E and Andre but just the back of a man's head.

E tapped on the door. "Tony, I'm here with Lito, from Antiqua. You busy?"

Tony opened the door. "Hey, Lito. How are you? Come in, E. Get some ice. Come in, pal." Lito walked in. Tony sensed he was not the happy-go-lucky guy he had met before at the casino.

"Tony, thanks for seeing me," he said.

"Well, of course I'd see you." The man's face was nearly gray, and his eyes had a strange look. "What's the matter, Lito? You look terrible," said Tony.

"Tony, I know you and Sam are good friends. I had no idea what Bobby was doing. I remember your visits, and then your brother, Charlie, came a few times. I guess I should have figured something was up, but I didn't get it," Lito said, then hung his head down and shook it slowly side to side. "Stupido, testa dura" (Stupid, thick head), said Lito.

"What are you talking about?" said Tony.

"Okay, I understand, but can you help me? Look, you and the other guys know I was there for Bobby, and I always made sure your group was okay. In fact, it was me that stayed up and watched the floor at the hotel to be sure no one came up that didn't belong, and I had two of my group there too. I watched your back. I always watched Bobby's back too, you know," said Lito.

"What happened?" said Tony, completely confused.

"You really don't know?" said Lito.

"I've been on the island for about three weeks and over here for one. It's hard even to get a weak radio program. I haven't heard anything," said Tony.

"Well, Bobby's got this game, Tony. A few weeks ago, he got a message to go back right away. He got to Jersey. I don't know what was up. He said something about some new guys coming in, and they needed him there for a few weeks about some other deal. I really didn't understand much. Then my cousin called me yesterday. They found Bobby in the trunk of a car with his hands cut off. They said one was shoved in his mouth, and the other up his ass or something. The rumor was he was stealing from the casino. Tony, I never knew. I got a grand a week and took care of one of my guys. That's all I ever got. Oh, I had a bungalow on the property, along with food and drink, and could bring anybody in. I even could cut a few hundred in chips to my friends once in a while. But I never got any cash that didn't belong to me. You gotta believe me," said Lito.

"Why are you telling me this?" said Tony.

"Come on. Please help me out here. As soon as my cousin told me, I got on the next plane here. I figure you can square me with Sam 'cause you know," said Lito.

"Hey, listen. Sam and I go back a long way, but I didn't stick my nose in his business. What can I do anyway?" said Tony.

"Can you find out what's happening back there? My cousin is afraid to talk to anyone just yet. He doesn't know if he's being watched," Lito said.

"Look, I'll try to find out something," Tony said.

"Can I stay here till you do?" said Lito.

"Well, I really don't have any place for you, but if you want to stay at the plant here, there's some small storage rooms off the back that some men use like bunk rooms. There's a shower back there too and a toilet," said Tony.

"Yeah, sure, that's fine. It'll do," said Lito.

"Okay. E will show you."

There was a tap at the door, Tony opened it, and E brought in a bottle of rum, a tray with glasses, and a pitcher with ice water.

"Here. Have a drink," said Tony, and he poured some rum into two water glasses.

Lito drank it down quickly. "Thanks. I needed that," said Lito.

"E, show Lito where the bunk rooms are in the back. He's going to stay with us for a few days," said Tony. The two men left.

"Can't you go through another line there? I've got to get that call to the States," Tony bellowed into the phone.

"I'll call you back, sir, once I get through," the local operator said. Phoning the States was no easy process. Sometimes it took hours to get through, sometimes more.

Tony heard the buzzer about an hour later and picked up the phone. "Tony, you hear me? It's Nicky."

"Yeah, I hear you," Nicky said. "What's up?"

"Well, I heard something about our friend and just didn't quite get the whole picture, you know. I think Mr. D was there and then not," said Tony.

"Oh, that's all done now, all done. You know, it's over," said Mike.

"So, I got this guy who came for work. Maybe I can find a spot. What do you think?" said Tony.

"Umm, does he know what to do?" said Nicky.

"No idea," said Tony.

"Let me call you tomorrow. I'm kinda busy now," said Nick.

"Okay, what time?" said Tony.

"Well, around three my time," said Nicky.

"Okay," said Tony. Since there was no way of knowing who might be listening in on a phone line, names were never said, and the conversations remained obscure.

That night, Tony had Lito and E and two other men come to his house near the plant for dinner. "Gregorio has this kid who gets these lobsters for fifty cents apiece. The kid always brings five or six, way more than we can eat anyway. Gregorio is a pretty good cook. He even chases Wilda out of the kitchen. She cooks and cleans here."

After the dinner, Tony beckoned for Lito. "Come outside here while they clean up. I got some Cuban cigars from Gregorio, and there's a bit of rum."

They sat out on a small porch. "I am having someone find out things, maybe soon. You got to tell me if you know anything else—anything," said Tony.

"Well, all I can figure is that it's that little rat Bennett. He hated Bobby and never liked me either. He would hang around the casino watching all the time. I didn't know why, but I think he was spying on Bobby and the pit bosses too. Guys from Boston would come down sometimes, maybe two or three of Bennett's people. They would keep to themselves. They wouldn't even have dinner or drinks with us very much and only made small talk. I think Bennett was reporting to them, and they went back to Sam and the other partners. That's all I can figure out. This last week, Bennett took a vacation. He's been there about five years and never left the island, except once. Then a week ago, he leaves. He told Bobby that his assistant will take care of the accounts and that he was going to Acapulco for a vacation. Then one of these Boston guys shows up and says he's there to help Bennett's guy. Bobby went back to the States two weeks before that, and I never heard from him again. This Boston guy is in the counting room every day. Then I hear about Bobby," said Lito.

"Hmmmm, looks like they knew things were wrong. Well, let's see what I hear," said Tony.

Three o'clock the next day, Tony heard the phone buzzer. "Yeah," said Tony.

"Hey, how bad is it down there?" said Nicky.

"Always the same, mideighties," said Tony.

"Well, no problem, it's all done. They got everything they need. The other one can do whatever he wants. His place is still there too. Okay?" said Nicky.

"Yeah, okay. I'll talk to you when you get back," Nicky said and hung up.

Tony walked back to the bunk rooms around the rear of the building. Lito was sitting outside with a machete cutting at a coconut. "Well, you won't need that. I just got word you're clear. They got everything they need. You got your job there too if you want to go back," said Tony.

"Really?" said Lito. "Tony, I owe you. Wow," said Lito. Tony detected a faint tear in one eye as Lito shook his hand. Then he stood up straight. "I'll never forget this, Tony. You stuck your neck out not knowing anything. I can't tell you how much I appreciate this, Pisano. I owe you," said Lito.

"It's okay, pal," said Tony.

Big Tony spent his time shuttling back between St. Lucia and New York.

CHAPTER 58

SUNDAY MORNING AT Prospect Storage usually meant black coffee with anisette at ten o'clock. There were usually half a dozen men gathered, and Tony would hold court. It was more a social gathering than business, although some matters were resolved on those mornings.

"Hey, E, want a pig knuckle sandwich with that coffee?" John McBratney joked. Everyone laughed. The Friday night when Nicky pulled up in his Oldsmobile, though, was one to remember. He was never flashy with money. In fact, he was always trying to remain inconspicuous and lived in a midpriced, brick rancher in a very nice upper-middle class neighborhood.

"Hey, Tony, I got to talk for a minute," said Nicky. "Listen, double check all the arrangements for our travelers, and I'll stop by tomorrow night. I want to keep all this between us. Tell John to button up on this one, okay?"

"Sure, you got it. No problem," Tony answered. He looked at Nick but never asked any questions.

"This is very important. Thanks. I'll see you." And with that, he left.

June 2 came, and the ship, the *Athena*, was docked at a main pier in the Naples dock district. Antonio Stravis, the captain, had been sailing the oceans for over forty years. He had seen every port imaginable and sailed in all kinds of weather. He enjoyed his Mataxa (Greek brandy) in his coffee each morning, and this one was no exception. He watched as the men loaded his vessel, which he had sailed in from southern Greece a few days before. By midday, there were thirty men working to fill the ship's hull. The *Athena* was twenty years old but in decent condition, with a spacious captain's quarters and ample room for a large crew and big cargo holds. There were twenty crew cabins, small but ample for one man. Two of the units could be conjoined.

Crew members would generally be assigned regularly to one ship, but it was not customary to add or change work gangs or ordinary seamen. The captain noted the men that came on board and got a crew registry. Generally, they came in one or two at a time. The three men who came in at ten o'clock signed in. Then shortly after, three more came aboard as well, all of them in their late twenties and early thirties. Antonio did not recognize any of them. Though the captain really had no reason to take notice, he thought it a little strange that this many younger men, who didn't look much like sailors, would be on board this one ship. But since it was none of his concern who the shipping line hired, he dismissed his suspicion.

The men eventually congregated. They formed a work crew, and finally, on departure day, the local workmen left, and the crew set out for New Orleans. There were twenty-six men aboard, including the captain and the first mate.

The men spoke Italian and rarely had anything to say to their ship-mates. The voyage was uneventful, and they arrived in New Orleans as scheduled. Just as they were docking, however, the vessel began to experience major electrical disruption. The mechanical crew had to be called to the generator room and saw black smoke smoldering. Water was pumped into the area, and eventually the crew learned the entire generator and connectors were damaged beyond repair. By three in the afternoon, the news had spread about the damage to the main office of the shipping line, the Scorpio Company based in Athens.

Each crew member was given a passage document and directed to a waterfront rooming house since the ship was unlivable without electricity. They cleaned up the areas as best they could, and the crew left a few hours later. The captain, first mate, and two others stayed on board, and the two were ordered to rotate a watch. A temporary dockside electrical line was hooked up so the captain and the three others had some power and the ship could be lit up at night.

The six men eventually gathered on a street corner near the dock.

"Antonio, che cosa da fare?" (What shall we do?) asked a tall, thin fellow.

"Andare" (Come), said Antonio. The men split into two groups of three about thirty yards apart and began a trek into the inner city. They finally reached the French Quarter. There was a bar on St. Charles Street, and Antonio beckoned to the others to follow him in.

"Hello," said Antonio to a big, brawny, baldheaded fellow behind the bar. "I am Antonio. I think someone has left a message for me and some of my friends." The big guy gave the foreigner the once over. He could tell by his accent that he was not entirely fluent in English.

"What did you say your name is?" inquired the big guy.

"Antonio," he answered.

"Okay, I got it. Wait here." The big guy went over to another fellow behind the bar, small, skinny, about fifty years old. Then he walked out from behind the bar to the back of the place, down a long hallway, and entered a door at the back of the building. Within a few minutes, he came back with another man who was dressed in a black jacket and well-tailored slacks.

They came to the bar. "I'm Jake. I was told you would be here. Here, this is an address just down the street. There are rooms there for you and your friends. Just let the guy at the door know that Jake sent you. Okay?" he said.

Antonio began to walk and looked at the address number. When they got to the address, he knocked and went in. There was a fellow reading a newspaper in a room just as he entered a long hallway. "Jake told me to let you know we are here for a few rooms. Okay?"

The old man looked up from his paper, reached over to a peg board, and took three keys with numbered tags off a wall board. "Here you go: 206, 207, 208. There's a little restaurant in the front here. You can get whatever you want to eat, and they can take messages at the bar," the old man said as he handed the men the keys. They picked up their bags and trudged up the stairs. Finally, their voyage was over, and their real work was to begin. The six gathered in Antonio's room and unpacked.

"Antonio, when do we get some food here—real food?" said Demetrios.

"Soon, we can go downstairs. I just want to check the weapons," said Antonio.

Within ten minutes, there were the parts of three rifles lying on the bed, all assembled except for the stocks. Donio was screwing the wood pieces together, and one by one, the weapons were assembled.

Antonio inspected the room and found the floorboards under a round rug to be nailed down. He took a small metal tool from a leather rolled-up kit and worked them loose. One by one, he wrapped the guns in sheets from the bed and stacked them under the floorboards, replacing them once he was done. The group left and reconvened at the bar downstairs.

"Hello, I'm Antonio. I have a room upstairs here." He showed his key. "My friends and I would like to have dinner."

The bartender handed him some menus and said, "I'll have someone take care of you right away."

The six men sat together at a back table. The bartender was a bit surprised that none of them spoke English. In fact, he couldn't make out their language at all. Their language sounded somewhat like Cajun but different. The six conversed in a Corsican dialect, French based and their island dialect, strange to anyone not from that island. Two men met at the Showbar, a block over and a few blocks down on Bourbon Street. One was a heavyset, balding man, who sat at a back table wearing a gray fedora cocked to one side. The other man was neatly dressed, sleek, and middle aged. This meticulously attired man was doing all the talking.

"These guys got here today. They need to be transported to the country and then need to be briefed on the locations we are reviewing. You have to keep them under wraps and move them out to where they will never be noticed. Once we have a layout, we can fine-tune the plan. We still have to decide on the location options. These guys need to practice with what they have; then get them to review the layout. You will have all the money you need to finance everything. We have guys to drop you dough at the bar. You should just give them cash from time to time. I'll get you more as it's needed, but here is ten grand. Our guys will let you know whatever you need to know, from time to time. We're counting on you. Okay, big guy?"

The bigger man lifted his head and nodded. "Yeah, John. Don't worry about a thing. I have it all down."

The next morning, Antonio got a tap on his door followed by a quick help. Antonio cracked the door open enough to peek through the crack. "What do you want?" he asked.

"I'm Piero. I have a truck here to pick you and your guys up," the man said. "Okay. I'll wait down at the bar. Just let me know when you're all set up, and I'll pull the truck around. Take all your stuff with you. You won't be back here."

Soon, the flat-body truck bumped along, and the city faded away from sight. All that was visible were thick stands of trees and heavy bush undergrowth. The five men were trying to make themselves comfortable on their duffel bags and mats in the back. About two hours later, Piero turned off the main road down a dirt road that was full of potholes, with underbrush scraping the truck as it lumbered along.

After fifteen minutes, the truck stopped. There was a large decrepit old house at the end of the road. The back of it led to a dock and a long, winding canal. There were four small boats tied to the end of a long pier. The men got out, and Piero said, "Well, this is it. Let's get all the stuff in. There are at least six bedrooms in this place, so you guys can pick a room. Mine is the first one at the top of the stairs. There's food in the kitchen and some clothes in the closets in the second-floor hall. Make yourselves comfortable."

Antonio went up the stairs to the second floor. He entered the back bedroom and found a bed, an old, big, metal-framed thing that smelled musty even though the linens were clean. He looked out the two windows overlooking the front porch roof. There was a wide expanse of fields and marshes all around the building beyond where the truck was parked.

In the middle of the night, the men heard a car coming toward the house. Half-asleep, they all got up and went to the porch and could see headlights bobbing up and down. Soon the figure of a black sedan was visible. Two men were sitting in the front with a dark figure in back. When the vehicle pulled up in front of the house, the driver got out and called to the men. "Govani, vene ca." (Young men, come here.) One by one, they walked into the headlights, and the driver shook their hands. "Vene," he said and pointed to the house. They walked into the large center room, and a few minutes later, a small, thin man came in. He was overdressed with a long brown raincoat and wide-brim fedora. It was difficult to see his face. He walked around the room and looked closely at each face. He then went back outside. The men, who had been sleeping, had only their trousers and sleeveless T-shirts on.

"Basta!" the man said to the dark figure sitting in the back of the car. "They're all there. It's okay."

Old man Carlos Marcello rolled his round, stumpy body out of the car and waddled into the house.

"Amici," he said, shaking each hand and kissing each man on the cheek. He explained his relationships to each one, his family, their ties in Italy, and their mutual businesses with the Corsicans and Sardinians. He then laid out their mission. They were to leave within three days after being briefed on their parts in the plan. They would have a driver, and when done with the mission, they would spend some time at a resort before going home. The driver would take them to Dallas where they would be given more instructions.

They would change the course of history. Tony Scotti had grown up knowing everything a New York City street kid needed to survive. He could use his fists to protect himself but only did so when his wit and smooth talk failed him. Growing up with his family and enjoying the structure of being connected gave Tony a sense of importance and even obligation. Now, as the leader of the Longshoremen's Union, he easily handled the men he knew. He strolled easily from the piers in Red Hook to the banquet rooms of the Waldorf Astoria in Manhattan. The downtown financial district was always the place where all kinds of deals were made in Manhattan. Tony Delmonte had his table at DelMonico's Steak House at the center of the downtown district. This was Delmonte's office, and it was open five days a week. One day, he noticed a few men walk in and mill about without ordering anything. One of the men went out and then came back in accompanied by Jimmy Hoffa, a short, chunky man, a celebrity in this town. Hoffa sat down after being directed to a table by the leader of the four men. Tony had met Hoffa during a number of union events in Manhattan and some political banquets they had attended there too. He nodded to the group before continuing his conversation with the shipping official from the Ming Shipping Line. He was solidifying a deal to handle all their damaged ship salvage on a consignment basis, with a large cut, a bribe, to this fellow, Mr. Wing.

"Hey, Tony. How are you?" Tony Scotti said as he rushed in past Delmonte's table. Scotti sat down at the big, round table in the rear of the dining room. Within a few minutes, the other four men had returned to the bar, and Scotti and Hoffa were deep in conversation.

"We got to get these guys off our backs. I got these guys in Vegas saying they are very nervous. We got to get your guys to move soon, before the end of the year. This little prick, Bobby Kennedy, won't stop. I talked to my connections. They tell me even Hoover can't talk to these guys. They hate each other. Bobby's ambition is so huge that there are no limits to what he will do," said Hoffa.

"I can tell you we got things in motion. My uncle told me that the connections with Marcello are pulling it together and expect to be able to finalize things once the campaign is over. They all have a stake in the cash flow in Vegas and want to keep things there problem-free. This Bobby Kennedy steps on everyone's toes, and he don't care. Even his brother can't or won't slow him down, the double-crossing bastard. We elect this guy, and he pisses on us, him, and his father, Joe, who really fucked us all. Well, someday the bill comes due," said Scotti. "Jimmy, this Mike Blarney is killing us. He's like a one-man show. He won't listen to us. Have you got any pull with him through any of your guys?" asked Scotti.

"No, in fact, he is making my guys in the locals nervous. They get complaints from their rank and file when they can't equal what this big mouth gets from the city for his transit workers," said Jim.

"Well, he's screwing up the order of things, and our people are fed up," said Scotti.

"The people in the Transit Workers Union love the guy. That Mick thinks he's St. Patrick now," said Hoffa.

Tony Delmonte watched them from the corner of his eye completing his own deal. "See that guy Delmonte over there?" Scotti said. "He's helping us. From time to time, he needs our help either with the docks or the trucking guys in the unit. He can always be counted on. My uncle gets his help here and there. I think you know him."

"Yeah, I've seen him around. I'll remember if it comes up," said Hoffa. "I got to go, Tony," he continued. "Keep me up to speed here. They got these feds up my ass." He got up and left.

Scotti went over to Tony's table. "I got word," he said. "Keep far away from this guy, Hoffa. He's on the feds' top hit list. He's our biggest problem. The old man and Paulie are going to need to talk to Ally for some help. I want you to set up a meeting and keep it low-key." Scotti knew he could trust Tony to do it then forget. He also knew Delmonte and his crew had eyes and ears everywhere in New York and could keep him informed if anything didn't seem right.

CHAPTER 59

GROWING UP IN the New York neighborhoods was a learning experience in and of itself.

Whether a kid never finished grammar school, or in the rare instance of actually graduating college, there was always another educational experience in the street and the neighborhood.

Filomena's Bar began filling up by late afternoon on Saturdays. By late April, Joe LaMorte, the owner, would leave the front door open since it was warm enough outside in the late afternoon to do so. The noise from the crowd talking, the jukebox, and the men yelling at the shuffleboard tables sounded like an orchestrated mock musical piece out on the street. The old wood bar had about fifty stools, and the little white ceramic tiles on the floor, with sawdust scattered here and there, made the sound bounce off the floor and ricochet off the tin ceiling twelve feet above. The place was over fifty feet wide and over a hundred feet deep. There were tables with ice-cream style bent wood chairs scattered all around the bar and back room area, which was fully opened to the bar. If you walked in the front door, you could see all of the activity, front to back of the place. Smoke from cigars, cigarettes, and pipes fumed out the front door and transom top.

The odor of beer, whiskey, and tobacco mixed with and competed with the aroma of marinara sauce and pizza dough being cooked in the kitchen. The old Italian guys drank their wine and spoke in their native tongue, as they felt more comfortable using their native language as to prevent the coloreds and drunks from hearing what they had to say.

The coloreds, the blacks that lived in their section of the New Brighton neighborhood, knew their place in Filomena's. They also were cautious when they ventured into other neighborhood bars and restaurants, which included Bovino's, Florence Garden, Westbrook Inn, and the Miami Club. These places were all owned by old-line Italian families. They tolerated some of the coloreds but were quick to discipline anyone who stepped out of line. They also tolerated the black women who occasionally came in, some looking for their husbands or sons, some to get food, and some to chase down their man for money before he blew it all on drinks.

There was a great paradox. These owners and patrons, primarily of Italian descent, and, in fact, many born in Italy, and the mix of Irish, Polish, and some Jews as well as Negroes were not considered the most tolerant of each other. From time to time, there were ethnic-motivated clashes but not as often as one would find elsewhere in the 1950s and 1960s in other parts of New York City or other ethnically diverse cities in the USA.

Crimes occurred occasionally, but mostly the participants were from the same ethnic group. Occasionally a fist fight or a knife fight broke out when a black guy in a white bar got juiced up and ran into an Italian who had a chip on his shoulder and drank as much as his black opponent. Sometimes it was over money that was borrowed or lost in a card game or shuffleboard.

If a local store was burglarized, the internal communication between the leaders of each community would be expected to find out if it was an outsider or a local who did the crime.

The black community had its traditional leaders. The old man, Sixty, might be called upon to discipline a young black because he pilfered some fruit from Joe the Fruitman's Fruit and Vegetable Store. Maybe some smart-alec Italian kid robbed some money or candy from Mr. Bluth's Jewish cigar and candy store; if so, he might be called on the carpet by Joe Black or even Joe LaMorte. If he was a regular at Westbrook Inn, just a few harsh words from Joe Mazzerella, who stood over six feet tall and weighed over 350 pounds, would put enough fear in this little thief that he would cower in fear and vow never to do it again.

The tenuous truce sometimes was broken, and the cops had to step in, particularly if a big brawl broke out or a serious crime became notable, such as a shooting or stabbing. There never was a known murder, but there were disappearances and many beatings. But if the rare occasion of a major disagreement occurred, it usually was over money, and someone was forced to pay. Armed robbery rarely occurred, and senseless murders were very few. Placing a bet was part of everyday activity in each shop and store; never was there a sex crime.

Fat Sol, the Jew whose immigrant Polish Jew parents owned the bakery, could be seen hour after hour scouring the race forms and sports pages and betting cash register money on the ponies or a game. Leblich's Bakery, however, made the best cakes and pastries anywhere, and their rolls and bread operation ran twenty-four hours a day. The place was a real moneymaker.

Contes Meat Market also served as a back-room betting parlor. You could buy a chicken and bet on the numbers at the same place. Of course, this was only a way station, a drop, for Joe Black's operation. He picked up the bets in the stores and shops, even in the A & P and at Borden's Milk Truck Garage and the NY Department of Sanitation Truck Barn, part of the city of New York's operations in Staten Island.

Even though the A & P was full-service, the many small markets thrived. Among them were Peppina Nashada's Fish Market, Joe's Fruit and Vegetable, Columbia Meat and Fish Markets, Leblich's Bakery, Bluth's Cigar Store, Deodatis Pharmacy, La Manna's TV shop, Bisognas Italian Bakery, Tom Vazzanas Delicatessen and Italian Market, the Malandro Brothers Fruit and Vegetable Market, Dondaros Liquor Store, Kleins Clothing, Campbells Country Store (The Southern Black Meat Market). All had a place and a following, as did the bars, restaurants, and clothing shops in this mixed community.

The traditional trades fell mostly along ethnic lines. The Jewish community was noted as seamstress specialists like Binders Corset Shop, Kleins Clothing and Levi Store, the Sunday Man Cloth and Dress Shop, and Cohens Clothing. The Italians had the bakery, butcher, fish, vegetable, and fruit markets, as well as the restaurants and bars. The blacks had a bar and a meat market for smoked southern meat specialties like raccoon, chitterlings, hog maws, pig snouts, smoked tongues, smoked ham, picnic pork smoked shoulders, country sausage, and collard greens. There were a few Irish too, and they had their watering holes.

The neighborhood was run, however, by the Italians. The Assumption Church on Brighton Avenue overflowed every Mass on Sundays and even was partially full every morning with the Italian ladies. But Sundays were traditional. Masses started at six thirty in the morning and ran every hour until noon Mass.

Throngs would come and go, then crowd Bisogna's Bakery for bread and *pastachotte* (pastry) for the Sunday meal.

A *salsa di pomodora* (the tomato sauce) was bubbling away by the time the Roman Catholic Mass was done at church, and families would have their first arguments over who broke off the heel of the *pane* (bread) and stole the meatballs before they were fully cooked (and slopped the floor with sauce, trying to rush out of the kitchen before Mama caught the brigand with her weapon, the wooden spoon).

The men sometimes would go visit *I pasani* (their relatives). Sunday-morning visits were expected. There was also espresso coffee shared, and the anisette bottle was put out on the table with lemon rind and biscotti. The men would dress in suit and tie. They wore their best fedoras and brought along their sons. The visits would end well before the traditional mealtime at midday. By that time, they were all back home ready to spend three or four hours at the table. Maybe a late-afternoon visitor would pop in but not very often. However, it was not unusual to invite relatives over for the Sunday meal or to go visit with pasani and share Sunday dinner. For most of these Italian families, work was a six-day event, and socializing occurred on Sundays.

When Freddie Barnes entered the Florence Gardens Restaurant, he was usually greeted with a turn of heads and a nod from those seated at the long bar. They acknowledged him in a way that was the last vestige of an old tradition. It was reminiscent of a courtier's bow or a peasant walking or working at a roadside stopping and bowing to a nobleman as he was passing, a sign of *respetto*, the respect due a person of position. Freddie was far from a blue blood or a member of the nobles, the nobility. He was a working member of the Gambini family. He was a lower-echelon mobster, a soldier who grew up in the neighborhood. He learned his craft on the streets but also in his father's house, an immigrant house that revered his good fortune of coming to I Stati Uniti, the United States, so many years ago. The old man, Frederico Bernardino, worked as a laborer, a construction worker. He had his skills, however. He knew the work of his forefathers, concrete and stone. He was an old man now but still physically strong. His back was bent over from carrying the loads of stone and mortar and bending over his work day after day, year after year, so that his spine fused into a forward curve that was an inflexible rod of bone and cartilage. He suffered a bit of pain because of it, and the arthritic calcium buildup continued to accelerate his inflexibility and his aching back. However, the stoic Italian bore his burden with little complaint. He, as his ancestors, bore his lot in life with the acceptance that this was simply how things were. The contrast between father and son was exceptionally dramatic when the two were seen together. The old man squinted because the bright sun peaked through the leaves of the fig trees from time to time as he slowly walked to his place, where his chair and metal table were under the shade of those trees.

His eyes were focused on the chains that had grown into the middle of the crooks in each tree, and the rusted metal with the S-hooks and circular hoop were now imbedded in the dark bark. One of the trees, the one on the north side, was half-dead, likely because the chain cut off the flow of sap, but part was still alive, still hanging onto life, much like he was. He remembered when the chain swung free and was hooked to the thick, heavy canvas hammock, a surplus from a World War II navy supply. It still had the faint blue markings, which were legal trade when he bought it so many years ago after the war.

The hammock was hung at his first home from a six-by-six post, tethered to the post with a rope and strung to the trunk of an oak tree that grew tall and up through the grape arbor in his backyard. The yard in that home in Staten Island was a memory now. Also a memory was the vision of his three sons arguing over whose turn it was to get in the hammock and who was to push and swing it for a turn.

The sun was warm. He set the bottle and a very small thick glass next to it onto the table and sat down. It was a relief to sit. His left leg was aching again, a remnant of an injury from an automobile accident many years ago. The pain was not unusual but was still a reminder of the accident. The old Ford soft-top touring car flipped over and over, and he was catapulted through the leather roof top and rolled onto the ground. When he looked up, only a rubble heap of metal was all that was left. Not only was the car indistinguishable as a 1935 Ford, but it was just crushed chunks of metal in a disoriented mound. He poured himself a drink from the clear glass bottle filled with the deep ruby-red liquor and replaced the cork in the bottle.

He had crafted the drink from the time-honored way his father had taught him, a recipe from the little Sicilian village and countryside where the roots of the family had begun ages before. The bottom of the bottle still had the thick black hue that was the little black cherries, *il cerrizine*, that gave the flavor to choke-cherry brandy. The little berries had come from one of the very trees he now sat under. He sipped the strong brandy and felt its sting on his lips and the warmth in his throat as it burned its way down. The aroma filled his nostrils, and he remembered the days he made this same drink along with the wine his father had taught him to make. He also recalled the days in his own backyard in Staten Island with his sons helping him to do the same. He knew his father, as a young man, along with four other brothers had gone through the wine- and spirit-making ritual with his grandfather in Sicily, and generations before did the same. Now that was just a memory. No more wine making. No more sons to teach. All had gone their separate ways now. Just Vincenzo stayed nearby. All the others had found their way elsewhere.

His son Frederico Jr was now known as Freddie Barnes. He was hardly an image of his father, although the family resemblances, facial features, height, coloration, even the deep green eyes, were all Bernadino genes. Those resemblances were the only similarities between the two.

The old man lived in a style and mentality that had its foundations in an ancient past.

Freddie, in contrast, was a manifestation of the neighborhood he grew up in. He was no immigrant. He felt no obligation to anyone. In fact, the reverse was true. Freddie's superiority complex stemmed from having risen from the inauspicious family background to being a made man in the Gambini family. He appreciated the old manners and understood respect. But now it was he who should be the object of that respect.

He had seen his father work himself into a broken, frail man, and though he loved him dearly, he vowed to himself he would somehow raise himself above menial labor and never have to work like a donkey to make his way in life, no matter what it took to do that.

Freddie worked at a number of tasks for the family. He was relied upon to bring bags of cash from the local bookies to the capo-regime, the boss of his crew. He also was the go-between to funnel money to political campaigns, sort of another kind of bag man but with an entirely different purpose. Unrecorded cash in political campaigns could be a huge factor in besting the competition. If an opponent felt you were underfunded, the entire campaign might feel comfortable by having less money and less effort.

Suddenly, when it was too late, a last-minute barrage of ads could tip the race, and the guy with less dough would also be holding a bag, an empty one.

So, Freddie's missions were very important. Especially to guys like George Carfieno. Georgie grew up with Freddie. They were neighborhood pals. They went to PS 11 (Public School #11) together as children and then to Curtis High School. They both dropped out around the same time. Freddie got a position as a numbers runner, and Georgie did the same.

There were little bars and "a shot and a beer" joints all over the neighborhoods they traveled. Some were a bit better. One place seemed to be a sort of crossroads, the Florence Gardens. It was likely because the owner was also the chef. He came over from Italy as a teenager but learned how to cook in Italy. No matter if it was a veal dish, pasta, or fish, the food was exceptional. So, from eleven o'clock in the morning, after the eight o'clock drunks had taken up half the bar, through the lunch hour and up until late night, the kitchen was always as busy as the bar.

Across town at the Westbrook Inn, Big Tony Mazzarella also did a swift business, and his veal cutlet and sausage sandwiches were as good as the Garden. But for some reason, the Florence Garden always drew the wiseguys and wannabes. Maybe because it was in the heart of the Italian neighborhood, not on the edge of the black neighborhood like Westbrook, or maybe because there was the nightclub a block or so down, the Miami Club, that was one of the hottest night spots on the island, like a little Copacabana with a floor show on the weekends and live entertainment six nights a week. Or maybe it was because you could run a tab at Florence Garden and pay once a month if you "got stuck." Or maybe because some of the *bella robbia* (slang for pretty dressed), meaning loose women, were found there, even some of the Miami Club's dancers. Or on a given afternoon, a few dozen guys at the bar might be entertained by an impromptu dance by Mushy Gush, a buxom brunette that was a part-time professional party girl, a stripper who also worked as a dancer at the Miami.

Mushy could be enticed with a handful of ten-dollar bills to do a strip on the bar. She would bounce around from man to man, rubbing her naked breasts against the guys' faces, then follow it up with a half squat and push her G-string cover in a face if another ten-dollar bill appeared. If there was more than ten dollars, she pulled the front cover aside and rubbed her pussy in the guy's face, hence the nickname Mushy Gush.

Florence Garden was also safe territory. Everybody knew everyone else, so if a stranger came in, the private conversation stopped, and the intruder would get a stare. Cops never frequented the Florence Garden unless they too were part of the neighborhood and could be trusted. Georgie saw to that by making sure his contacts, particularly Congressman Murphy, influenced the precinct captain at the 102 in St. George to assign friendly cops who were on the pad to the neighborhood. Freddie knew them all as well, and they helped Murphy get reelected time after time.

CHAPTER 60

GEORGE GOT UP, stood at the podium, and looked around the room solemn faced. He began to read through the notes in hand. "What do these guys know about real life? It's so easy for them. They were born with money. They grew up with money. They never had to scratch for a nickel. Our people, on the other hand, were born into a world of adversity. They were born into nothing and had nothing but a craving to do better, be better. The parents, even without education, wanted more for their children, so they worked to make a difference for their kids. When they finally had a loaf of bread under one arm, they still had fear. The fear would disappear but again, and they would be back to scratching and digging in the hard dirt for the next buck. These politicians don't have any idea about that. They don't know about getting up at five in the morning and working the second job till nine at night and on Saturdays and many Sundays too. They have no idea why on a Sunday the Catholic church on the corner is packed to overflowing. What are these people doing there? They pray! They pray for work. They pray for their family's health. They pray to ease the pain. And sometimes, they pray just to thank their God for life and the opportunity. Can you imagine? The opportunity for what? To kill themselves for another work week. To look forward to five nights a week of eating pasta and bread and maybe a glass of wine and an orange. Maybe to soak their feet in water warmed on a twenty-year-old stove. And get some cool water from a twenty-year-old ice box. And they are the pride of their race. These Italians, these wops, are stupid, ignorant slobs, aren't they? They make shoes, they clean streets; they deliver coal and ice and make bread. There isn't a spark of intelligence in any of them, these greaseballs, these greenhorns, these *whyl yos*,

Managia America! But they don't know the real background of these imports, the real fiber of these strange people who trust no one, our people. These people weren't born in the Lower East Side of New York City; they walked off a ship and ended up there, carrying children born on the other side as well. They found a tenement to live in through a *comparde* who tried to help those wretched, poor Sicilians coming from his old piaese, from old country, from his town. He helped them get work; he cleaning a slaughter house, she as a seamstress. There was a crippled woman who looked after half a dozen kids in the building, too young to take care of themselves. They paid her what they could and sometimes shared some food with her.

Congressman John "Jackie" Murphy

"We learned our lessons on the streets in New York City, on Hester Street in Manhattan, and in the Bronx, in Brooklyn, and in Queens. Each place had a Little Italy and other ethnicities as well.

"The politicians and their sons tried to reach these folks to get them to register and get their vote. Only when our people understood the power of the system, beyond *e* Mafioso as ruler of the streets, did we emerge from the squalor. That's when we lifted the boot off our necks and could, at last, stand up. I tell you now it is so important to keep our people moving forward by being sure we keep supporting our friends in a solid block. We vote for Democratic Jackie Murphy. He knows how we feel, and he is the only guy in Congress to get the government on our side. He grew up like us, hardworking Irish immigrant parents with seven children. They build houses and roads, they build a life. Frank, Joe, Mary, and the rest worked like our people worked. Now we need this guy to help our people, for all of us, for the best of America. Thank you all, and God bless."

George looked out over the crowd. Then there was avid applause. The speech was like every other he had been giving to these local folks for the last ten years, nearly the same words. But he also went door-to-door. Every business, every house in the neighborhood knew his knock on the door and big smile.

George was a scrawny boy with a big mouth. He never shut up even when he was a baby. He went from incoherent babble to understandable babble to political babble but still never said too much. Along the way, he acquired a taste for rye whiskey. Now each day started with a large cup of black coffee, laced with a bit of Four Roses. At lunch, he had a little sandwich or, once in a while, a plate of pasta washed down with some Four Roses. Over the years, his eyes turned to a faded blue-gray. The alcohol kept him going but also kept him from being anything more than a neighbor political hack. He always had some sort of no-show city job that paid a weekly salary. Some concocted position that paid enough to keep him and his wife alive. He also took a little cream off the political donations he took in for Murphy and a piece of every fundraiser he ran.

His daily routine of going door-to-door through the business section of New Brighton and West Brighton was really a business pursuit more than a political effort. George was also the local numbers runner with a territory that was part of a city-wide organization, mostly run by the Gambini and Bonanni families. George had his own small territory in Staten Island. This was his reward, in a sense, for both his political as well as his street skills. In fact, it was, as the higher-ups knew, not a dual loyalty but merged at the top by the secret organization for Cosa Nostra. To get political power in the late 1950s in the Democratic Party in any part of New York City, you had to be in with the in guys, and the in guys were connected to New York and New Jersey's work organizations and the family organizations, the mob.

George grew up as part of that culture, and though he never finished high school, he was clever enough to work his way up to positions he now held. This numbers racket gave him total financial independence. He would start at nine in the morning and could zip through the pickup spots, get all his numbers, and be done by noon, just in time for lunch at Florence Gardens or Lucio's, where he would pick up even more business.

The neighborhood bars were the hub for many kinds of business. The concrete contractor placed a bet, got a sandwich and a beer, and maybe made a deal to do work with another contractor on a job. The daily menu, with the special, was the best buy in town, no matter what town you found yourself in on the side of the island. Florence Garden might have a veal and peppers or *salsiccia* sandwich. If you were near the docks, you always found a good lunch at Mazzio's, maybe "macs and knucks" (macaroni in thick red sauces with two big, whole pig's knuckles and a side of hot cherry peppers) and a chunk of Italian bread.

Georgie was careful with his bets. He would scratch down every number on a postage-stamp-size scrap of paper and turn every one into his book, Joe Black. If George could not be around on a specific day, Joe might make the major stops. Being careful with the number turn-ins means avoiding going into your own pocket if someone hit. The number, the last three digits of the daily handle at Aqueduct Race Track, printed daily in the newspapers, could not be manipulated, and it was recognized city-wide as the number. Everyone had their favorite number; maybe it was an address or a birth date or related to some special event. If, for example, a noted black guy in the neighborhood died, there would be lots of bets on 002. No one knew how it came about, but that was a local superstition bet, maybe a parting gesture by the deceased to his neighborhood friends. In any case, there was an uncanny number of hits on such superstitious bets, especially if a notable black leader was a respected guy in the neighborhood.

If there was a problem with the police, the first place they looked for a collar was the low-level numbers runners. It could be a signal that some cops didn't get proper tribute. Lots of cops supplemented their income by participating in protecting the gambling and other operations of the organized guys. Just ignoring what they knew were illegal operations was sufficient enough to earn a spot on the weekly pad. Thus, a small scrap of paper could be easily swallowed if a runner thought he might be collared. No evidence, no crime.

But, if you were Joe Black, you never wrote anything down. He memorized thousands of bets and never missed one. Only Joe Black could do that. The others would drop the bets after several stops and then go out for more.

Georgie, on the other hand, needed to keep a written record. Sometimes he used the inside of a matchbook cover, folded, so if he had to light his cigarette suddenly, the matchbook would flare up and burn the list. Again, no evidence. He turned his bets into Joe Black daily. Joe would wait for the daily pickup by one of the men the Priest sent to collect. The Priest, also known as Ally Dessio, was a nephew of Don Carlo Gambini, who had a large concrete building in a street near a West Side dock entrance road. This was his headquarters for his vending machine business. It was also the drop and counting room for all the booking operations on the entire island and the areas of New Jersey controlled or in cooperation with the Gambini organization. Ally and his two brothers, Nicky and Johnny, ran all the operations. The legitimate business consisted of vending, jukeboxes, cigarette wholesale, and vending soda and candy. No one else was permitted to put any machines on Staten Island or in the New Jersey docks at Port Socony or Port Newark. It was all Gambini territory.

Ally was an imposing figure with a dense crop of reddish-brown hair on his big head and a bulky torso that made him appear the size of a small refrigerator. His brisk speech, rasping orders to men, made him sound like an old army general.

However, his closest contact with the army was when he and his deceased brother, Joey, were drafted. Ally turned out 4-F because of a punctured eardrum in the left ear and complete deafness in the right ear, an injury he got as a kid. Joey ended up an army private and was killed on D-day, gun in hand, on June 6, 1944, at age nineteen, in the first wave of troops at Normandy, France. His body was shipped home and buried in the family plot at Moravian Cemetery in the shadow of the famous Hormann Mausoleum. The Hormanns were one of the most famous and wealthy families to settle on the island. They founded the Moravian Church there, but more important, they founded R&H Beer Company, with a huge brewery in Stapelton, which employed thousands during its many years of operation. Being buried near this famous family's resting place added a certain importance to the young man's death.

The Dessio family, in tribute to Joey and another Staten Islander, John Scabetti, formed an American Legion VFW post called the Dessio-Scabetti Post. Island-wide events were sponsored by the "Post" located in the middle of the island at Clove Road and Richmond Road, one of the busiest intersections.

Ally and his brother were proud of their lost brother, and his loss actually gave their family name a special aura of being the ultimate patriots. Even the cops and politicians recognized this notoriety.

Congressman Jackie Murphy depended on the Gambini family and its organization and street-level people to help fund his campaigns and to get the votes out for him and his associates on Election Day. The Murphy family had a longstanding business relationship with the Gambinis. Their fortune was made by securing local government contracts for construction. City roads, curbs, sidewalks, and bridges— construction contracts all somehow went through Murphy's hands and through their connections in Tammy Hall and its Democratic leader, Congressman Carmine De Sapio. But there was a catch. The subcontractors and supplies were always those chosen specifically for each job. Sicilian Paving got most of the roads, Post Construction got the concrete work, and so on. Each one had a deal cut with percentages kicked back to the boys on every contract. Papa Johnny Murphy had started his connection in the business with the boys in the twenties. Now they took it to a bigger level. Frankie was the oldest and the brains of the operation. Jackie was the pretty boy with piercing, steely blue eyes and a gregarious personality. He was charming enough and clever enough to become the darling of his teachers in school. Frank and the old man, in true Irish political tradition, slated Jackie to become an elected office holder and open further government doorways into the municipal pots of gold that government work offered. He accompanied Congressman Jackie Murphy to all the events and the campaign sessions and felt proud that everyone knew he was in Jackie's inner circle. "Hey, Georgie, I got a problem getting my cousin a green card. He came from Italy two years ago and needs to get a union card so he can get full-time as a longshoreman," said "Woodchuck" Charlie Brita.

"Okay, I'll see what I can do. You gotta let me know his background is clear, and I'll need a grand to oil the wheels," said Georgie. A grand was a sizeable piece of change, but spread around to the right people, it could buy that green card.

The schedule of payments for such services was roughly known to each person along the way. Murphy's office would set up the meeting with one of the people they had placed in a job with the Immigration and Naturalization Service Agency. The contact got two hundred dollars. One hundred for him and one hundred to donate to the next racket that Georgie would run. Next, the New York City cops had to clear the prospective citizen's record, no criminal activity. Another hundred dollars went to one of the cops that was placed on the job by one of the Murphys. There was another hundred for incidentals, and then Jackie got five hundred dollars, and Georgie got his one hundred or so.

For each segment of government where there was a public need, there was a fee to get it done. A driver's license was another example. The driver's test was held in Tompkinsville, starting in the middle of Bay Street, a very wide avenue. The driving test included a road test. The test officer/monitor had you drive around for a half hour, turn, park, and test general driving skills. Georgie would arrange that a friendly monitor would be assigned to one of his new drivers. A small envelope with twenty dollars in it for the monitor was to be placed folded into the paperwork and presented before the test. If there were ten tests in a day, a young man likely would not pass if he didn't have a connection. These instructors with the city had ultimate authority. If there was a pretty girl, and she charmed the instructor, there was a good chance she'd pass without the grease.

If you needed to get an approval for cutting a curb for your businesses for a new parking lot, you needed a city permit. Georgie could arrange it for five hundred dollars. Building permits, sewer tie-ins, road paving, streetlights, guardrails—any license at all had a price and a connection, and all paid tribute to Jackie and company and all those down the line.

The Murphys all had their responsibilities. Frank, the brains, under Papa's watchful eye, and with his help with the boys, ran the construction business and made the deals. Jackie cleared the legal way with his New York City law school connections and political pull with the mayor's and governor's offices. He endeared himself to the national Democratic Party with large cash infusions and his commanding presence in local street politics throughout the city. Mary was the Murphy Company's chief bookkeeper; Tommy the tough guy was the construction crew general manager; Rose was the courier, taking care of going from bank to bank, buying gifts and running all over town on a million errands; and Robbie, a rotund, burly guy, was not too bright, so Frankie kept tabs on him so he wouldn't get in trouble. Frankie had his heavy equipment chief, Lenny, teach Robbie how to operate a cement truck and put a little Italian guy, Pete Moro, with him in the truck to keep an eye on him. Louise, the youngest, stayed at home to help her mother, Ida. Frankie, dressed in a black Italian knit shirt, Palm Beach checkered sport jacket, and gray slacks with brown brogues, was known as a classy dresser. He walked into Capelli's Restaurant and went over to the maître d'. "Hey, Mario I want the round table over there," he said, pointing to the end of the room in a secluded corner.

"Yes, Mr. Frankie," the maître d' responded before accompanying him to the table.

"I have some people coming here to meet me, and we need to talk quietly," said Frankie as he handed Mario a ten spot. Mario knew that whatever business was about to be transacted was very private and would be sure not to sit anyone nearby so the conversations could not be overheard.

Capellis was a place where major commerce occurred, especially at lunchtime. It was in the middle of the more populated areas of Staten Island and at a crossroads of two major roads, Richmond Road and Clove Road, not far from other thoroughfares on the expanding island.

Mario set up the table for six and put out bread, olives, cheese, and crackers. Two men in business suits, the gray uniforms, came in. "Commissioner," Frankie called out, "over here." The two men walked over. Commissioner Michael Riley was one of New York City's Mayor Robert Wagner's right-hand men. He ran the New York City Department of Transportation with strict authority.

"Frankie, this is Assistant Commissioner Bob Reed," said Riley. They shook hands.

"Have a seat." Mario came over and took drink orders and scurried to the bar. It was twelve fifteen on a Wednesday, and the place began to fill up with about half the tables taken, but the bar was already full.

A serious-looking young man in a black suit walked in. He looked around the room, standing at the maître d' stand, scanning the crowd slowly, then walked out. A few minutes later, he walked back in followed by two other men. Tom Leonard, the US secretary of commerce, a tall, slim man, well dressed in a blue suit with a bright red tie, arrived with Congressman Murphy at his side. The three walked over to the table.

"Mr. Secretary, welcome to New York. Good to see you again," said Commissioner Riley. "Bob told me to tell you what a great job you're doing and how much he appreciates the help you and the president have given him in these tough times in the city."

"Thank you, Mike."

"Hello, Mike," said Murphy. After the handshakes, Mario stepped in again with a tray of drinks and took more orders. The fellow in the black suit, who was obviously the secretary's bodyguard, stood several paces away from the table and kept a close eye on the comings and goings. Few people even noticed the little group at the table.

One short, squat fellow at the bar dressed in a cashmere sweater and slacks occasionally glanced over as he sipped his scotch on the rocks. Johnnie Dessio kept one eye on the activity in the back of the room and the other on the front door. Dessio was a regular, and there was some talk that the Dessio family, after lending Cappelli money to feed a bad gambling habit, now owned a piece of the joint. So Johnnie kept an eye on the place and the action that might be important.

"Mr. Secretary, you are aware that Staten Island is growing by leaps and bounds and that the traffic situation is nearly gridlocked. The commerce through the island and the new Verrazano-Narrows Bridge project to Brooklyn demands the type of limited-access super highway construction to be completed as soon as possible. The federal appropriations are nearly complete. The need to get the roads and infrastructure finished is a top priority," said Riley.

Jack Murphy added, "I'm sure you're aware of the entire situation. Also, my brother Frank and my father have the knowledge and experience to get the job done. They have also been supporters and part of our team on the local, state, and national levels. Forest Oak Construction and its subsidiaries will devote the time and experience to do a class A job in an expedient time frame. The mayor, as Commissioner Riley will tell you, is on board. We will commit three percent of the gross contract to his coffers. The DNC or anyone you designate will get seven percent. We have a commitment to the unions for five percent, and our friends, who will be sure we have everything we need, as well as protection, union peace, and other incidentals, will get ten percent. This is a fair sharing of the entire deal. Phase one is already approved at four hundred million. You know those big cats in Washington are salivating over this deal. We know you need to appease them. We think our structure of the deal is within reason. We simply need the information on the other bidders and the influence of your folks to get the bids up. Mr. Secretary, this can be a great win for everyone," Murphy finished.

Leonard said nothing for a moment, then slowly nodded his head as if each bit of information was being analyzed with each nod. "Yes, I think you are correct here. I like it, and I will recommend the deal," said Leonard. The Murphys smiled broadly, as did Riley. Dessio, still at the bar, noted that these men seemed to be agreeable.

"Okay, now let's see what Johnnie Cappelli can do in that kitchen," said Jackie. He beckoned to Mario, who scurried over. "Tom, what would you like? Anything at all," said Jackie. They ordered steaks, and when they were done eating, after another round of handshakes and back pats, Leonard and his security man and Riley departed.

Jackie was sipping coffee when Johnnie Dessio came over to the table. "Jack, you're looking very happy. All is well I take it," said Johnny.

"It's great, John. We got the expressway deal locked up. Now here's the plan. We need to get additional heavy excavation machinery to do the road bedding and lots of concrete. We need the union guys to lay off on this. We'll give them a big piece, but we need some of our own guys in on this. I'm sure you know what to do," said Jack. Dessio nodded.

Frank added, "I'm gonna need to set up a deal to lease all this equipment. I'll have Gene Ferranti set me up a company to do the leasing for Forest Construction. We can lease the equipment with no money down and sublease to Forest. I'll get Tony Stones to do part of the concrete with his crew and a piece to Sicilian paving. They can kick back ten percent each to cover our expenses with Leonard. You know the way we work it with change orders and such, so we'll have no problem. There will be plenty of federal money to spread around. These contracts are solid gold. Because of that, we will go to Chemical Bank or First America and take a loan out to finance our end. If we work it right and get some surpluses, we can lend out to the subs, in house. Ferranti can set us up a loan organization. We can make a big buck in interest but also keep tabs on the cash flow as well." They all nodded.

The Staten Island Expressway was to be the main highway to the new Verrazano Bridge. During the course of land acquisition, the Murphys helped to manipulate the land deals for the acquisition of the expressway roadbed and exit locations through Murphy with his connections to the Boro president, Allie Manicuso, and Allie's real estate buddy, Kenny Wilton. They got their many surrogates to acquire most of the land necessary for the project. The land was then sold to the Expressway Commission at a huge profit. All these deals went forward quietly, but there were rumblings with some Staten Island guys who recently had come in to invest. These fellows were from Brooklyn, and though some were associated with the Profaci and Bonanni mob organizations, others also were with the Luchese and Colombo Mafia families. Thus, the families all were satisfied by getting a piece, a tribute.

The rumor circulated that the lesser families were being slighted. The concern was that if all this money and control was vested in a deal between Joe Bonanni's guys and old man Gambini and his crews, and it fattened the pockets of the Profacis and their other associates, the power shift already seen in Gambini's running the garment industry, construction union, long salesmen union, garbage and sanitation, and so many politicians and judges, with guys like Murphy and Sapio and others in their fold calling the shots, other families would be that in name only, relegated to being low-level street hoods, otherwise water boys for the big guys. However, since the big guys were satisfied, they made sure no one else complained.

There was a great interest in these goings-on by another group, the FBI, headed by its curious federal director, J. Edgar Hoover. Hoover was a very dangerous guy. He seemed to have his ears on everything of major importance in the country and was particularly interested in mob finances. His knowledge of the deals between the mob and various political figures made him invincible in Washington. Every president had an uneasy feeling about what Hoover knew, and they were right to. Hoover found ways to get information on every import- ant political and business figure as well as criminal elements in the United States and elsewhere.

"Mr. Director, Special Agent Franz is here now."

"Show him in," said the director.

The man in a black suit sat in front of the director. "I have some interesting information on the meeting Secretary Leonard had in New York," said Tony. Then, over the next two hours, he briefed Hoover on what had happened. Although he was several paces away, he had stayed within listening range or could read their lips.

When Franz concluded, Hoover, leaning back in his chair, said calmly, "You know this Congressman Murphy and his family are the kind of cancer our society suffers from, corruption in the guise of being a man of the people. These folk's greed is only surpassed by their blatant disregard for the respect of elected office." Hoover was already investigating several congressmen and senators as well as other national figures. His investigation and intense surveillance of the Murphys thus began while transformation of Staten Island was fully underway, with the woodlands becoming highways, accompanied by a building boom spread across the island. Expressway construction had begun with great fanfare, but it was followed by an eerie slowdown and then silence. Months passed, and no more progress was made.

"Georgie, can you believe what's going on?" said Jimmy Conte, the butcher on Jersey Street. He had the *Staten Island Advance* newspaper open to the headlines, "FOREST IS LOST IN THE WOODS." The story related the collapse and bankruptcy of Murphy's company and had pictures of a harried Frank pointing at a deep cavern in the earth. The "forest through the trees" comment stung the law enforcement community, which was blamed for laxity.

Indeed, Frank had a big problem, but it was one of his own making. The Murphys decided that they couldn't get the federal monies in fast enough to hold off the boys who had been financed, in part, by the collapsing Murphy empire. So, Frank sold off the heavy equipment. The problem was that Forest didn't own the equipment. The multimillions from selling off the equipment went directly into Frank's pocket. The materials and the labor of the subcontractors who were not connected, which left the partially built expressway in limbo, were the obligation of the Forest Group, Inc., not personally, so they were all left holding the bag. The big guys got their cut, and Frank and Papa felt it was time to call it quits and retired to Florida. Congressman Jackie took a little heat but survived without much problem. He was still an important asset to both the Democratic Party and the boys.

With the Murphy Construction operations out of action, Jackie was now forced to make his own way. Frankie "the Brain" only visited infrequently now, and the rest of the family followed into retirement in Florida with the big money Frankie got from skimming the Forest Company, then taking all the saleable assets.

Jackie still needed to make a buck, though. Hoover knew of the insatiable Murphy avarice and the superiority complex of the congressman. He was a man of privilege, confident of presidents and senators, organizer of political power in New York City's Democratic organization and power broker in national politics. He commanded a huge war chest for political patronage. Jackie's problem was his own personal finances. He could not show any personal benefit from the Forest scam and the roughly $100,000 he got between congressional salary, law office, and such just didn't pay the bills. When he was contacted to talk to some foreigners about assisting them in a number of business matters, which required the help of a US congressman, he was all for it.

Sheik Omar Kahlid had one of his emissaries contact Murphy's New York office. The Kahlid family said they had billions of dollars from their ownership of oil fields spread throughout the Middle East. The sheik spent a great deal of time in New York City where he and his formal associates interacted with financial institutions handling the Kahlid billions and promoting various interests in the US.

The first meeting between the sheik, his entourage, and Murphy was as near a Hollywood script as could be. Murphy was asked to come to the sheik's suite in the Waldorf-Astoria. He arrived and was greeted by two bodyguards at the hotel lobby entrance and escorted to the penthouse suite. There in lavish splendor was the sheik, wearing traditional Arab garb and dark, round sunglasses, seated in the center of a semicircle of throne-like high-back chairs. In an awkward gesture, Murphy sort of half-bowed and put his hand out. The sheik extended his hand for a moment, touched Murphy's fingertips, and withdrew back to his seat. A chair was drawn up for Murphy in front of this assemblage.

Murphy said, "It is a great pleasure to meet you, Your Eminence. Our government is grateful for your friendship and the longstanding relationship your family has had with the United States."

The sheik stroked his beard and moustache and hesitated for a long moment, then spoke. "Congressman, I am told you are a senior person in your government and enjoy a great deal of power and prestige. I have a number of, what shall I say, delicate matters that, if they could be resolved, could be financially beneficial to my family's interest and also to those who can assist us. Do I make myself clear?"

"Yes, I understand," said Murphy with a quizzical look back at the sheik.

"I need the help of someone who can keep a strict confidence and can accomplish our aims without a bit of notoriety. I have a number of my people who I need here to assist me in the ongoing business of my family. They have been refused visas and entry for frivolous reasons. I seek to get a petroleum supply contact with your Department of the Navy. We know the highest prices paid and seek to secure those contracts. We are also exploring new sites for oil fields in three locations in Saudi Arabia, Iraq, and Texas. Due to the way our finances are structured, we are known to these owners of the areas involved but seek to be behind the scenes in those negotiations. Therefore, we have set up an organization, a company called Oil Aramis Petrol, an American company. We seek funding from your government to do the necessary oil exploration in Texas so as not to expose our family's interest, which will drive up the prices of the oil lease rights. I am prepared to pay five hundred thousand American dollars to those who can help us in these matters. Forgive me for being blunt, but much time has passed, and we are concerned that our opportunity may be lost. We have had my man Mr. Wahlid discuss some of these concerns with you in the past. Now you know more precisely what is needed. Are you prepared to help?" asked the sheik.

"Yes. Yes, I can take care of these things for you," said Murphy. The sheik smiled, and Murphy nodded his head.

"Well then, you can let Mr. Wahlid know your progress, and he will give you some details," said the sheik.

"I may need some front money to start things forward, probably one hundred thousand," said Murphy.

"I will contact you once we have a deposit for you, Mr. Murphy," said the sheik. "Now I must go. Thank you very much, sir."

Murphy rose and, with a taut smile, headed to the elevator with one of the sheik's men as escort.

Murphy could not believe his good fortune. A half-million dollars falling into his lap even though he wasn't entirely sure he could deliver on any or all of the promises. Two weeks later, he was again summoned to the Waldorf.

"So, Congressman Murphy, we have agreed on our deal," said the sheik, this time with only two others sitting by on a sofa across the room.

Murphy said, "Yes, now let's discuss the specifics again," and the Sheik outlined each problem to be solved.

"We are agreed that you will receive five hundred thousand American dollars upon the production of the contract; we shall present you with additional funds," said the Sheik. Murphy saw the stacks of bills emerge from a cloth bag and being piled on the coffee table in front of him.

"Very well," he said. He did not press the issue of the suggested one hundred thousand, perhaps thinking a bird in the hand was worth two in the bush when he saw that there was just fifty thousand in cash.

In a cubicle built at the center of the wall behind that hotel living room was a sound-proofed, walled area with a camera and an audio tape machine rolling. Three men watched carefully through a two-way mirror as Murphy restacked the money and put it in his briefcase. Later that evening, one of the three men observing Mr. Murphy's exit picked up a telephone that was hooked up inside the cubicle. "Mr. Director, we have it on video and audio tape. It is of excellent quality. Mr. Murphy took the fifty thousand dollars and placed it in a briefcase in perfect view of our camera, sir. We can proceed as you instructed."

The headlines blared across the front pages of the New York City newspapers first, then in Washington, and eventually across the nation. "US Congressman Indicted," the story of how Murphy greedily scooped up money under the recording eye of an FBI camera and how a phony sheik, actually an FBI agent, had duped this pillar of society into the admission on the record that he was merely a thief willing to sell his office.

"The man is going down, Georgie. Stay away from him, and for now keep a low profile. I'll have someone contact you if I need to talk to you. Let's keep things on the Q-T till this plays out. Capisce?" said Ally Dessio to Georgie Carfano.

Dessio stepped out of the phone booth and checked up and down the street before he got in his car. "Angelo, shut Georgie out of everything for now. He was too close to Murphy, and they might be watching or listening to him. Have one of our guys keep an eye out and ear out for his comings and goings and see if he's being tailed. Let's circle the wagons with all our guys. Put the word out to take precautions," said Ally.

In order to avoid further embarrassment for himself and his family, and knowing he was caught red-handed with marked bills, Murphy pleaded with the federal prosecutor's office to make a deal. Unfortunately, a copy of the film had already gotten out and made its way through to the national news. Besides being branded a thief, he was a laughing stock, duped by what clearly appeared on tape to be a fake sheik in what one commentator said looked like a cheap Halloween costume.

Once Murphy took the fall, the Gambini family had lost one of its closest allies and entrée to various segments of the government as well as some influences with a few unions. They still had much of Manhattan and parts of other boroughs locked in, but the loss of Murphy in the city and in Washington was really damaging.

CHAPTER 61

"**NICKY, THE OLD** man wants to sit with us. Tell John that Paulie Castellucci called and set us up for eleven o'clock at the house on Fingerboard Road. You should come together and keep it low-key. Capisce?" said Ally. He struggled to get out of the phone booth. Each year it seemed he added ten more pounds and five more inches on his waist.

Jackie, who was somewhat slim, would yell to Ally now and then, "Hey, Five-by-Five." Ally didn't respond. He had an extremely low boiling point. He knew his size was somewhat comical, but he refused to deprive himself of anything he liked, particularly food, wine, and women. After all, what was making all that money for anyway? It was to enjoy. And enjoy he did. He could devour a five-pound steak and then have pastries before he bedded one of his several *cumades*, the *bella-robbe* he sponsored. These women were treated to rent-free apartments, cash stipends, gifts, sometimes stolen fur coats, jewelry, TVs, booze, or whatever was pilfered from the ships when they were unloaded or hijacked trucks, and Ally got plenty of this stuff. These ladies were expected to be available day or night. Usually it was a phone call, an hour or two roll in the hay, a bite to eat, then home to the wife or back to work. Occasionally, if there were reasons to go out of town, they might meet their man at a motel or hotel for one or two days. If there was a social event, a golf outing, or a special party, they might be treated to several days at a swanky Miami Beach hotel and make the rounds at all the clubs and restaurants on the arm of the man, being sure to fawn all over him. His associates would do the same.

The night of the sit-down, Ally was all business. He had set up the Fingerboard Road house as his family residence. However, when he had the house built, he had a concrete bunker room built below the ground. The walls were twelve inches thick, and he installed a two-foot-thick vault door as the only entrance. It was heated and air-conditioned and without a single window. Surely no device could eavesdrop on that room.

The guests began arriving, one or two at a time, from about nine thirty until eleven. Nicky arrived with John. Paulie's driver and bodyguard, Tommy Bottelli, arrived with Paulie. A few moments later, Claudio arrived as well. Claudio had recently come to the United States from Sicily. He was a member of the highly regarded Sicilian Mafia family there and was part of a group of new recruits sent from Italy.

Ally closed the door. The sound was like the sealing of an ancient tomb. Paulie said, "Listen, we got problems now that Jackie got burned. This Kennedy thing is a mess, and our boy Hoffa has leaked stuff all

Calogero "Carlos Marcello" Minacore

over his organization. We have a friend out there in the Midwest. He knows a guy very close to Hoffa. If Hoffa gets arrested and is forced to sing, our whole organization in Vegas is going to crumble. I think you are going to get a car from the Midwest to deal with it. It may have one or two large packages in the trunk. I need it crushed and disposed of very quickly. Also, I need one of your best shooters to find a quiet place out west, maybe in Fort Worth, Texas. He will be out there for about a month. Once he's there, let Tommy know when he can be contacted by some of our people out there. He will be working for old Carlo with some other people."

Ally and Nicky just listened and said, "Okay."

Johnnie asked about funding. "Don't worry about money. Just do it, and it will all be worthwhile."

"Okay, see you later," Paulie said, before walking to the door. Everyone followed him out.

Ally got a call three weeks later from Tommy. "Hey, there is a car coming to you tonight. Keep the yard open." Ally's junkyard had a big car crushed, and it was part of his claim to fame that his machine was a foolproof disposal for anything, including a dangerous national union leader.

No evidence related to the death or disappearance of Jimmy Hoffa was ever found. His old friend and bodyguard, Hank, was rumored to have admitted he shot Jimmy and put the body in the trunk of a car. No evidence was ever found. Other rumors abound even that Hoffa was buried at Yankee Stadium.

Paulie and Tommy met their end on a street in Manhattan in front of a restaurant. Some say it was orchestrated by an ambitious underling who was drunk with power. Others say a long-emerging Manhattan-based plot was hatched when the old man Carmie Gambini died and named Paulie, his brother-in-law, as his successor. Paulie allegedly did not have the brains or the balls to be a "Capo di Tutti Capi," and the southern faction headed by the ailing Don Carlos Marcello set the plan in motion. He also ordered the hit on President John Kennedy and gathered shooters from several cities to plant themselves around Dallas in places like Fort Worth until the opportune time to set these men up in a plan for the final solution to the Bobby Kennedy's crime investigation problem of the mob. He allegedly also arranged foreign assassins to be brought in from the obscure island of Corsica, people who could not be traced, as part of the plot to get JFK.

The old man, Carlos, also put together a secret death squad to eliminate everyone who knew about the Hoffa and Kennedy hits. One by one, everyone who could be a threat or who had knowledge of the plots disappeared. There were rumors that some politicians and law enforcement at the highest levels were implicated, even the vice president, Lyndon Johnson.

Frank Costello
(Francesco Castiglia)

The New York mobs were the largest and most capable of carrying out the most difficult assignments, especially getting rid of high-profile politicians. They especially were concerned when certain politicians were using crime-busting headlines to enhance their careers. Bobby Kennedy's crusade against so-called organized crime was of grave concern not only to those mob organizations but many others who had associated with the organization both in business, unions, and the government itself. Indeed, old Joe Kennedy was known to have had a working relationship with these same organized crime families and their associates when making his fortune early on in life by partnering with the likes of Frank Costello, a key mob boss in the illicit liquor trade during Prohibition. This relationship with Costello, who headed the biggest of New York's five organized crime families, eventually lead old man Kennedy to connections with all the families.

Born Francesco Castiglia in Cababria, Italy, he immigrated to the United States in 1895. He became part of Charles "Lucky" Luciano's inner circle. When Prohibition was enacted, Costello was a major partner in the illicit business, and old Joe Kennedy was an associate. Costello went on to run the entire organization when Luciano was jailed then deported; Kennedy kept close ties to Costello and also many of his associates, who became part of his influence network.

During the Kefauver Crime Commission era, the mob was exposed, but it hardly touched day-to-day operations. But now the mob in New York City was already under some heat. The investigations spurred by Bobby Kennedy, after his brother won the presidency, with a little help from his father's mob friends, really created turmoil. The Gambini clan and the other leaders in New York were seething over the double-cross and laid blame on Bobby. The way they saw it, the old man, Joe Kennedy, with whom they had made deals during Prohibition in the whiskey business with Frank Costello, made this deal with their guys to elect his son, John, and then give the organization a pass. This was a United States president bought and paid for by the mob. They organized all over the country when Santo Grancanto of Chicago and his crew put the word out to all the major families in the country to pull out all the stops to get John Kennedy elected.

They didn't like Dick Nixon anyway. He was seen as a white bread and mayonnaise WASP who had an extreme dislike for all criminals. He had made his mark politically in California politics as an anticommunist crime buster. Kennedy was at least a Catholic, and his father had made many deals with Costello and some of the old New England and New York crowd, the Buffalinos in Boston, Costello and even Charley Luciana in New York, as well as Meyer Lansky from Brooklyn. He also had ties to and helped other associates in the Great Lakes and California. In the old days when the Parker family ran the Jeris Hair Tonic operation, Kennedy made connections with the New York guys to get them pure alcohol to make good whiskey from the Parkers, who had licenses for alcohol and supposedly used all that alcohol to make hair tonic. The gin it made might make your hair stand straight up but only if you gulped it down. Kennedy also was a known supplier in the Massachusetts cities during Prohibition. Indeed, he even started his operation selling booze to his fellow students at Harvard University.

Joe Kennedy was a known guy, if not completely trusted; so why not make a deal. At least they could be in play with someone that close to the next president.

The election results in West Virginia and key precincts in Illinois, near Chicago, and a few other key locations were bought and paid for by the mob guys. Richard Daley, mayor of Chicago, saw to it to hold his guys in line along with Santo's help. Old mob boss Jack Dragna's people in California brought in LA and so on around the country in key areas. Even the Hollywood crowd was led by the so-called chairman of the board, ole blue eyes himself, Frank Sinatra. Frank pushed hard for Jack Kennedy's election. After all, he was a drinking and carousing buddy. Now Frank and company, and the Rat Pack, could bring their shenanigans to the White House. Frank had set Senator Kennedy up with fun times in Vegas—booze and showgirls.

But now it was all over. Bobby turned out to be a snake. All the goodwill between old Joe and the guys he tapped to help the son was out the window. When the old man ended up with a stroke and basically confined to a wheelchair, the Boston connection completely died. Bobby went full steam ahead against all of his father's former connections. There was a rumor that the old man was behind it all anyway, trying to build a legacy for his sons by pumping up their images and distancing himself and his former mob ties by this antimob crusade. Who would consider that they, the royal Kennedys, had the mob buy the election if they were responsible for destroying the mob? A great strategy, but it was also very dangerous. They even disowned Sinatra and the Hollywood crowd that contributed to their reputations as well as time and a lot of money. Sinatra was seething as well. Didn't he even get actress Marilyn Monroe to meet and ultimately to go to bed with Jack? Even Bobby Kennedy had been fucking her as well. Rumor was that she was a danger to Bobby, so she had conveniently overdosed on pills and died almost on cue. Bobby, at the time, had her under twenty-four-hour surveillance, and he got the first call about her death.

Later it was verified he was one of the first to know of her death and sent someone to the scene.

Old Carlos Marcello and the leaders around the country were furious. How could they be had like this? They were all smart guys. How could old Joe have roped them in? They felt they had lost face, especially with the younger, eager guys in their organizations. They were supposed to be the leaders; now their leadership could be questioned. This whole thing was a problem, a big problem. It needed a solution, and they needed it now.

Nicky had another deal and needed Tony's help. "Nicky, can we be sure about the cigarette stamps?" asked Tony. "The feds have been all over us lately. Tony Scotti has been on the TV complaining about the feds' accusations against him. Our guys on the docks tell us they see these suits checking out all the big-money loads now and question all the guys. Even the shape-up guys need to have some pedigree before the crew bosses put them on because they're afraid they're plants. The federal government agents were looking for illegal traffic in unstamped cigarettes that avoided taxes," said Tony. Nicky was always looking for a money-making deal.

"Hey, Tony, don't worry. Pretty soon, things'll work out. Our guys won't let this go on forever. The stamp thing needs some time anyway. We got this restaurant supply deal for now, and maybe some cargo stuff from North River piers now and then, and there's always loads from the airport. We'll eat okay. Carlo has been communicating with some other guys too. He wanted me to ask you about arranging a trip for some guys from Italy on one of the freighters coming in. We need your connection to get six guys on a boat from Italy to the States without anybody the wiser. Can you do that?" Nicky asked.

"Sure, that's easy to arrange. We just put them on as crew till we get to port. When in port, we develop some mechanical problem that shuts down the generators and electrical so we got to get the crew off to stay at a land-based spot. When the boat is fixed, we substitute the six other guys to go back; they never check these guys out. We do it all the time. Where do you want these guys to land?" asked Tony. "Miami or New Orleans?"

"In fact, New Orleans is best," Nicky Dessio answered.

"I'll find out about what's around and see how to arrange it. We may need some serious money to buy a big load in Italy. Probably Naples is fastest to locate a freighter that we can get one of our connections to. I am still doing things with Onassis. We helped him with the unions here, so he always is willing to help us," said Tony.

"Okay, I'll tell Carlos to line up his guys in Naples, and you let me know what kind of time frame you can get for these guys to get to New Orleans. Call me when you know more. In the meantime, we'll get this other thing going. I'll see you at Frankie's on Friday night. They got a dinner for Monsignor O'Mara for some kind of fundraiser or something for kids. Ally and the congressman will be there too. Some of our other guys are coming. I told Johnnie the food better be good or we will throw it at him." Nicky laughed. So did Tony.

Tony made his phone calls. Since it was already Wednesday, he needed to make the arrangements by Friday. If he could do that, he knew Carlos would be impressed.

"Hey, big Nick, what are you doing?" Tony Delmonte yelled into the phone.

"Muzzi, what do you want? You got something good?" the guy at the other end answered. John McBratney grew up on the streets of Manhattan much like Tony, but his Irish Catholic family had a made enough to send John to New York University. He ended up in the shipping industry fresh out of college and worked his way up from a dispatch desk to vice president in charge of bookings for the Onassis Export Shipping Lines. He liked the street guys, especially party guys like Tony Delmonte who always had a big roll of dough. When John went out with Tony and his friends, he always had a ball. Then he worked some very lucrative deals together. John would alert Tony to certain shipments coming in on his line. Tony would get Tony Scotti, the boss of the longshoremen's union, to send a special crew to loot the cargo when it got unloaded so everybody got a cut.

Calling Tony by the nickname Muzzi, short for Mussolini, was John's way of teasing Tony in one way and showing him respect in another. John knew Tony was tough but a smart guy. He had done hundreds of deals, and Tony always came through, usually with a wad of cash, thousands at a clip.

"I need to know what we can do for accommodations if I need them for six guys in Naples who don't want a cruise ship crossing, if you know what I mean. They have to land in New Orleans, the sooner the better, and then six other guys will need to return. But I will arrange that. We can buy a load in Naples, anything to make a shipment—olive oil, Italian marble, whatever," Tony said.

"Muzzi, for you, anything. Give me a little time, and I'll get back to you. Does the departure time from New Orleans make any difference?" said John.

"Well, I thought the ship might develop a problem in the Port of New Orleans and have to stay over to repair a generator for a while, so our transfers would get lost in the city for a while. When the crew returns, who knows who? You know?" said Tony.

"I get it. That could cost a few bucks, you know," said John.

"Well, whatever few bucks it takes, just see what you can do as soon as you can," said Tony. "Hey, why don't you come over to Frankie's Chateau Rivera on Friday night? They have this dinner for Monsignor O'Mara. It's gonna be a good time. I'll meet you over there, okay?"

"Okay, Tone. I'll be there. See ya," said John.

By five o'clock on Friday evening, the parking lot at the Chateau had already filled up. Every valet guy was jumping, and the Lincolns and Caddies were lining up. Men in sharkskin suits with silk ties and black nosepicker dress shoes were streaming into the bar. By six o'clock, the bar was six deep.

"Hey, Tony," Nicky yelled as he was walking in. There were about seventy-five guys at the bar already, and the few couples who were just there for dinner were being hustled into a side dining room so they wouldn't interfere with the main group there for the monsignor's dinner.

The monsignor, resplendent in black and red robes, sat at the bar with a glass full of scotch in one hand and a Cuban cigar in the other, laughing with Frankie and Poppy "Cee." Tony said, "Nicky, I'm waiting for my friend McBratney. He called me about that travel thing and said he had it worked out and would tell me the details tonight. I'll get the lowdown and arrange it."

"Oh, great, Tone. Whatever you need on the dollar end is covered. Just let me know. Carl will be happy to hear that," Nicky said, and patted Tony on the back as he smiled from ear to ear. "Great, Tony, just great."

John McBratney walked into the bar. He already had a red face from sharing a liquid lunch with some of the shipping line executives at a downtown Manhattan waterhole.

"Muzzi!" he yelled across the bar room and walked over.

Tony turned around and grinned. "Hey, how you doing? Let's have a touch over here," he said to the bartender.

"Scotch rocks, JB, and what's yours, Tone?" said John.

"The same is fine," said Tony.

"I got your guys lined up, Naples on June 2 and into New Orleans about June 10 or 11. They will take two or three days to load at Naples, and they already had a big load booked. I also think June 10 or 11 could be delayed, as this rust bucket has had generator trouble already this week, if you get what I mean. The name of this ship is the *Athena*," said John.

"Hey, John, great. This is going to really help, and when it's done, I'll make sure you're happy," said Tony.

"Hey, John," said E, who came out from the men's room around the corner, "how you doing?" E smiled from ear to ear, his face was red as a beet, and his eyes were just slits. His hair was as disheveled as his suit and tie.

"Oh fine, Emiliano, just fine. You look well rested," said John as he burst out laughing. "What the hell are you on?"

E just grinned. Tony looked at him. "E is a substance garbage can. Booze and drugs of any kind, anything to get high. That's E."

E stayed mostly straight during most of the workday, but past five o'clock, he was beginning to fly. Tony looked at him, disgusted. "You're a fucking degenerate. Go clean yourself up or leave, you fucking punk." E sulked off to the men's room again. The reason he stayed straight during the day was to avoid being beaten by Tony.

The rest of the party filed in. Johnny "Cee" wouldn't stay long; he had his own restaurant to close. Paulie Castellucci came over from Brooklyn. He was, in fact, looking for a house in Staten Island. Charlie

Pizza owned a beer and liquor distribution company and race horses. The Denyen brothers were there. They owned a beer garden and restaurant and also ran a book. "Black Jack" John Murphy, the congressman who was under indictment, and his brother Frank, Borough President Al Maniscalci, the New York Assemblyman Louis Lascio, State Senator Joe Marchese, and several other politicians and local judges showed up as well. It was one big, happy family.

Tony was talking to McBratney when he noticed Gino Gambini walk in and go over to Nicky. "Cugino, how are you," said Gino to Nicky.

"Fine, Gino, thanks. And I'm very happy to see you. How's Pop doing?" asked Nick.

"You know, he has his good days and his bad ones. He has to watch his ticker all the time," Gino said as he tapped his chest. It was rumored that Carlos had a bad heart and was in and out of hospitals at least four or five times a year. However, having a medical history also could keep a guy from appearing in court on doctor's orders, so many of these guys had "heart conditions."

Anthony Delmonte

"Well, I think we have a problem solved. My friend Tony Delmonte has the transport problem arranged for the beginning of June. You have your Corsican friends get to Sardinia and get credentials with our guy there, and then we can get a fishing boat to take them to Naples. From there, it's easy—just sailors, Italian seamen on board. The boat is named the *Athena*. The captain and mate are already clued in through New York to take on more crew for a big load, and these guys know what to do. When they get to the States, our friend in New Orleans, Marcello, will take over. It's all arranged," Nicky said. Carlos Marcello worked close with Gene on a number of business deals, particularly in Brooklyn and Manhattan.

Tony sensed that something major was up for Gene to come in from Brooklyn but was astute enough not to inquire. The bartenders were spinning back and forth as fast as they could. This bar had the distinction of hosting the biggest drinkers on the island, and probably the most expensive.

Big Marcy Hegeman waltzed in. This big Dutchman, six feet six and over three hundred pounds, drank between one and two bottles of rum a day. "Tone!" he yelled and grabbed Tony Delsante in a half bear hug and headlock. He wore a $400 suit that looked like he slept in it. He had gravy stains on a $50 tie and spots all over his white-on-white broadcloth cotton shirt.

"Hey, Marcy, where have you been?" said Tony.

"Oh, I was in New York for a few days. I bought out a bakery on Forty-Sixth Street and had to pull out all the stuff to the warehouse. It took three days to complete the deal, and I had to stick around so the local neighbors didn't rob me blind. I already have orders in the islands for a lot of the stuff. Maybe when you go down again, we'll go together," said Marcel.

"Maybe. I think I have to go soon, so we'll talk. I have ship containers going down there. What do you need?" asked Tony.

"Oh, probably enough room for twenty big pieces—baker's ovens, dough mixers, big stuff," said Marcy.

Marcy had a hand in several different pies. He wholesaled wine, imported and exported, and he sold all kinds of commercial machinery. Usually his firm refurbished old stuff and sold it under his own manufacturing label for new in third world countries. He bought and sold anything—textiles, metals, food stuffs, even coffee beans.

For Tony, he was an unlimited source of information to sell off goods, straight stuff and swag.

"Marcy, I am going to be getting a lot of top-quality restaurant goods, number ten cans of tuna, bulk fresh-ground coffee in bags, stuff like that. Let me know if you have someone for that stuff. I can sell it all to one guy, but we can make some friends if we spread it around a little and if you got someone who'll buy other stuff as well. Okay?"

"Sure, that kind of stuff is easy to move. I'll call a few of the Greeks. They'll take it."

Marcy was drinking a triple shot of rum neat and was on his second one when he saw E standing next to the end of the bar. He eased over to him but not so that he faced him. E was talking to a young man to his left. Marcy backed up to E's leg and with a little force exploded some gas so that it resonated. Marcy roared, and the six or seven men around him moved away. "Jez," said E. "Marcy, you're unbelievable." Marcy continued to laugh. Tony and John saw the activity and began to laugh as well.

E was red faced to begin with but now got a bit upset since he saw that the others around him also noticed and were chuckling as well. He purposely tipped his glass and spilled some of his drink right on Marcy's pants, at zipper height. The others around saw that, and soon most of the place was roaring in laughter as Marcy, with his big mitts, was trying to brush the liquid off his pants at the zipper.

Then the jokes started. "Hey, Marcy, you shouldn't be playing with yourself at the bar," and, "Marcy, when you shake it too much, you're going to go blind." "Hey Marcy, try the toilet next time instead of the barstool when you gotta take a leak." Marcy took it all in stride and laughed. Then he turned again and backed up to E's lap, pinned him against the bar with his ass, and farted again, even louder than the first time. Barrrupp!

The entire place erupted in laughter, and even E, who was pissed off, had to laugh.

The bartenders and Tinker couldn't stand up straight. Even the monsignor joined in. "God bless you, Marcy, my boy. You sound the trumpet in fine style. Can you reach the high C?" The room cracked up again.

There was a young couple who had just walked in when the second blast occurred. The young man, obviously on a date, trying to impress the young lady with him by bringing her to the classy Riveria Chateau, looked at the red-faced girl whose eyes widened. She just smiled, and he put both his hands in the air. The girl, sensing the humor of the moment, began to join in the laughter as well.

There was a large banquet room with an entrance just off to the end of the bar. The dais was set with an array of flowers, candles, bottles of wine, cut-glass water pitchers, and twenty chairs. A banner with a gold embroidered cross hung behind the dais. The politicians and the monsignor took their places along with Nicky, Frankie, and a few of the judges. Nicky was the first to speak. In turn, several of the speakers spoke of the good works of the Children's Center headed by the monsignor and how many orphans and poor that were helped that year.

There were more than 150 people in the room. Now that they were all seated, eating, and drinking, he lowered the house light. Then over the PA system where soft music had been playing, suddenly the sound of march music came on a bit loud, and an announcement: "And now the Riviera Chateau, in honor of our esteemed guest, Monsignor O'Mara, proudly presents our main course."

With that, the waiters, all decked out in tuxedos with huge silver platters held high over their heads, paraded around the dining room. On the platters were perfected, browned, whole roasted suckling pigs lit with a dozen candles and festooned with ferns and ribbons. The pigs had an apple in the mouth, black bow ties around their necks, and pink bow ribbons on their tails.

The room erupted in applause and laughter.

The pigs were set in line, fifteen in all, before the dais, and the waiters began to carve them and serve each table.

By this time, between the whiskey and wine, no one was feeling any pain.

Marcy was sitting at Tony's table with Nicky, John, Gene, John McBratney, E, and a councilman, Ned Curran.

Marcy could still feel the dampness in his crotch where E had spilled his drink. He was close enough to the dais area to reach over to the platter nearest him and grab the nearest pig head. E was turned talking to New York City Councilman Ned Curran as Marcy slowly rose up and walked around to E's side of the table. With measurable force, he deposited the slimy roasted pig's head directly in E's lap, spattering his shirt, tie, suit, and face. E leaned back in shock, with his hands over his head.

The others at the table were momentarily startled. Then Marcy began to roar out loud, and he was joined by Tony, then the others. E could not decide if he should stand or stay seated. E looked down at the pig's head in his lap, then looked back up at Marcy, who by now was nearly doubled over in laughter, his big belly shaking. He took the pig's head in both hands and threw it at Marcy. Marcy had noticed that E was about to remove the pig's head from his lap, and he turned away. The pig head flew right past Marcy and landed on the monsignor's plate, splattering him with mashed potatoes and gravy and the vegetables on his plate.

The monsignor sat back in his chair, quite confused as to what had just happened but also befuddled due to having consumed nearly a half bottle of Johnnie Walker Scotch by himself already. When he realized what happened, his face went blank. The room quieted, except for Marcy and Tony, who were still roaring. The monsignor slowly made the sign of the cross. E was rigid. He was trying to focus on the priest. He surely had too much whiskey but also had filled his nose twice during the evening as well during his trips to the bathroom.

Slowly the priest finished his hand gesture and seemed to be resting his hands on the table, but with one swift movement, he grabbed the pig's head off his plate and in an underhanded toss, threw it right at E's face some ten feet away. E seemed to be watching this action in slow motion. Suddenly he realized the pig's head was coming straight at him. He was pinned between his chair and the table, and though he tried at the last second to move out of the way, he was struck full-face, nose to nose, by the pig.

Well, that started an uproar of laughter. Suddenly, another pig's head flew across the room. Within three minutes, each pig head had begun making the rounds, tossed from table to table. The scene was completely surreal.

The elite and powerful, all dressed in their tailored suits, tossing pig heads. The owner, Frankie, started to yell to stop. The carpet and the walls of the fine Chateau were being splattered with the pigs' juices. The scene was accompanied by laughter, yelling, and screaming as guests from the three other dining rooms peered in out of curiosity; they too were welcomed by a toss of a pig's head.

"E, you see what you started," yelled Tony. That just started Marcy roaring again, and everyone at the table again joined in.

Later, that event would be remembered as the Flying Swine Night.

Frankie never got over the mess these so-called elites made of his dining room. It cost him thousands to have the carpets and draperies cleaned. Every upholstered chair needed to be shampooed and cleaned. He fumed at the mention of Swine Night. He even banned Marcy, E, and even Tony for weeks. Even the cleanup expense was no major amount compared to the money Tony's crew spent there. Years later, the place would be completely destroyed in a suspicious fire. It was rumored that Frankie's wife, who helped in the office, had forgotten to pay the fire insurance, and they lost everything.

CHAPTER 62

TONY SCOTTI HAD a real problem facing him with the advent of Sea-Land Container Company finally making the deal with several major local pier facilities. The city of New York had the control to bring the new era of a containerized cargo system into New York ports. The impact on union labor would be immense.

George's restaurant was bustling at noon as Scotti walked in and walked back to Anthony's table. "Hey, how are ya?" asked Tony. Three men were with Anthony, including the chief manager of American Export Isbransten Shipping Line.

"Hey, Tony," said George McNell. Anthony put his hand out, and Tony shook it.

"Anthony, I need a drink. Johnnie Walker Black, rocks. Lot of pressure." The other two men, E and Junior, were given instructions and left on their mission.

George said, "What's up, Tony? You look like shit."

"Well, you'll probably hear it on the late news tonight. Hoffa's gone missing. You know we all thought after JFK got hit, then his brother got it, life would slow down some and things were going to be a little normal. This Sea-Land deal has to kill us, not to mention the new Port Newark and Port Socony dock operations in Jersey. Sam the Plumber over there said he feels heat all over the place there with the construction unions, and he has felt heat from the unions, both in construction and longshoreman as well. Now with Hoffa gone, that's going to raise a lot of questions. It seems like a lot of this is unraveling. I'd give my right arm to have one-tenth of my uncle Albert's power or my uncle Tony's respect on the docks."

Tough Tony Anastasia was a legend on the docks of New York's waterfront. Big men would shake in fear when he walked on the pier. His reputation was well earned. "I'm hearin' that Hoffa was grabbed to keep his mouth shut because of the money connections in Vegas with the Union trust funds and pension funds. Then I heard he had inside knowledge of the Kennedy hit too. Of course, the New York families all did things with Jimmy and the union. Anyway, if you ask me, he's pushing up daisies. I think he's long gone. We made him and unmade him."

Anthony Delmont had already heard the story. In fact, there was a rumor that some guy looking a lot like Hoffa was put in a derelict Lincoln, and it went through one of Nicky D's car crushers. Someone put four bullets in the back of his head after a drive to a supposed meeting. Jimmy went to meet some of Sam DeCavalcanti's guys from the waterfront at a diner near Chicago. It was arranged that his driver and the guys he met ended his life, then shipped him in the back of that same car cross country to Staten Island. The AFL-CIO was in turmoil, trying to figure out what to do next. Who would run the show? Many did not like Mr. Fitzsimmons, the elected VP, so most locals were just trying to mark time until things got sorted out. Hoffa's disappearance made Fitzsimmons a suspect as well as the mob.

"Tony, what is the next step if Hoffa is gone?" his men were asking.

"We've got to move on. Likely we may never learn about just what happened to the guy. Life goes on," said Anthony, not revealing that the information he already had was just reaffirmed. Hoffa was a risk; he just knew too much about too many people. Brooklyn's reputation as a tough town never wavered. Regardless of where it was, who it was, or what it was in this place, it was never easy. The Brooklyn Dodgers continually fought their way into baseball's upper echelon. Ebbitt's Field looked more like a penitentiary than a ballpark. Was it little wonder then that guys like Joey Gallo, Carlo Gambini, Big Paulie Castellucci, even the Anastasias and Capones had roots there? Joe Bonanni and his relationship through his son's marriage to a Profaci girl intermingled old-time mob family. Brooklyn was like no other place. It was indeed an anomaly. At once a rancid, poverty-ridden ghetto of blacks, Jews, and foreigners and yet a bucolic strip of neighborhood after neighborhood with tomato and zucchini gardens, huge oak and locust trees, ball fields and country-like dirt paths leading through expansive backyards. In some neighborhoods, it resembled some middle-class Midwestern town. Then there was Coney Island and a series of beaches that teemed with visitors in the summer and were nearly totally isolated in the winter, a true seasonal resort. Even the Jews fought each other there. The Hasidim had their two factions constantly arguing over who was more of a heretic and blasphemer while accepting the gentiles' degraded existence, and indeed they were not only tolerant but curious about "the others." The Sixty-Ninth Street ferry to Staten Island, the Brooklyn Battery Tunnel, the BQE (Brooklyn Queens Expressway), the Brooklyn Bridge, the Red Hook Section, the Atlantic Avenue Piers and Brooklyn Waterfront, Downtown Court Street, Crown Heights, Bay Ridge, Canarsie, Brighton Beach, each place offered its own version of typical Brooklyn. Also, Fort Greene and the Fort Greene Market was its own business neighborhood.

"Hey, is Paulie in?" yelled Junior.

"Yeah, he's in the cooler with someone. He'll be right out," said some young heavyset guy standing by the office door at the top of the steps. Junior took out a pack of Chesterfields and sat on the running board of the big Ford refrigerated box truck. He puffed away as he looked up and down the street. There were four or five other meat wholesalers on the block. Paulie specialized in chickens and other poultry and veal. Junior waited patiently.

"Hey, Paulie, how are you? Anthony sent me over to pick up some stuff," Junior said after Big Paul Castellucci had said his goodbye to a short, thin older man who got in a black Buick parked next to his truck.

"Junior, I'll have somebody take care of you in a minute," said Paul.

Junior walked up really close and said, "Anthony said to tell you that his deal in St. Lucia is going good, and he'll be shipping out a lot of chicken parts soon. He met your friends in Antigua, and they are setting him up with the hotels and casino there. The guy from Jersey says hello."

"Good. Tell Anthony I'll see him in a few days."

Junior waited, and another older fellow came out dressed in the same butcher's white, long coat. "Hey, June, open up, and we'll load you." Soon, wheeled dollies with thin wood crates held together by wire were rolling onto the loading platform and into the truck. Case after case of iced chickens were stacked in. Then came four quarters of veal and pairs of legs of veal wrapped in white cotton stockinette over paper.

Junior was given a bill and wrote out the check he had in his pocket. He drove back to the Sixty-Ninth Street ferry terminal. The new bridge from Brooklyn to Staten Island would be done soon, but until then, the ferry system was still the shortest way to Staten Island from the city, either Brooklyn or Manhattan. Junior pulled the big truck off the ferry and headed south. When he got to the turn into the street leading up to the warehouse, he saw a commotion. Cop cars with their lights blinking, black, unmarked cars pulled across the roadway to block traffic, and uniform cops and other guys dressed in suits were all over the street. He backed the truck up, drove off down the road, and pulled into the parking lot next to the Stapleton Chop House Restaurant. He got out and walked into the bar and started for the phone booth at the back.

"Junior," someone called from the back end of the bar. "Come 'ere." The fellow was a short, stocky guy in his sixties with thick shocks of white hair. "Junior, they got trouble. My guys saw the feds over there. They're opening up everything. One of my guys was walking up from the piers, down the street, and saw them pull up with their guns drawn. He came to tell me. I figured somebody would show up here. I guess the liquor shipment a few days ago caught their interest. We must have had them watching the unloading. You better take off." The little fireplug of a man with the bulldog face was Alex Briggani, Uncle to the Ds (Dessios).

"Yeah, I got a load of iced-up chickens and veal on the truck. I got to drive it somewhere," said Junior. "Maybe I'll go see Capelli or his father. They got big cooler space. I'll tell them what happened. Better yet, I can go see the Demyan boys. They have plenty of cooler space. They'll help. It's closer than the Tavern." The Hofbrau was not far, just a couple of miles. Tavern on the Green was across town. Junior left.

"Look, it was just a big mistake. When the pallets came off the ship, there were cases of canned tomato and olive oil. We were supposed to get that stuff. The guy driving the hi-lo went to the wrong stack of pallets—that's all. He loaded the wine and liquor in, then the other guy loaded in the tomatoes. We didn't even know that stuff was in the trailers," said E to the two suits who just nodded and half-smiled in total disbelief of the story.

"Yeah, and I guess the paperwork just blew away, and the canary won't sing," said the FBI guy. Anthony just sat there and said nothing. "We want to know who arranged the deal. We want the guy on the pier and in the union. You help us, and we'll help you. We want to know who else is involved, your Gambini buddies. We watched your plant for months. We have a who's who of wiseguys connected to this place. You are all going to take a big fall if you're stupid," said the agent.

"Look, we're in business. Lots of people come here to buy stuff, ship stores, meat, fish, salvage, whatever. We don't ask who they are or what they do. It's cash and carry. We didn't know no Gambarini or Garbini guys, whatever name you said; we just run a business here," said E.

Agent Gilroy's face got a bit red anytime he got a little annoyed. "You guys are really dumb; the meat wagon is on its way. You could cooperate and make it easier on yourself," he said.

Finally, Anthony turned to the agent. "We really don't have anything to say to help you, Agent. Why don't you cool your heels?"

Moments later, a tall, large man walked in. He had on a dark suit, red tie, and big diamond pinky ring. He held a black briefcase. "I'm Gene Feranti, legal counsel to these men. Do you have a search warrant?" said Feranti in a brisk voice.

Gilroy pulled papers from his chest pocket and waved them. "Your clients were given a copy. I'm now arresting them based on our inspection of the contents of the trucks outside there," said the agent.

Ferranti whispered in Anthony's ear and then said, "Fine, let's go then. I'll have these men released in less than twenty minutes."

Another agent walked in and nodded to Gilroy. "Okay, boys, let's go," he said. With that, he snapped handcuffs on the two men and led them outside. An old truck with a metal box with screening and bars on the windows pulled alongside the loading dock steps. Two men in a small van ran over. One with a large camera started snapping pictures, while the other man started asking questions. "Fucking reporters. Who tipped them off?" said E, knowing full well it was the feds. Anthony put his hands in front of his face as best he could with the manacles twisting into his wrists.

Feranti bumped into the camera man purposely, nearly knocking him off his feet, and his camera fell to the ground. "Get out of the fucking way," he hissed. The doors to the rear of the paddy wagon closed, and they drove off. Anthony watched as the reporter picked up the pieces of his camera.

They were booked in downtown Manhattan, and Feranti had them out of jail after arranging a quick hearing before the federal judge later that day. It was exactly twenty minutes when a bail bondsman, Art Fletcher, was present. Bail was set at $100,000 for Anthony and $50,000 for E. The judge originally asked several questions of the federal prosecutor for the FBI. They had asked for $500,000 and $100,000 respectively; Ferranti argued that the charges were merely suspicion of receipt of stolen goods since no connection had been made between the two men and the actual theft. The FBI had been looking for the stevedore's gang boss, Tommy Rosa. They had evidence that he had met on the pier with three of the tractor trailer drivers who drove the swag load from the pier to the warehouse. They had waited to see if more stuff was going to be taken that morning or if anyone would show up at the warehouse since both places were under heavy surveillance. They missed Rosa, who apparently walked from one end of the docks to the other before being driven away unseen. They also missed the truck drivers who got lost in the afternoon crowd when they broke for lunch on the piers. The next morning, photos hit the front page of the *Staten Island Advance*. Two of the city papers carried the story but only a small clip, just a few sentences, in the middle of the paper. However, they all carried their names.

"Shit. That fucking *Advance*. The feds are up someone's ass there. They blast bullshit all over the front page," said Junior as he sat the next morning in the office with Anthony and E.

"They had been arrested for bookmaking. They keep putting out stories like the stolen golf balls and Nicky's dealing with that. Somebody has to do something about those clowns," said E.

Anthony said nothing for a while. "Listen," he finally said, "this thing is a problem in a lot of ways." The New York City Police Department had long kept records of the various factions in each of the known organized crime families. There were at least three separate divisions tracking the movement of the mob, but it was very complicated. The interaction of business and political figures, judicial power, union influence, various fraternal and religious groups, and charitable organizations created an entwined web of interaction between these various group subcultures.

While the federal law enforcement had known of some similar interactions, the city of New York, in particular, and (to a lesser degree) other major metropolitan areas were definitely influenced by the ebb and flow of the subtle pressure exerted but distantly connected as well as closely connected power brokers. The wild card in this order of disorder was public opinion and the media treatment.

At once, the young Turk, Joey Gallo, became a Broadway favorite (if not a Hollywood character), a celebrity who flaunted his lifestyle and his nefarious reputation. The media interest spurred public interest. However, such exposure and even some positive press embarrassed the local law enforcement who had been so lax in putting pressure on anyone who chose celebrity over cautious anonymity. Even J. Edgar Hoover directed his agency in a varying degree of intensity when it came to the captains of big business, political power, and their connections to the mob. He had his private communications system with mob leaders when he needed to do so.

It was speculated by several factions, including those political and those who controlled major business interests, that Hoover's concepts were complex, but there was a pattern. It was thought J. Edgar recognized that a certain order had emerged in organized crime, and the interconnection with other segments of the society were intricately affected by this order and likewise had influence on the activities of these crime bosses. The belief was that there would be disorder due to multiple crime factions who were autonomous. It would simply attract more people to criminal careers if there was no control by some organized, strong groups. Some believed that J. Edgar was an intermittent contact with all these factions in some fashion, sometimes directly and sometimes through the least expected surrogates. In general, the FBI theory was that if the organized and known mob structure was attacked, others would replace these individuals, who would then be known and untraceable. Further, and as much a concern, eliminating the Italian mob might create a vacuum surely to be filled by some other worse criminal elements or more vicious foreign gangs. The Italian or European mob had a certain measure of perverse morality. Most of these men at least grew up with some knowledge of a Christian ethic. They had a deeply rooted tradition of family. The perversion of incorporating a family concern within a Romanesque hierarchy of levels of authority and combing a military-like pecking order with rules of personal, sexual, religious, and ethical conduct earned a certain respect from some law enforcement. The families were somewhat predictable in their operations and attitudes. In earlier days, certain taboos, such as dealing in the use of drugs by any member by his family or his associates, were absolute. The trading in various illegal activities was a day-to-day concern. These men took their positions of control, at all levels, very seriously. If someone stepped out of line on any major rule, they were dealt with harshly, sometimes more as an example to others than for the offense. It was thought that Hoover would rather have an orderly hierarchy conduct these illicit activities than a mishmash of rogue interests creating havoc in society. The concerns about the old street gangs that emerged at the turn of the century in places like New York City's Five Points—emerging uncontrolled in every US city, much like in many cities and countries in the world where there was a chaotic, nonstructured order to criminal elements—may have been justifiable.

When an individual brought the spotlight on any part of this underworld, it was a huge problem. History, as it is said, repeats itself.

The Gallo boys, Joey in particular, grew up in the cauldron of the mob, Brooklyn. All things seem more extreme in that part of the city, and the effect on the personalities of its inhabitants seem even more eccentric.

The old Profaci family members were first-generation Italians transplanted to Brooklyn; so were their mentors, the leading New York family, the Bonannis. The Gallos emerged as boyhood toughs to a small neighborhood gang that eventually recognized that they needed to associate with the known order in their community. The neighborhood kids learned early in the streets that there was a structure and order to each illegal activity, a boundary with rules.

The problem with Joey Gallo was that in order to rise up, he had to distinguish himself and be recognized. His ego demanded it, and the influence in his neighborhood helped create the persona as a tough guy. Surely being the most dangerous was high on the list; being tough, if not the toughest, too was important. Being accepted as a local product had its advantages. Even if your family was not considered local, one could reach that criteria in a number of ways. Being streetwise might not mean you were PhD material but that you knew the neighborhood, the people, the ruled order, the big shots, and you fit in with all that. Being intelligent was an extra, A plus. But being wise to the street helped you survive.

The younger guys had to dress sharply. The older men, particularly those of the position, dressed appropriately—translated guinea-chic. This could mean a hundred-dollar Italian knit shirt and pleated, pegged pants for a young guy with either flapjacks black leather shoes or nosepickers highly polished, sharply pointed, Italian leather laced shoes.

Evening, especially Friday night and Saturday night, meant dressing to the teeth. A typical uniform of the night was a black mohair suit, white-on-white shirt, and silk tie. Those who had little money still were not excused from the dress code if they expected to mingle with those at the clubs in the nightlife districts of Brooklyn or the upper crust in Manhattan or Long Island.

One could find two or three major clubs in Bay Ridge or around Red Hook or Atlantic Avenue in Brooklyn areas that had a notable, if not noted, band. Joey D at the Peppermint Lounge in Manhattan, Chubby Checker at the late-night clubs in Brooklyn, and the older crowd at the San Sou See in Long Island, or the Copacabana in Manhattan. The Copa featured every big star from the well-known icons like Frank Sinatra and Dean Martin to the new young Turks like Bobby Darin and Bobby Rydell, all of whom had been products of their Italian heritage.

Joey Heatherton, a hot, lively young singer who was a new sex symbol, whose dad, Ray, was TV's Merry Mailman, might be sitting at the bar there in Long Island along with singer Lou Monte doing his humorous Italian songs. Perhaps a local like Frankie Roma or Connie Francis was headlining as well.

Joey Gallo wanted to be a guy who was first and foremost recognized and totally respected and feared. Joey was the older; Larry and Albert the younger. His cousin, Joey G (Joseph S. Gallo), was a short, slightly built, wiry, and athletic guy. The lack of height and bulk was offset by the sense of pressure. He was quick witted and threw money around, not big dollars but enough to appear like there was more where that came from. However, while Joey Gallo had an obsessive nature, Joey S. had a certain reserve and maturity; he was even classy. When the news stories broke about Joey Gallo having a pet lion in his basement, ostensibly to deal with deadbeat debtors, he not only bragged about how ferocious this creature was, but he put it on a chain leash and paraded down President Street, his home turf, with the beast in tow.

Benjamin "Bugsy" Siegel

He was rumored to have people witness a terrifying vignette. He would get a big chunk of bloody meat and open the door to the basement. He would wave the meat and call down to the animal he did not feed regularly. The lion would smell the meat and shake the house with his roar. Then Joey would walk down a few steps, far enough to throw his pet the meat. The sound of the roaring was frightful enough, but the sound of the lion devouring huge chunk of meat was enough to make any would-be deadbeat pledge payment immediately.

The newspapers had a field day. The city haute couture loved it. Joey boasted that he bedded Broadway and Hollywood babes, some just as a ticket to see his pet. Even some of the lower-end political types and Brooklyn mob types were impressed by this guy. He was sort of a reincarnation of the legendary Bugsy Siegel who charmed Hollywood and the media. Ben Siegel built the first mega casino in Las Vegas, the Flamingo. But it ended up costing him his life when he was accused of squandering the mob's money that financed the Flamingo.

However, the upper-level mob guys had a different opinion of Joey. They thought he was nuts. He hung around with his Italian crew but also accepted blacks and others as business associates, some even on the same level as his own men. He gave interviews at parties to the local New York newspaper columnists and rubbed elbows with movie people who were constantly seeking publicity photographs. The police were alerted to his antics, particularly loan-sharking, hijacking, fencing, and, when necessary, murder.

Brooklyn had its fill of wiseguys. Carmine Persico and his brother Allie Boy were midlevel mob newbies. Joseph Columbo had taken over the old Profaci gang and, in alliance with the others, carved out a new family for himself with the help of an aging and dying Vito Genovese.

The mantle of leader, bosses of bosses, had long ago fallen to Carlo Gambini. Carlo was a private and quiet man. He shunned the spotlight and admonished those who did not. When Joe Columbo went national with his Italian American League group and started antagonizing the FBI's suggestion that there was a Cosa Nostra, the heat intensified. He defied the FBI in the media, claiming Italians were being persecuted just as the African Americans and others by the FBI and the government.

The New York City Police could at most times be predictable and somewhat reserved in their intensity in enforcement against the mob.

The apparent ongoing truce between the mob and the FBI was jeopardized by guys like Gallo and Columbo. Having public rallies and having newspapers and the media splashing mob guy stories all over the national scene was not good for business. Suddenly, federal agents were all over New York, then Boston and even Philadelphia and New Jersey, cramping business operations.

Cousin Joey S sat at the bar at Milton's, down at the Great Kills waterfront and beach. He was nattily dressed in a medium-gray Italian silk suit with a gray knit Italian shirt, sipping the expensive, aged Johnnie Walker Swing scotch. It was late for that crowd for food, but the bar was filling up. A small, thin fellow came in the porthole door. He looked the room over and then spotted Joey S at the front end of the bar. Joey S's main source of income was bookmaking. He had a slow and easy way about him and was likened to Richard Widmark, Kirk Douglas, and Frank Gorshin all rolled into one.

The thin fellow with receding black hair walked directly over to Joey S. "Hey, Joey. I'm Carmine Frantanno. I'm a friend of Johnnie D from New Dorp Beach. My cousin just called me when I was on my way to Shoals Bar. He said Joey Gallo was shot dead in Little Italy an hour ago outside of Umberto's Clam House. The cops are all over it. I thought you needed to know. Johnnie said you hang out here and sent me to tell you."

Joey S shook his head. He seemed to be expecting the news. The word on the street was they identified the black guy who shot Joe Columbo; he knew his cousin Joe was implicated. It was known that Crazy Joe, as he was dubbed by the New York daily newspaper, associated with the blacks and did business with them utilizing black enforcers. What was not known was that Joe Columbo's high profile caused the old guy, Carlo Gambino, to react. Having a guy like Gallo, an eccentric who could not be trusted, could easily be explained away as the ambition of an unstable character. Convincing the Persicos that Joey had to go would be easy enough if they were offered his territory. The Persicos were, at least, a bit more. If need be, they would not be missed in the mob hierarchy if the old man decided they were a liability as well. It also helped that they were fearless. They had no hesitation, even if it meant having to defend themselves if any of the

Gallos' crew sought revenge. Fact was the few inner core left in the Gallo crew were neither in a position, members-wise, nor had such a death-wish loyalty to Crazy Joe that they would risk their lives for revenge or vendetta.

"Crazy Joe had it coming is what's being said, for what he did to Columbo," Carmine whispered to Joey S. Joey S did not respond. He knew that his cousin had been far too visible for far too long. He even had tried, at the suggestion of several of his guys, to calm Crazy Joe's flamboyant public display—to no avail. Then when Columbo was shot, Crazy Joe strutted around town, daring a reprisal.

Joey S whispered back, "Carmine, tell them I know why, and I understand the problem that was created. My boys are sorry for Joey, but these things happen. He just got way too far out there. Thanks for coming by." Carmine nodded, stood up, and walked out. He could get word back now through the Staten Island faction of the Gallos that there would be no trouble, no reprisals.

Joe Columbo took a bullet to the head at the Columbus Day rally, organized by the Italian American Unity League. He remained in a vegetative state until he passed several years later. His sons, Anthony and Joseph Jr., were made to realize that those in control would not and could not tolerate a public display by anyone in the life. The mob bosses would not have the organized order embarrass law enforcement so that it demanded that the boys straighten out this brazen, irritating loudmouth. Thus, he was silenced, and the clever fox, Carlo the Boss, got rid of two headaches at once. In fact, the boys were fearful that someone might come after them, thinking they would seek revenge and also step into their father's shoes. Instead, they pulled up stakes from Brooklyn and moved to Upstate New York outside of Newburgh and left the Columbo family management.

The Columbos and Gallos faded away, and their importance in the wider pecking order eventually faded as well. Some of their associates defected to other families, and remnants of their organizations all but disappeared. However, history of the mob shows that they sought to promote themselves to the leadership. Carlo understood that any sight that an individual had, had to be dealt with swiftly and permanently. When a message is sent to change your ways, and it goes unheeded, the consequence is laid at the feet of the offender. Those who show weaknesses in any way when they are in a position of leadership are vulnerable to being deposed. Carlo was too perceptive and experienced to allow these unruly upstarts to upset the order of things. He also felt the heat of law enforcement when the Columbos and Gallos went public. The old man kept a tight rein on all his people, and when a statement was necessary to be made when someone did not toe the line, he acted with emphasis. Hence the end of the Italian American Unity One and the Columbos and the public antics of Crazy Joe.

When the old man got ill, he and those around him withdrew, but his shadow was cast across the city and beyond. The mistake Carlo made was, in his last days, considering the mob as more a corporate operation than a criminal organization. The need for ruthless and vigilant leadership was paramount to holding the order together. He put his brother-in-law in the line to succession because he was a relative, the husband of his sister, and a respected organizer. But Big Paulie Castelluci lacked the visceral timbre to command respect and fear at the same time. Being an earner always was held in high regard, but leadership absolutely demanded the main ingredients, raw power and fear.

Thus, it allowed another boisterous, publicity-seeking, ruthless character to emerge. The antics of Joe Gallo and Joe Columbo did not rise to the savage progression of the Gotti crew. John Gotti essentially murdered his way to prominence in the order of things, and Paulie Castellucci was either too preoccupied or too weak to do what surely his predecessor would have done—dealt with in the same manner as the Gallo and Columbo problem, elimination. Gotti's very public behavior and ruthlessness might have had the reverse effect on Castellucci. Paul chose not to deal with it, and that attitude led, eventually, to elimination not of the upstart but instead the weak sister. No one could ever think about taking on Carlo. The fear of retribution was just too big a risk. But as Big Paul withdrew during his legal and personal problems, and having lost the one man who could hold this thing together, Neal Della Croce, he squandered his preeminence.

Aniello Neal Della Croce was the senior statesman of the mob, a structured guy who was perceived to be tough and smart and, in fact, the natural choice to succeed the old man, Carlo. John Gotti, a Della Croce protégé, resented that Neal was passed over.

True to the code, however, Neal did not create too many waves when he was passed over. Instead, he pledged loyalty, and when critical issues ended up before him, he responded. No one guessed Neal would die in bed of cancer. His death was the signal for the resurgence of dissatisfaction with Big Paulie by Gotti. He wasn't leading; it was said he was just sucking up money, money that did no one else any good. Paulie, however, had made a close association with Roy DeMeo. Roy was known to be a ruthless murderer. His reputation for brutality struck fear by the mere mention of his name. DeMeo operated out of a club in Brooklyn, the Gemini Lounge. Roy and his crew not only murdered their victims but cut up the bodies and disposed of them so that no evidence was ever found. Indeed, Roy and his crew became infamous for performing the Gemini treatment. They would lure their victim into the apartment just behind the club. There they would shoot the victim, drain the blood from the body in a bathtub, dismember it, and place pieces in plastic bags that ended up scattered in dumpsters around the city. Eventually, however, Roy's expanding interests fueled by the money he got from murder for hire came to the attention of law enforcement. He ran an auto-theft ring that involved millions of dollars. He was dealing drugs and loan sharking. Eventually, Castellucci learned that the feds were on Roy's trail and were about to indict him. Fearing he would turn on him, Paulie ordered Roy's execution. Since Roy was Paulie's main hit man and others knew it, Paulie was feared. Once Roy was gone, John Gotti was emboldened and felt he could take Paulie out without retribution. When he made the move, it was shocking, but the manner, the public execution, the newspaper spreads and the venue, the streets of Manhattan, impressed his friends and foes alike. It reinforced his ruthless image. However, this kind of public letting of blood was acceptable in an earlier era. It was no longer tolerable to anyone, not the hierarchy of law enforcement or the business-minded mob guys. It was *too* public, *too* press worthy, and eventually the publicity without stealth and shadows spelled the end or the power of the organized crime empire, which reigned for nearly a century.

Big Paulie and his enforcer, Tommy Bottelli, were gunned down on a Manhattan street outside of Sparks Steakhouse. This Wild West style murder was meant as a message to the rest of the New York Mafia chiefs that Gotti was taking over. The answers to who, what, when, and where may have presented even more questions than it answered, but it was clear who was the new boss almost immediately. Thus were the people and the times that the Delmontes were part of, even if not as notable as the front-page news reported of the others. Perhaps they chose the lesser roles, which warranted less scrutiny. The high-profile pecking order brought high-profile reactions. The fact was these men learned these ways as kids.

CHAPTER 63

ANTHONY "DELMONT" DELMONTE was the undisputed leader of the younger kids. He was stronger, faster, and more aggressive than all the others and clever to boot. Once he convinced his cousin Tutti to steal his father's car keys while they were at a family barbeque in the park. Tutti got the keys. Anthony propped himself up in the seat and started the car. Tutti was shocked but said nothing as it lurched forward and down the dirt road. He drove for over a half hour, then went back to the party. No one else saw this except three other cousins who caught a glimpse of him on the way back.

From that day forward, Anthony was seen as someone to respect. And so it happened at another family event, this time a wedding. "Look, Tutti. There's the door to the downstairs, probably the kitchen. Let's go," said Anthony. Tutti and the others hesitated but soon followed. There on the counter were huge trays of Italian pastries, cream puffs, cannoli, pane di grano, sfogiadella, and more. Anthony grabbed one and stuffed it in his mouth. Soon all the others were gorging themselves. Anthony took three cream puffs filled with yellow cream and went behind a refrigerator. He pitched it directly at Tutti's head, and it spattered across his face. Everyone laughed. Tutti grabbed a cannoli and fired back, hitting the refrigerator and spattering two of his cousins. Then they all grabbed pastries, and the fight was on. Within a few minutes, entire serving trays were emptied in what was to be known from then on in the family as the Battle of the Cannolis. Anthony heard voices, and everyone froze. Quietly, they all exited as the chefs and waiters came down the front stairs.

Little was said to the bride's father, except that there was an accident in the kitchen. Somehow no one ever knew the extent of the accident. The chef had an additional stock of pastries for another event and separated half of them and brought them to the party. The kids, however, did not get away unscathed. The bride's mother was asked to tell her husband he was needed in the kitchen for a moment. He was directed downstairs to the scene of the crime. He figured out where all the boys from both families had disappeared to when no one saw them. Each parent eventually was tipped off to the event, and each kid who participated in the battle was eventually punished. None, however, regretted the day, and Anthony, the ringleader, would remain the chief.

Anthony enjoyed the opportunity to meet with the relatives and friends at the engagement party. He sat with Big Tony Delmonte for most of the time. Over the last few years, the older Delmonte had suffered from deteriorating health from diabetes, stomach ulcers, and then a stroke. The stroke impaired his speech and his mental capacity as well. As his ability to operate the business functions diminished, Anthony took over. He moved some of the more urgent operations over to his own company. He set up an automatic cash transfer fund that paid all of the old man's expenses and provided his caretaker, an old friend, Joe Marto, with cash whenever he asked for it.

The old man eventually even stopped inquiring about the operation of the business. He also felt comfortable that Anthony was there, took charge, and was very capable. Anthony scaled down operations and, in time, sold off the meat and food product division as well as the real estate but took back a mortgage with a hefty interest rate. He also remained as the insurance agent. He installed a young nephew, Danny, who had become a CPA, as chief financial officer of his company and accountant for the old man's former company as part of the sale deal, though he had firsthand knowledge of all the business finances. He also found a pair of brothers in Brooklyn, old family friends, to take over the meat business.

The Terrace was an expansive supper club and had been retrofitted with expensive touches. A granite-topped bar, deep-cushion rugs, expensive upholstered chairs, etched-glass mirrors with elaborate figures of seminude women and vineyards made the place a very attractive location.

"Mr. D, how are you?" the man behind the bar greeted Anthony as he walked in.

"I'm good, Tommy, very good," said Anthony.

He sat at the bar, and Tommy, without asking, poured Johnny Walker Black into a rocks glass over ice, rimmed the glass with lemon rind, and added just a slight splash of imported sparkling water. He put it in front of Anthony. "Thanks, Tom," he said. "Louie here?"

"He's in the office doing some paperwork. He'll be right out—unless you want me to buzz him?"

"No, thanks. I'll talk to him later," Anthony said.

Five young men walked in and came over to Anthony. "Mr. Delmont, thanks for inviting us." Three of them were the Scalisce brothers, Dominick, Vito, and Michael, and the other two were John Botti and Frank Sinesgali, relatives of the Scalisces. Soon several others came, the Merendino boys, the Marinos, and the Cellas. Others included members of the families of Castelli, and the Caterini, who were related to the Delmontes, Russo, Castelluci, Abarno, Albano, Palamara, Arcari, Delassandro, Fusco, Biondi, Arini, Vazzana, and Visconi. The men represented several different business backgrounds and were really the heirs of the next generation of leaders in the area's business community. Many were either related or were from the same paese and had old family friendships.

There were large round tables set with opulent tablecloths. Each one had a bucket of ice and a few large bottles of sparkling water. There were also two bottles of wine, one red and one white, and several stem glasses.

Victor made his rounds of the room and got all the business cards from each one of the over thirty-five men there.

"It is really a great evening to see all of you gathered here with me tonight. We are here to celebrate our guest of honor, Victor," said Anthony. All applauded, and a few hoots could be heard. "Now anyone who has a Victor story is welcome to come to this microphone and share it with all to us."

Jimmy Albano stood up. He took the microphone from Anthony said, "I'm Jim Albano, and I grew up living next door to Vic. He I had a great time, Vic getting in trouble, me getting blamed."

The group laughed, and then he continued. "Vic decided he wanted to skip school, steal some wine from his uncle's wine cellar, and he and our little gang, all thirteen years old, would have a wine party. We snuck into the wine cellar through a trapdoor window and found a small keg. This little barrel already had a spigot socked in, so we filled the two-gallon jug we had and took off for the woods. Once there, we passed out paper cups, and Vic filled them to the top. We began drinking when I noticed an extremely sour and harsh taste. 'Hey, Vic, this ain't wine; it's vinegar.' Everyone spit it out, except Vic. 'No, no it's just a little turned. It's good,' he said nonchalantly, before drinking the whole cup full. He pours a second. We all look at him. He downs two more. Suddenly, he doesn't look so good. We all start to chuckle, and then he erupts, puking all over everyone," said Jim.

The crowd made a sound almost in unison, "Ooooooh."

"It gets worse. He gets done puking, and we get leaves and wipe ourselves off. Suddenly this look comes over his face; he turns from green to red and fumbles, trying to get his pants down. He grabs a tree, and red shit diarrhea gushes out of his ass," Jim says.

The crowd looks at each other, their faces twisted in laughter and pain, yelling, "No, no, no more."

Vic, standing there next to Jim, bumps him with his elbow. "You got to remember that stuff. It's over twelve, maybe fourteen years, and you remember?" said Vic.

"Oh yeah, I remember." The room roared.

"Okay, anyone else?"

A few more guys came up and told stories of the distant and more recent past as a Sinatra soundtrack played quietly in the background.

Finally, Anthony got back to the microphone. "I'm glad you are enjoying this at Vic's expense. We all know how much we really love this guy. So now I will tell you Vic has agreed to come to work for me in my real estate and insurance operation." They all applauded.

"We are also expanding our financial management and business consulting operation and still doing insurance brokerage *and* food brokerage.

"Now, I know most of your families and some of you since you were born. As we have grown, we are looking to bring in people we know, people we trust.

"I am going to be calling some of you over the next few weeks to come talk to me about yourselves. Our operations have spread out globally; we now have a division in Europe, Italy and England, as well as several operations here in the States and in the Caribbean, the US Virgin Islands and St. Maarten. It is likely your businesses are compatible with the many things we do. We will find out, and if you want, I would also be interested in talking to those of you about other opportunities with us. For tonight though, let's all have a good time," Anthony closed.

There was applause, and then the room started buzzing. Many of these young men were just embarking on careers or making their way through the first stages of the business world after finishing school. Very few of them realized that Anthony had accumulated such a vast network of contacts and was doing so well financially.

The next day, his secretary received some twenty-six phone calls, and he instructed her to set up appointments over the next few weeks. He had the appointments arranged in an order he prescribed, knowing which ones he wanted to see first, those whose education and work operations had been checked by his staff. The others he would see later. They all underwent the same vetting process before they met. Delmont began his master plan.

He put together a team of five people whose knowledge, education, and background was carefully checked. Each had a specific talent or ability. A psychologist, a medical expert, a financial consultant with professional accounting credentials, a criminal forensics expert, and finally a genealogist. This was the brain trust.

Each was unaware of the other's existence, and they all conducted their own research independently.

Sir Anthony Eden

When Anthony interviewed one of the chosen individuals, they were advised that any other interviews would be kept strictly confidential. Anthony was careful to have each one understand the nature of the interviews and the presumed purpose, simply a verification of various points of their character and ability. In fact, the review was an intense profiling. The psychologist Herman Glockensfeld had been brought in from Berlin. He was in his late seventies and had worked with some of Europe's most noted experts in the field of psychiatry and personality evaluation. He was the retired chief of the research group that vetted NATO commanders. The European affiliates in Italy and England had contracts with NATO for supplies, and the connection there led to finding the man in retirement and bringing him in as a consultant in this project. Of course, he was offered substantial compensation and was treated with utmost respect.

The medical expert, Doctor Scott Rushman, was the relatively young physician who verified the condition of professional athletes who were about to be given multimillion-dollar contracts for the NFL, MLB, NHL, and NBA. He was the most sought-after physician, whose testing techniques could detect even the rarest defects and obscure medical conditions.

Thomas Herzfolder was a financial genius. He had headed several government financial think tanks and become a Wall Street legend. In fact, he had a weekly financial column in the *Wall Street Journal* and authored a few books on finance. The criminal forensic consultant, Frank DiCarlo, was a retired agent who was the Washington, DC, station manager of the CIA. His unit did international criminal profiling and could do instantaneous criminal identification. It was rumored that if someone's great-grandfather had a traffic ticket, Frank would find out by noon. His sister was married to a Delmonte cousin.

Hans Louis was a Belgian who lived in London. He was unofficially a consultant to the royal family and a European liaison between the many European royal families. He was a go-between in verification and background information sought when inquiries were made as to the background of any individual who was, in some cases, to marry into royalty or associate in business. For many years, he was a close friend of Sir Anthony Eden, a former British prime minister who had used his talents to check the background of Mr. Delmonte, whom he learned had ties to many worlds, both legitimate and otherwise, but was never accused or convicted of wrongdoing. Thus, it was surmised that he was both cautious and discreet. So too was his nephew, Anthony Delmont. And, having the advantage of being educated, Delmont learned ways to accomplish goals with reducing risk. The trick was to balance caution and risk and determine key elements that could weigh on the side of success or failure. Determining timing, location, financing, cooperation, sufficient assistance, and that innate feeling for any venture was evaluated in parts and from various angles and points of view to gauge success. Over the years, he developed a pattern of preplanning, one that he modified and altered to adhere directly to a venture or project at hand. He possessed a very keen analytical sense, which permitted him to access a situation fairly quickly but with great intensity and render a well-thought-out decision, based on what others might think was less than a fully-thought-out perspective. He welcomed various opinions before arriving at any conclusions of his own.

The current case in point was the team he assembled. Those he gathered would assist him in his ultimate plans going forward, setting the foundation on which all else would rest. From this solid and dependable foundation, one could build—and build he did.

He chose a cousin, Francisco Scalise, as his personal assistant. Frankie was smart, college educated, and ambitious. He was also very confident, though he still understood his limitations. He was an accomplished negotiator but bored by statistics and figures. His background was in public relations and venture coordination. Sitting at financial reviews for the stock market company he once worked for on Wall Street was a necessary part of the job but extremely boring to him. He enjoyed research, personal interaction, and negotiating deals. He was talented in bringing expert analytical teams together to assess a purchase of a company, buying real estate or partnering in a venture. This knowledge, ability, and versatility did not go unnoticed by Anthony. It complemented Anthony's own abilities, and it also helped that Frankie was trustworthy. While he enjoyed the nightlife as the bachelor, he was also restrained and cautious. If he drank at all, it was not to excess. He enjoyed many female friends but never became much entangled with anyone except his own family.

"Frankie," Anthony told him, "you are my second in command. We will have the able assistance of two others. Although Uncle Anthony is debilitated, he still has a great deal of knowledge that comes from real experience. He is, after all, one of the patriarchs of our families, and he still enjoys their respect. He has his limitations, but he is still someone from whom we can learn.

"Also, Don Carlo Scalise, even at advanced age, is still mentally a vast storehouse of information. That Sicilian blood is still thick, and he's the kind that's still going to be around to see his one hundredth birthday. He's built like a fireplug and can still bust heads if he is pushed too far. He has his limits in this new dynamic, however, as we all do. He is a leader in the pack. However, we need to create a new form of leadership forged from the old but set for the future.

"Here is how we do that. First, there is the formation of the core, our inner circle with Uncle Anthony, Don Carlo, you, and me. There is Giacomo Senisgali, the accountant. He graduated from Wharton

School of Economics and is a financial scholar. He was related to the Terranovas. He is a low-profile guy who worked for the Internal Revenue Service for years as a senior analyst and sectional manager. He started as an IRS agent for the feds, then got a great deal with the Halliburton Corporation. We will make him a better deal." Anthony Delmont had been working on his plan for years. He made sure to keep in touch with all those who had been Big Tony's contacts and added those of other family members.

Another great asset was Mario Bonanti. He had been involved with a political public relations firm who did work in several states, including New York, New Jersey, Florida, and California. His company, of which he was a full partner, worked for the highest bidder regardless of party. They had ex-senators and congressmen as their consultants and lobbyists and had a line on nearly everything political from the statehouse to the courthouse, including those in Washington.

"Also, we may from time to time need the help of Dick Hosering. Dick is an old friend of my father and me and is very close with Ray Kinsor. Ray has been assistant state police commissioner in New York state, then went with the National Security Agency, and he was posted with the International Service as chief liaison of immigration with Interpol. Ray is a friend, and we need that connection as well, but not as the member of *il cuore*. This we reserve for the few I mentioned. Ray has access to the worldwide intelligence-gathering organizations.

"The next ring is our insulation and shield, La Forza. Dick, Ray, and Tony Marino, the ex-police commissioner of New York City, will be important. So too will Tony Romanello. He knows the players and has access to the Wall Street moguls and bankers as well. He started when Bank of America was beginning to expand and then started his own company in financial management in New York. Our friendships over the years have built trust. We always came through when we were asked a favor.

"Ossie Ocassio is a very savvy guy who will be helpful as well. He had been a midlevel manager for New York City Transit and then became a vice president of Weld Transportation. He sold his interest a few years ago for a lot of money and has since retired as a consultant.

He also did a lot of work as a liaison with several unions for both city and state leaders.

"Tom Tabone has worked in the entertainment industry for many years. Any big shows in any major city somehow have Tom's thumbprint on them. He started with the William Morris Agency before branching out on his own. He brought in people from all over the country from the best agencies, including the legal experts who represent performers and the investors, some who had interest in theater chains, concert venues, and media. Clever guy, Tom, and well respected. He is known as Handshake Tom. You shake his hand once, and it's a deal. His word is gold, something rare in that industry.

"Bobby Pinto is a freelance journalist who has written op-ed pieces, features, and was nominated three times for a Pulitzer Prize. He has a creative genius and insight to view an issue, then writes about it, capturing the attention of the reader almost in a hypnotic way. His only problem is the booze. He binge drinks, and when he does, it's a problem. He can be controlled, however, and is willing to work to finish any project so his drinking doesn't interfere. His wife, Edie, is a saint. She puts up with his mood swings and boozing, but he loves her, and she him. He has a kid in high school, Sophia, and is very attentive to her. He can really be helpful in certain situations that require a creative press treatment.

"Ralphie Credenzo grew up in Red Hook. His stepfather, Joey Girazzi, was a club fighter. Ralphie was well trained and reached a level just below the top-ten ranking. He just didn't have enough talent to break into the big time. Joey got financed by some union guys in the longshoremen's union. Some of the higher-ups gave Joey work when he retired due to eyesight problems.

"Ralphie became a staff member of the union as well, and he was a fairly smart guy. He even got to finish his second year at Brooklyn Polytechnic with straight As before he went full-time as a boxer. The union local had him as recruiter and strike organizer. He was also the unannounced enforcer. If someone stepped out of line, Ralphie and a few of his boxing cronies would pay the offender a visit. If talking to someone did not resolve the problem, a bit of force always seemed to work. After all, that was Brooklyn. But even in Manhattan or Newark,

Ralphie had a reputation. He was hired also as a consultant by other locals on special projects when the cooperation between unions was mutually beneficial. He also had friends in the New York Police Department and state police, and a few of them ended up in the FBI as well.

"Tito Alvarez moved to Miami from Panama, a business hub for many of the companies who did business in the Southern Hemisphere, several years ago. He had originally worked as the assistant to the minister of commerce and helped in trade deals throughout Central and South America. He then split the company into three separate entities, putting his brother, brother-in-law, and cousin as the respective heads, overseen by a holding company, Chesna International. He moved Chesna headquarters to Miami and then opened a division in Manhattan at 2 Broadway. Chesna is still a privately owned company and one of the biggest players in commerce in North and South America. This economic power created political power as well, and Tito was often invited by the hierarchy of many countries to attend events and consult in business relations. He was also engaged from time to time by some of Washington's most influential lobbyist firms and knew his way around K Street very well. He could influence elections by assembling the financial and commercial world as an ally to a candidate, which in most cases assured the candidate a victory. Or, conversely, he could arrange a formidable opposition and prevent a landslide from securing either financial or logistical support, which would be essential in various elections. He had influence with unions and organizations as well as government and could create formidable opposition in the form of strikes, media pieces, and boycotts. He had his fingers in many pies in the Southern Hemisphere.

"In typical Latin style, he was a gregarious fellow with abounding energy. He was an accomplished speaker and an entertaining host. He stood five feet eight inches but always appeared much taller, thanks to the special shoes he had built that provided another four inches. His father, through political connections, had gotten a job as chief assistant to the Panamanian government's delegation representation to the United Nations. Thus, he and his sister and mother spent a great deal of time in New York, though both finished high school in

Panama. His father, Juan, saw to it that his son and daughter got a good education, and eventually Tito had his sister, Rosa, two years his junior, follow him to New York University. Both were good students and very popular with their college friends. They also attended many diplomatic functions both at the UN and in Washington, and that was an education in itself. While Juan was not a wealthy man, his children did qualify to have their education paid for by the Panamanian government under a government student-exchange program.

"Juan's ability to be effective with the diplomatic corps of the UN and in Washington created a very high regard for him in Panama's diplomatic circles. Hence, even when the political winds changed, he was always included in any new outlook in direction and accepted by new leaders as essential. Indeed, as ambassadors came and went, Juan was truly the mainstay as chief assistant. He made deals for his country that no one else was capable of since he had the connections and stature to do so. Indeed, he was the chief consultant for this government when negotiating the return of the Panama Canal to Panama with the Carter administration. That move was enough to give him lifetime security in his position if he chose to stay."

Anthony Delmont recognized Tito as a real force to ally himself with when he was dealing with him and his import-export company in New York and Miami and Uncle Anthony's company that supplied ship stores to companies that did business with Alvarez. The piers in the New York area were greatly influenced in their operations by the union leadership. Through Anthony Delmonte, his uncle, and their other contacts, Alvarez and his associates were given preferential treatment, and the relationship was reciprocal when the unions needed support. However, Anthony's relationship with Tito went even deeper than just business.

"Frankie, you know that I do business with Tito Alvarez. You saw him when we were at the piers in Manhattan and then had dinner with his group. Tito is a very vivacious guy. One night, a bunch of us finished work and decided to catch a Tito Puente Band performance at a Manhattan club. Tito and some of his friends invited me and one of my guys to go with them. My friend was Johnny Polista, a New York City cop who was also doing security for our company. Well, we got to this place, and it was jammed, really hopping. The men were dressed in fancy suits with colorful shirts, and the women in high-end sexy dresses and stiletto heels. We got a table, and soon he had a little group of ladies join us. Tito made his rounds of the place. He's a real charmer. We danced the Latin dances, and the girls were all giggles. One girl in particular caught Tito's eye. I think her name was Lorena. Black hair, green eyes, slim with a lot of cleavage revealed, and very flirty. She, from time to time, rubbed herself against Tito on the dance floor in a most enticing way, and she was a helluva dancer. Tito was drinking rum cocktails and was downing a whole one every fifteen minutes or so. The more he drank, the more animated he got, but with all the noise going on in that place, it was hardly noticeable. Well, one thing led to another, and Tito whispered something to this girl, and he got me aside. He said he was going out to his limo with this girl for a private conversation, but he would return. They left. About a half hour later, I noticed a couple of the club's bouncers rushing out the front door. I really didn't think anything of it, and Johnny and I continued to drink with the others. Then we saw two NYPD cops come in. Johnny looked at me and said maybe he ought to check this out. In a few minutes, he returned and said the cops had Tito outside in the parking lot. We rushed out and saw three cop cars, lights blazing and a bunch of cops next to Tito's limo. They had him against the car in handcuffs. Johnny knew one of the cops, and he said he was with Tito and could he talk to him. 'What happened?' Johnny asked Tito. 'Well, this bitch got real arrogant with me and started punching and kicking me. She's crazy or something. I don't know. I slapped her back,' said Tito. There were spots of blood on Tito's cream-colored shirt. Johnny looked in the limo. The girl in the back seat was trying to pull together the torn top of her dress and bra, but her breasts were sticking out of the dress. Her lip was swollen and cut, and she had blood on her face. Johnny had pulled the slightly opened door wide open to look in. She fussed with the dress for a while and finally stuffed her breasts into the cloth and tied the ripped sleeve around her neck. She realized then that Johnny was looking in and I was right behind him. She yelled, 'What the fuck are you looking at? This is no strip show; get the fuck out of here.' Johnny closed the door. He went over to the cop he knew. They talked for a while, and

Johnny pulled something out of his pants pocket and put it in his top pocket. The two of them turned around, and the other cop started nodding. They returned. 'Take the cuffs off this guy. Hey, Jimmy, come here. We're gonna write this up as a domestic squabble. No one was injured here. Hang on while I talk to the girl.' He knocked on the door, and the voice inside said, 'Yes?' He got in the car and closed the door. In about ten minutes, he got out. 'The girl said they were arguing, and she started to run back to the club, tripped, fell, bit her lip, and ripped her dress on the curb,' and hence, Lorena came out. 'Isn't that right, Miss Mendez? You fell while you were running?' 'Yes, Officer, I fell. Yeah, I fell. Now I'm out of here,' and she hurried back to the club.

"Johnny looked at me and raised an eyebrow. 'Well, that's it. Thanks, guys,' said Johnny. And the cops left.

"Tito didn't quite realize what really went on, but he knew Johnny and me got him out of the mess and began thanking us and calling us his brothers.

"The next day, he called me. We talked about business, and after the discussion, he said, 'What can I do for you and Johnny? Anything, anything you want.'

"'Hey, Tito, we're brothers. We help each other, that's all. Forget it. We're glad we got there in time to help. No problemo,' I said.

"'Thanks, amigo. I will not forget,' he said.

"From that time on, we became good friends and never mentioned the incident again. So, when we need Tito, we can count on him. Capisce?"

"Yeah, I got it," said Frankie.

"Now you see how I have this constructed—the inner core, the middle ring, and the outer ring. The outer ring is only those on a need-to-know basis. None of these members needs to know who else is involved, only who we seek to interact with on some matter. The middle ring is both contact and protection. These members know the outer ring and assist in keeping them protected while overseeing these operations. Then there is us, the inner core, the heart. We are the operators, the motivators, and administrators. So now we fill in the rest. I want you to talk to my vetting team members and arrange for this list of people to be interviewed." He handed Frankie a list. "Once you memorize it, destroy it."

Terranovas, Scalices, Georgios, Delmontes, Pumilias, Bonnanis, Merendinos, DiSimones, Castelluccis, Abanos, Garberini, Vazzanas, Piccottos, Vitarossas, Morellis, Biondis, Donofrios, and more. There were over forty names. He was familiar with nearly every name on the list, relatives, relations of relatives, friends. Some were generational friends, people who knew each other and their families for over a hundred years. Frankie did not question the purpose, but he was curious why thy would be interviewing so many. So, one by one, he contacted the names on the list and kept a coded diary without names. He devised a number and letter system to aid his memory, and he attached a sort of score for each interview and category of expertise.

Anthony monitored the progress as the weeks went by. He would occasionally attend by way of a two-way mirror hidden in places in the various interview rooms. After some three months, the forty odd candidates were reduced to twenty, and as the vetting wound down, the vetting team was asked, individually, to continue as consultants from time to time and although separate and anonymous to one another join in a chat room online to review and discuss either a person, a theory, or a project. The participants enjoyed the flexibility of the format as well as the money they were paid when a deal came along.

So Anthony created his semiperpetual think tank. Sometimes he would add someone with a specific knowledge. Each was supplied a code, generally three numbers and two letters, and a password. Frankie was 242XA. Anthony was 300XX and so on. It was in this way that the organization Anthony designed began to take form, from the time Joseph Valachi decided to cooperate with federal law enforcement and identified the then organization of the La Cosa Nostra *cause celebre* for law enforcement to attack, with sufficient information that there was an international cooperation between the American mob and that in Europe and elsewhere.

The watershed event gave the law enforcement community an opportunity to demand resources and expansion in sectors from the FBI to state police to local metropolitan police forces. Forensic teams and investigative divisions were formed to combat and destroy the organization. Federal agencies grew in time to include new and expanded manpower, authority, and legal accommodations, including the RICO Act (Racketeer Influenced and Corrupt Organizations).

One by one, these organizations, "families" as it were, were the object of intense scrutiny. In the early 1960s, Robert Kennedy, the US attorney general, in an opportunity to gain huge notoriety for himself and his brother's administration, burst upon the scene with a declaration of war against the Mafia and proclaimed that this corrupt and devious organization was priority for the government to rid it from existence.

It was ironic that decades later, the very organization despised by Kennedy was chronicled as the single most important factor that turned the defeat of John Kennedy's presidential effort against Richard Nixon into a victory. There were revelations that the Kennedy clan, headed by Joseph Kennedy, the family patriarch, noted as a former associate in the illegal liquor trade during Prohibition, had enlisted Mafia forces to tip the election in West Virginia and in Illinois to his son, thus completely changing the outcome of the election by a razor-thin margin.

Old Joe Kennedy knew, to some degree, the way the Mafia could find ways to get things done, from experience. His business dealings and his involvement on many levels in both politics and the manipulation of business forces gave his sons insights into the future of Americans leading institutions, even recent ones.

After being uncovered at the Appalachian meeting where dozens of Mafia chieftains were found to be assembling and were arrested and identified, there was a massive attempt to get out of the spotlight. When Joseph Columbo, the head of a New York crime family, decided he wanted a public platform and formed the Italian American Anti-Defamation Organization and began a public campaign, it irked a lot of Mafia bosses, including Carlo Gambino, Capo di Tutti Capi, head of the American organized crime hierarchy. He had his motives to remove Columbo, and Columbo's actions caused others to sanction his removal.

So, in a very public display, this news hound Columbo, who had organized a mass rally in Manhattan at Columbus Square on Columbus

Day, was shot in the head in the middle of the entire affair. He was never to recover and remained in a vegetative state until his death.

Again, it was a media field day. It served to remove one impediment to those who saw Columbo as one who sought to expand his power and chose to clip his wings but created a firestorm in law enforcement. In a sense, this very public act helped create a new intensity to rid New York of the plague, the Mafia, altogether. That inspired a new national commitment, and what was seen as a period of subsiding interest by law enforcement rekindled the Kennedy-inspired quest, a war against the Mafia. The organized crime strike force teams became well funded, semiautonomous entities within law enforcement, charged with a singular mission: nab the mob. And nab them they did. The nearly inexhaustible resources prevailed, and these forces resulted in decimating one crime family after another. When one line of leadership was found conducting criminal activity, they were tried and jailed. The next line of leadership was carefully monitored as well, and they were found out and jailed. While the national syndicate became more scattered, individual gangs, who had really no resemblance to the power structure and connected predecessors, had other issues to deal with. Attracting new members was very difficult. Families experiencing the demise of their fathers and grandfathers sought to distance themselves from the life. And the times were changing too. The sons and daughters of Mafia families were sent to the better schools; they became educated and sought financial gain in legitimate businesses, no longer needing or wanting to join the nefarious clicks and ambitious new leaders who had little loyalty and less knowledge, missing the tutelage of their predecessors. One could not trust anyone anymore. Turning state's evidence became a common avenue to save one's skin. Omerta gave way to the Witness Protection Program. The structure itself, once last of the old traditions, disintegrated into a gang mentality devoid of the very rules that had sustained the organization and held it together.

The Jamaicans moved into the drug trade in New York, Miami, and other major cities, and they were soon followed by the Colombians and Mexicans. The Russians were noted to be even more ruthless than the Italians, and their methods were hardly kept secret even in America. Russian mobsters were a fearsome lot and well financed. So it was that the huge void that these enterprising foreigners took advantage of in a swift and ruthless manner became the new wave of crime.

Anthony Delmont had watched the progression and understood the concept of the Oriental philosophy that every yin had a yang. He studied these groups and their effects. In short order, these new entrepreneurs began warring with each other for territory. Each had its own strongholds.

In the big metropolis, New York, the Russian mob settled in Brooklyn, while the Jamaicans had a long-term influence in the Bronx and Manhattan. The Chinese had held their ground in Manhattan.

Now the rest of the country was seeing the rise in Latino gangs. Most notable was the expansion of the Bloods and Cripps and others. There were enclaves of Hells Angels that filled the drug market gap as well, and then there were the drug cartels from Mexico, some transplanted units into Arizona and other areas of the Southwest.

One by one, Anthony put each of his new soldiers in position, not to confront these groups but to engage them in a dialogue for profit. What they lacked was the connections that the Italian Mafia prized, the same ones that could make them successful.

If you had legal problems, they had prosecutors and judges who had reason to deal with the new order. If you had problems with other groups, could they be solved without bloodshed?

If financing was needed, he had access to some of the more progressive and, not less importantly, legitimate loan situations to meet needs. If there were union problems, no problem. He had open communication with unions. If there was legislation creating an impasse, they had politicians who would be sympathetic so that a business venture could go forward.

Anthony had created a multifaceted service-oriented organization that could resolve many problems with little fanfare. Thus, the leaders he chose enjoyed the support of the others, knowingly or not. While the organizations that filled the void left as the Mafia disintegrated, they lacked a key element that the Mafia had.

The Scalisces and the Gobeos once again found that mutual cooperation and interaction could serve both families well, as did all the other families when mutual business interests intersected.

Anthony began inserting the individuals he had gathered into positions to replace the old order of influence. He had chosen his operatives carefully.

Old Paulie from Brooklyn had met his demise when going to a sumptuous steak dinner at his favorite restaurant with his lieutenant, Tommy Bottellii. The two were gunned down as they were getting out of the car and died instantly. The scene looked like a Hollywood horror movie. People witnessed the event on the street, but it happened so quickly no one could identify the shooters, the driver, or any of the license plates. It was rumored that a disgruntled mob leader had boldly ordered the hit. The leader, Johnny Gotti, was again one of the "I am a star" mob guys and after several years in the limelight was permanently sent to "college" for life, where he died from cancer.

The void he left was enormous since no one would seek to challenge the once ruthless and maniacal Gotti clan. Many Gotti associates also went to jail, and huge parts of the organization in New York disengaged so that it was not much more than a group of the surviving members with a go-it-alone attitude. Anthony Delmont provided a solution to the void by interacting with judges, unions, politicians, and even friendly law enforcement when the opportunity arose, and he did so with an aura of legitimacy.

If a construction contract with the city was a viable venture, the multi-forces in this new alignment were summoned each for their part. By satisfying all factions and sharing the wealth, deals were made, and peace prevailed.

Charlie Gobeo would do his part. John Scalisce was one of the Terranovas and would cover his end until all bases were touched and the deals made. Everyone got what they wanted, and the new alignment derived the power to go to even greater heights. Delmont and his associates grew in stature with every new deal.

Candidates for office from the legislative to the judicial knew the strength that certain individuals had and sought them out for support and guidance. Few people ever suspected that such an effort was motivated by the arrival of a new group. No one even knew that there were multiple forces interacting in a master plan to reach an ultimate goal, election or appointment, with the beneficiary being beholden to only one or two of the alignments members.

When some Turkish officials sought trade agreements with some businesses in Manhattan and their Islamic background was in question, there were those who could resolve the issue by assuring those who were in positions of power to inform the State Department that these moderates offered no threat, and hence the deal was sanctioned. When eyebrows were raised in some governmental security agencies, the concerns were quietly quelled by exposing the cooperation of those who aligned with the functionaries, the elected, judicial, and local law enforcement vouching as to the integrity of those involved. This was accomplished through a very complex web of interconnected contacts.

During World War II, both army and navy intelligence sought every avenue available to them to gather information on a broad scale. Prior to the invasion on D-day and the subsequent invasion of Italy, army intelligence operatives had made it clear that they would pay any reasonable price (and even more) for certain kinds of information. Salvatore "Lucky" Luciano came into contact with a US Army intelligence group that had operatives in Mussolini's Italy. His organization knew exactly where the Axis forces, primarily those set up by Hitler, were located in Italy. He also had observers at all the major port installations, both in Italy as well as others in the Mediterranean Sea ports. The close ties between his Mafia organization in the States and the longshoremen's union as well as many of the shipping companies provided invaluable information to American naval forces. Luciano was credited with saving hundreds of thousands of lives and was given a new and much-appreciated view by the government. Some of those who worked with Luciano were also accorded special treatment by American intelligence.

Those lines of communication between US intelligence and the Mafia continued well after the war. J. Edgar Hoover had been involved in the operations in the States. He created his own communication network with members of various mob families throughout the country. The Military Intelligence Organization eventually created a unit for international information gathering and spying, the CIA. Other security agencies were formed as well. The operatives and informants became the core of a worldwide network. Since the Mafia had communication sources in Europe as well as the United States, trading information, indeed cooperating when it suited both parties, grew into an ongoing relationship that continued for generations. Thus, when Delmont needed to get help from an elected official or someone in law enforcement, having some high-level intelligence operative in the CIA could open many doors. It also had the power to shut down speculation and inquiries.

CHAPTER 64

MORTALITY SEEMS A remote consequence of an action previously undertaken. Anthony Delmonte Sr. never even contemplated the possibility, nor did his subordinate.

"Mr. Delmonte?" The question was asked as Anthony lifted the phone.

"Yes."

"This is Sergeant Tom Feldon of the Dade County Sheriff's Department. We have a situation here. We found a person, a man, who expired in the Fort Lauderdale area along Route 10. Apparently, from the officer on the scene, it appears to have been drug related. His identification indicates he is one Emilio Vallani, age fifty-eight, and he is employed by your company, Bay Company/Coastal Purveyors. His business cards and yours were also with his effects."

Delmonte was momentarily stunned. "Really, well, that is sad news," responded Anthony. He gave the officer information and indicated where Emilio's brother, Val, could be contacted. Within days, arrangements were made, and the body was flown back to New York.

Pietrangelo's Funeral Parlor on Richmond Road in Staten Island was the site of the final transition for those whose Italian background held the need for a traditional wake. There was a general protocol of a two-day wake with a receiving line during each session by family members, friends, and others. The overbearing scent from the multiple floral pieces was normal. On the last day, day three, there was a short ceremony at the funeral parlor and then the finality of burial. If the deceased was from the Bronx or Manhattan, arrangements would be made with the Cinquemani Funeral Parlor on Allerton Avenue and White Plains Road in the Bronx. These funeral homes were run by the same families, generation after generation, and could be counted upon to have all the arrangements made with the same respect accorded a member of their own family. In fact, some were related.

Once E's funeral was over, Delmonte and half-dozen others who knew E gathered at Tony's office. Anthony poured out shots of scotch. "What an asshole! He killed himself with junk. He had so much cocaine in him that the body turned blue."

They looked at each other. "Such a fool."

"Now we will have my nephew take over the things E was handling. So if you need to call him, know he is directly under me. Capisce?" They all nodded, including Delmont. Delmonte envisioned that he would eventually incorporate this operation into his own.

As transitions go, this one was very simple. Delmont already knew all the players and had been around enough that the new tasks were no great challenge. The deal making, buying, selling, directing men, and, most importantly, controlling money was a daily exercise in training since Delmont first began working in the operation. However, having been through college and having Delmonte as a mentor as well, Anthony had a really good set of skills. He also had a sense of organization. Within weeks, he reorganized the communications of the operations. He already had his own operation running smoothly.

A phone was installed with an automated message system that could be accessed by simply dialing a code. Delmont divided the men into crew units. Each had a crew boss answerable only to the two top men. The crews were purposely separated and only communicated when there was a combined operation. As time went on, Delmonte did less and less daily management and more outside contract work. Delmont had freed him from much of the operational tasks, so now he was able to travel and seek a wider field of operation.

As the crew bosses grew more experienced, Delmont also found more time to devote to expansion and making new contacts. He also reached out to some of the old timers, and those still around introduced him to their heir apparents as well.

When the call came to Delmont, he seemed resigned to acceptance. He and Delmonte had spoken about what to do if something unforeseen occurred. The caller was rather clinical, one of Delmonte's doctors.

"Mr. Delmont, I was asked to call you to notify you that Anthony Delmonte suffered a stroke. He is here at Staten Island Hospital and is being treated and evaluated. I am Dr. Manzanna, and I will be caring for him." Delmont paused, jotted down a phone number and room number, and thanked the doctor.

Delmont had played out his actions in his mind. He contacted his crew bosses first. Then the lawyer was called. Documents had already been in Ferranti's file to initiate the transition for Delmont to take over the company. All had been preplanned. Delmonte remained in critical condition for weeks, and then with some treatment, he began to walk with a walker. Gradually he was able to regain some speech, but it was limited. He had lost a great deal of his mental capacity; however, his mind was clouded by the fact he was still living and breathing while many others he knew were long gone. Eventually all mention of business by Delmont's conversations with the boss ended, and his visits were purely social and familial.

Four years later, Delmonte suffered a fatal heart attack. Delmont's inevitable takeover was as seamless as it could be. Young Delmont was intelligent and quickly understood how to operate.

The old ways in business were giving way to a more precise and calculated direction. The use of cellular phones, computers, fax machines, and other machines provided a new speed. Delmont had been brought up in the old world of business, and as he grew, he evolved with the new as well. Moving with change was the vehicle for survival. Delmont had learned early on that planning and learning really boosted good luck. Though he was not averse to taking calculated risks, he tried to envision all aspects of the risk instead of going off blindly. He did so in several ways. Some seemingly offhand conversations might really be more than that. A chance meeting might have been meticulously orchestrated. A simple deal agreement might have much more far-reaching results than it initially appeared to have. He always looked for the signs.

Delmont was at once the student and the teacher. He would sometimes sit alone and go back mentally through the years to recall events and conversations. His memory was vivid, and in those moments, he would seek to find information and clues to unanswered questions in his own mind. Even images or phrases seemed to come forward with frequency that could be comical or very cutting!

"Are you a wiseguy or a boy scout?" was a Delmonte favorite expression. It could have meant different things depending on who it was said to and under what circumstances. "Cafone!" could be an insult or just a singular jibe. *Capo doste* or *testa dura*, stubborn or hardheaded, could be said of a monetary condition or a lifelong affliction. *Babbo* or *stupido*, dumb or stupid, surely was not a word anyone wanted to be called. *Slick* could mean smart or conniving. *Juice* equaled power. *Compadre* was originally the connotation of a godfather in the relationship of the Roman Catholic Church's requirement to have "spirited overseer and guide" who looks after the religious health of a newborn child at first and then too at Communion and Confirmation, those who stand up for you. It could also mean a close friend.

The Goomba slang word developed, but those who were bestowed the honor of being named godmother and godfather denoted a very special, lifelong relationship to the youngster, one that carried with it the obligation under church law to see to it that the youngster followed through with the religious obligations required to be a good Roman Catholic. The relationship was recognized by the recipient as having an extra caretaker, a special envoy. Indeed, more than a simple relation, such as an uncle or cousin who was related just by blood, the godfather and godmother were *chosen* because of some special reasons. So, all their life, one had a second advocate.

Thus these images and the experiences were weaved through the memories and experiences of Delmont. It gave him a sense of grounding and provided a sense of inner confidence and stability, the feeling of standing on the shoulders of others from the past and the basis for a continuous but optimistic view of the future. Considering all the obstacles that others of his heritage had to overcome and did, there was reason for one to think they too could succeed. Further, there were really no boundaries, merely obstacles, to achieving what was sought after, all within reason. Delmont was a pragmatist with a will and spirit to use his talents and those he associated with to achieve goals. Inevitably, once a goal was reached, he would reset the bar even higher. He reveled in his successes but never let them define finality. There was always more to do.

The transport of oil from the Middle East had been for many years controlled by the Greek shipping magnates that, as a closed cartel, controlled much of this. Now some of the original magnates like Onassis had died off, and others fell on hard times.

Christina Onassis, who was a very smart business woman in her own right, began to lose interest in being the day-to-day hands-on operator of an empire. Having lost her brother in a plane crash and suffering from both depression and some other physical problems, not to mention a misdirected love life, she was open to the assistance of Anthony's people stepping in and assisting in arrangements and contracts with major oil refineries in the United States. She trusted Delmont but knew the others in the United States who worked for her father could not be trusted. When Ms. Onassis suffered a heart attack and died on a vacation in Brazil, Delmont was able to continue his cooperation with the heirs to the Onassis operation.

Over a few years, the gaping holes left by the removal of the power bases of organized crime families, financial giants they helped support like banks, unions, politicians, law enforcement, commerce, and indeed much in the international realm of commerce and thus politics, began the emergence of a legally construed operation. While some of the tactics were extremely brutal and ruthless, care was taken to cover the legal and public perceptions so there could be no public knowledge, legal or otherwise, and no vocal protest.

Anthony found that his loyalist troop could act with autonomy and saw to it that all controversial matters were kept quiet. "You know we have an issue with the idea that the city administration wants to shut down all the downtown markets and eventually move everything up to the Bronx. The Bronx! Can you believe it?" said Anthony.

"Yeah, I know. They argue the city congestion makes the need urgent. Also, that part of the food supply, the fish market on the East Side and meat and vegetable on the West Side, really isn't efficient."

"Well, if they are hell-bent on doing this, then let's be sure that we have enough controversy stirred up so that it will be an easy sell for our contractor friends to get the construction contracts and our friends in the markets get sweetheart deals to move," said Anthony.

"It's in the works, boss. It's all been worked out and with little resistance at that," Frankie responded.

"Good, very good," Anthony said with relief. "This political climate is really strange. It seems that we might not totally ignore some of what's going on but instead stand back while the warring forces in the region battle it out to the end and then align our people on the side of the winner. The problem is knowing who will ultimately end up as the power brokers in the Tri-State area. Washington is in such a state of disarray that we can only be extremely cautious and deal one-on-one with those folks who we hold confident in their loyalty."

"Yeah, I know. Cousin Tom Terranova and his brother-in-law, Richie Bonelli, have been keeping their team on their toes. His company, Police-tech Surveys, have brought in some very influential politicians, and as a lobbyist group, they have an excellent reputation."

"While we hope to have more juice there, it's at least a situation of having a good working relationship in areas where it counts most," said Frankie.

"Okay, let's have dinner next Sunday at the shore house with the family. We have your cousins coming over, and it will be good for the kids to be with each other."

"Okay, I'll tell Mary and my brother," said Frank.

The Delmont house at the Jersey Shore was an imposing beach-front structure. It was surrounded by a wall and fences and took up three lots. The building itself dated back to the 1930s and had been renovated and updated, yet its Mediterranean stucco and clay tile roof retained the original features. There was one side yard with a Hollywood-era swimming pool and cabana surrounded by an elaborate flower garden, a replica of an ancient garden from a palazzo in Rome. Fruit trees dotted the perimeter, and a large stand of fig trees led to a grape arbor.

Sunday morning began with those family members who had stayed the night scurrying around to get ready for the nine o'clock Mass at the nearby Saint Caroline-by-the-Sea Church. The neighborhood came alive with people pouring out of their homes and onto the sidewalks on their way to the large old church.

The Delmonts took the same pew up in the front when they were in town, which was often on weekends. Escaping the congestion of the Staten Island community to the serenity of Cape Island was something Delmont felt was important. He recalled many years before when he was a small boy, the age of some of his grandchildren, how the family would pack up on Sunday for a drive from one side of Staten Island to the far side where his grandfather, Vincenzo, had a beach house compound in Great Kills.

That compound consisted of two houses with a high wooden fence and huge backyard. The front yard was actually the beach. There it was another world. The boat docks were a block down, and the fishing pier was always an exciting place to go, either to fish, swim, or check out the catch from the pleasure boats coming in. There were ice cream stands and hot dog carts. And then there was Milton's. Milton's was a beach grill on the beach side and a bar and restaurant on the other.

From early morning when the fishermen would catch breakfast at five o'clock to the night crowd who would dance to the piano player or the jukebox until three in the morning, Milton's never seemed to close. Indeed, during the summer, it hardly did close, only for a cleanup and reset.

Kids would be all over from the beach to the docks to the reappearing beachfront sandbar, which appeared at low tide and was covered by the sea at high tide.

On the next cove down was yet another series of docks and the huge Shoals Restaurant and Nightclub. This was a full-service three-hundred seat restaurant and club set in the midst of several piers and docks. Visitors would dock their yachts and large boats and dine and dance at Shoals. There was even an outdoor dance floor overlooking the bay. Just further down the coast was the Island Yacht Club, a private club. Anthony Delmonte had been an owner-partner for many years. Before the club began, it was an inauspicious series of docks and piers but a hotbed during Prohibition. The ships containing whiskey and wine from Europe and Canada would lay anchor offshore while fishing boats would transfer their cargo to the clubhouse sheds on the pier. From there, the cases were trucked to spots in New York City as well as Staten Island and New Jersey. The more commerce, the more warehousing sprung up. It was great memories.

The Delmont house at the Jersey Shore also afforded a private place where the comings and the goings of visitors was little noticed or not unusual in this weekend retreat town.

The early summer weekends usually meant a rush to the shore, and this season was no different. The traffic from all points north going south was extreme. The cosmopolitan areas in New York City, North Jersey, and Philadelphia accounted for the majority of weekend warriors. Further down the shore, these folks were known as shoobies, though they really were not exactly the true definition of the term. Back in the day, true shoobies were those who traveled to the shore as day trippers. They took the train or the bus, shoebox in hand with their lunch and snacks. Thus they were identified as shoobies.

The Delmont tradition of traveling to a retreat away from the everyday location of regular life really had its roots long before in their ancestors. The Delmontes in Corleone were an industrious business people. They were shop owners and land owners. They were patrones, owners of vast expanses of lands that grew everything from fruits and vegetables. They had vineyards and pasta-manufacturing businesses. The meat market in the town was supplied by the animals they raised in the countryside nearby.

Not far from this mountain town, the Delmonte farm was once a place to raise animals and grow various items but also a retreat, albeit a rustic one. Just some four or five miles from the edge of Corleone, the hillside farmlands and vineyards were quiet and serene places where the family could pack off to in horse and carriage on a Saturday night or Sunday morning to enjoy bucolic surroundings. The hills here grew everything, and the wild rabbits, quail, and other creatures flourished. Here too were grazing areas for the lambs and goats raised for the butcher shop and sheep's milk, and the small cattle herd, some housed in ancient stone barns, provided the scarce cow's milk.

Access to the house was from a dusty, rut-ridden dirt road whose hard scrabble base was worn into two deep ruts carved by the centuries of the wagon wheels that pounded the earth and stone into a hard surface. Here the donkey carts, laden with harvest from the fields, would be brought to the main center of the farm and barns and house. Here too was the only real access by road, which also afforded a bit of security as well. The building compound stood on a plateau with an extremely steep terrain on all three sides, which had small footpaths beaten and winding pastures where the goat herders and sheepherders had brought animals up to fenced-in graze lands for centuries. The modest stone house afforded a view from three sides. The rolling hills and vineyards could be seen for miles, and one could see any movement on and off the rustic roadways in all directions. Thus, too, it was a safe haven when controlling factions of Mafia clashed, ending in violence and vendetta.

The Delmontes would arrive and have the farmhands that lived in the small houses on the farm prepare the house. There was a high mountain spring that had been used to bring water to the house utilizing the ancient viaduct technology founded by the Romans. The flow of water, though slow from the spring, gathered in a system of clay pipe cisterns and stone support, so there was a strong flow when the catch basins were partially opened by movement of carefully cut stone stops. The flow was diverted to the basins and fields below.

The house had been constructed of the local materials available on the countryside. The rounded stones were cut and fitted then sealed by mortar and were nearly two feet thick. The density provided resistance from the heat of summer when the windows were covered. It also maintained heat when it turned cool at night, and a small fireplace radiated heat throughout the house. There was a nearby granite quarry, and the floor was made from various-size slabs of the reddish stone laid carefully to a perfect flat surface but with no visible seam between the slabs. The stone walls had been cut flat inside and covered with a thick, textured plaster with niches and alcoves for storage of jars and vases. There were five small bedrooms.

The patriarch would go to the lamb or goat herd and select an animal for slaughter for the day's meal. Perhaps too a pig had been slaughtered, and the ingredients for pork sausage were assembled the day prior for making sausages. Fruits and vegetables had been gathered by the farm families and brought to the kitchen. The lamb, slaughtered and butchered, was slowly roasted over the charcoal fire. The afternoon would be relaxed with perhaps a mandolin serenade and a walk in the flowering fields.

The more ambitious men might, on occasion, walk the countryside with shotguns and provide the dinner table with some wild rabbit as well.

Here, too, family matters might be sorted out and decisions made.

Thus it was with this shore house Anthony sought to use as a place where he could assemble his organization heads and discuss business in complete privacy.

The grape arbor outdoor dining room was the perfect location, one where his men could discuss their business in a quiet and relaxed atmosphere after the afternoon meal. This particular afternoon, Frank, his brother, and three other families had enjoyed a dinner alfresco.

"Frank, we here must prepare to move quietly when the word is given about some action that is about to take place in Washington. I have received word that some major turmoil is about to occur. The president, Mr. Carrington, is traveling in Asia. I have information that there will be a fatal plane crash and thus the vice president, such as he is, Mr. Bodine, will need to act quickly to put the nation at ease with the upcoming transaction. He is not the most popular or respected guy in the country. He is seen by most as a loudmouth and by some as a figure of ridicule. Now the selection of a new vice president is crucial once all this happens.

"Senator John Minardi is someone who has considerable power and support. He also controls a powerful wing of the Democratic Party. He enjoys a good working relationship with some Republican leaders as well, so he could be getting help there as well. His main opponents are Senator Charles Dobbs and Senator Donald Sizemore. Dobbs's support from his state of Connecticut has reaches in the rest of the northern New England area from Massachusetts to Maine, Sizemore from New York has the mid-Atlantic region. Minardi has the South and, being from Nevada, the West. He also has support in California, where his cousin Tom Contadina, the Republican congressman, has managed to consolidate some influence in both parties since the two senators there and some of the more radical congressional members supported the Carrington Financial Plan, which caused the economic depression we are in.

"If we can maneuver Minardi's position with our friends in politics and business, he will have enormous power in Washington. In part, it's not unlikely Bodine, who is so unpopular before this change occurs, will be even more unpopular. He's to blame for the economic chaos as well.

"So, there is a need to get all of our people in position now. Frankie, I need you to get to Washington and meet with our people there without explaining much. Just get the information in a meeting as to where all their influential people are. See who is doing what with our K Street operation. We are really going to need them as soon as this breaks. See if you can get together, maybe a casual lunch or dinner, with that Bud Norbeth who heads the political desk at the *Washington Sentinel* newspaper. Maybe touch base with Corey Jessel, the girl at the WBS-TV News. Our guy there, Tom Christo, should be able to give you an immediate reaction, so be sure he is easily accessible the moment the news breaks. Maybe arrange daily review meetings with him by midweek so you know he'll be around.

"There are assignments in New York, California, and Florida. Joey Corbo was dispatched to Rome already to meet with friends in Europe about our business there. He also will get a sense of the reaction and have our business people prod the European politicians in the EU to back Minardi. We have Bishop Cattaggio in Rome, who will help us with the Vatican. After all, Minardi is a Catholic, and Dobbs is a Lutheran, and Sizemore is a Jew. There should be a worldwide move by the Catholics to promote Minardi. When he visited Rome a few months ago, Pope Francesco, who he has consulted for years, discussed how the finances in America had impacted the church. Minardi suggested that the government's ability to look carefully at any church-related real estate that was being offered for sale might be perfect for government locations. This is a powerful friend. Pope Francesco is extremely well respected and powerful worldwide. His friendship with Minardi is important."

While the espresso and dolce were being brought to the table, Anthony reviewed the worldwide plan to these, his closest brain trust members.

"This is the most important thing we'll ever do. If we are successful, it will set up a kind of control of our own destiny and for generations to come. If you need to talk to me directly, you have a number to leave the code so that I can return your message."

The code set up was Anthony's date of birth and the date of birth of the caller followed by middle initial. Once the code was received, Anthony would have a disposable burner phone, and his contact would have the same. There was a set time, the eleventh hour, for all such calls, unless it was an emergency. Frank and the others had a coded website to communicate any immediate emergency, and each had it noted in their Blackberry as an alert message. Thus, the event was set in motion and all the arrangements set like wheels of a clock. One movement set another and then another until the final turn occurred.

The news flashes began, but they were inconclusive.

Reports stated that Air Force One had been lost by radar somewhere between Tokyo and the end of the Japanese archipelago. There were no early reports that the plane crashed or exploded. Then, a Reuters News Service report stated, "Wreckage of a plane, which was in the vicinity of the last reported radar location of Air Force One, has been spotted." Then finally: "The wreckage of a plane in the ocean off the coast of a small atoll at the end of the Japanese archipelago, which has been identified as Air Force One, the US aircraft that President Robert Carrington was aboard, has been identified by a US-Japanese team." The grim news followed reports from numerous sources in and around the site of the wreckage. "They found Air Force One, the plane on which the president and his entourage were traveling, but have not found any survivors."

Internet descriptions of the scene showed various-sized vessels combing the sea, picking up pieces of seats and cloth. Reporters then explained, "There have been no reports of any bodies found, nor has the main portion of the plane or the black box been found."

It seemed that each newscast was more desperate than the last. Other than finding evidence of the wreckage, little else could be reported since nothing was immediately found. As night fell, the reports trailed off.

Frankie got a message that simply said in text BBX—code that the first event occurred.

Minardi, who had been in Bethesda, Maryland, at a naval conference, was rushed to Washington. There in an underground bunker, he went on television with a brief statement. Minardi was chairman of the Senate Intelligence Committee and the closest person to act as a spokesman since the vice president was traveling by plane to California. "I have been notified that remnants of the plane on which President Carrington was traveling in Asia, US Air Force One, has been found in the South China Sea area. There is no further information at this time regarding the president or the cause of the plane's downing. I have sent numerous investigative teams, and we are working with Japanese officials and their navy to locate survivors if they exist. Seven US submarines and other vessels are also converging on the area as well as four squadrons of planes with various types of equipment. I will give updates as we learn more," said Minardi.

There was a call to the chief justice of the Supreme Court, Anthony Salerno, and he was alerted to be available to get brought to the bunker for a briefing. The entire government alert system placed several in security mode. Those in the lineage for succession to the presidency, including the Speaker of the House and others, were taken to safe houses around Washington. A squadron of jet fighters was dispatched to intercept and escort Vice President Bodine's plane to an air force base in Nevada.

Crews of divers equipped with special lighting worked through the night.

Then at dawn, announcements came.

"The main fuselage and the engines were found along with a long stretch of debris. There is evidence of some kind of explosion, based on what has been found thus far and the pattern of the debris. It is unknown if this was accidental or if the plane was hit by a missile or destroyed by a bomb." The next few days, the news reports were endless. The remnants of the plane were slowly retrieved. The chief justice in concert with the leadership of the Senate and Congress did not wait. As that process continued, after forty-eight hours, Minardi was convinced there was no hope that Carrington survived. He called a conference, and the leadership agreed with an immediate transfer of power. They went to their respective branches of government and advised of the time and place of the transfer.

At high noon on the third day, an assembly of members of Congress, Senate, Supreme Court, and joint chiefs of staff converged on the Capitol. The only absent official was the Speaker of the House, who watched the process from a secure location.

Minardi's staff had already alerted every news outlet to keep a constant review of emergency releases.

Minutes before the actual transfer of power, all the television, radio, and internet outlets were put on a public address system mode. "This is a national alert. All media standby for an important information from the United States Capitol," the announcement came.

"My fellow Americans, this is Senator John Minardi. President Carrington and his staff, crew, and some news reporters were en route from Japan to Indonesia aboard Air Force One. I have received confirmation that the plane went down and there are no survivors. Following a meeting with the leaders of Congress and the chief justice of the US Supreme Court, I have been asked to assemble the Congress, Supreme Court, and joint chiefs here at the Capitol, and as prescribed by the Constitution of the United States, the presidency will be transferred to Vice President Bodine. It is with great regret and a heavy heart I announce the transfer of the presidency. Thank you, and God bless America." As soon as he completed his statement, he was escorted to the congressional chamber. It was nearly noon. There, Vice President Bodine and over one hundred dignitaries were assembled.

The great hall was unusually quiet. There was a slight buzz of whispered voices as he entered and walked directly to the center of the room. The chief justice was standing there with Bodine's wife, Rita, and his son, Jake. As his wife held the Bible, he was administered the oath of office.

Anthony Delmont was in a locked room at the Willard Hotel with Frank and two of the Merendino boys, watching the television. "So now it's complete, and we move forward," said Anthony.

Over the past two days, Anthony had dispatched his emissaries to key positions in the US and to several foreign countries. They all presented a message from him that he would be in Washington at the request of Senator John Minardi.

Now, they would revisit their contracts again and be advised that following the transfer of power, President Bodine had called a group of the trusted advisers and would rearrange the cabinet. At that meeting, several of these advisers would be appointed as liaisons to each cabinet secretary and would report directly to the president. The next day, a group of Democratic senators and congressmen concurred and agreed to submit the name of Senator Minardi as vice president. Considering the negative public opinion of Bodine, they had decided to fast-track Minardi's elevation. A special meeting of Congress was called, and within forty-eight hours, Minardi was elected by Congress and sworn in as vice president. He already was a popular figure, and the reaction nationally was extremely positive.

Anthony Delmont was asked to act as special liaison to the secretary of commerce. In that capacity, and at Minardi's suggestion, the president would direct Delmont to present his directives to the secretary in advance of meetings. Thus, Delmont became the conduit for information to the secretary publicly, but privately he would confer with Minardi, and the actions of the Bodine administration would have a distinctive cooperation with Delmont's advisers and council.

After several days, a definite cause was assigned to the downing of Air Force One, and Minardi again commanded the airwaves. "After an extensive investigation, it has been determined that an explosion occurred inside Air Force One. While the exact location cannot be determined, it was roughly at midplane between the front seating area and the president's quarters near the area where the plane's wings join the fuselage. The explosion ignited the jet fuel and instantly destroyed the plane. The evidence is clear that the initial explosion was not accidental or due to a mechanical event. The plane was sabotaged. The full force of the United States government has been engaged to determine the perpetrator or perpetrators of this horrific act. We will not rest until these people are captured and brought to justice." Minardi sounded outraged as he delivered his statement.

As the weeks went by, reports surfaced that a terrorist group with ties to a number of international groups in the Middle East were being investigated and were the chief focus of a blue-ribbon investigative group formed by Minardi, consisting of CIA, FBI, Interpol, NSA, senators on the Intelligence Committee and Naval Intelligence, along with a subgroup of Japanese law enforcement.

Minardi began his transition and one by one substituted his loyal people in positions previously held by Carrington loyalists. This was done slowly over the next two months with little fanfare. Resignations came, at Minardi's suggestion, and replacements were made nearly immediately, appointed as temporary until, as some required, approval of Congress.

Minardi began the process by announcing a national day of mourning two weeks after the tragedy, and memorials were held in Washington and around the country. Leaders from around the world attended services at the national cathedral. A month later, a huge outdoor service was held on the Mall, where the service was open to the public.

It was announced that over one million people attended, but that figure was exaggerated, as the numbers were closer to 350,000. Carrington was far from the most popular figure in America. Even his martyrdom did little to increase his popularity. Minardi, however, sought to pay proper homage to the fallen leader of the free world. He also took the opportunity, under the threat of terrorism, to solidify his support by both parties and quiet any media speculation or dissent. It worked well. His approval rating soared to the midseventies within a month and a half. Thus, he was seen as a powerhouse in Congress, and he got little opposition. Bodine was forced to defer to Minardi as he solidified his support in Washington. Aged seventy-four, he had been chosen by Carrington as vice president because he was nonthreatening.

Bodine was the senior member of the Senate, and the liberal wing of the party knew he would never win the nomination after the Carrington presidency. They had in mind to bide their time until the next opportunity to put one of their own in place.

He had a history of heart disease and suffered a near fatal heart attack only two years earlier. He had undergone a four-way bypass surgery and managed to recuperate. The turmoil that followed the death of Carrington and the transfer of power, though, took its toll on Bodine. His schedule changed from basically a ceremonial figure to one who attended meetings and conferences on a tight schedule. Indeed, an election was coming up as well, and he was obliged to attend fundraisers for his party all over the country. After a month, he began looking gaunt and exhausted but refused to slow down as advised. He truly believed he could redeem his image and be nominated by his party.

On a trip bound for Dallas, Bodine was on Air Force One (a new plane commissioned after Carrington's death). He was reviewing a speech with his press secretary when he suddenly fell over. Members of his staff rushed to revive him but could not. He died of a heart attack.

Vice President Minardi got word directly from John Colandro, a member of Bodine's staff, minutes after the president collapsed. He had been one of Minardi's staff members in the Senate when Bodine arranged his presidential cabinet. Colandro was also a close friend of the Delmonte family. He also was a former partner of Big Tony Delmonte. He had been educated at George Washington University and continued his studies in political science and earned a master's degree. He was then hired as an aide to Minardi when Minardi was elected some eighteen years earlier.

Once the plane landed, Bodine was rushed to the hospital where he was pronounced dead. Though efforts were made to revive him, it was to no avail. Minardi ordered that Air Force One be flown back with Bodine's body to Washington that evening. The question as to cause of death became an immediate matter at speculation. Was this another assassination? Was there a conspiracy? No one knew. Minardi had an autopsy done that night at the Bethesda Medical Center. He appointed an old colleague of his, a fellow senator, Dr. Louis Carpaccio, to do the autopsy. The results were made public the next morning: heart attack. At a quiet ceremony at the Capitol, Minardi was sworn in as president by midnight.

He had already chosen a professional team when he became vice president.

Also to his credit, he had chosen an inner circle of advisers who had great skills in working out problems with both legislation and directives. His popularity rose as, assisted by a very positive media relationship, he projected the image that showed a proper and heartfelt respect for the fallen presidents. But also there was the expectation that he was the catalyst for a new direction. This enabled him to gain substantial power with the US Senate even as a successor by fate, not by vote. He was indeed part of the Senate's old boys' club. To begin with, he had worked in the system for three terms and was headed to a fourth when he became the compromise candidate that the party nearly forced Carrington to accept. His actions when leading the nation in mourning both Carrington and Bodine just made him more popular.

Carrington had wide support among moderates and independents alike, but he shunned some more traditional views of government. He was not seen as a tax reformer, while Minardi was. Senators Dobbs and Sizemore represented, essentially, the more liberal wing of the party, and each had been battling the other for control. Dobbs had sought the presidency in the primary process when Carrington was seen as a weak frontrunner. Sizemore had negotiated a deal with Dobbs, albeit reluctantly, to accept the vice presidential spot when Dobbs won. Thus, the huge coffers that the two commanded from New England to nearly the end of New Jersey were formidable.

Carrington, from California, cobbled together groups from the West Coast, the South, and the heartland and painted the Dobbs team with a much visible Sizemore, as left, and more left. Carrington's people also brought to light that Dobbs's father, himself a former senator from Connecticut, had been forced to leave office after five terms. Indeed, he retired and did not seek a sixth term, as a federal indictment was looming for bribery and conspiracy. Several of his associates, including his campaign manager and his chief of staff, were indicted, tried, convicted, and jailed. His six terms in the Senate as a member of the old boys' network earned him a "get out of jail free" card. He used his personal connections and his knowledge of some of his fellow senators' foibles as the collateral to get the pending indictments quashed with a promise to step down. Six years later, the same organization he held together over the years was used to elect his son Charles. The senior Dobbs, known to his friends as Timmy, became an adviser to the son and even took a penthouse apartment at the Watergate in Washington, DC, and began hosting elaborate parties for his old cronies and the shakers and movers. He orchestrated streams of power within the party and with the big donors. His penchant for wheeling and dealing that nearly put him in jail for twenty years was now focused on capturing the White House for his son. He even brought back his old chief of staff after he received twenty-six months in a country club prison.

To his chagrin, the Minardi connections with the media were overlooked. The newspaper story broke in the *Washington Express Chronicle*. It was front page, just two weeks before the primary season began in earnest in February. Documents showed Timmy had accepted not only bribes from various companies to vote favorably on legislation that benefited them but also accepted campaign donations from numerous foreign companies who benefited from Timmy's vote on the Commerce Committee. Some of the contributions were from regimes who were to be on the US Terrorist Watch List and included some of the leading rulers from the oil-producing Arab nations. He had a compound at the Connecticut shore near Mystic with three houses, one a huge mansion reminiscent of those in Newport, Rhode Island, built by the old robber barons at the turn of the century as summer homes, but more as monuments to wealth and power. Records showed that the contractors used to build and expand the compound with its two swimming pools, tennis courts, two boat houses, docks, and cabana were the very same ones that were favored with multimillion-dollar federal construction contracts through the years. And there was no accounting for payment for over 75 percent of the work. Eventually one vice president of Con-Build, Inc., the contractor, offered up the information on the Dobbs matter to beg leniency after he was indicted on another case where he had been caught in an FBI sting operation. The national and international press had a field day. Minardi and his friends, including Delmont, made sure of it. Some of the same people involved in that matter were on Senator Charles Dobbs's payroll. The association and linkage was clear. There were so many interlocking schemes, in fact, that it became difficult to decipher whether it was a Timmy deal or the Charles in charge. For his part, Sizemore ducked for cover. He had benefited from the association with the Dobbs and, in turn, received hefty donations from their donors, some of whom faced indictments. Indeed, some of the contractors and business connections were setups by companies in Milan, Rome, Athens, and Barcelona, all of them with close ties to Delmont.

The long-term plan of wresting control from these titans played upon their greed. Their lust for money made them an easy target for bribery. The foreigners who did their work from shadow companies and obscure offshore financial institutions could not be held responsible under US law, and it was difficult, if not impossible, to track who sent these funds and from where. Accounts from various places in Europe, Japan, and Morocco passed through banks in the Caribbean islands. Funds were transferred from Barbados to Panama City and Bogata, Colombia, to Mexico. The trail was dizzying. Delmont had been very cautious in his plans and had kept both his dealings and his personal life very much inconspicuous. Indeed, few people knew he had a wife, Nancy, or six children. The eldest, baptized Guielmo Delmont, "Will," was a strong, handsome lad who was educated at the finest schools and excelled in sports as well as his studies. He had an exceptionally keen and analytic mind. He graduated from Notre Dame in the top 10 percent of his class before moving on to Wharton Business School, and then to Rome, where after only four short years, he became a partner in an international finance firm, Entaterra, Ltd. The firm administered much of the funds of large companies both in Europe and worldwide; it also administered a vast amount of funds for the Vatican. Will had brought in Fiat, Nestlé, and Greco Petroleum and formed associations with Barclays Bank worldwide as well as Banco Populare.

His sibling Alexander Delmont had graduated from Liberty University, where he became quarterback for their football team as a freshman. Then after law school, he joined the West Coast law firm of Wilson-Catania P. C., which had seventeen offices in major US cities, Grenada, Central and South America, and Europe. They also formed associations with law firms in the Middle East, in Saudi Arabia, Israel, and Hong Kong and had connections in Athens and the Ukraine. Alex was part of what was known as the foreign desk where he coordinated not just legal matters but also was responsible to monitor the political watchdog team of the firm. He was often consulted by the CIA.

James Delmont enrolled in MIT, where he was most known for his work as an engineer and architect, graduating summa cum laude. Within three years, he headed the Signal Group, the professional technology group that designed the NASA space exploration program and military satellite system at the Johnson Space Center in Texas. It was likely that he too would end up on the West Coast. The youngest sibling, Nicholas, was admitted to Harvard and was elected to the Harvard Law Review. He carried a double major in law and medicine and played trumpet in a Dixieland jazz group.

Although Anthony Delmont yearned to have his boys nearby, he knew that their long-term careers and futures rested on their education and their business pursuits. He also needed trusted allies in places of particular importance. What better than to have his own in-house positions. Anthony Delmont still had Lucia and Maria Bella at home in local Catholic schools, and then there was Carolina. She was the second child, and her natural ability as an artist was evident even at a very young age. She was an accomplished oil painter from the age twelve, and after finishing graduate school at Yale, she was invited to work with an art group at the Sorbonne in Paris, both teaching and learning. She had married a young man from Malta, but after only two years together, the young man, Christo, was lost at sea when a sailboat he and a friend took out for a day's sail ran into a freak storm and both were lost. The vessel was never found.

Delmont had placed his family in his plan and in control of the inner circle. Paramount in his plans were loyalty and secrecy. His bloodline, going back generations to that small town in Sicily, embraced those two concepts as his forebears did before him—traditions in "la famiglia."

CHAPTER 65

MINARDI'S INVESTIGATIVE TEAM had success in the several months following the Carrington assassination. An important conspiracy was uncovered. A reporter, Richard Condroy, who had traveled with the press corps, had recently gotten an assignment with the presidential press corp by his company, Amalgamated Press International (API). The service was a worldwide network based in Washington, DC. Condroy had not gotten on Air Force One that fateful day.

He had traveled there with the press corps on the plane and had taken a room in a hotel across the street from where President Carrington had stayed during his stay in Tokyo. He was found dead in his hotel room in Tokyo a day later.

The Japanese had brought his body to a local morgue and contacted the United States consulate. It appeared that he had died of natural causes, since his body was found in bed with no signs of foul play and the door was locked with a Do Not Disturb sign on the handle.

Minardi's investigative team came across this information several days later as the body was shipped back to Washington, DC. Strangely, no family could be found, but the API (a press service) assumed care for the body when it arrived. It was put in the Washington, DC, morgue.

There was some confusion over authority and responsibility, since the death occurred in a foreign country and Condroy listed his address as an apartment in Washington, DC, but held residency in a house in nearby Alexandria, Virginia.

The body was finally autopsied three weeks after death.

Immediately, the coroner noted a strange configuration in the lungs of the deceased. They appeared convulsed and oddly discolored, and blood vessels had burst parts of lung tissue, revealing that minute particles of a foreign substance had been inhaled. Further investigation revealed the substance tracked from the mouth through the windpipe into the lungs. The substance was so obscure that it took another few weeks to actually pinpoint what it was. It was finally discovered that it was a compound containing snake venom, likely a combination of venoms. The compound was mixed with some other inert substance, including talc, and compressed into an aerosol container and propelled by noxious oxide gas, laughing gas, used by dentists. The compound likely was administered by forcing the victim's mouth open and, with a funnel-like attachment to an aerosol device, spraying the contents down the victim's throat. This caused the lung passages to seize up and close, suffocating the victim, leaving no outward signs. Indeed, Mr. Condroy was the victim of a very professional murder.

He then became the focus of investigations. It was discovered that he had originally come aboard Air Force One with one suitcase and a laptop computer, which he carried. His suitcase was in the room when he was found, and the description and photos taken while the plane was being loaded matched the suitcase. The laptop and its leather case, however, were missing. The suitcase and its contents were then taken to the FBI laboratory for inspection. Inside was a memory stick from the laptop computer. Upon intense testing, traces of a plastic explosive were found on the top of the memory stick. FBI and CIA analysts were able to find the origin of the laptop and determine its manufacturer and model, as it had been recently purchased by Cordroy at a Washington, DC, shop and paid for with a credit card. The investigators theorized that Cordroy had carried the laptop to the airport. He then removed it from the case, and it was scanned as he walked through the body scan, but he left the case on the conveyor behind the laptop. The scan on the conveyor would not have detected any materials in the leather case as explosive. Later, Condroy loaded the explosives inside the case of the laptop sometime during the flight and set a timing mechanism he had installed in the laptop in the overhead compartment above his seat, and then he deplaned in Tokyo. The plane was under twenty-four-hour surveillance, and, therefore, no secondary security check was necessary. In part, two of the president's bodyguards actually stayed on the plane for the day and a half that the president visited in Tokyo, taking shifts.

The investigation into Condroy revealed this forty-one-year-old journalist had worked for API for some seven years and had been with the foreign desk nearly the entire time. He had spent the last five years in the Middle East and Far East. They tracked his family. His mother died at childbirth, and he had no siblings. His father was not married to the mother, and he was given the mother's maiden name. The hospital record in Bethesda, Maryland, listed the father as a noncitizen Hari Abib. There was no history on Abib, so it was considered he was an illegal alien, likely from either Yemen or Syria, since some records were discovered from a Swiss Air record database of a person of that name traveling to the US via Switzerland and then to Yemen and Syria on several occasions. Investigation also was done at Cordroy's house and apartment. They found a file cabinet at his home and traced credit card records of trips from Israel to Grand Cayman Islands and back. After a considerable effort by the CIA with Cayman officials, the numbered bank account secrecy regulation was bypassed. There was no revelation as to exactly how it was tracked, but Condroy had left some sort of evidence that led them to the account through his home computer. There they found a deposit of $5 million in the account number Condroy had. The money transfer took weeks to track from Panama City to London, then to a Syrian connection. The funds came from an organization, El Hal. The organization was later traced as a front for Jihad El, a terrorist group with ties in Pakistan, Jakarta, and Tokyo.

Now Interpol as well as the CIA and other US agencies and security agencies from Indonesia and other countries, including Israel, were alerted, and headquarters were set up in Rome. There, Will Delmont received secret briefings as to the progress of the investigation. The leadership of the groups was traced to a village outside Jakarta, Indonesia. A strike team was dispatched that consisted of eight US Navy Seals in a covert operation. They were flown from Rome to a military base in Jakarta and then converged on the location. Upon entering the house, they found three male bodies, all of them shot in the back of the head. Two were identified as brothers from Yemen, and the other a Saudi.

Again, CIA and FBI as well as the Massad and Interpol scanned their records. Photos of these men with others popped up at several places, including airports and train stations. Four others were immediately identified, and the tracking continued. Some weeks later, one of the men, a Syrian, was identified on a review at an airport in Jakarta.

The team of Navy Seals was again dispatched, as well as several undercover CIA agents. The photo of the man was identified by a bank teller as a Minister Kalil. Profiling of the man revealed he was Harri al Khohani, the leader of a terrorist group known as Jihad Al. They brought in a huge contingent of undercover agents and local informants. Allocations of bribe money moved swiftly. An informant identified a house about thirty miles outside of Jakarta as the place where this man and others had been seen.

A coordinated team consisting of US Navy Seals, CIA, Indonesia Secret Service, and Massad under the direction of US Lieutenant Colonel John Litting converged upon the house. Surveillance revealed five males inside the house with two armed men standing guard on a wood porch outside. After surrounding the house, a call went out to the occupants to surrender. It was met with wild gunfire in all directions. The instant response was heavy gunfire at the house, and its occupants were all killed. Five bodies were recovered as well as some materials that were connected to the banking trail that led back to Condroy. They also retrieved two laptop computers, phones, and notebooks.

After the computers and cell phones had the information secured from them, the experts were able to pinpoint transmissions from an area near the Pakistan border with Afghanistan and a location on the edge of Athens in Greece. Again, teams were rushed to these sites.

Accompanied by Interpol and Turkish and Greek Special Forces, a team surrounded an apartment house in a densely populated area. Fortunately, in the morning hours, most occupants of this three-story building were out, likely at work. Only two apartments contained people once infrared scans were done. There were two people in one unit and one in another. They were able to determine that the one person was a woman. One of the Greek Special Forces was given a package and posed as a delivery person. He went to the building, and then directly to the first-floor unit and tapped on the door. A middle-aged woman answered. To her surprise, the man quickly grabbed her, put his hand over her mouth, and pushed her back into the apartment and closed the door. As she struggled, he was able to pull out his military credentials and told her to calm down and he would release her. When he was confident she would not scream, he released her. He told her that they had to leave because the men on the floor above were terrorists. Still a bit confused, she complied, and he led her out of the building.

As soon as she was out of sight, several men entered the house. The men were in the kitchen near the middle of the unit. There was no other alternative but to go in through the front door. Deftly, the front door was unlocked, and a signal to men on the roof to propel down was given. The timing was perfect. As three men came down the hallway, six more men repelled down to windows on three sides of the building. However, a voice from the opening of one of the windows alerted the two who had automatic weapons next to them in the kitchen, which they grabbed. They then turned toward the hallway and moved toward the voice at the back of the house. In an instant, the three team members took arm, and as the men entered the hall, looking down the hall with their backs to the front, one yelled in Arabic, "Drop your weapons." They began to wheel around, pointing their weapons as the three opened fire instantly, killing both of them.

It took two days and some thirty men in a similar team to reach a remote area in Pakistan. Here there was no question that the terrorists would be warned of an approach through lookout points and locals. But along with the men, a cadre of six helicopter gunships and two fighter jets along with very sophisticated satellite and other imagery pinpointed the group in a compound halfway up a ravine, with steep mountain terrain protecting the place. Here, they detected six men. At a given signal, they all converged, first with a strafing blitz that killed four. One set off a ground-to-air missile, and it destroyed a helicopter and three men.

Next, the ground troops went in, and a gun battle ensued that lasted over two hours before both were killed inside the stone house.

The team used restraint, as they did not want to bomb and thus destroy evidence. It was hoped that trying to wound and incapacitate one of the band would result in the capture of a live assassin, but all of them were dead. One of the Pakistanis identified one of the men in a house as Harri Kahili, the leader of the major terrorist movement. He had been sought for many years by six different governments for acts of terror.

Thus they got every known conspirator, or at least it was thought so. Once the computers and documents from the house were reviewed, they were able to piece together the plot. In the following weeks, arrests in Palestine of some fifteen coconspirators were made by the Moussad. While protests and riots broke out, meetings between Israelis and the Palestinians gave an opportunity to show that fifteen were involved in the blowing up of Air Force One. The more moderate elements were able to get the information out quickly, and the uproar died out. In the weeks and months ahead, the meeting led to higher-level talks, and the result was a demarcation of land set near the Israeli border with Egypt with an open international corridor controlled by the Israelis, which proved safe passage to the holy sites in Jerusalem. President Minardi himself met with leaders from both sides, both in Washington and in Israel. The Egyptians also assisted and created an international gate at a crossroads between the three borders. A high-level Vatican emissary and a British diplomat assisted thus on the one hand, providing protection for Catholics in the region and providing an international monetary fund coordinated by Barclays Bank, five Middle East oil producers, national and the European Economic Union and the World Bank.

The event was marked by the signing of documents at the international gate and attended by leaders from some twenty-five nations. Prominent in the accolades was President Minardi, who was seen as the catalyst for the pact. The advent of this peace mission and the evidence that some five terrorist groups were involved in coordinating the explosion of Air Force One created a positive reaction to antiterrorists, but just a few months later, a high-ranking Saudi sheik was kidnapped and killed.

Thus nations either turned against the terrorists who were in their country or refused to protect them, permitting border crossings by forces chasing them. Three shared intelligence enclaves were uncovered and wiped out. This led to a sort of international force where several nations sent their people to act together to hunt down terrorist bands.

Back home in each of these nations, the authorizations and interaction created a constant flow of contact and with it higher-level diplomatic meetings and interaction. Eventually this also led to high-level talks on several subjects, including oil supply, weapons proliferation, nuclear power, technology sharing, trade, immigration practices, and even human rights, food supplies, medical care, and more. A new era began.

The Minardi government with assistance from the Vatican, the Saudi king, and the Israeli prime minister and the British prime minister began holding international conferences. Suddenly many nations sought to interact with this new order. The French president and German leader, not wanting to be left out, insisted on being a main partner, which caused the rest of the European nations to participate.

This new international trade consortium eventually opened a headquarters and clearinghouse in Rome. Minardi saw to it that Guilemo Delmont became chief administrator because of his financial and diplomatic background. He was proposed by the pope himself. A chief of trade was appointed as well. It was Marcus Stavros, the nephew of the late Aristotle Onassis. A ceremony for the formal creation of the consortium and installation of its directors was held in Rome.

Anthony Delmont was invited, and he had his youngest daughter, Lucia, act as his chief of staff in arranging for his entire family and some business associates to attend. He was also being recommended as one of the sixteen international directors.

Thus the families made plans to attend, including the Merendinos, the Scalisces, the Pumilias, the Viscones, the Terranovas, the Castleluccis, the Vazzanas, the Perinos, the Donofrios, the Schellenginas, the Cellas, Garbarinos Marinos, Russos, and Palamaras. The event was akin to a royal conclave. Heads of the Gervasi, Rittaco, Zizolfo, and Perricone, heads of state, monarchs from every nation, and even some less desirable leaders—dictators and tyrants—were permitted to attend. Even the Chinese communists sent a high-level delegation.

Only a few countries were advised that they were unwelcome, and only one representative was permitted. North Korea and Venezuela decided not to send anyone, while Cuba did send its third-ranking politician, a commerce diplomat.

The events took some twelve days, and during that time and for weeks later, the groundwork for economic cooperation was laid. It also included military safety pacts whereby nations agreed to protect the means of commerce and cease any aggressive acts as a caveat to staying as a member in good standing.

One late August weekend, the Delmont compound at the Jersey Shore became a beehive of activity. Tents were set up, and the two houses nearby became part of the compound. Delmont had asked his two neighbors on either side to assist him, as he was to have a special visitor over the weekend and needed additional quarters for a Secret Service team. The guest was President Minardi. No one refused the request, especially when it came with a rental offer of $100,000. Not more than a few miles away, Delmont had invested in a beachfront hotel. He arranged for the hotel and its one hundred rooms to be closed to the public from the last week in August through the Labor Day holiday weekend. The president was scheduled for an unprecedented four-day stay.

Thus, on a sunny, warm Sunday afternoon, the tables were set, and the guests from all the families arrived for Sunday dinner, Sicilian-style. The wine and cheese and grapes were laid out, and a well-known actor, Dominic Chianti, was engaged to play his mandolin and sing old Italian folk songs. A string band was flown in from a Sicilian mountainside village. They came in full costume, plus a mouth harp and a strange array of instruments, many handcrafted in the very village where Delmonte lived for centuries.

The Meredinos and Scalices enjoyed the festivities, and the old-timers related stories of first coming to the new country. Only a few were left now; even the second generation were senior citizens. The Terranovas, Scalisces, and Marinos and all the other families were invited. The invitations graciously offered transportation and accommodations for a week's stay. Delmont's inner circle, Frankie, the Merendino brothers, and others helped prepare the events weeks in advance. Each was to bring a list of all family members, past and present—a bloodline.

On Friday about noon, several black SUVs rolled down the residential street to the Delmont compound. For weeks prior, Secret Service had set up their headquarters next door, and there were several conspicuous men in dark suits surrounding the area. Minardi emerged from the first vehicle. He wore a thin tan sport jacket and white trousers, tan loafers, and a gold-colored open-collar shirt. His wife, Joan, accompanied him. She wore a flowered summer dress with blue and yellow flowers dotting the bloused-out shirt and puffy sleeves. The cloth rose and fell with just the slightest breeze, due to the thin material. She wore no jewelry. She was average height and thin but had an intense and sincere manner. Anthony strode over to her, took her hand, and kissed it. "Welcome, Madam First Lady. It is an honor and a privilege for the Delmonts to have you here. My wife, Nancy, here has been so excited about your visit." Nancy, who had just been greeted by the president, took Joan's hand and escorted her to the house. Delmont took Minardi's hand. "Charlootz, it's wonderful to have you here. Come, come," said Anthony. He led him to the rear of the property where tents and tables were set. There under a heavily leafed grape arbor sat Delmont's inner circle, his sons, his daughters, Frankie, the Merendinos, and the others. One by one, Anthony introduced them, although Minardi had met some of them through the years. However, he had never met Guielmo.

"Will, it is my pleasure to introduce you, finally, to our friend President Charles Minardi," said Delmont.

"Mr. President, it is an honor," said Will. The Italian band began playing.

Minardi shook his hand and pulled him close so he could in a low voice tell him, "Will, I know what great work you have done for your country and for us. Thank you. While we are here and out of earshot to my security, please call me Uncle Charles or Compare. After all, I am your godfather." Will looked up rather surprised and turned to his father. Delmont just smiled and nodded his head.

After the introductions, Anthony ordered that the wineglasses be filled, and there under the arbor, he ordered a toast.

"May we all continue to be blessed by God and enjoy the fruits of our labor. May the Lord keep safe and protect our friend and our president, Charles Minardi, and may all of you enjoy long life and the joy of many children. Cent' anni." He raised his glass, and they all drank. Then Anthony led Minardi to the back-fence area of the compound.

There were five vines of grapes flourishing and climbing up the wood trellis. They had bunches of still unripe grapes hanging down.

"Charlootz, see these vines? I had the shoots of vines from my great-grandfather's vineyard in Corleone brought over to me. I kept close watch and tended to them, and they grew here on American soil, much as our founders did. See how rich and robust the grape and the vine grow? It is like how we here are prospering. But lest we forget our roots, we are the product of all those who have gone before us. We were given the tasks to ensure the best life for our families and our friends, and it seems we have done that. Perhaps we have gone beyond that and have touched other people as well, *buona fagista*." And they hugged and sipped their wine.

Soon all assembled around the tables under the tent. The waiters began bringing out the salads and bread. Each place had a wineglass and a small long metal box with the presidential seal atop of it.

President Minardi and Anthony Delmont were placed at the head of a wide table and could look down to the many family and friends on either side. A photographer stood inconspicuously near the Secret Service men. The popping of corks caused everyone to smile, and waiters began filling glasses with Asti Spumante, the Italian version of festive champagne.

The president asked all to rise and take their glasses.

"Ladies and gentlemen, it is my honor and my pleasure to be here with my old friend Anthony Delmont—or is it *Antonio Delmonte*? Tony has been my friend and ally and my brother since we were children. We always looked out for each other and for our families—and now our nation.

"Over the last two and a half years as president of the United States, I have had the help and support of Tony and all of you. I literally could not have done it without you.

"Now the nightmare of the death of President Carrington is becoming more a bitter memory, but we were able to eliminate his assassins, vindicate our efforts to promote peace, and perhaps prepare for a period of prosperity without conflict.

"Anthony had a great deal to do with this, and for his efforts, I am eternally grateful. I am sure he shares that success with all of you, his loyal friends and associates.

"And now I have an important announcement to make here and soon to the world.

"Out of respect to the memory of President Carrington, I have held in place his appointees for some period of time. One by one, some have chosen to leave the administration of their own accord since they were my predecessor's close advisers and went on to work to ensure his legacy. Others remained for longer periods. Recently, I met with Ambassador Michael Bolare. He was appointed by President Carrington and has been an effective ambassador and a loyal friend. He has asked that he be reassigned. He knew that my emissary to the Vatican, Carl Bunz, asked to be replaced because of his advanced age, and Mike wishes to fill that position. Thus, there was a vacancy about to occur for Mr. Bolarsi's position.

"Just before I left Washington, I drafted a proposal that has been forwarded to the United States Senate. The proposal is contained in that little silver box next to your glass; along with the proposal is a document approving my proposal from the majority leader of the Senate and my vice president, Nicholas Novant.

"I will read a portion of the proclamation.

"So it is with our advice and consent that Anthony C. Delmont is approved as ambassador to the Republic of Italy." Minardi turned, glass raised, and looked at Anthony. "To Ambassador Delmont." They all sipped the wine and then began applauding and yelling. Anthony smiled, a bit overwhelmed. His wife, Nancy, came to his side, squeezed his hand, and kissed him on the cheek. Minardi rested his glass, took Anthony by both shoulders, and hugged him and kissed him on the other cheek.

Cameras snapped all around him. Tony's lifelong aspiration of returning to his roots was met in a fashion he could not have ever imagined. The Italian band played the Italian anthem and then the "Star-Spangled Banner" and other Italian folk music.

After the meal was served, Anthony led Minardi, Will, his brothers, and Frankie to his study. There the walls were lined with a conglomeration of books, magazines, sculptures, photographs, music albums, and movies. While there was little order to the items, Anthony seemed to know precisely where things were. He pulled out a book with a red cover, *The History of the Roman Empire.* He laid it down on the table and then opened a globe to reveal a bottle and several shot glasses. He carefully set out several glasses and filled them from a cut-glass canister. The liquor was deep red in color.

"This is cherry brandy. The little berries come from my father Salvatore's tree. He and my mother, Caroline"—he looked at Will—"your grandmother, were close to the earth. She could grow anything, and he could as well. He taught me and my brother Vincent how to make this brandy. So here we are about to sip a drink and acknowledge our ancestors. And it is befitting that this book, which chronicles what our ancestors accomplished in the Roman Empire, be laid before us both as a symbol of the pride in our culture and a warning as well. For as long as the Romans stayed true to the democracy that they created under the emperor of Rome and as long as they followed Roman law, they prospered. The Sicilians learned much from them but kept their own customs and their own council. However, when the Romans became complacent and ignored their own foundation and permitted decadence to prevail, they crumbled. Thus, we raise our glasses to those who passed and wish to go forward in mind of who we are and what we stand for. We will not permit those who would lead us to a decadent and crumbling society to prevail. While some may disagree with the methods we must employ to reach the goals, they do not disagree with the outcome. The end has, in fact, justified the means. May we be judged by our Lord in that light, and may he bless us all. Here we raise these glasses of red brandy wine, the same drink our ancestors used to toast the great events that occurred for our heritage, a symbol of our cherished Sicilian tradition generation after generation, *sangue di sangue*—blood to blood." As he finished his words, each raised a glass and then drank. And the music played.